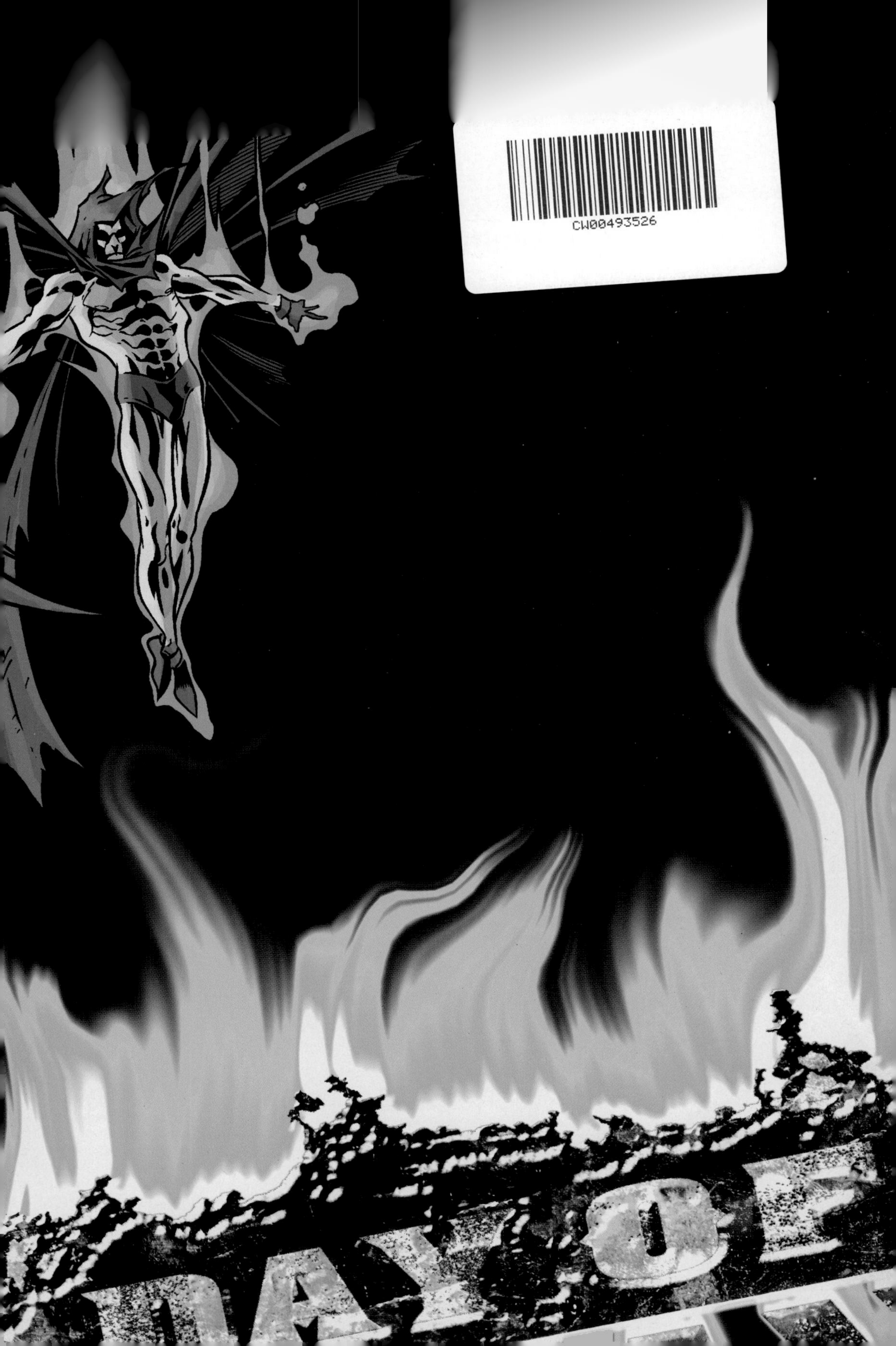
DAY OF

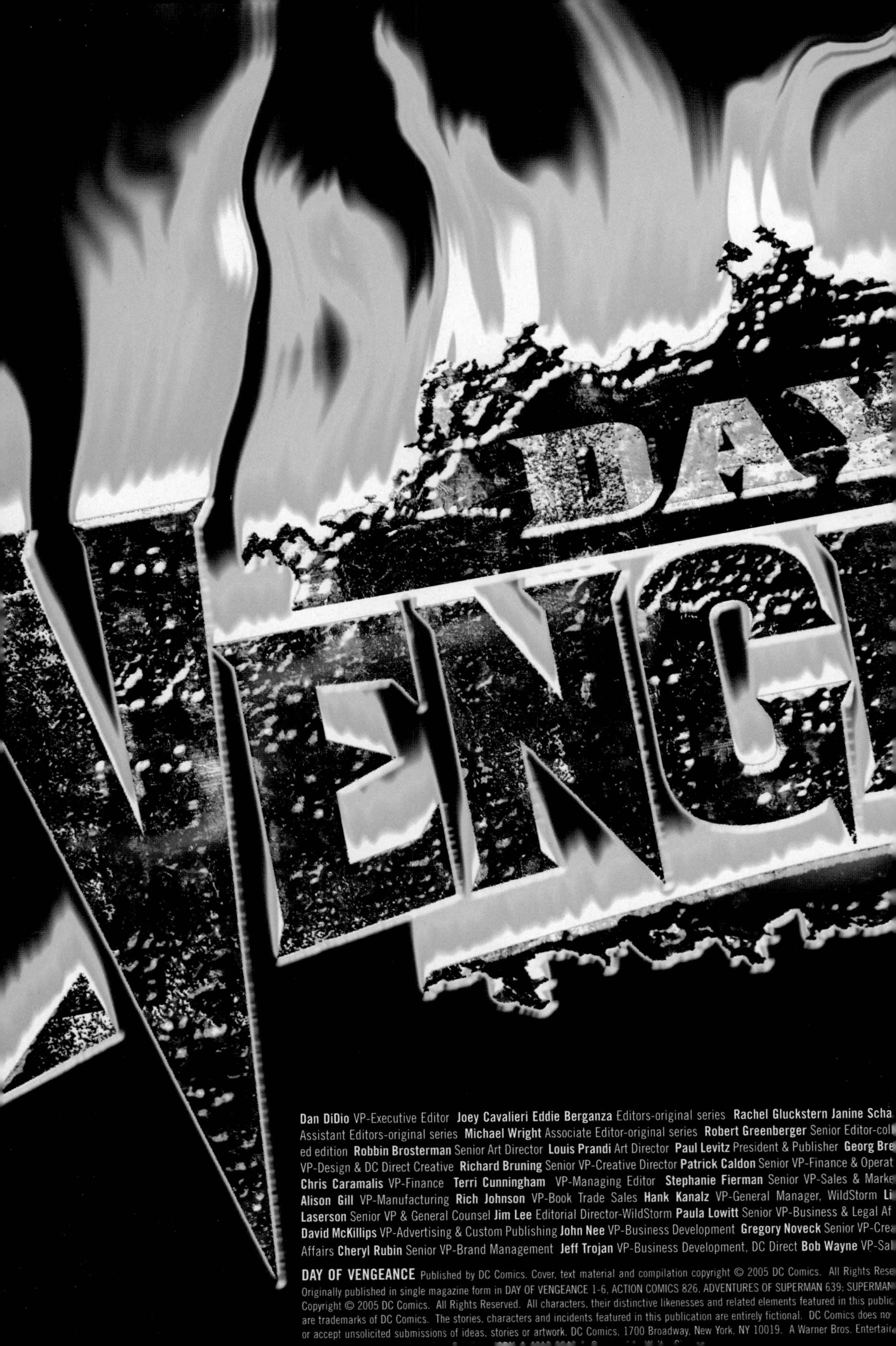

Dan DiDio VP-Executive Editor **Joey Cavalieri Eddie Berganza** Editors-original series **Rachel Gluckstern Janine Scha**
Assistant Editors-original series **Michael Wright** Associate Editor-original series **Robert Greenberger** Senior Editor-coll
ed edition **Robbin Brosterman** Senior Art Director **Louis Prandi** Art Director **Paul Levitz** President & Publisher **Georg Bre**
VP-Design & DC Direct Creative **Richard Bruning** Senior VP-Creative Director **Patrick Caldon** Senior VP-Finance & Operat
Chris Caramalis VP-Finance **Terri Cunningham** VP-Managing Editor **Stephanie Fierman** Senior VP-Sales & Marke
Alison Gill VP-Manufacturing **Rich Johnson** VP-Book Trade Sales **Hank Kanalz** VP-General Manager, WildStorm **Li**
Laserson Senior VP & General Counsel **Jim Lee** Editorial Director-WildStorm **Paula Lowitt** Senior VP-Business & Legal Af
David McKillips VP-Advertising & Custom Publishing **John Nee** VP-Business Development **Gregory Noveck** Senior VP-Crea
Affairs **Cheryl Rubin** Senior VP-Brand Management **Jeff Trojan** VP-Business Development, DC Direct **Bob Wayne** VP-Sal

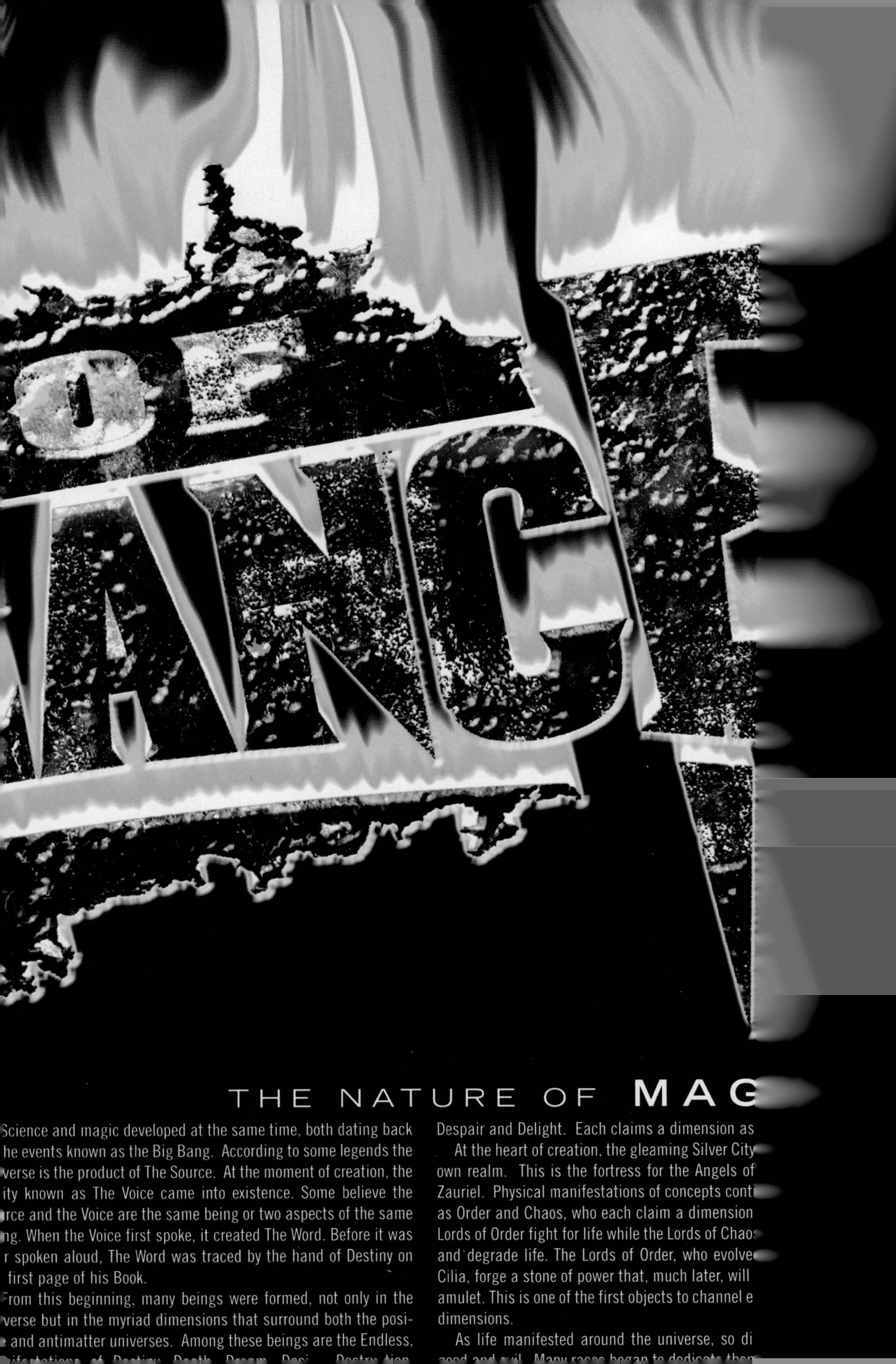

THE NATURE OF MAG

Science and magic developed at the same time, both dating back he events known as the Big Bang. According to some legends the verse is the product of The Source. At the moment of creation, the ity known as The Voice came into existence. Some believe the rce and the Voice are the same being or two aspects of the same ng. When the Voice first spoke, it created The Word. Before it was r spoken aloud, The Word was traced by the hand of Destiny on first page of his Book.

From this beginning, many beings were formed, not only in the verse but in the myriad dimensions that surround both the posi- and antimatter universes. Among these beings are the Endless,

Despair and Delight. Each claims a dimension as

At the heart of creation, the gleaming Silver City own realm. This is the fortress for the Angels of Zauriel. Physical manifestations of concepts conti as Order and Chaos, who each claim a dimension Lords of Order fight for life while the Lords of Chao and degrade life. The Lords of Order, who evolve Cilia, forge a stone of power that, much later, will amulet. This is one of the first objects to channel e dimensions.

As life manifested around the universe, so di

ng the balance between good and evil. One such being, picked by the Lord of Heaven, was Aztar, who was the first Wrath of God. Eons later, Aztar was replaced by Eclipso.

Soon after, for reasons beyond mortal comprehension, Lucifer Morningstar, the Lightbringer, rebelled against the leadership of Heaven and was cast down in the Chaoplasm with his rebellious underlings. The Chaoplasm became Hell, and Lucifer, its leader. Around this same period, Shathan came into existence as one of Hell's rulers. There will be many such demons, all giving rise to Hell's Hierarchy.

Beings who wield tremendous powers in comparison with other lifeforms around the universe were considered gods. When they died during a battle known as Ragnarok, the Godwave was formed and began its periodic tour of the universe, forever altering life on the worlds it touches.

After its formation, the sun known as Sol gave life to several of its planets. The third one, dubbed Earth, is for unknown reasons a focal point for beings of science and for magic. Adam was created as an androgyne giant, a hermaphrodite. God (or the Source) divided Adam into two beings, and Adam and Lilith were created. The two coexisted in Eden. When Lilith refused to be sexually submissive, she was cast out of Eden and formed her own garden. There, Lilith mated with demons from other realms and conceived many children, including Mazikeen. Lilith was believed to be the first vampire, and all who followed consider her their Queen.

As life developed on Earth, creatures of science known as the Oans attempted to collect the bulk of all magical energy in the universe and store it away, in order to prevent it from causing harm. This concentration of collected energy, imprisoned in the center of a blazing sun, becomes the Starheart.

Yggdrasil, the World Tree, gained sentience, and the Parliament of Trees grew in a sacred South American grove. The Parliament created a race of plant/Earth elementals to protect the planet. Other elemental forces created their own parliaments, including Water, Air, Fire, and Stone. Through the years, each has had avatars among humans on Earth.

The Homo magi, an offshoot of the evolving human race with access to magic, emerged some 500,000 years ago. During this so-called "Golden Age," races of mystic beings and sorcerers transformed much of the planet into a world of enchantment, deriving their power from a dimension known as the Darkworld. The shining, mysti-

years later. A group of Atlantean magicians formed the Twelve Crystals of the Zodiac (also known as the Twelve Gems) with magical properties to help differentiate power and status. The gems contain unparalleled power and were never kept together.

Unknown to the Atlanteans, the entire Earth has been submerged in water, the work of the then-current Spirit of Wrath known as Eclipso. Having "overreached himself," Eclipso was eventually banished into the prison of a black diamond, not to be unleashed until recent times.

The first Terrestrial "gods" appeared around 33,000 B.C., marking the beginning of the Third World. The earth spirit Gaea emerged, mated with the sky god Uranus, and the Titans of Myth were born. The Titans and their fellow beings formed the pantheon of gods known today through Greek mythology, stories filled with their couplings with humans and interference in mortal affairs.

In Canaan, a young boy named Jebediah was given a magic word, *Vlarem*, by one such pantheon of gods to become a hero named the Champion, who possessed the strength of Voldar, the wisdom of Lumiun, the speed of Arel, the power of Ribalvei, the courage of Elbiam, and the stamina of Marzoah. The hero was seduced by a demoness and sired twins destined to be known as Blaze and Lord Satanus. The Champion later defeated Terror, Sin and Wickedness, the Three Faces of Evil and, in the process, created the Rock of Eternity. For 3,000 years as Jebediah grew older, until the gods he knew were forgotten by all save himself, he became a great wizard, taking the name Shazam. Residing in the Rock of Eternity, Shazam then granted his powers to select mortal champions for the next several millennia.

In outer space during what humans called the 15th century, a super nova sent violent emanations across the galaxy. Major zodiacal alignments were shifted and Earth, once a great epicenter of magic concentrations, began to lose its magic. The masters of Twelve mystic houses, each named after a gemstone, fled to another dimension and founded Gemworld.

And since then, a small but growing number of humans learned about magic, how to harness its energies and how to use it. Some can be corrupted by it while others are destined to use it for greatness.

But watching from their various realms are angels and demons, order and chaos, and other manifestations of will that use men and women as their pawns, each with a separate agenda. When the conflicts occur, the human race can suffer.

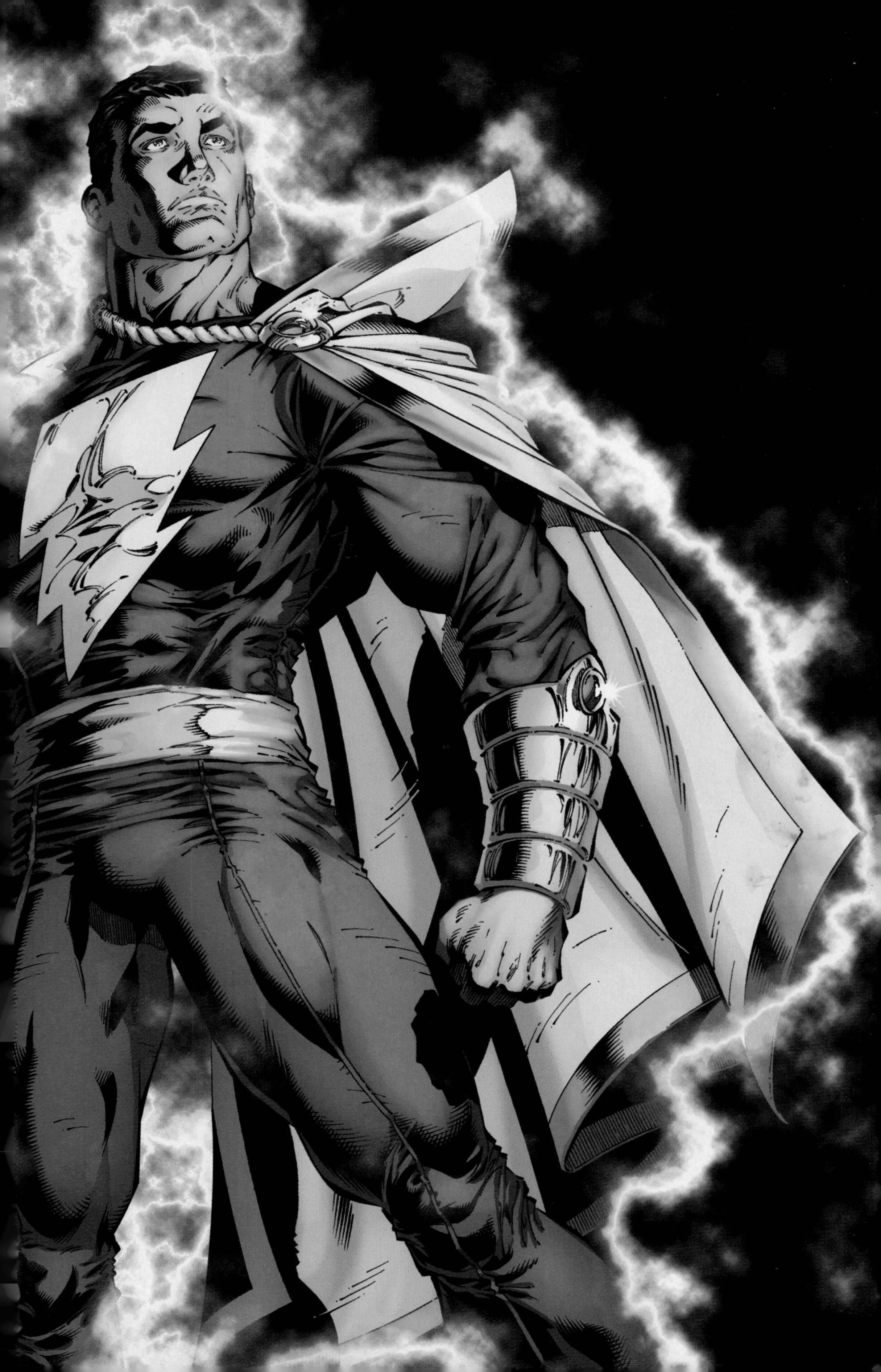

LIGHTNING STRIKES TWICE

Judd Winick WRITER
Ian Churchill PENCILLER
Norm Rapmund INKER
Beth Sotelo COLORIST
Richard Starkings LETTERER
Ian Churchill, Norm Rapmund &
Dave Stewart
ORIGINAL SERIES COVERS

SUPERMAN created by
JERRY SIEGEL & JOE SHUSTER

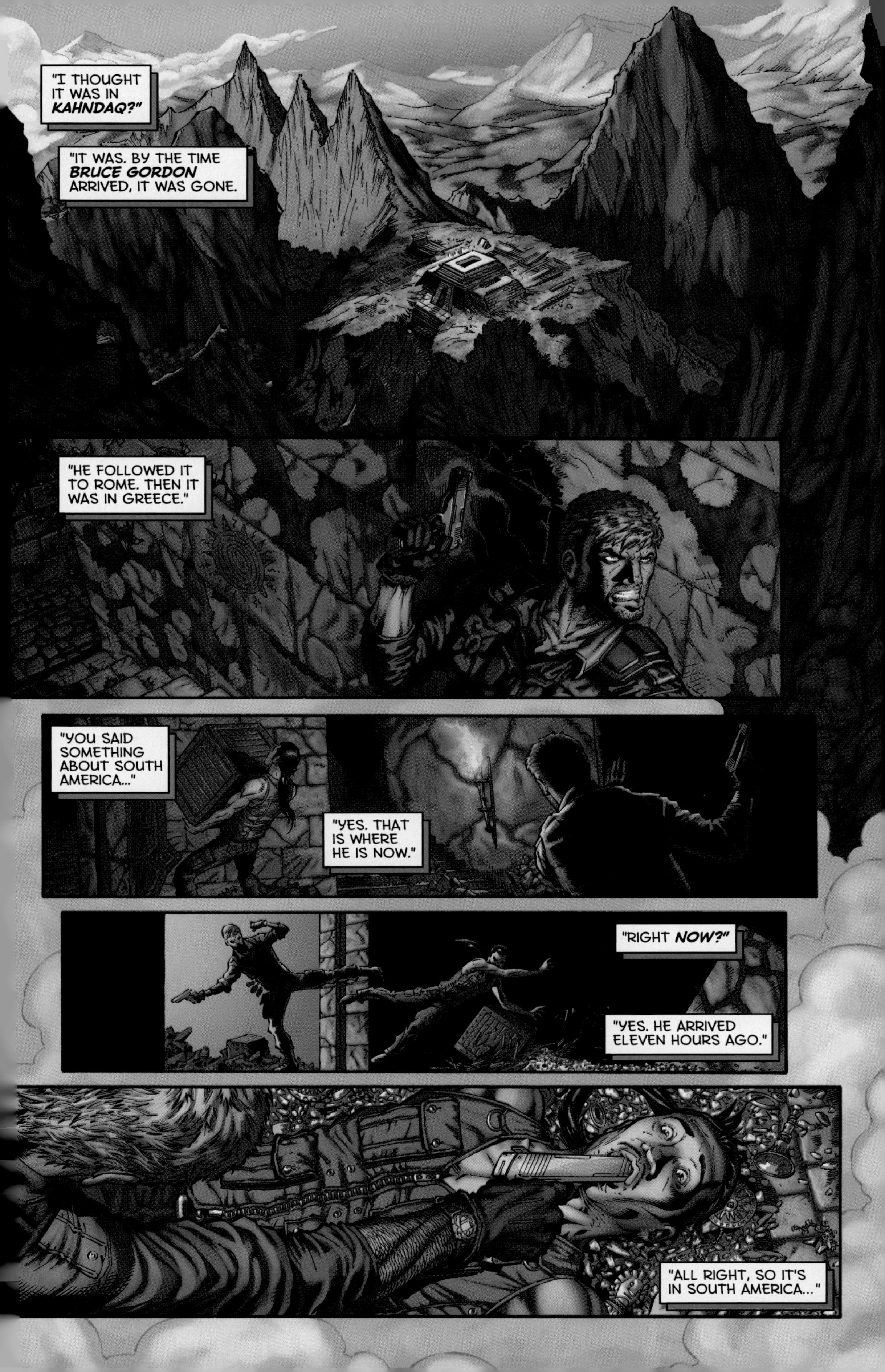
"I THOUGHT IT WAS IN ***KAHNDAQ?"***
"IT WAS. BY THE TIME ***BRUCE GORDON*** ARRIVED, IT WAS GONE.
"HE FOLLOWED IT TO ROME. THEN IT WAS IN GREECE."
"YOU SAID SOMETHING ABOUT SOUTH AMERICA..."
"YES. THAT IS WHERE HE IS NOW."
"RIGHT ***NOW?"***
"YES. HE ARRIVED ELEVEN HOURS AGO."
"ALL RIGHT, SO IT'S IN SOUTH AMERICA..."

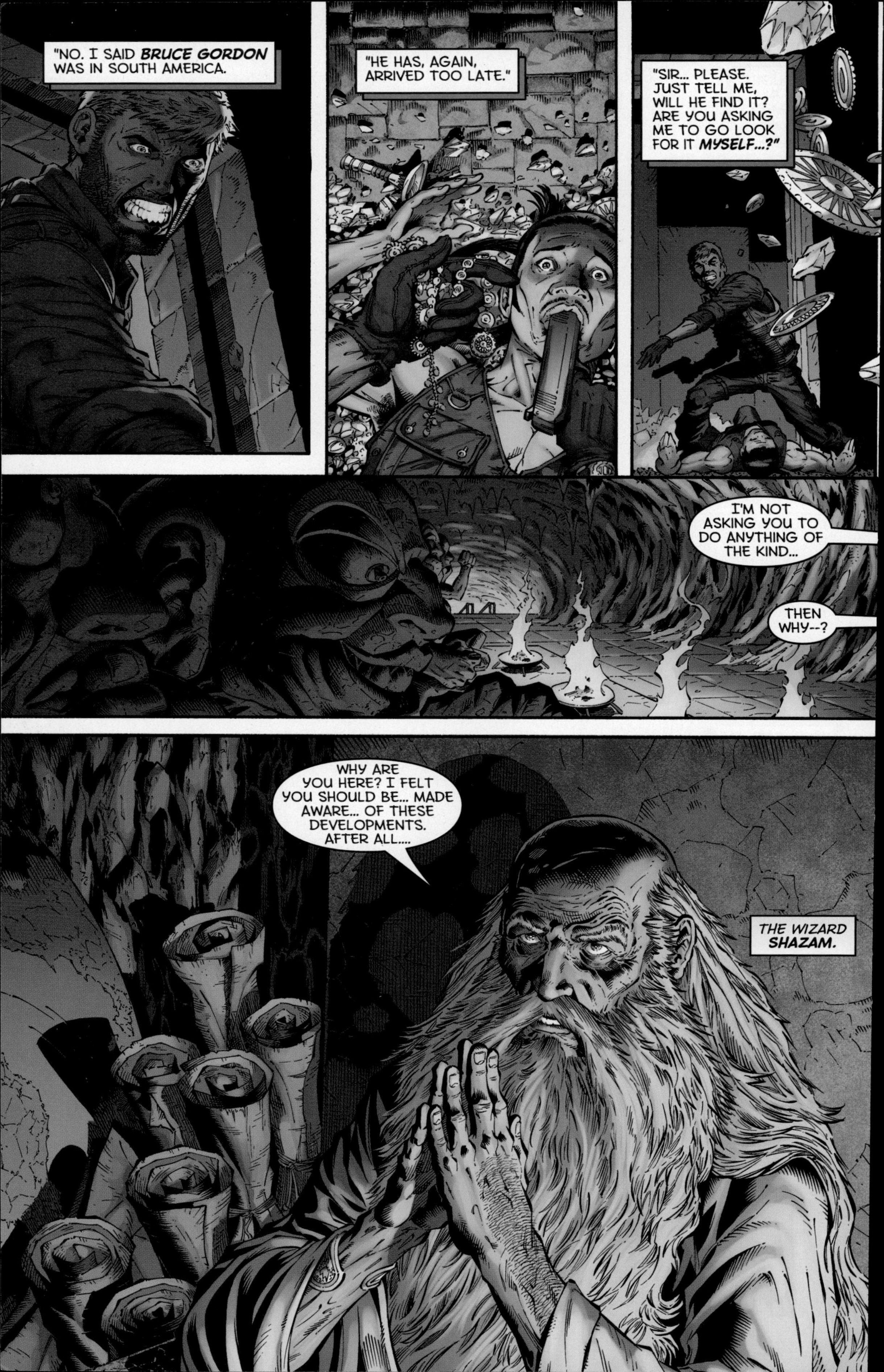
"NO. I SAID **BRUCE GORDON** WAS IN SOUTH AMERICA.
"HE HAS, AGAIN, ARRIVED TOO LATE."
"SIR... PLEASE. JUST TELL ME, WILL HE FIND IT? ARE YOU ASKING ME TO GO LOOK FOR IT ***MYSELF...?"***
I'M NOT ASKING YOU TO DO ANYTHING OF THE KIND...
THEN WHY--?
WHY ARE YOU HERE? I FELT YOU SHOULD BE... MADE AWARE... OF THESE DEVELOPMENTS. AFTER ALL....
THE WIZARD **SHAZAM.**

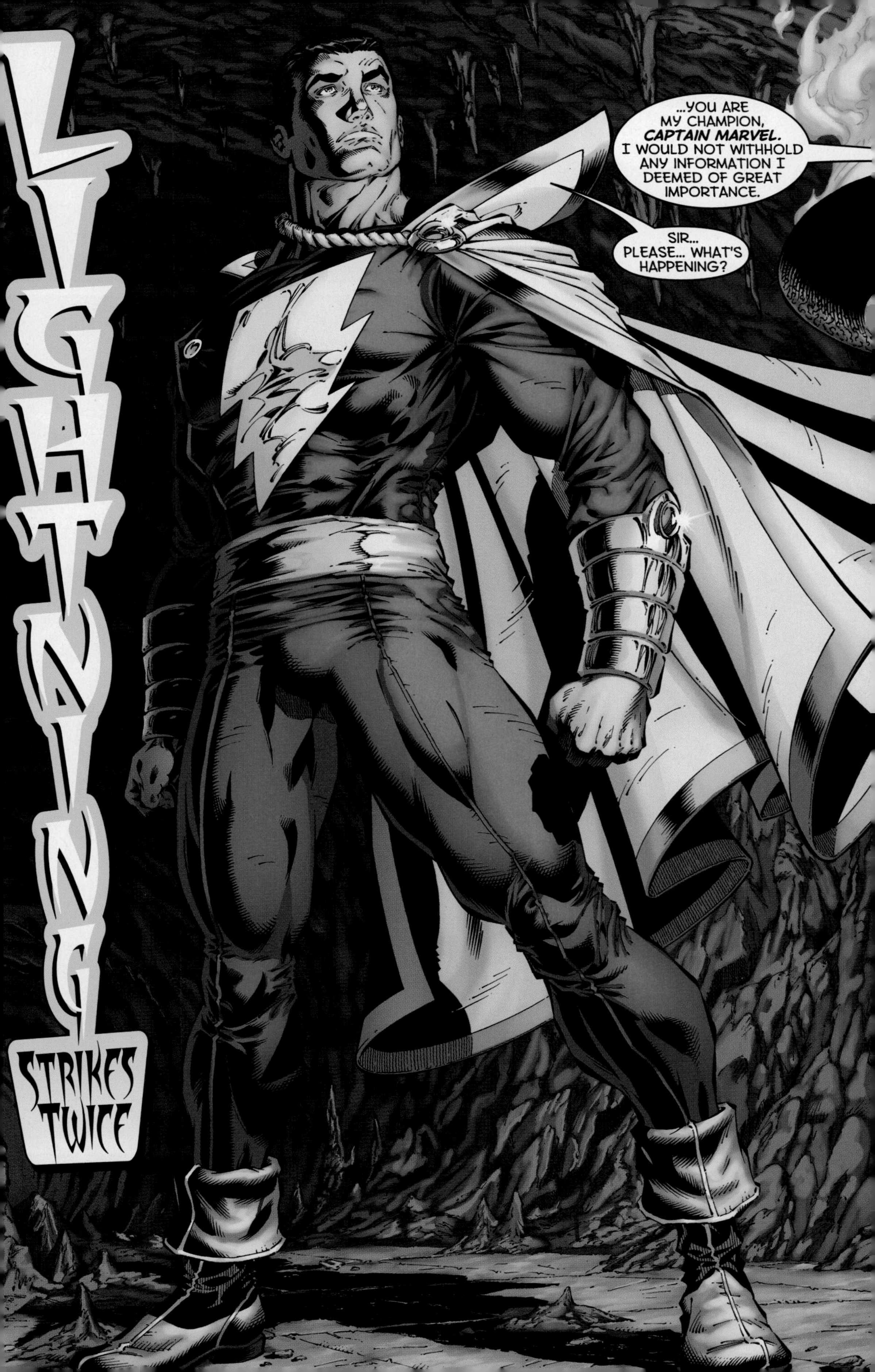
LIGHTNING
STRIKES TWICE
...YOU ARE MY CHAMPION, **CAPTAIN MARVEL.** I WOULD NOT WITHHOLD ANY INFORMATION I DEEMED OF GREAT IMPORTANCE.
SIR... PLEASE... WHAT'S HAPPENING?

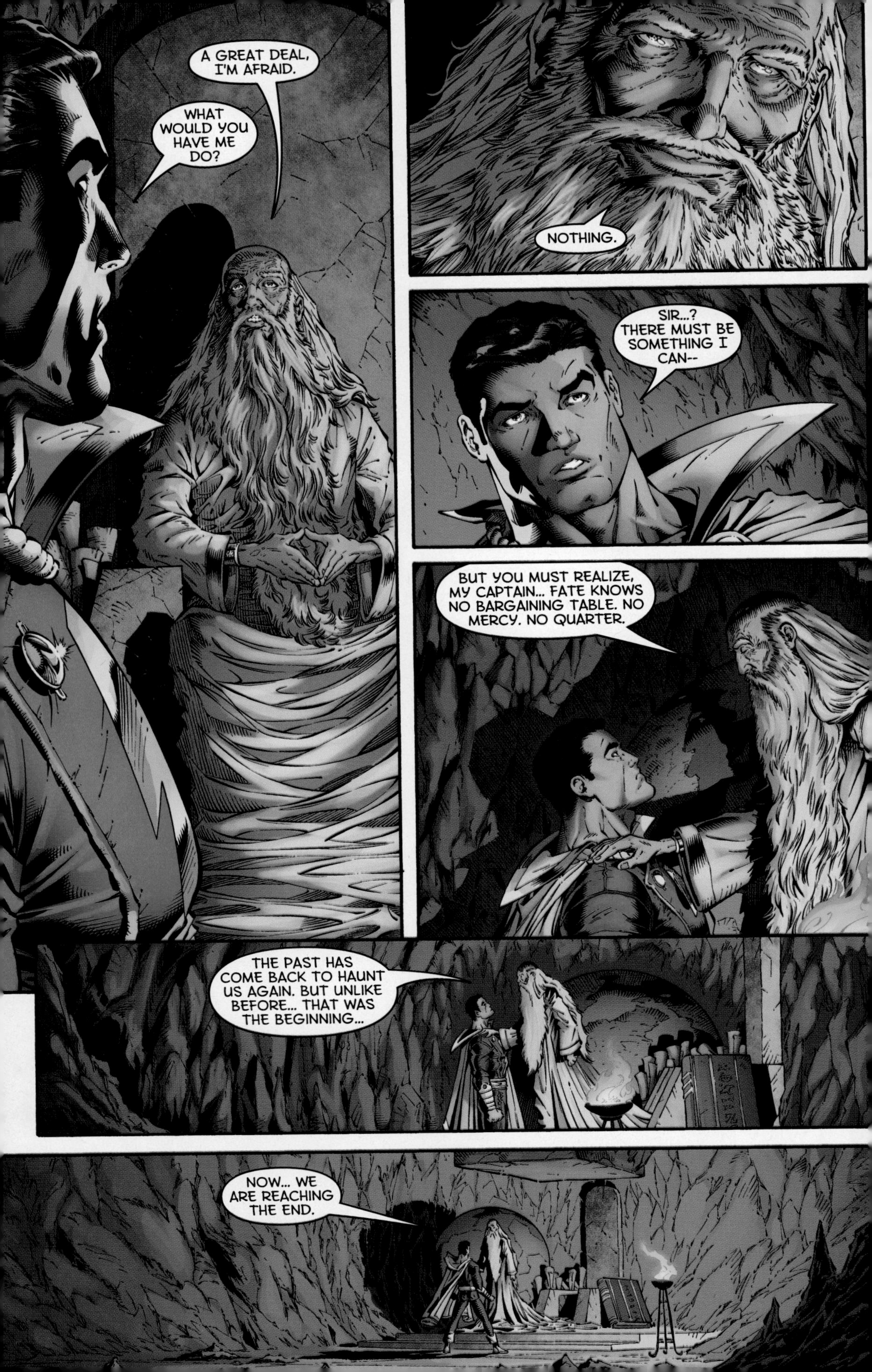
A GREAT DEAL, I'M AFRAID.
WHAT WOULD YOU HAVE ME DO?
NOTHING.
SIR...? THERE MUST BE SOMETHING I CAN--
BUT YOU MUST REALIZE, MY CAPTAIN... FATE KNOWS NO BARGAINING TABLE. NO MERCY. NO QUARTER.
THE PAST HAS COME BACK TO HAUNT US AGAIN. BUT UNLIKE BEFORE... THAT WAS THE BEGINNING...
NOW... WE ARE REACHING THE END.

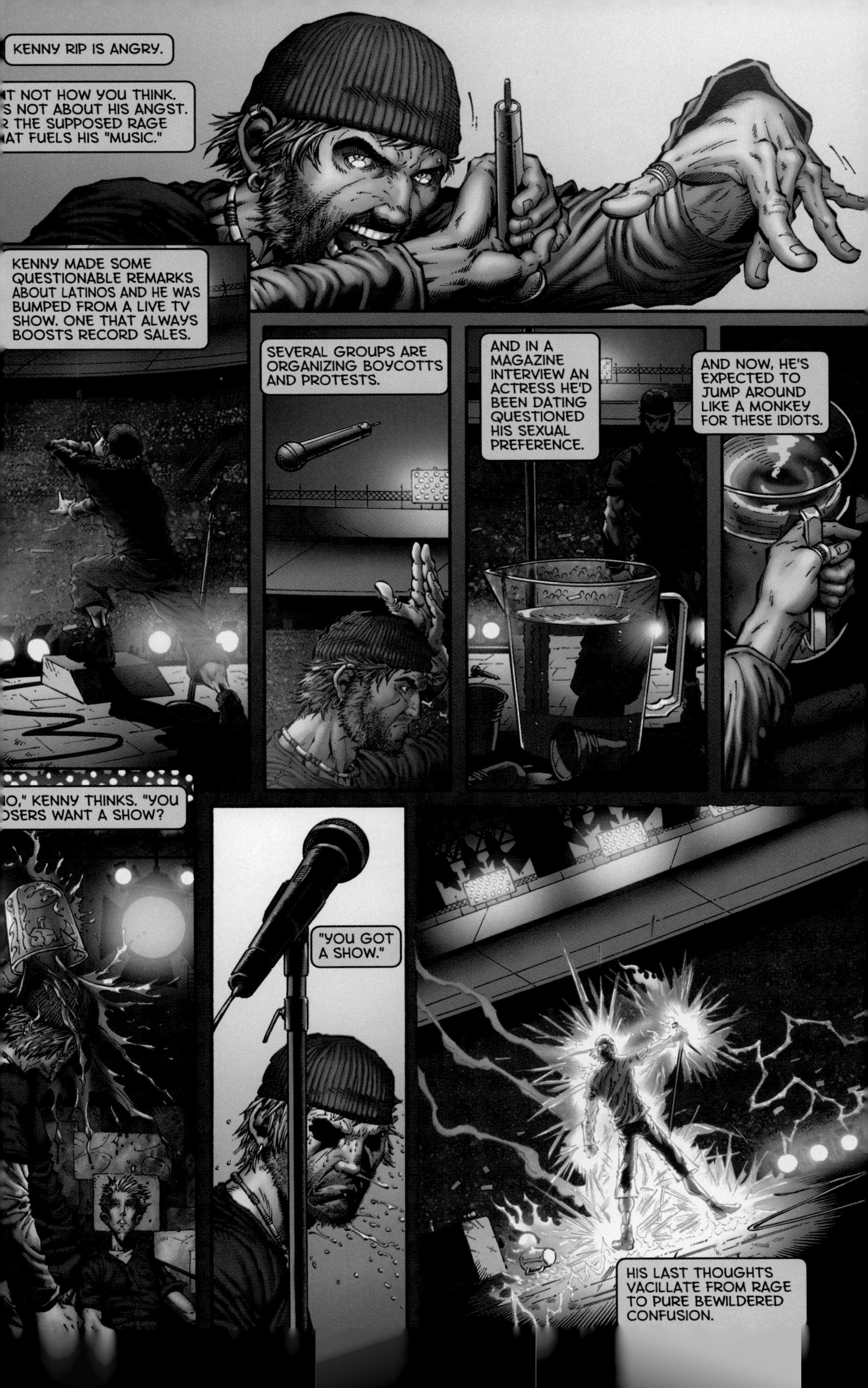
KENNY RIP IS ANGRY.
T NOT HOW YOU THINK. S NOT ABOUT HIS ANGST. R THE SUPPOSED RAGE AT FUELS HIS "MUSIC."
KENNY MADE SOME QUESTIONABLE REMARKS ABOUT LATINOS AND HE WAS BUMPED FROM A LIVE TV SHOW. ONE THAT ALWAYS BOOSTS RECORD SALES.
SEVERAL GROUPS ARE ORGANIZING BOYCOTTS AND PROTESTS.
AND IN A MAGAZINE INTERVIEW AN ACTRESS HE'D BEEN DATING QUESTIONED HIS SEXUAL PREFERENCE.
AND NOW, HE'S EXPECTED TO JUMP AROUND LIKE A MONKEY FOR THESE IDIOTS.
O," KENNY THINKS. "YOU OSERS WANT A SHOW?
"YOU GOT A SHOW."
HIS LAST THOUGHTS VACILLATE FROM RAGE TO PURE BEWILDERED CONFUSION.

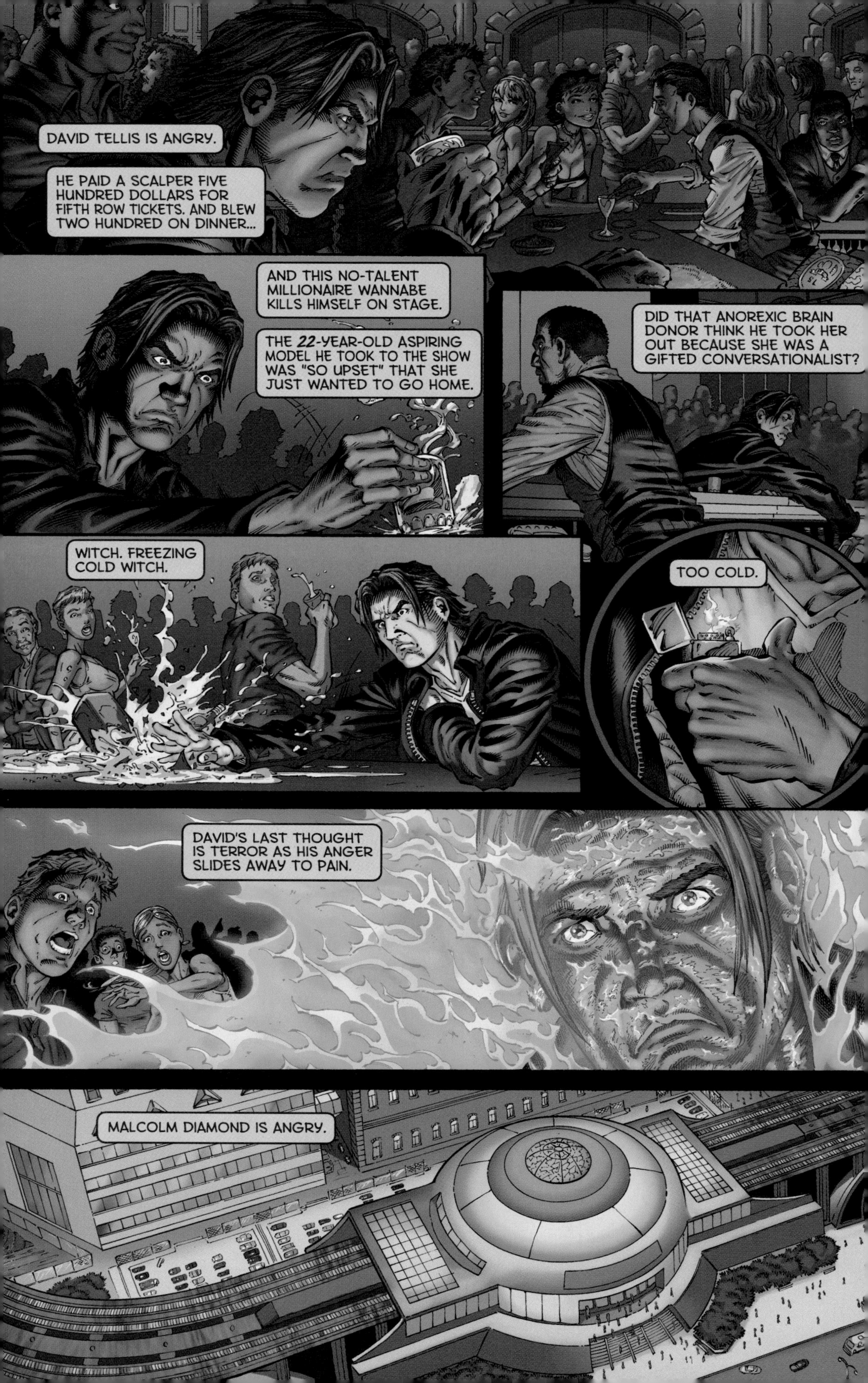
DAVID TELLIS IS ANGRY.
HE PAID A SCALPER FIVE HUNDRED DOLLARS FOR FIFTH ROW TICKETS. AND BLEW TWO HUNDRED ON DINNER...
AND THIS NO-TALENT MILLIONAIRE WANNABE KILLS HIMSELF ON STAGE.
THE 22-YEAR-OLD ASPIRING MODEL HE TOOK TO THE SHOW WAS "SO UPSET" THAT SHE JUST WANTED TO GO HOME.
DID THAT ANOREXIC BRAIN DONOR THINK HE TOOK HER OUT BECAUSE SHE WAS A GIFTED CONVERSATIONALIST?
WITCH. FREEZING COLD WITCH.
TOO COLD.
DAVID'S LAST THOUGHT IS TERROR AS HIS ANGER SLIDES AWAY TO PAIN.
MALCOLM DIAMOND IS ANGRY.

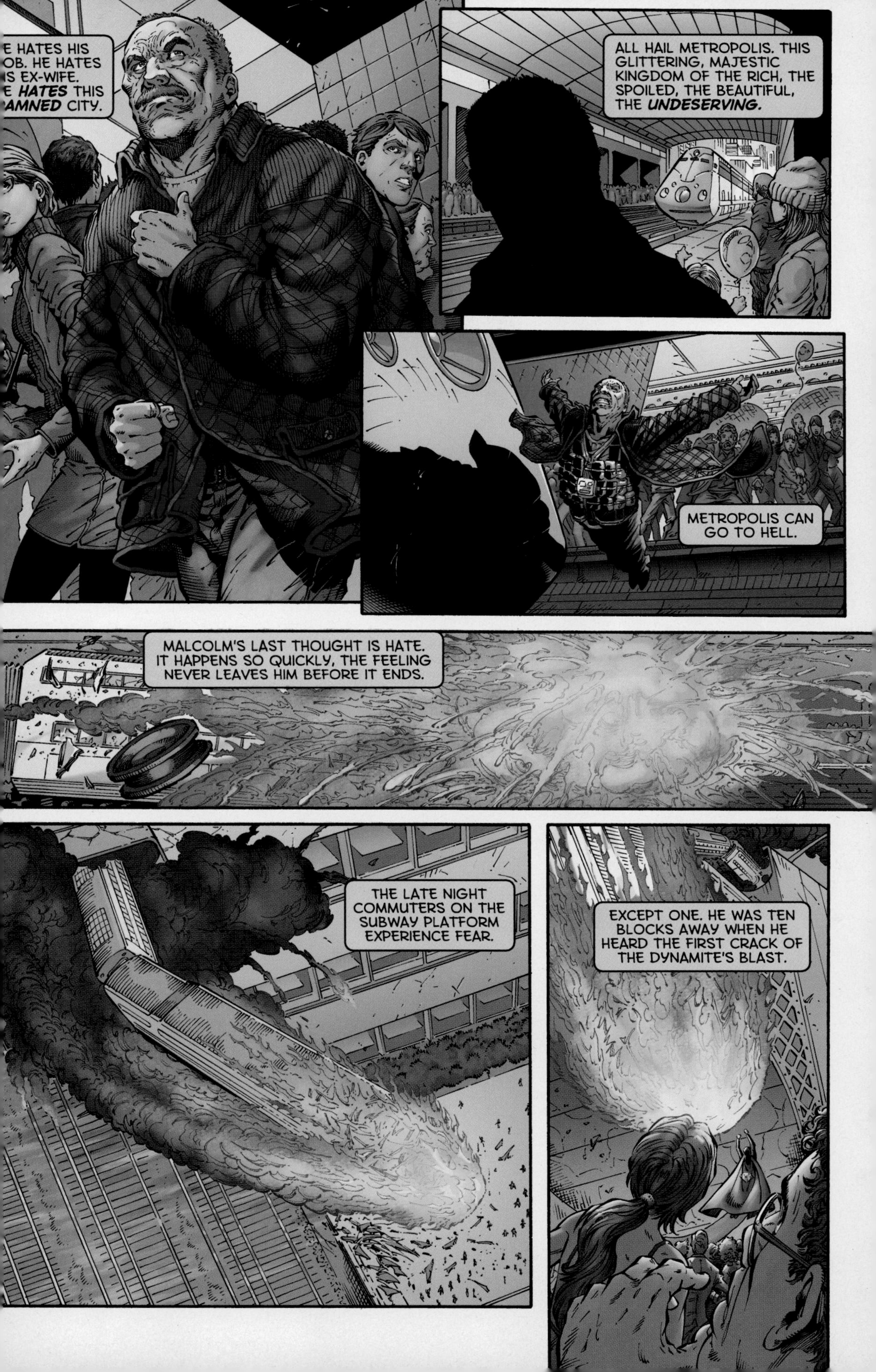
E HATES HIS
OB. HE HATES
S EX-WIFE.
E HATES THIS
AMNED CITY.
ALL HAIL METROPOLIS. THIS GLITTERING, MAJESTIC KINGDOM OF THE RICH, THE SPOILED, THE BEAUTIFUL, THE UNDESERVING.
METROPOLIS CAN GO TO HELL.
MALCOLM'S LAST THOUGHT IS HATE. IT HAPPENS SO QUICKLY, THE FEELING NEVER LEAVES HIM BEFORE IT ENDS.
THE LATE NIGHT COMMUTERS ON THE SUBWAY PLATFORM EXPERIENCE FEAR.
EXCEPT ONE. HE WAS TEN BLOCKS AWAY WHEN HE HEARD THE FIRST CRACK OF THE DYNAMITE'S BLAST.

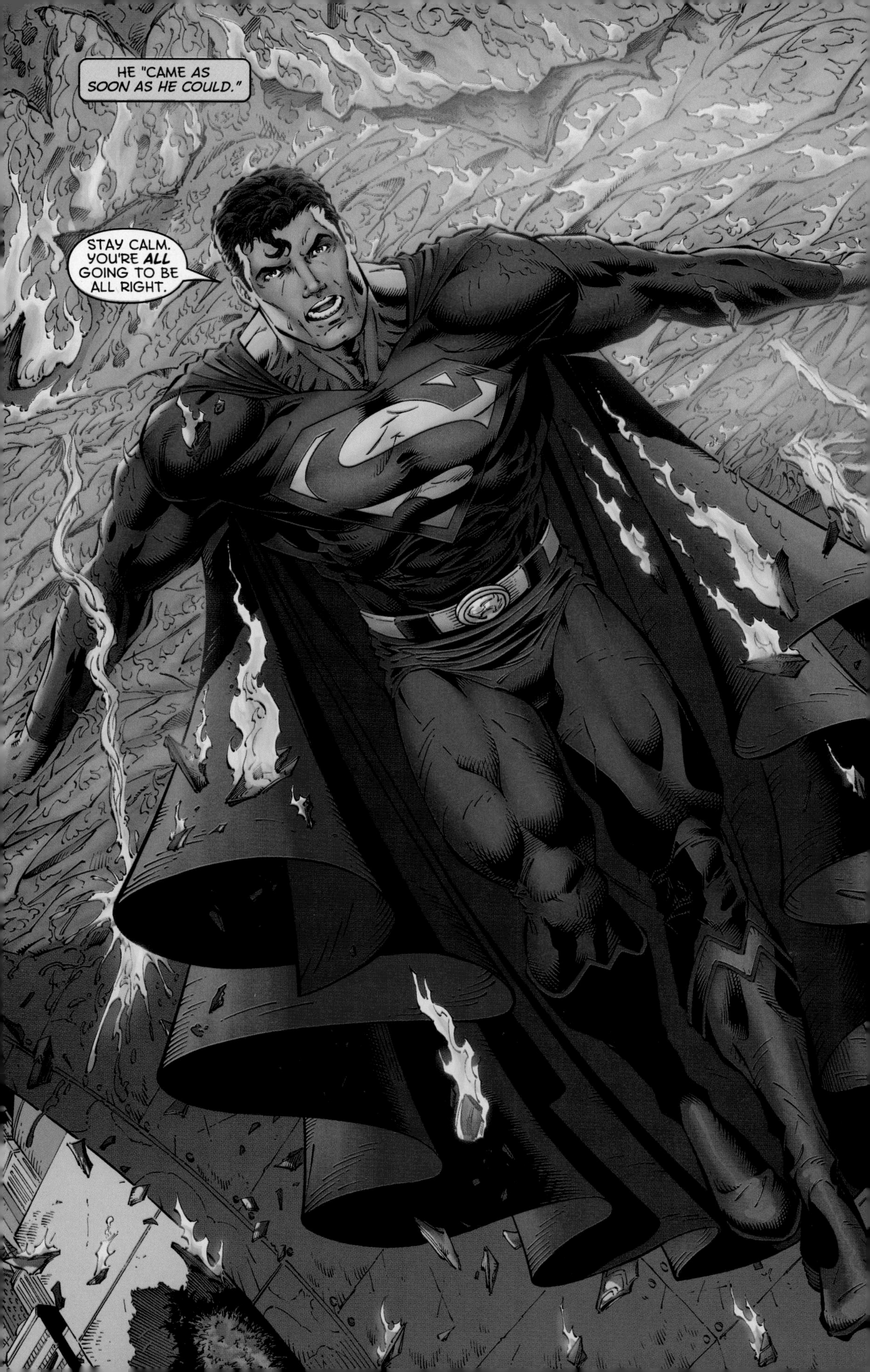
HE "CAME AS SOON AS HE COULD."
STAY CALM. YOU'RE ALL GOING TO BE ALL RIGHT.

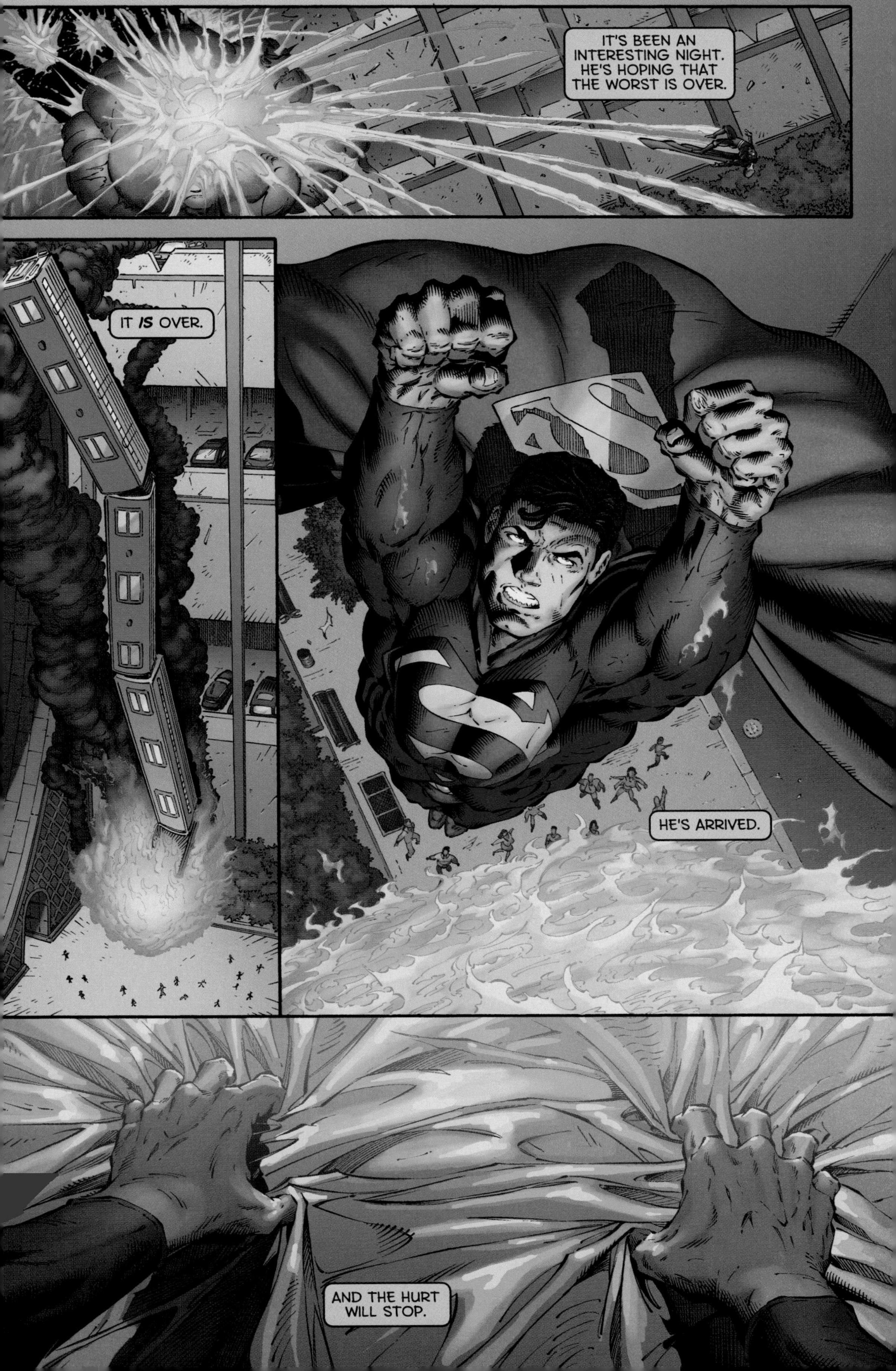
IT'S BEEN AN INTERESTING NIGHT. HE'S HOPING THAT THE WORST IS OVER.
IT *IS* OVER.
HE'S ARRIVED.
AND THE HURT WILL STOP.

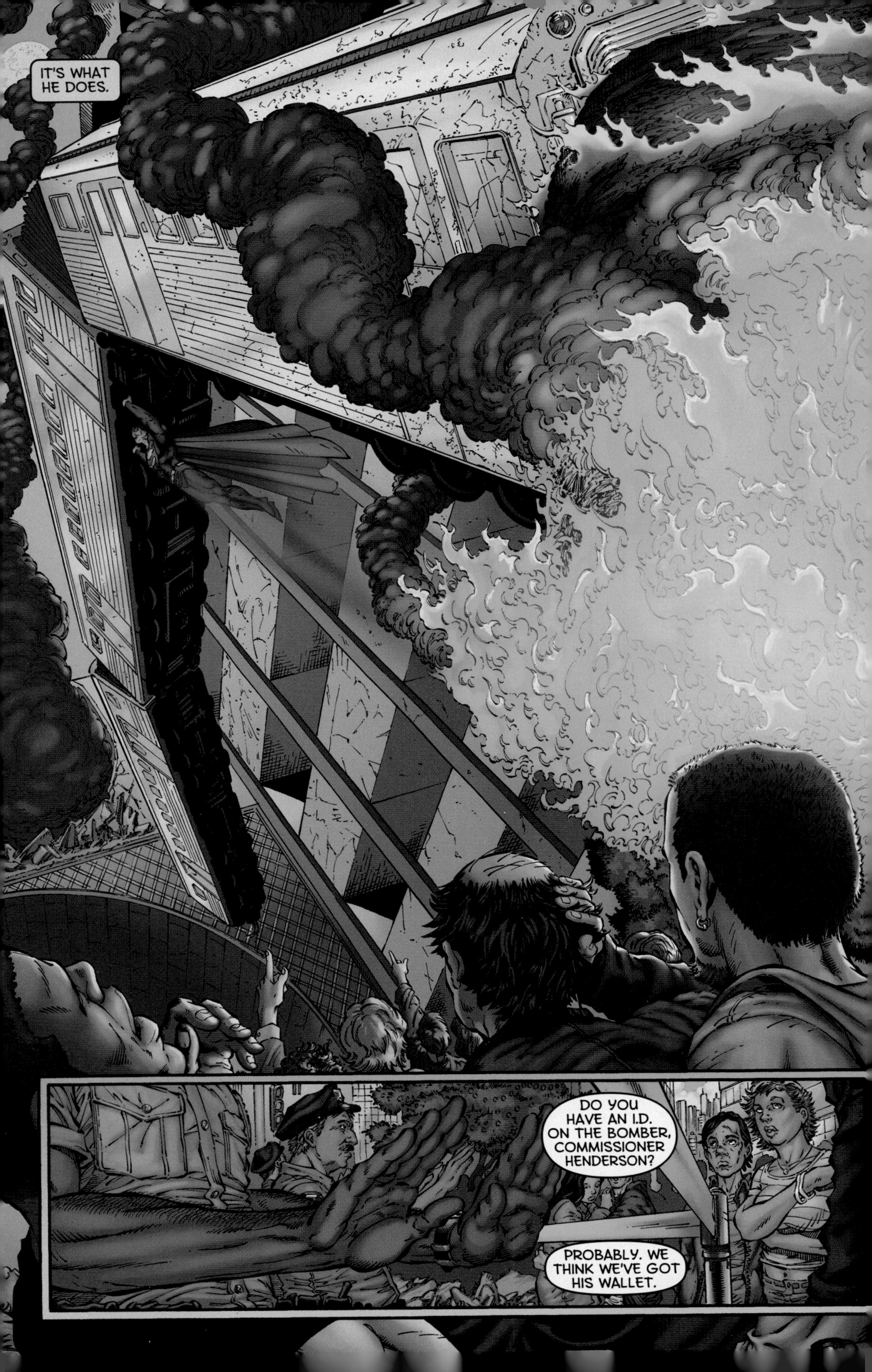
IT'S WHAT HE DOES.
DO YOU HAVE AN I.D. ON THE BOMBER, COMMISSIONER HENDERSON?
PROBABLY. WE THINK WE'VE GOT HIS WALLET.

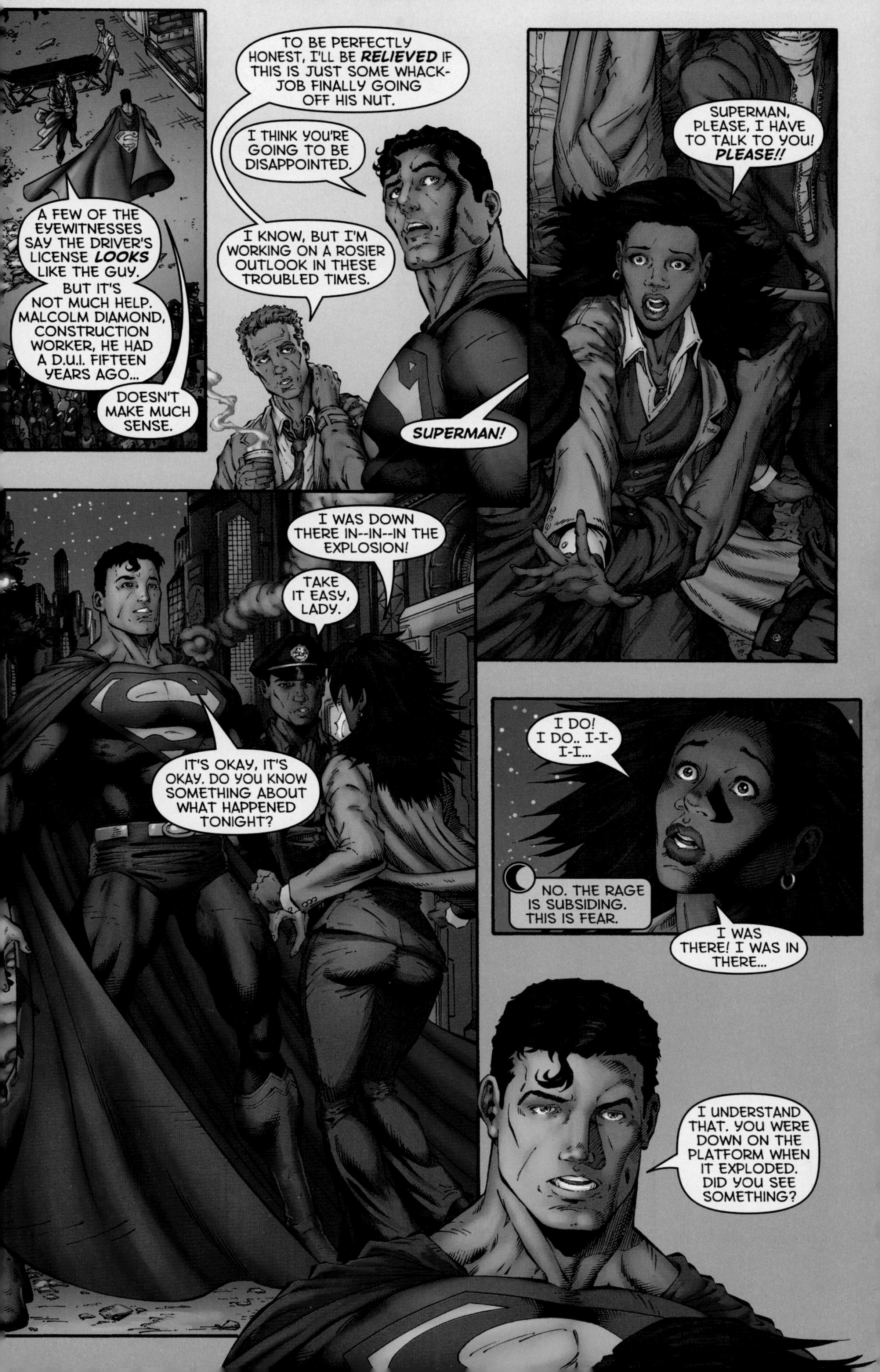
A FEW OF THE EYEWITNESSES SAY THE DRIVER'S LICENSE *LOOKS* LIKE THE GUY.
BUT IT'S NOT MUCH HELP. MALCOLM DIAMOND, CONSTRUCTION WORKER, HE HAD A D.U.I. FIFTEEN YEARS AGO...
DOESN'T MAKE MUCH SENSE.
TO BE PERFECTLY HONEST, I'LL BE *RELIEVED* IF THIS IS JUST SOME WHACK-JOB FINALLY GOING OFF HIS NUT.
I THINK YOU'RE GOING TO BE DISAPPOINTED.
I KNOW, BUT I'M WORKING ON A ROSIER OUTLOOK IN THESE TROUBLED TIMES.
SUPERMAN!
SUPERMAN, PLEASE, I HAVE TO TALK TO YOU! *PLEASE!!*
I WAS DOWN THERE IN--IN--IN THE EXPLOSION!
TAKE IT EASY, LADY.
IT'S OKAY, IT'S OKAY. DO YOU KNOW SOMETHING ABOUT WHAT HAPPENED TONIGHT?
I DO! I DO.. I-I-I-I...
NO. THE RAGE IS SUBSIDING. THIS IS FEAR.
I WAS THERE! I WAS IN THERE...
I UNDERSTAND THAT. YOU WERE DOWN ON THE PLATFORM WHEN IT EXPLODED. DID YOU SEE SOMETHING?

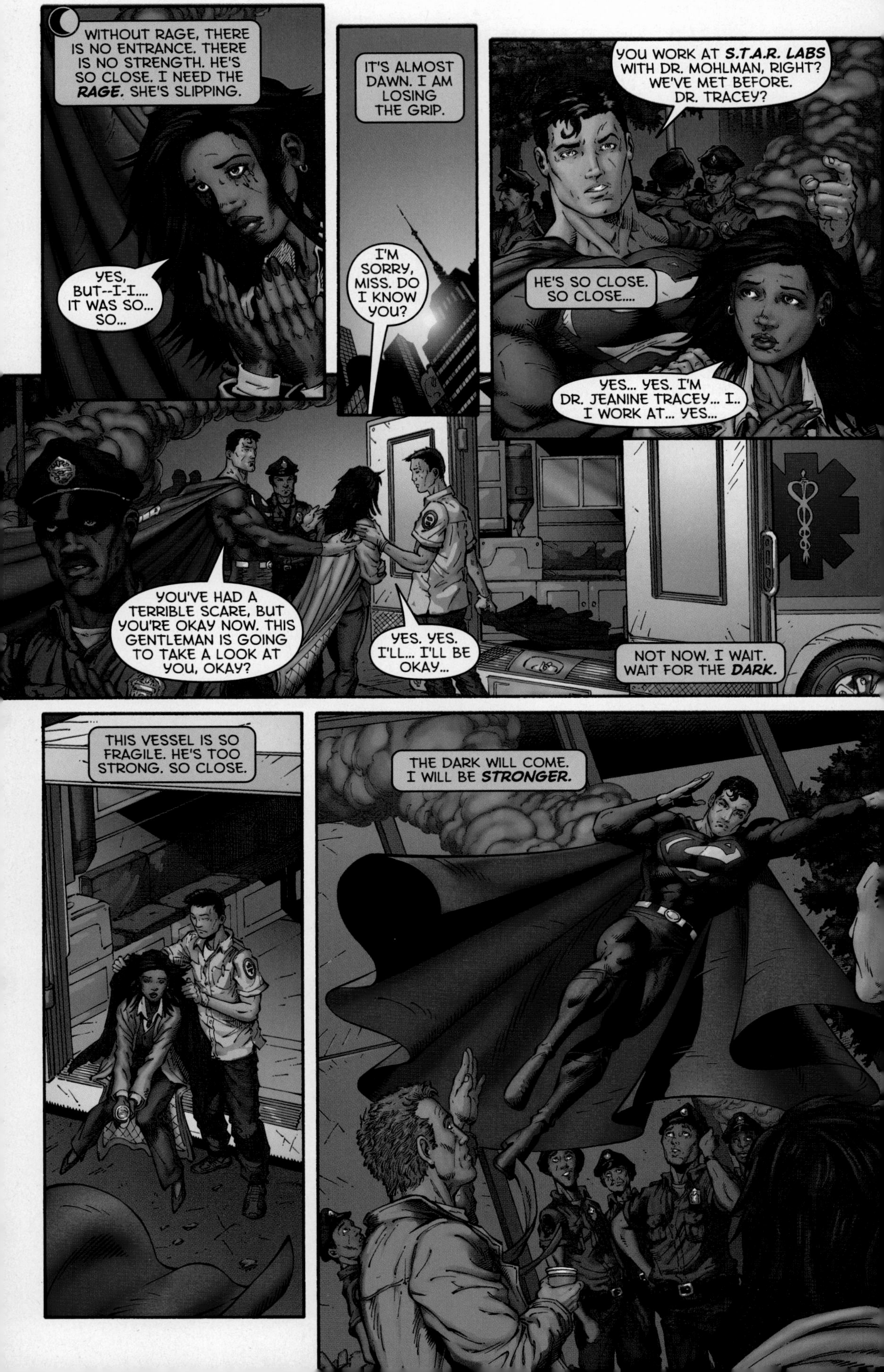
WITHOUT RAGE, THERE IS NO ENTRANCE. THERE IS NO STRENGTH. HE'S SO CLOSE. I NEED THE RAGE. SHE'S SLIPPING.
YES, BUT--I-I.... IT WAS SO... SO...
IT'S ALMOST DAWN. I AM LOSING THE GRIP.
I'M SORRY, MISS. DO I KNOW YOU?
YOU WORK AT S.T.A.R. LABS WITH DR. MOHLMAN, RIGHT? WE'VE MET BEFORE. DR. TRACEY?
HE'S SO CLOSE. SO CLOSE....
YES... YES. I'M DR. JEANINE TRACEY... I.. I WORK AT... YES...
YOU'VE HAD A TERRIBLE SCARE, BUT YOU'RE OKAY NOW. THIS GENTLEMAN IS GOING TO TAKE A LOOK AT YOU, OKAY?
YES. YES. I'LL... I'LL BE OKAY...
NOT NOW. I WAIT. WAIT FOR THE DARK.
THIS VESSEL IS SO FRAGILE. HE'S TOO STRONG. SO CLOSE.
THE DARK WILL COME. I WILL BE STRONGER.

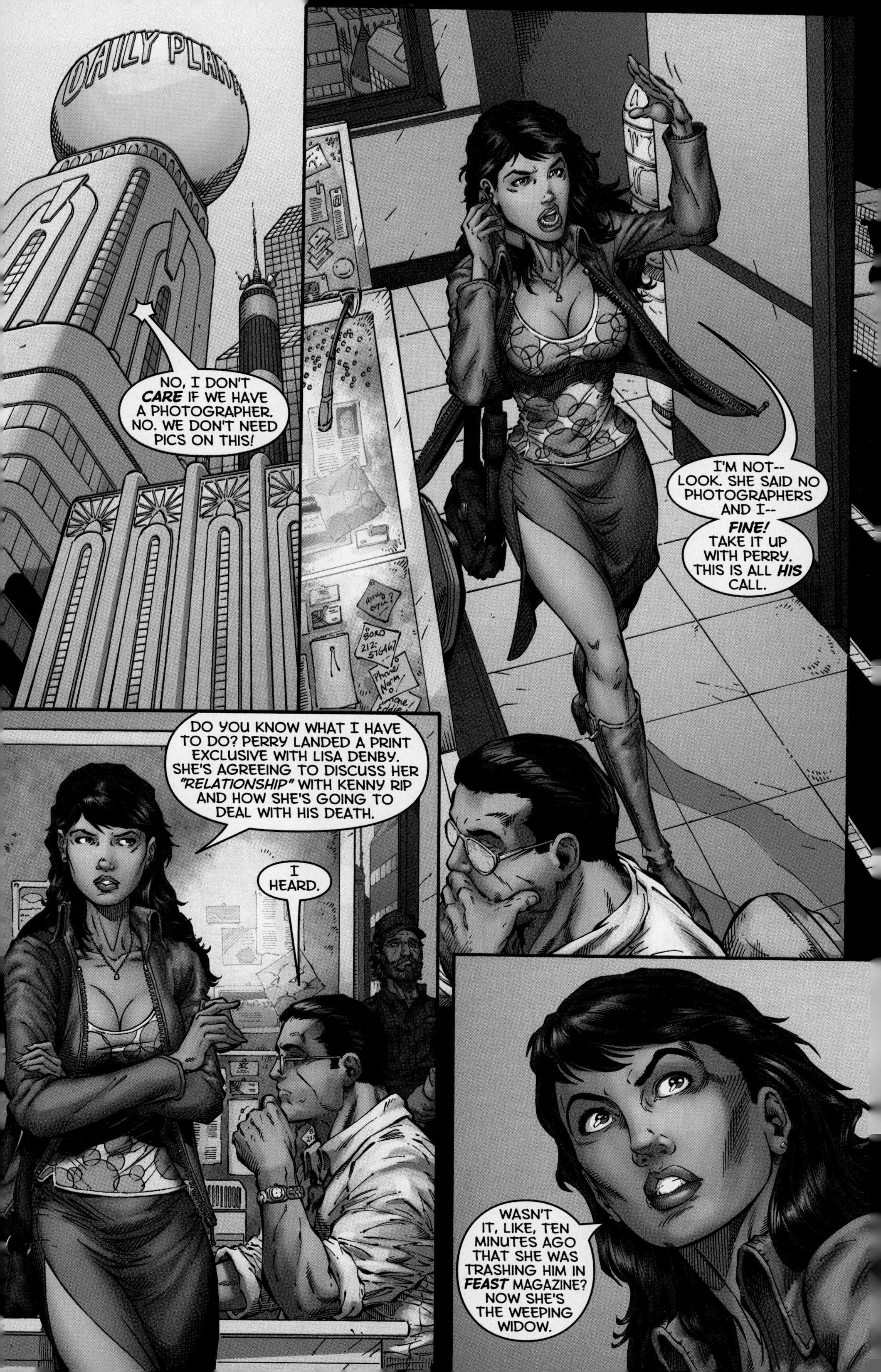

NO, I DON'T **CARE** IF WE HAVE A PHOTOGRAPHER. NO. WE DON'T NEED PICS ON THIS!
I'M NOT-- LOOK. SHE SAID NO PHOTOGRAPHERS AND I-- **FINE!** TAKE IT UP WITH PERRY. THIS IS ALL **HIS** CALL.
DO YOU KNOW WHAT I HAVE TO DO? PERRY LANDED A PRINT EXCLUSIVE WITH LISA DENBY. SHE'S AGREEING TO DISCUSS HER *"RELATIONSHIP"* WITH KENNY RIP AND HOW SHE'S GOING TO DEAL WITH HIS DEATH.
I HEARD.
WASN'T IT, LIKE, TEN MINUTES AGO THAT SHE WAS TRASHING HIM IN **FEAST** MAGAZINE? NOW SHE'S THE WEEPING WIDOW.

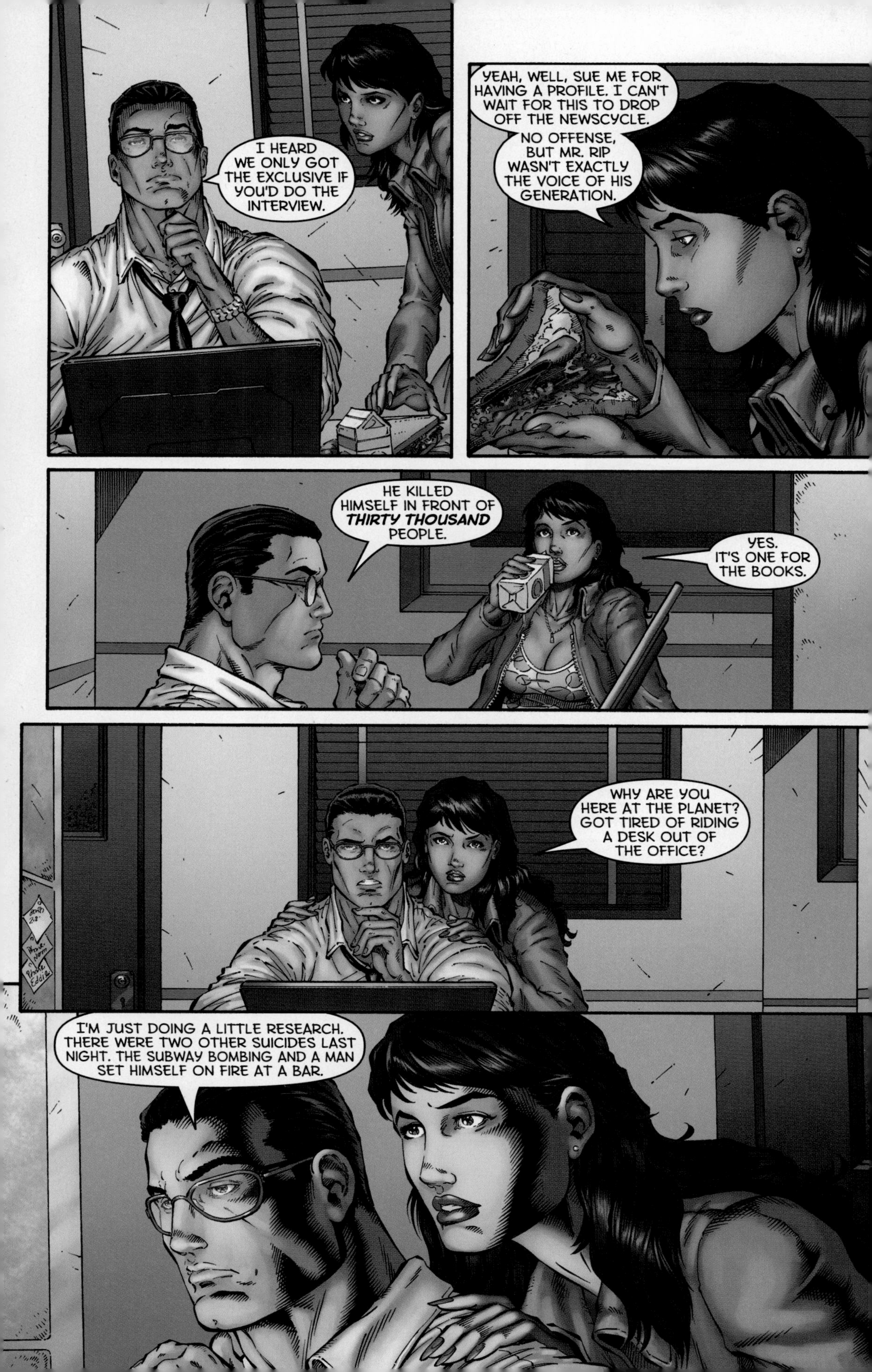
I HEARD WE ONLY GOT THE EXCLUSIVE IF YOU'D DO THE INTERVIEW.
YEAH, WELL, SUE ME FOR HAVING A PROFILE. I CAN'T WAIT FOR THIS TO DROP OFF THE NEWSCYCLE.
NO OFFENSE, BUT MR. RIP WASN'T EXACTLY THE VOICE OF HIS GENERATION.
HE KILLED HIMSELF IN FRONT OF ***THIRTY THOUSAND*** PEOPLE.
YES. IT'S ONE FOR THE BOOKS.
WHY ARE YOU HERE AT THE PLANET? GOT TIRED OF RIDING A DESK OUT OF THE OFFICE?
I'M JUST DOING A LITTLE RESEARCH. THERE WERE TWO OTHER SUICIDES LAST NIGHT. THE SUBWAY BOMBING AND A MAN SET HIMSELF ON FIRE AT A BAR.

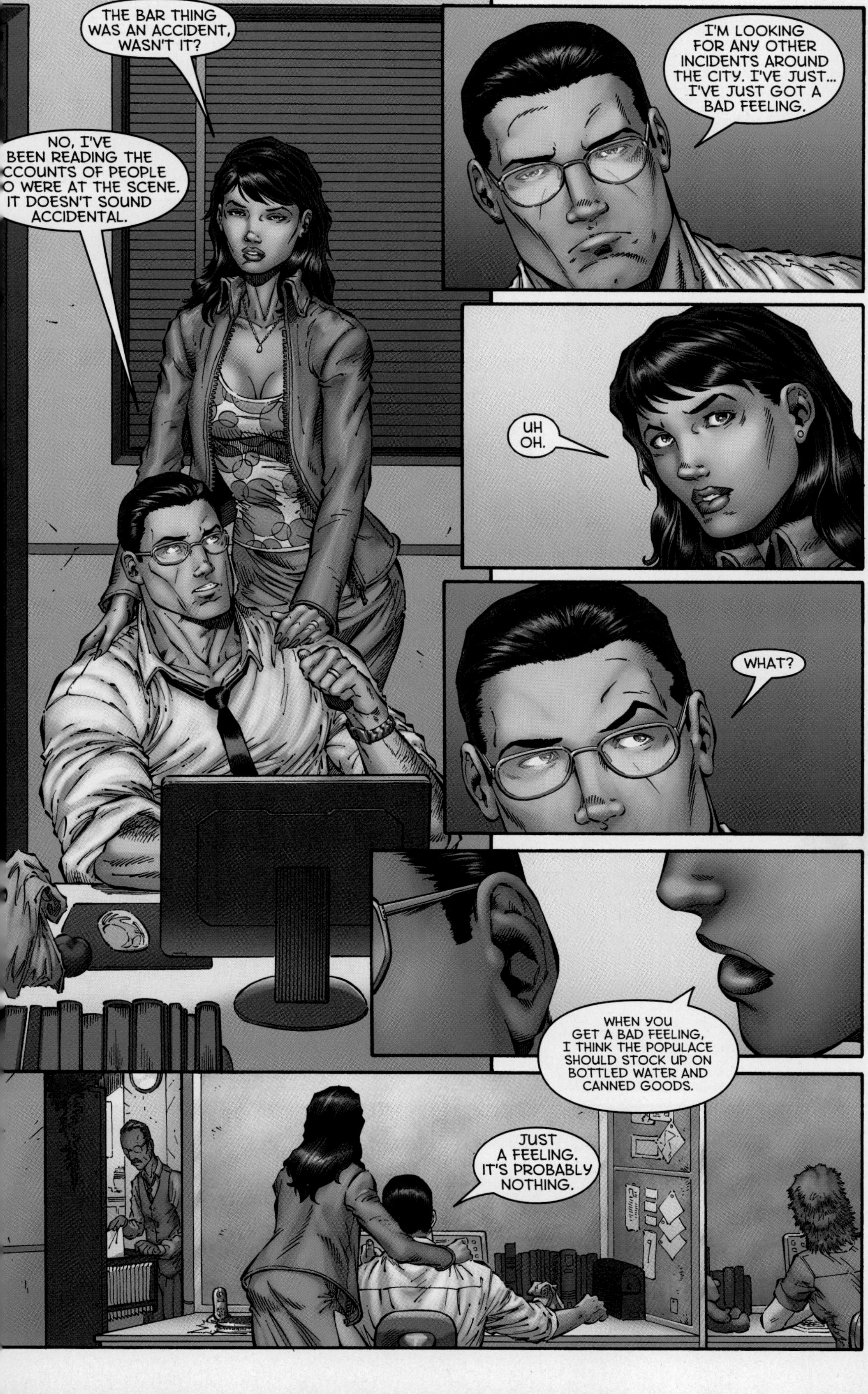
THE BAR THING WAS AN ACCIDENT, WASN'T IT?
NO, I'VE BEEN READING THE CCOUNTS OF PEOPLE O WERE AT THE SCENE. IT DOESN'T SOUND ACCIDENTAL.
I'M LOOKING FOR ANY OTHER INCIDENTS AROUND THE CITY. I'VE JUST... I'VE JUST GOT A BAD FEELING.
UH OH.
WHAT?
WHEN YOU GET A BAD FEELING, I THINK THE POPULACE SHOULD STOCK UP ON BOTTLED WATER AND CANNED GOODS.
JUST A FEELING. IT'S PROBABLY NOTHING.

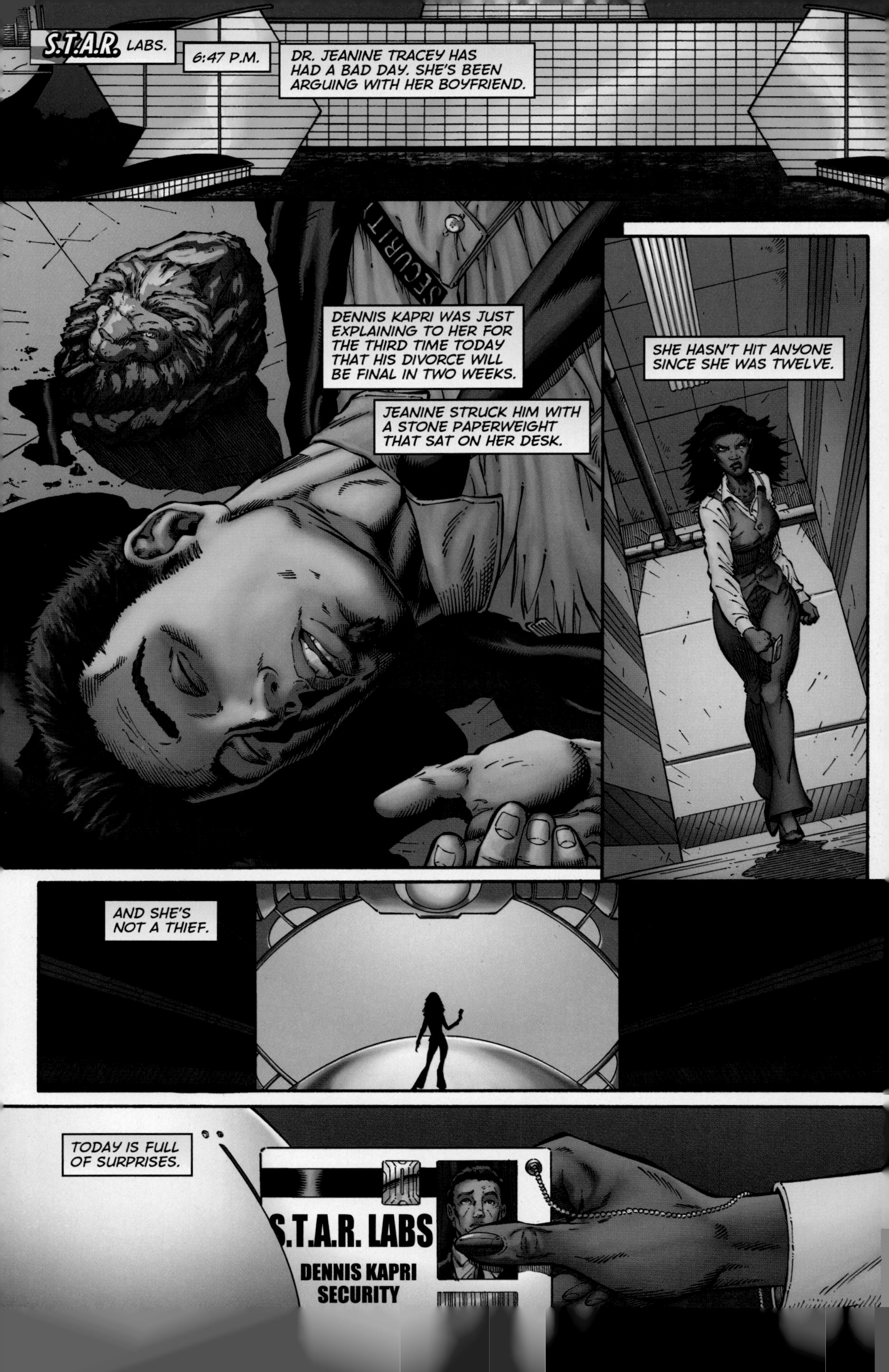
S.T.A.R. LABS.
6:47 P.M.
DR. JEANINE TRACEY HAS HAD A BAD DAY. SHE'S BEEN ARGUING WITH HER BOYFRIEND.
SECURITY
DENNIS KAPRI WAS JUST EXPLAINING TO HER FOR THE THIRD TIME TODAY THAT HIS DIVORCE WILL BE FINAL IN TWO WEEKS.
JEANINE STRUCK HIM WITH A STONE PAPERWEIGHT THAT SAT ON HER DESK.
SHE HASN'T HIT ANYONE SINCE SHE WAS TWELVE.
AND SHE'S NOT A THIEF.
TODAY IS FULL OF SURPRISES.
S.T.A.R. LABS
DENNIS KAPRI
SECURITY

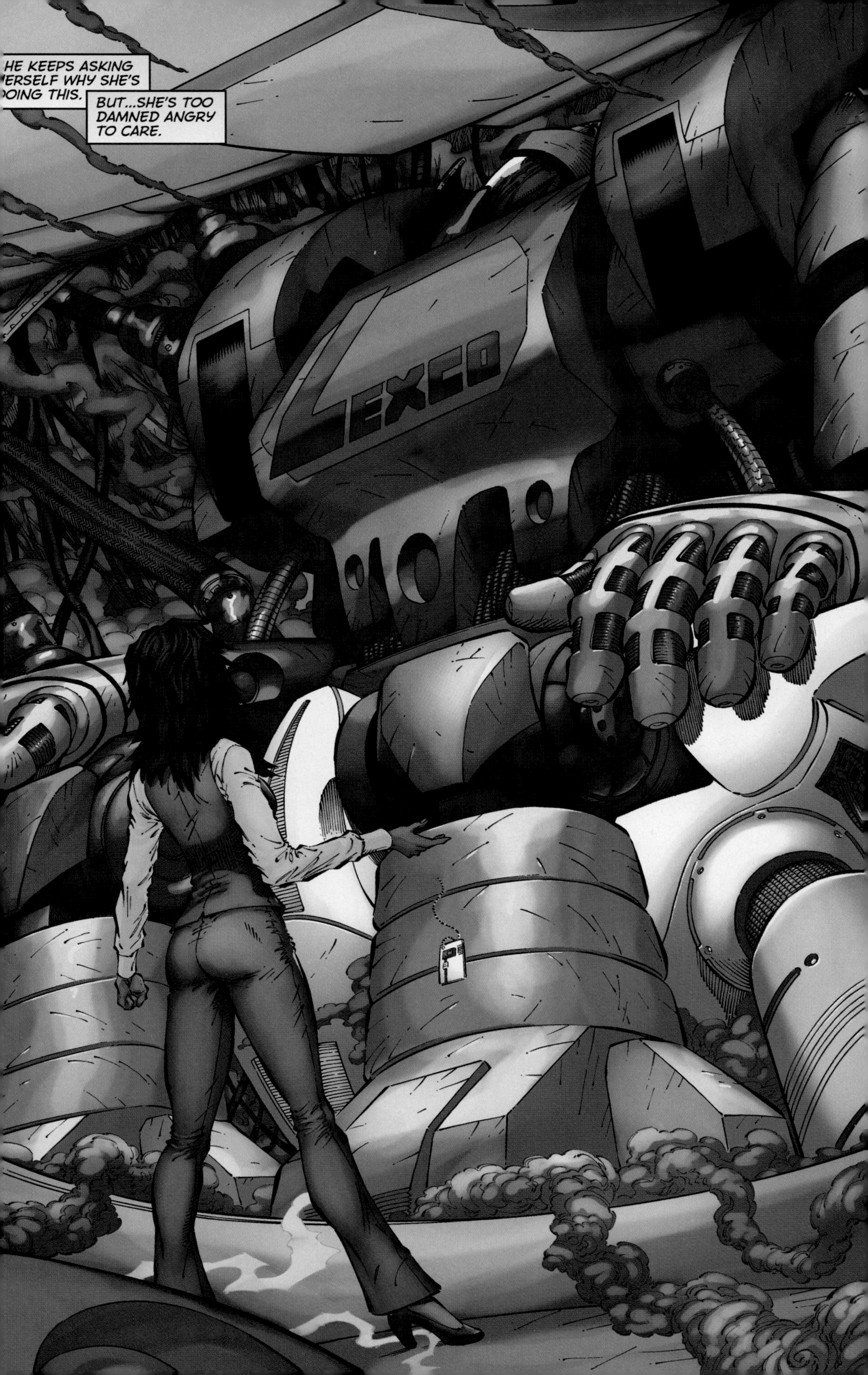
HE KEEPS ASKING
ERSELF WHY SHE'S
OING THIS.
BUT...SHE'S TOO DAMNED ANGRY TO CARE.

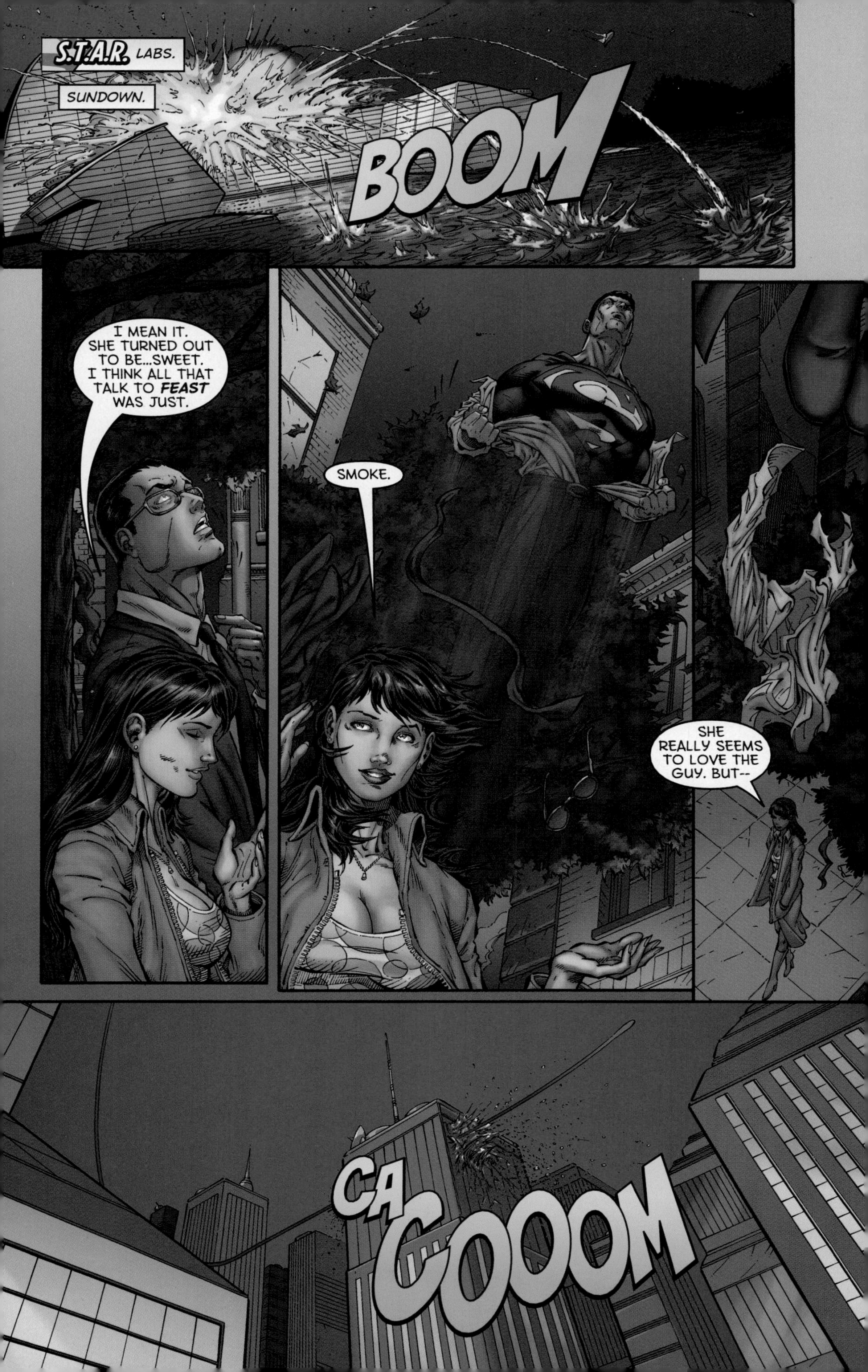
S.T.A.R. LABS.
SUNDOWN.
BOOM
I MEAN IT. SHE TURNED OUT TO BE...SWEET. I THINK ALL THAT TALK TO FEAST WAS JUST.
SMOKE.
SHE REALLY SEEMS TO LOVE THE GUY. BUT--
CA COOOM

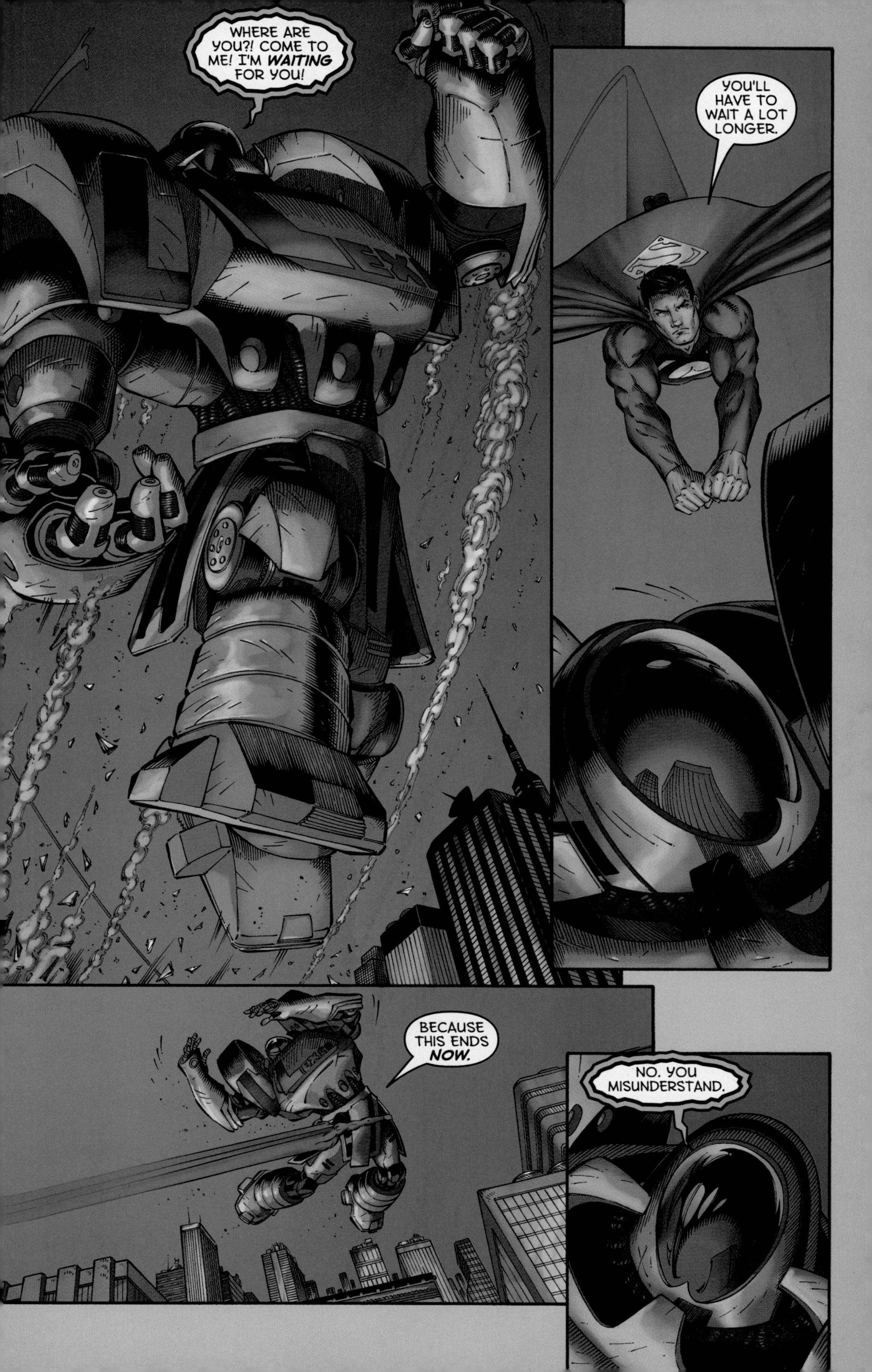
WHERE ARE YOU?! COME TO ME! I'M *WAITING* FOR YOU!
YOU'LL HAVE TO WAIT A LOT LONGER.
BECAUSE THIS ENDS *NOW.*
NO. YOU MISUNDERSTAND.

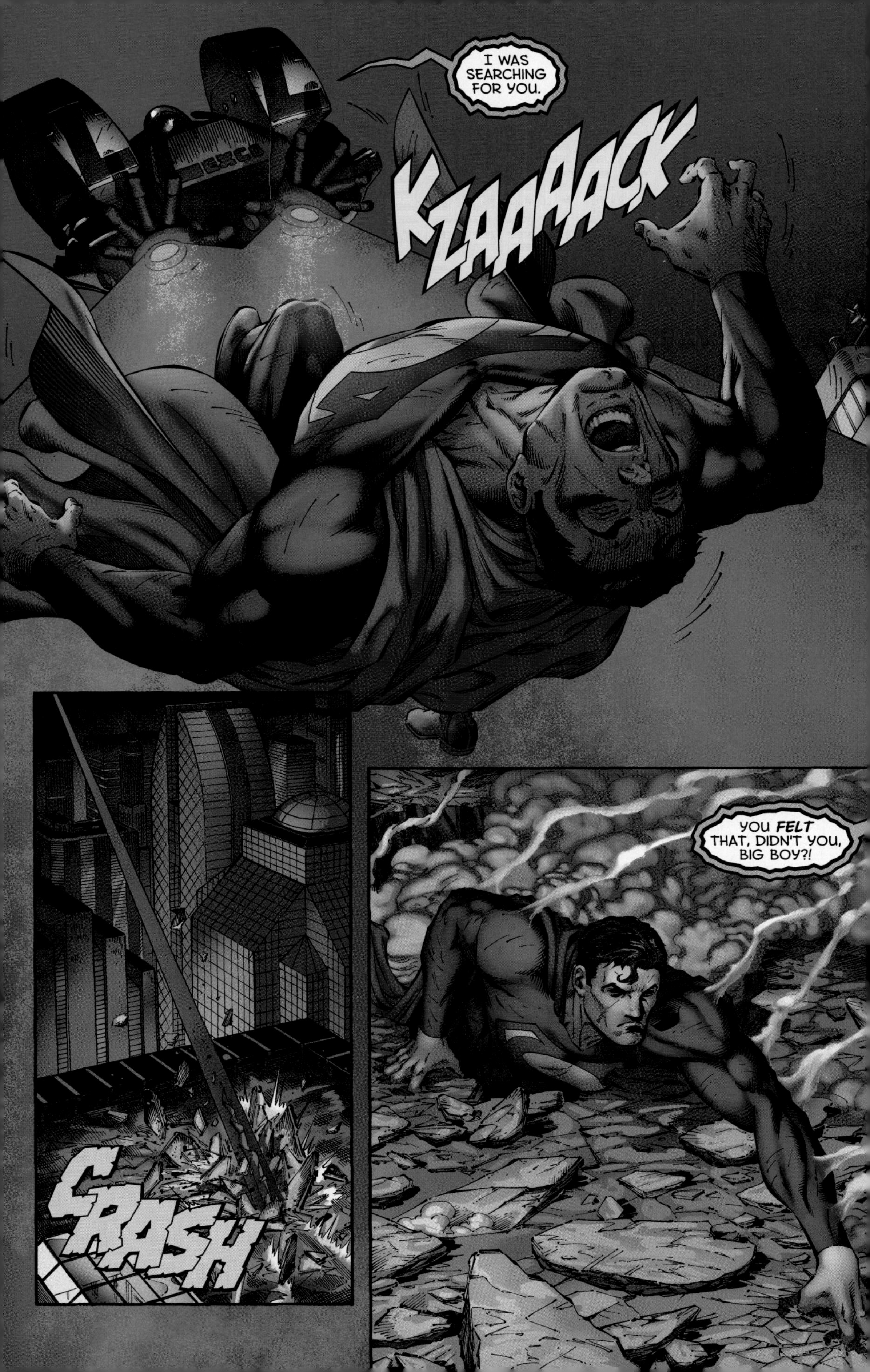
I WAS SEARCHING FOR YOU.
KZAAAACK
CRASH
YOU **FELT** THAT, DIDN'T YOU, BIG BOY?!

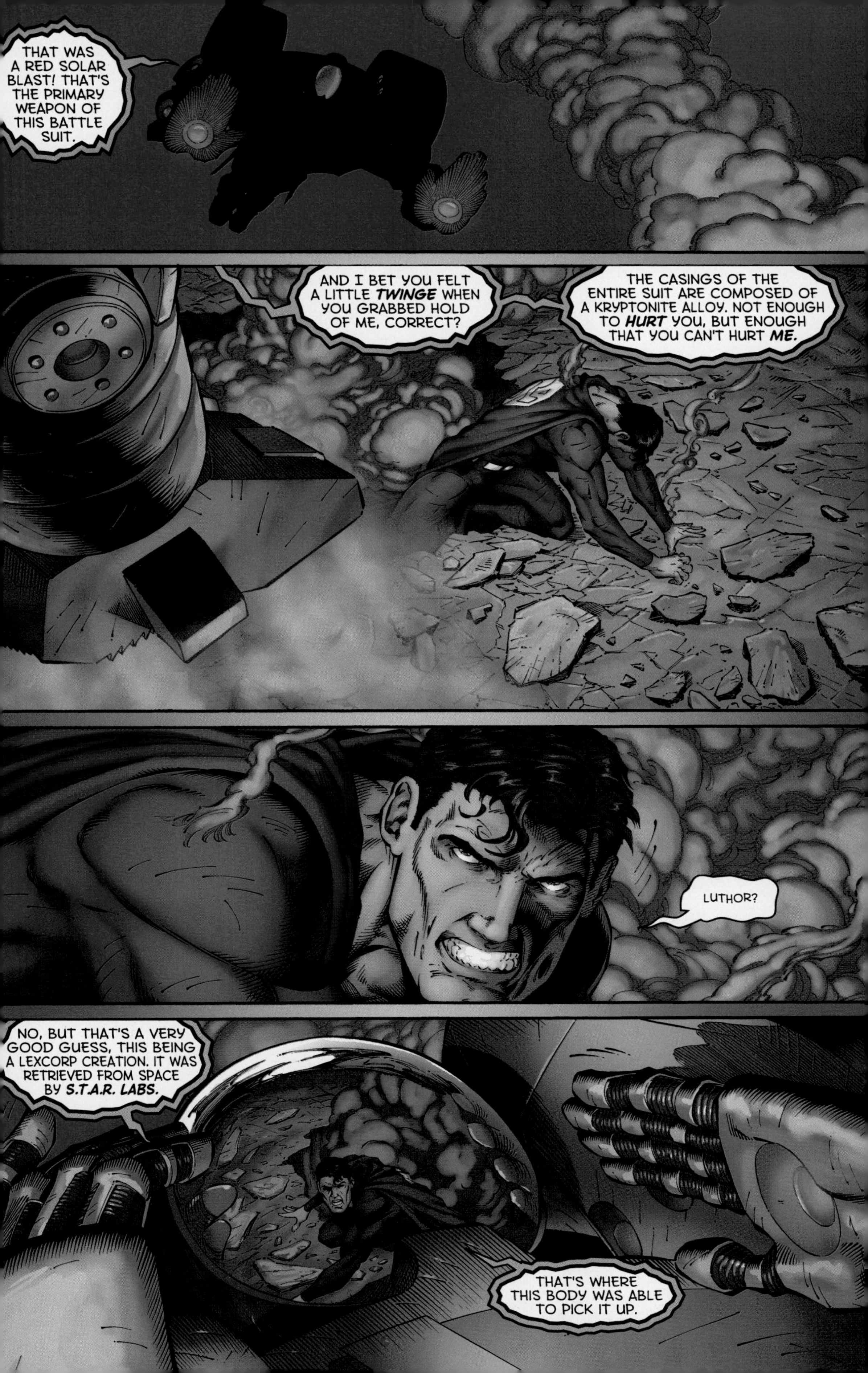
THAT WAS A RED SOLAR BLAST! THAT'S THE PRIMARY WEAPON OF THIS BATTLE SUIT.
AND I BET YOU FELT A LITTLE **TWINGE** WHEN YOU GRABBED HOLD OF ME, CORRECT?
THE CASINGS OF THE ENTIRE SUIT ARE COMPOSED OF A KRYPTONITE ALLOY. NOT ENOUGH TO **HURT** YOU, BUT ENOUGH THAT YOU CAN'T HURT **ME.**
LUTHOR?
NO, BUT THAT'S A VERY GOOD GUESS, THIS BEING A LEXCORP CREATION. IT WAS RETRIEVED FROM SPACE BY **S.T.A.R. LABS.**
THAT'S WHERE THIS BODY WAS ABLE TO PICK IT UP.

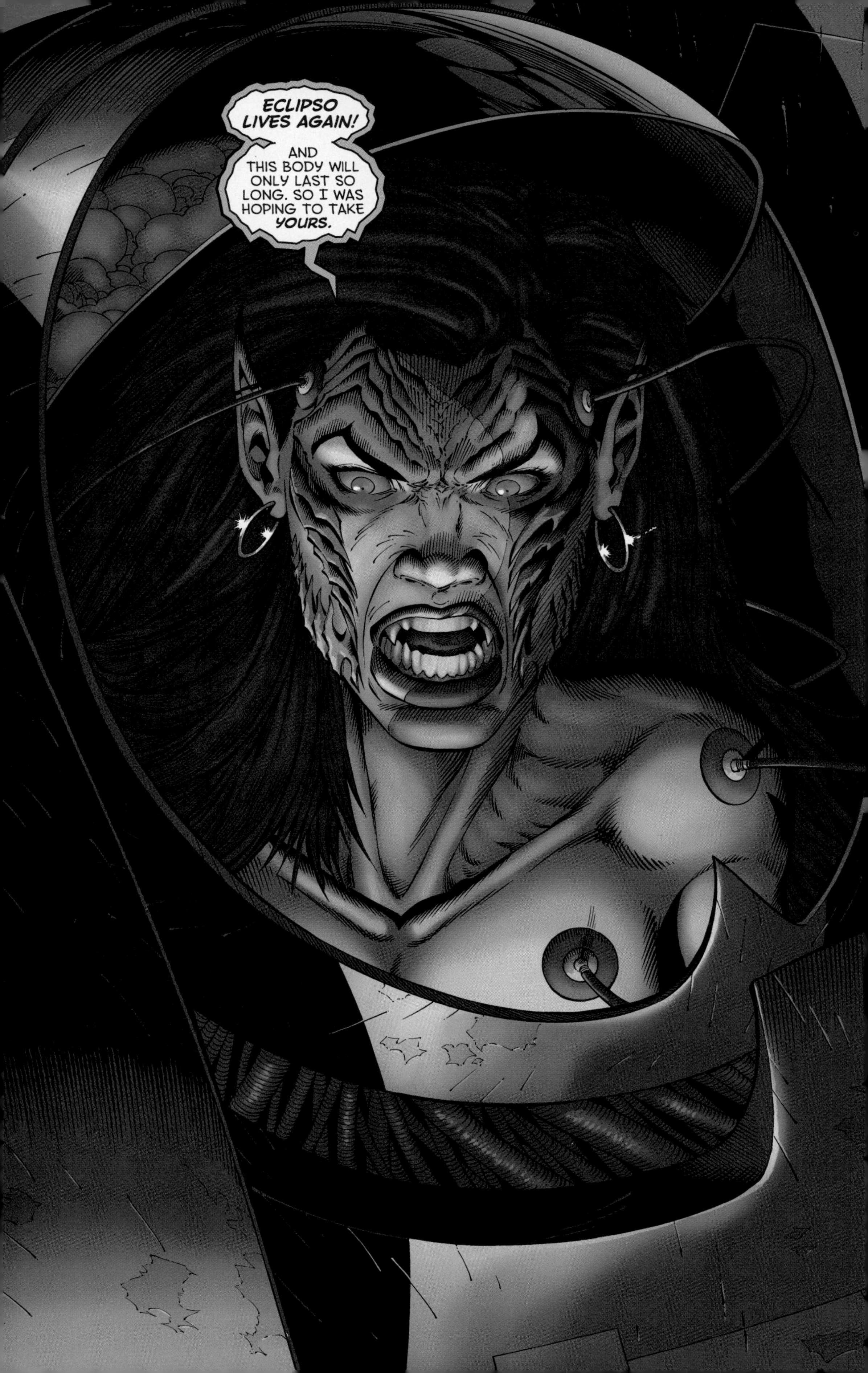
ECLIPSO LIVES AGAIN!
AND THIS BODY WILL ONLY LAST SO LONG. SO I WAS HOPING TO TAKE YOURS.

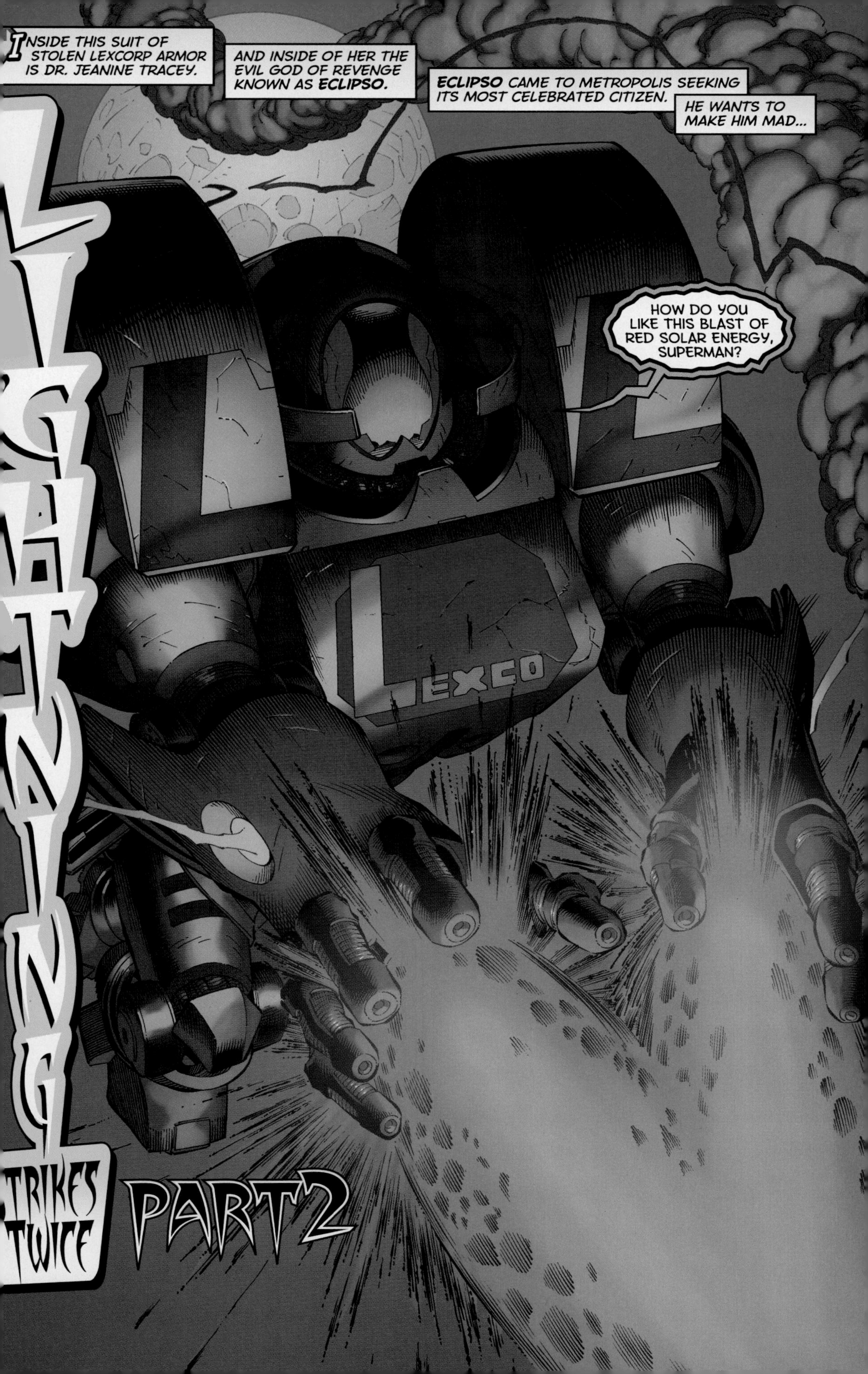
INSIDE THIS SUIT OF STOLEN LEXCORP ARMOR IS DR. JEANINE TRACEY.
AND INSIDE OF HER THE EVIL GOD OF REVENGE KNOWN AS ECLIPSO.
ECLIPSO CAME TO METROPOLIS SEEKING ITS MOST CELEBRATED CITIZEN.
HE WANTS TO MAKE HIM MAD...
HOW DO YOU LIKE THIS BLAST OF RED SOLAR ENERGY, SUPERMAN?
LIGHTNING
STRIKES TWICE
PART 2

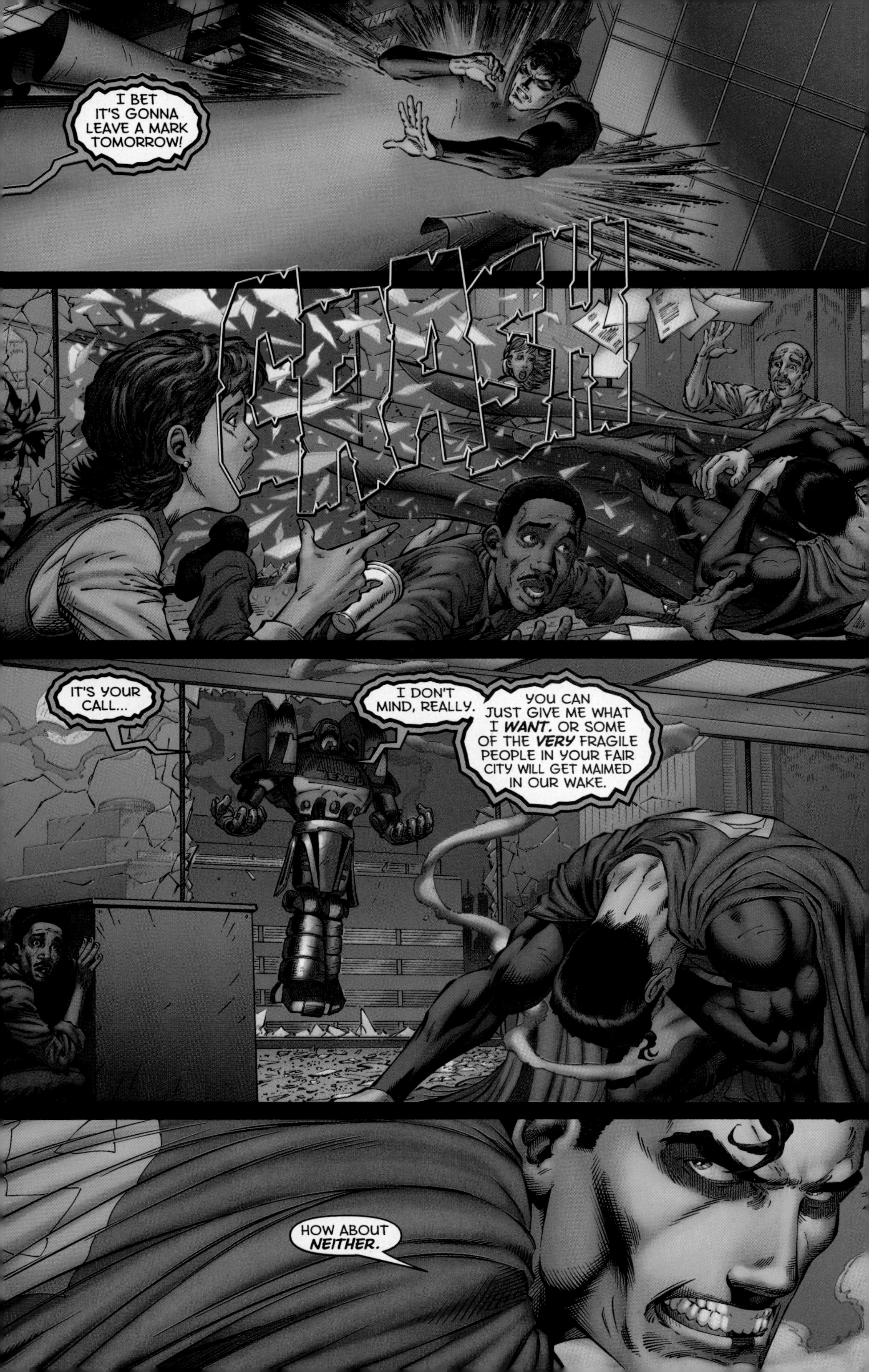
I BET IT'S GONNA LEAVE A MARK TOMORROW!
CRASH
IT'S YOUR CALL...
I DON'T MIND, REALLY.
YOU CAN JUST GIVE ME WHAT I **WANT.** OR SOME OF THE **VERY** FRAGILE PEOPLE IN YOUR FAIR CITY WILL GET MAIMED IN OUR WAKE.
HOW ABOUT **NEITHER.**

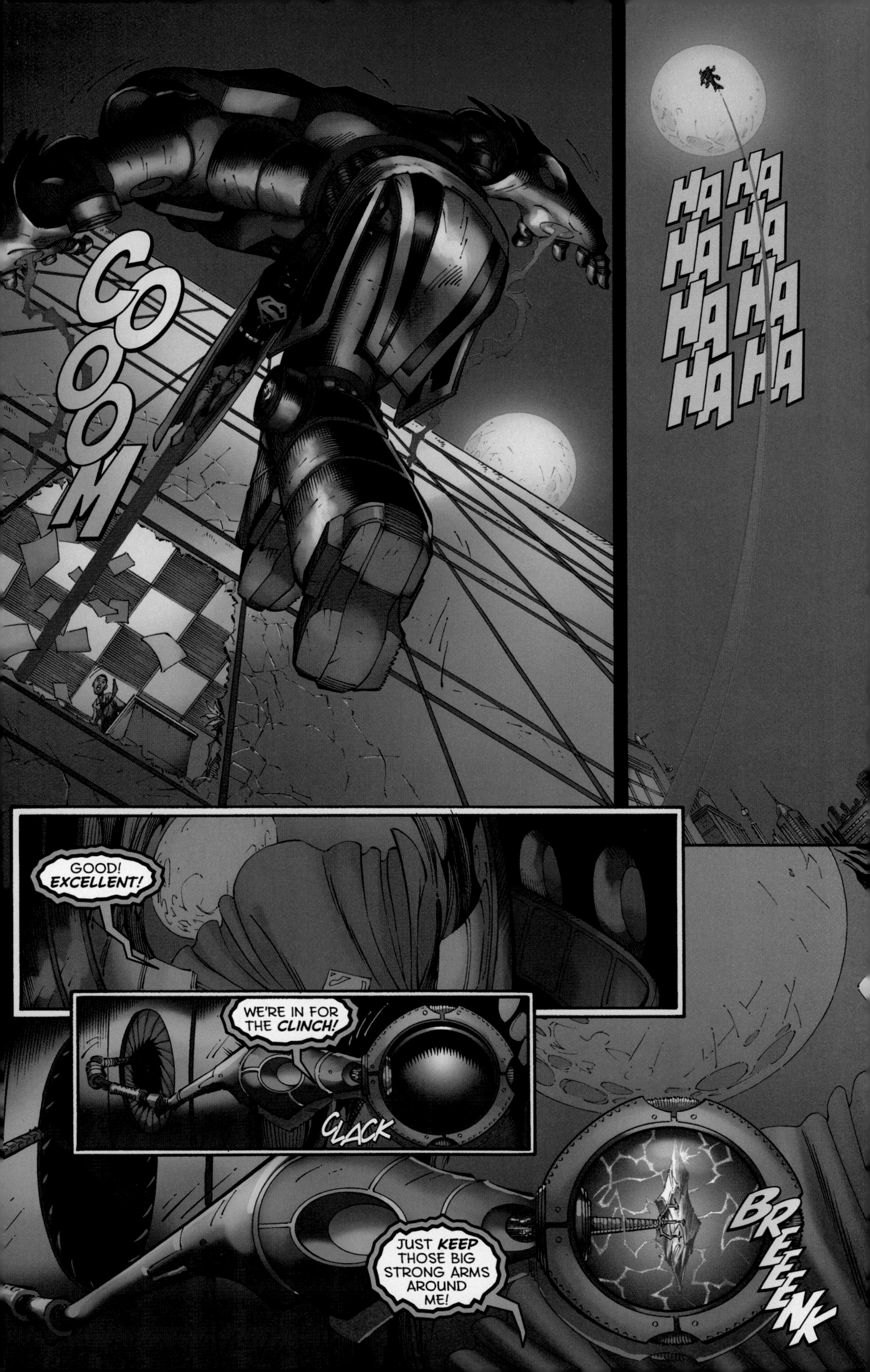
COOOM
HA HA HA HA HA HA HA HA
GOOD! EXCELLENT!
WE'RE IN FOR THE CLINCH!
CLACK
JUST KEEP THOSE BIG STRONG ARMS AROUND ME!
BREEENK

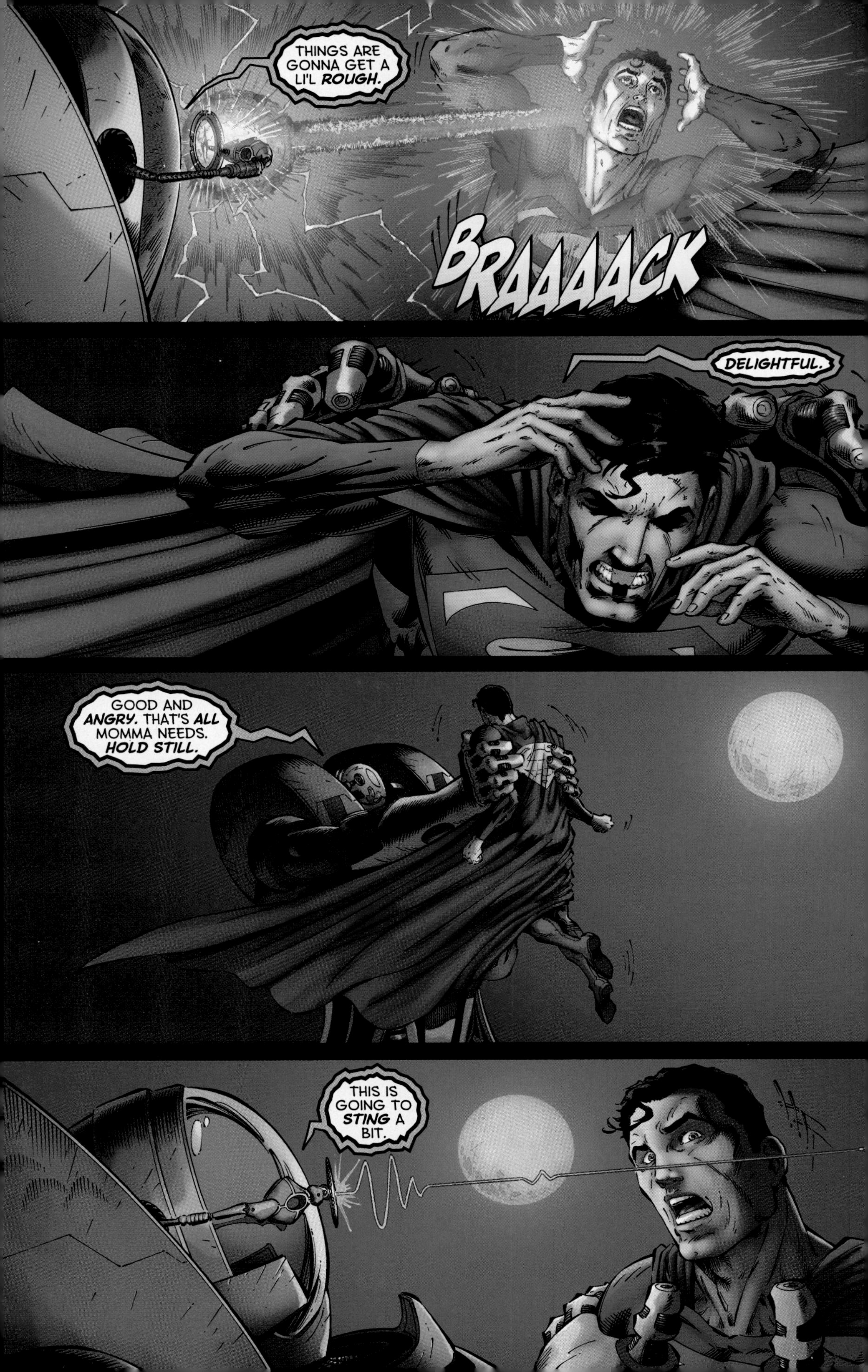
THINGS ARE GONNA GET A LI'L ROUGH.
BRAAAACK
DELIGHTFUL.
GOOD AND ANGRY. THAT'S ALL MOMMA NEEDS. HOLD STILL.
THIS IS GOING TO STING A BIT.

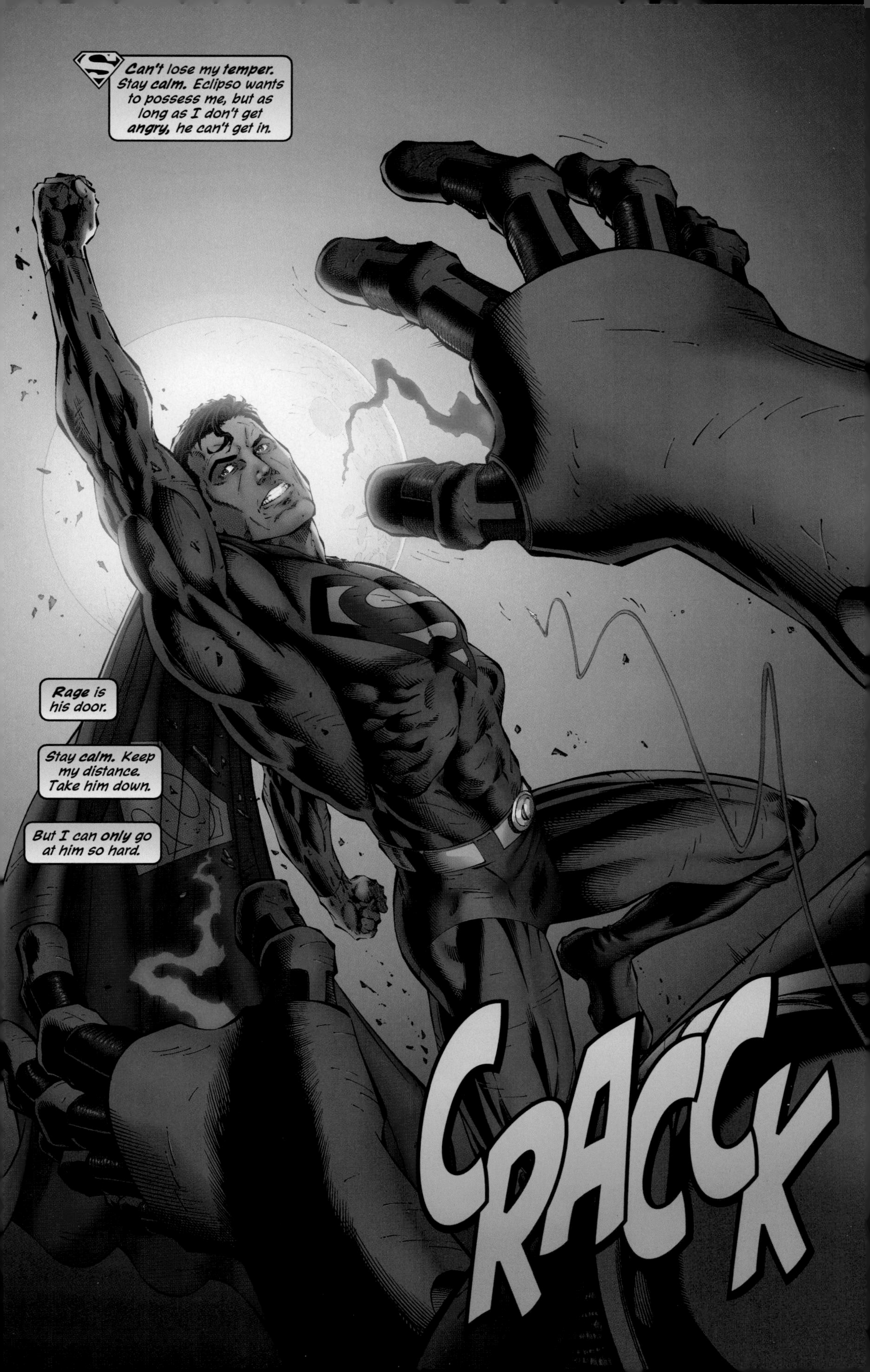
Can't lose my temper. Stay calm. Eclipso wants to possess me, but as long as I don't get angry, he can't get in.
Rage is his door.
Stay calm. Keep my distance. Take him down.
But I can only go at him so hard.
CRACCK

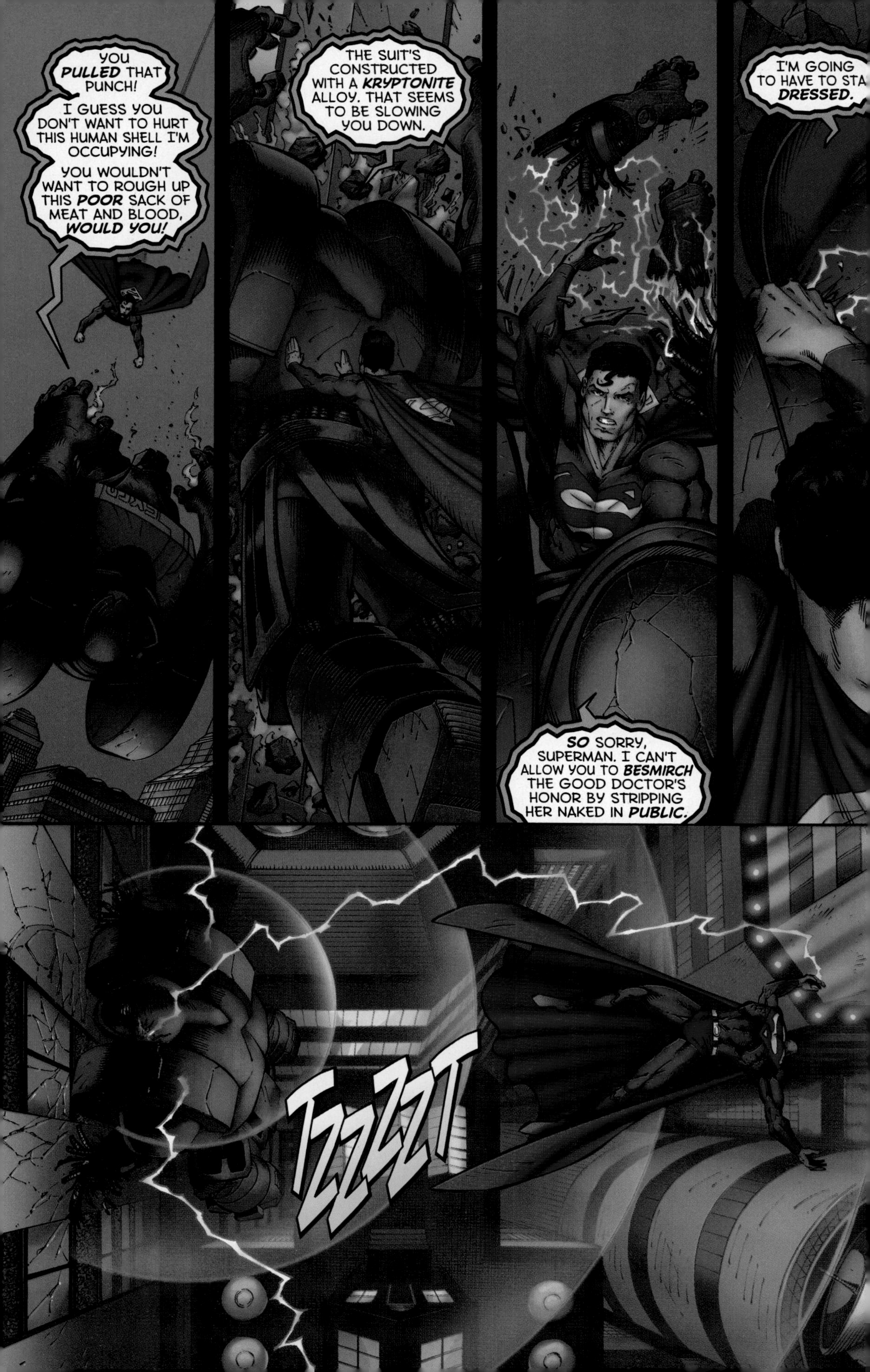
YOU PULLED THAT PUNCH!
I GUESS YOU DON'T WANT TO HURT THIS HUMAN SHELL I'M OCCUPYING!
YOU WOULDN'T WANT TO ROUGH UP THIS POOR SACK OF MEAT AND BLOOD, WOULD YOU!
THE SUIT'S CONSTRUCTED WITH A KRYPTONITE ALLOY. THAT SEEMS TO BE SLOWING YOU DOWN.
SO SORRY, SUPERMAN. I CAN'T ALLOW YOU TO BESMIRCH THE GOOD DOCTOR'S HONOR BY STRIPPING HER NAKED IN PUBLIC.
I'M GOING TO HAVE TO STA DRESSED.
TZZZZT

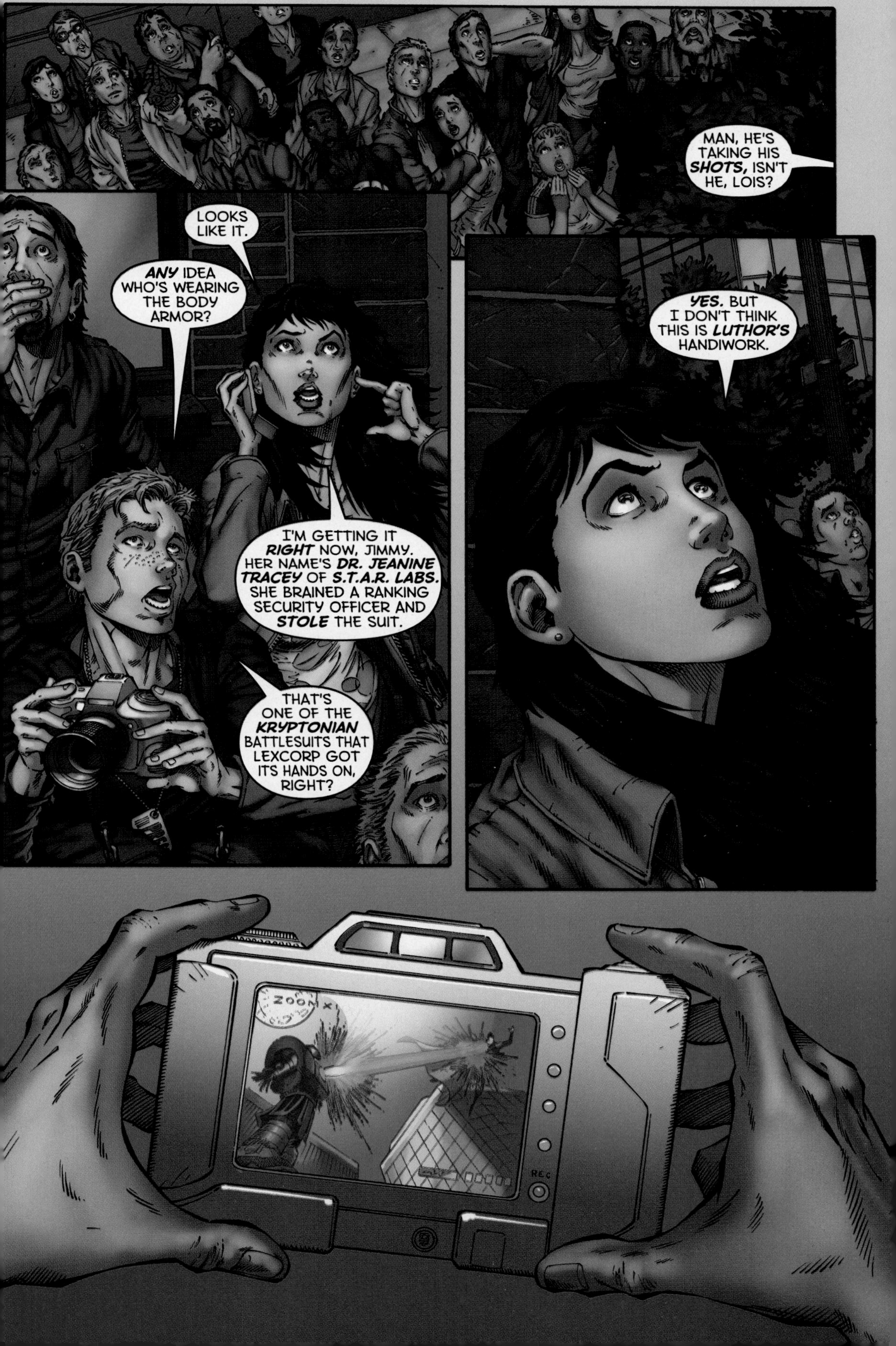

MAN, HE'S TAKING HIS **SHOTS,** ISN'T HE, LOIS?
LOOKS LIKE IT.
ANY IDEA WHO'S WEARING THE BODY ARMOR?
I'M GETTING IT **RIGHT** NOW, JIMMY. HER NAME'S **DR. JEANINE TRACEY** OF **S.T.A.R. LABS.** SHE BRAINED A RANKING SECURITY OFFICER AND **STOLE** THE SUIT.
THAT'S ONE OF THE **KRYPTONIAN** BATTLESUITS THAT LEXCORP GOT ITS HANDS ON, RIGHT?
YES. BUT I DON'T THINK THIS IS **LUTHOR'S** HANDIWORK.
ZOOM X
REC

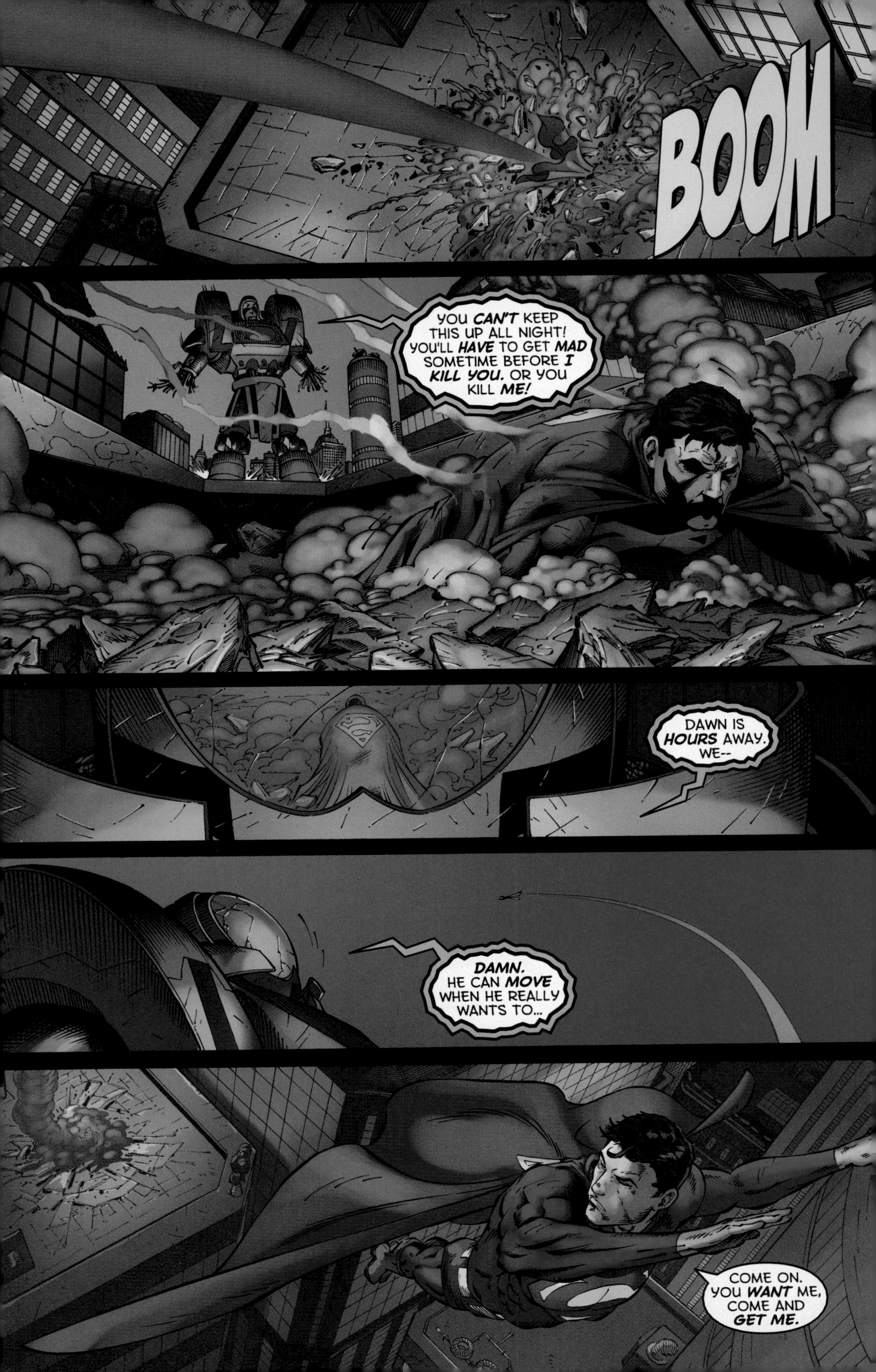
BOOM
YOU CAN'T KEEP THIS UP ALL NIGHT! YOU'LL HAVE TO GET MAD SOMETIME BEFORE I KILL YOU. OR YOU KILL ME!
DAWN IS HOURS AWAY. WE--
DAMN. HE CAN MOVE WHEN HE REALLY WANTS TO...
COME ON. YOU WANT ME, COME AND GET ME.

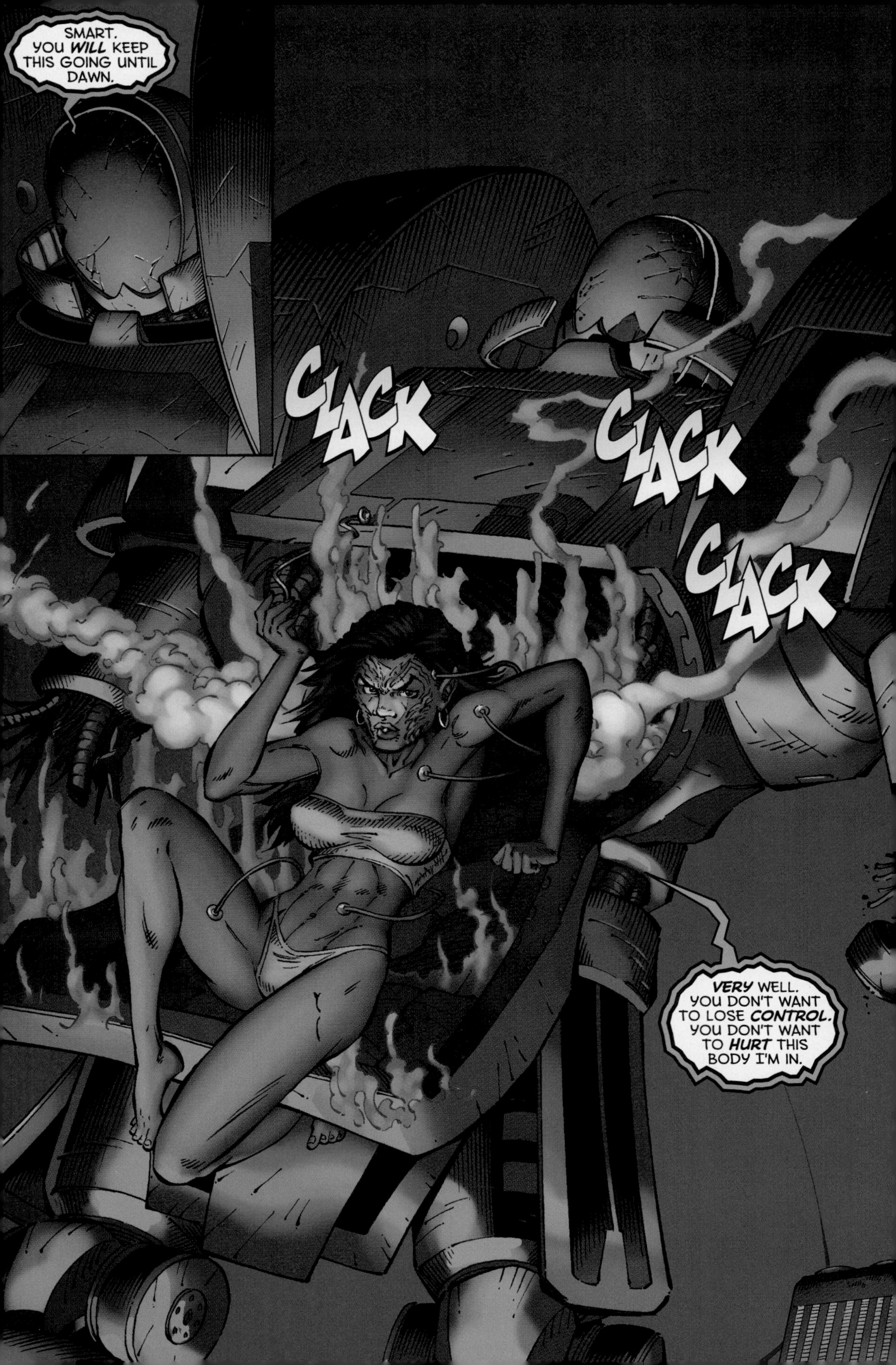
SMART. YOU WILL KEEP THIS GOING UNTIL DAWN.
CLACK
CLACK
CLACK
VERY WELL. YOU DON'T WANT TO LOSE CONTROL. YOU DON'T WANT TO HURT THIS BODY I'M IN.

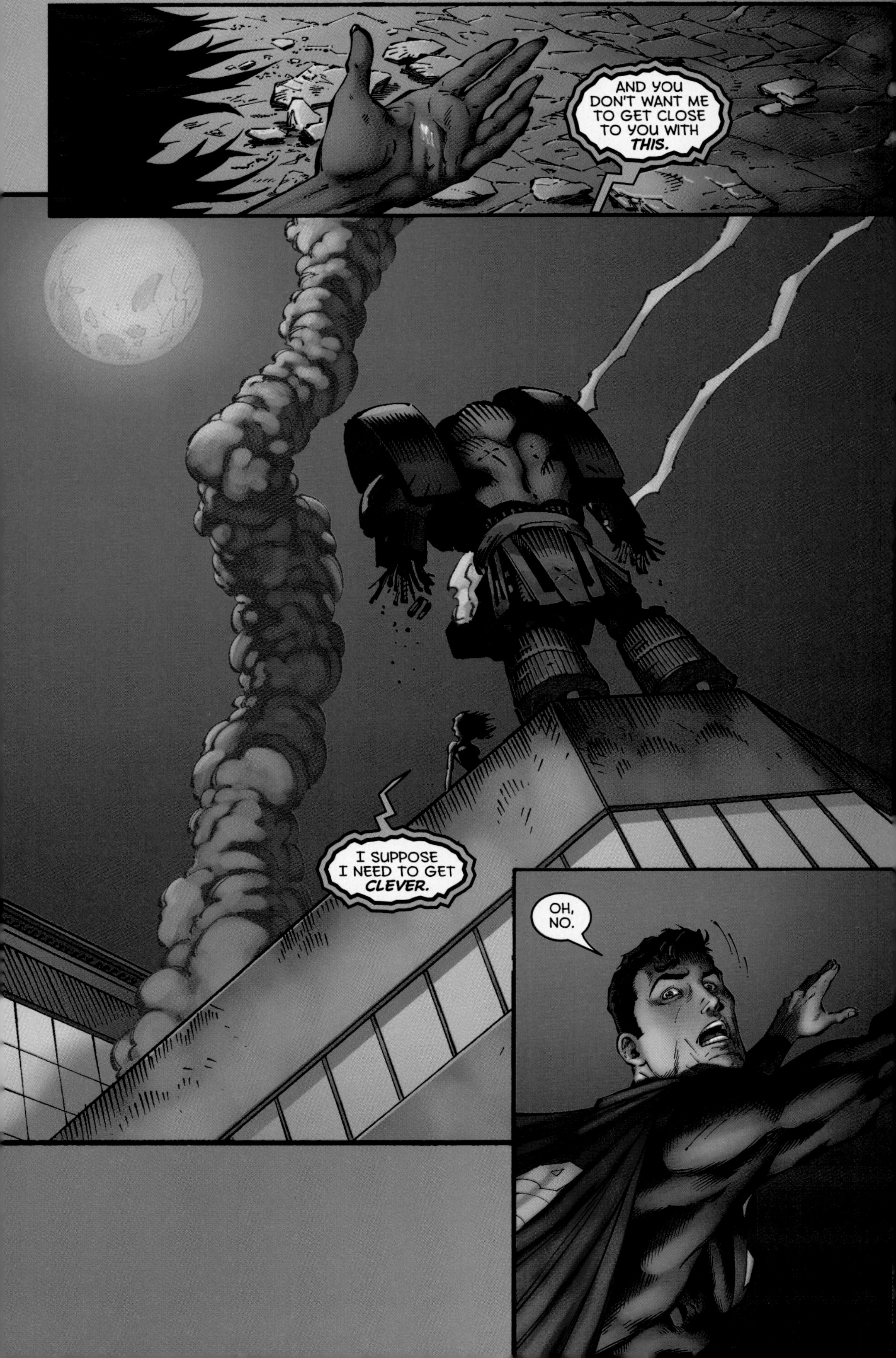
AND YOU DON'T WANT ME TO GET CLOSE TO YOU WITH *THIS.*
I SUPPOSE I NEED TO GET *CLEVER.*
OH, NO.

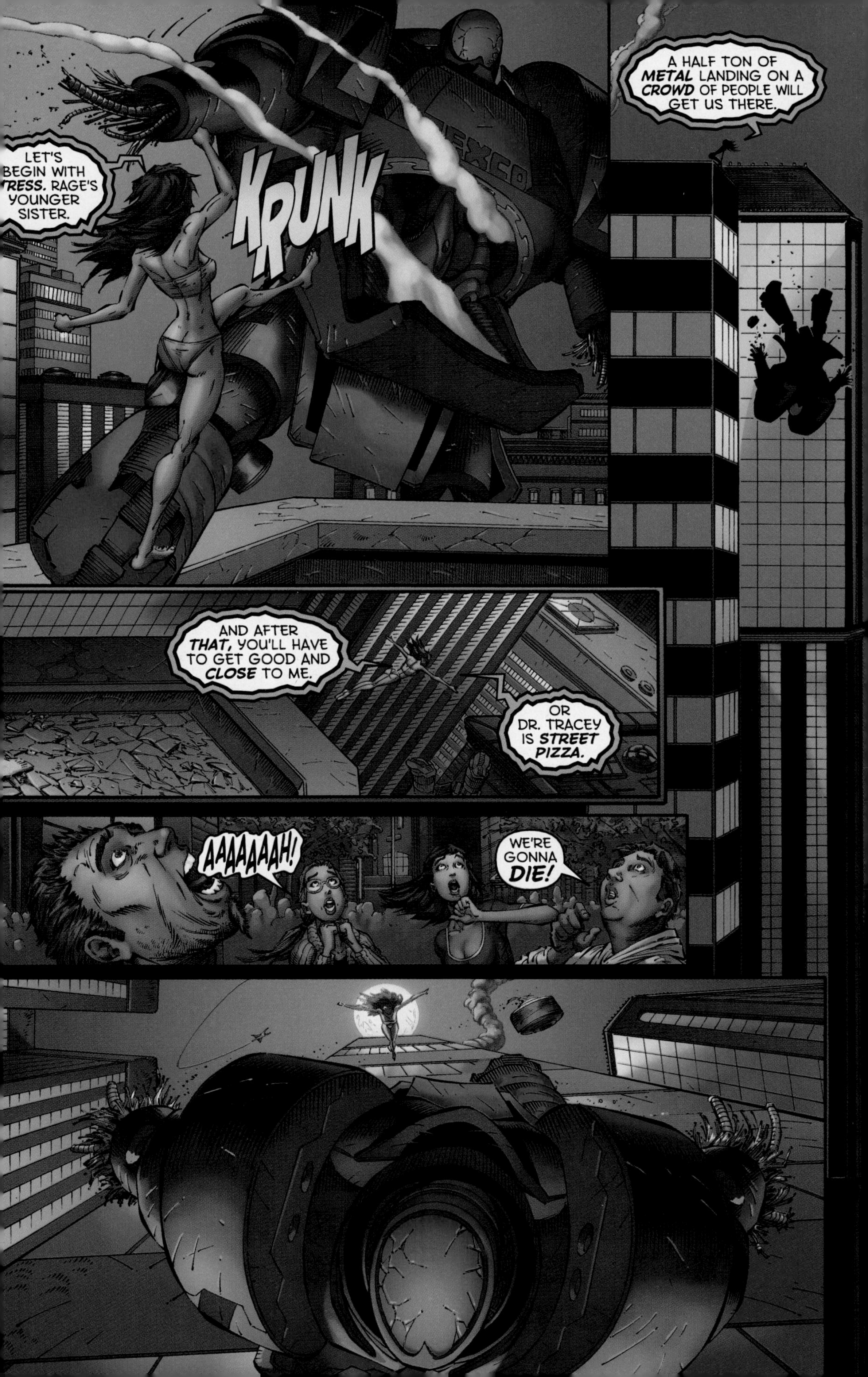

LET'S BEGIN WITH TRESS. RAGE'S YOUNGER SISTER.
KRUNK
A HALF TON OF METAL LANDING ON A CROWD OF PEOPLE WILL GET US THERE.
AND AFTER THAT, YOU'LL HAVE TO GET GOOD AND CLOSE TO ME.
OR DR. TRACEY IS STREET PIZZA.
AAAAAAAH!
WE'RE GONNA DIE!

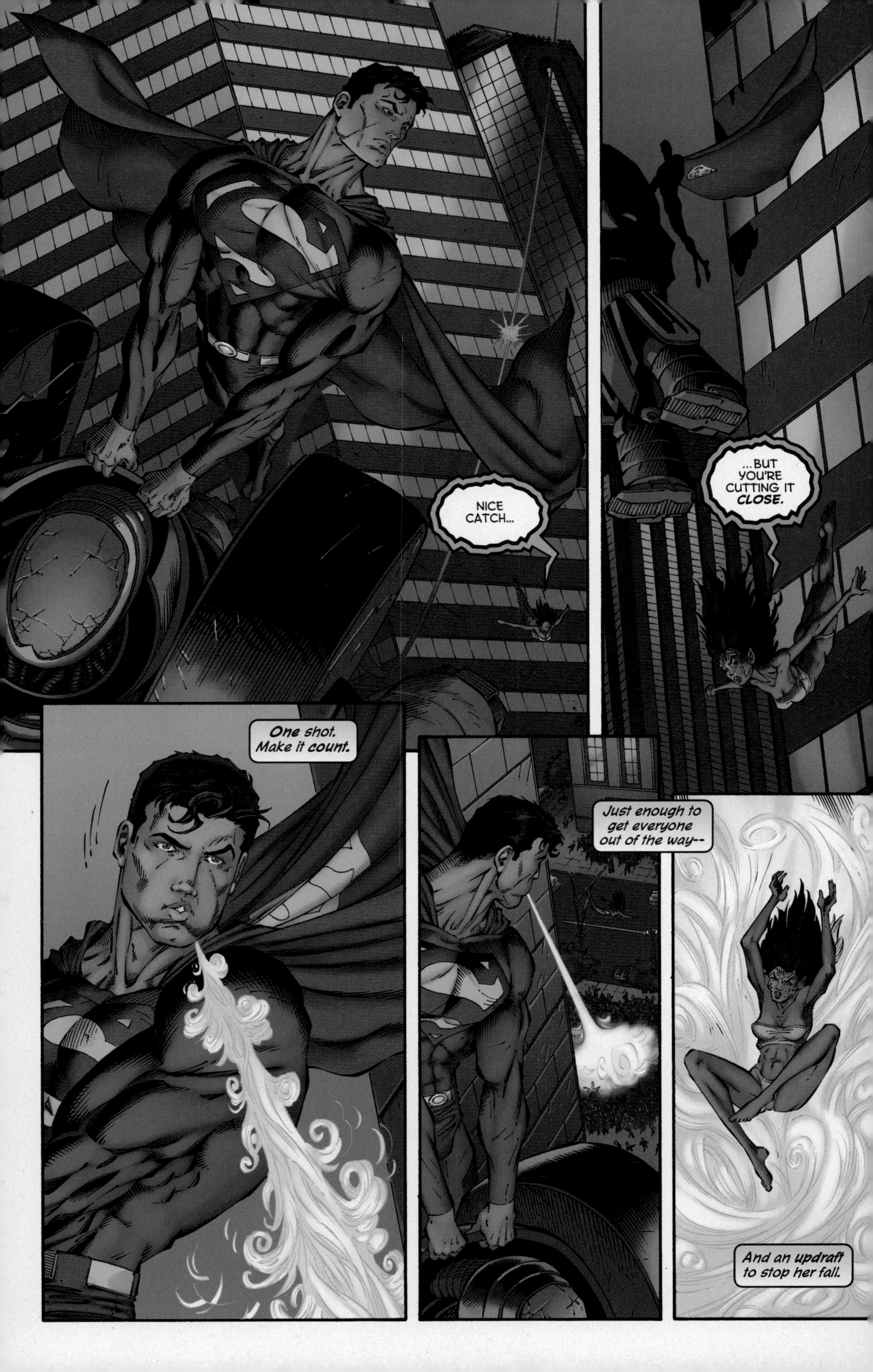
NICE CATCH...
...BUT YOU'RE CUTTING IT CLOSE.
One shot. Make it count.
Just enough to get everyone out of the way--
And an updraft to stop her fall.

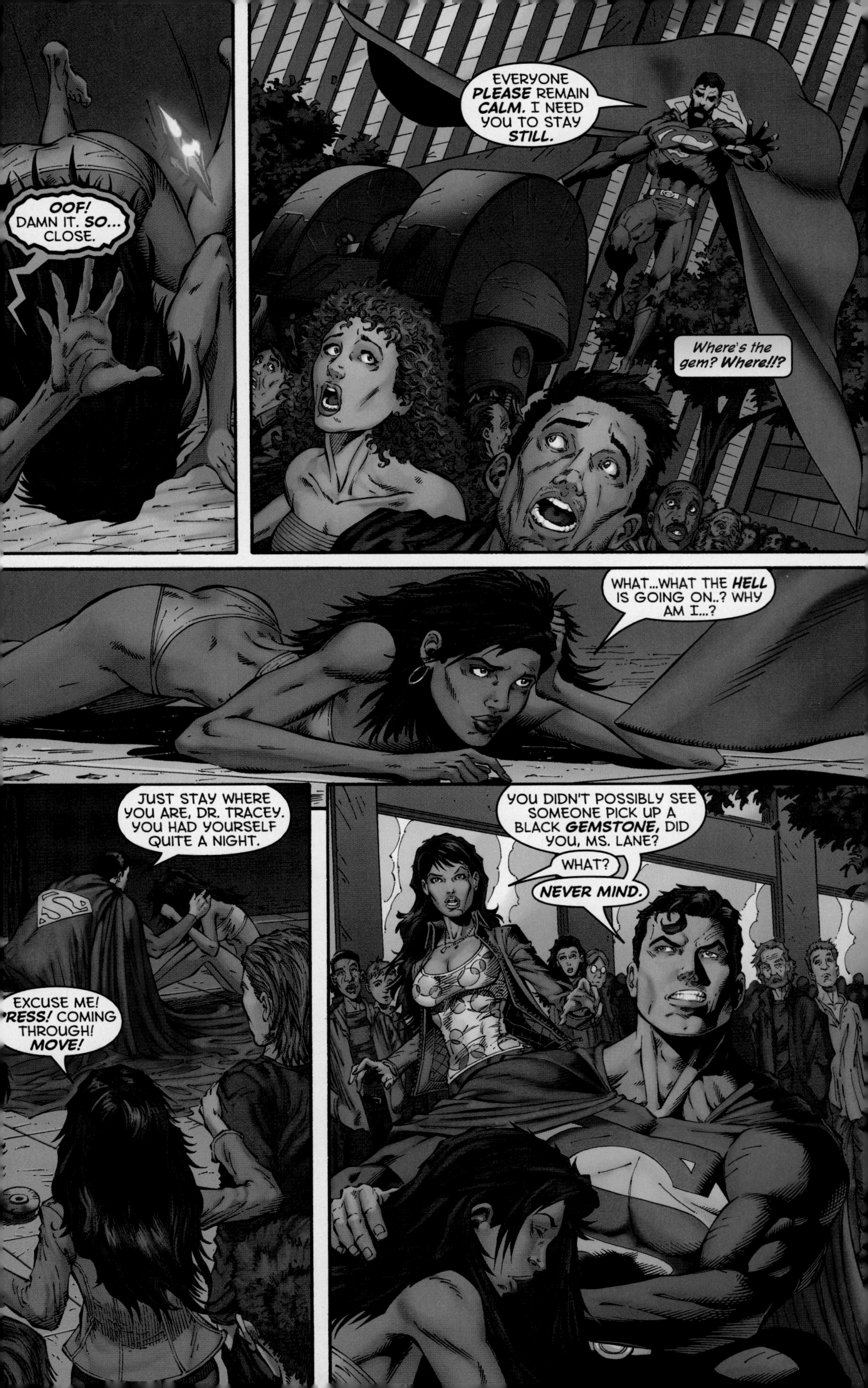
OOF! DAMN IT. SO... CLOSE.
EVERYONE PLEASE REMAIN CALM. I NEED YOU TO STAY STILL.
Where's the gem? Where!!?
WHAT...WHAT THE HELL IS GOING ON..? WHY AM I...?
JUST STAY WHERE YOU ARE, DR. TRACEY. YOU HAD YOURSELF QUITE A NIGHT.
EXCUSE ME! PRESS! COMING THROUGH! MOVE!
YOU DIDN'T POSSIBLY SEE SOMEONE PICK UP A BLACK GEMSTONE, DID YOU, MS. LANE?
WHAT?
NEVER MIND.

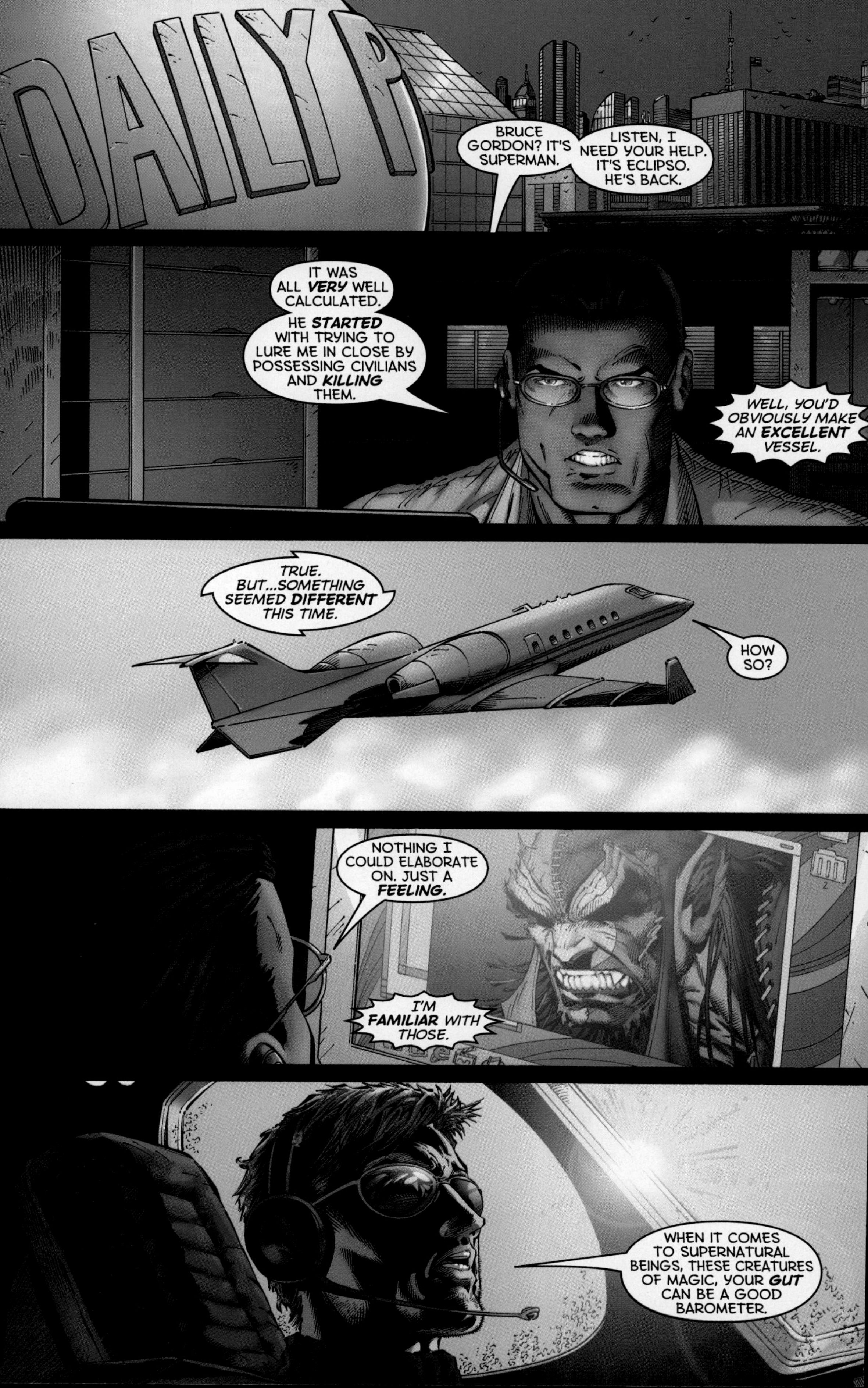
DAILY P
BRUCE GORDON? IT'S SUPERMAN.
LISTEN, I NEED YOUR HELP. IT'S ECLIPSO. HE'S BACK.
IT WAS ALL **VERY** WELL CALCULATED.
HE **STARTED** WITH TRYING TO LURE ME IN CLOSE BY POSSESSING CIVILIANS AND **KILLING** THEM.
WELL, YOU'D OBVIOUSLY MAKE AN **EXCELLENT** VESSEL.
TRUE. BUT...SOMETHING SEEMED **DIFFERENT** THIS TIME.
HOW SO?
NOTHING I COULD ELABORATE ON. JUST A **FEELING.**
I'M **FAMILIAR** WITH THOSE.
WHEN IT COMES TO SUPERNATURAL BEINGS, THESE CREATURES OF MAGIC, YOUR **GUT** CAN BE A GOOD BAROMETER.

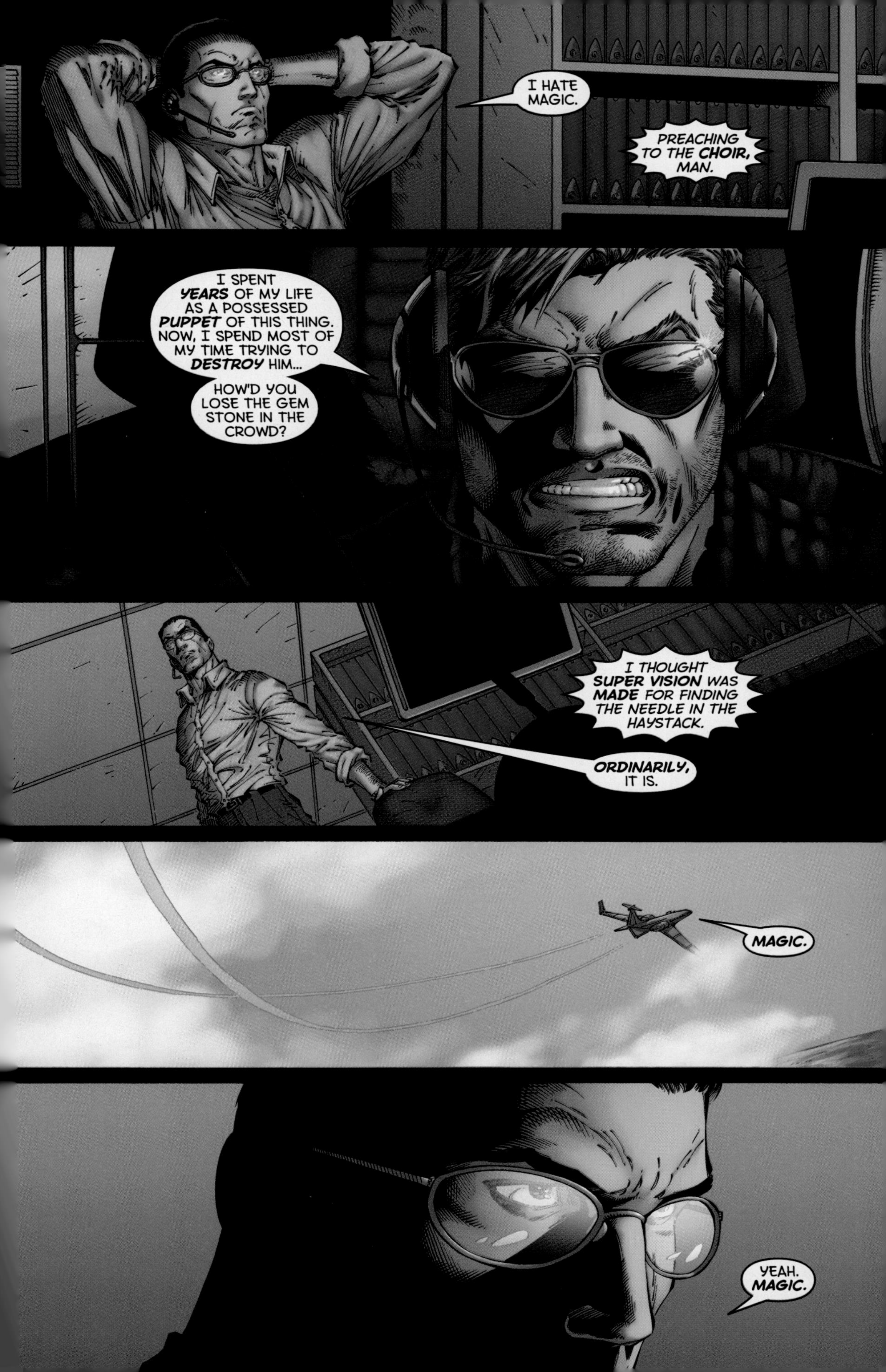
I HATE MAGIC.
PREACHING TO THE CHOIR, MAN.
I SPENT YEARS OF MY LIFE AS A POSSESSED PUPPET OF THIS THING. NOW, I SPEND MOST OF MY TIME TRYING TO DESTROY HIM...
HOW'D YOU LOSE THE GEM STONE IN THE CROWD?
I THOUGHT SUPER VISION WAS MADE FOR FINDING THE NEEDLE IN THE HAYSTACK.
ORDINARILY, IT IS.
MAGIC.
YEAH. MAGIC.

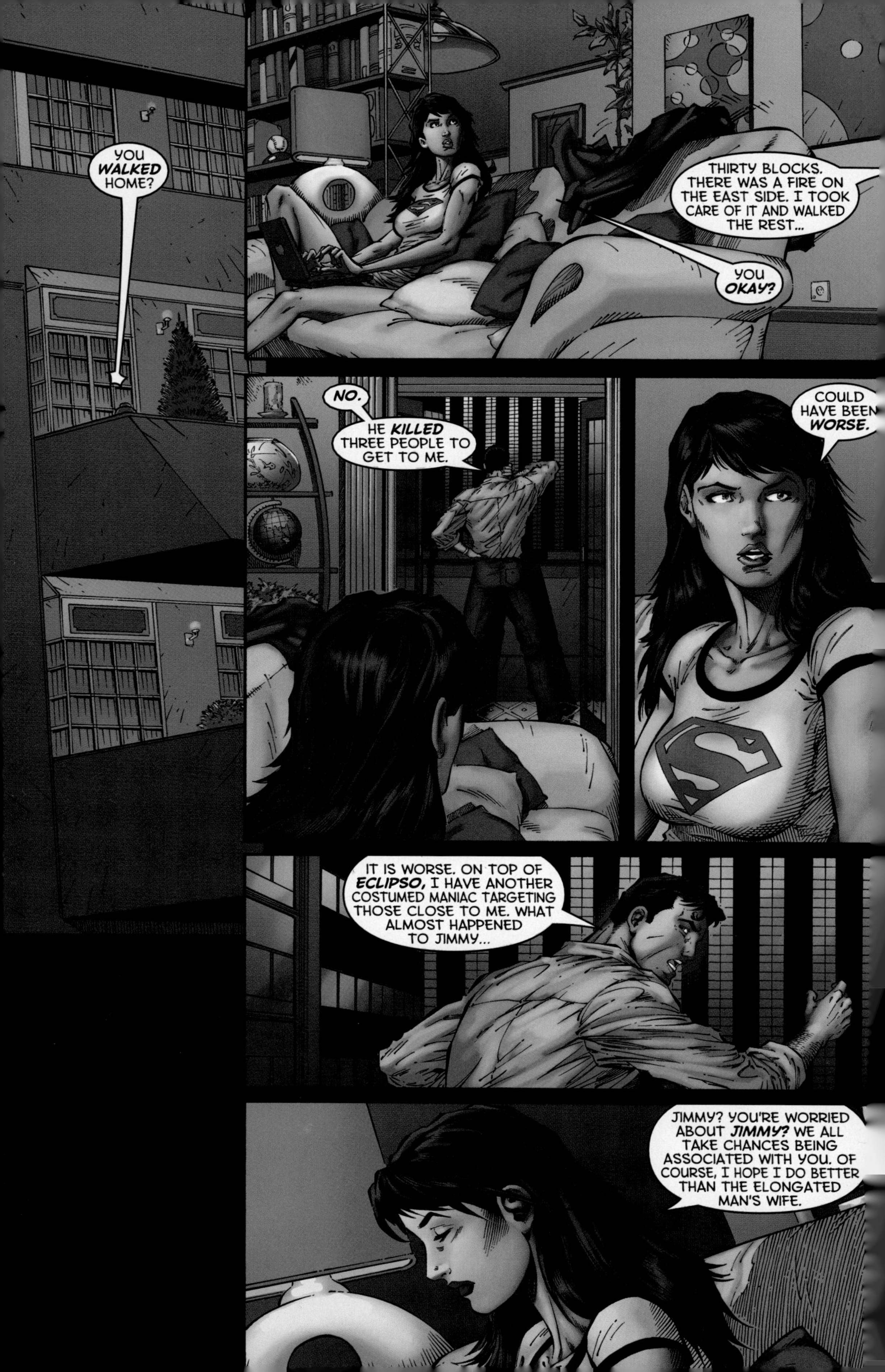

YOU **WALKED** HOME?
THIRTY BLOCKS. THERE WAS A FIRE ON THE EAST SIDE. I TOOK CARE OF IT AND WALKED THE REST...
YOU **OKAY?**
NO.
HE **KILLED** THREE PEOPLE TO GET TO ME.
COULD HAVE BEEN **WORSE.**
IT IS WORSE. ON TOP OF **ECLIPSO,** I HAVE ANOTHER COSTUMED MANIAC TARGETING THOSE CLOSE TO ME. WHAT ALMOST HAPPENED TO JIMMY...
JIMMY? YOU'RE WORRIED ABOUT **JIMMY?** WE ALL TAKE CHANCES BEING ASSOCIATED WITH YOU. OF COURSE, I HOPE I DO BETTER THAN THE ELONGATED MAN'S WIFE.

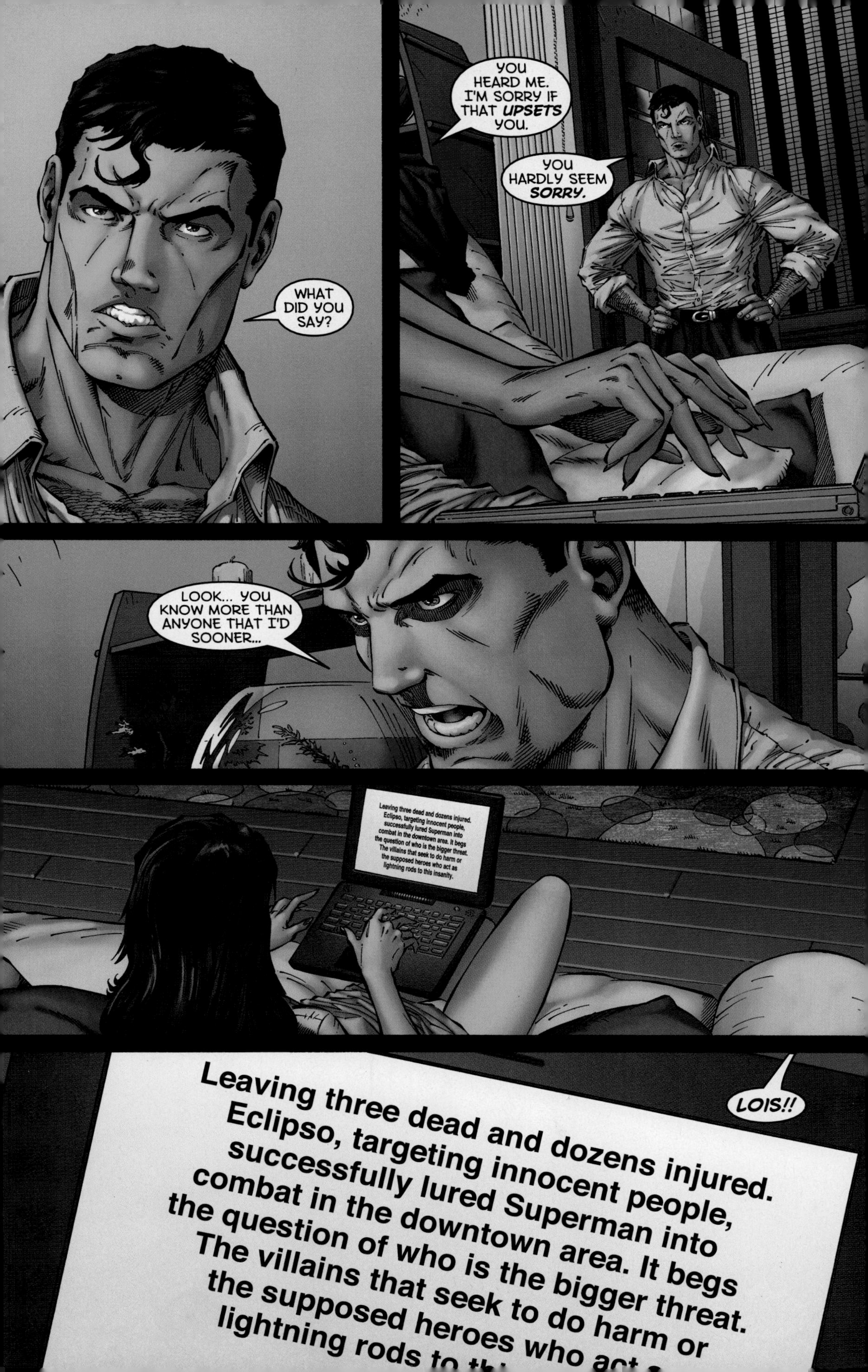

WHAT DID YOU SAY?
YOU HEARD ME. I'M SORRY IF THAT UPSETS YOU.
YOU HARDLY SEEM SORRY.
LOOK... YOU KNOW MORE THAN ANYONE THAT I'D SOONER...
Leaving three dead and dozens injured. Eclipso, targeting innocent people, successfully lured Superman into combat in the downtown area. It begs the question of who is the bigger threat. The villains that seek to do harm or the supposed heroes who act as lightning rods to this insanity.
Leaving three dead and dozens injured. Eclipso, targeting innocent people, successfully lured Superman into combat in the downtown area. It begs the question of who is the bigger threat. The villains that seek to do harm or the supposed heroes who
lightning rods to
LOIS!!

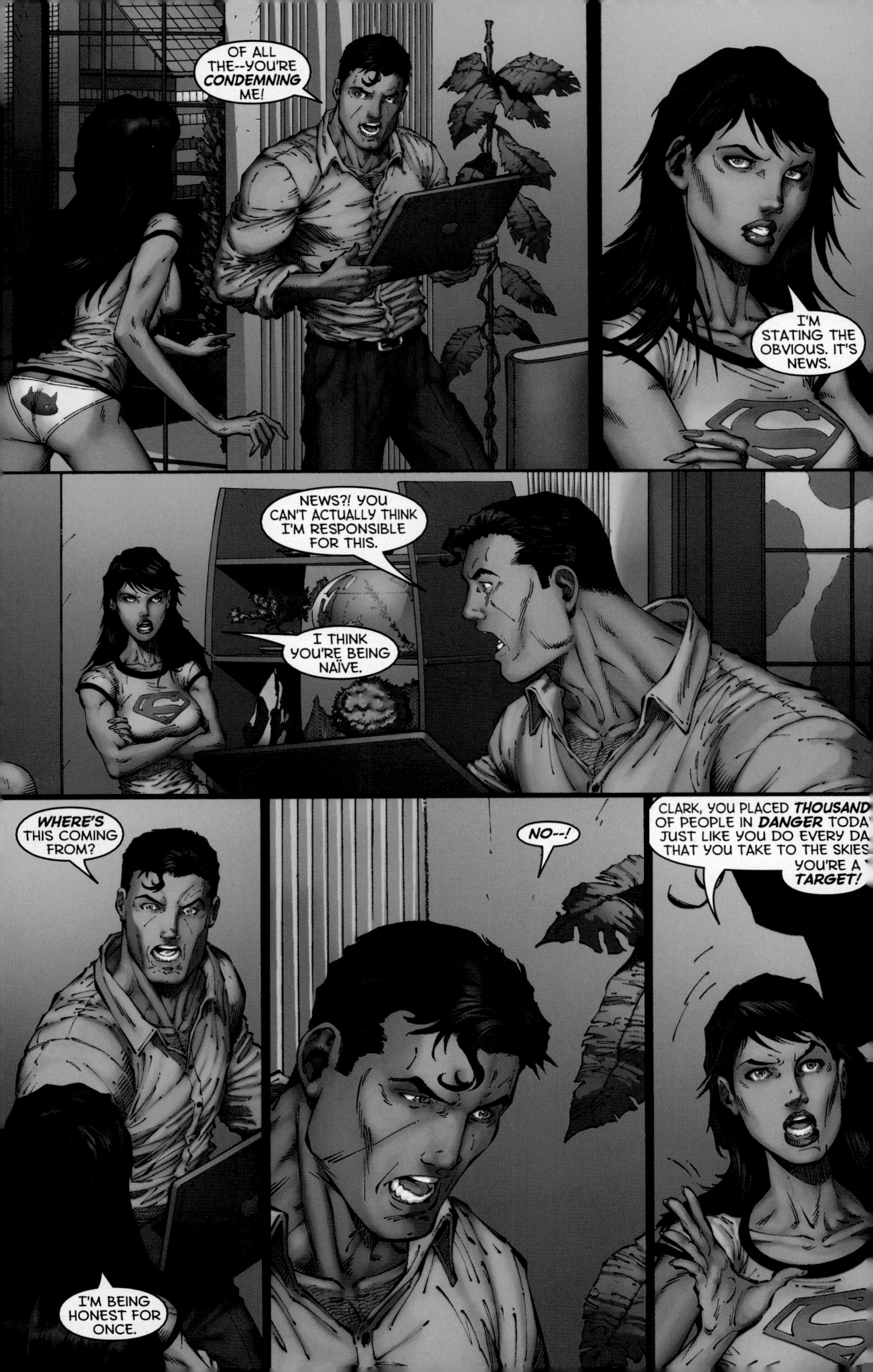
OF ALL THE--YOU'RE CONDEMNING ME!
I'M STATING THE OBVIOUS. IT'S NEWS.
NEWS?! YOU CAN'T ACTUALLY THINK I'M RESPONSIBLE FOR THIS.
I THINK YOU'RE BEING NAÏVE.
WHERE'S THIS COMING FROM?
I'M BEING HONEST FOR ONCE.
NO--!
CLARK, YOU PLACED THOUSAND OF PEOPLE IN DANGER TODA JUST LIKE YOU DO EVERY DA THAT YOU TAKE TO THE SKIES YOU'RE A TARGET!

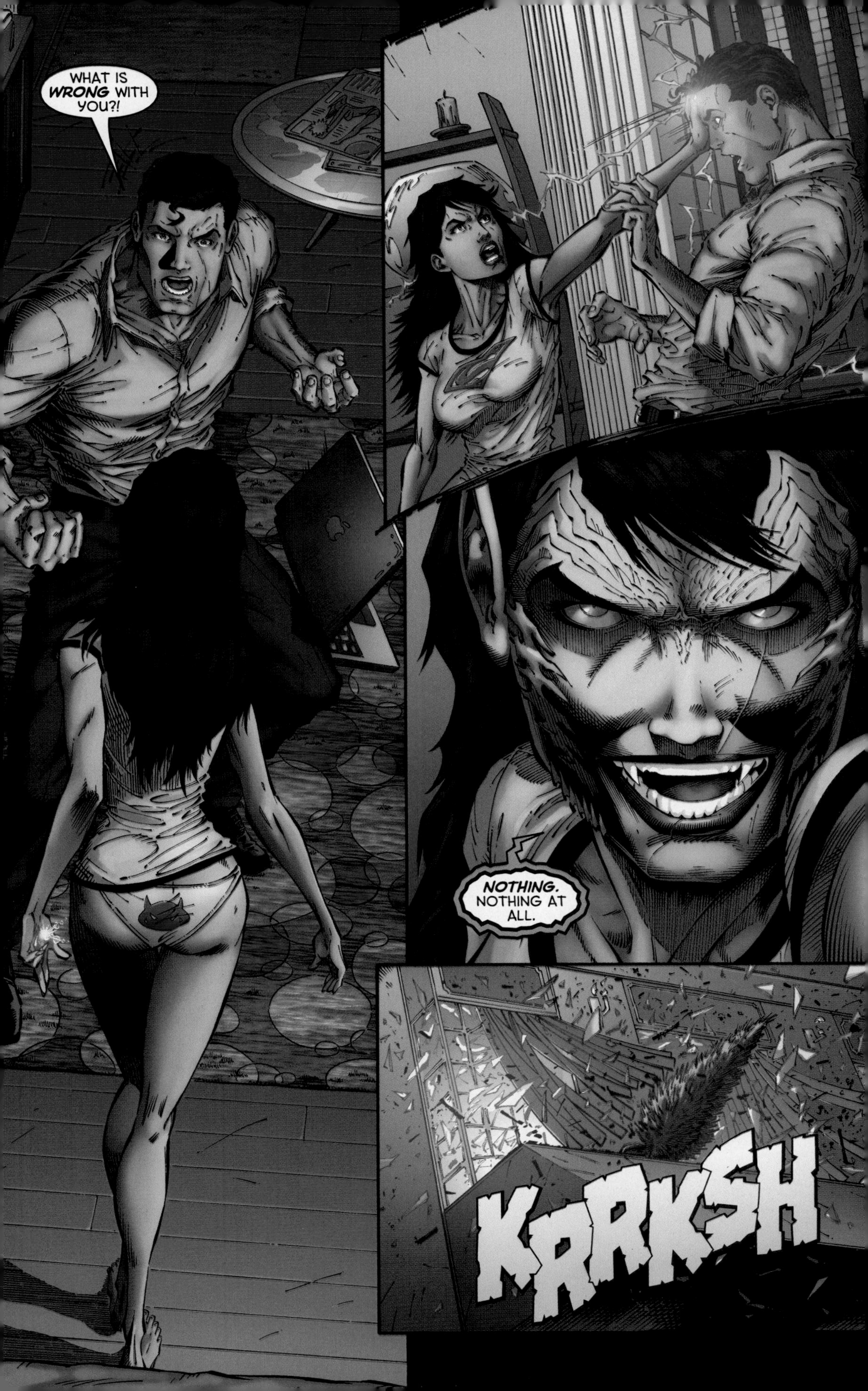
WHAT IS *WRONG* WITH YOU?!
NOTHING. NOTHING AT ALL.
KRRKSH

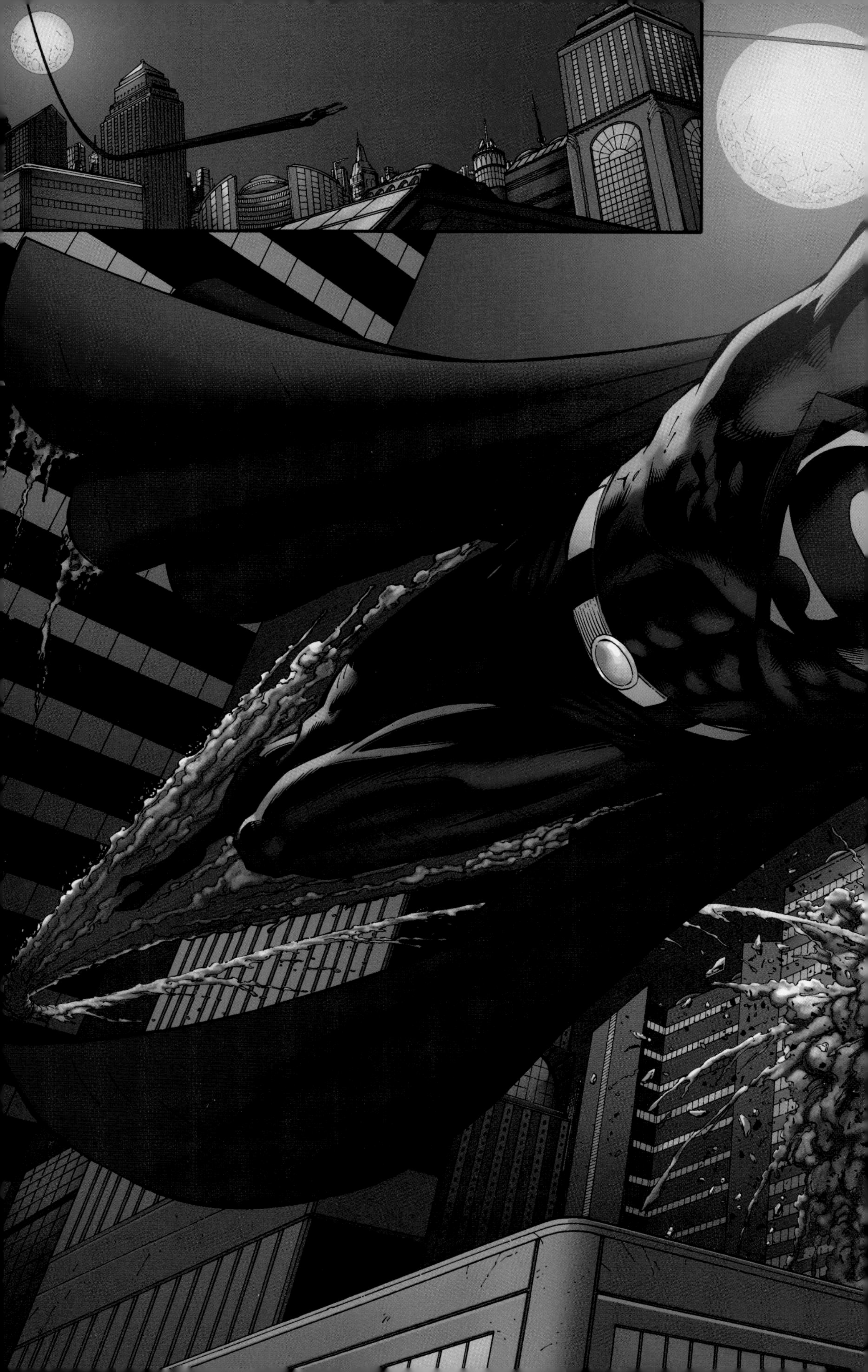

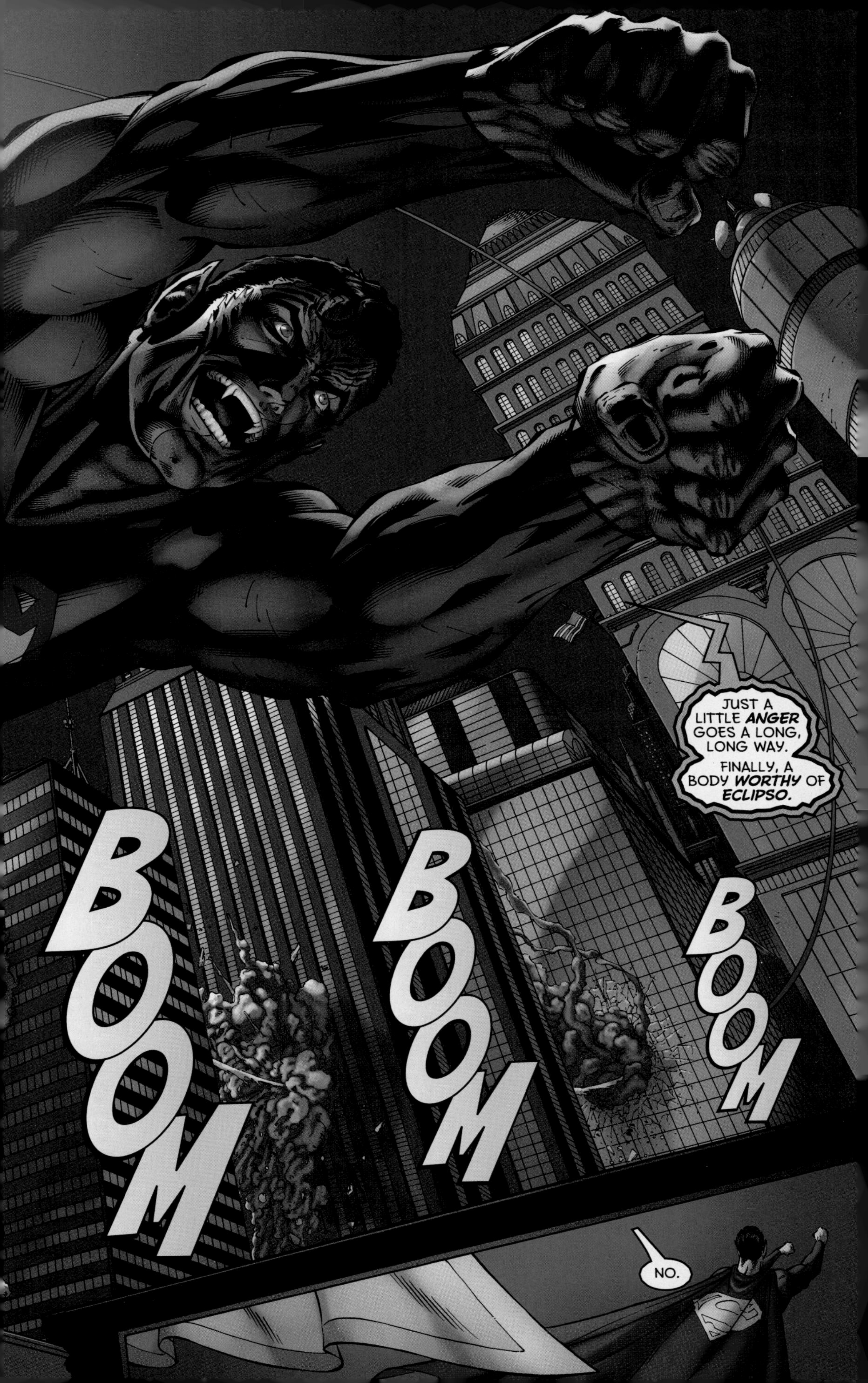
JUST A LITTLE ANGER GOES A LONG, LONG WAY.
FINALLY, A BODY WORTHY OF ECLIPSO.
BOOM
BOOM
BOOM
NO.

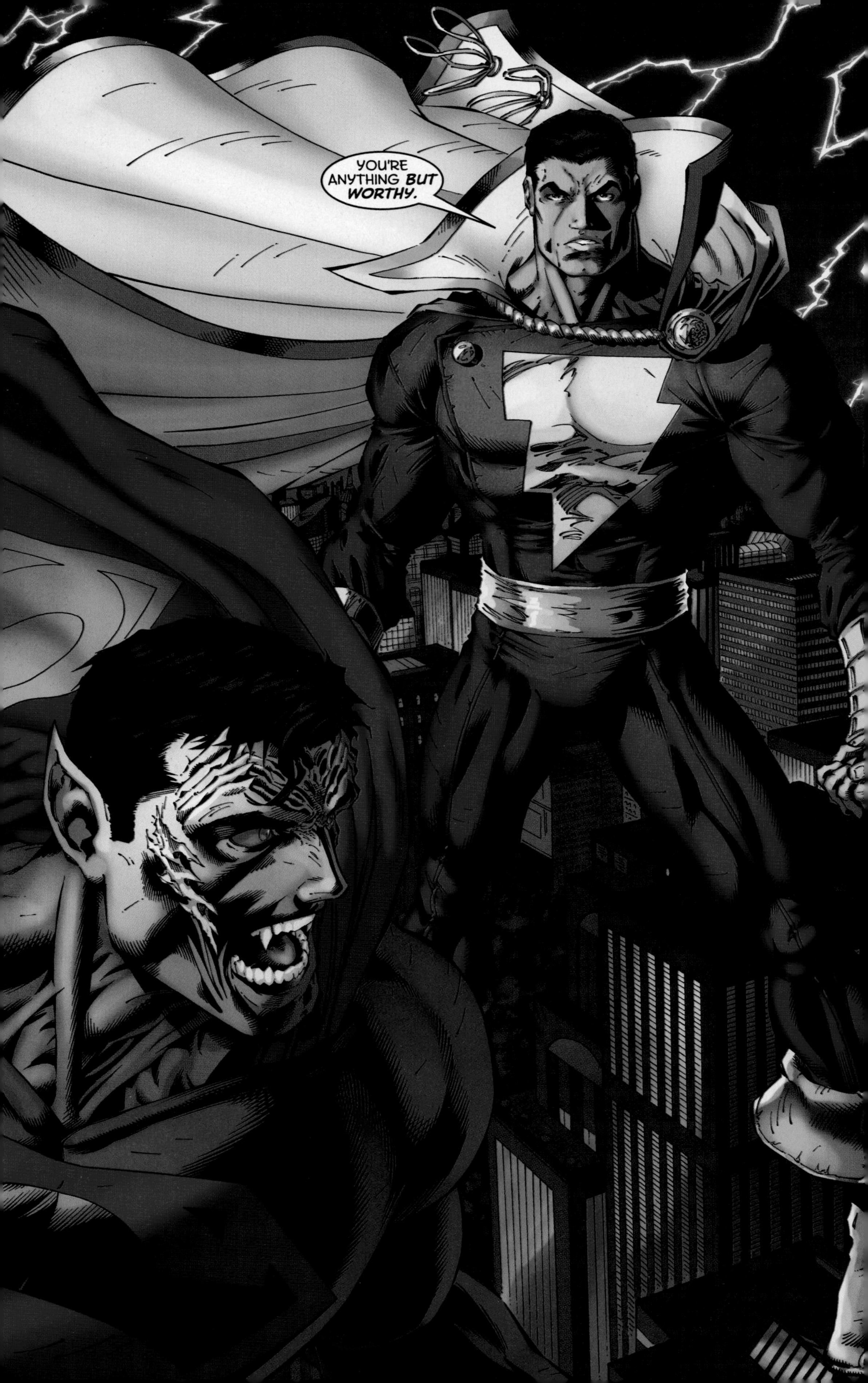
YOU'RE ANYTHING **BUT** **WORTHY.**

OUR UNIVERSE IS A MECHANISM OF **BALANCE.** PUSH AND PULL. POSITIVE AND NEGATIVE. LIFE AND **DEATH.**

GOOD AND **EVIL.**

TO MAINTAIN THE EQUILIBRIUM BETWEEN THE ACTIONS OF **DARKNESS** AND THE ACTIONS OF **VIRTUE,** THE UNIVERSE CREATED A BEING TO CARRY OUT ITS WILL.

AN AGENT OF **RETRIBUTION.** A SPIRIT OF **VENGEANCE.**

IT WAS CALLED **ECLIPSO.**

UNFORTUNATELY, ECLIPSO DID NOT BEHAVE ACCORDING TO ITS DESIGN. IT WAS NOT **TETHERED** TO A **LIVING HOST,** SO IT SOUGHT OUT A **VESSEL.**

IT **POSSESSED** CREATURES AT THE TIME OF THEIR GREATEST **WEAKNESS.** WHEN THEY WERE LOST TO **RAGE.**

IT **FED** OFF THEM.

EVENTUALLY, **ECLIPSO** BECAME TRAPPED WITHIN A BLACK DIAMOND, THE **HEART OF DARKNESS** -- CORRUPTING ONLY THOSE THAT FELT ITS TOUCH.

AND THE UNIVERSE RESPONDED, AS IT **ALWAYS** DOES, WITH **ANOTHER** CREATION.

THE SPECTRE. FOREVER BOUND TO LIVING SENTIENT HOSTS, THE SPECTRE DOLES OUT **VENGEANCE** FROM THE GREAT ORDER OF CREATION, BUT WITH THE **COMPREHENSION** OF **COMPASSION** THAT CAN **ONLY** COME FROM LIVING BEINGS.

A BALANCE EXISTS **BETWEEN** THESE TWO BEINGS.

ONE FOLLOWS **ORDER.**

THE OTHER THRIVES IN **CHAOS.**

BUT TODAY, **CHAOS** HAD A MOMENT OF **CLARITY.**

IT FOUND A **VESSEL** THAT SERVES ITS PURPOSES ON **SO MANY LEVELS.**

AT THE VERY **LEAST...**

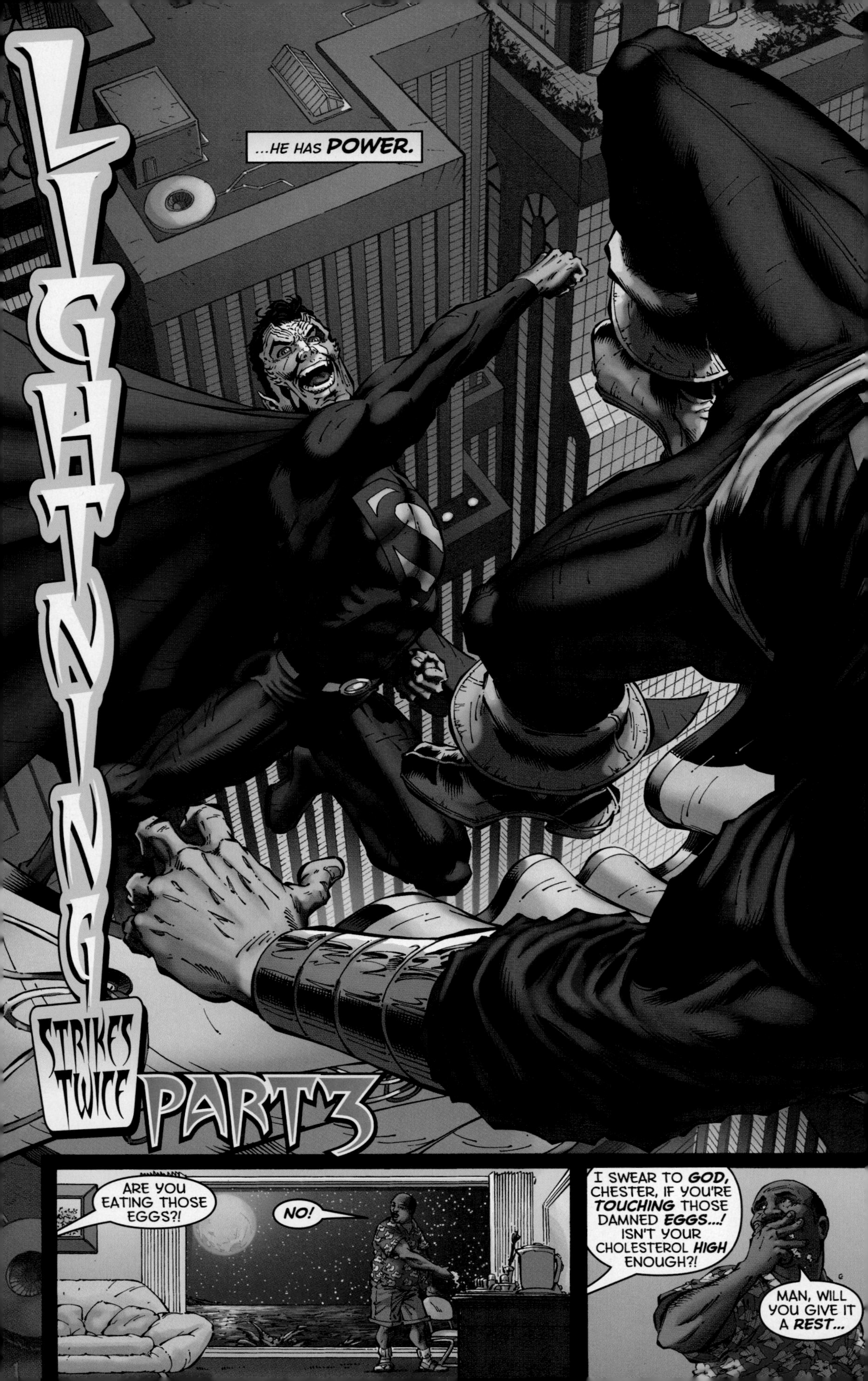
...HE HAS POWER.
LIGHTNING STRIKES TWICE PART 3
ARE YOU EATING THOSE EGGS?!
NO!
I SWEAR TO GOD, CHESTER, IF YOU'RE TOUCHING THOSE DAMNED EGGS...! ISN'T YOUR CHOLESTEROL HIGH ENOUGH?!
MAN, WILL YOU GIVE IT A REST...

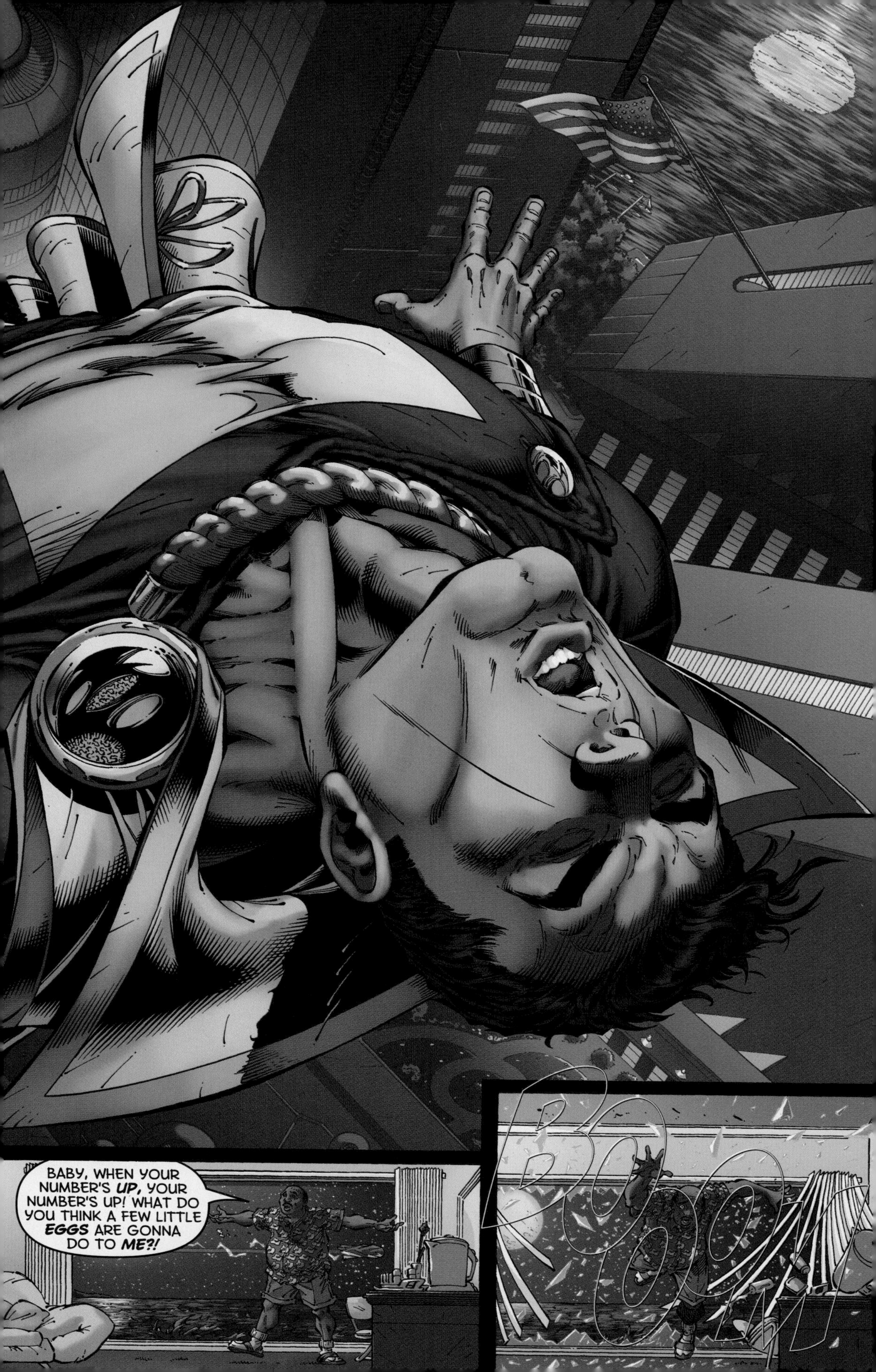
BABY, WHEN YOUR NUMBER'S **UP**, YOUR NUMBER'S UP! WHAT DO YOU THINK A FEW LITTLE **EGGS** ARE GONNA DO TO **ME?!**
BOOOOM

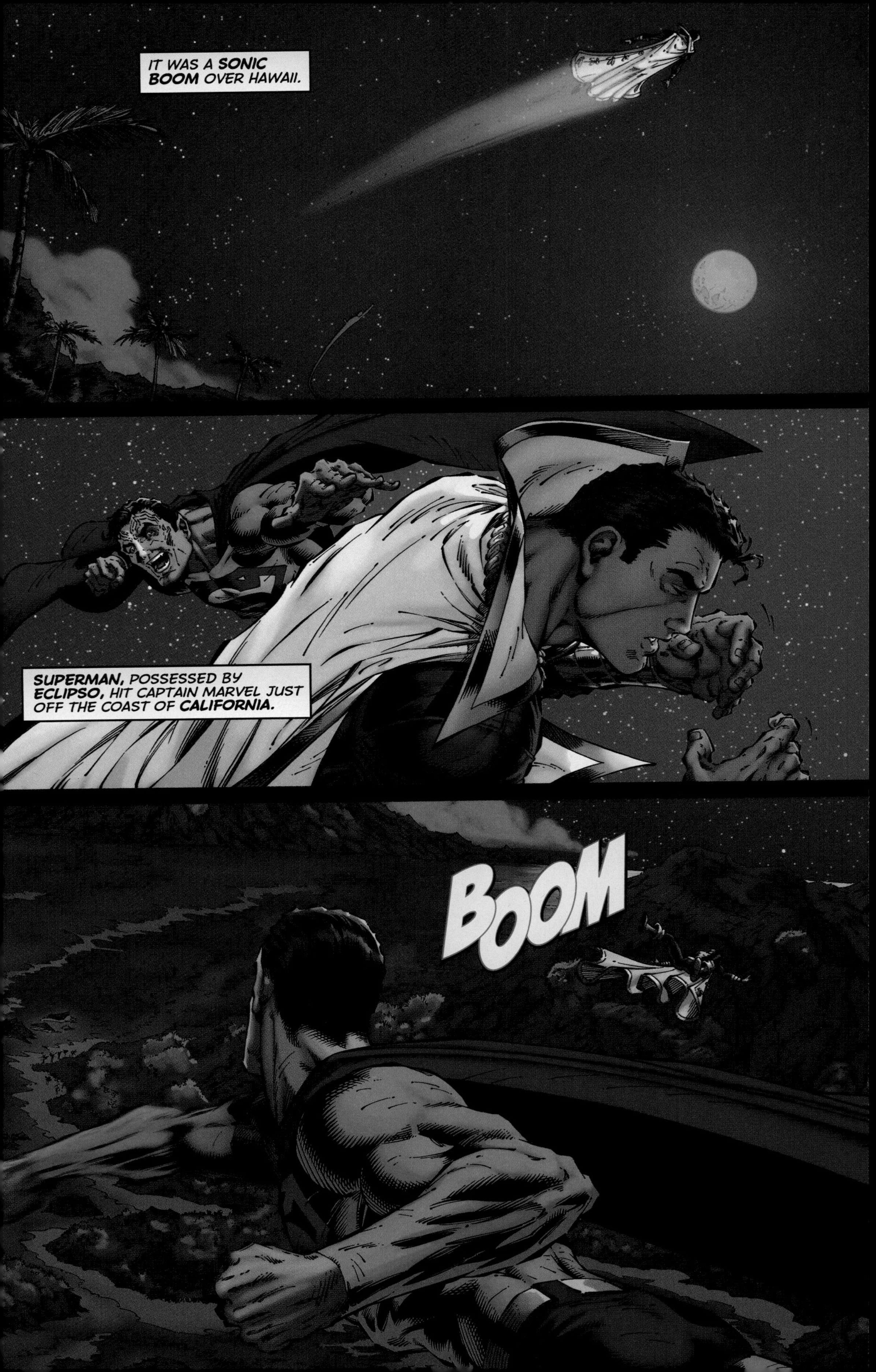
IT WAS A SONIC BOOM OVER HAWAII.
SUPERMAN, POSSESSED BY ECLIPSO, HIT CAPTAIN MARVEL JUST OFF THE COAST OF CALIFORNIA.
BOOM

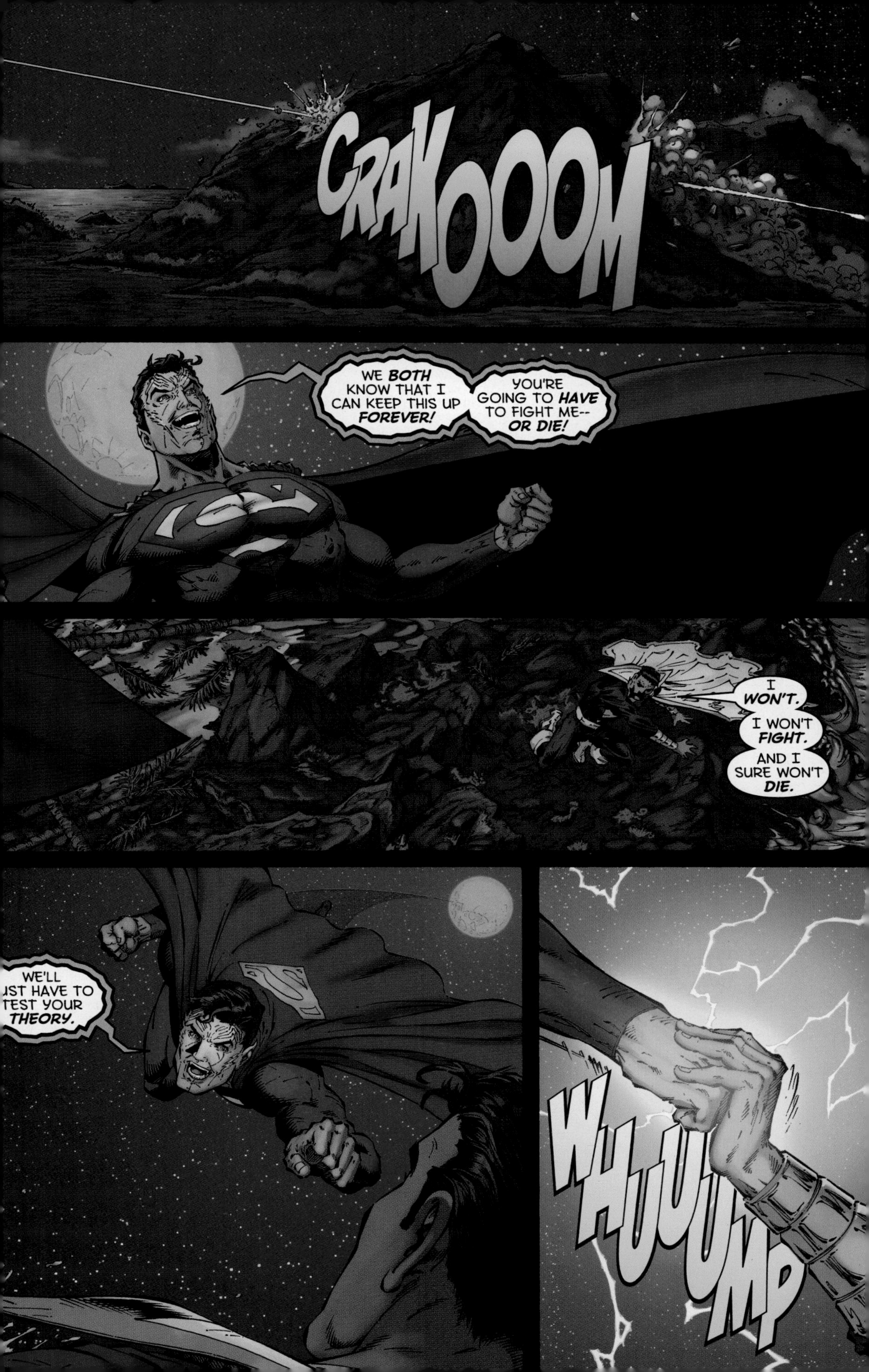
CRAKOOOM
WE BOTH KNOW THAT I CAN KEEP THIS UP FOREVER!
YOU'RE GOING TO HAVE TO FIGHT ME-- OR DIE!
I WON'T.
I WON'T FIGHT.
AND I SURE WON'T DIE.
WE'LL JUST HAVE TO TEST YOUR THEORY.
WHUUUMP

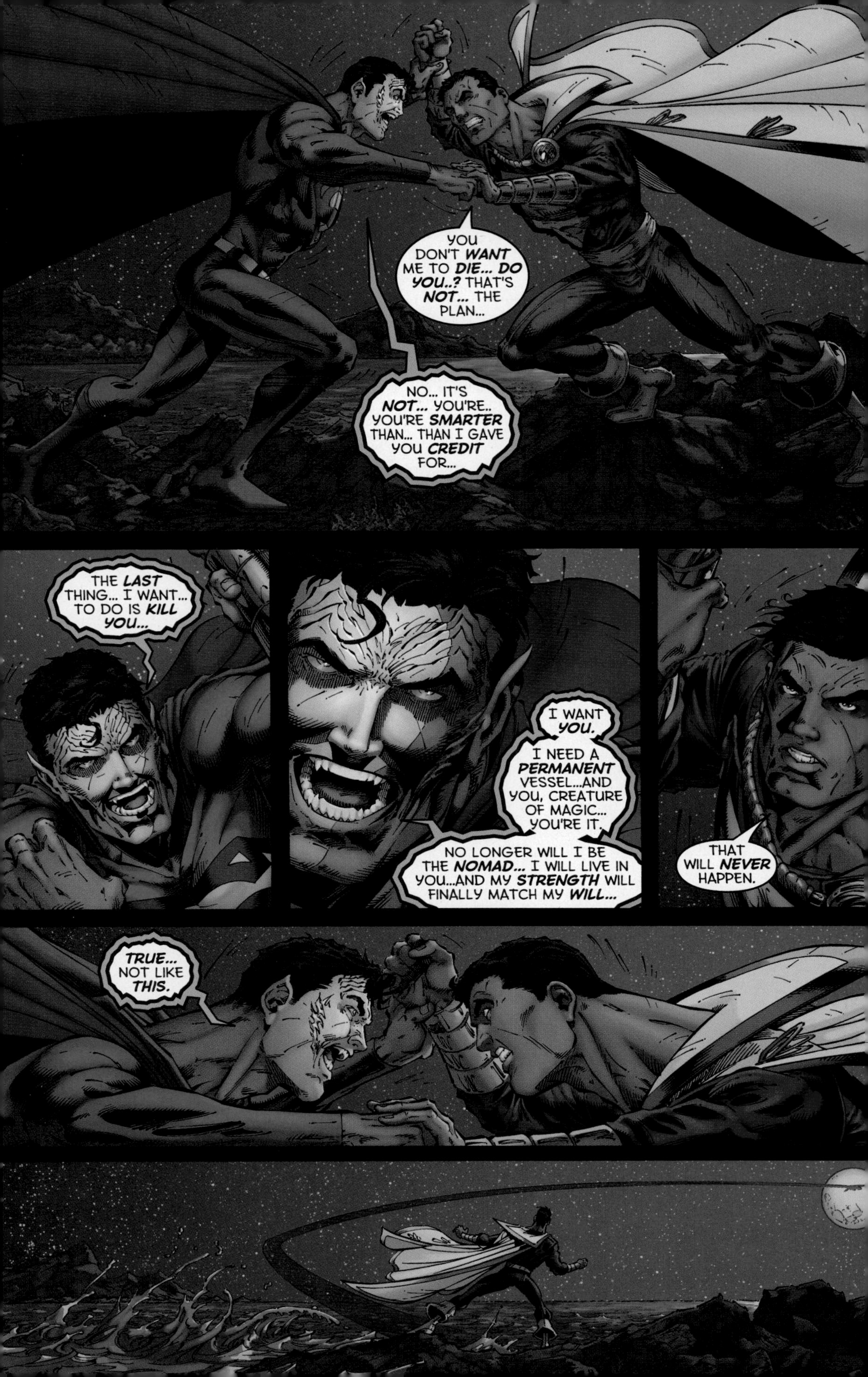
YOU DON'T WANT ME TO DIE... DO YOU..? THAT'S NOT... THE PLAN...
NO... IT'S NOT... YOU'RE.. YOU'RE SMARTER THAN... THAN I GAVE YOU CREDIT FOR...
THE LAST THING... I WANT... TO DO IS KILL YOU...
I WANT YOU.
I NEED A PERMANENT VESSEL...AND YOU, CREATURE OF MAGIC... YOU'RE IT.
NO LONGER WILL I BE THE NOMAD... I WILL LIVE IN YOU...AND MY STRENGTH WILL FINALLY MATCH MY WILL...
THAT WILL NEVER HAPPEN.
TRUE... NOT LIKE THIS.

SO, WE GO TO PLAN B.

YOU WILL GIVE ME POSSESSION OF YOUR BEING *WILLINGLY*.

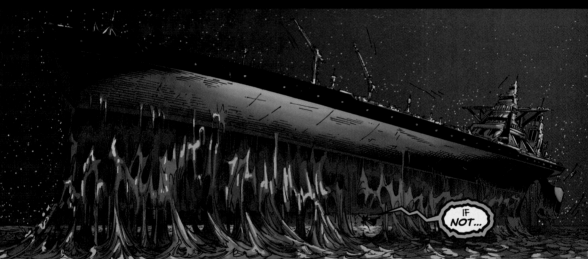

IF *NOT*...

NO.

WE CAN JUST WAIT UNTIL THE *BODY COUNT* GETS HIGH ENOUGH THAT YOU *RECONSIDER*.

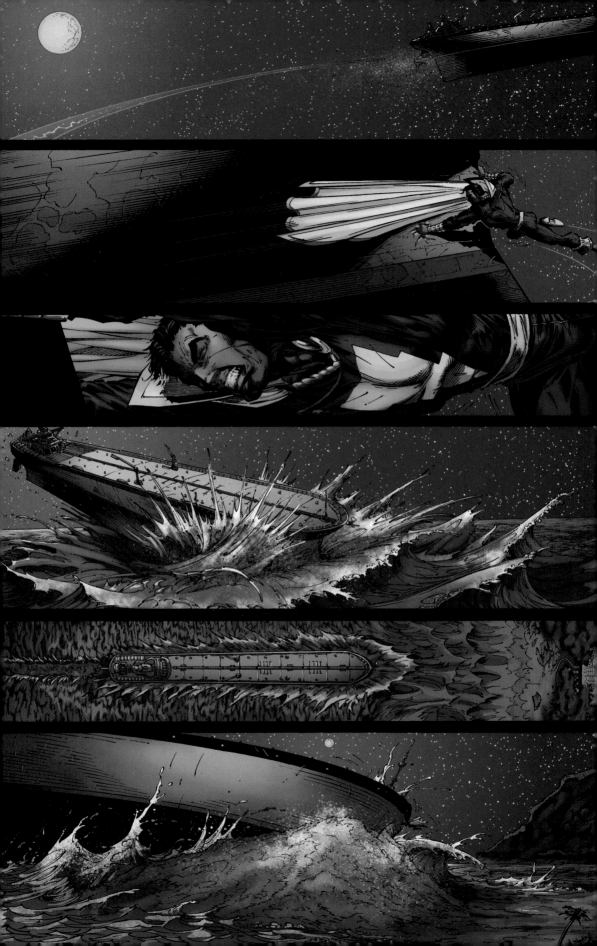

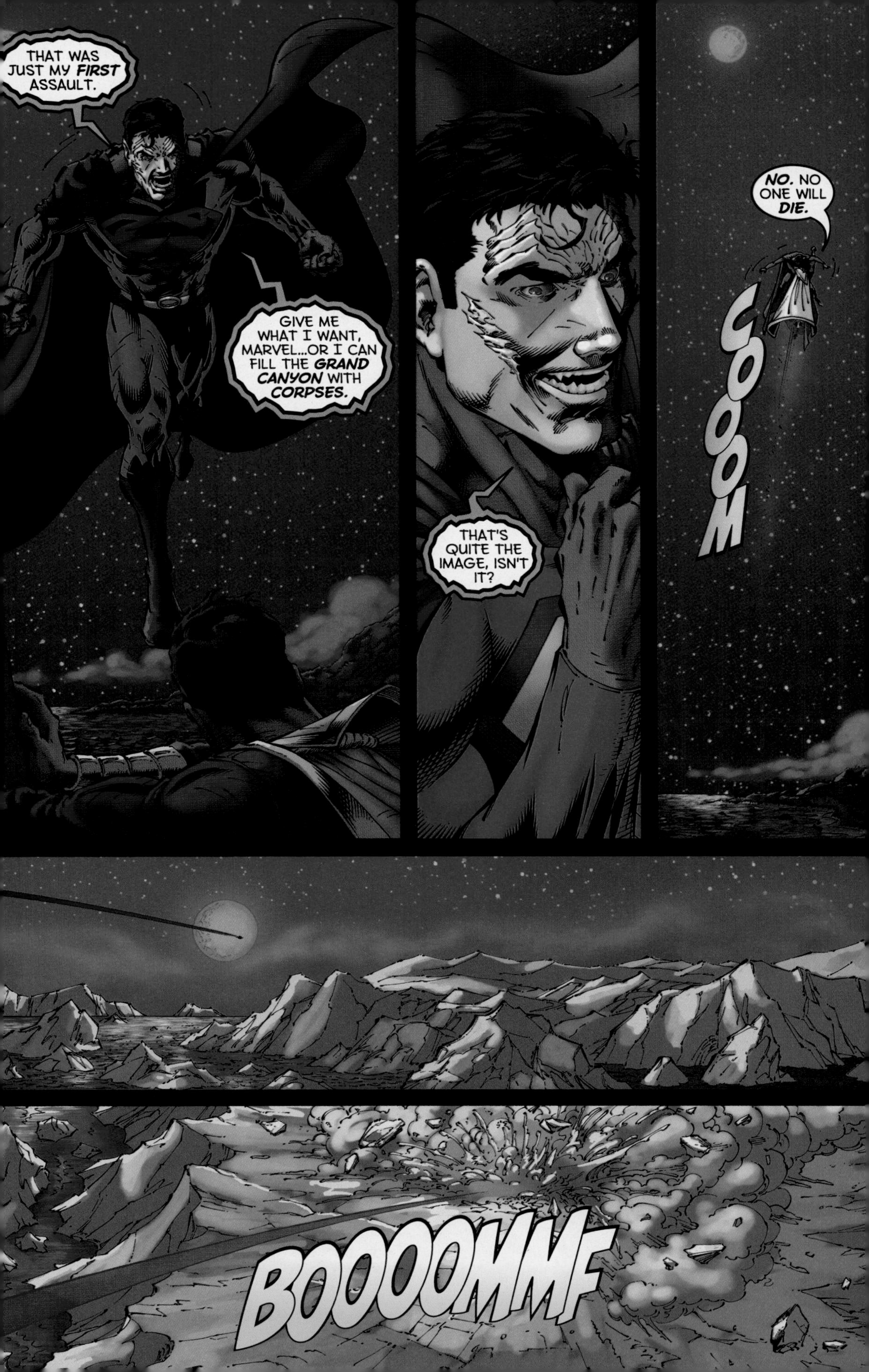
THAT WAS JUST MY FIRST ASSAULT.
GIVE ME WHAT I WANT, MARVEL...OR I CAN FILL THE GRAND CANYON WITH CORPSES.
THAT'S QUITE THE IMAGE, ISN'T IT?
NO. NO ONE WILL DIE.
COOOOM
BOOOOMMF

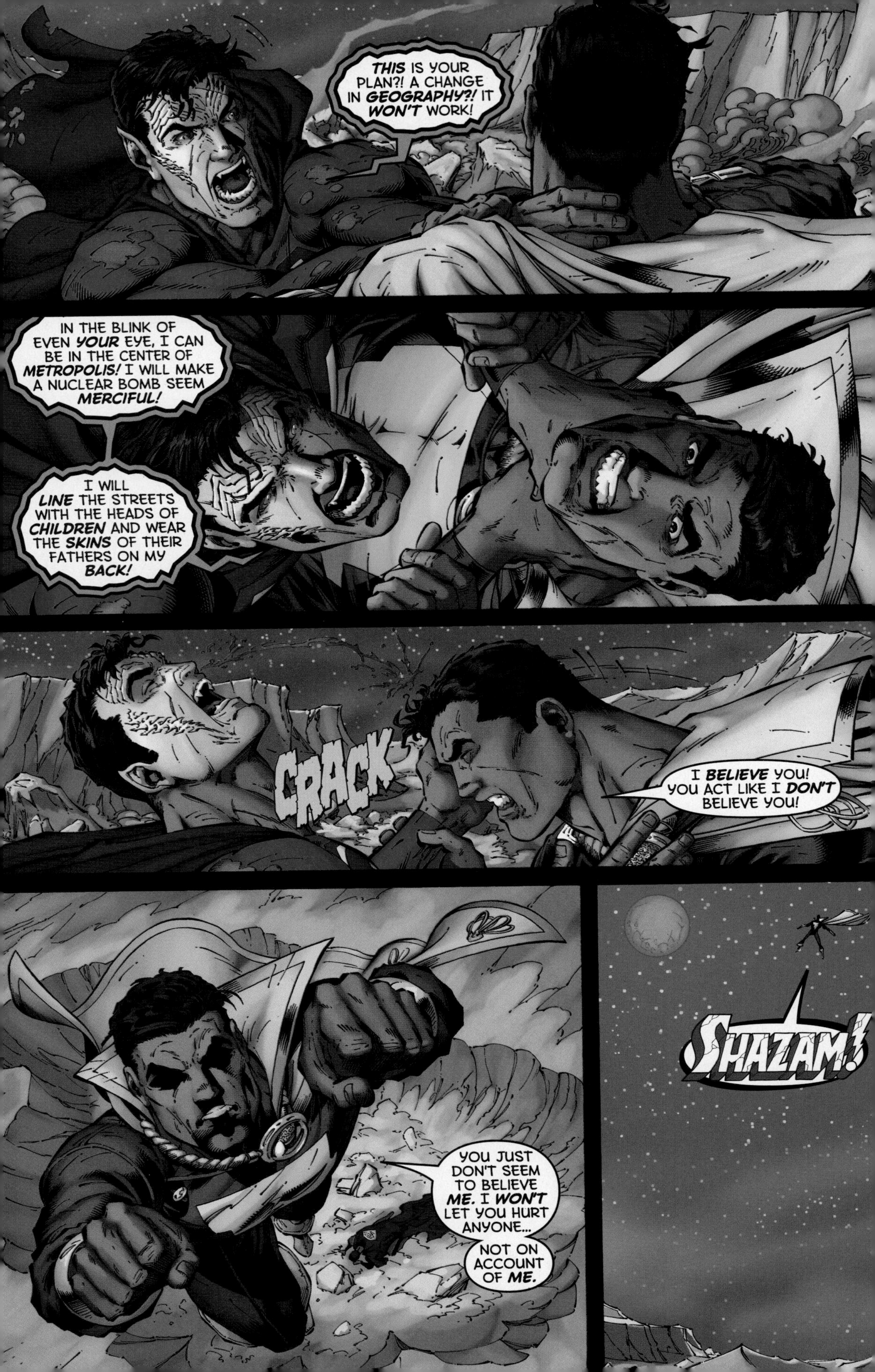
THIS IS YOUR PLAN?! A CHANGE IN GEOGRAPHY?! IT WON'T WORK!
IN THE BLINK OF EVEN YOUR EYE, I CAN BE IN THE CENTER OF METROPOLIS! I WILL MAKE A NUCLEAR BOMB SEEM MERCIFUL!
I WILL LINE THE STREETS WITH THE HEADS OF CHILDREN AND WEAR THE SKINS OF THEIR FATHERS ON MY BACK!
CRACK
I BELIEVE YOU! YOU ACT LIKE I DON'T BELIEVE YOU!
YOU JUST DON'T SEEM TO BELIEVE ME. I WON'T LET YOU HURT ANYONE...
NOT ON ACCOUNT OF ME.
SHAZAM!

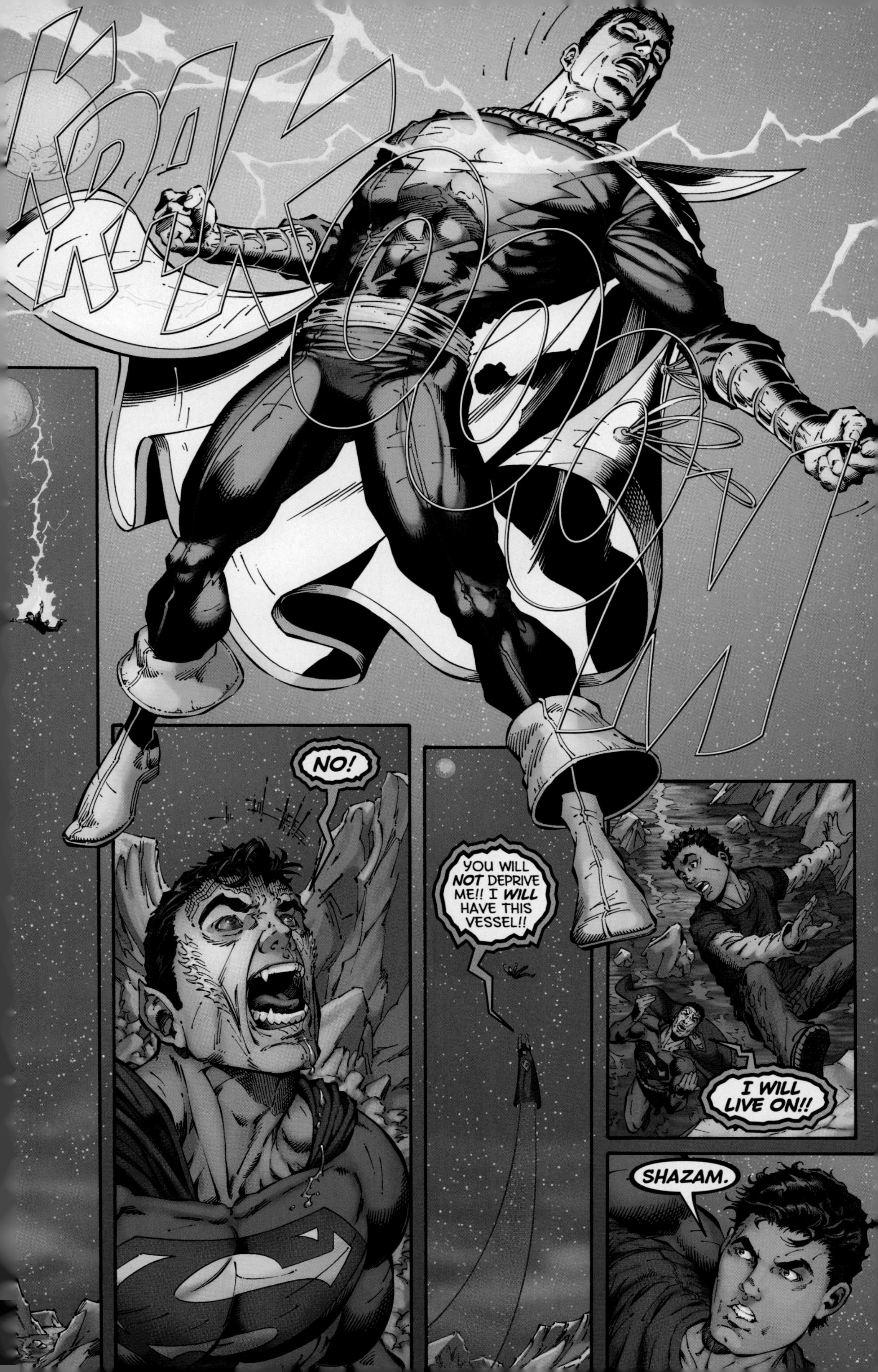
NO!
YOU WILL NOT DEPRIVE ME!! I WILL HAVE THIS VESSEL!!
I WILL LIVE ON!!
SHAZAM.

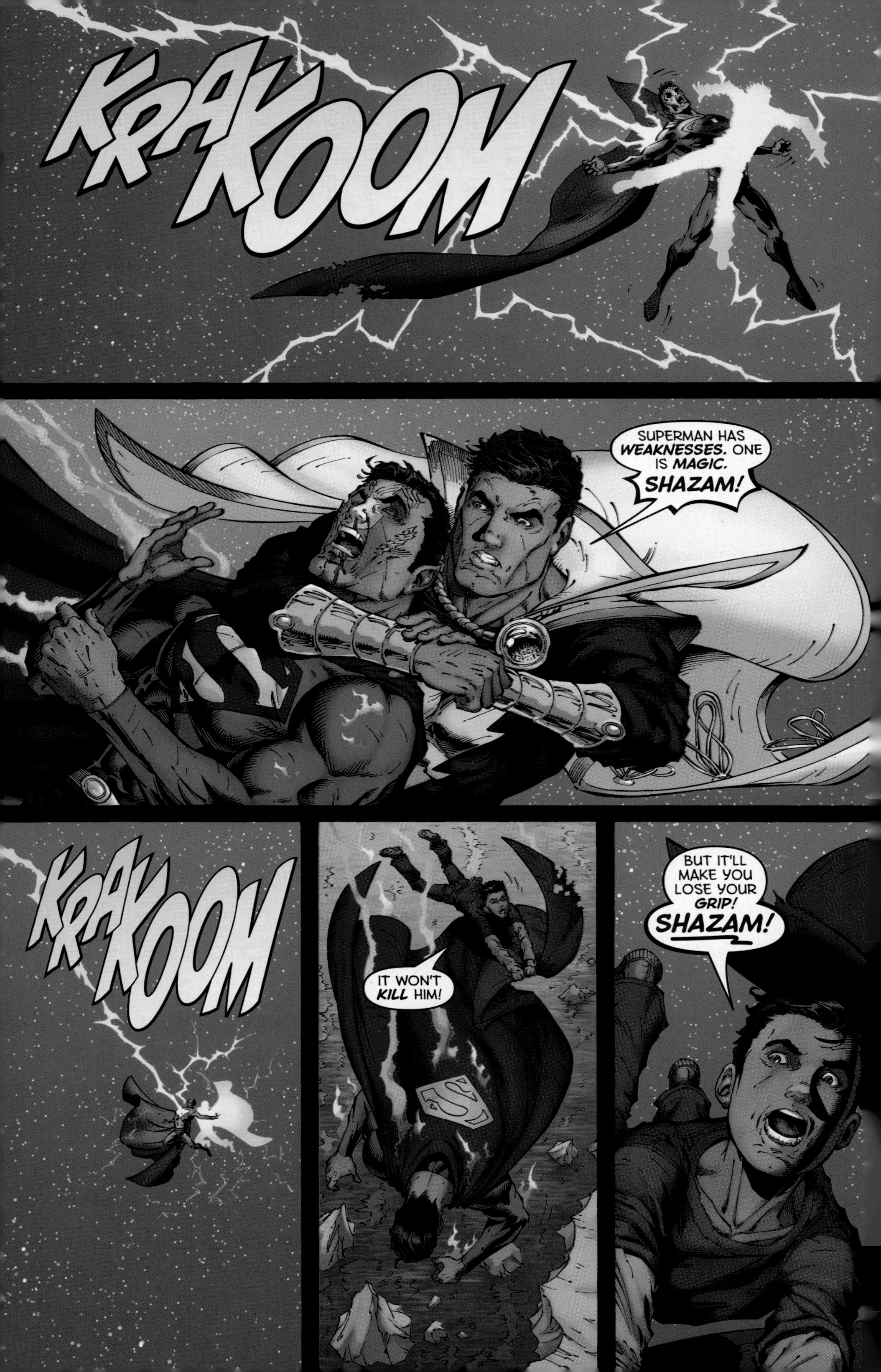
KRAKOOM
SUPERMAN HAS WEAKNESSES. ONE IS MAGIC. SHAZAM!
KRAKOOM
IT WON'T KILL HIM!
BUT IT'LL MAKE YOU LOSE YOUR GRIP! SHAZAM!

IT'S ...T... IT'S **NOT** ...WORKING...

SUPERMAN...?

ECLIPSO... HAS **TOO** STRONG A GRIP... I **CAN'T** BREAK... I **CAN'T**...

KILL ME...

I **KNOW** THAT'S NOT **SUPERMAN** TALKING, ECLIPSO.

AND YOU **KNOW** I CAN'T **KILL** HIM.

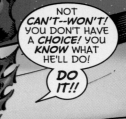

NOT **CAN'T**--**WON'T!** YOU DON'T HAVE A **CHOICE!** YOU **KNOW** WHAT HE'LL DO!

DO IT!!

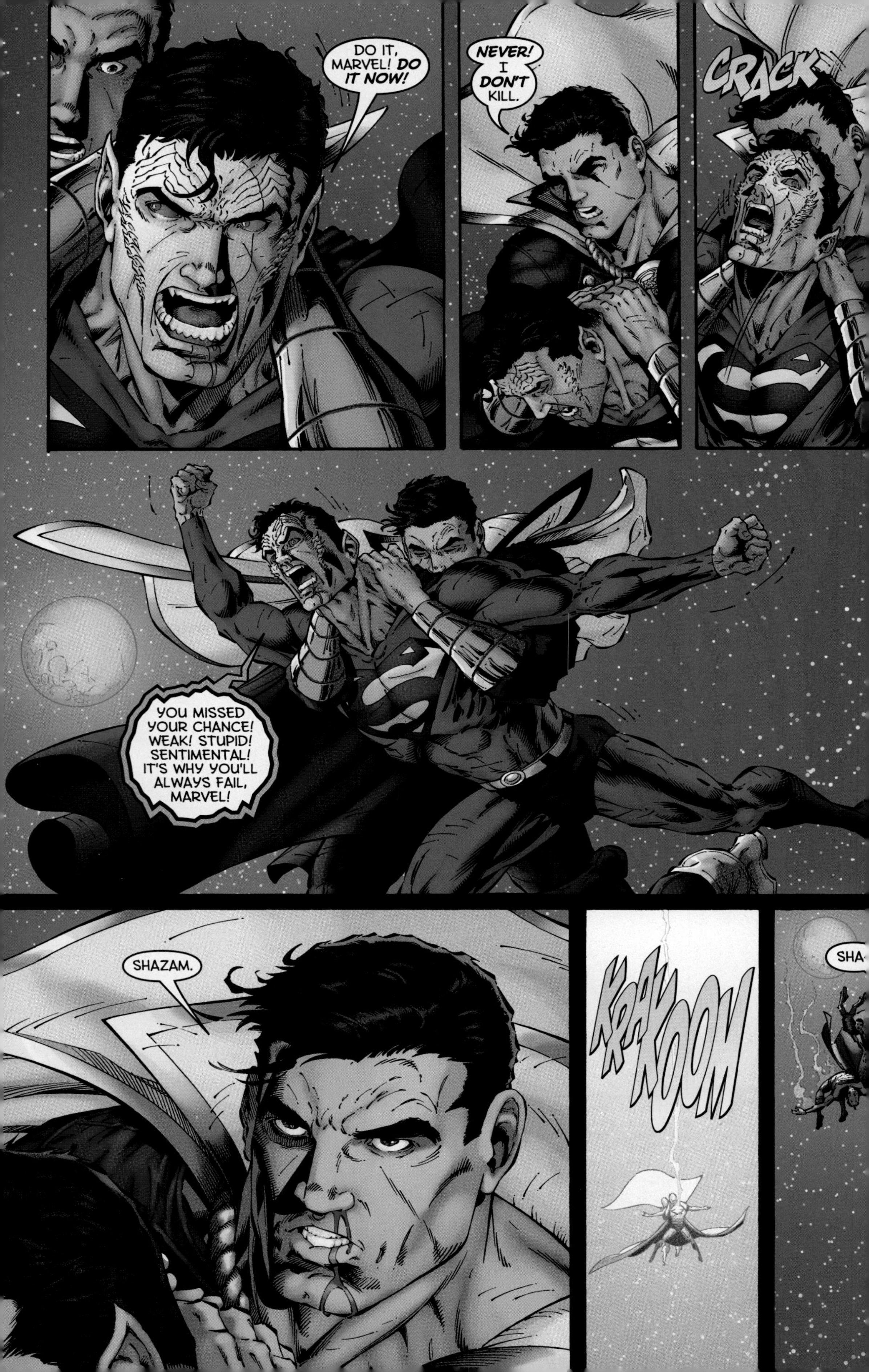
DO IT, MARVEL! DO IT NOW!
NEVER! I DON'T KILL.
CRACK
YOU MISSED YOUR CHANCE! WEAK! STUPID! SENTIMENTAL! IT'S WHY YOU'LL ALWAYS FAIL, MARVEL!
SHAZAM.
KRAKOOM
SHA

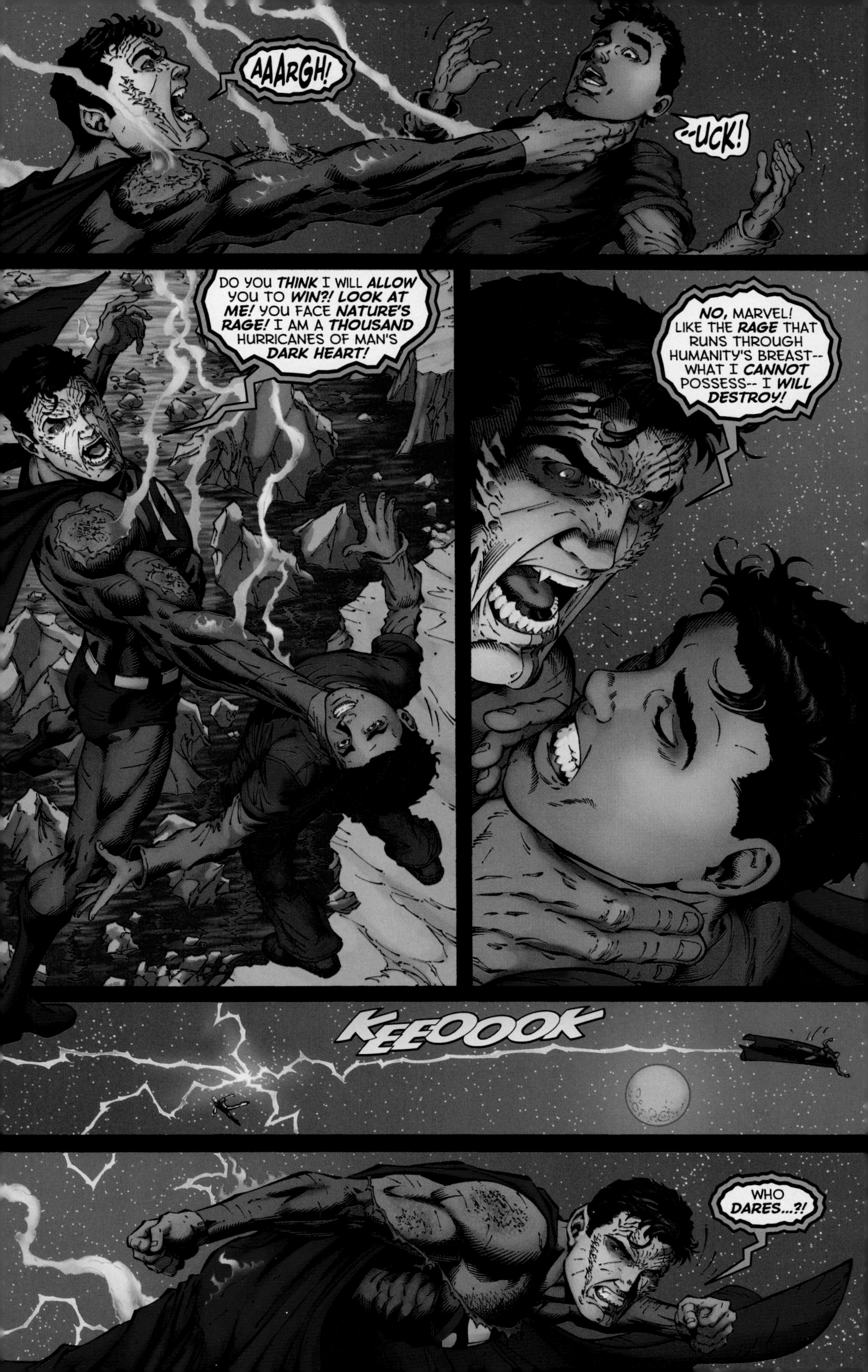
AAARGH!
--UCK!
DO YOU THINK I WILL ALLOW YOU TO WIN?! LOOK AT ME! YOU FACE NATURE'S RAGE! I AM A THOUSAND HURRICANES OF MAN'S DARK HEART!
NO, MARVEL! LIKE THE RAGE THAT RUNS THROUGH HUMANITY'S BREAST-- WHAT I CANNOT POSSESS-- I WILL DESTROY!
KEEOOOK
WHO DARES...?!

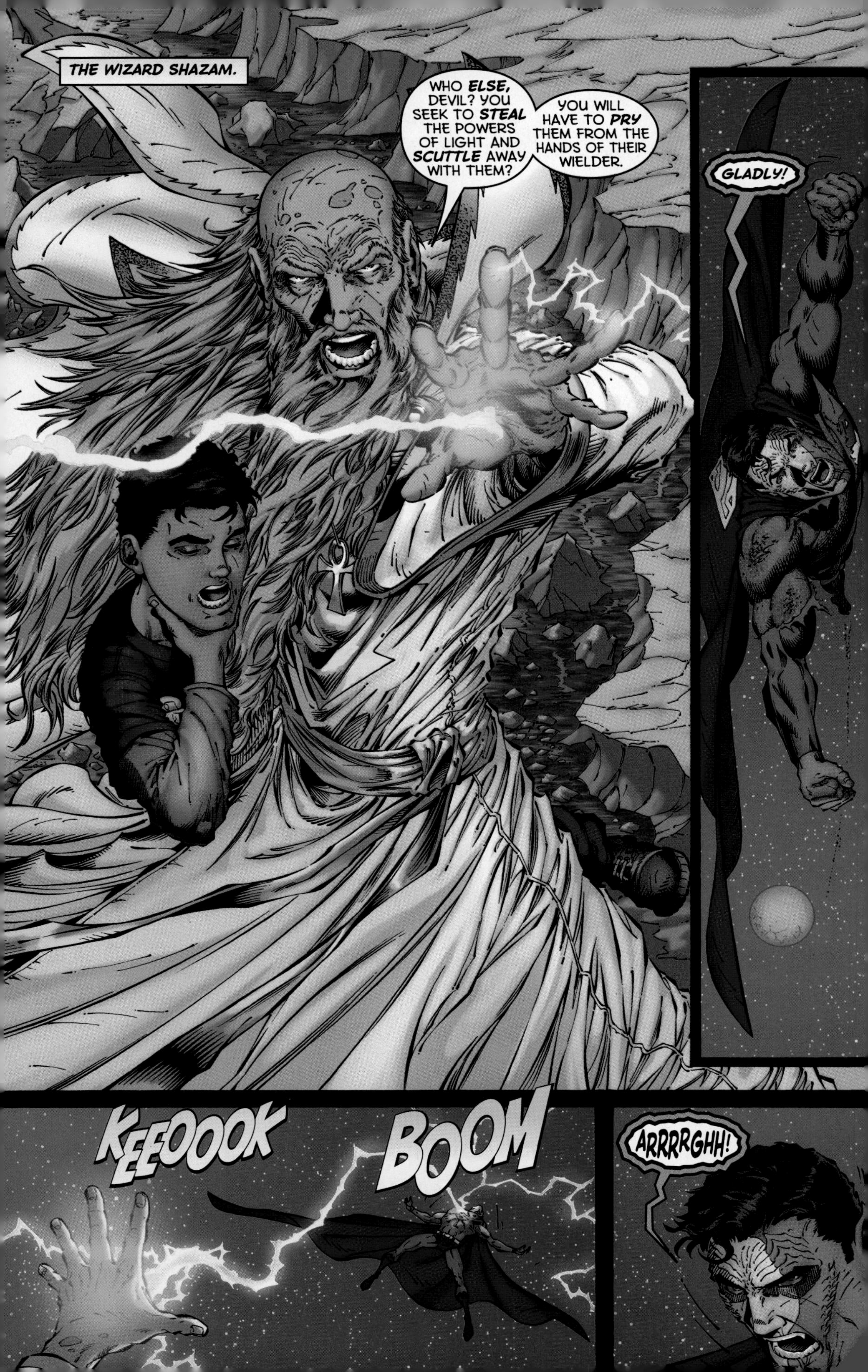
THE WIZARD SHAZAM.
WHO ELSE, DEVIL? YOU SEEK TO STEAL THE POWERS OF LIGHT AND SCUTTLE AWAY WITH THEM?
YOU WILL HAVE TO PRY THEM FROM THE HANDS OF THEIR WIELDER.
GLADLY!
KEEEOOOK
BOOM
ARRRRGHH!

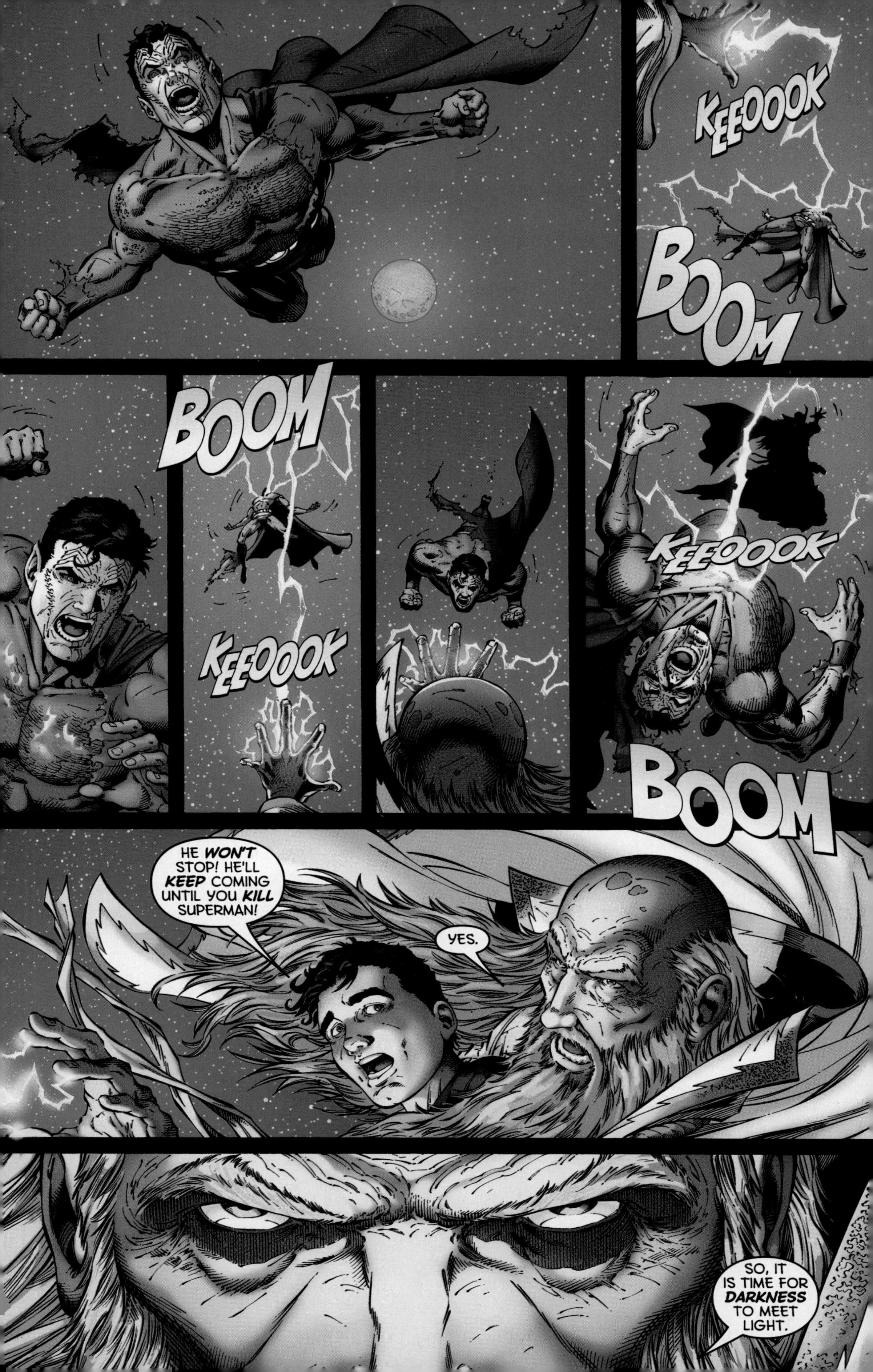
KEEOOOK
BOOM
BOOM
KEEOOOK
KEEOOOK
BOOM
HE **WON'T** STOP! HE'LL **KEEP** COMING UNTIL YOU **KILL** SUPERMAN!
YES.
SO, IT IS TIME FOR **DARKNESS** TO MEET LIGHT.

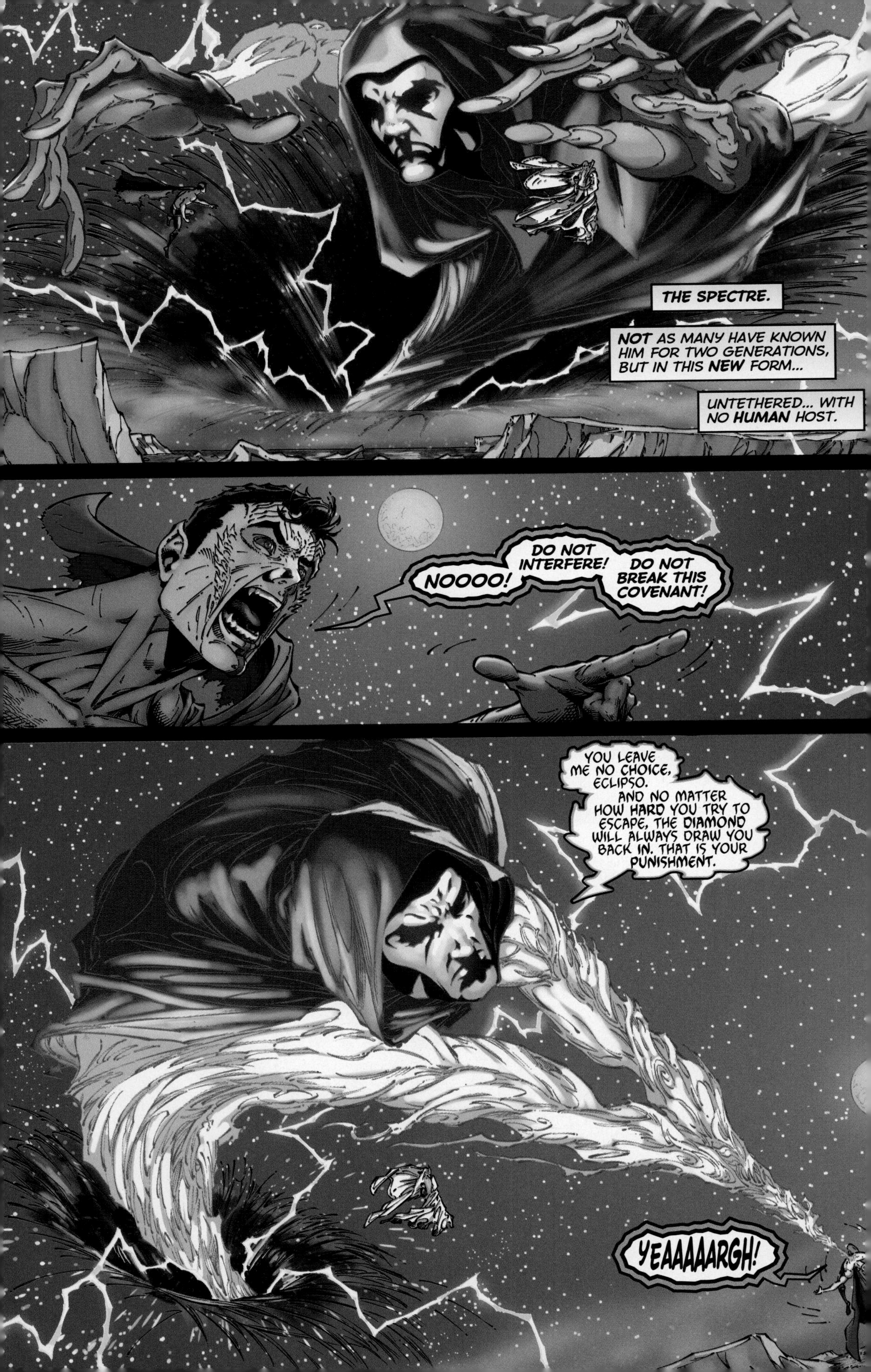
THE SPECTRE.
NOT AS MANY HAVE KNOWN HIM FOR TWO GENERATIONS, BUT IN THIS NEW FORM...
UNTETHERED... WITH NO HUMAN HOST.
NOOOO!
DO NOT INTERFERE!
DO NOT BREAK THIS COVENANT!
YOU LEAVE ME NO CHOICE, ECLIPSO.
AND NO MATTER HOW HARD YOU TRY TO ESCAPE, THE DIAMOND WILL ALWAYS DRAW YOU BACK IN. THAT IS YOUR PUNISHMENT.
YEAAAAARGH!

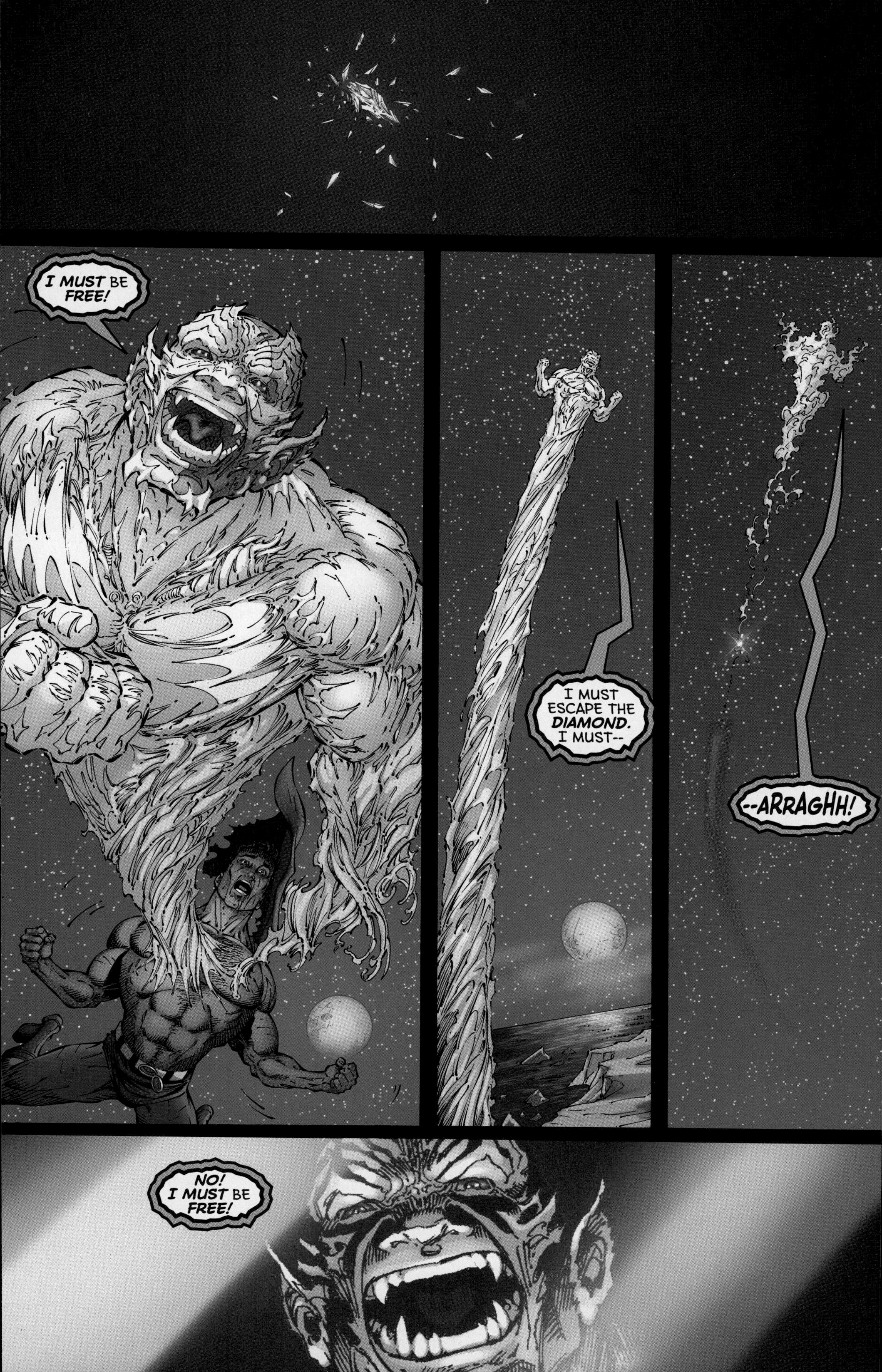

I MUST BE FREE!
I MUST ESCAPE THE DIAMOND. I MUST--
--ARRAGHH!
NO! I MUST BE FREE!

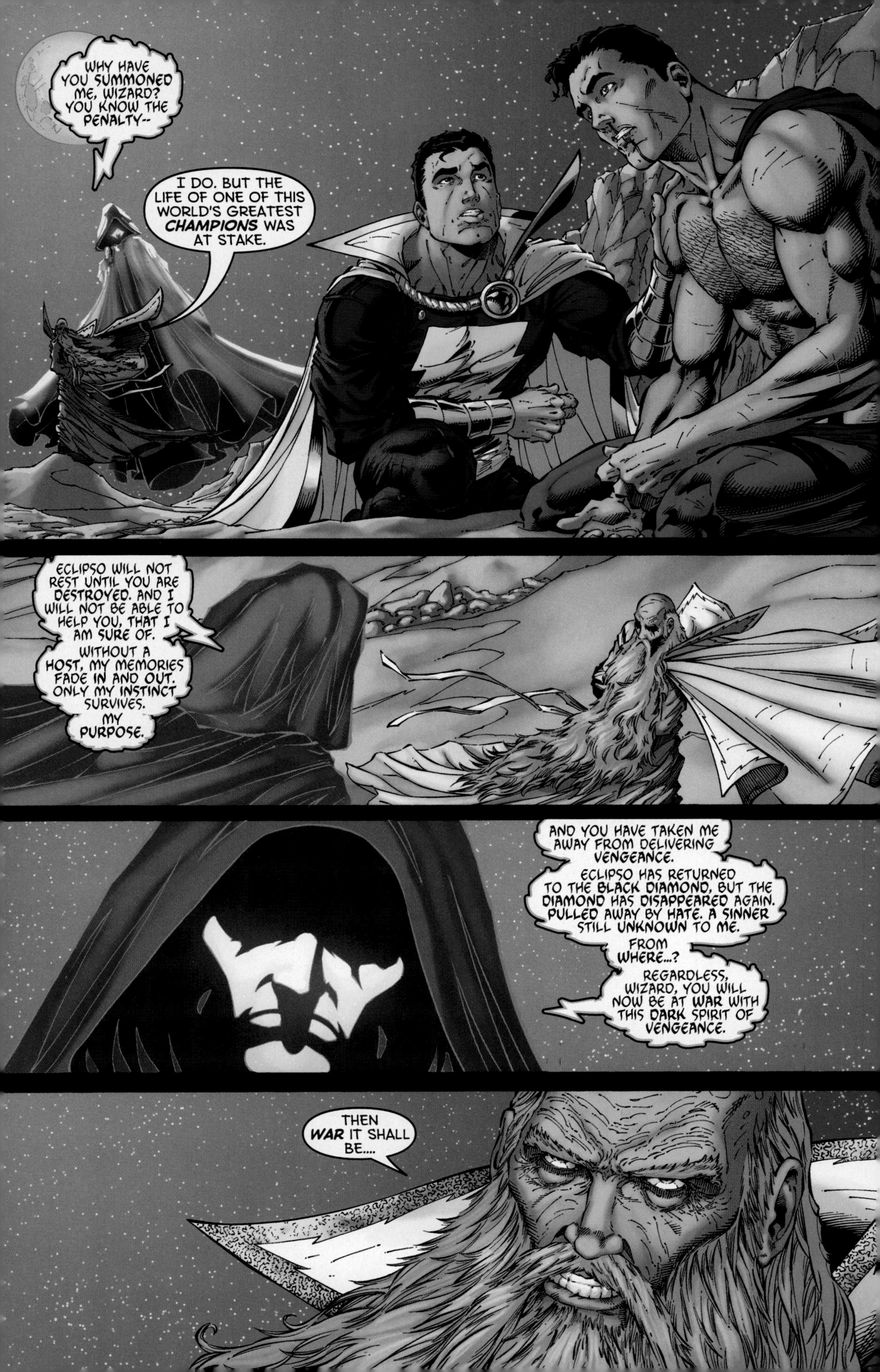
WHY HAVE YOU SUMMONED ME, WIZARD? YOU KNOW THE PENALTY--
I DO. BUT THE LIFE OF ONE OF THIS WORLD'S GREATEST CHAMPIONS WAS AT STAKE.
ECLIPSO WILL NOT REST UNTIL YOU ARE DESTROYED. AND I WILL NOT BE ABLE TO HELP YOU, THAT I AM SURE OF.
WITHOUT A HOST, MY MEMORIES FADE IN AND OUT. ONLY MY INSTINCT SURVIVES. MY PURPOSE.
AND YOU HAVE TAKEN ME AWAY FROM DELIVERING VENGEANCE.
ECLIPSO HAS RETURNED TO THE BLACK DIAMOND, BUT THE DIAMOND HAS DISAPPEARED AGAIN. PULLED AWAY BY HATE. A SINNER STILL UNKNOWN TO ME.
FROM WHERE...?
REGARDLESS, WIZARD, YOU WILL NOW BE AT WAR WITH THIS DARK SPIRIT OF VENGEANCE.
THEN WAR IT SHALL BE....

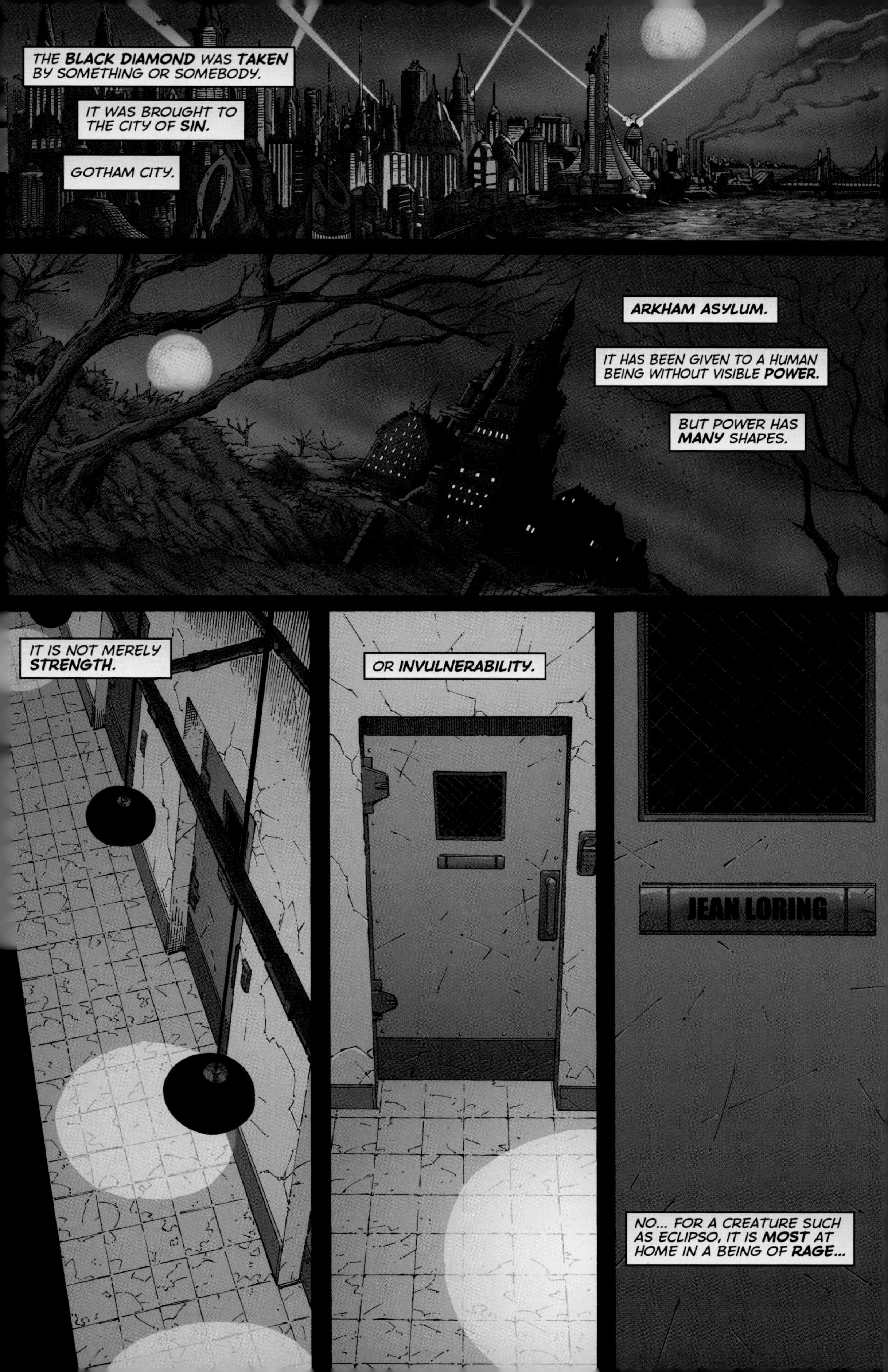
THE BLACK DIAMOND WAS TAKEN BY SOMETHING OR SOMEBODY.
IT WAS BROUGHT TO THE CITY OF SIN.
GOTHAM CITY.
ARKHAM ASYLUM.
IT HAS BEEN GIVEN TO A HUMAN BEING WITHOUT VISIBLE POWER.
BUT POWER HAS MANY SHAPES.
IT IS NOT MERELY STRENGTH.
OR INVULNERABILITY.
JEAN LORING
NO... FOR A CREATURE SUCH AS ECLIPSO, IT IS MOST AT HOME IN A BEING OF RAGE...

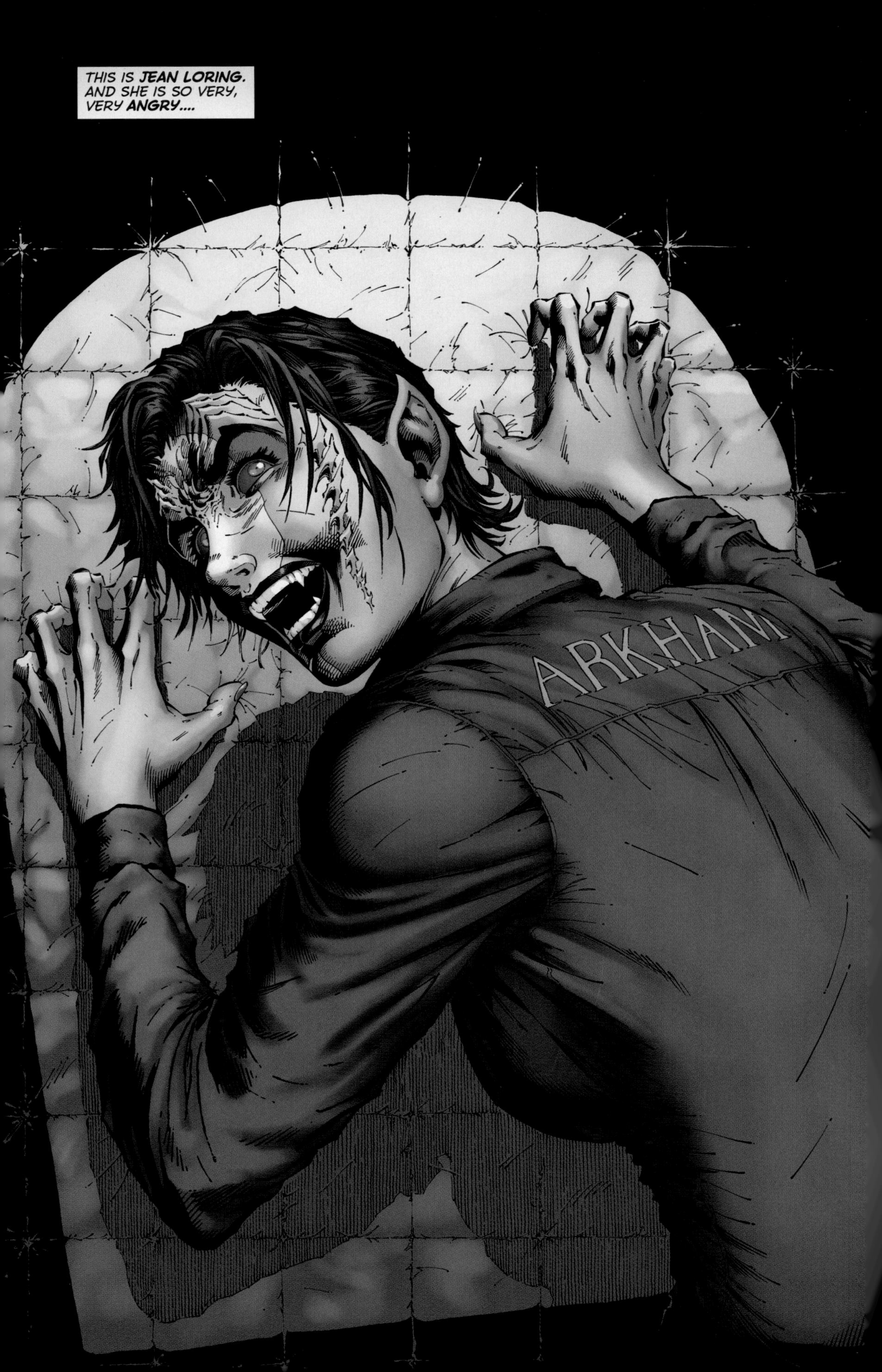
THIS IS JEAN LORING. AND SHE IS SO VERY, VERY ANGRY....
ARKHAM

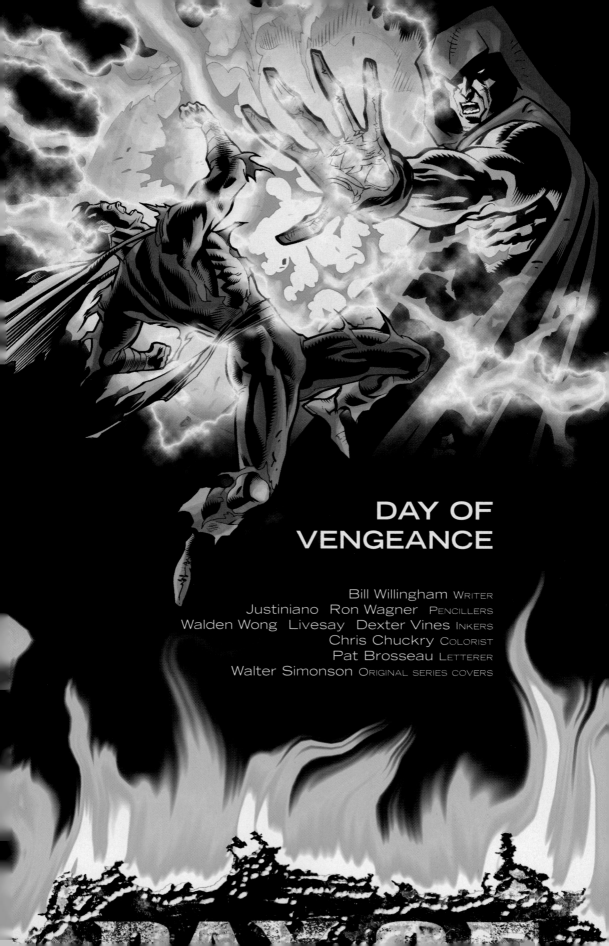

DAY OF VENGEANCE

Bill Willingham WRITER
Justiniano Ron Wagner PENCILLERS
Walden Wong Livesay Dexter Vines INKERS
Chris Chuckry COLORIST
Pat Brosseau LETTERER
Walter Simonson ORIGINAL SERIES COVERS

THE WORLD OF HEROES AND SORCERERS

While many mortals gained powers and abilities far beyond those of their peers ever since the first man was turned immortal, the concentration of such beings was never greater than it is today. It could be that Earth, the universe and the allied dimensions need so many champions. Or it could all be an experiment at the whim of Order and Chaos or the denizens of the Silver City or a fluke from the passing Godwave. No one may ever know.

But many of these super-heroes and super-villains also try to lead something resembling a normal life. They have siblings, parents and loved ones. But being the partner of a super-being has its risks.

In one such case, scientist Ray Palmer found himself married to lawyer Jean Loring, the love of his life. But Ray's duties at Ivy University and The Atom's obligations as a member of the Justice League of America left Jean lonely. And she found solace in the arms of another man and the marriage died.

Jean discovered over time that she missed Ray, missed being part of the super-hero community and wanted him back. It all seemed so simple at first, use one of Ray's size-changing belts to reduce her mass and threaten Sue Dibny, wife of the Elongated Man. But it all went horribly wrong and Sue died. The heroes were devastated and while they searched for the supposed murderer, they also drew their dearest ones closer, ironically part of Jean's plan. And Ray drew Jean close and a dormant romance was rekindled…

…Until the scientists and detectives among the heroes determined the culprit was Jean. Driven to the brink of madness, Jean was uncontrollable and Ray found himself grief-stricken, consigning her to Arkham Asylum for the Criminally Insane. And that is where the hostless Eclipso found her.

So begins the story, but first let us introduce you to the dramatis personae…

BLUE DEVIL

An encounter with the demon Nebiros left stuntman Daniel Cassidy permanently bonded with the costume he was wearing for his new movie, and he soon became known as Blue Devil. Daniel frantically tried to find ways out of the suit before eventually resigning himself to his fate. Rather than perform before the camera, he fell back on becoming a special effects supervisor. Still, his mystical transformation also seemed to have turned him into a "weirdness magnet," and he found himself spending his time fighting demons, criminals and a freaked-out public. Eventually tiring of the constant battles, he made a deal with the demon Neron in exchange for becoming a successful actor. He learned too late that his success would come at the expense of other human life, as well as his being transformed into a true demon. Blue Devil was subsequently killed in combat with the second Mist. During the Day of Judgment, the magician Faust resurrected Daniel and helped him evolve into a powerful demon. Blue Devil also obtained the fabled trident of Lucifer and now strides the Earth, locating demons and banishing them back to Hell.

ENCHANTRESS

secret passage in Terror Castle led June Moone to a eature named Dhazmor, who revealed her destiny to ecome a magical defender. By uttering the name Enchantress," June acquired awesome powers, hich she used to thwart mystical menaces. Years ter, Dhazmor summoned June and told her that an stral alignment would empower her to cleanse the arth of evil. But Power Girl prevented the alignment moving the real Moon, denying June her destiny. nbittered, June lost control of her alter ego and the nchantress turned to villainy. Jailed for her crimes, e Enchantress was given amnesty as a member of e U.S. government's Suicide Squad. June's fight th the Enchantress ended when the son of Felix ust sacrificed her to reignite the fires of Hell. though the Enchantress appeared to have died, eeing June, the sacrifice merely further split her syche. She returned, disguised as demoness Anita oulfeeda during a Justice League mission. After arrowly losing to the JLA, this third personality took ot and June shared the evil Enchantress's personal- with its mirror persona, Soulsinger. Right now, e Enchantress personality appears to be dominant.

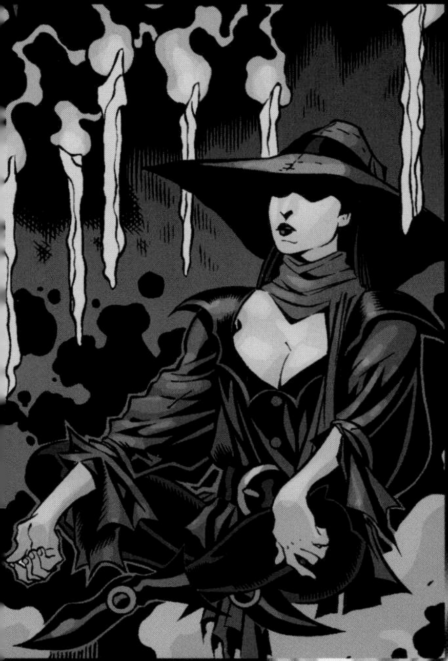

NIGHTMASTER

In the late 1960s, Jim Rook, lead singer of rock band The Electrics, entered a strange New York City shop called Oblivion, Inc. with his fiancée Janet and found himself transported to the alternate dimension of Myrra, a land of knights and sorcerers. Rook learned that he was the descendant of a Myrran warrior and took up his ancestor's magic Sword of Night. At that moment, Jim Rook became the Nightmaster. Reluctant to play a chivalrous role that he found slightly ridiculous, Nightmaster nevertheless freed Myrra from the grip of evil warlocks and returned with his fiancée to Earth. Over the next two decades he opened a bookstore in the Oblivion Inc. location and led a quiet life, until persuaded to help the Leymen of Primal Force defeat the cult called the August. An encounter with Swamp Thing convinced Rook that his Myrra experiences had been an hallucination, but the truth seems to have won out. For reasons unexplained, Oblivion, Inc. has morphed into the pandimension Oblivion Bar where mystics from across space and time can congregate in relative peace.

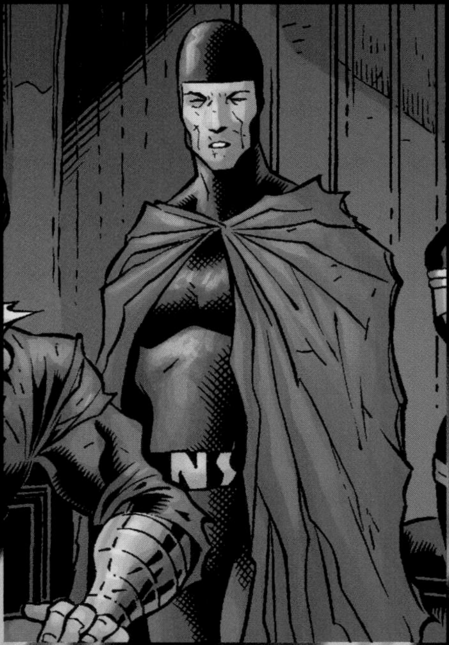
NS

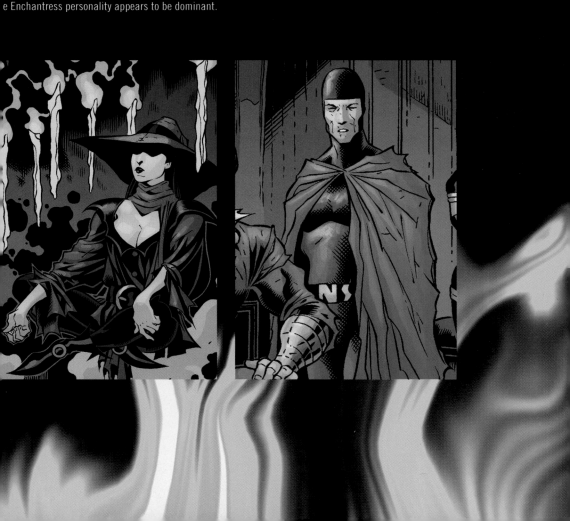

Eve's mother, Maureen, was Queen of the Land of the Nightshades, a mystic dimension. Maureen took Eve and her brother Larry to the Nightshade world and Maureen was attacked by the Incubus, a vile being that abducted Larry. Eve promised her dying mother that she would find Larry and take him back to Earth. Eve became the government agent Nightshade, training at first with King Faraday and then joining the Suicide Squad. On a mission to the Nightshade world, Eve discovered that Larry had been possessed by the Incubus. Squad member Deadshot killed Larry, and the Incubus also died. Nightshade had romances with the Squad's Rick Flag and Nemesis, assisted Captain Atom on several occasions, worked with the extraterrestrial strikeforce InterC.E.P.T. for a time and recently adopted a new look shortly before her participation in a massive metahuman conflict involving Superman and Batman in Washington, D.C.

DETECTIVE CHIMP

Bobo tells his story better than anyone, and you'll find it four chapters in.

To protect themselves from persecution, the Jews of 16th century Prague animated a soulless golem from river clay. Wary of the monster they created, the Council of Rabbis decreed that the Golem should be replaced with a human defender. The Rabbis chose rags to clothe their new champion who, like the Golem, was empowered by a verse in the Kaballah. Thus, the "Ragman" was first woven to guard over the Warsaw Ghetto. During World War II, Jerzy Reganiewicz took up the patchwork mantle of the Ragman to protect Warsaw's Jews from the Nazis. Tragically, Jerzy failed to spare his people from the horrors of the Holocaust. Years later, Jerzy, renamed Gerry Regan after emigrating to the United States, passed down the Ragman's suit to his son, Rory, who first wore it to defend the oppressed denizens of Gotham City's slums. From his "Rags 'n' Tatters" junk shop, Rory continues to add new rags — each containing a piece of a corrupted soul — to the garish garment of the "Tattered Tatterdemalion," Ragman. Though working alone more often than not Ragman has paired with other modern day mystics as a Sentinel of Magic or a customer at the Oblivion Bar.

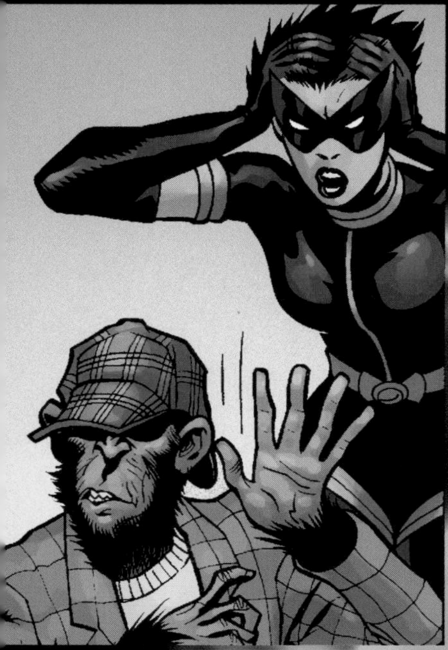

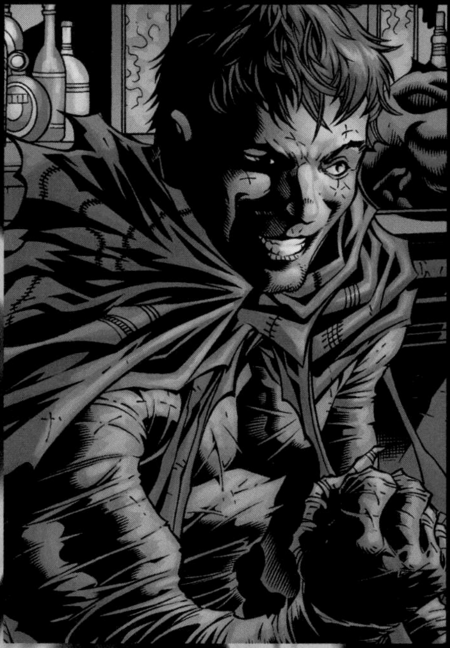

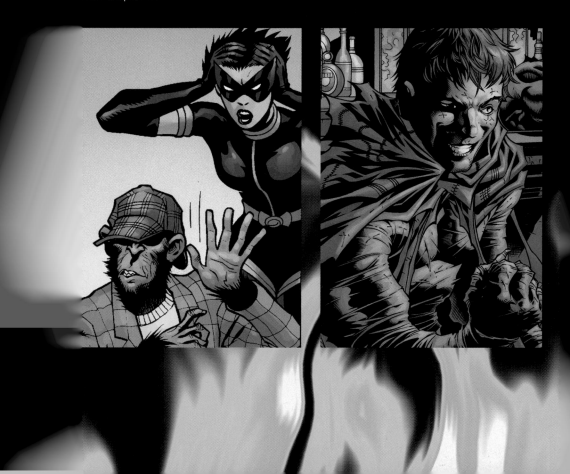

PROLOGUE:
A CONVERSATION IN A DARK PLACE

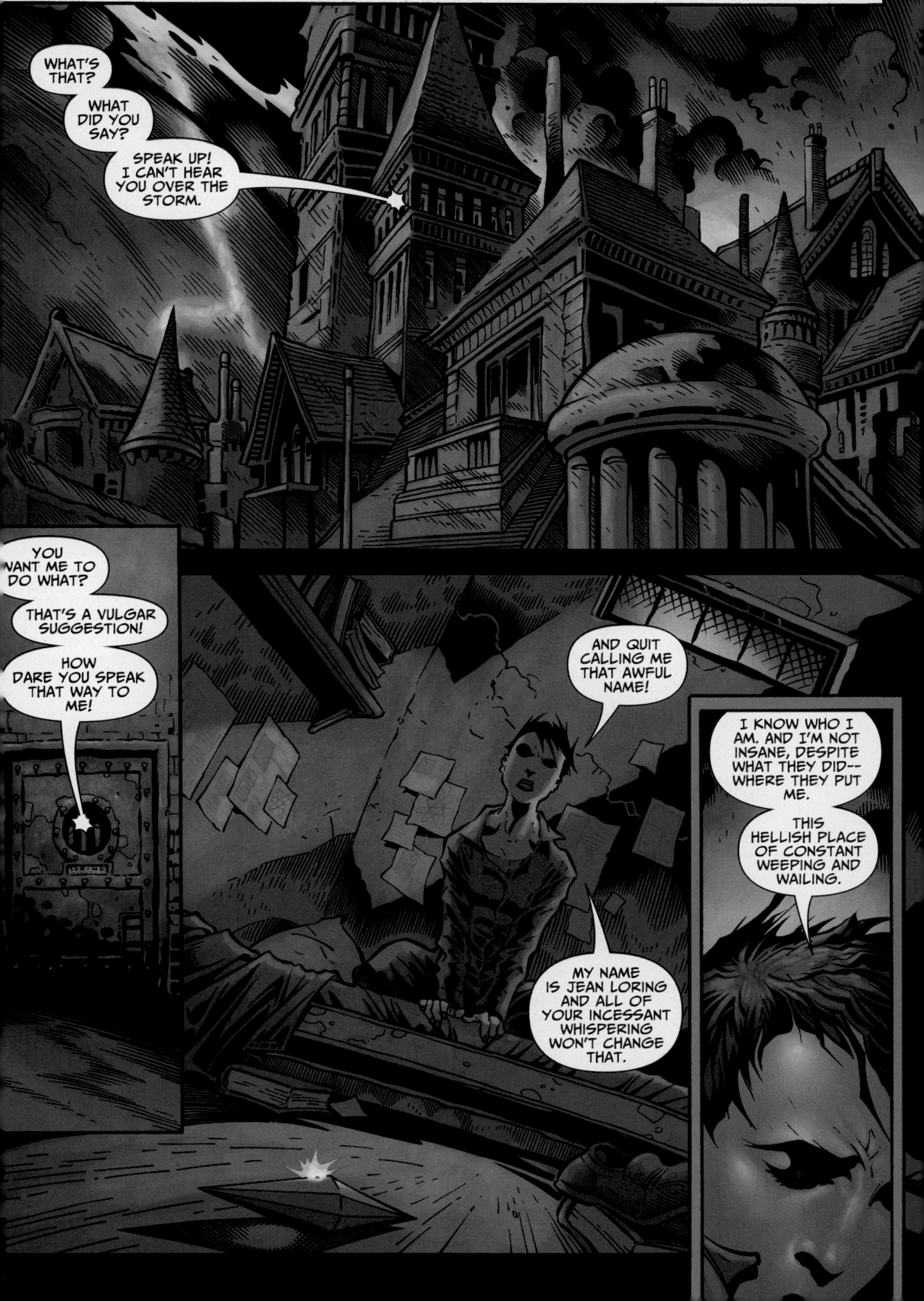

WHAT'S THAT?
WHAT DID YOU SAY?
SPEAK UP! I CAN'T HEAR YOU OVER THE STORM.
YOU WANT ME TO DO WHAT?
THAT'S A VULGAR SUGGESTION!
HOW DARE YOU SPEAK THAT WAY TO ME!
AND QUIT CALLING ME THAT AWFUL NAME!
MY NAME IS JEAN LORING AND ALL OF YOUR INCESSANT WHISPERING WON'T CHANGE THAT.
I KNOW WHO I AM. AND I'M NOT INSANE, DESPITE WHAT THEY DID-- WHERE THEY PUT ME.
THIS HELLISH PLACE OF CONSTANT WEEPING AND WAILING.

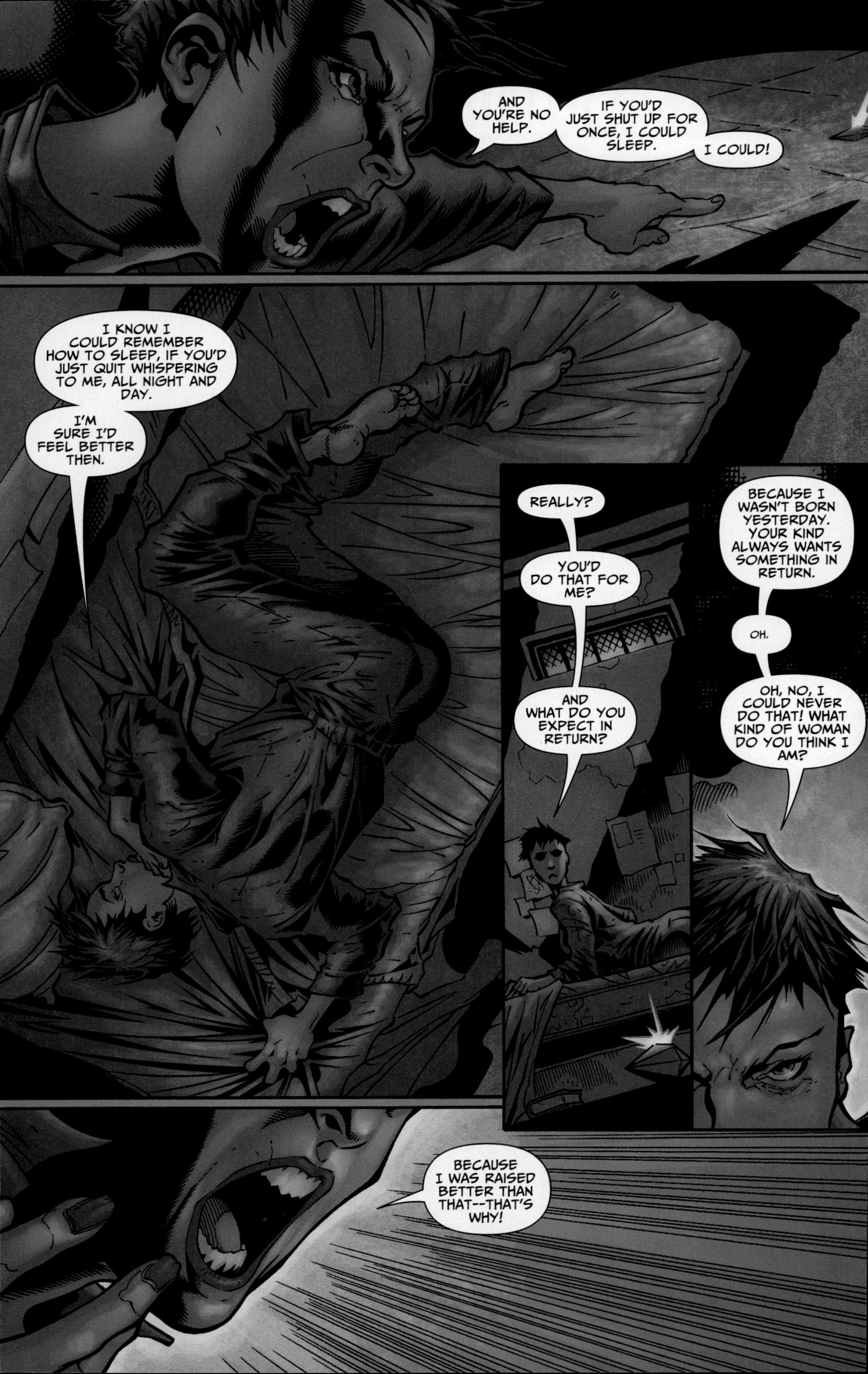
AND YOU'RE NO HELP.
IF YOU'D JUST SHUT UP FOR ONCE, I COULD SLEEP.
I COULD!
I KNOW I COULD REMEMBER HOW TO SLEEP, IF YOU'D JUST QUIT WHISPERING TO ME, ALL NIGHT AND DAY.
I'M SURE I'D FEEL BETTER THEN.
REALLY?
YOU'D DO THAT FOR ME?
AND WHAT DO YOU EXPECT IN RETURN?
BECAUSE I WASN'T BORN YESTERDAY. YOUR KIND ALWAYS WANTS SOMETHING IN RETURN.
OH.
OH, NO, I COULD NEVER DO THAT! WHAT KIND OF WOMAN DO YOU THINK I AM?
BECAUSE I WAS RAISED BETTER THAN THAT--THAT'S WHY!

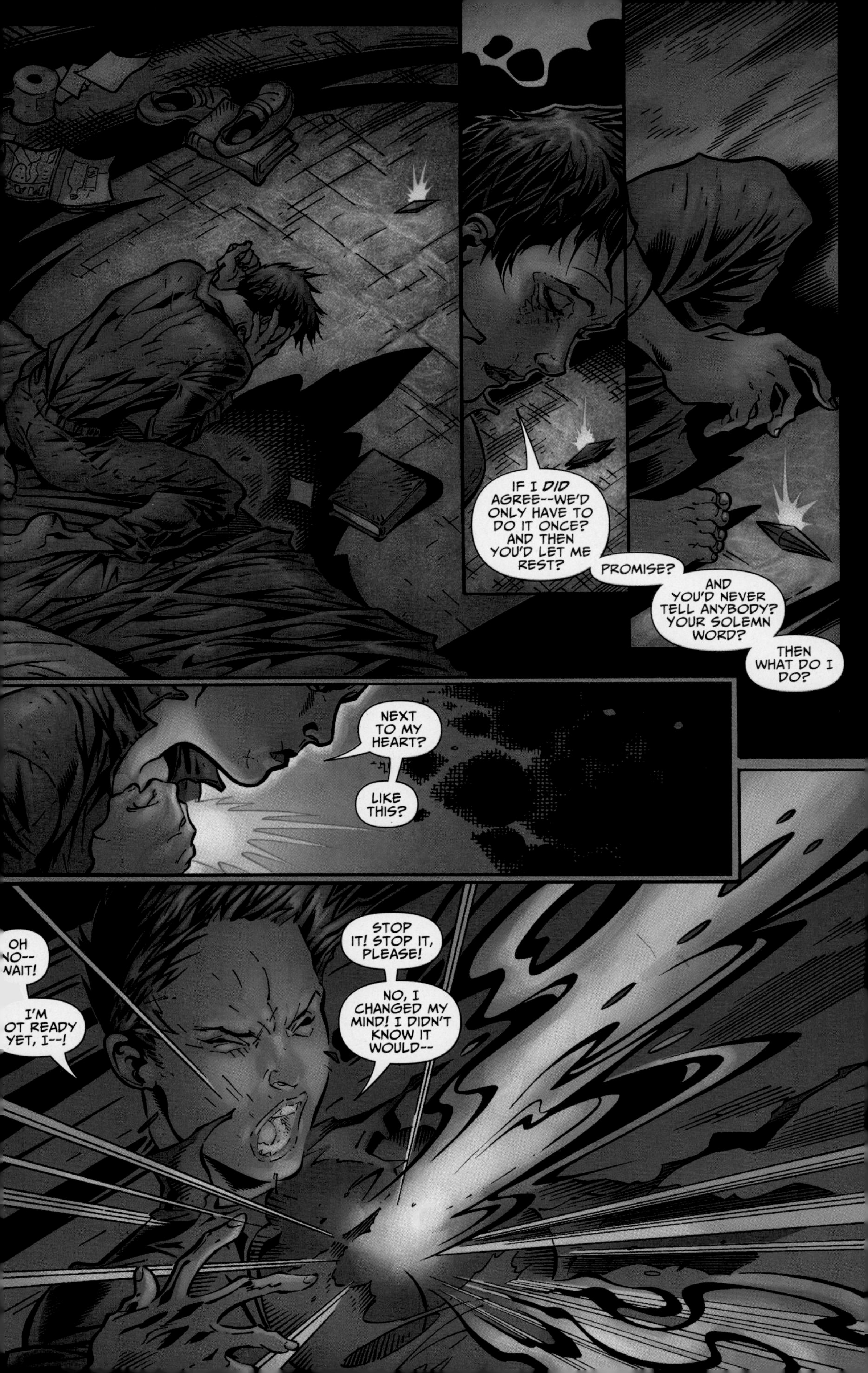
IF I *DID* AGREE--WE'D ONLY HAVE TO DO IT ONCE? AND THEN YOU'D LET ME REST?
PROMISE?
AND YOU'D NEVER TELL ANYBODY? YOUR SOLEMN WORD?
THEN WHAT DO I DO?
NEXT TO MY HEART?
LIKE THIS?
OH NO--
I'M
YET, I--!
STOP IT! STOP IT, PLEASE!
NO, I CHANGED MY MIND! I DIDN'T KNOW IT WOULD--

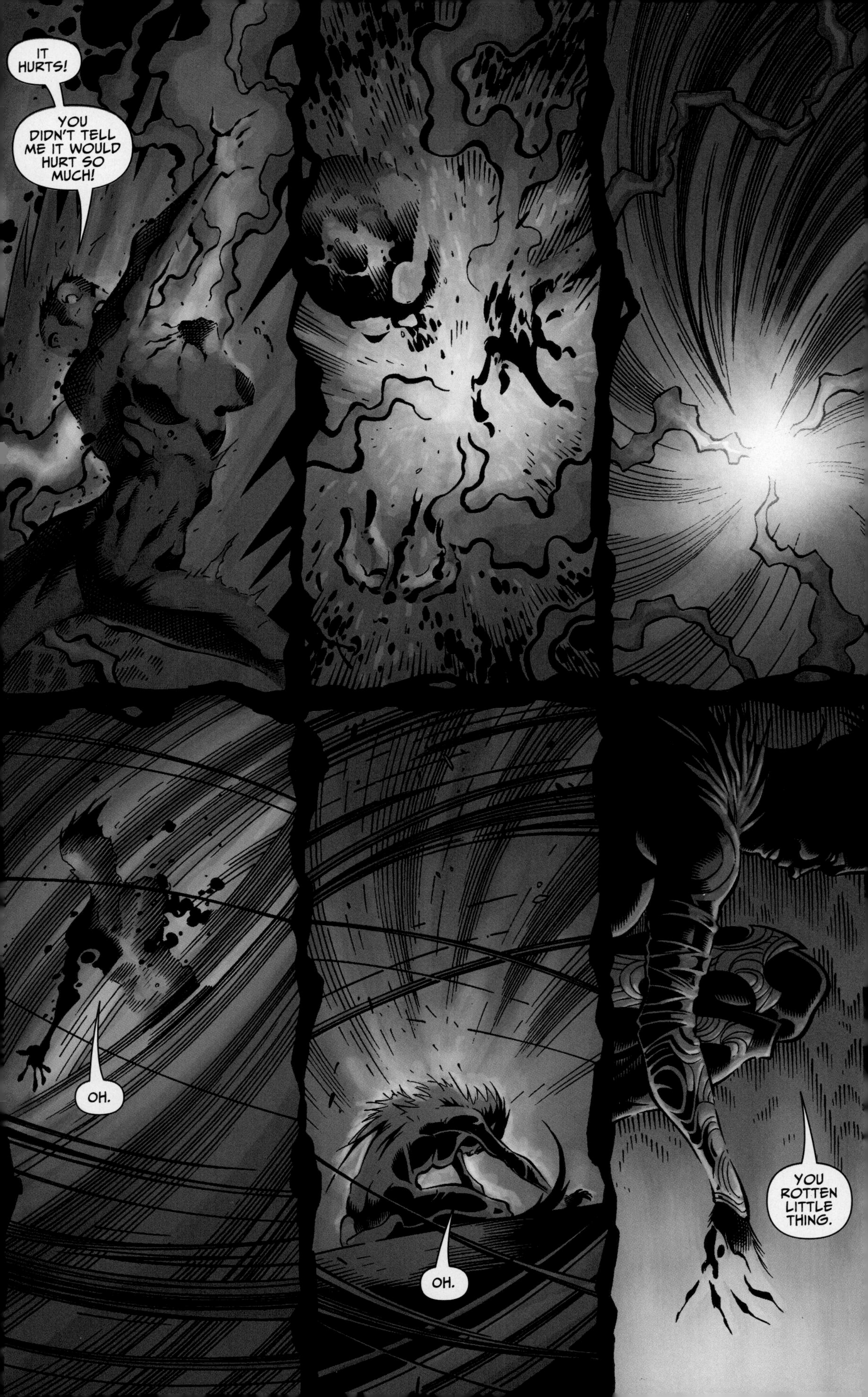
IT HURTS!
YOU DIDN'T TELL ME IT WOULD HURT SO MUCH!
OH.
OH.
YOU ROTTEN LITTLE THING.

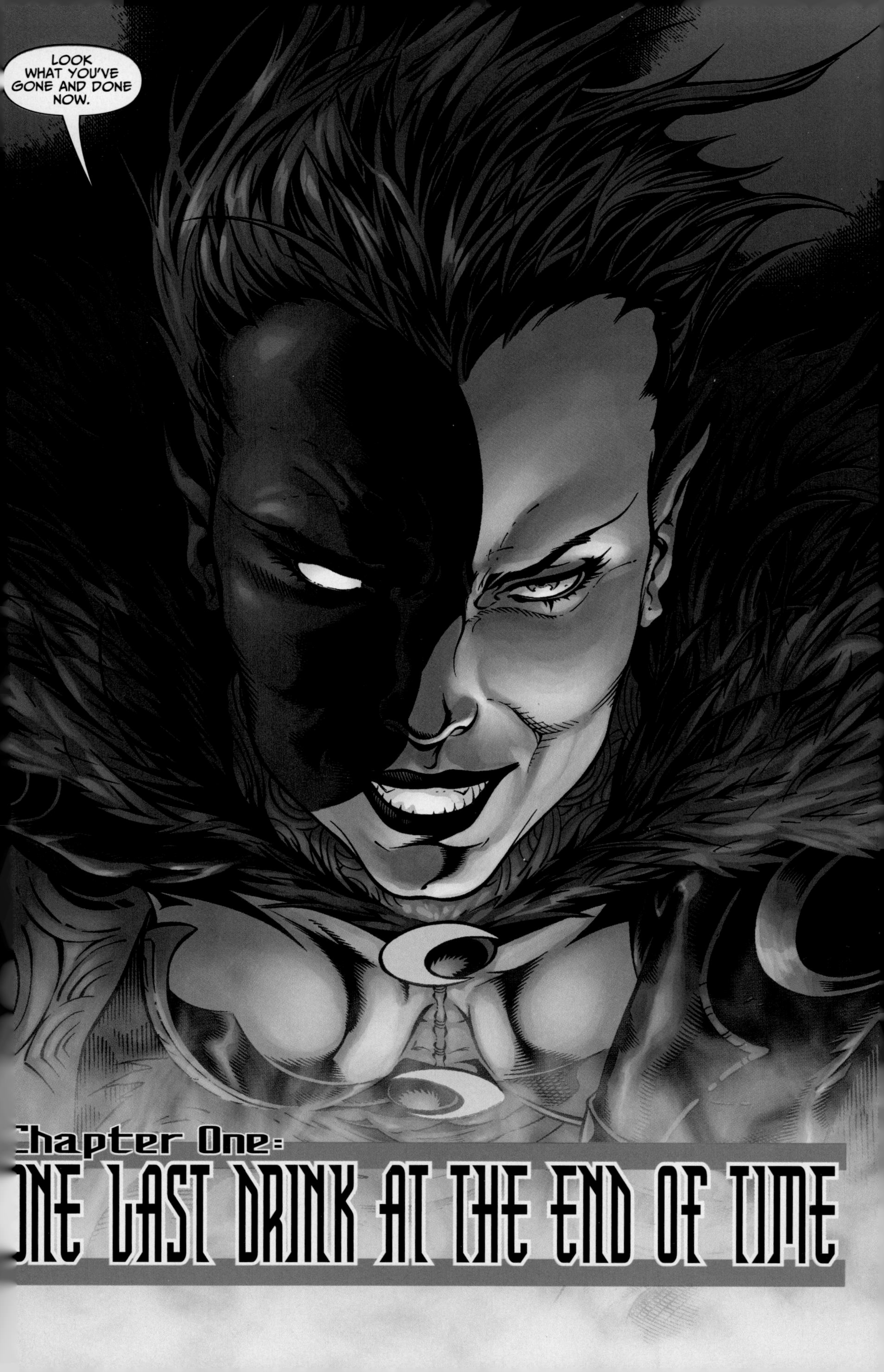
LOOK WHAT YOU'VE GONE AND DONE NOW.
Chapter One:
ONE LAST DRINK AT THE END OF TIME

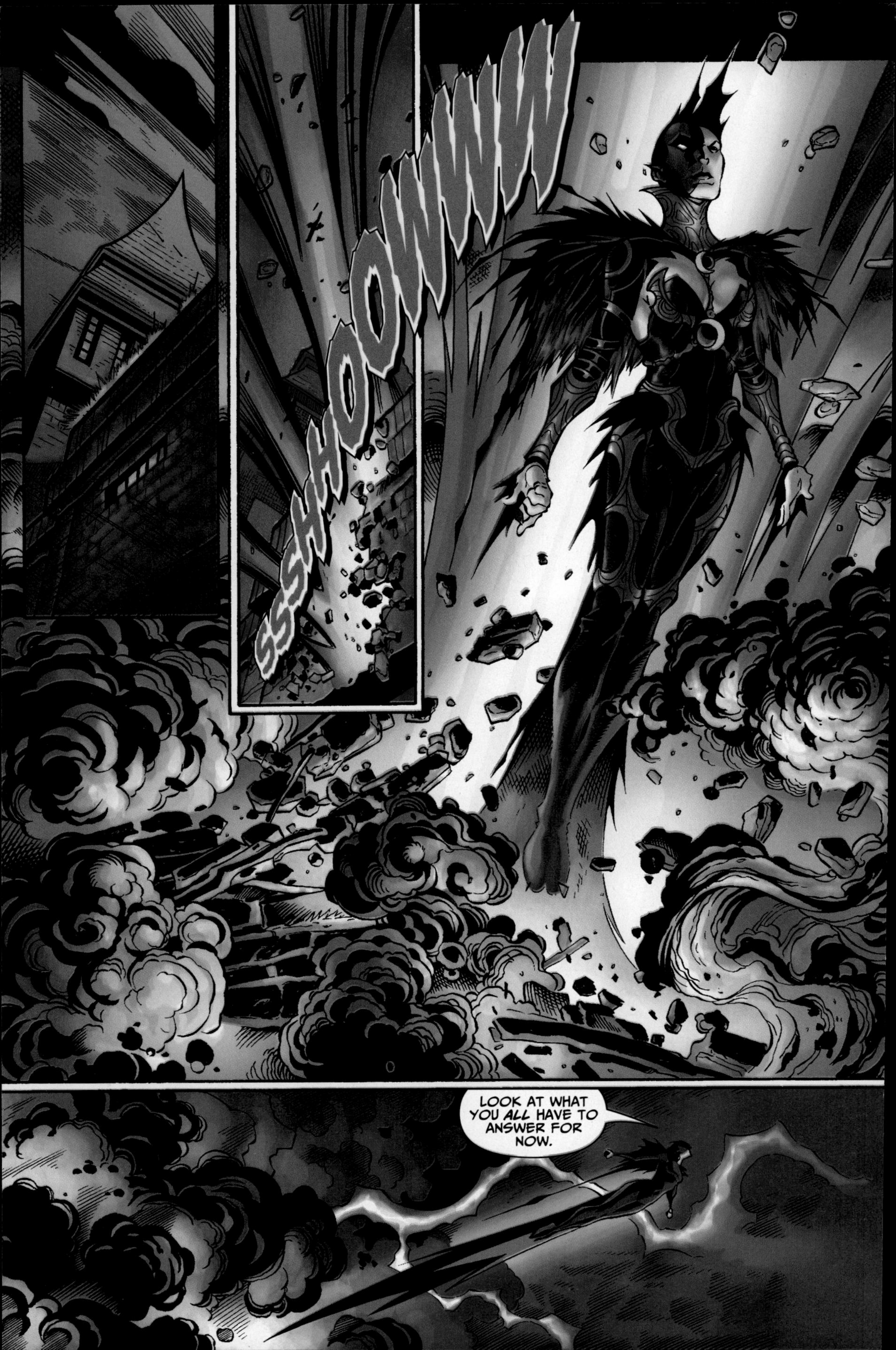
SSHOOWWWW
LOOK AT WHAT YOU ALL HAVE TO ANSWER FOR NOW.

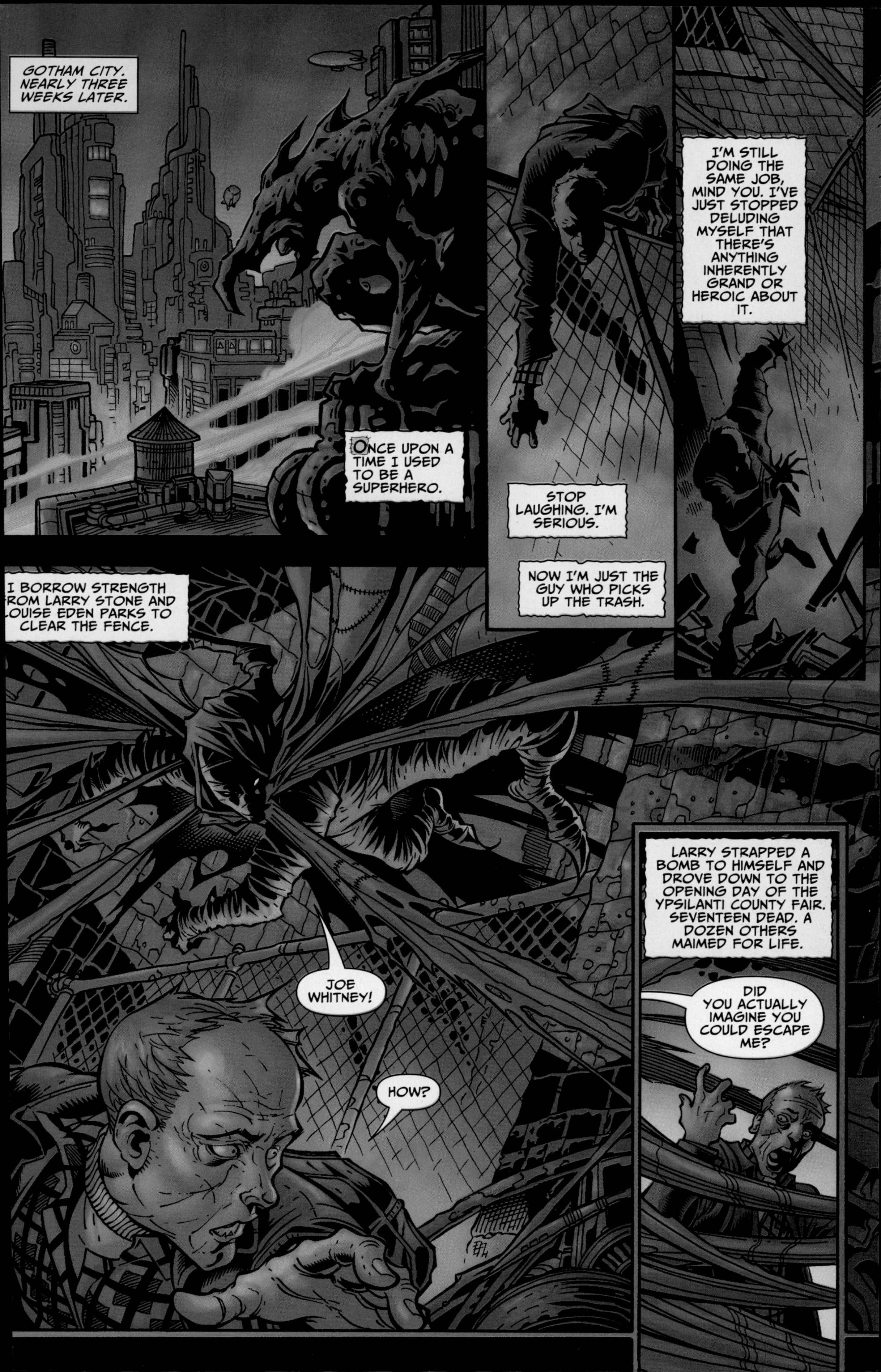
GOTHAM CITY. NEARLY THREE WEEKS LATER.
ONCE UPON A TIME I USED TO BE A SUPERHERO.
STOP LAUGHING. I'M SERIOUS.
NOW I'M JUST THE GUY WHO PICKS UP THE TRASH.
I'M STILL DOING THE SAME JOB, MIND YOU. I'VE JUST STOPPED DELUDING MYSELF THAT THERE'S ANYTHING INHERENTLY GRAND OR HEROIC ABOUT IT.
I BORROW STRENGTH FROM LARRY STONE AND LOUISE EDEN PARKS TO CLEAR THE FENCE.
JOE WHITNEY!
HOW?
LARRY STRAPPED A BOMB TO HIMSELF AND DROVE DOWN TO THE OPENING DAY OF THE YPSILANTI COUNTY FAIR. SEVENTEEN DEAD. A DOZEN OTHERS MAIMED FOR LIFE.
DID YOU ACTUALLY IMAGINE YOU COULD ESCAPE ME?

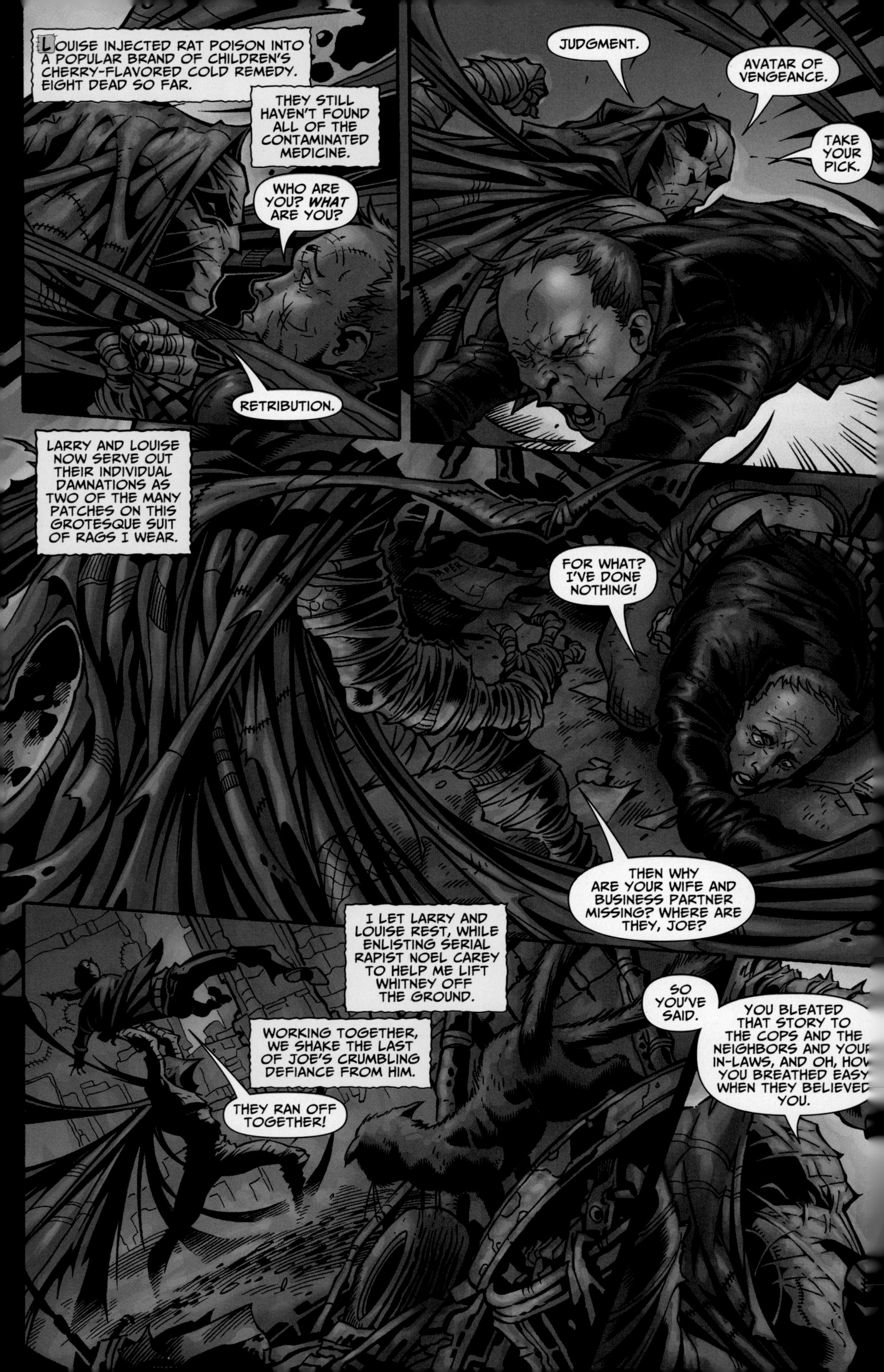
LOUISE INJECTED RAT POISON INTO A POPULAR BRAND OF CHILDREN'S CHERRY-FLAVORED COLD REMEDY. EIGHT DEAD SO FAR.
THEY STILL HAVEN'T FOUND ALL OF THE CONTAMINATED MEDICINE.
WHO ARE YOU? *WHAT* ARE YOU?
RETRIBUTION.
JUDGMENT.
AVATAR OF VENGEANCE.
TAKE YOUR PICK.
LARRY AND LOUISE NOW SERVE OUT THEIR INDIVIDUAL DAMNATIONS AS TWO OF THE MANY PATCHES ON THIS GROTESQUE SUIT OF RAGS I WEAR.
FOR WHAT? I'VE DONE NOTHING!
THEN WHY ARE YOUR WIFE AND BUSINESS PARTNER MISSING? WHERE ARE THEY, JOE?
I LET LARRY AND LOUISE REST, WHILE ENLISTING SERIAL RAPIST NOEL CAREY TO HELP ME LIFT WHITNEY OFF THE GROUND.
WORKING TOGETHER, WE SHAKE THE LAST OF JOE'S CRUMBLING DEFIANCE FROM HIM.
THEY RAN OFF TOGETHER!
SO YOU'VE SAID.
YOU BLEATED THAT STORY TO THE COPS AND THE NEIGHBORS AND YOUR IN-LAWS, AND OH, HOW YOU BREATHED EASY WHEN THEY BELIEVED YOU.

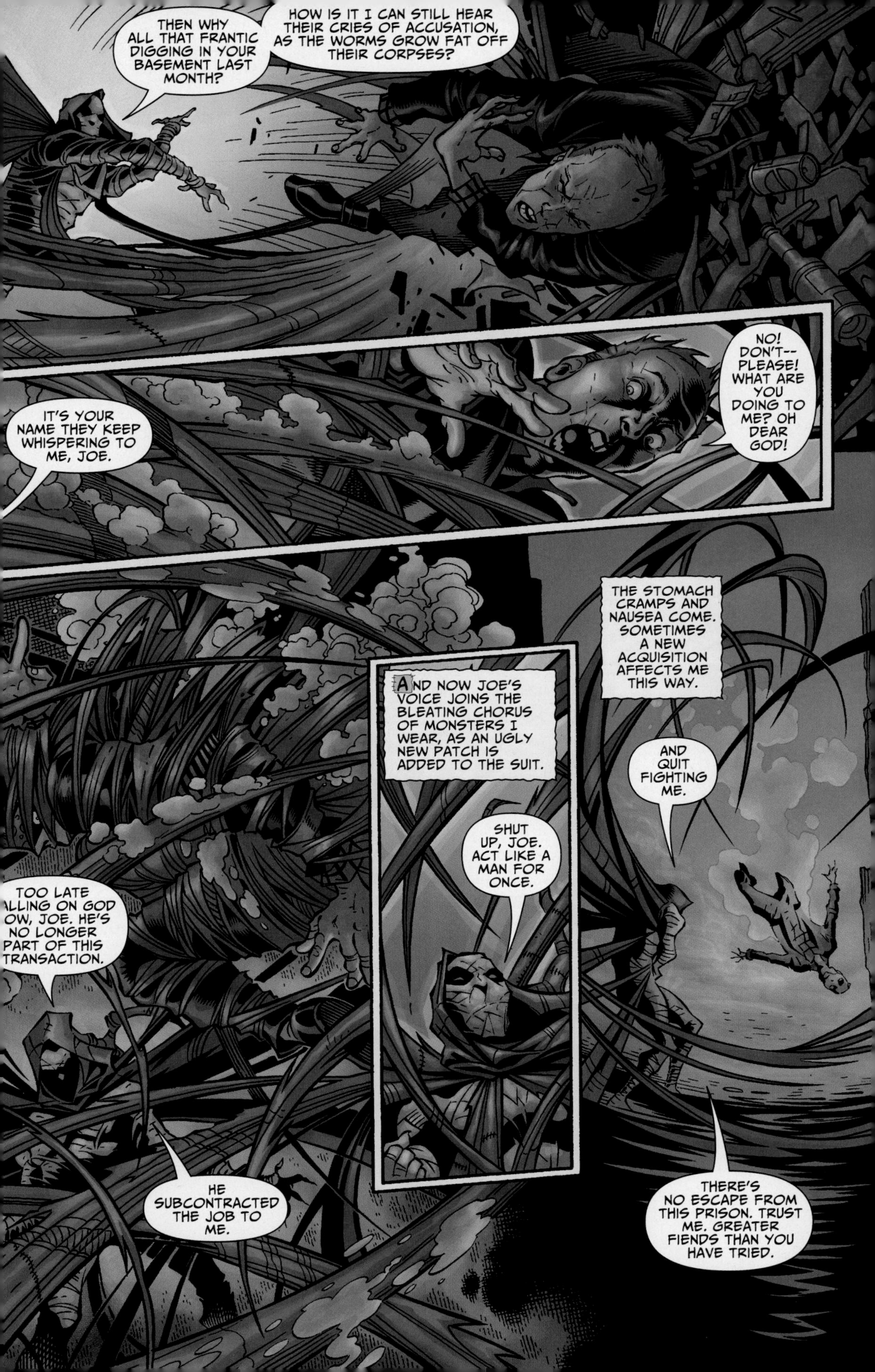
THEN WHY ALL THAT FRANTIC DIGGING IN YOUR BASEMENT LAST MONTH?
HOW IS IT I CAN STILL HEAR THEIR CRIES OF ACCUSATION, AS THE WORMS GROW FAT OFF THEIR CORPSES?
IT'S YOUR NAME THEY KEEP WHISPERING TO ME, JOE.
NO! DON'T-- PLEASE! WHAT ARE YOU DOING TO ME? OH DEAR GOD!
TOO LATE ...LLING ON GOD ...OW, JOE. HE'S NO LONGER PART OF THIS TRANSACTION.
HE SUBCONTRACTED THE JOB TO ME.
AND NOW JOE'S VOICE JOINS THE BLEATING CHORUS OF MONSTERS I WEAR, AS AN UGLY NEW PATCH IS ADDED TO THE SUIT.
SHUT UP, JOE. ACT LIKE A MAN FOR ONCE.
THE STOMACH CRAMPS AND NAUSEA COME. SOMETIMES A NEW ACQUISITION AFFECTS ME THIS WAY.
AND QUIT FIGHTING ME.
THERE'S NO ESCAPE FROM THIS PRISON. TRUST ME. GREATER FIENDS THAN YOU HAVE TRIED.

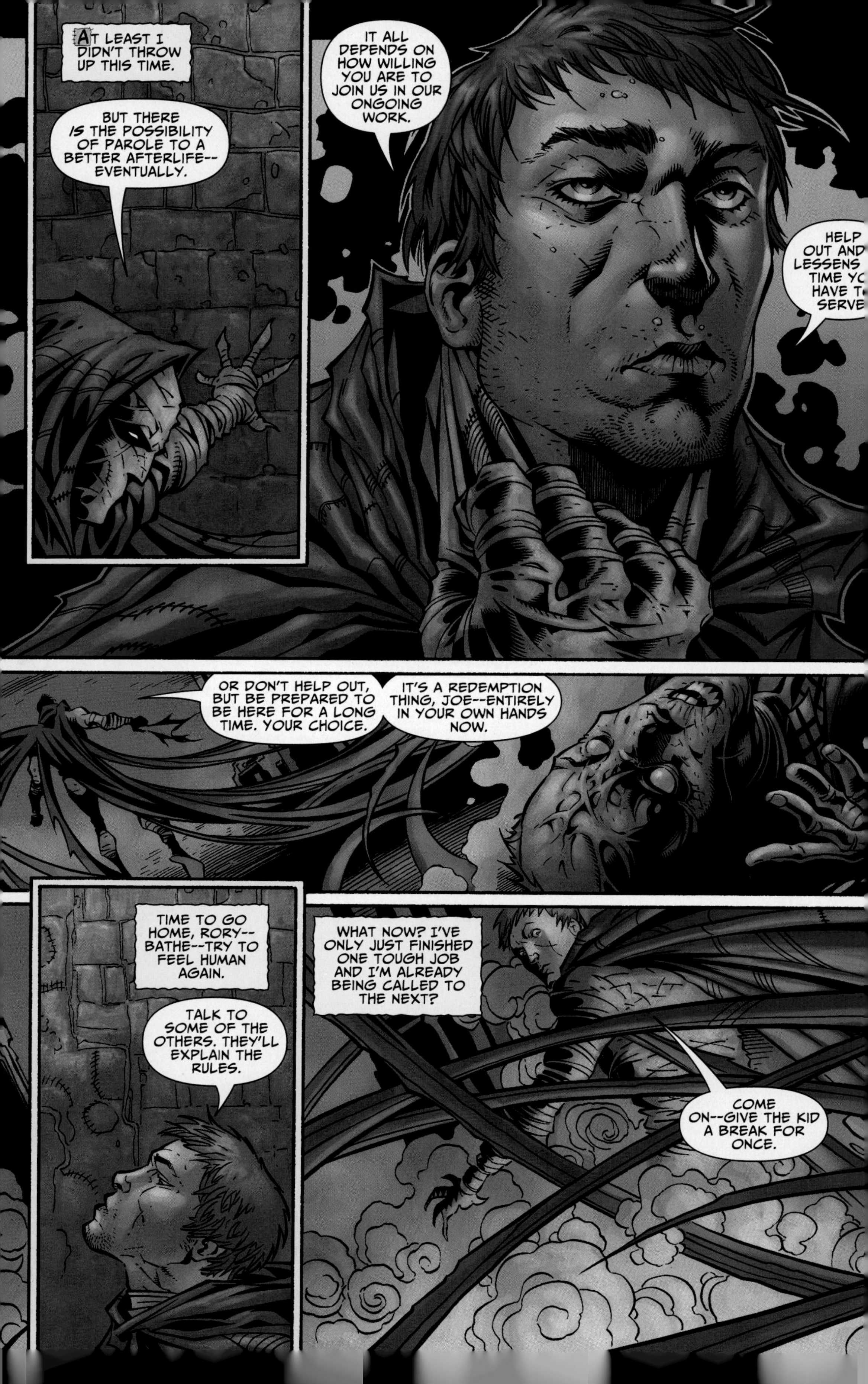
AT LEAST I DIDN'T THROW UP THIS TIME.
BUT THERE *IS* THE POSSIBILITY OF PAROLE TO A BETTER AFTERLIFE--EVENTUALLY.
IT ALL DEPENDS ON HOW WILLING YOU ARE TO JOIN US IN OUR ONGOING WORK.
HELP OUT AND LESSENS TIME YO HAVE T SERVE
OR DON'T HELP OUT, BUT BE PREPARED TO BE HERE FOR A LONG TIME. YOUR CHOICE.
IT'S A REDEMPTION THING, JOE--ENTIRELY IN YOUR OWN HANDS NOW.
TIME TO GO HOME, RORY--BATHE--TRY TO FEEL HUMAN AGAIN.
TALK TO SOME OF THE OTHERS. THEY'LL EXPLAIN THE RULES.
WHAT NOW? I'VE ONLY JUST FINISHED ONE TOUGH JOB AND I'M ALREADY BEING CALLED TO THE NEXT?
COME ON--GIVE THE KID A BREAK FOR ONCE.

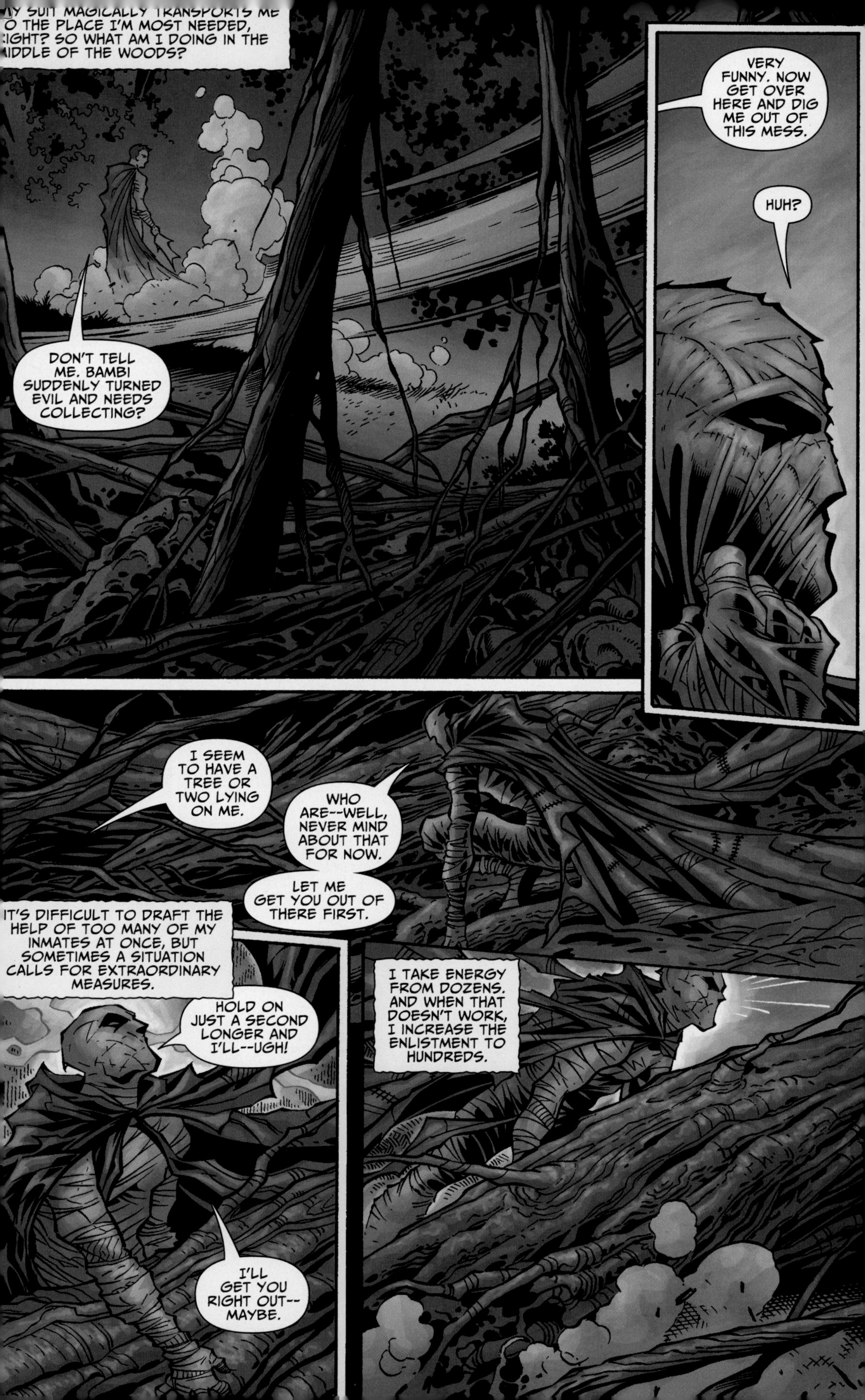
Y SUIT MAGICALLY TRANSPORTS ME O THE PLACE I'M MOST NEEDED, IGHT? SO WHAT AM I DOING IN THE IDDLE OF THE WOODS?
DON'T TELL ME. BAMBI SUDDENLY TURNED EVIL AND NEEDS COLLECTING?
VERY FUNNY. NOW GET OVER HERE AND DIG ME OUT OF THIS MESS.
HUH?
I SEEM TO HAVE A TREE OR TWO LYING ON ME.
WHO ARE--WELL, NEVER MIND ABOUT THAT FOR NOW.
LET ME GET YOU OUT OF THERE FIRST.
IT'S DIFFICULT TO DRAFT THE HELP OF TOO MANY OF MY INMATES AT ONCE, BUT SOMETIMES A SITUATION CALLS FOR EXTRAORDINARY MEASURES.
HOLD ON JUST A SECOND LONGER AND I'LL--UGH!
I'LL GET YOU RIGHT OUT-- MAYBE.
I TAKE ENERGY FROM DOZENS. AND WHEN THAT DOESN'T WORK, I INCREASE THE ENLISTMENT TO HUNDREDS.

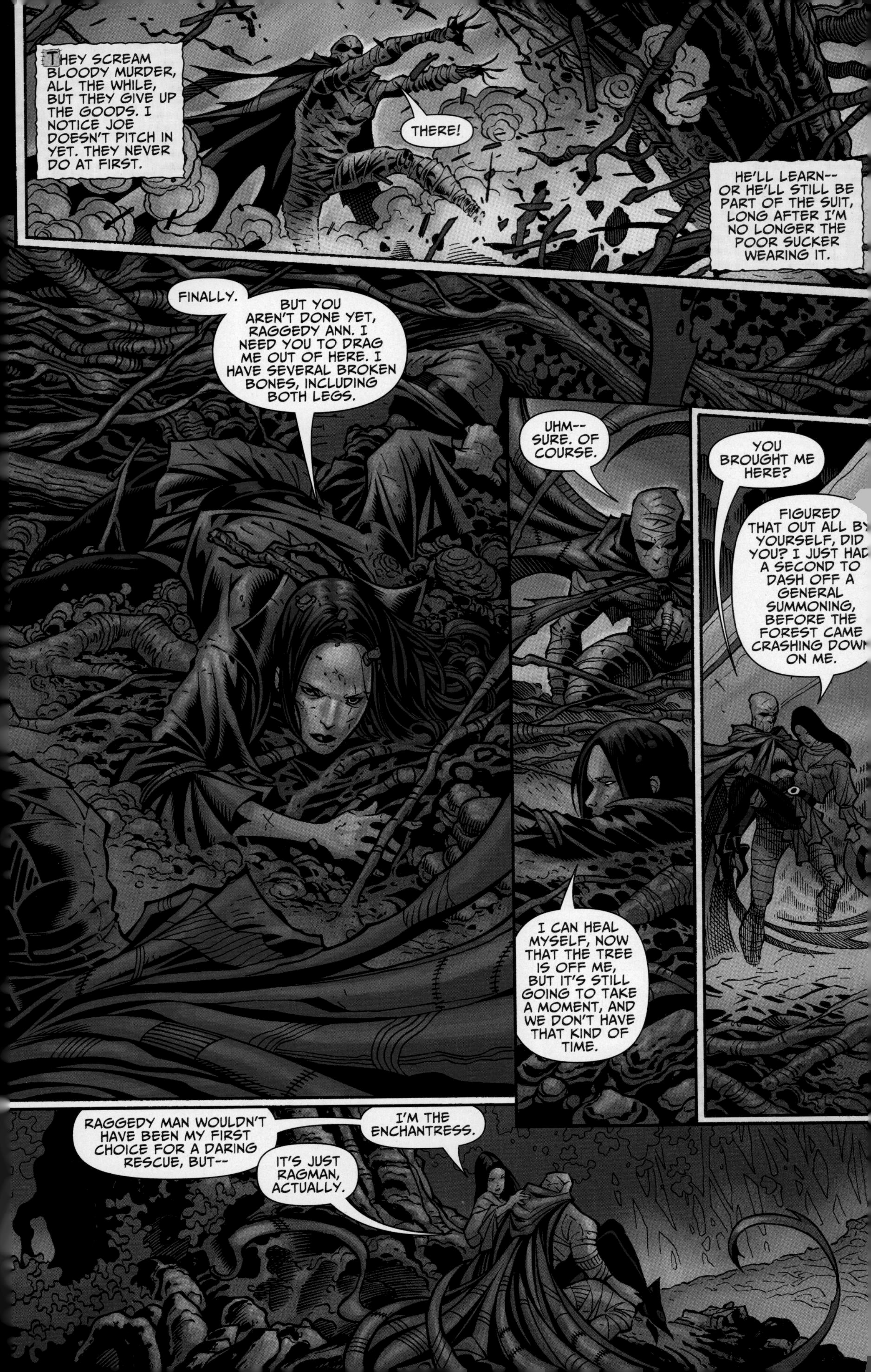
THEY SCREAM BLOODY MURDER, ALL THE WHILE, BUT THEY GIVE UP THE GOODS. I NOTICE JOE DOESN'T PITCH IN YET. THEY NEVER DO AT FIRST.
THERE!
HE'LL LEARN-- OR HE'LL STILL BE PART OF THE SUIT, LONG AFTER I'M NO LONGER THE POOR SUCKER WEARING IT.
FINALLY.
BUT YOU AREN'T DONE YET, RAGGEDY ANN. I NEED YOU TO DRAG ME OUT OF HERE. I HAVE SEVERAL BROKEN BONES, INCLUDING BOTH LEGS.
UHM-- SURE. OF COURSE.
I CAN HEAL MYSELF, NOW THAT THE TREE IS OFF ME, BUT IT'S STILL GOING TO TAKE A MOMENT, AND WE DON'T HAVE THAT KIND OF TIME.
YOU BROUGHT ME HERE?
FIGURED THAT OUT ALL BY YOURSELF, DID YOU? I JUST HAD A SECOND TO DASH OFF A GENERAL SUMMONING, BEFORE THE FOREST CAME CRASHING DOWN ON ME.
RAGGEDY MAN WOULDN'T HAVE BEEN MY FIRST CHOICE FOR A DARING RESCUE, BUT--
I'M THE ENCHANTRESS.
IT'S JUST RAGMAN, ACTUALLY.

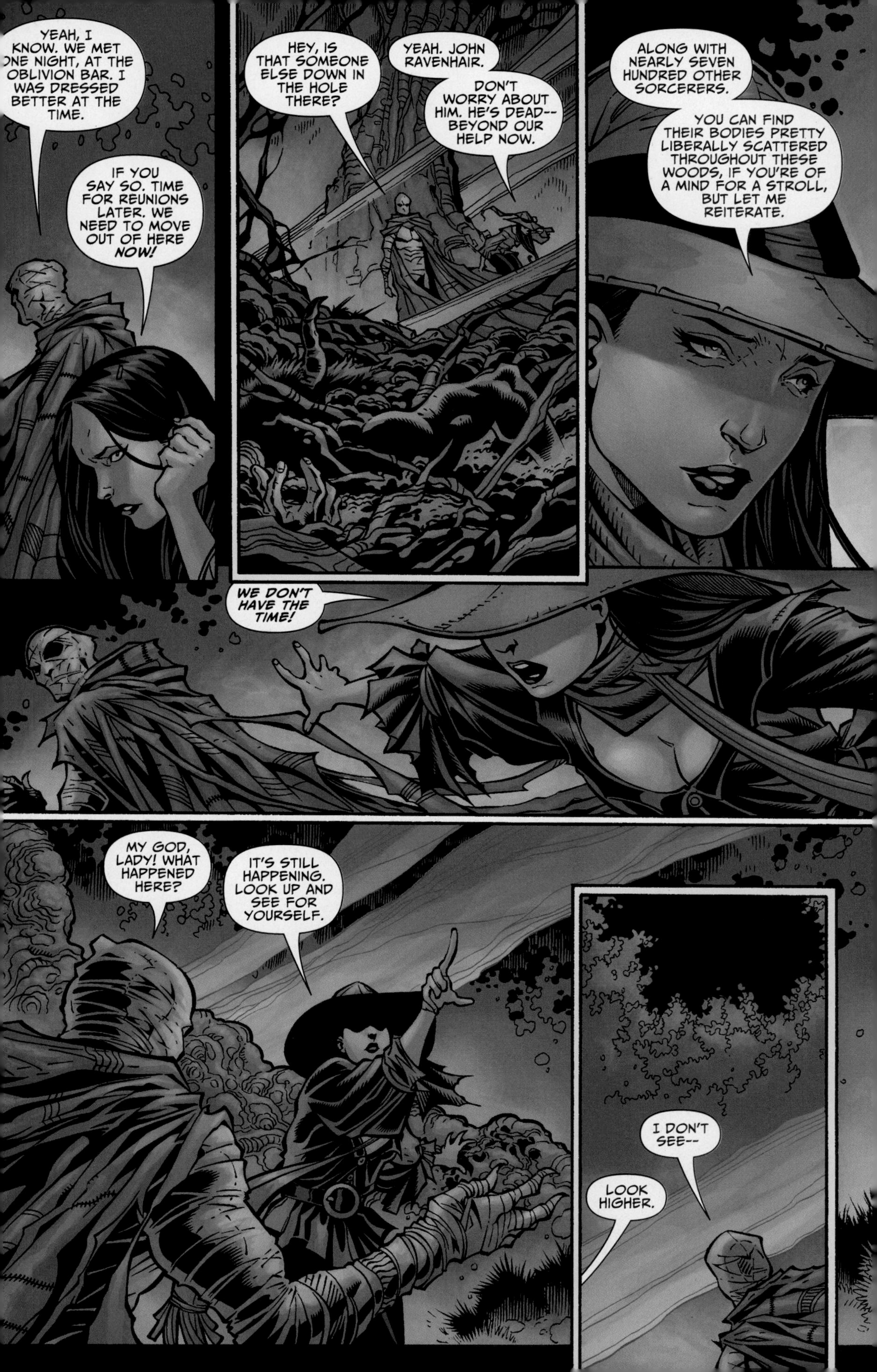
YEAH, I KNOW. WE MET ONE NIGHT, AT THE OBLIVION BAR. I WAS DRESSED BETTER AT THE TIME.
IF YOU SAY SO. TIME FOR REUNIONS LATER. WE NEED TO MOVE OUT OF HERE *NOW!*
HEY, IS THAT SOMEONE ELSE DOWN IN THE HOLE THERE?
YEAH. JOHN RAVENHAIR.
DON'T WORRY ABOUT HIM. HE'S DEAD-- BEYOND OUR HELP NOW.
ALONG WITH NEARLY SEVEN HUNDRED OTHER SORCERERS.
YOU CAN FIND THEIR BODIES PRETTY LIBERALLY SCATTERED THROUGHOUT THESE WOODS, IF YOU'RE OF A MIND FOR A STROLL, BUT LET ME REITERATE.
WE DON'T HAVE THE TIME!
MY GOD, LADY! WHAT HAPPENED HERE?
IT'S STILL HAPPENING. LOOK UP AND SEE FOR YOURSELF.
I DON'T SEE--
LOOK HIGHER.

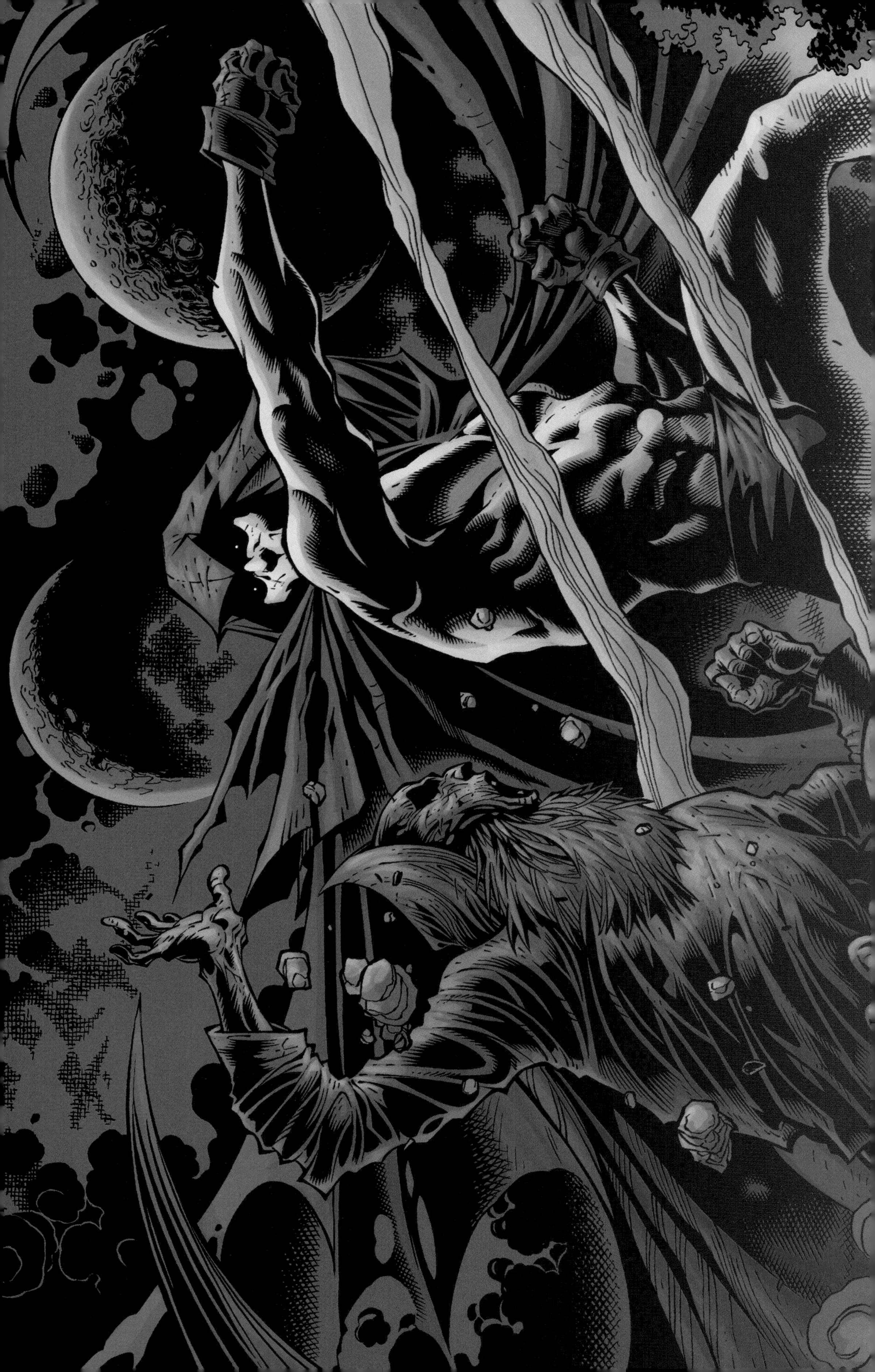

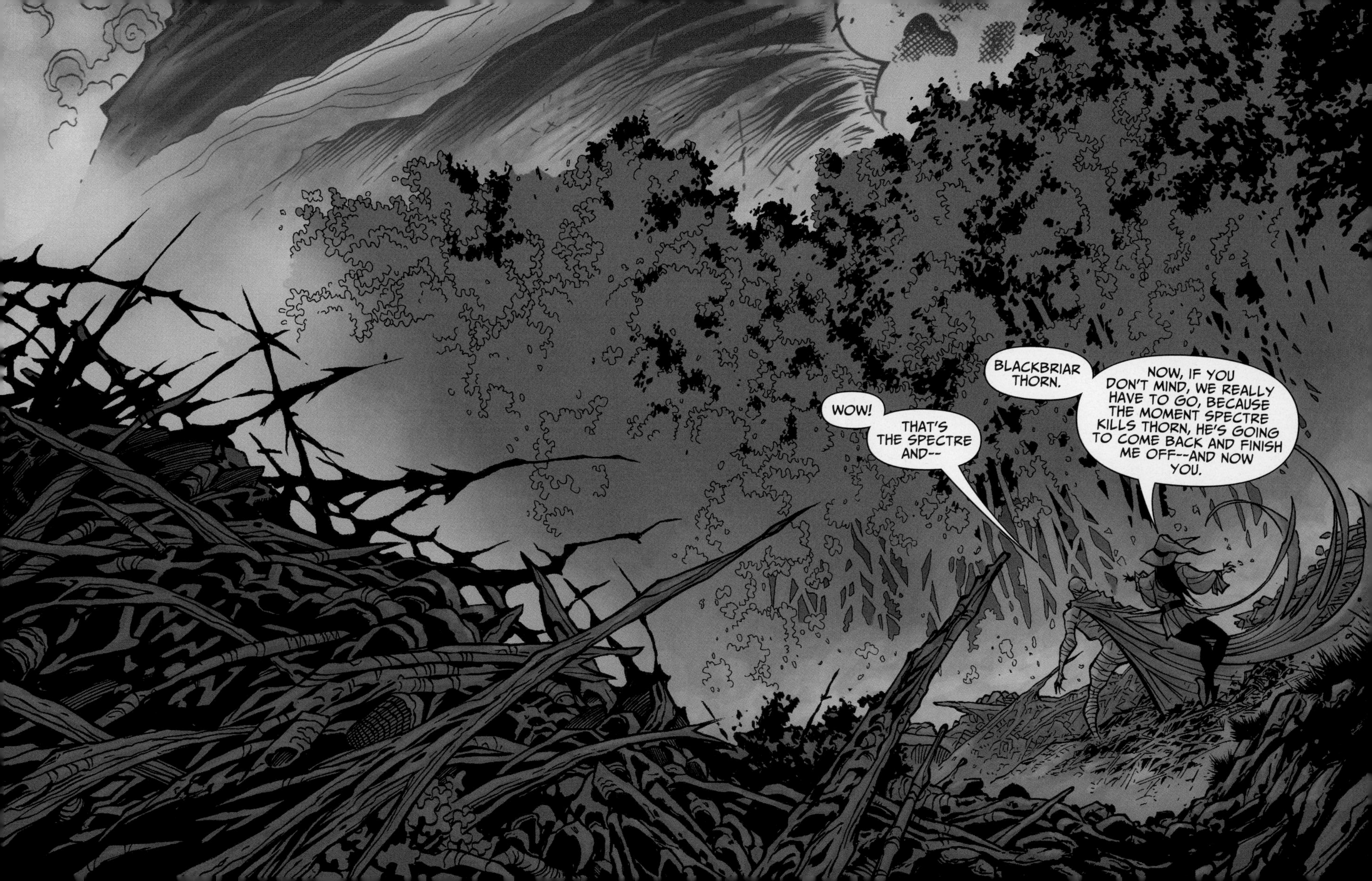
WOW!
THAT'S THE SPECTRE AND--
BLACKBRIAR THORN.
NOW, IF YOU DON'T MIND, WE REALLY HAVE TO GO, BECAUSE THE MOMENT SPECTRE KILLS THORN, HE'S GOING TO COME BACK AND FINISH ME OFF--AND NOW YOU.

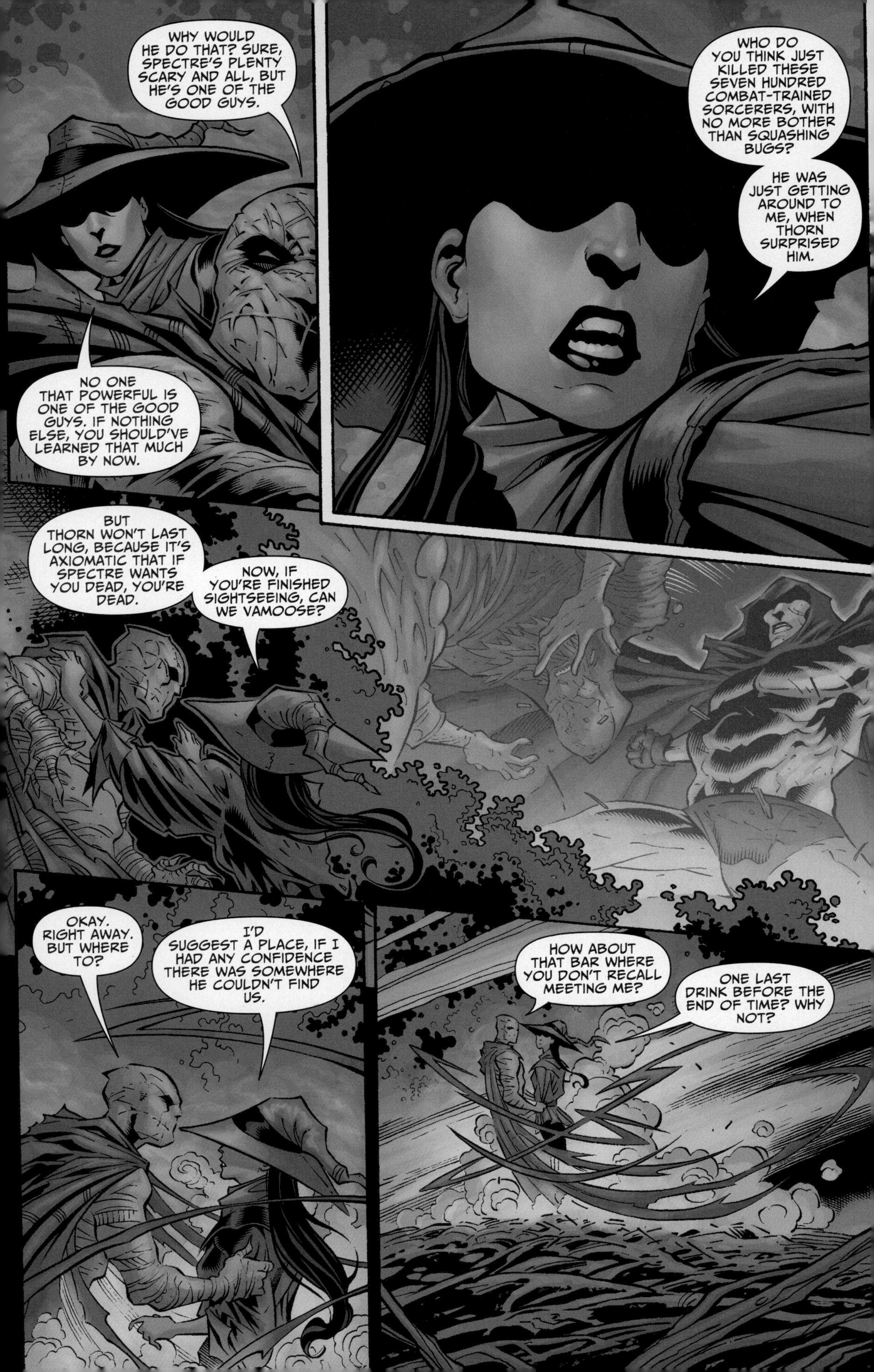
WHY WOULD HE DO THAT? SURE, SPECTRE'S PLENTY SCARY AND ALL, BUT HE'S ONE OF THE GOOD GUYS.
NO ONE THAT POWERFUL IS ONE OF THE GOOD GUYS. IF NOTHING ELSE, YOU SHOULD'VE LEARNED THAT MUCH BY NOW.
WHO DO YOU THINK JUST KILLED THESE SEVEN HUNDRED COMBAT-TRAINED SORCERERS, WITH NO MORE BOTHER THAN SQUASHING BUGS?
HE WAS JUST GETTING AROUND TO ME, WHEN THORN SURPRISED HIM.
BUT THORN WON'T LAST LONG, BECAUSE IT'S AXIOMATIC THAT IF SPECTRE WANTS YOU DEAD, YOU'RE DEAD.
NOW, IF YOU'RE FINISHED SIGHTSEEING, CAN WE VAMOOSE?
OKAY. RIGHT AWAY. BUT WHERE TO?
I'D SUGGEST A PLACE, IF I HAD ANY CONFIDENCE THERE WAS SOMEWHERE HE COULDN'T FIND US.
HOW ABOUT THAT BAR WHERE YOU DON'T RECALL MEETING ME?
ONE LAST DRINK BEFORE THE END OF TIME? WHY NOT?

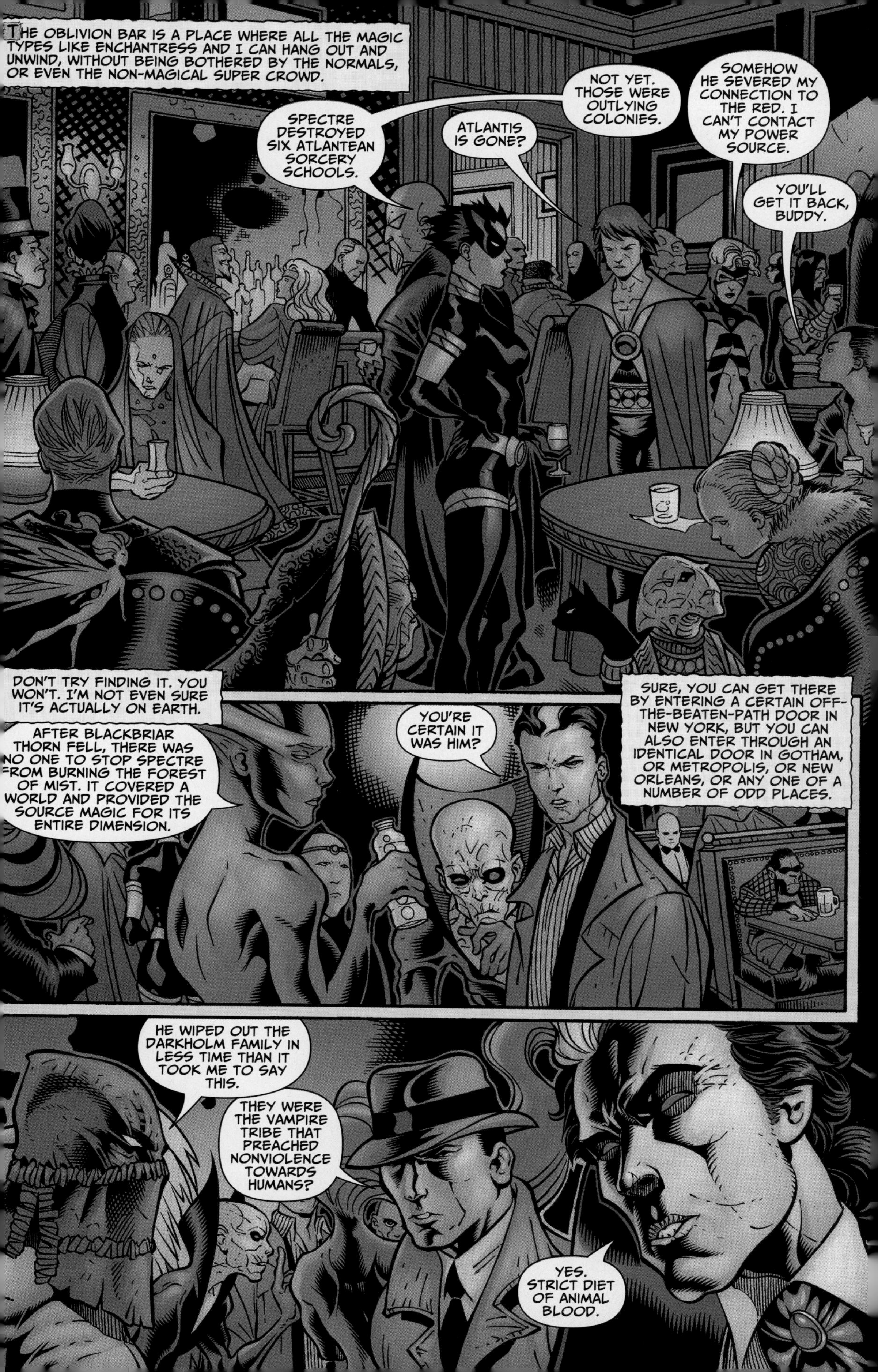
THE OBLIVION BAR IS A PLACE WHERE ALL THE MAGIC TYPES LIKE ENCHANTRESS AND I CAN HANG OUT AND UNWIND, WITHOUT BEING BOTHERED BY THE NORMALS, OR EVEN THE NON-MAGICAL SUPER CROWD.
SPECTRE DESTROYED SIX ATLANTEAN SORCERY SCHOOLS.
ATLANTIS IS GONE?
NOT YET. THOSE WERE OUTLYING COLONIES.
SOMEHOW HE SEVERED MY CONNECTION TO THE RED. I CAN'T CONTACT MY POWER SOURCE.
YOU'LL GET IT BACK, BUDDY.
DON'T TRY FINDING IT. YOU WON'T. I'M NOT EVEN SURE IT'S ACTUALLY ON EARTH.
AFTER BLACKBRIAR THORN FELL, THERE WAS NO ONE TO STOP SPECTRE FROM BURNING THE FOREST OF MIST. IT COVERED A WORLD AND PROVIDED THE SOURCE MAGIC FOR ITS ENTIRE DIMENSION.
YOU'RE CERTAIN IT WAS HIM?
SURE, YOU CAN GET THERE BY ENTERING A CERTAIN OFF-THE-BEATEN-PATH DOOR IN NEW YORK, BUT YOU CAN ALSO ENTER THROUGH AN IDENTICAL DOOR IN GOTHAM, OR METROPOLIS, OR NEW ORLEANS, OR ANY ONE OF A NUMBER OF ODD PLACES.
HE WIPED OUT THE DARKHOLM FAMILY IN LESS TIME THAN IT TOOK ME TO SAY THIS.
THEY WERE THE VAMPIRE TRIBE THAT PREACHED NONVIOLENCE TOWARDS HUMANS?
YES. STRICT DIET OF ANIMAL BLOOD.

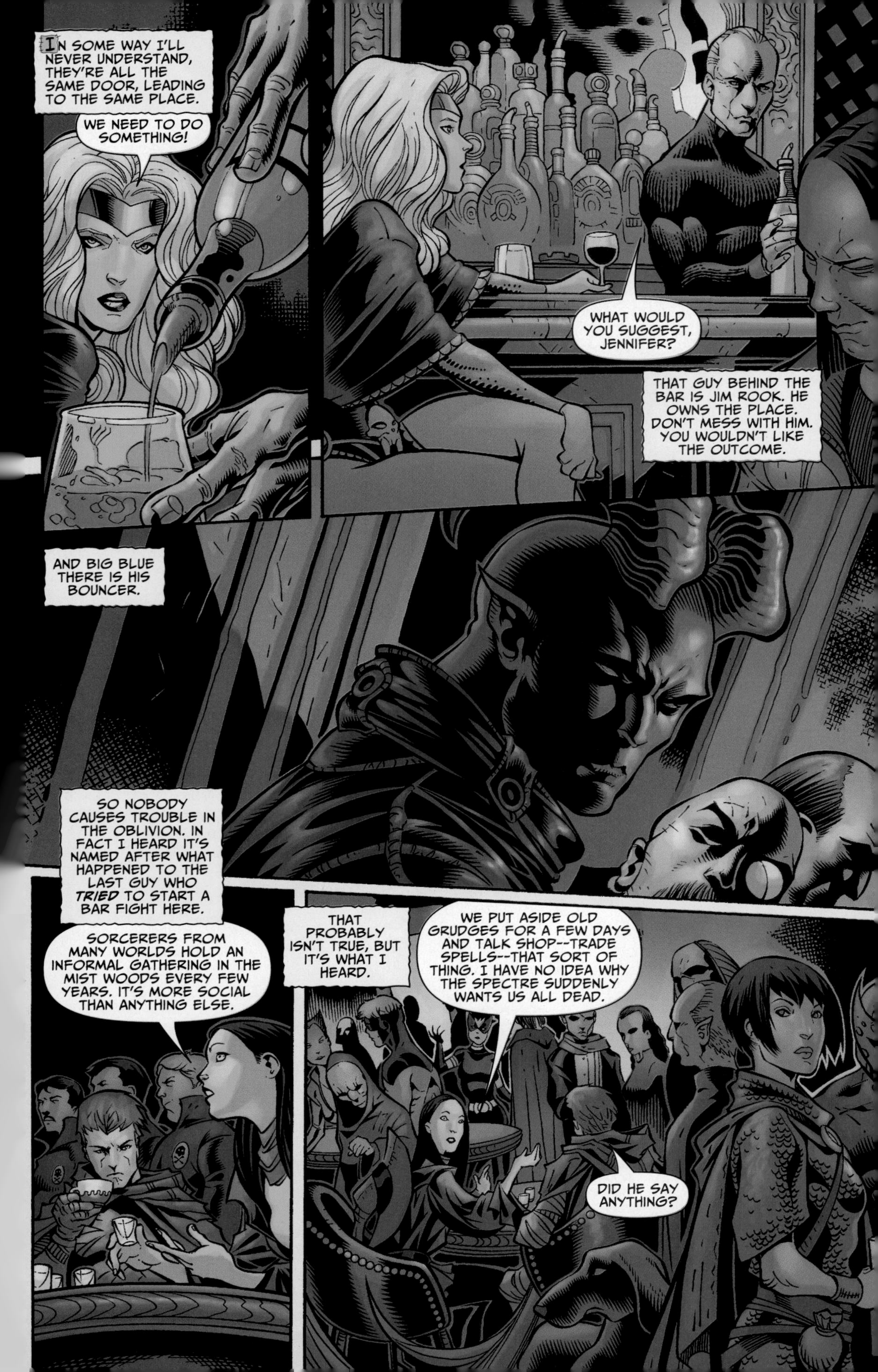
IN SOME WAY I'LL NEVER UNDERSTAND, THEY'RE ALL THE SAME DOOR, LEADING TO THE SAME PLACE.
WE NEED TO DO SOMETHING!
WHAT WOULD YOU SUGGEST, JENNIFER?
THAT GUY BEHIND THE BAR IS JIM ROOK. HE OWNS THE PLACE. DON'T MESS WITH HIM. YOU WOULDN'T LIKE THE OUTCOME.
AND BIG BLUE THERE IS HIS BOUNCER.
SO NOBODY CAUSES TROUBLE IN THE OBLIVION. IN FACT I HEARD IT'S NAMED AFTER WHAT HAPPENED TO THE LAST GUY WHO *TRIED* TO START A BAR FIGHT HERE.
SORCERERS FROM MANY WORLDS HOLD AN INFORMAL GATHERING IN THE MIST WOODS EVERY FEW YEARS. IT'S MORE SOCIAL THAN ANYTHING ELSE.
THAT PROBABLY ISN'T TRUE, BUT IT'S WHAT I HEARD.
WE PUT ASIDE OLD GRUDGES FOR A FEW DAYS AND TALK SHOP--TRADE SPELLS--THAT SORT OF THING. I HAVE NO IDEA WHY THE SPECTRE SUDDENLY WANTS US ALL DEAD.
DID HE SAY ANYTHING?

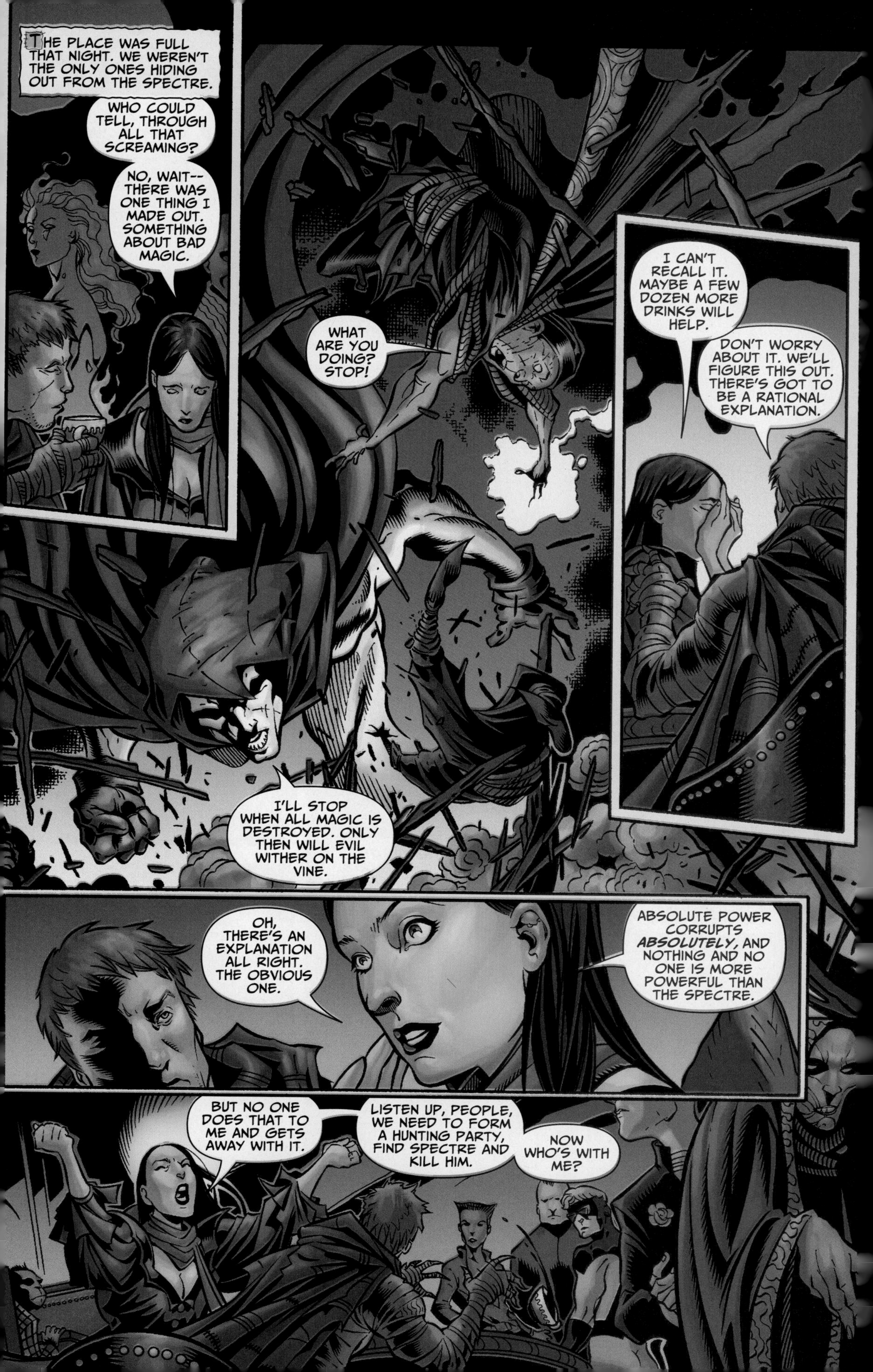
THE PLACE WAS FULL THAT NIGHT. WE WEREN'T THE ONLY ONES HIDING OUT FROM THE SPECTRE.
WHO COULD TELL, THROUGH ALL THAT SCREAMING?
NO, WAIT-- THERE WAS ONE THING I MADE OUT. SOMETHING ABOUT BAD MAGIC.
WHAT ARE YOU DOING? STOP!
I'LL STOP WHEN ALL MAGIC IS DESTROYED. ONLY THEN WILL EVIL WITHER ON THE VINE.
I CAN'T RECALL IT. MAYBE A FEW DOZEN MORE DRINKS WILL HELP.
DON'T WORRY ABOUT IT. WE'LL FIGURE THIS OUT. THERE'S GOT TO BE A RATIONAL EXPLANATION.
OH, THERE'S AN EXPLANATION ALL RIGHT. THE OBVIOUS ONE.
ABSOLUTE POWER CORRUPTS *ABSOLUTELY*, AND NOTHING AND NO ONE IS MORE POWERFUL THAN THE SPECTRE.
BUT NO ONE DOES THAT TO ME AND GETS AWAY WITH IT.
LISTEN UP, PEOPLE, WE NEED TO FORM A HUNTING PARTY, FIND SPECTRE AND KILL HIM.
NOW WHO'S WITH ME?

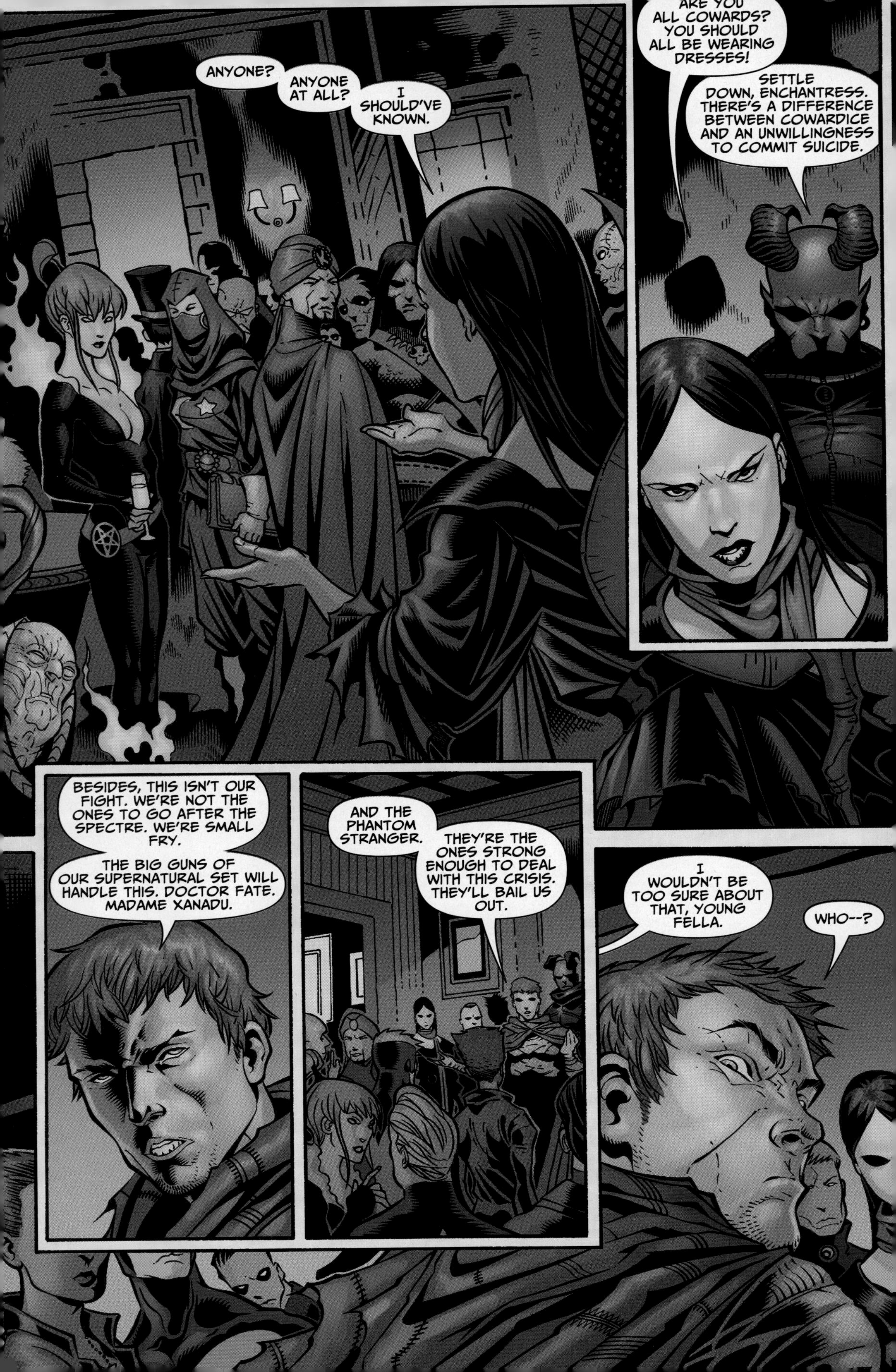
ANYONE?
ANYONE AT ALL?
I SHOULD'VE KNOWN.
ARE YOU ALL COWARDS? YOU SHOULD ALL BE WEARING DRESSES!
SETTLE DOWN, ENCHANTRESS. THERE'S A DIFFERENCE BETWEEN COWARDICE AND AN UNWILLINGNESS TO COMMIT SUICIDE.
BESIDES, THIS ISN'T OUR FIGHT. WE'RE NOT THE ONES TO GO AFTER THE SPECTRE. WE'RE SMALL FRY.
THE BIG GUNS OF OUR SUPERNATURAL SET WILL HANDLE THIS. DOCTOR FATE. MADAME XANADU.
AND THE PHANTOM STRANGER.
THEY'RE THE ONES STRONG ENOUGH TO DEAL WITH THIS CRISIS. THEY'LL BAIL US OUT.
I WOULDN'T BE TOO SURE ABOUT THAT, YOUNG FELLA.
WHO--?

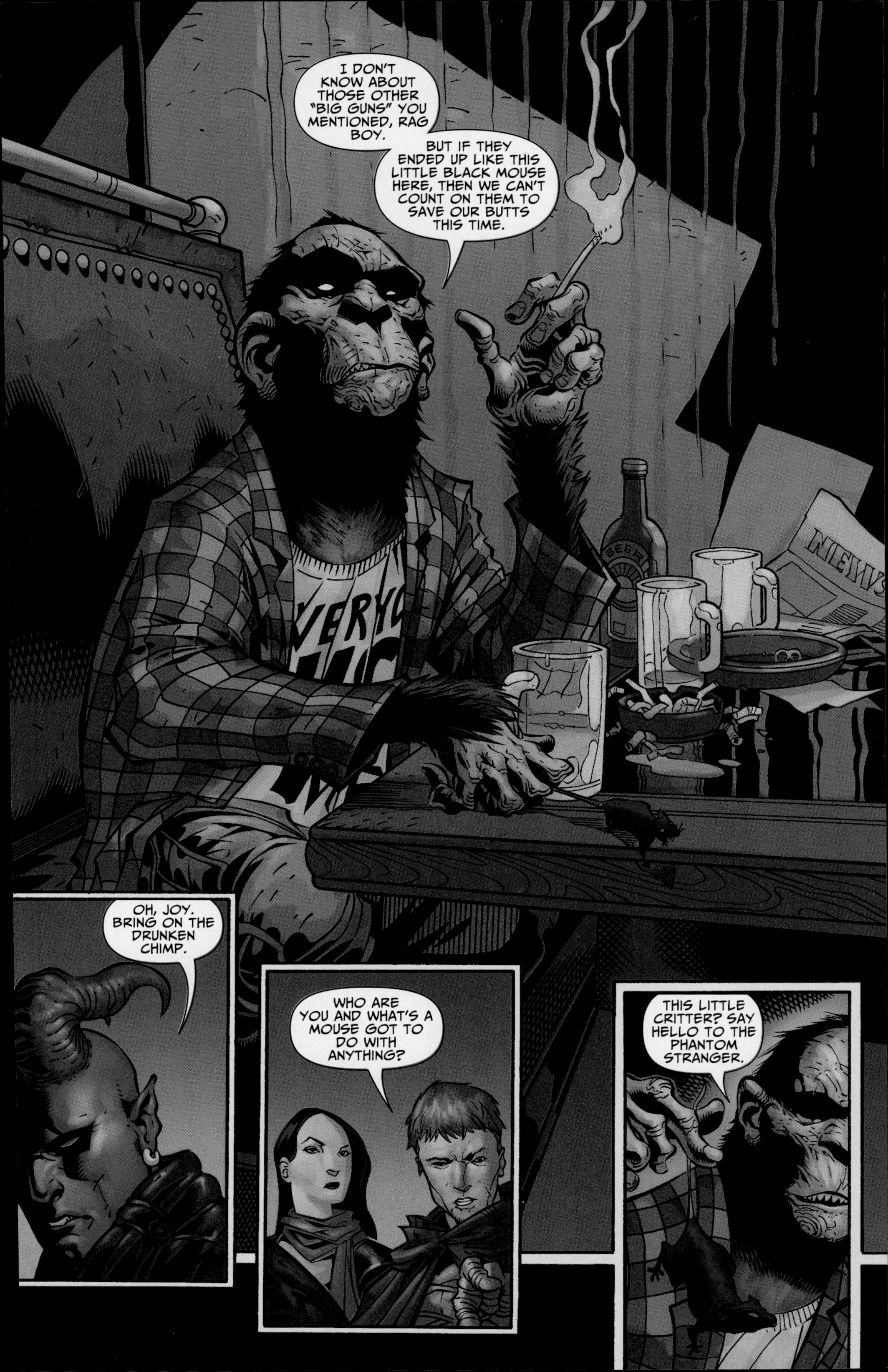
I DON'T KNOW ABOUT THOSE OTHER "BIG GUNS" YOU MENTIONED, RAG BOY.
BUT IF THEY ENDED UP LIKE THIS LITTLE BLACK MOUSE HERE, THEN WE CAN'T COUNT ON THEM TO SAVE OUR BUTTS THIS TIME.
BEER
NEWS
OH, JOY. BRING ON THE DRUNKEN CHIMP.
WHO ARE YOU AND WHAT'S A MOUSE GOT TO DO WITH ANYTHING?
THIS LITTLE CRITTER? SAY HELLO TO THE PHANTOM STRANGER.

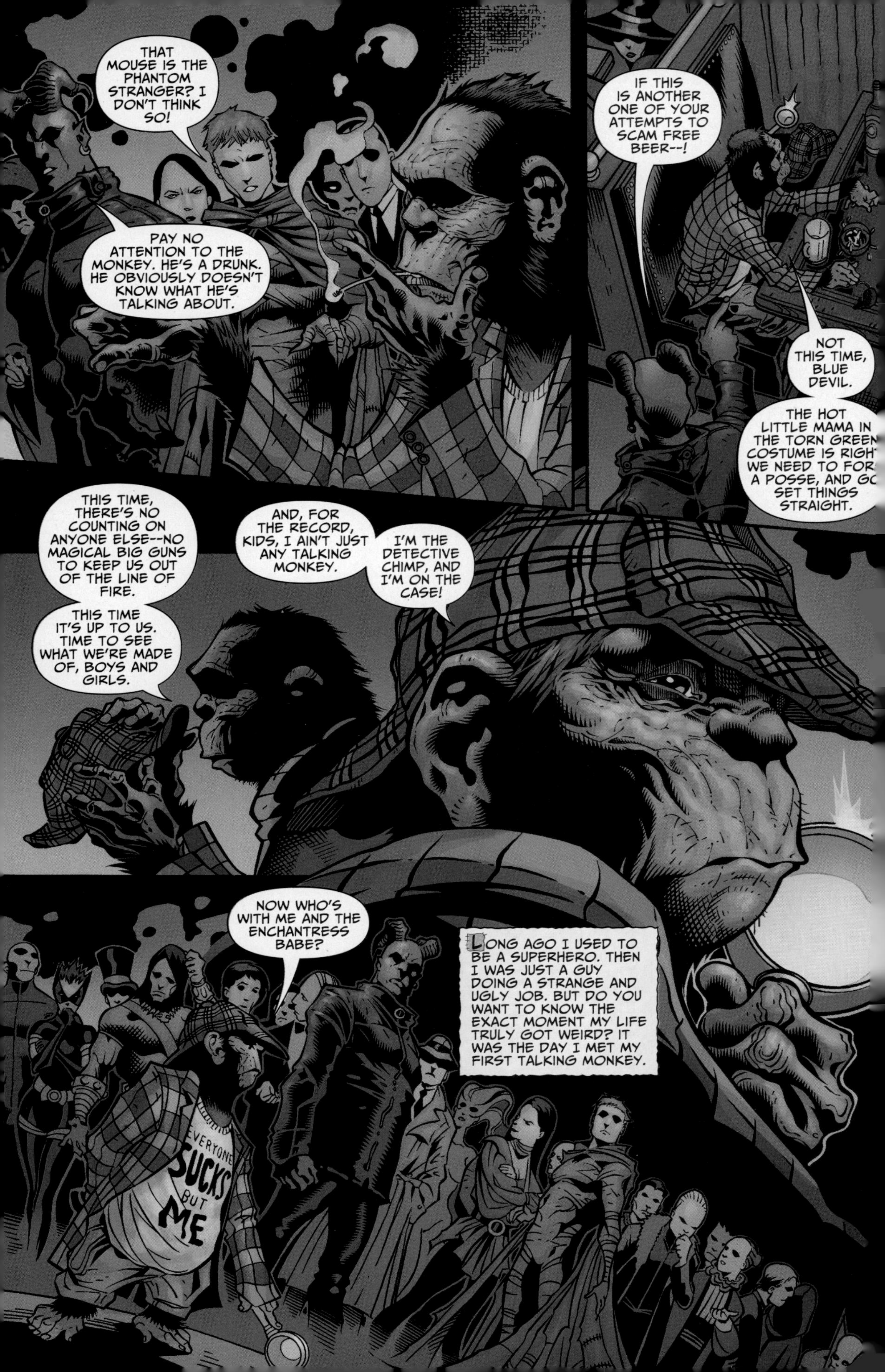
THAT MOUSE IS THE PHANTOM STRANGER? I DON'T THINK SO!
PAY NO ATTENTION TO THE MONKEY. HE'S A DRUNK. HE OBVIOUSLY DOESN'T KNOW WHAT HE'S TALKING ABOUT.
IF THIS IS ANOTHER ONE OF YOUR ATTEMPTS TO SCAM FREE BEER--!
NOT THIS TIME, BLUE DEVIL.
THE HOT LITTLE MAMA IN THE TORN GREEN COSTUME IS RIGHT. WE NEED TO FORM A POSSE, AND GO SET THINGS STRAIGHT.
THIS TIME, THERE'S NO COUNTING ON ANYONE ELSE--NO MAGICAL BIG GUNS TO KEEP US OUT OF THE LINE OF FIRE.
THIS TIME IT'S UP TO US. TIME TO SEE WHAT WE'RE MADE OF, BOYS AND GIRLS.
AND, FOR THE RECORD, KIDS, I AIN'T JUST ANY TALKING MONKEY.
I'M THE DETECTIVE CHIMP, AND I'M ON THE CASE!
NOW WHO'S WITH ME AND THE ENCHANTRESS BABE?
LONG AGO I USED TO BE A SUPERHERO. THEN I WAS JUST A GUY DOING A STRANGE AND UGLY JOB. BUT DO YOU WANT TO KNOW THE EXACT MOMENT MY LIFE TRULY GOT WEIRD? IT WAS THE DAY I MET MY FIRST TALKING MONKEY.
EVERYONE SUCKS BUT ME

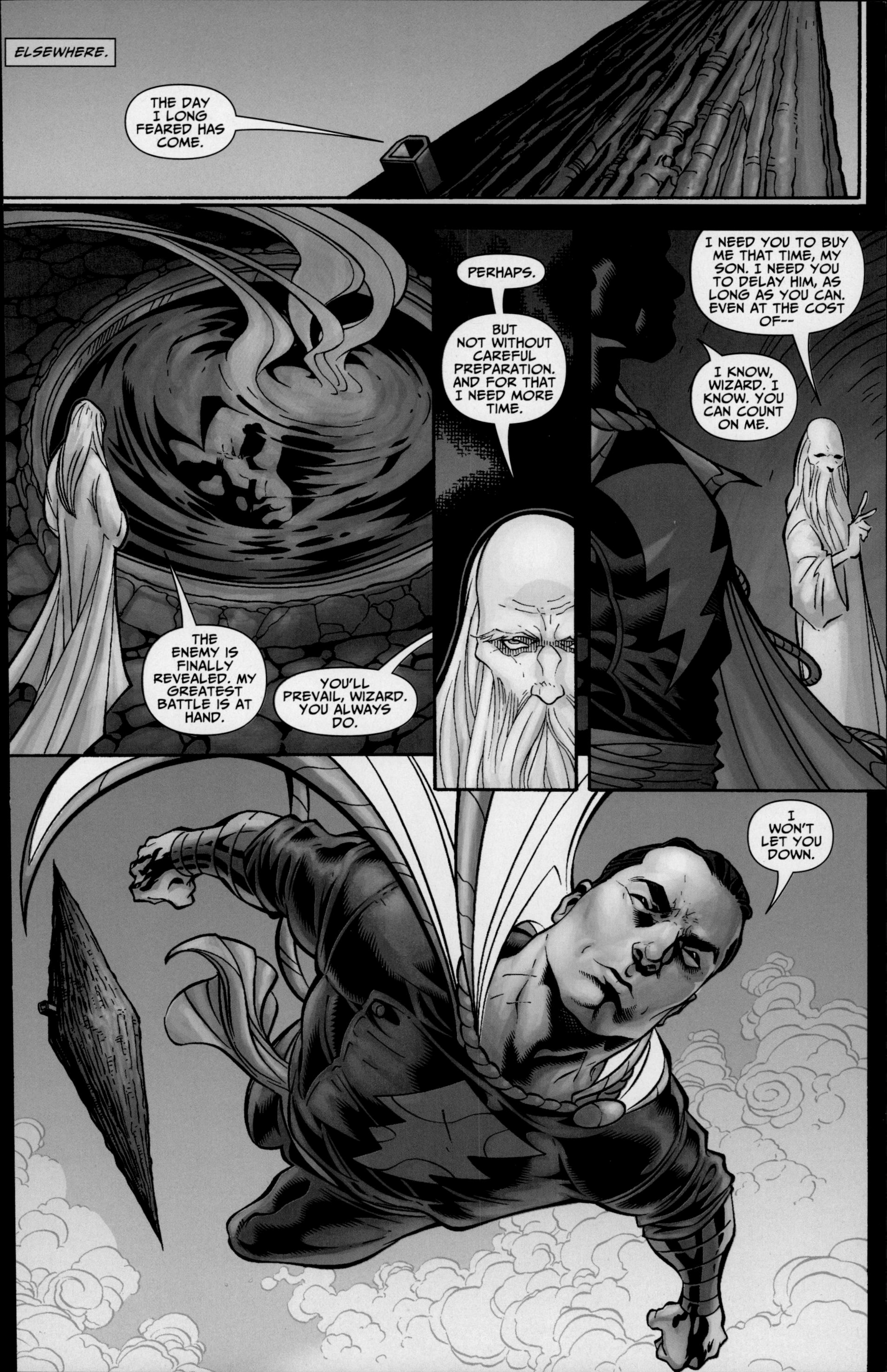
ELSEWHERE.
THE DAY I LONG FEARED HAS COME.
THE ENEMY IS FINALLY REVEALED. MY GREATEST BATTLE IS AT HAND.
YOU'LL PREVAIL, WIZARD. YOU ALWAYS DO.
PERHAPS.
BUT NOT WITHOUT CAREFUL PREPARATION. AND FOR THAT I NEED MORE TIME.
I NEED YOU TO BUY ME THAT TIME, MY SON. I NEED YOU TO DELAY HIM, AS LONG AS YOU CAN. EVEN AT THE COST OF--
I KNOW, WIZARD. I KNOW. YOU CAN COUNT ON ME.
I WON'T LET YOU DOWN.

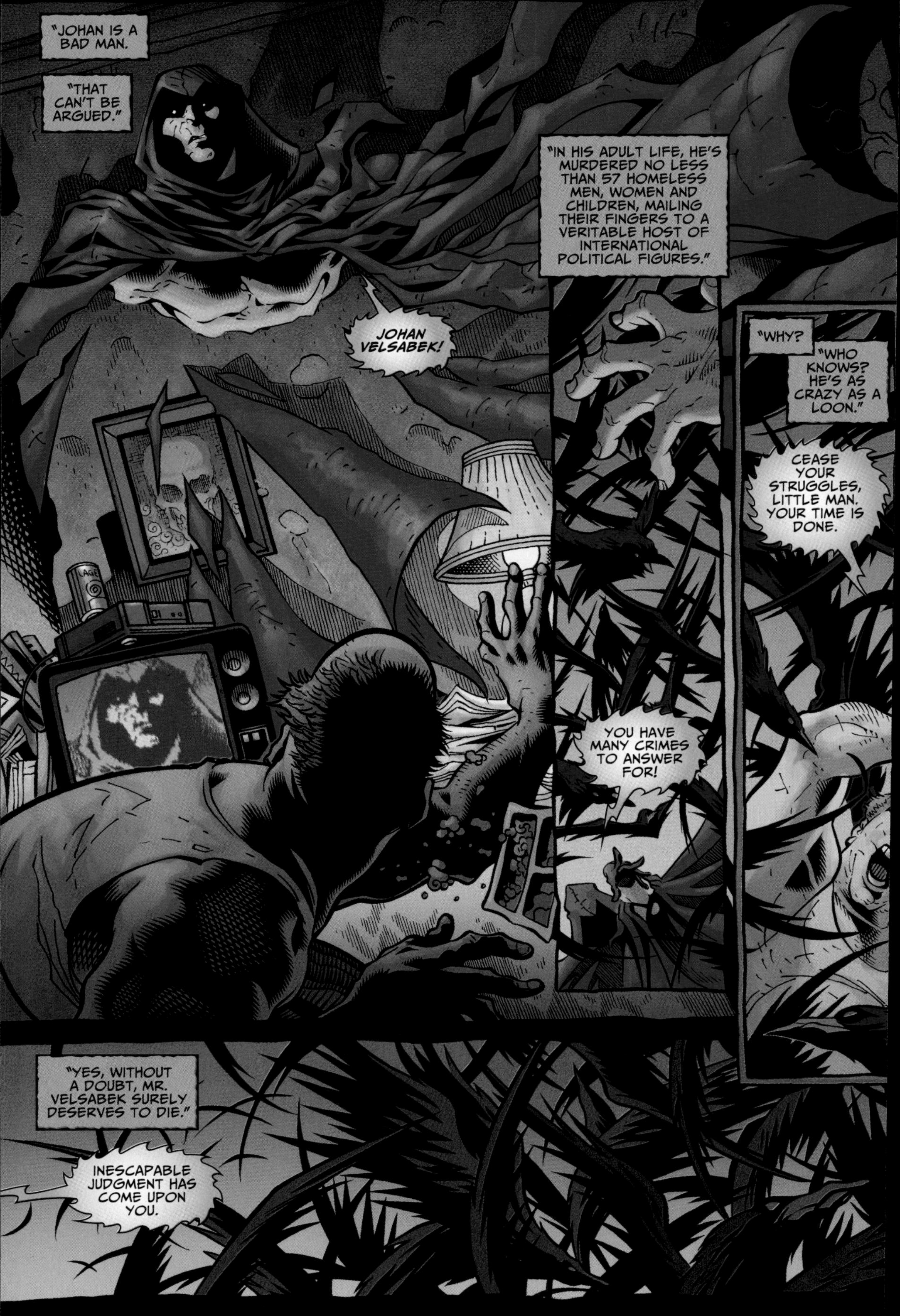

"JOHAN IS A BAD MAN.
"THAT CAN'T BE ARGUED."
JOHAN VELSABEK!
"IN HIS ADULT LIFE, HE'S MURDERED NO LESS THAN 57 HOMELESS MEN, WOMEN AND CHILDREN, MAILING THEIR FINGERS TO A VERITABLE HOST OF INTERNATIONAL POLITICAL FIGURES."
YOU HAVE MANY CRIMES TO ANSWER FOR!
"WHY?
"WHO KNOWS? HE'S AS CRAZY AS A LOON."
CEASE YOUR STRUGGLES, LITTLE MAN. YOUR TIME IS DONE.
"YES, WITHOUT A DOUBT, MR. VELSABEK SURELY DESERVES TO DIE."
INESCAPABLE JUDGMENT HAS COME UPON YOU.

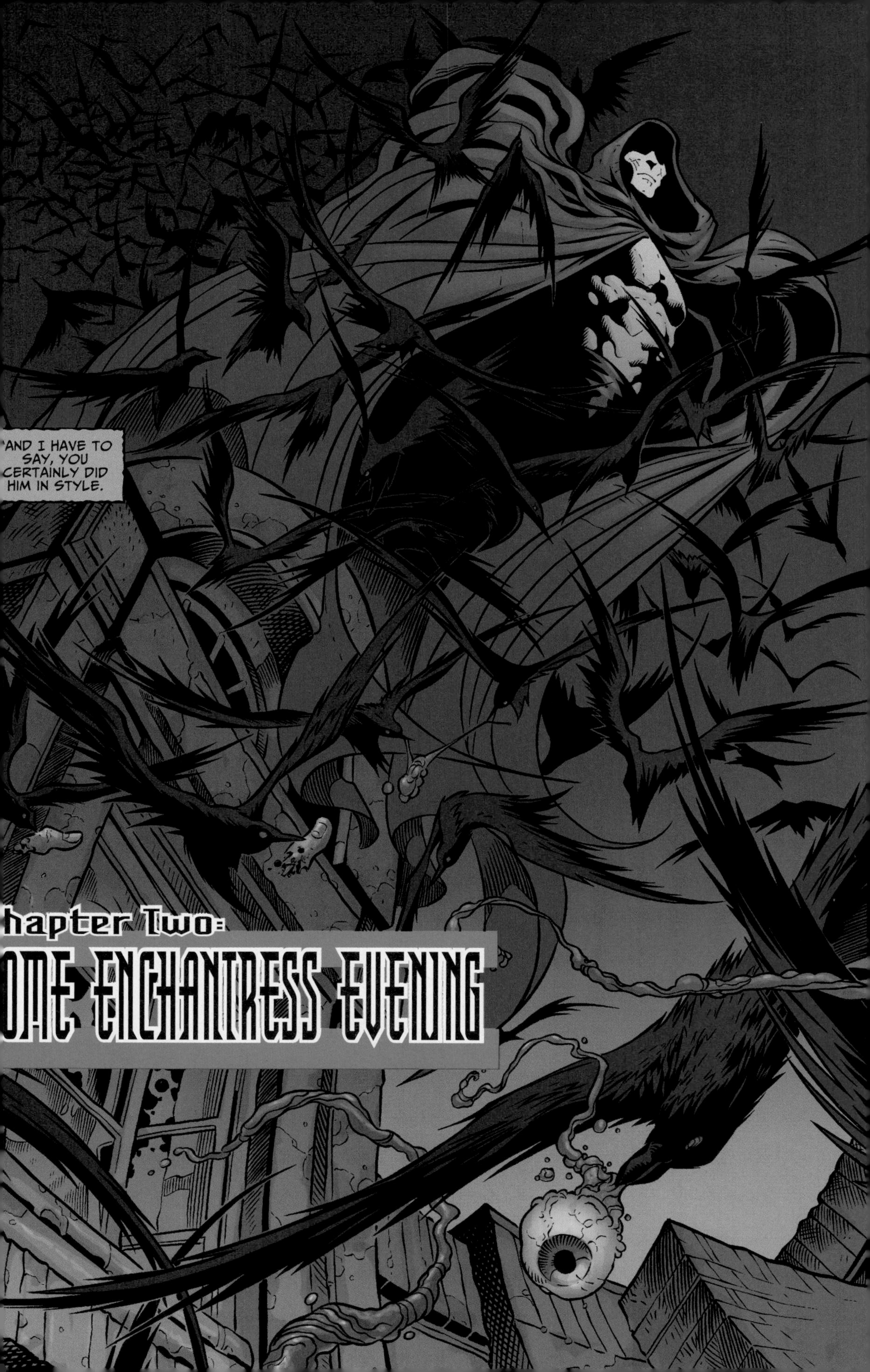
"AND I HAVE TO SAY, YOU CERTAINLY DID HIM IN STYLE.
hapter Two:
OME ENCHANTRESS EVENING

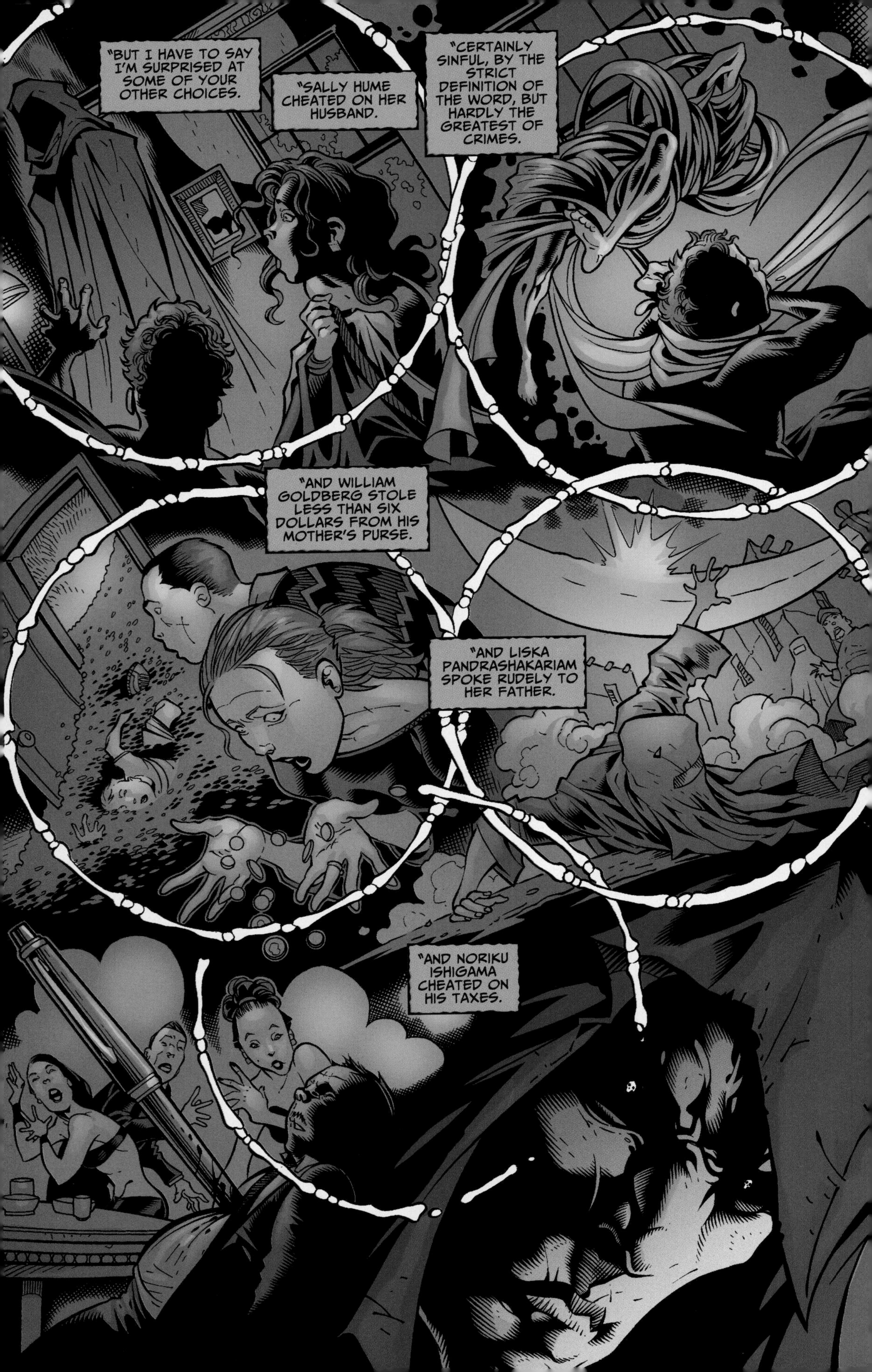
"BUT I HAVE TO SAY I'M SURPRISED AT SOME OF YOUR OTHER CHOICES.
"SALLY HUME CHEATED ON HER HUSBAND.
"CERTAINLY SINFUL, BY THE STRICT DEFINITION OF THE WORD, BUT HARDLY THE GREATEST OF CRIMES.
"AND WILLIAM GOLDBERG STOLE LESS THAN SIX DOLLARS FROM HIS MOTHER'S PURSE.
"AND LISKA PANDRASHAKARIAM SPOKE RUDELY TO HER FATHER.
"AND NORIKU ISHIGAMA CHEATED ON HIS TAXES.

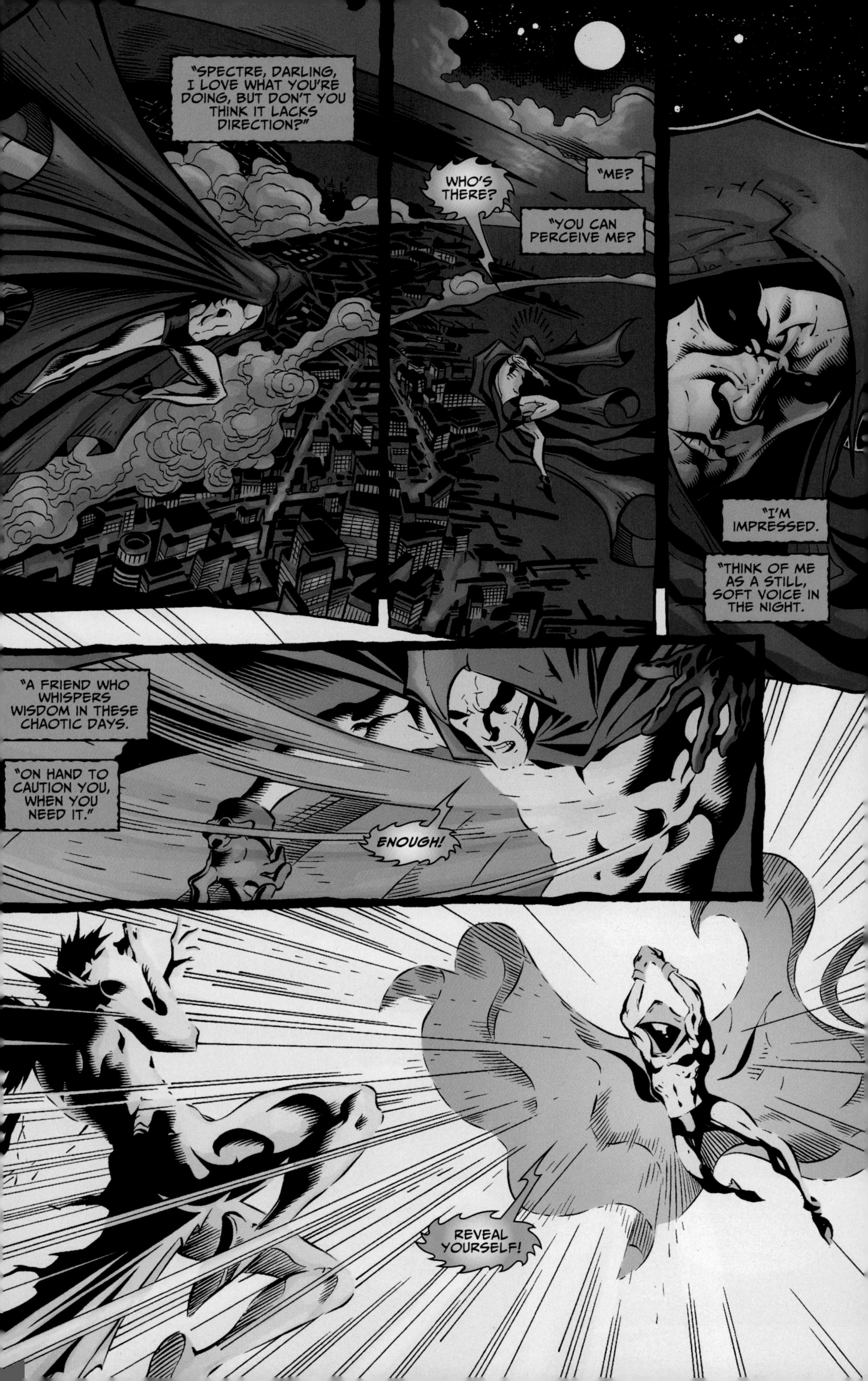
"SPECTRE, DARLING, I LOVE WHAT YOU'RE DOING, BUT DON'T YOU THINK IT LACKS DIRECTION?"
WHO'S THERE?
"ME?
"YOU CAN PERCEIVE ME?
"I'M IMPRESSED.
"THINK OF ME AS A STILL, SOFT VOICE IN THE NIGHT.
"A FRIEND WHO WHISPERS WISDOM IN THESE CHAOTIC DAYS.
"ON HAND TO CAUTION YOU, WHEN YOU NEED IT."
ENOUGH!
REVEAL YOURSELF!

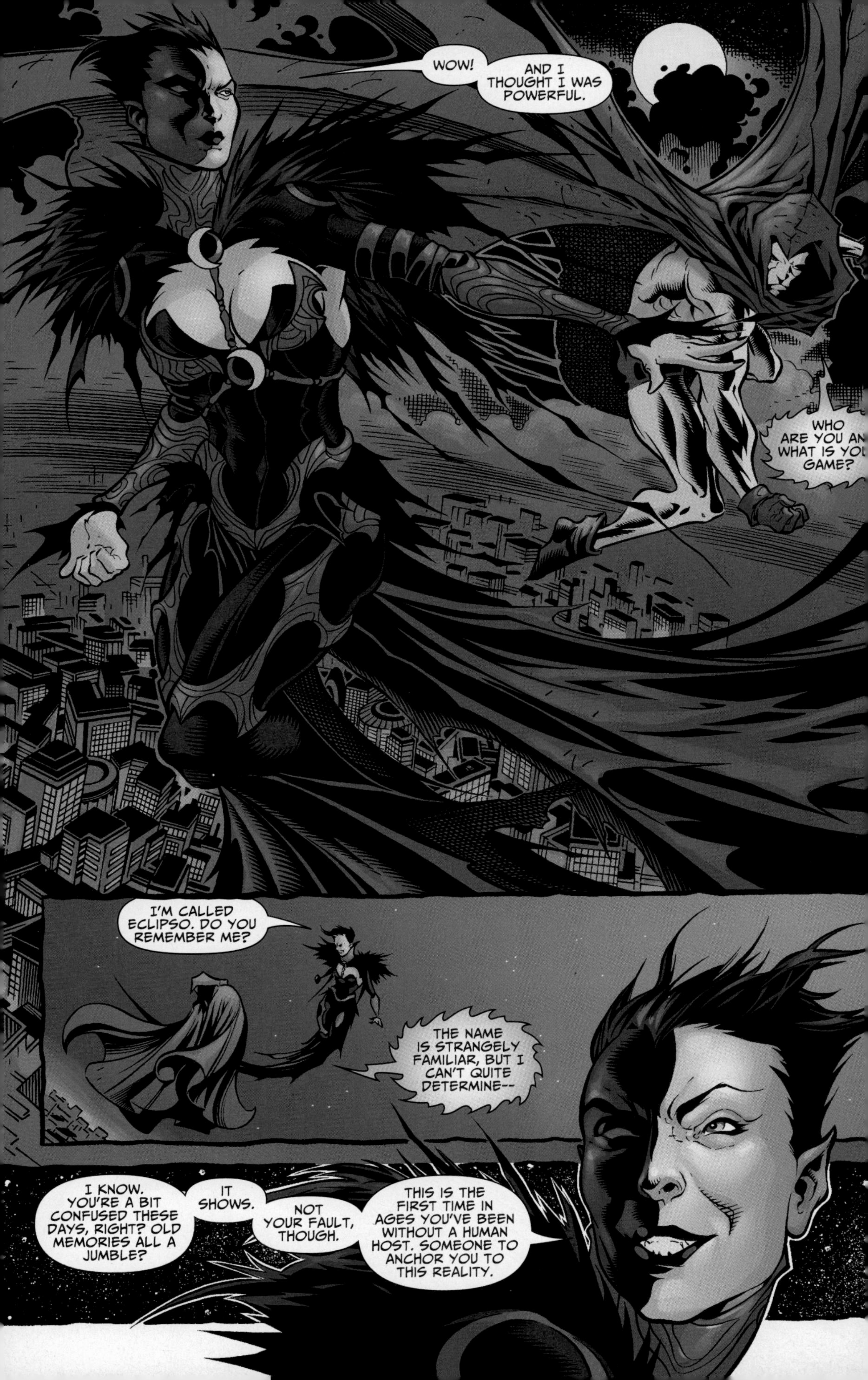
WOW!
AND I THOUGHT I WAS POWERFUL.
WHO ARE YOU AN WHAT IS YOU GAME?
I'M CALLED ECLIPSO. DO YOU REMEMBER ME?
THE NAME IS STRANGELY FAMILIAR, BUT I CAN'T QUITE DETERMINE--
I KNOW. YOU'RE A BIT CONFUSED THESE DAYS, RIGHT? OLD MEMORIES ALL A JUMBLE?
IT SHOWS.
NOT YOUR FAULT, THOUGH.
THIS IS THE FIRST TIME IN AGES YOU'VE BEEN WITHOUT A HUMAN HOST. SOMEONE TO ANCHOR YOU TO THIS REALITY.

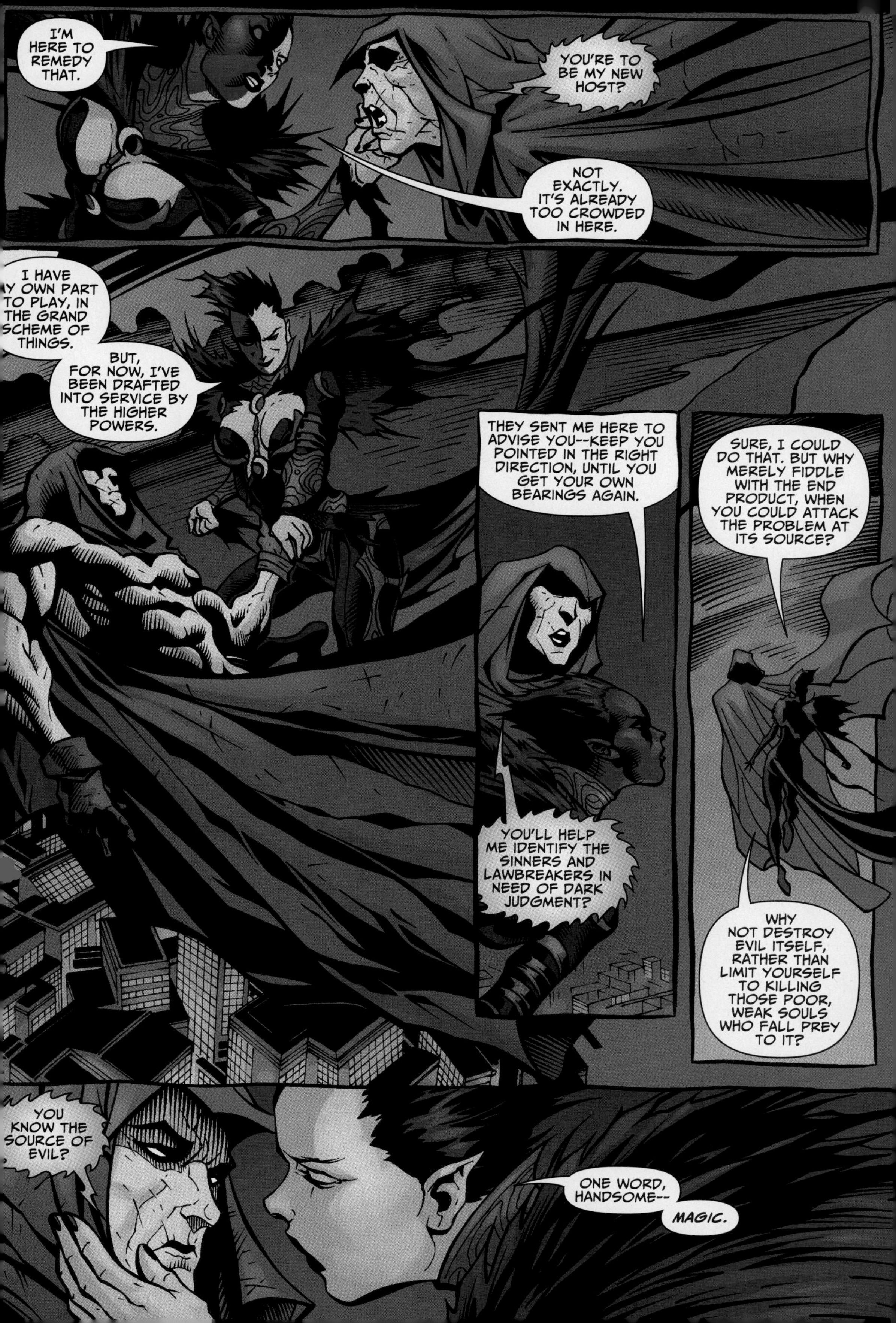
I'M HERE TO REMEDY THAT.
YOU'RE TO BE MY NEW HOST?
NOT EXACTLY. IT'S ALREADY TOO CROWDED IN HERE.
I HAVE MY OWN PART TO PLAY, IN THE GRAND SCHEME OF THINGS.
BUT, FOR NOW, I'VE BEEN DRAFTED INTO SERVICE BY THE HIGHER POWERS.
THEY SENT ME HERE TO ADVISE YOU--KEEP YOU POINTED IN THE RIGHT DIRECTION, UNTIL YOU GET YOUR OWN BEARINGS AGAIN.
YOU'LL HELP ME IDENTIFY THE SINNERS AND LAWBREAKERS IN NEED OF DARK JUDGMENT?
SURE, I COULD DO THAT. BUT WHY MERELY FIDDLE WITH THE END PRODUCT, WHEN YOU COULD ATTACK THE PROBLEM AT ITS SOURCE?
WHY NOT DESTROY EVIL ITSELF, RATHER THAN LIMIT YOURSELF TO KILLING THOSE POOR, WEAK SOULS WHO FALL PREY TO IT?
YOU KNOW THE SOURCE OF EVIL?
ONE WORD, HANDSOME--
MAGIC.

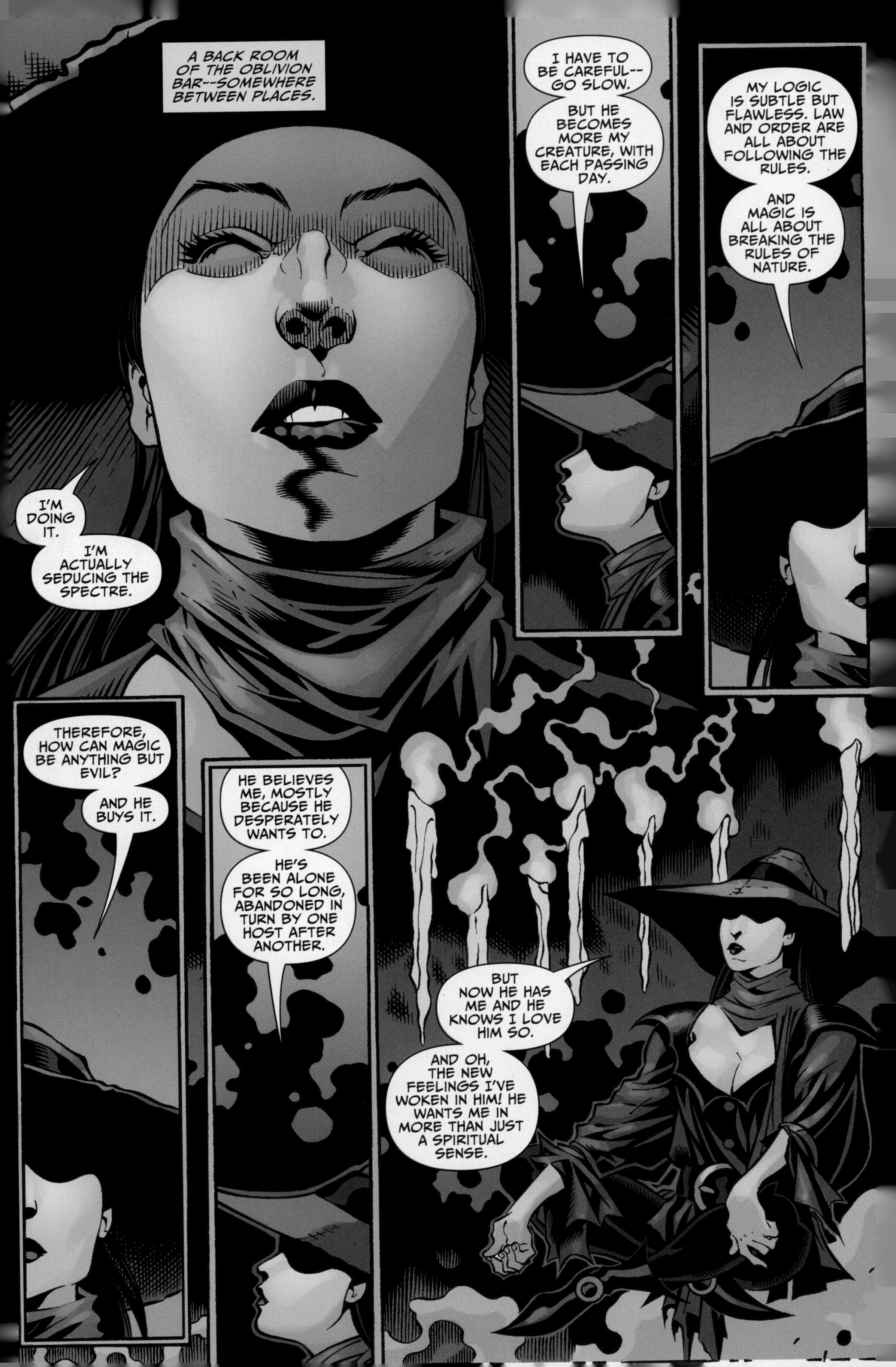
A BACK ROOM OF THE OBLIVION BAR--SOMEWHERE BETWEEN PLACES.
I'M DOING IT.
I'M ACTUALLY SEDUCING THE SPECTRE.
I HAVE TO BE CAREFUL--GO SLOW.
BUT HE BECOMES MORE MY CREATURE, WITH EACH PASSING DAY.
MY LOGIC IS SUBTLE BUT FLAWLESS. LAW AND ORDER ARE ALL ABOUT FOLLOWING THE RULES.
AND MAGIC IS ALL ABOUT BREAKING THE RULES OF NATURE.
THEREFORE, HOW CAN MAGIC BE ANYTHING BUT EVIL?
AND HE BUYS IT.
HE BELIEVES ME, MOSTLY BECAUSE HE DESPERATELY WANTS TO.
HE'S BEEN ALONE FOR SO LONG, ABANDONED IN TURN BY ONE HOST AFTER ANOTHER.
BUT NOW HE HAS ME AND HE KNOWS I LOVE HIM SO.
AND OH, THE NEW FEELINGS I'VE WOKEN IN HIM! HE WANTS ME IN MORE THAN JUST A SPIRITUAL SENSE.

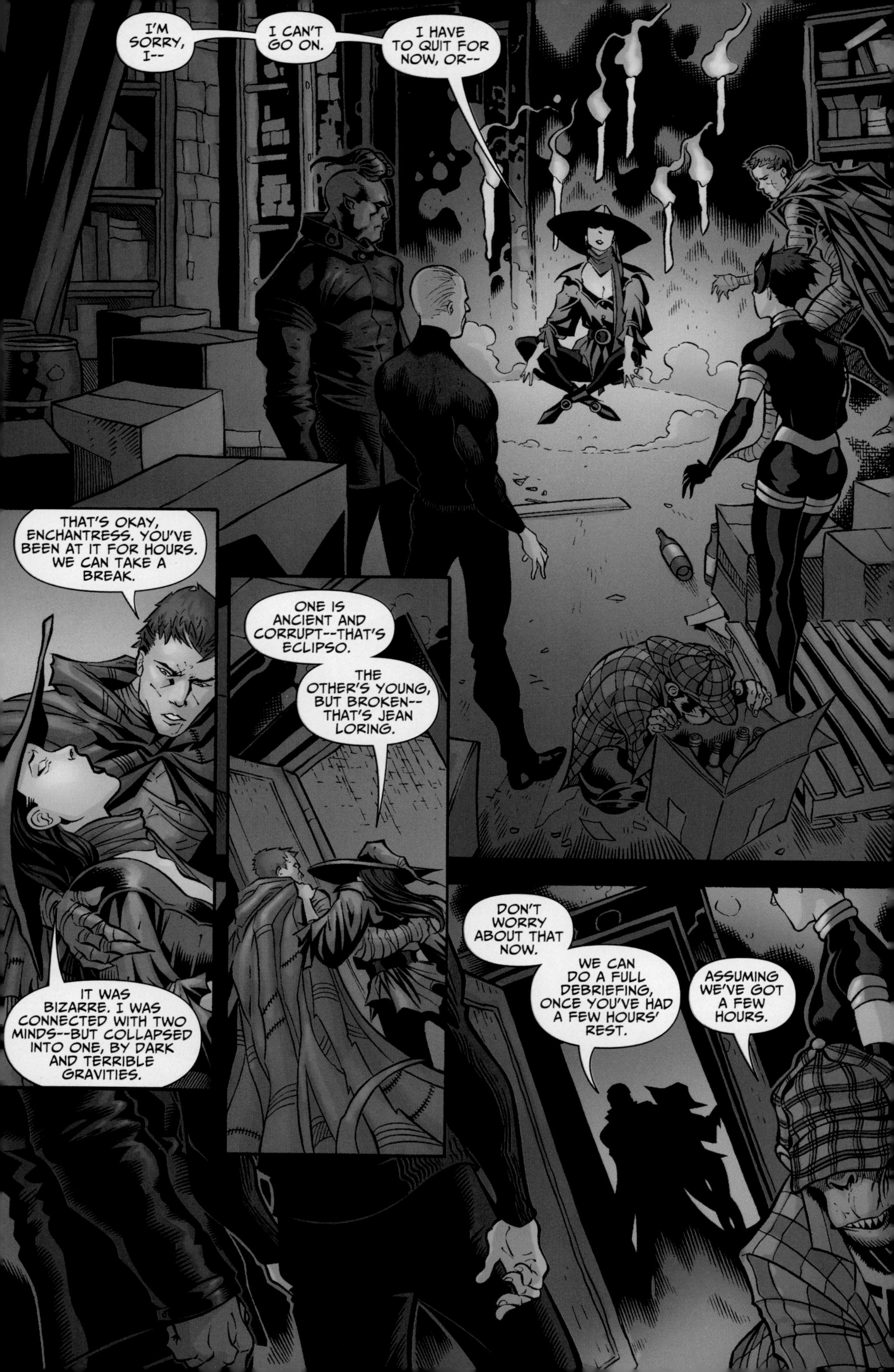

I'M SORRY, I--
I CAN'T GO ON.
I HAVE TO QUIT FOR NOW, OR--
THAT'S OKAY, ENCHANTRESS. YOU'VE BEEN AT IT FOR HOURS. WE CAN TAKE A BREAK.
IT WAS BIZARRE. I WAS CONNECTED WITH TWO MINDS--BUT COLLAPSED INTO ONE, BY DARK AND TERRIBLE GRAVITIES.
ONE IS ANCIENT AND CORRUPT--THAT'S ECLIPSO.
THE OTHER'S YOUNG, BUT BROKEN--THAT'S JEAN LORING.
DON'T WORRY ABOUT THAT NOW.
WE CAN DO A FULL DEBRIEFING, ONCE YOU'VE HAD A FEW HOURS' REST.
ASSUMING WE'VE GOT A FEW HOURS.

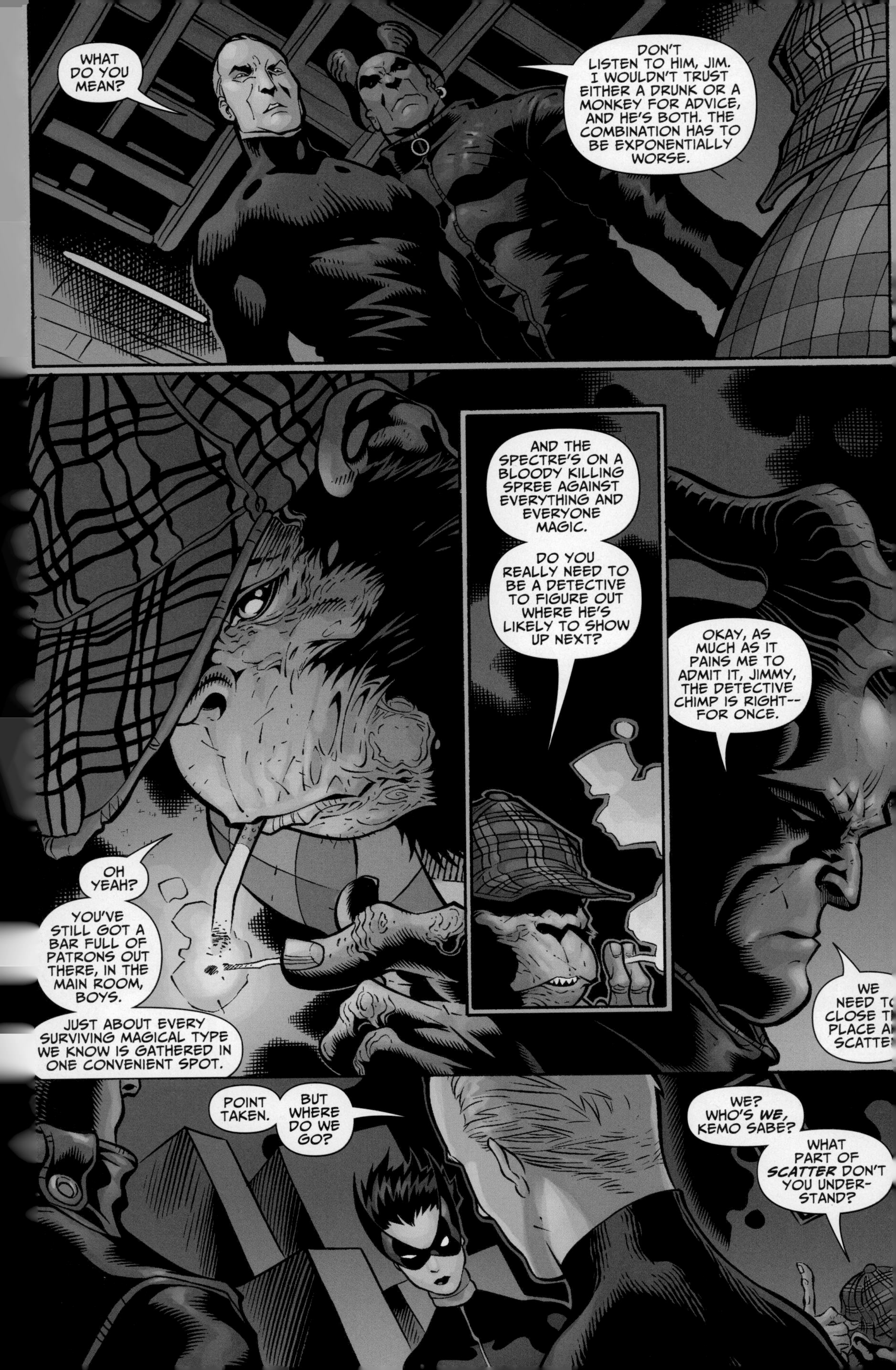
WHAT DO YOU MEAN?
DON'T LISTEN TO HIM, JIM. I WOULDN'T TRUST EITHER A DRUNK OR A MONKEY FOR ADVICE, AND HE'S BOTH. THE COMBINATION HAS TO BE EXPONENTIALLY WORSE.
OH YEAH?
YOU'VE STILL GOT A BAR FULL OF PATRONS OUT THERE, IN THE MAIN ROOM, BOYS.
JUST ABOUT EVERY SURVIVING MAGICAL TYPE WE KNOW IS GATHERED IN ONE CONVENIENT SPOT.
AND THE SPECTRE'S ON A BLOODY KILLING SPREE AGAINST EVERYTHING AND EVERYONE MAGIC.
DO YOU REALLY NEED TO BE A DETECTIVE TO FIGURE OUT WHERE HE'S LIKELY TO SHOW UP NEXT?
OKAY, AS MUCH AS IT PAINS ME TO ADMIT IT, JIMMY, THE DETECTIVE CHIMP IS RIGHT-- FOR ONCE.
WE NEED TO CLOSE T PLACE A SCATTE
POINT TAKEN.
BUT WHERE DO WE GO?
WE? WHO'S *WE*, KEMO SABE?
WHAT PART OF *SCATTER* DON'T YOU UNDER-STAND?

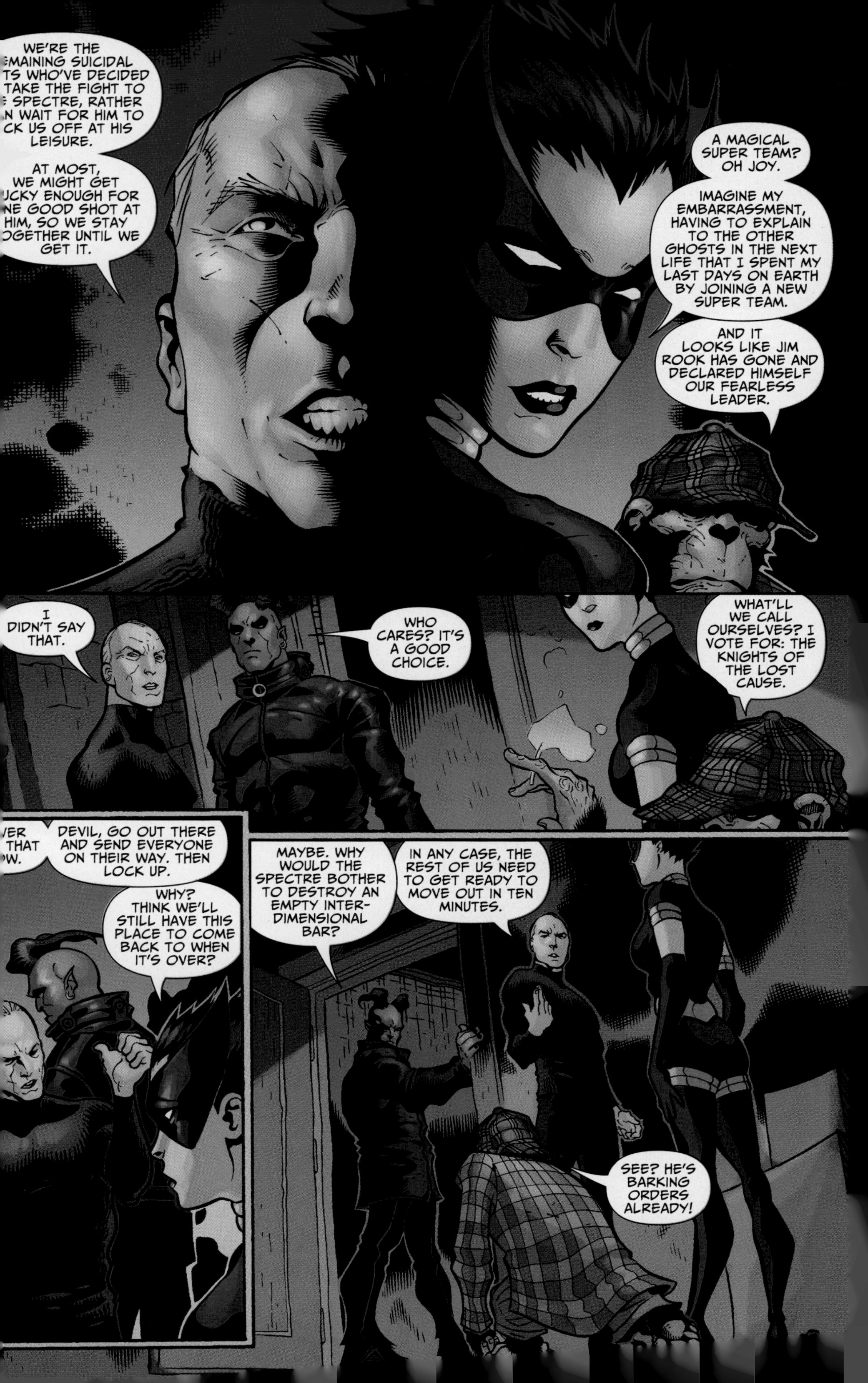

WE'RE THE
EMAINING SUICIDAL
TS WHO'VE DECIDED
TAKE THE FIGHT TO
E SPECTRE, RATHER
N WAIT FOR HIM TO
CK US OFF AT HIS
LEISURE.
AT MOST,
WE MIGHT GET
UCKY ENOUGH FOR
NE GOOD SHOT AT
HIM, SO WE STAY
OGETHER UNTIL WE
GET IT.
A MAGICAL SUPER TEAM? OH JOY.
IMAGINE MY EMBARRASSMENT, HAVING TO EXPLAIN TO THE OTHER GHOSTS IN THE NEXT LIFE THAT I SPENT MY LAST DAYS ON EARTH BY JOINING A NEW SUPER TEAM.
AND IT LOOKS LIKE JIM ROOK HAS GONE AND DECLARED HIMSELF OUR FEARLESS LEADER.
I DIDN'T SAY THAT.
WHO CARES? IT'S A GOOD CHOICE.
WHAT'LL WE CALL OURSELVES? I VOTE FOR: THE KNIGHTS OF THE LOST CAUSE.
VER
THAT
W.
DEVIL, GO OUT THERE AND SEND EVERYONE ON THEIR WAY. THEN LOCK UP.
WHY? THINK WE'LL STILL HAVE THIS PLACE TO COME BACK TO WHEN IT'S OVER?
MAYBE. WHY WOULD THE SPECTRE BOTHER TO DESTROY AN EMPTY INTER-DIMENSIONAL BAR?
IN ANY CASE, THE REST OF US NEED TO GET READY TO MOVE OUT IN TEN MINUTES.
SEE? HE'S BARKING ORDERS ALREADY!

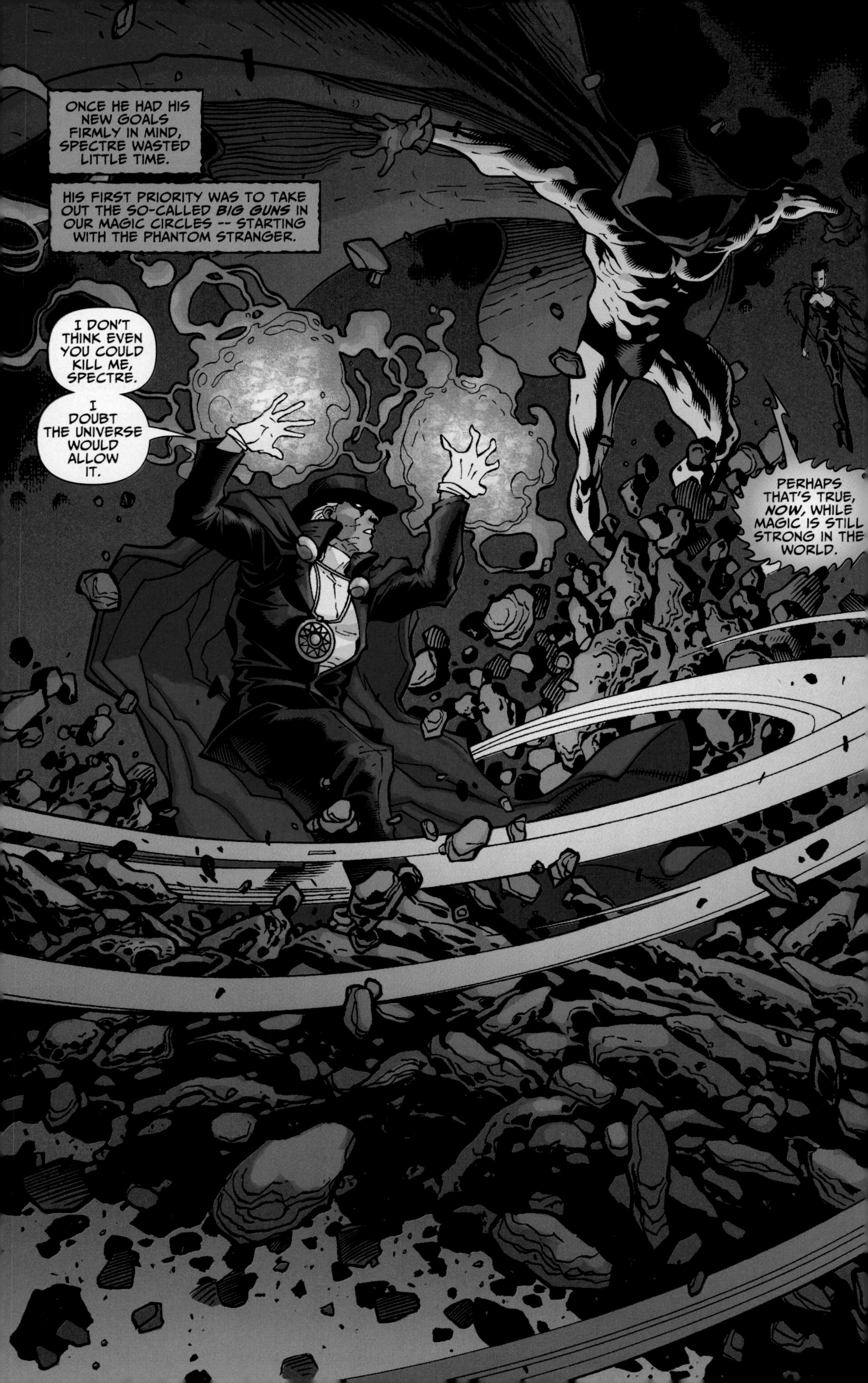
ONCE HE HAD HIS NEW GOALS FIRMLY IN MIND, SPECTRE WASTED LITTLE TIME.
HIS FIRST PRIORITY WAS TO TAKE OUT THE SO-CALLED *BIG GUNS* IN OUR MAGIC CIRCLES -- STARTING WITH THE PHANTOM STRANGER.
I DON'T THINK EVEN YOU COULD KILL ME, SPECTRE.
I DOUBT THE UNIVERSE WOULD ALLOW IT.
PERHAPS THAT'S TRUE, ***NOW,*** WHILE MAGIC IS STILL STRONG IN THE WORLD.

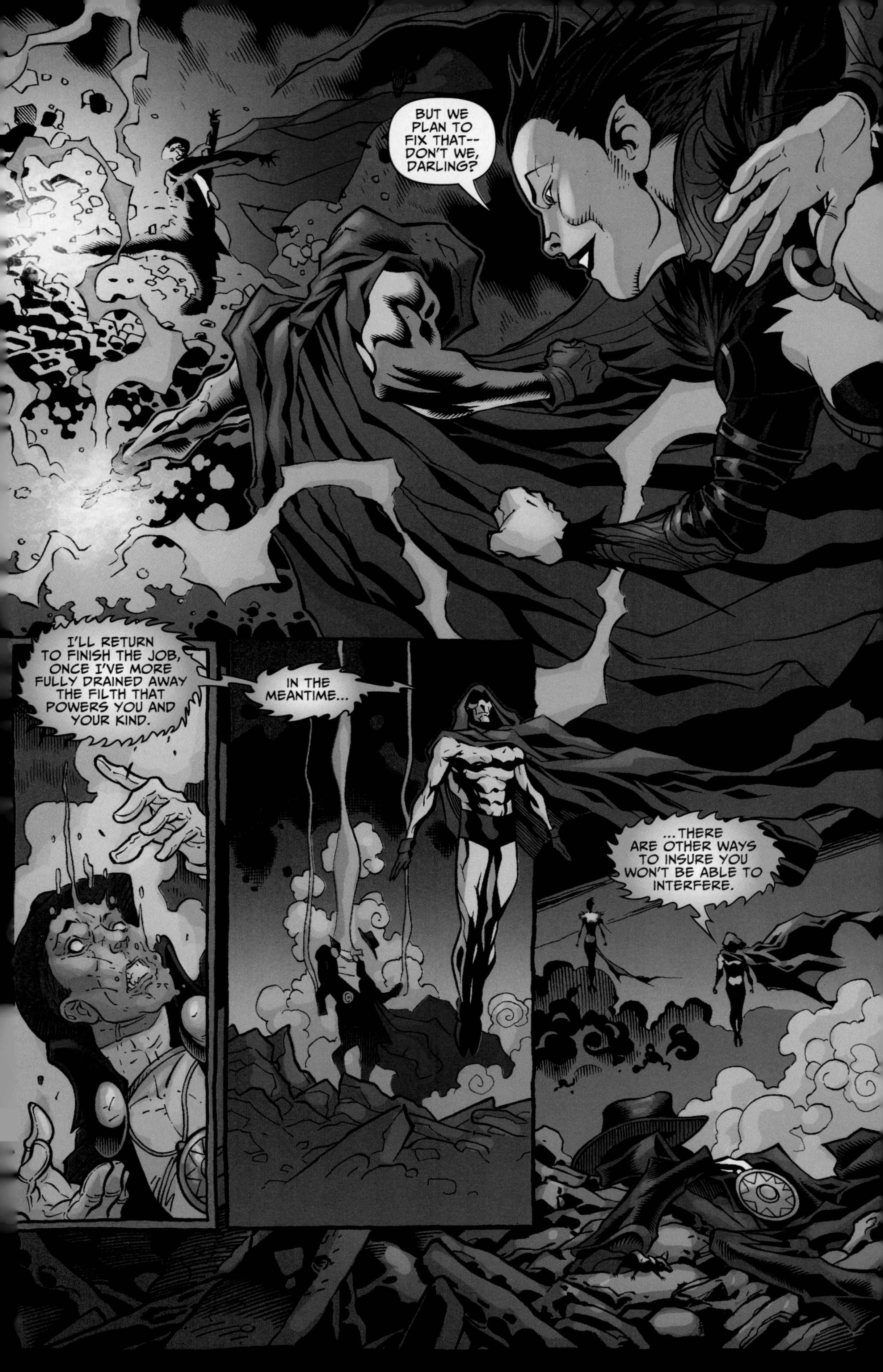

BUT WE PLAN TO FIX THAT-- DON'T WE, DARLING?
I'LL RETURN TO FINISH THE JOB, ONCE I'VE MORE FULLY DRAINED AWAY THE FILTH THAT POWERS YOU AND YOUR KIND.
IN THE MEANTIME...
...THERE ARE OTHER WAYS TO INSURE YOU WON'T BE ABLE TO INTERFERE.

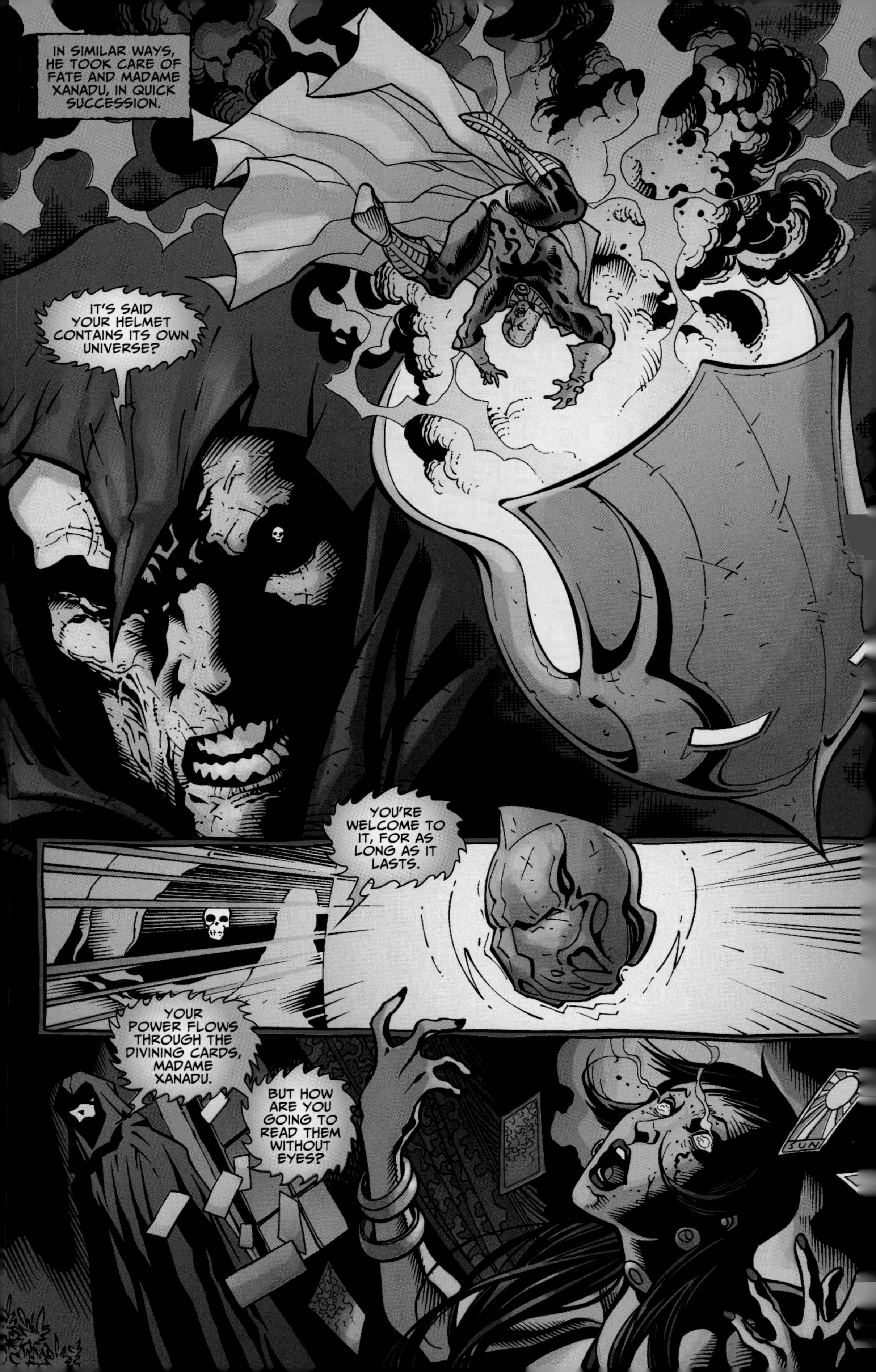
IN SIMILAR WAYS, HE TOOK CARE OF FATE AND MADAME XANADU, IN QUICK SUCCESSION.
IT'S SAID YOUR HELMET CONTAINS ITS OWN UNIVERSE?
YOU'RE WELCOME TO IT, FOR AS LONG AS IT LASTS.
YOUR POWER FLOWS THROUGH THE DIVINING CARDS, MADAME XANADU.
BUT HOW ARE YOU GOING TO READ THEM WITHOUT EYES?
SUN

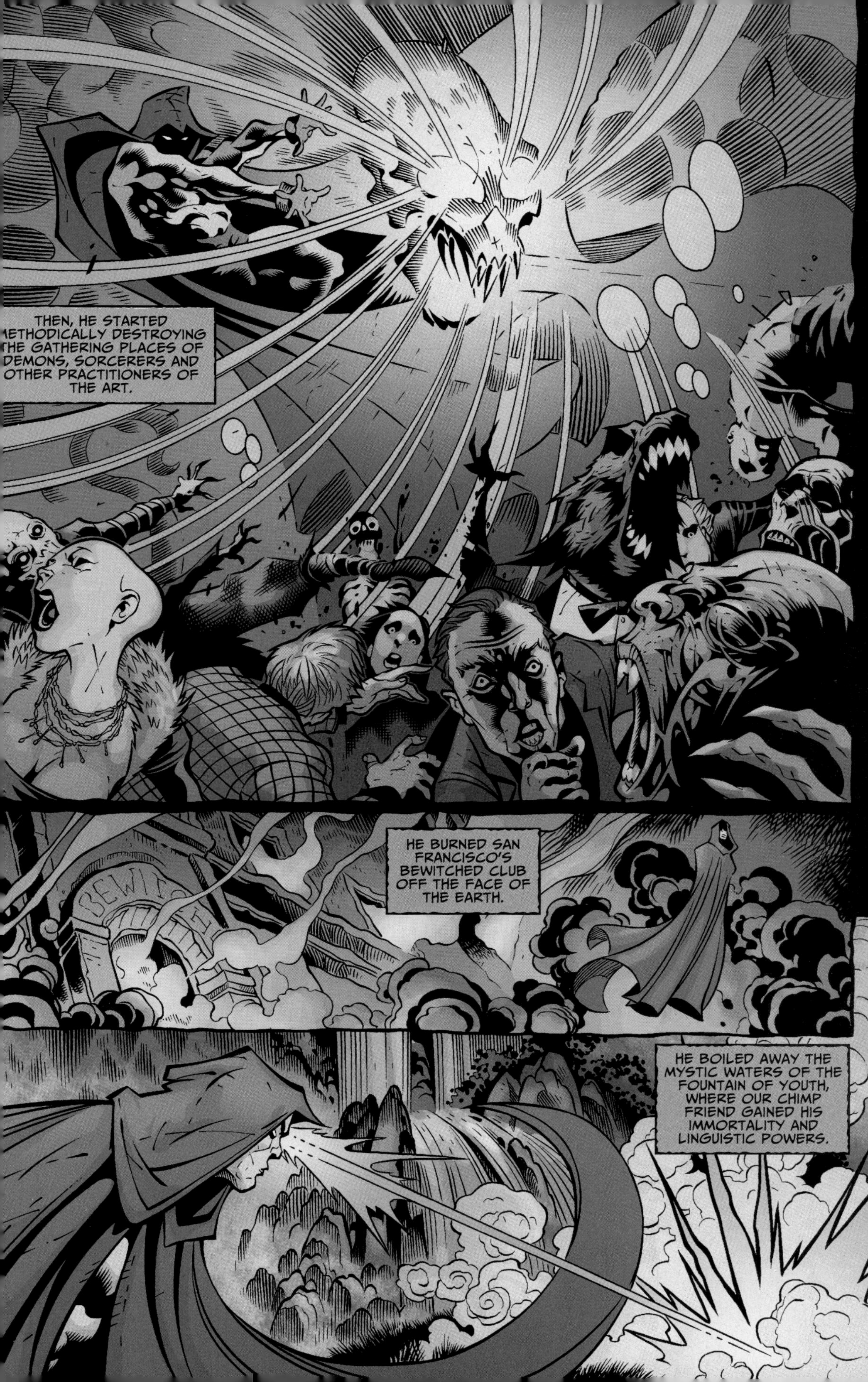
THEN, HE STARTED METHODICALLY DESTROYING THE GATHERING PLACES OF DEMONS, SORCERERS AND OTHER PRACTITIONERS OF THE ART.
HE BURNED SAN FRANCISCO'S BEWITCHED CLUB OFF THE FACE OF THE EARTH.
HE BOILED AWAY THE MYSTIC WATERS OF THE FOUNTAIN OF YOUTH, WHERE OUR CHIMP FRIEND GAINED HIS IMMORTALITY AND LINGUISTIC POWERS.

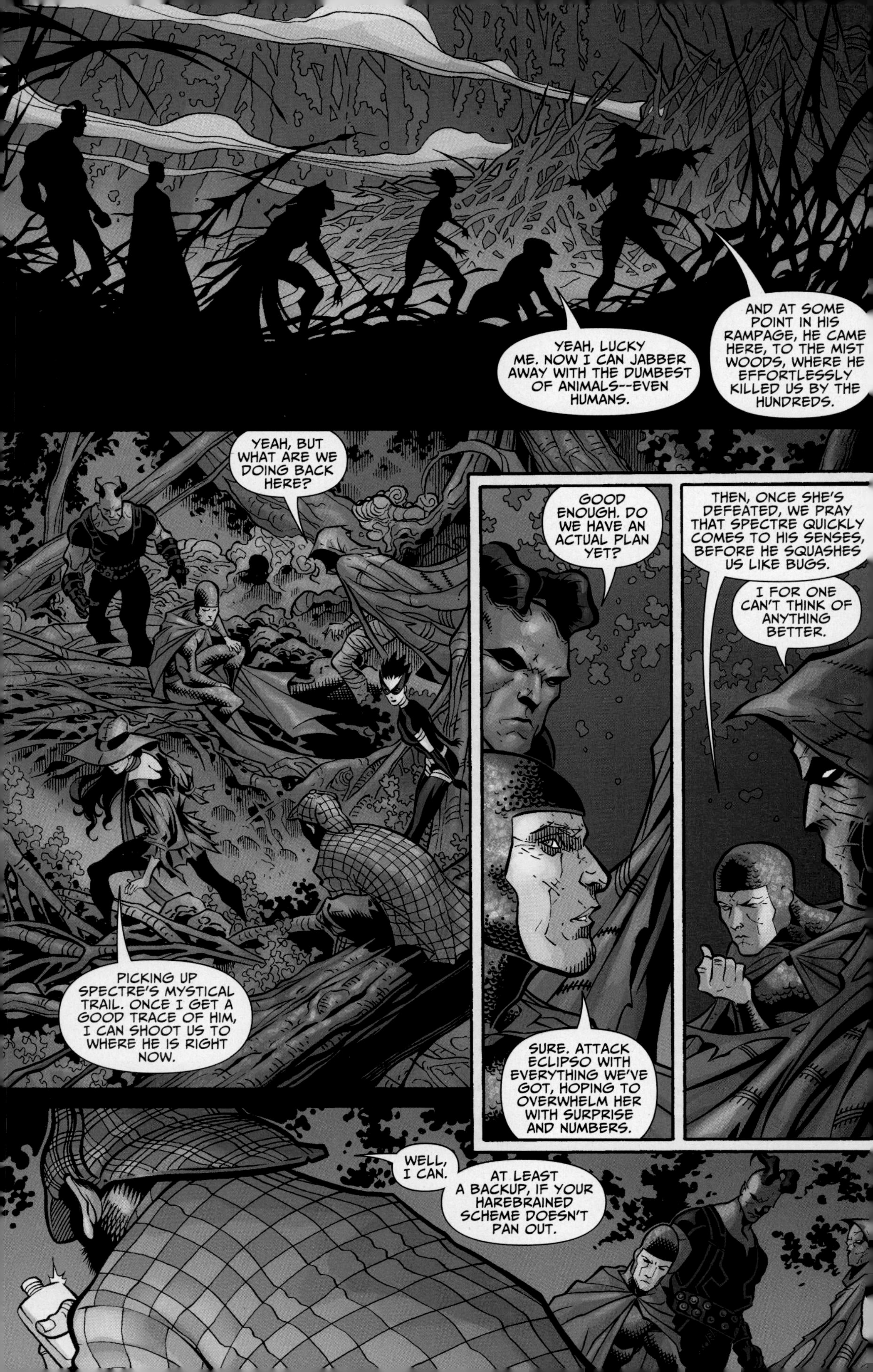
YEAH, LUCKY ME. NOW I CAN JABBER AWAY WITH THE DUMBEST OF ANIMALS--EVEN HUMANS.
AND AT SOME POINT IN HIS RAMPAGE, HE CAME HERE, TO THE MIST WOODS, WHERE HE EFFORTLESSLY KILLED US BY THE HUNDREDS.
YEAH, BUT WHAT ARE WE DOING BACK HERE?
PICKING UP SPECTRE'S MYSTICAL TRAIL. ONCE I GET A GOOD TRACE OF HIM, I CAN SHOOT US TO WHERE HE IS RIGHT NOW.
GOOD ENOUGH. DO WE HAVE AN ACTUAL PLAN YET?
SURE. ATTACK ECLIPSO WITH EVERYTHING WE'VE GOT, HOPING TO OVERWHELM HER WITH SURPRISE AND NUMBERS.
THEN, ONCE SHE'S DEFEATED, WE PRAY THAT SPECTRE QUICKLY COMES TO HIS SENSES, BEFORE HE SQUASHES US LIKE BUGS.
I FOR ONE CAN'T THINK OF ANYTHING BETTER.
WELL, I CAN.
AT LEAST A BACKUP, IF YOUR HAREBRAINED SCHEME DOESN'T PAN OUT.

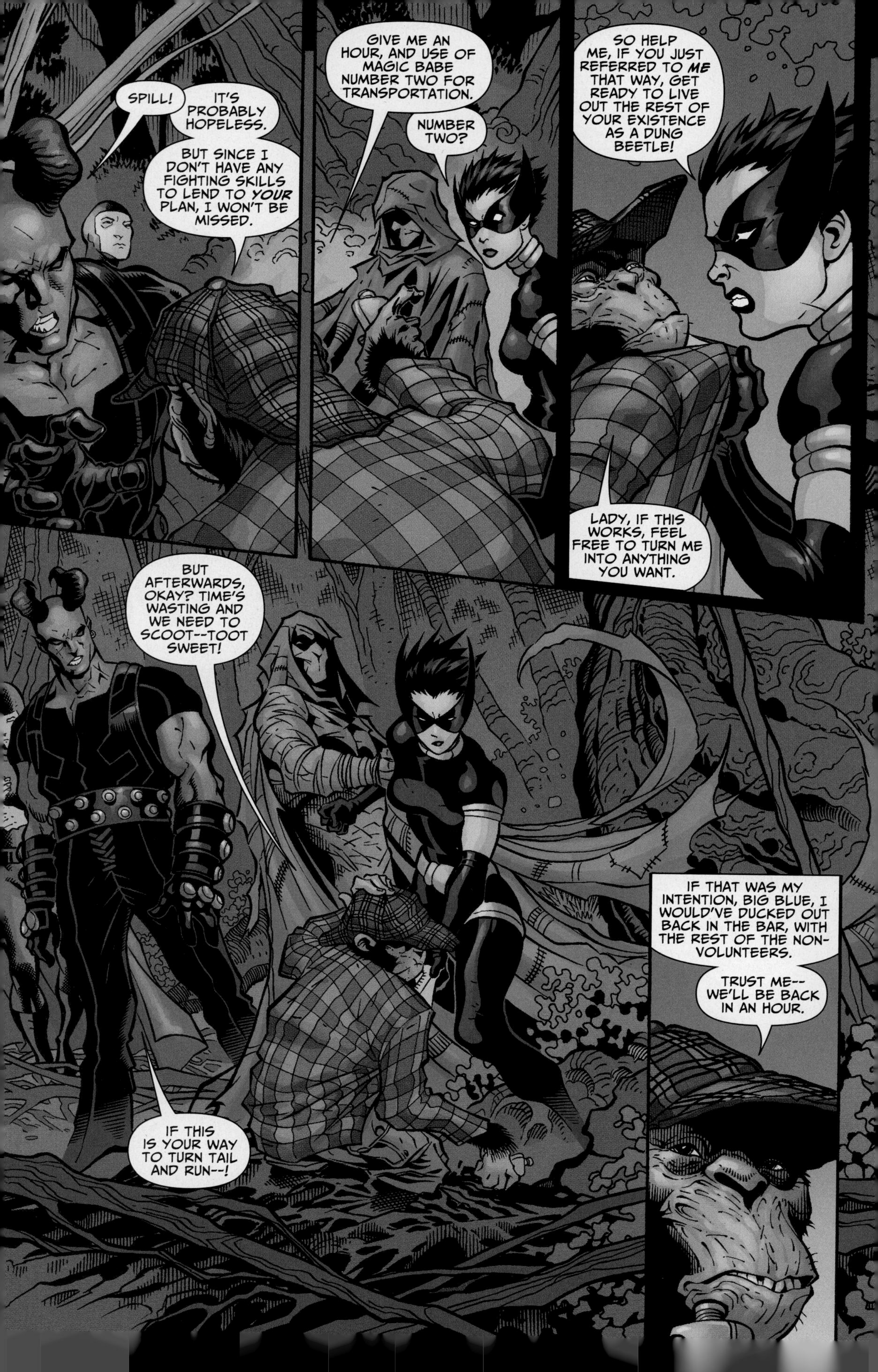
SPILL!
IT'S PROBABLY HOPELESS.
BUT SINCE I DON'T HAVE ANY FIGHTING SKILLS TO LEND TO *YOUR* PLAN, I WON'T BE MISSED.
GIVE ME AN HOUR, AND USE OF MAGIC BABE NUMBER TWO FOR TRANSPORTATION.
NUMBER TWO?
SO HELP ME, IF YOU JUST REFERRED TO *ME* THAT WAY, GET READY TO LIVE OUT THE REST OF YOUR EXISTENCE AS A DUNG BEETLE!
LADY, IF THIS WORKS, FEEL FREE TO TURN ME INTO ANYTHING YOU WANT.
BUT AFTERWARDS, OKAY? TIME'S WASTING AND WE NEED TO SCOOT--TOOT SWEET!
IF THIS IS YOUR WAY TO TURN TAIL AND RUN--!
IF THAT WAS MY INTENTION, BIG BLUE, I WOULD'VE DUCKED OUT BACK IN THE BAR, WITH THE REST OF THE NON-VOLUNTEERS.
TRUST ME--WE'LL BE BACK IN AN HOUR.

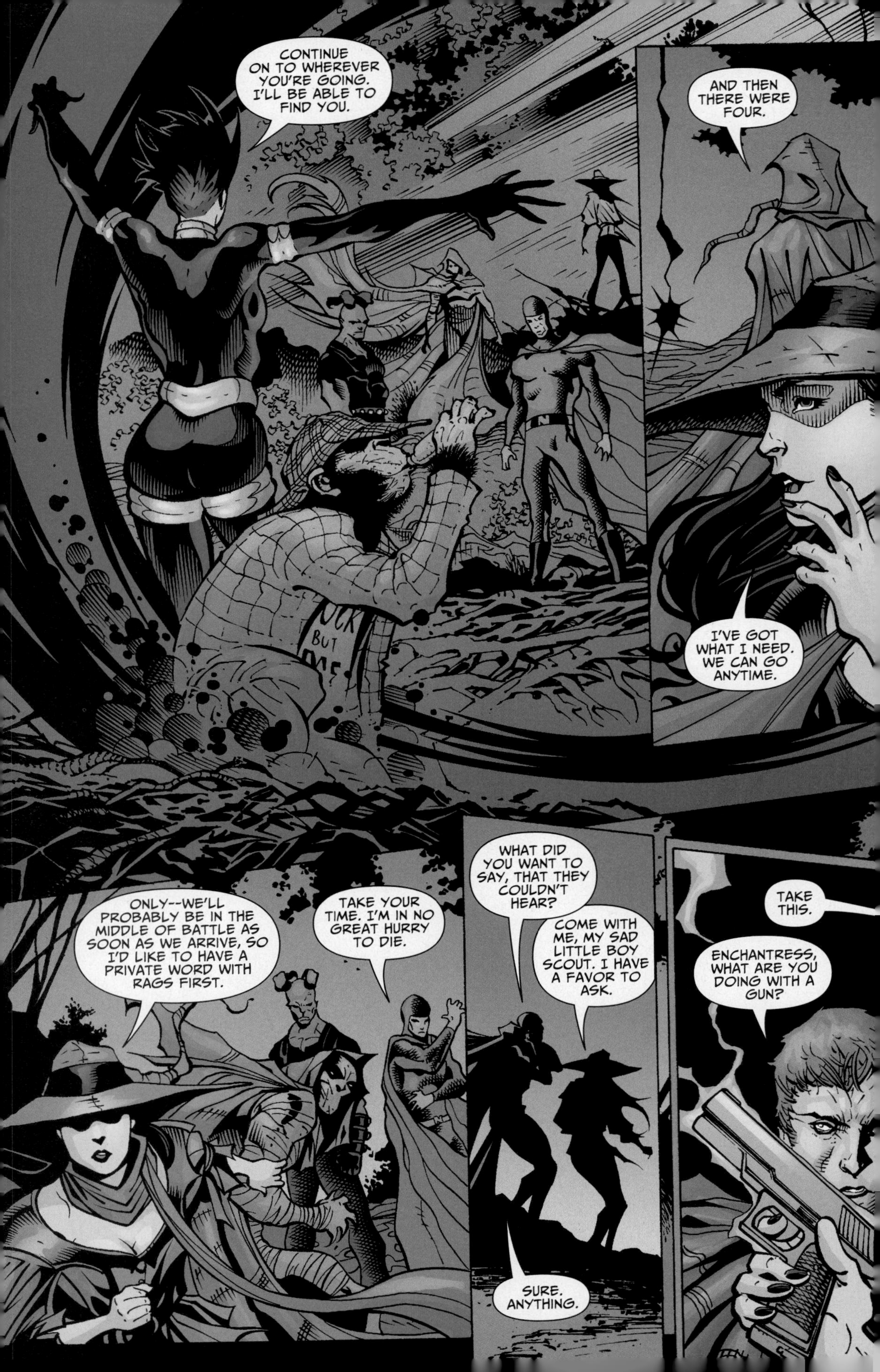
CONTINUE ON TO WHEREVER YOU'RE GOING. I'LL BE ABLE TO FIND YOU.
AND THEN THERE WERE FOUR.
I'VE GOT WHAT I NEED. WE CAN GO ANYTIME.
ONLY--WE'LL PROBABLY BE IN THE MIDDLE OF BATTLE AS SOON AS WE ARRIVE, SO I'D LIKE TO HAVE A PRIVATE WORD WITH RAGS FIRST.
TAKE YOUR TIME. I'M IN NO GREAT HURRY TO DIE.
WHAT DID YOU WANT TO SAY, THAT THEY COULDN'T HEAR?
COME WITH ME, MY SAD LITTLE BOY SCOUT. I HAVE A FAVOR TO ASK.
SURE. ANYTHING.
TAKE THIS.
ENCHANTRESS, WHAT ARE YOU DOING WITH A GUN?

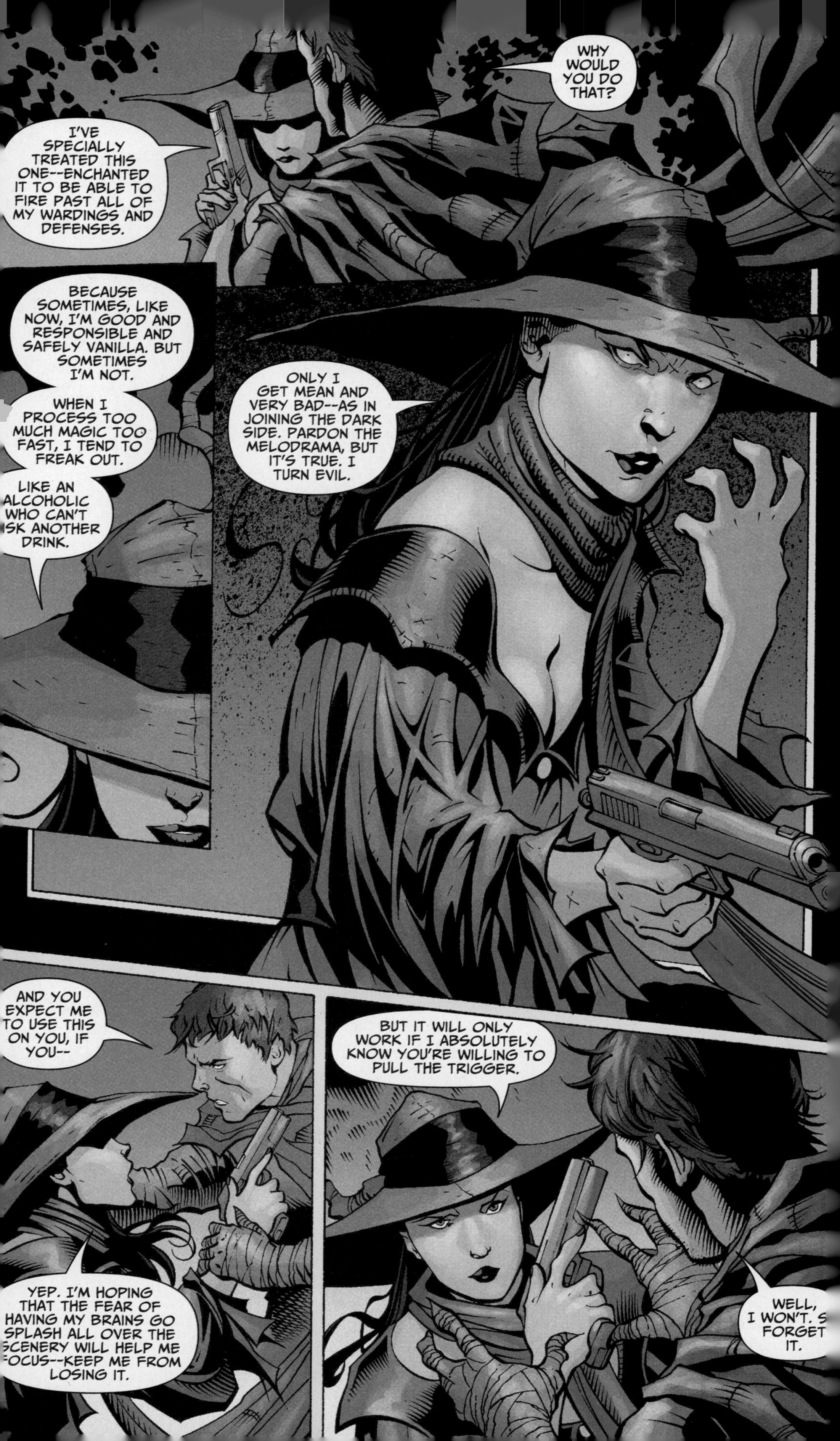
I'VE SPECIALLY TREATED THIS ONE--ENCHANTED IT TO BE ABLE TO FIRE PAST ALL OF MY WARDINGS AND DEFENSES.
WHY WOULD YOU DO THAT?
BECAUSE SOMETIMES, LIKE NOW, I'M GOOD AND RESPONSIBLE AND SAFELY VANILLA. BUT SOMETIMES I'M NOT.
WHEN I PROCESS TOO MUCH MAGIC TOO FAST, I TEND TO FREAK OUT.
LIKE AN ALCOHOLIC WHO CAN'T
DRINK.
ONLY I GET MEAN AND VERY BAD--AS IN JOINING THE DARK SIDE. PARDON THE MELODRAMA, BUT IT'S TRUE. I TURN EVIL.
AND YOU EXPECT ME TO USE THIS ON YOU, IF YOU--
YEP. I'M HOPING THAT THE FEAR OF HAVING MY BRAINS GO SPLASH ALL OVER THE SCENERY WILL HELP ME FOCUS--KEEP ME FROM LOSING IT.
BUT IT WILL ONLY WORK IF I ABSOLUTELY KNOW YOU'RE WILLING TO PULL THE TRIGGER.
WELL, I WON'T.
FORGET
IT.

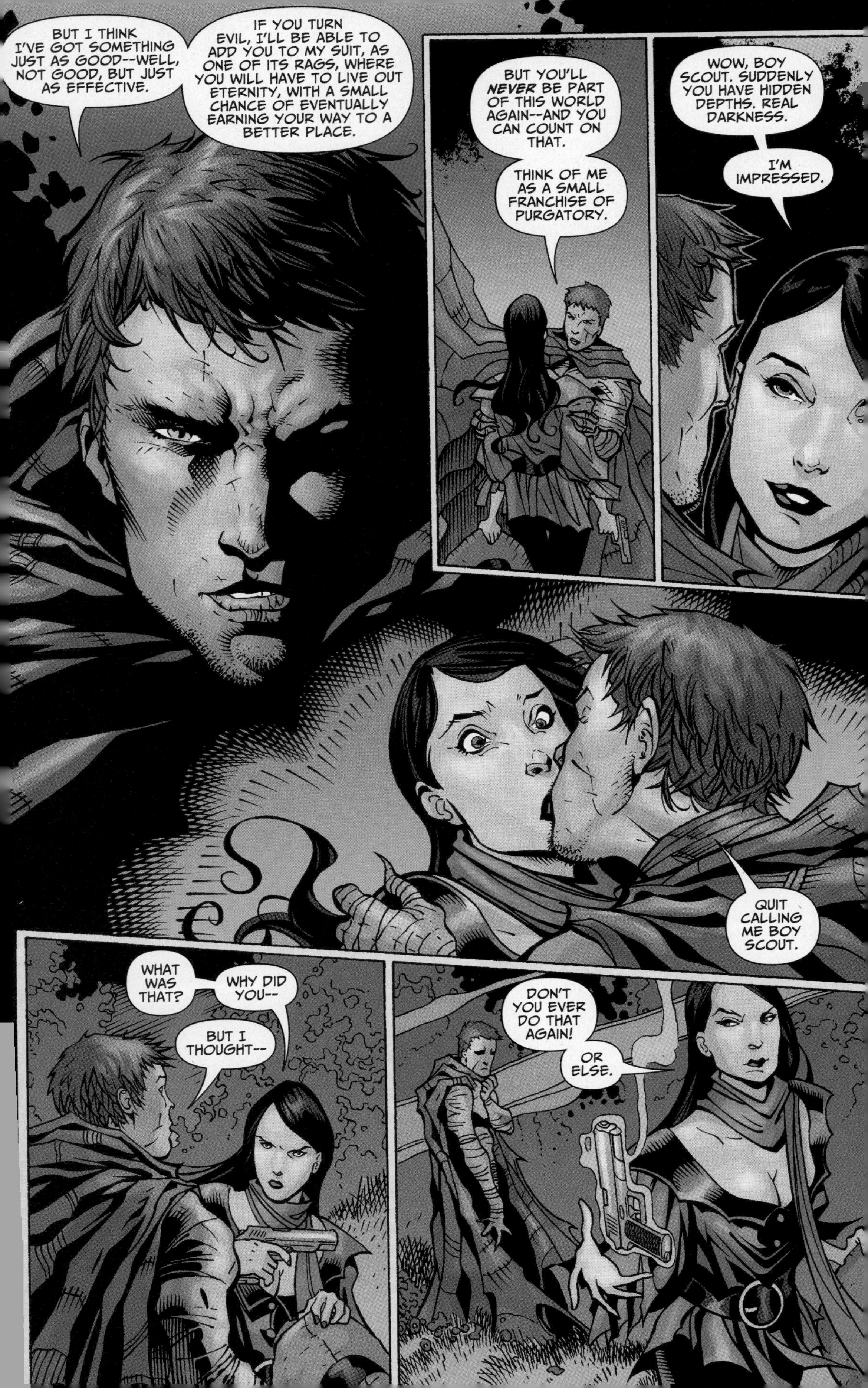
BUT I THINK I'VE GOT SOMETHING JUST AS GOOD--WELL, NOT GOOD, BUT JUST AS EFFECTIVE.
IF YOU TURN EVIL, I'LL BE ABLE TO ADD YOU TO MY SUIT, AS ONE OF ITS RAGS, WHERE YOU WILL HAVE TO LIVE OUT ETERNITY, WITH A SMALL CHANCE OF EVENTUALLY EARNING YOUR WAY TO A BETTER PLACE.
BUT YOU'LL NEVER BE PART OF THIS WORLD AGAIN--AND YOU CAN COUNT ON THAT.
THINK OF ME AS A SMALL FRANCHISE OF PURGATORY.
WOW, BOY SCOUT. SUDDENLY YOU HAVE HIDDEN DEPTHS. REAL DARKNESS.
I'M IMPRESSED.
QUIT CALLING ME BOY SCOUT.
WHAT WAS THAT?
WHY DID YOU--
BUT I THOUGHT--
DON'T YOU EVER DO THAT AGAIN!
OR ELSE.

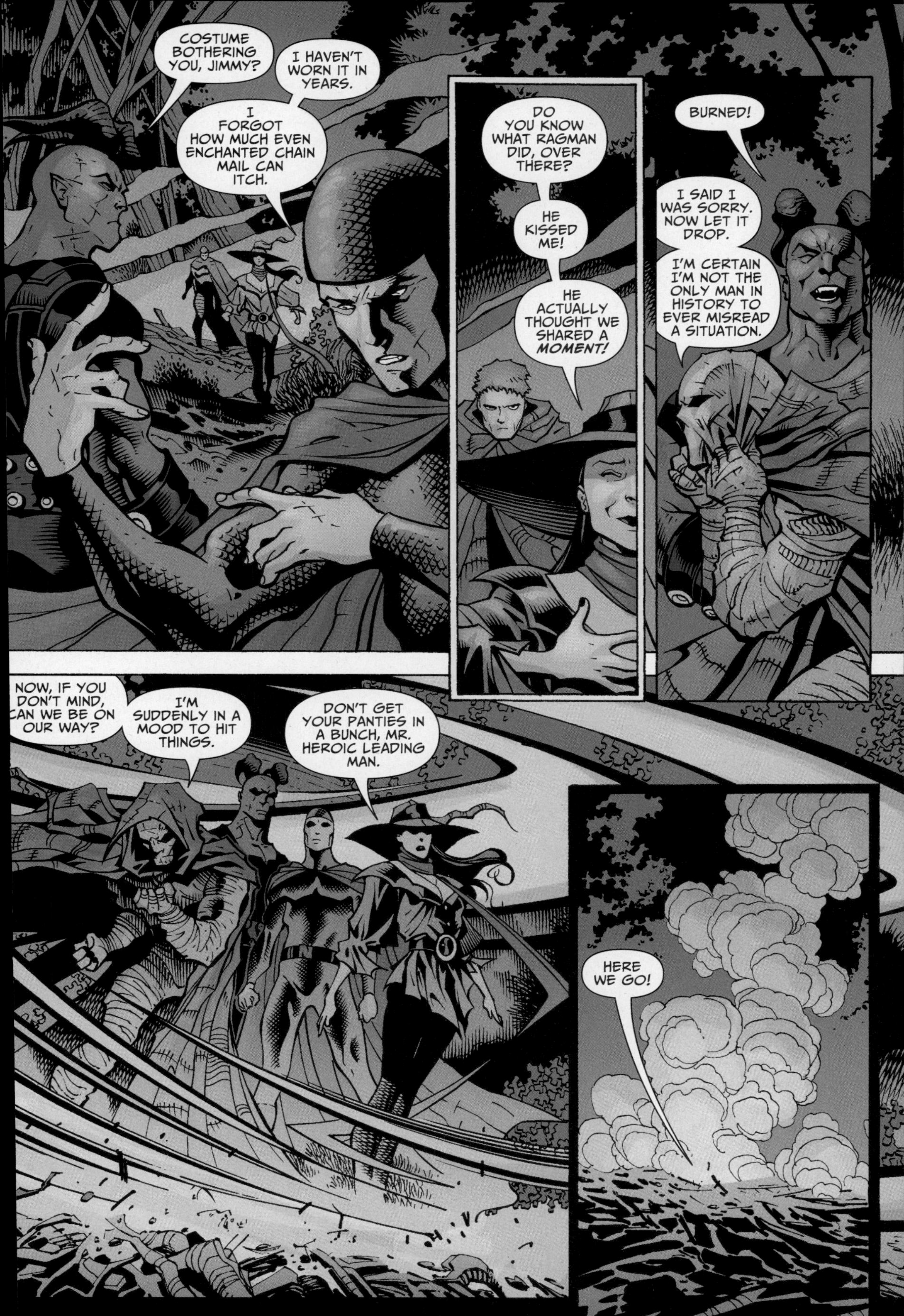
COSTUME BOTHERING YOU, JIMMY?
I HAVEN'T WORN IT IN YEARS.
I FORGOT HOW MUCH EVEN ENCHANTED CHAIN MAIL CAN ITCH.
DO YOU KNOW WHAT RAGMAN DID, OVER THERE?
HE KISSED ME!
HE ACTUALLY THOUGHT WE SHARED A *MOMENT!*
BURNED!
I SAID I WAS SORRY. NOW LET IT DROP.
I'M CERTAIN I'M NOT THE ONLY MAN IN HISTORY TO EVER MISREAD A SITUATION.
NOW, IF YOU DON'T MIND, CAN WE BE ON OUR WAY?
I'M SUDDENLY IN A MOOD TO HIT THINGS.
DON'T GET YOUR PANTIES IN A BUNCH, MR. HEROIC LEADING MAN.
HERE WE GO!

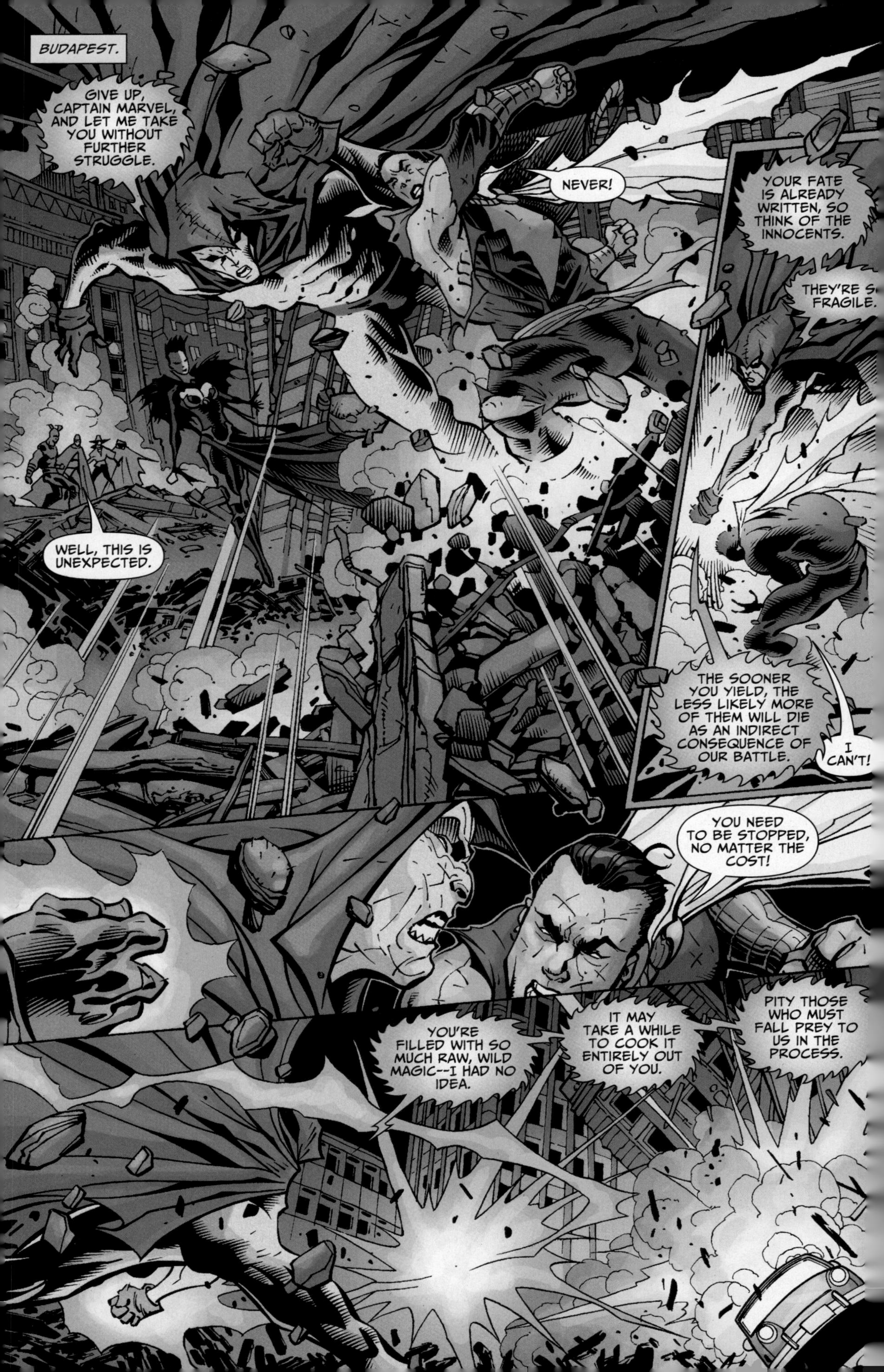
BUDAPEST.
GIVE UP, CAPTAIN MARVEL, AND LET ME TAKE YOU WITHOUT FURTHER STRUGGLE.
NEVER!
WELL, THIS IS UNEXPECTED.
YOUR FATE IS ALREADY WRITTEN, SO THINK OF THE INNOCENTS.
FRAGILE.
THE SOONER YOU YIELD, THE LESS LIKELY MORE OF THEM WILL DIE AS AN INDIRECT CONSEQUENCE OF OUR BATTLE.
I CAN'T!
YOU NEED TO BE STOPPED, NO MATTER THE COST!
YOU'RE FILLED WITH SO MUCH RAW, WILD MAGIC--I HAD NO IDEA.
IT MAY TAKE A WHILE TO COOK IT ENTIRELY OUT OF YOU.
PITY THOSE WHO MUST FALL PREY TO US IN THE PROCESS.

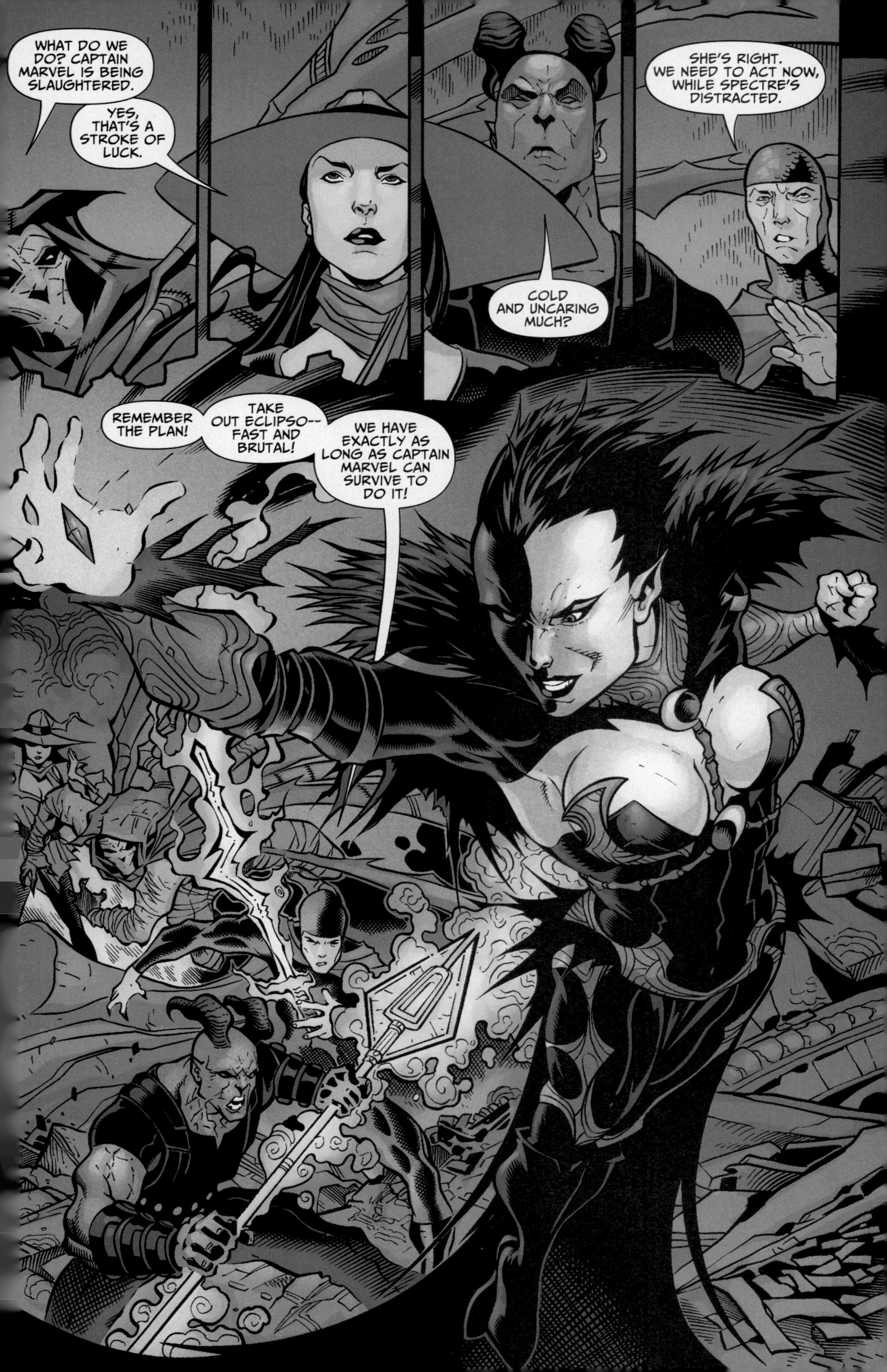
WHAT DO WE DO? CAPTAIN MARVEL IS BEING SLAUGHTERED.
YES, THAT'S A STROKE OF LUCK.
COLD AND UNCARING MUCH?
SHE'S RIGHT. WE NEED TO ACT NOW, WHILE SPECTRE'S DISTRACTED.
REMEMBER THE PLAN!
TAKE OUT ECLIPSO-- FAST AND BRUTAL!
WE HAVE EXACTLY AS LONG AS CAPTAIN MARVEL CAN SURVIVE TO DO IT!

DAY OF VENGEANCE

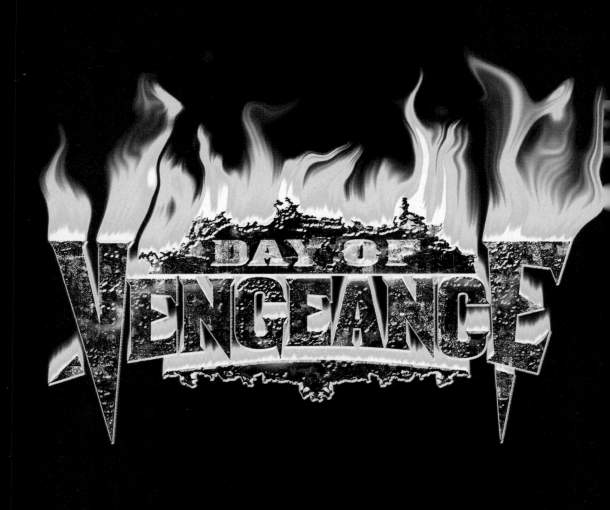

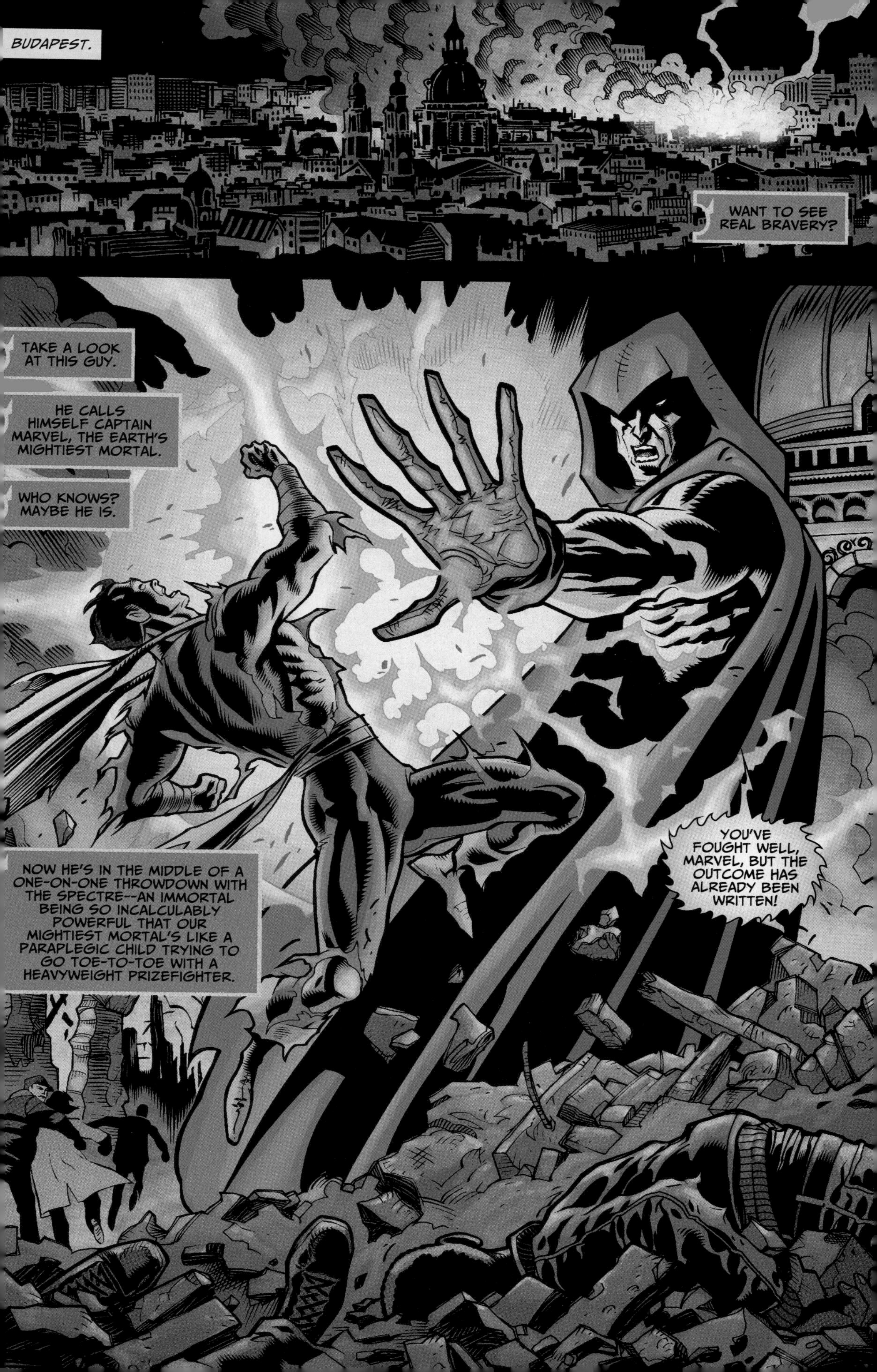
BUDAPEST.
WANT TO SEE REAL BRAVERY?
TAKE A LOOK AT THIS GUY.
HE CALLS HIMSELF CAPTAIN MARVEL, THE EARTH'S MIGHTIEST MORTAL.
WHO KNOWS? MAYBE HE IS.
NOW HE'S IN THE MIDDLE OF A ONE-ON-ONE THROWDOWN WITH THE SPECTRE--AN IMMORTAL BEING SO INCALCULABLY POWERFUL THAT OUR MIGHTIEST MORTAL'S LIKE A PARAPLEGIC CHILD TRYING TO GO TOE-TO-TOE WITH A HEAVYWEIGHT PRIZEFIGHTER.
YOU'VE FOUGHT WELL, MARVEL, BUT THE OUTCOME HAS ALREADY BEEN WRITTEN!

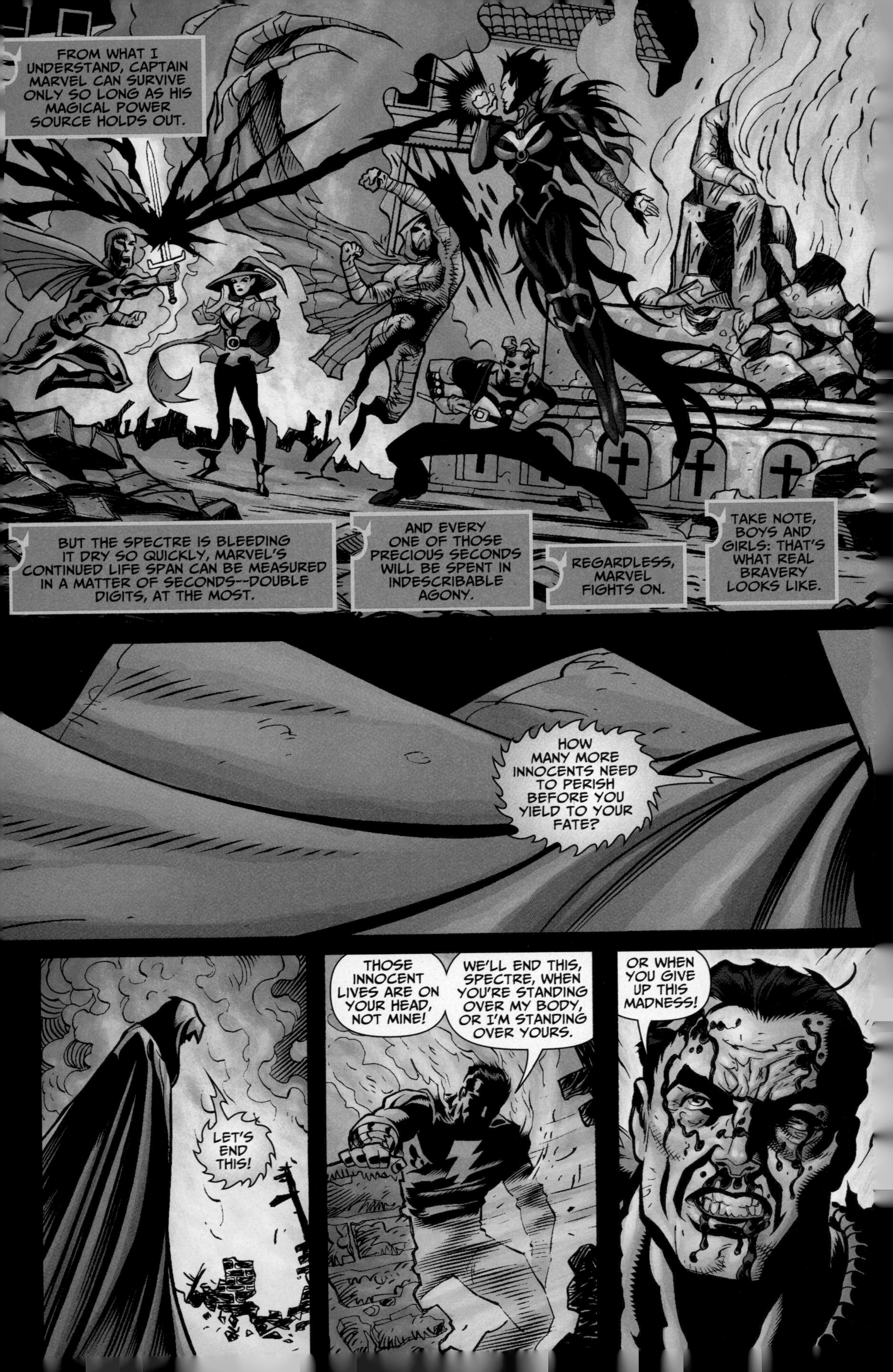
FROM WHAT I UNDERSTAND, CAPTAIN MARVEL CAN SURVIVE ONLY SO LONG AS HIS MAGICAL POWER SOURCE HOLDS OUT.
BUT THE SPECTRE IS BLEEDING IT DRY SO QUICKLY, MARVEL'S CONTINUED LIFE SPAN CAN BE MEASURED IN A MATTER OF SECONDS--DOUBLE DIGITS, AT THE MOST.
AND EVERY ONE OF THOSE PRECIOUS SECONDS WILL BE SPENT IN INDESCRIBABLE AGONY.
REGARDLESS, MARVEL FIGHTS ON.
TAKE NOTE, BOYS AND GIRLS: THAT'S WHAT REAL BRAVERY LOOKS LIKE.
HOW MANY MORE INNOCENTS NEED TO PERISH BEFORE YOU YIELD TO YOUR FATE?
LET'S END THIS!
THOSE INNOCENT LIVES ARE ON YOUR HEAD, NOT MINE!
WE'LL END THIS, SPECTRE, WHEN YOU'RE STANDING OVER MY BODY, OR I'M STANDING OVER YOURS.
OR WHEN YOU GIVE UP THIS MADNESS!

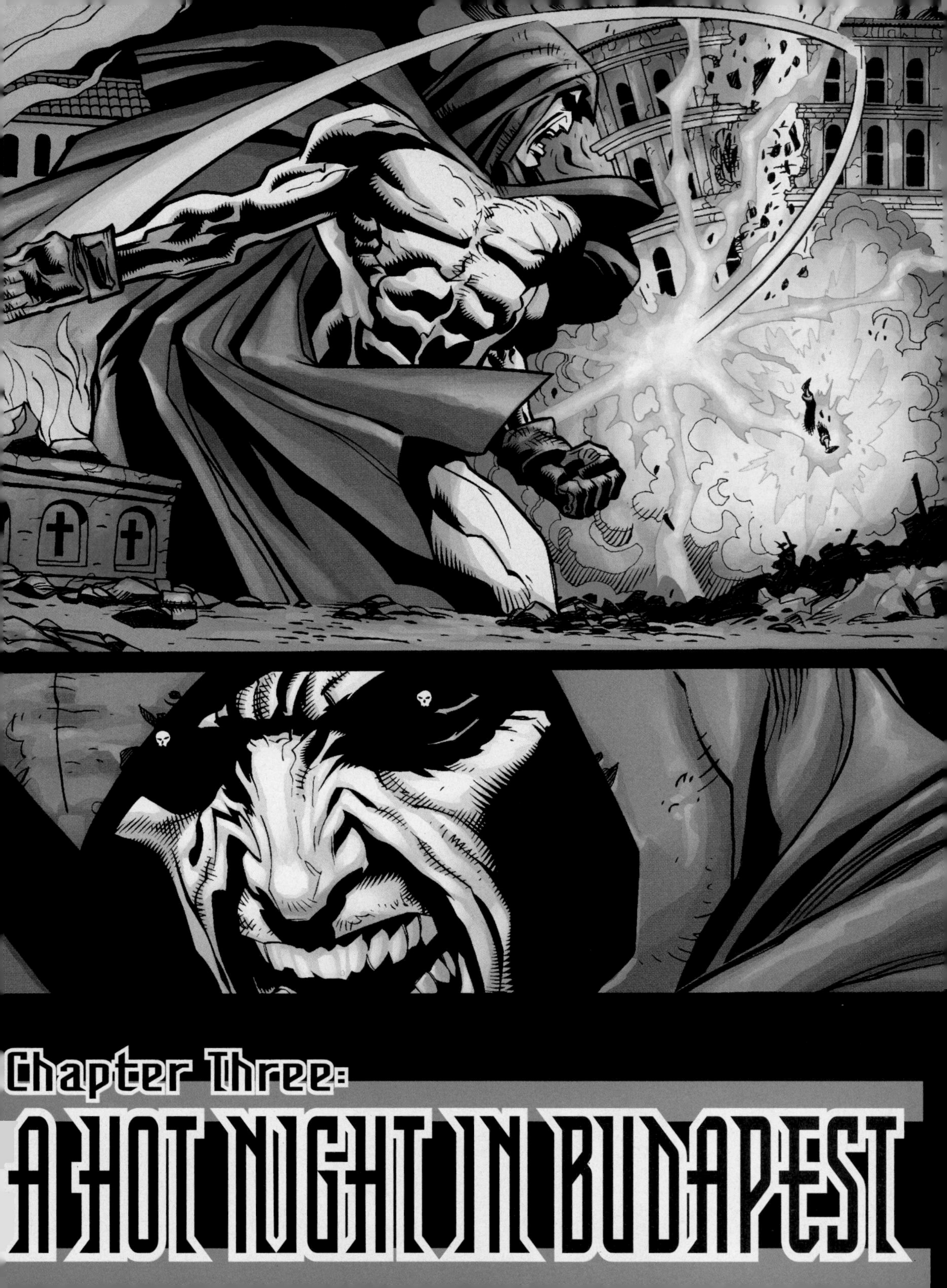

Chapter Three:
A HOT NIGHT IN BUDAPEST

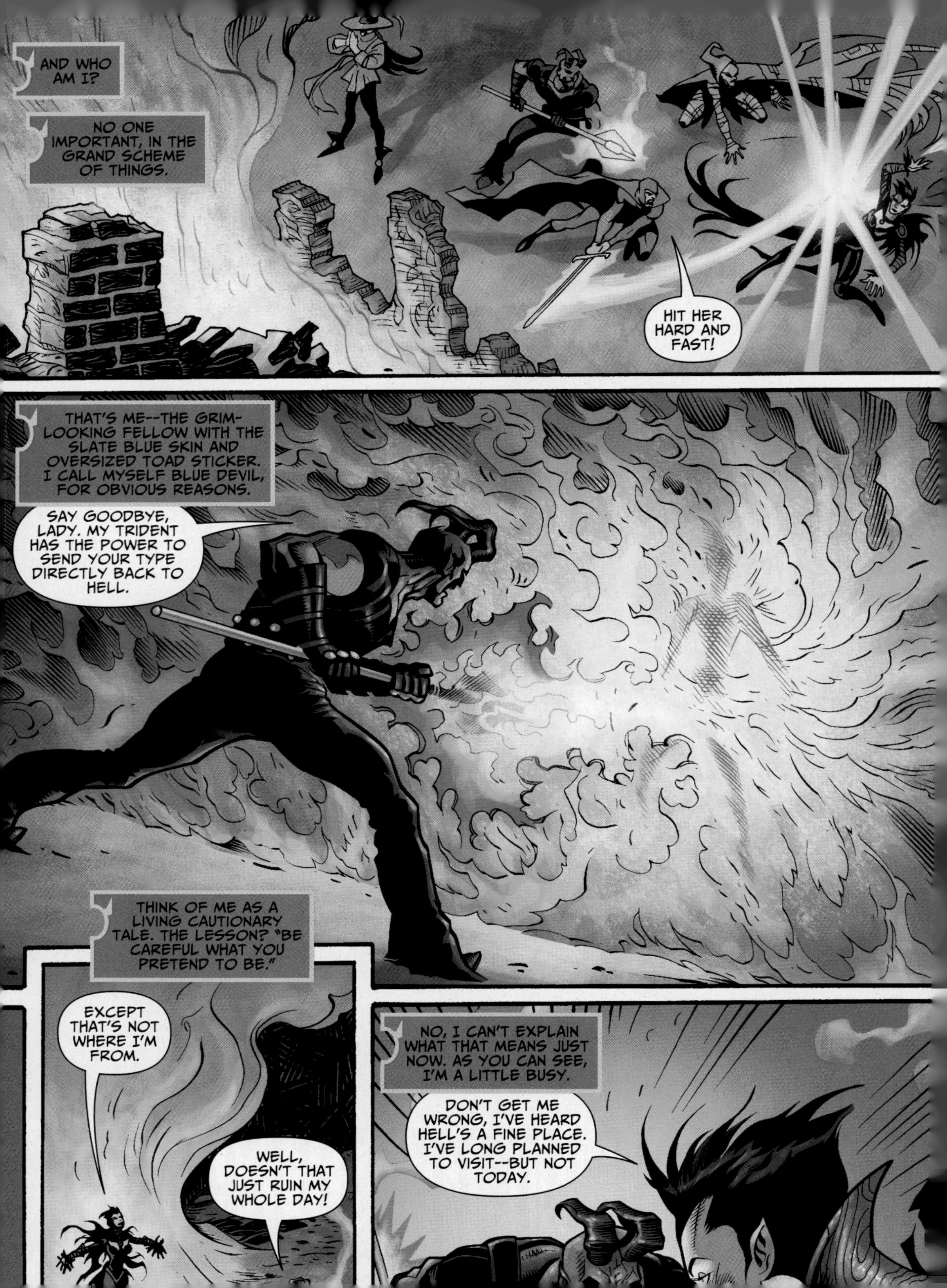
AND WHO AM I?
NO ONE IMPORTANT, IN THE GRAND SCHEME OF THINGS.
HIT HER HARD AND FAST!
THAT'S ME--THE GRIM-LOOKING FELLOW WITH THE SLATE BLUE SKIN AND OVERSIZED TOAD STICKER. I CALL MYSELF BLUE DEVIL, FOR OBVIOUS REASONS.
SAY GOODBYE, LADY. MY TRIDENT HAS THE POWER TO SEND YOUR TYPE DIRECTLY BACK TO HELL.
THINK OF ME AS A LIVING CAUTIONARY TALE. THE LESSON? "BE CAREFUL WHAT YOU PRETEND TO BE."
EXCEPT THAT'S NOT WHERE I'M FROM.
WELL, DOESN'T THAT JUST RUIN MY WHOLE DAY!
NO, I CAN'T EXPLAIN WHAT THAT MEANS JUST NOW. AS YOU CAN SEE, I'M A LITTLE BUSY.
DON'T GET ME WRONG, I'VE HEARD HELL'S A FINE PLACE. I'VE LONG PLANNED TO VISIT--BUT NOT TODAY.

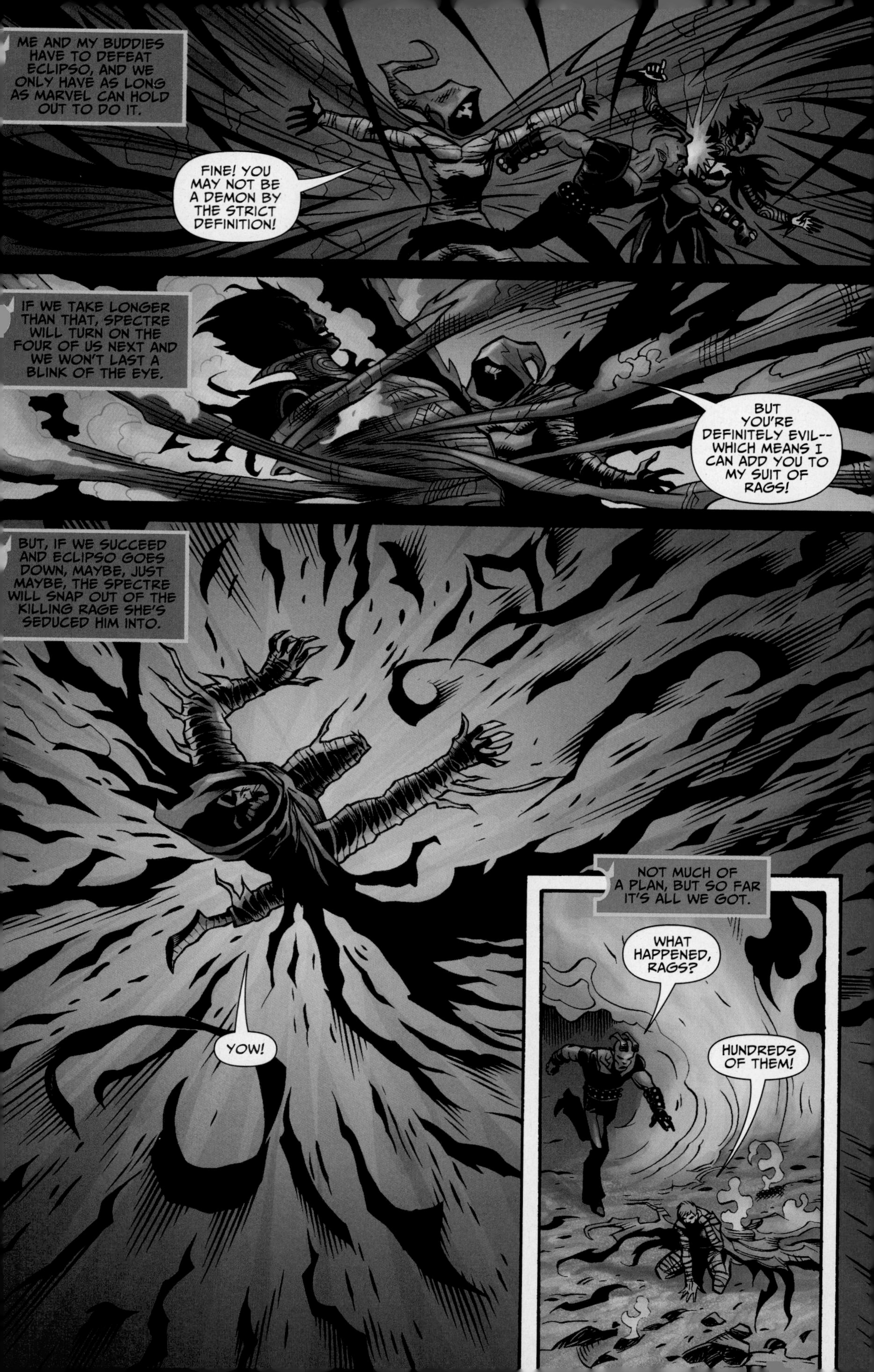
ME AND MY BUDDIES HAVE TO DEFEAT ECLIPSO, AND WE ONLY HAVE AS LONG AS MARVEL CAN HOLD OUT TO DO IT.
FINE! YOU MAY NOT BE A DEMON BY THE STRICT DEFINITION!
IF WE TAKE LONGER THAN THAT, SPECTRE WILL TURN ON THE FOUR OF US NEXT AND WE WON'T LAST A BLINK OF THE EYE.
BUT YOU'RE DEFINITELY EVIL-- WHICH MEANS I CAN ADD YOU TO MY SUIT OF RAGS!
BUT, IF WE SUCCEED AND ECLIPSO GOES DOWN, MAYBE, JUST MAYBE, THE SPECTRE WILL SNAP OUT OF THE KILLING RAGE SHE'S SEDUCED HIM INTO.
YOW!
NOT MUCH OF A PLAN, BUT SO FAR IT'S ALL WE GOT.
WHAT HAPPENED, RAGS?
HUNDREDS OF THEM!

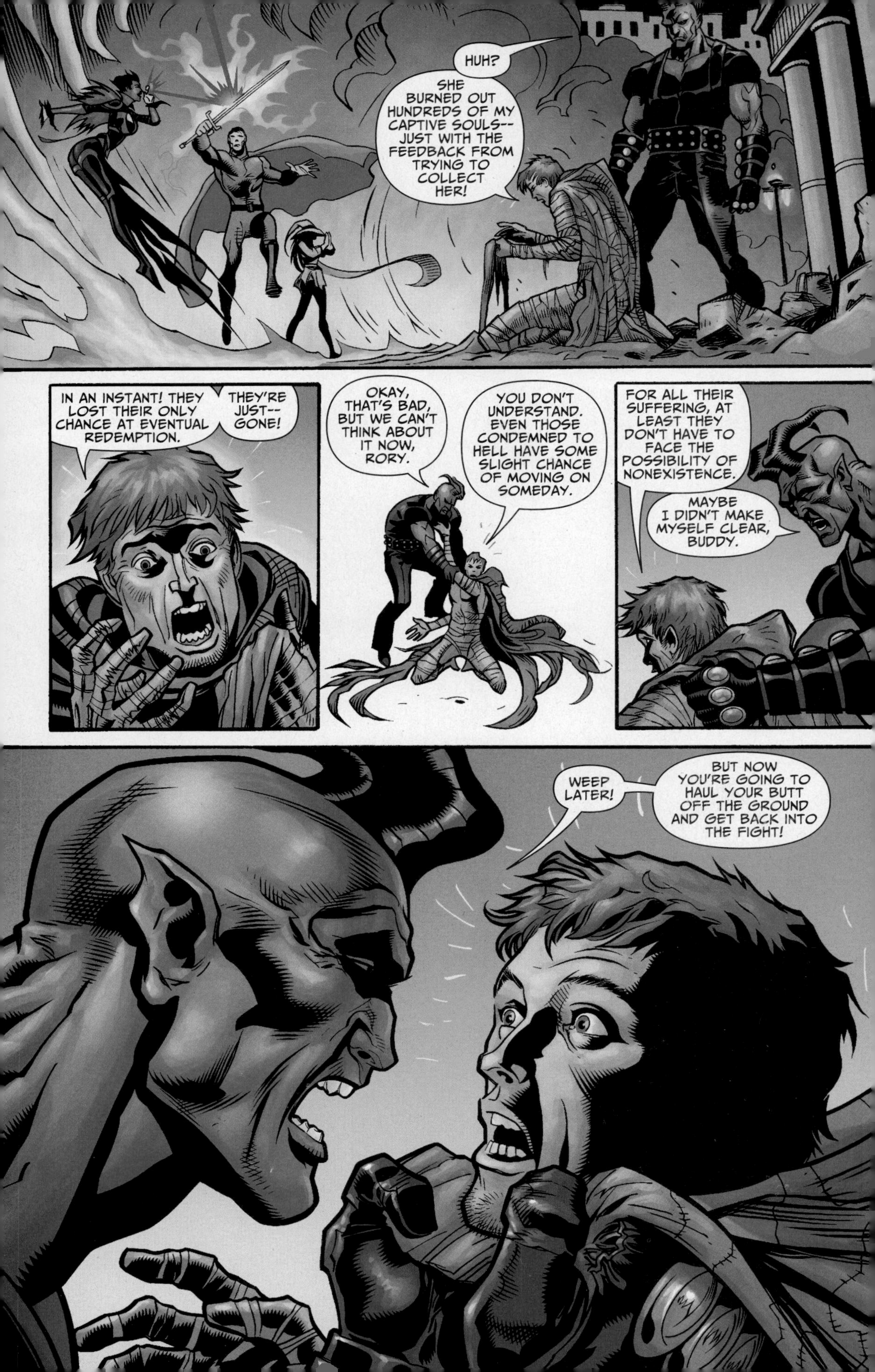
HUH?
SHE BURNED OUT HUNDREDS OF MY CAPTIVE SOULS-- JUST WITH THE FEEDBACK FROM TRYING TO COLLECT HER!
IN AN INSTANT! THEY LOST THEIR ONLY CHANCE AT EVENTUAL REDEMPTION.
THEY'RE JUST-- GONE!
OKAY, THAT'S BAD, BUT WE CAN'T THINK ABOUT IT NOW, RORY.
YOU DON'T UNDERSTAND. EVEN THOSE CONDEMNED TO HELL HAVE SOME SLIGHT CHANCE OF MOVING ON SOMEDAY.
FOR ALL THEIR SUFFERING, AT LEAST THEY DON'T HAVE TO FACE THE POSSIBILITY OF NONEXISTENCE.
MAYBE I DIDN'T MAKE MYSELF CLEAR, BUDDY.
WEEP LATER!
BUT NOW YOU'RE GOING TO HAUL YOUR BUTT OFF THE GROUND AND GET BACK INTO THE FIGHT!

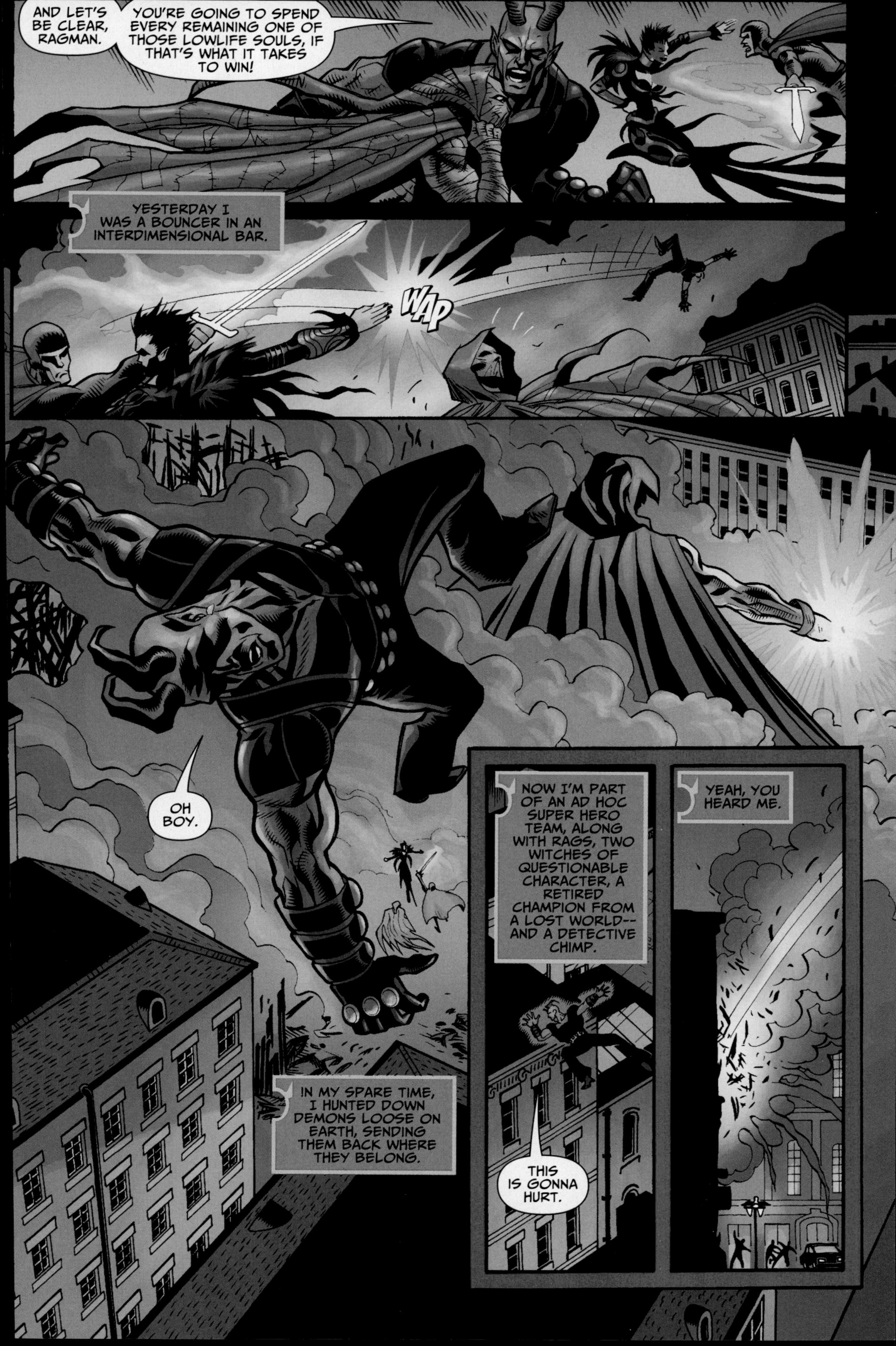
AND LET'S BE CLEAR, RAGMAN.
YOU'RE GOING TO SPEND EVERY REMAINING ONE OF THOSE LOWLIFE SOULS, IF THAT'S WHAT IT TAKES TO WIN!
YESTERDAY I WAS A BOUNCER IN AN INTERDIMENSIONAL BAR.
WAP
OH BOY.
IN MY SPARE TIME, I HUNTED DOWN DEMONS LOOSE ON EARTH, SENDING THEM BACK WHERE THEY BELONG.
NOW I'M PART OF AN AD HOC SUPER HERO TEAM, ALONG WITH RAGS, TWO WITCHES OF QUESTIONABLE CHARACTER, A RETIRED CHAMPION FROM A LOST WORLD-- AND A DETECTIVE CHIMP.
THIS IS GONNA HURT.
YEAH, YOU HEARD ME.

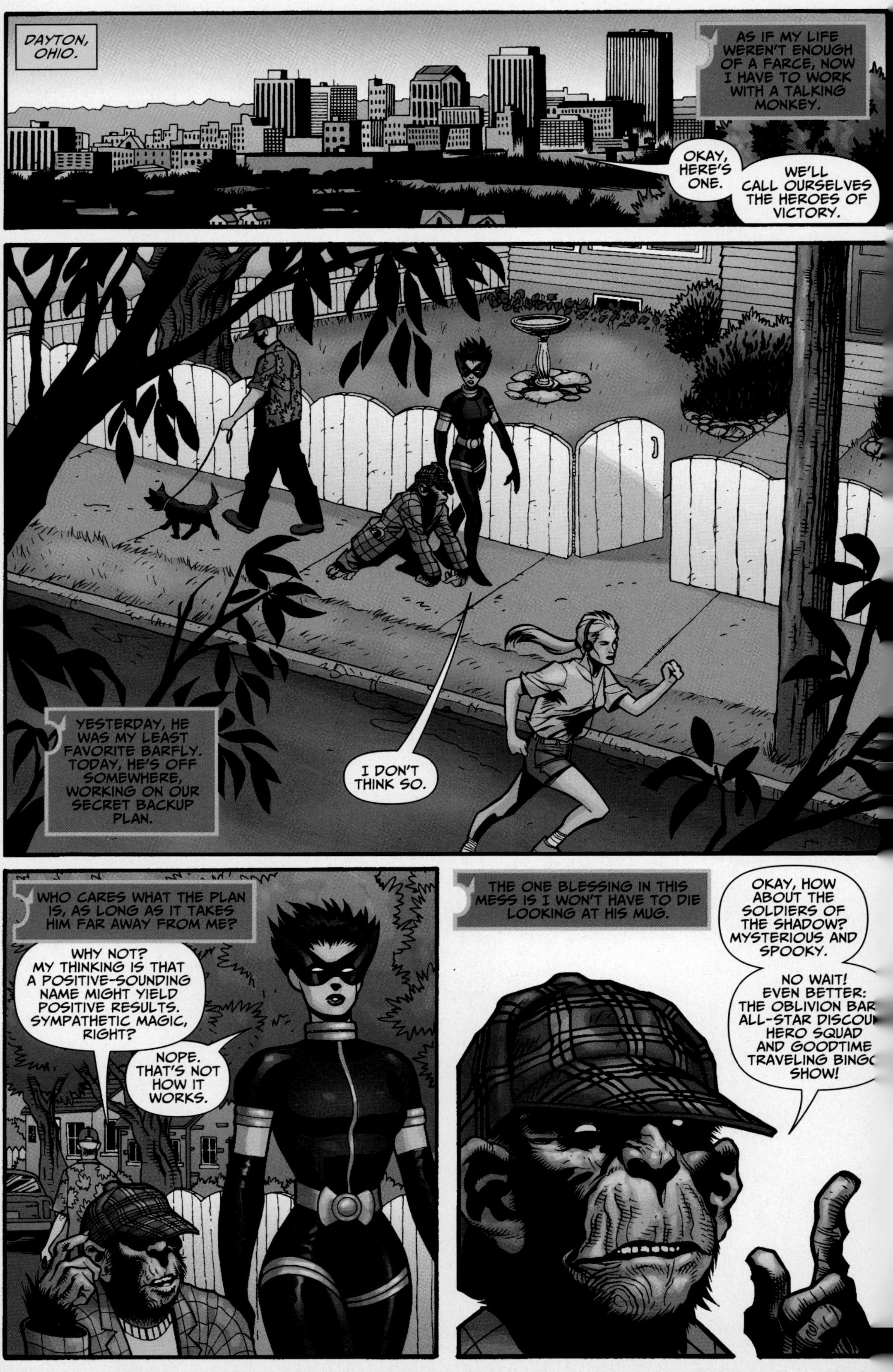
DAYTON, OHIO.
AS IF MY LIFE WEREN'T ENOUGH OF A FARCE, NOW I HAVE TO WORK WITH A TALKING MONKEY.
OKAY, HERE'S ONE.
WE'LL CALL OURSELVES THE HEROES OF VICTORY.
YESTERDAY, HE WAS MY LEAST FAVORITE BARFLY. TODAY, HE'S OFF SOMEWHERE, WORKING ON OUR SECRET BACKUP PLAN.
I DON'T THINK SO.
WHO CARES WHAT THE PLAN IS, AS LONG AS IT TAKES HIM FAR AWAY FROM ME?
WHY NOT? MY THINKING IS THAT A POSITIVE-SOUNDING NAME MIGHT YIELD POSITIVE RESULTS. SYMPATHETIC MAGIC, RIGHT?
NOPE. THAT'S NOT HOW IT WORKS.
THE ONE BLESSING IN THIS MESS IS I WON'T HAVE TO DIE LOOKING AT HIS MUG.
OKAY, HOW ABOUT THE SOLDIERS OF THE SHADOW? MYSTERIOUS AND SPOOKY.
NO WAIT! EVEN BETTER: THE OBLIVION BAR ALL-STAR DISCOU HERO SQUAD AND GOODTIME TRAVELING BINGO SHOW!

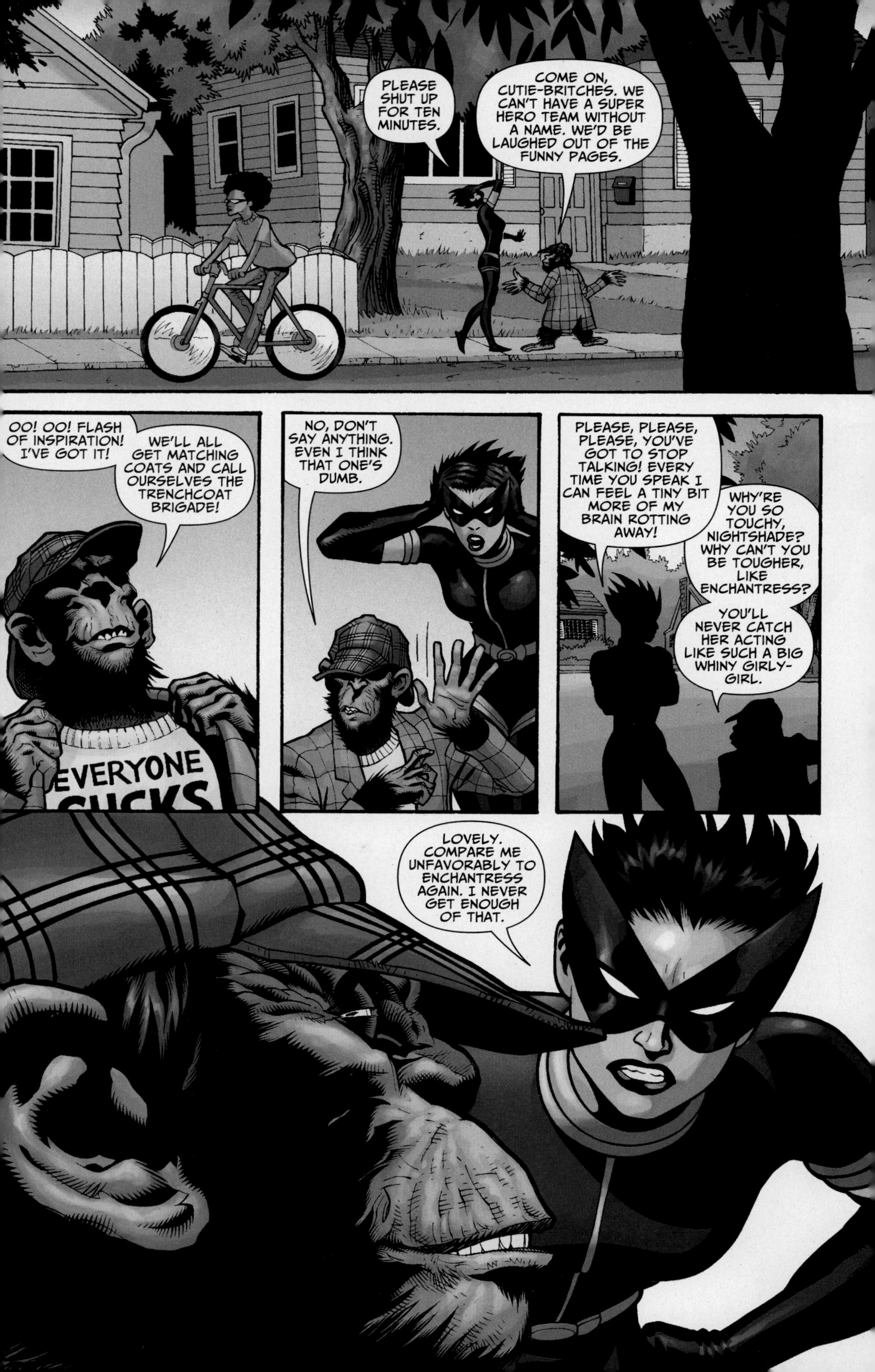
PLEASE SHUT UP FOR TEN MINUTES.
COME ON, CUTIE-BRITCHES. WE CAN'T HAVE A SUPER HERO TEAM WITHOUT A NAME. WE'D BE LAUGHED OUT OF THE FUNNY PAGES.
OO! OO! FLASH OF INSPIRATION! I'VE GOT IT!
WE'LL ALL GET MATCHING COATS AND CALL OURSELVES THE TRENCHCOAT BRIGADE!
EVERYONE
NO, DON'T SAY ANYTHING. EVEN I THINK THAT ONE'S DUMB.
PLEASE, PLEASE, PLEASE, YOU'VE GOT TO STOP TALKING! EVERY TIME YOU SPEAK I CAN FEEL A TINY BIT MORE OF MY BRAIN ROTTING AWAY!
WHY'RE YOU SO TOUCHY, NIGHTSHADE? WHY CAN'T YOU BE TOUGHER, LIKE ENCHANTRESS?
YOU'LL NEVER CATCH HER ACTING LIKE SUCH A BIG WHINY GIRLY-GIRL.
LOVELY. COMPARE ME UNFAVORABLY TO ENCHANTRESS AGAIN. I NEVER GET ENOUGH OF THAT.

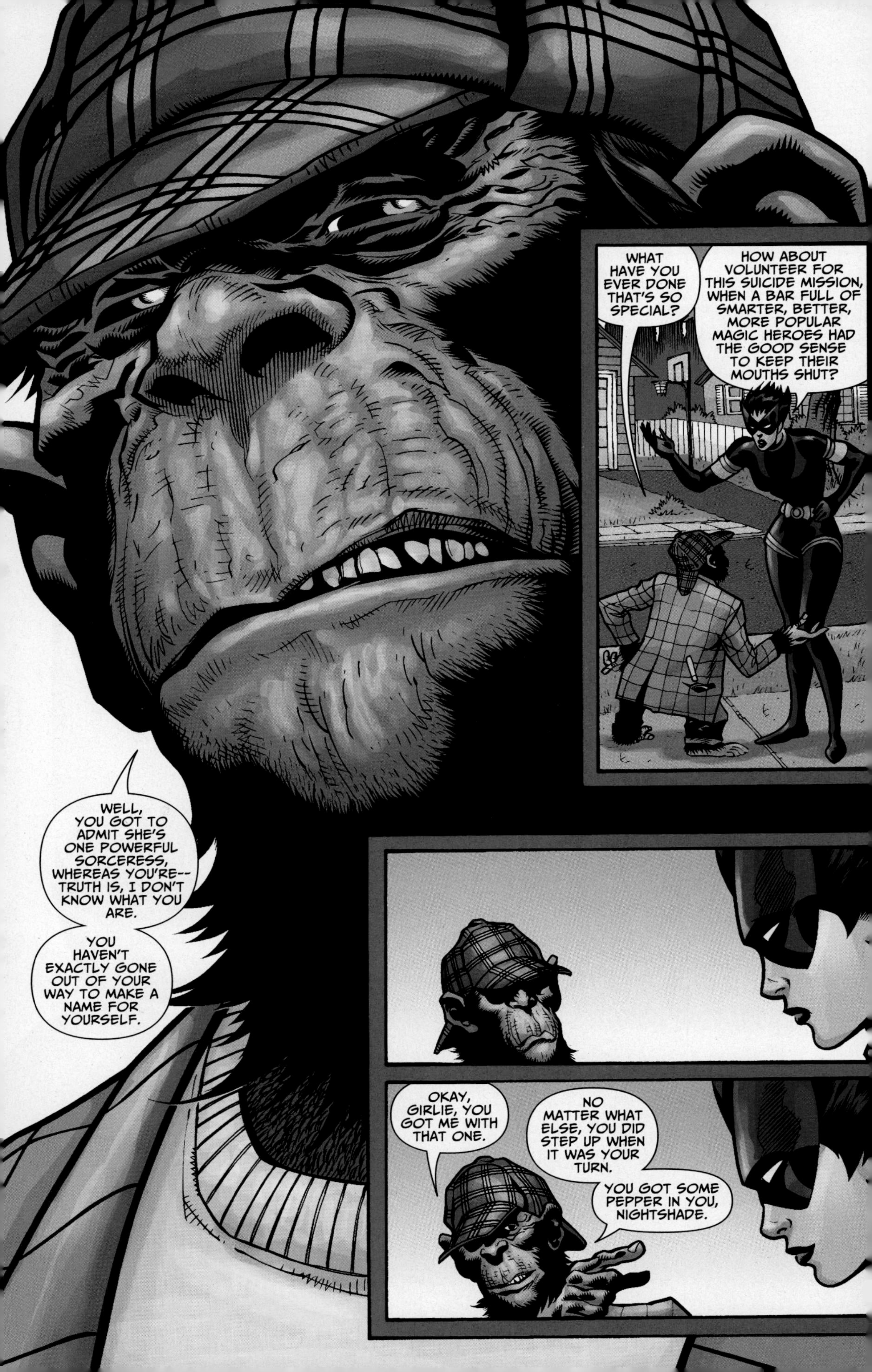
WHAT HAVE YOU EVER DONE THAT'S SO SPECIAL?
HOW ABOUT VOLUNTEER FOR THIS SUICIDE MISSION, WHEN A BAR FULL OF SMARTER, BETTER, MORE POPULAR MAGIC HEROES HAD THE GOOD SENSE TO KEEP THEIR MOUTHS SHUT?
WELL, YOU GOT TO ADMIT SHE'S ONE POWERFUL SORCERESS, WHEREAS YOU'RE-- TRUTH IS, I DON'T KNOW WHAT YOU ARE.
YOU HAVEN'T EXACTLY GONE OUT OF YOUR WAY TO MAKE A NAME FOR YOURSELF.
OKAY, GIRLIE, YOU GOT ME WITH THAT ONE.
NO MATTER WHAT ELSE, YOU DID STEP UP WHEN IT WAS YOUR TURN.
YOU GOT SOME PEPPER IN YOU, NIGHTSHADE.

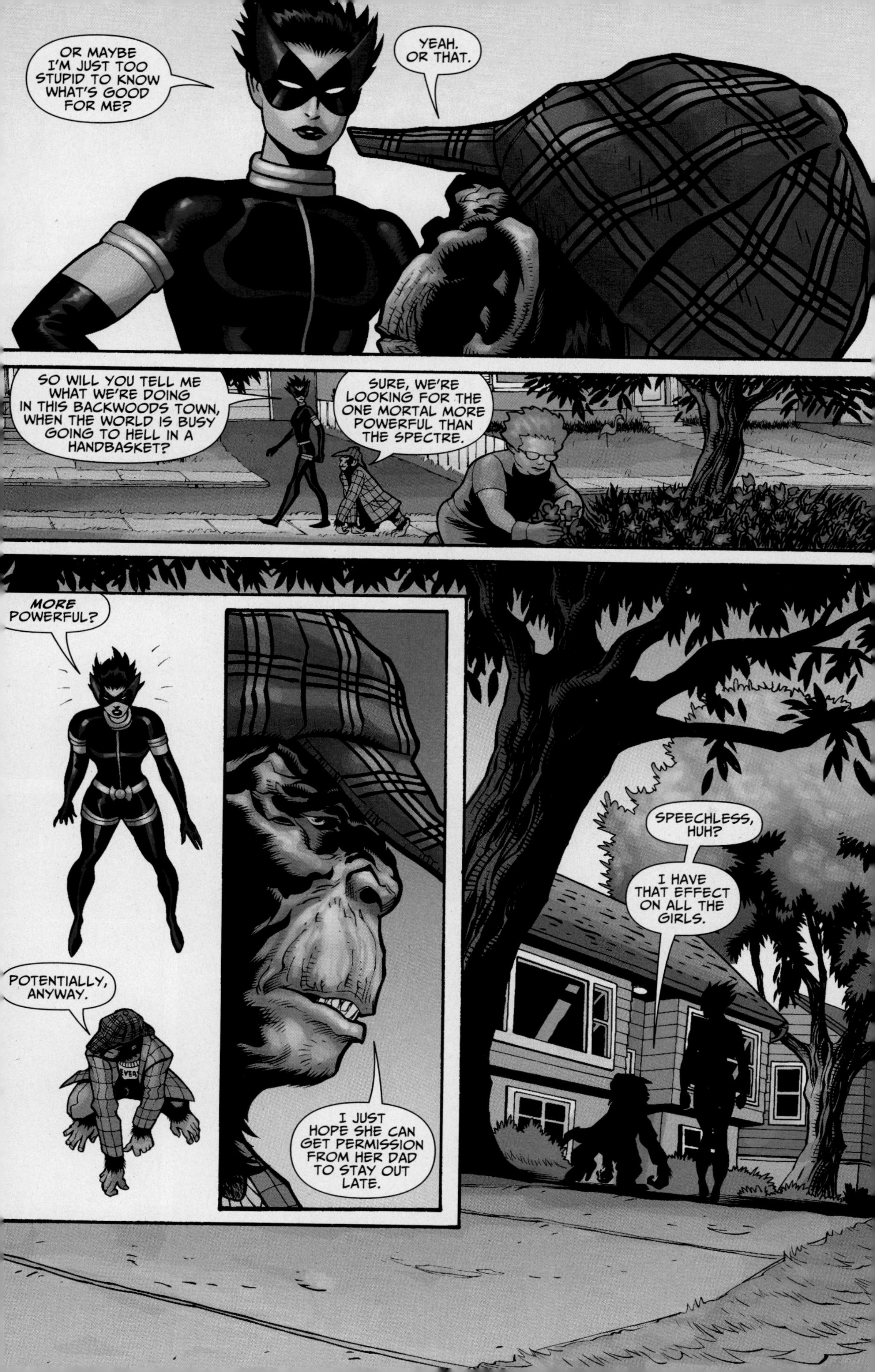
OR MAYBE I'M JUST TOO STUPID TO KNOW WHAT'S GOOD FOR ME?
YEAH. OR THAT.
SO WILL YOU TELL ME WHAT WE'RE DOING IN THIS BACKWOODS TOWN, WHEN THE WORLD IS BUSY GOING TO HELL IN A HANDBASKET?
SURE, WE'RE LOOKING FOR THE ONE MORTAL MORE POWERFUL THAN THE SPECTRE.
MORE POWERFUL?
POTENTIALLY, ANYWAY.
I JUST HOPE SHE CAN GET PERMISSION FROM HER DAD TO STAY OUT LATE.
SPEECHLESS, HUH?
I HAVE THAT EFFECT ON ALL THE GIRLS.

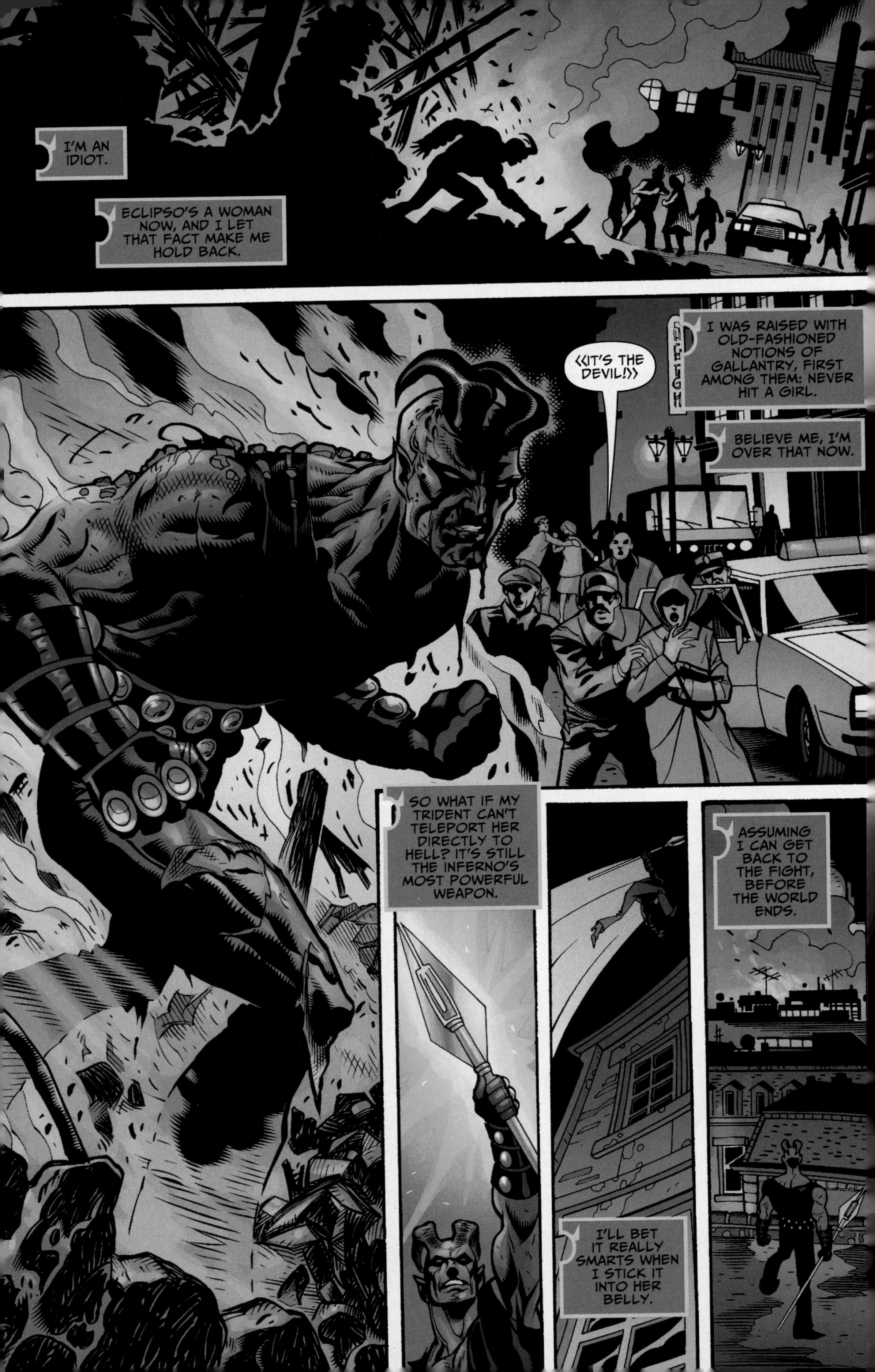
I'M AN IDIOT.
ECLIPSO'S A WOMAN NOW, AND I LET THAT FACT MAKE ME HOLD BACK.
<<IT'S THE DEVIL!>>
I WAS RAISED WITH OLD-FASHIONED NOTIONS OF GALLANTRY, FIRST AMONG THEM: NEVER HIT A GIRL.
BELIEVE ME, I'M OVER THAT NOW.
SO WHAT IF MY TRIDENT CAN'T TELEPORT HER DIRECTLY TO HELL? IT'S STILL THE INFERNO'S MOST POWERFUL WEAPON.
I'LL BET IT REALLY SMARTS WHEN I STICK IT INTO HER BELLY.
ASSUMING I CAN GET BACK TO THE FIGHT, BEFORE THE WORLD ENDS.

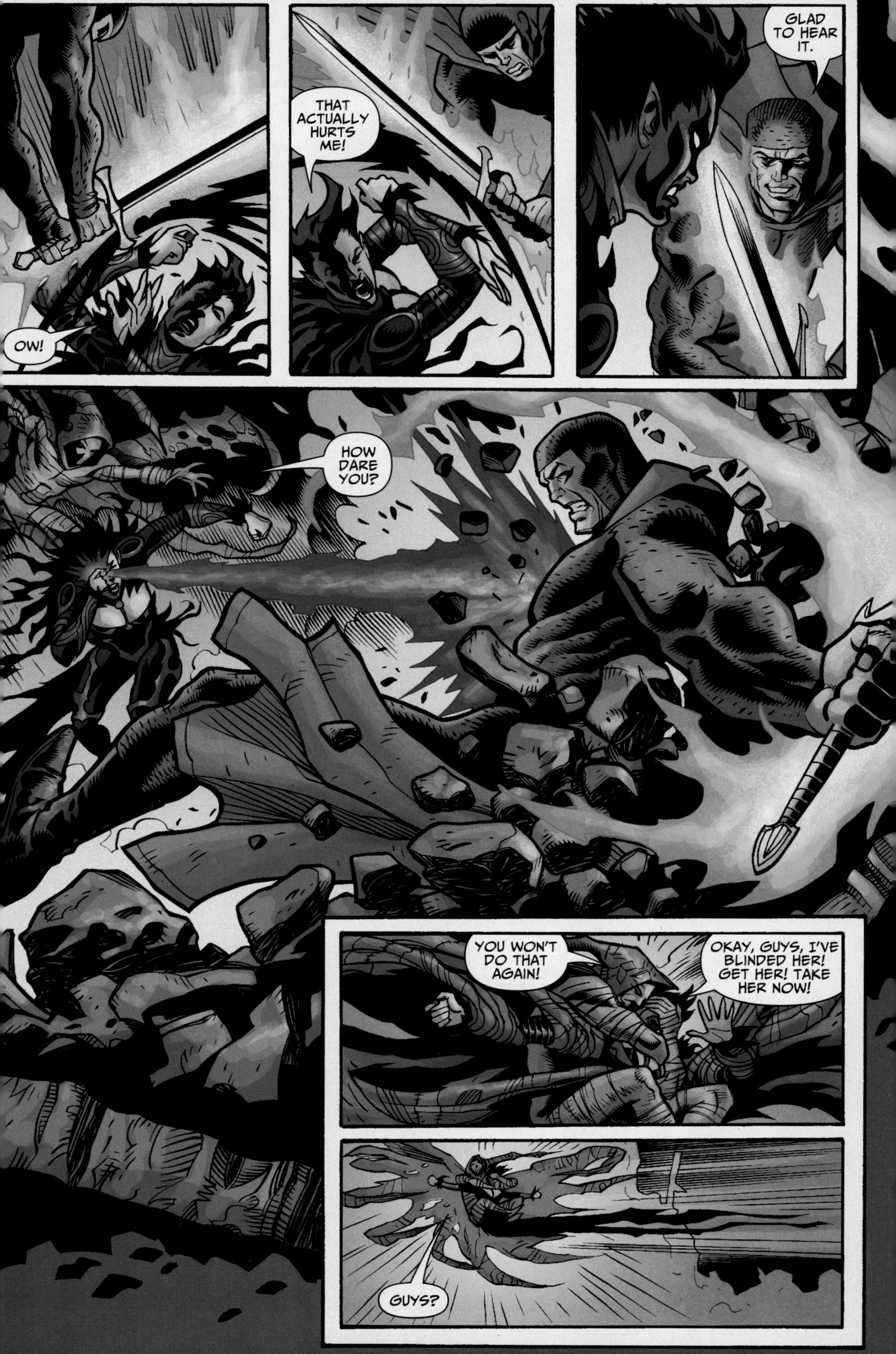
OW!
THAT ACTUALLY HURTS ME!
GLAD TO HEAR IT.
HOW DARE YOU?
YOU WON'T DO THAT AGAIN!
OKAY, GUYS, I'VE BLINDED HER! GET HER! TAKE HER NOW!
GUYS?

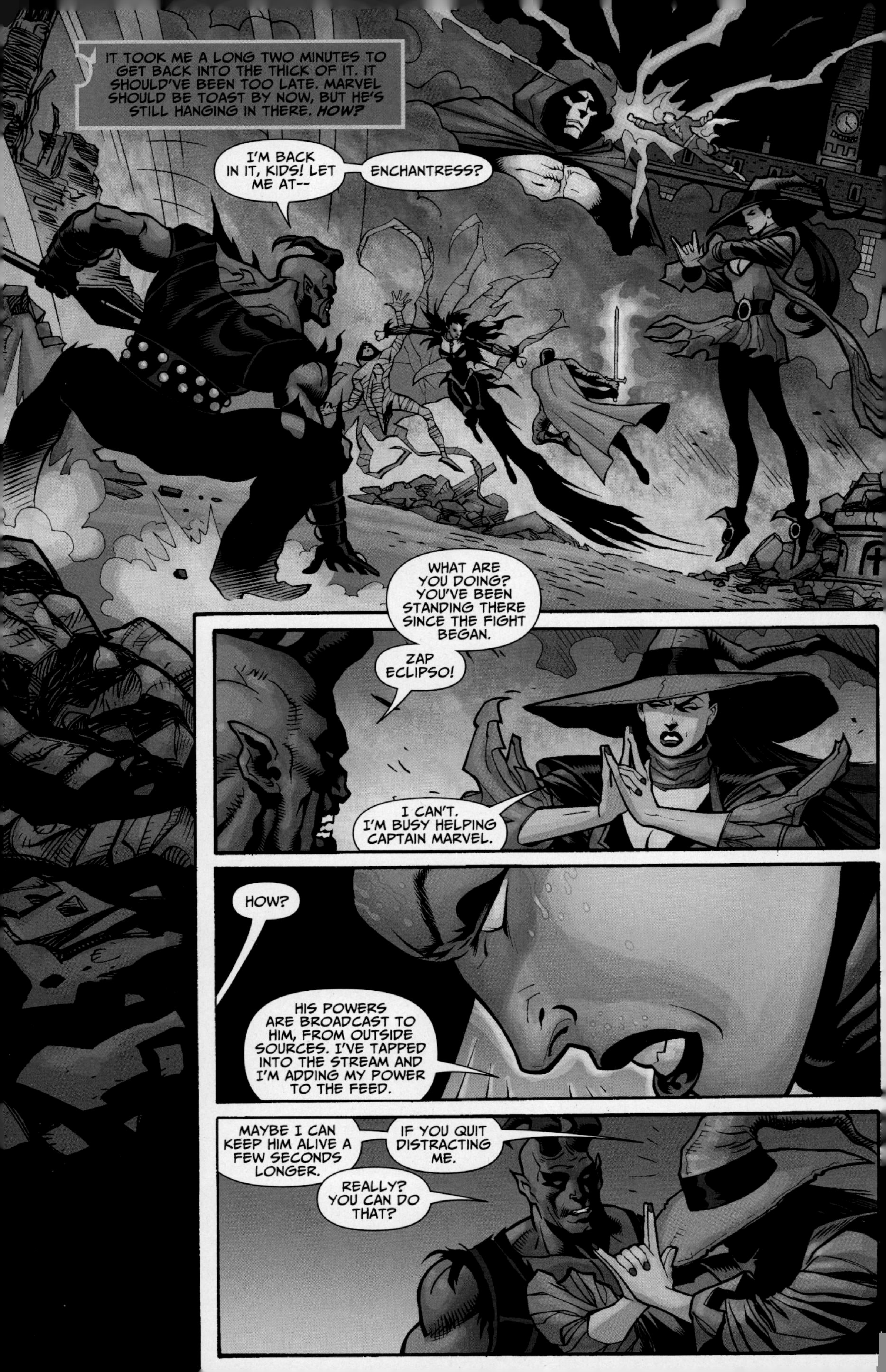

IT TOOK ME A LONG TWO MINUTES TO GET BACK INTO THE THICK OF IT. IT SHOULD'VE BEEN TOO LATE. MARVEL SHOULD BE TOAST BY NOW, BUT HE'S STILL HANGING IN THERE. *HOW?*
I'M BACK IN IT, KIDS! LET ME AT--
ENCHANTRESS?
WHAT ARE YOU DOING? YOU'VE BEEN STANDING THERE SINCE THE FIGHT BEGAN.
ZAP ECLIPSO!
I CAN'T. I'M BUSY HELPING CAPTAIN MARVEL.
HOW?
HIS POWERS ARE BROADCAST TO HIM, FROM OUTSIDE SOURCES. I'VE TAPPED INTO THE STREAM AND I'M ADDING MY POWER TO THE FEED.
MAYBE I CAN KEEP HIM ALIVE A FEW SECONDS LONGER.
IF YOU QUIT DISTRACTING ME.
REALLY? YOU CAN DO THAT?

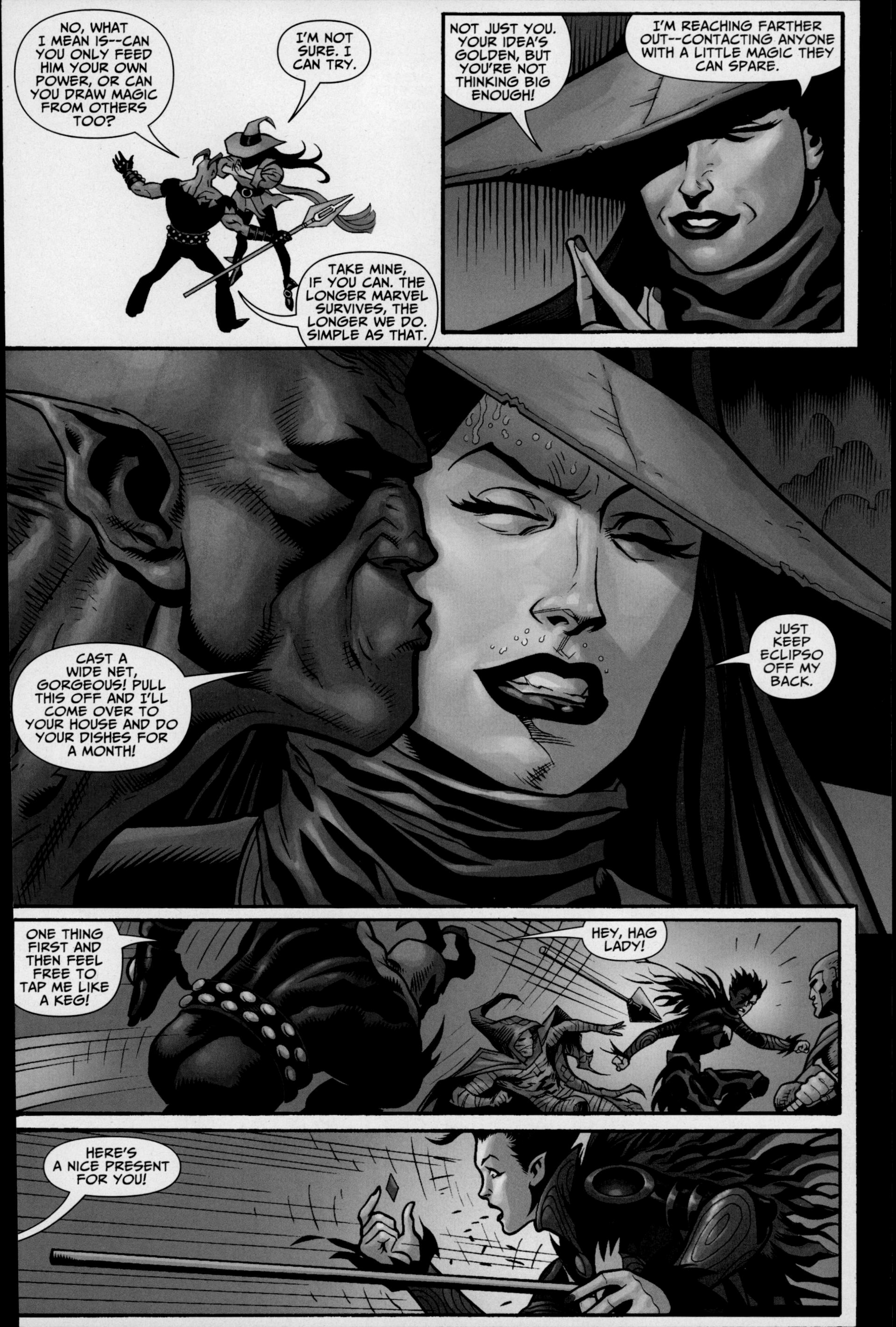
NO, WHAT I MEAN IS--CAN YOU ONLY FEED HIM YOUR OWN POWER, OR CAN YOU DRAW MAGIC FROM OTHERS TOO?
I'M NOT SURE. I CAN TRY.
TAKE MINE, IF YOU CAN. THE LONGER MARVEL SURVIVES, THE LONGER WE DO. SIMPLE AS THAT.
NOT JUST YOU. YOUR IDEA'S GOLDEN, BUT YOU'RE NOT THINKING BIG ENOUGH!
I'M REACHING FARTHER OUT--CONTACTING ANYONE WITH A LITTLE MAGIC THEY CAN SPARE.
CAST A WIDE NET, GORGEOUS! PULL THIS OFF AND I'LL COME OVER TO YOUR HOUSE AND DO YOUR DISHES FOR A MONTH!
JUST KEEP ECLIPSO OFF MY BACK.
ONE THING FIRST AND THEN FEEL FREE TO TAP ME LIKE A KEG!
HEY, HAG LADY!
HERE'S A NICE PRESENT FOR YOU!

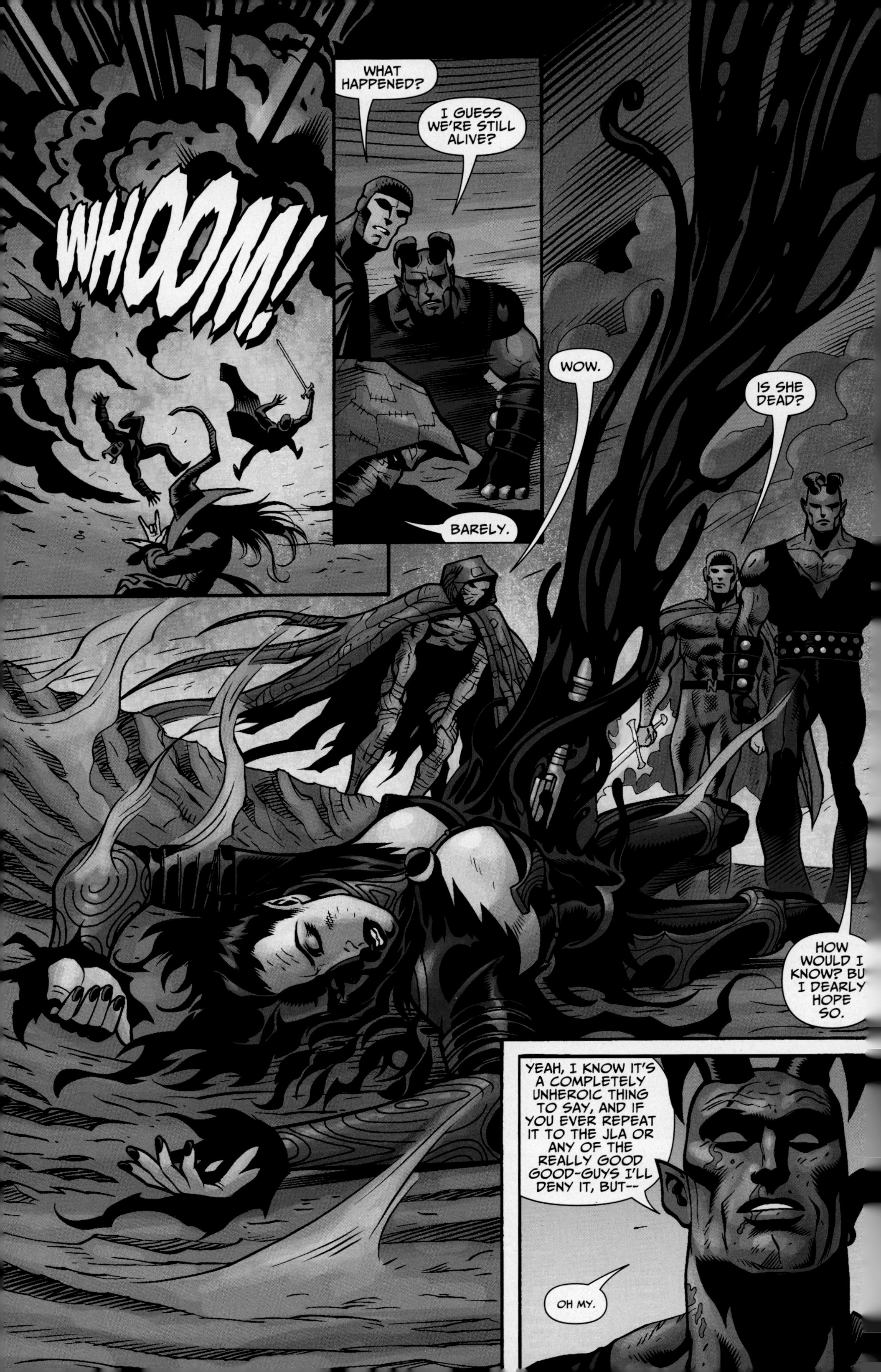
WHOOM!
WHAT HAPPENED?
I GUESS WE'RE STILL ALIVE?
BARELY.
WOW.
IS SHE DEAD?
HOW WOULD I KNOW? BU
I DEARLY HOPE SO.
YEAH, I KNOW IT'S A COMPLETELY UNHEROIC THING TO SAY, AND IF YOU EVER REPEAT IT TO THE JLA OR ANY OF THE REALLY GOOD GOOD-GUYS I'LL DENY IT, BUT--
OH MY.

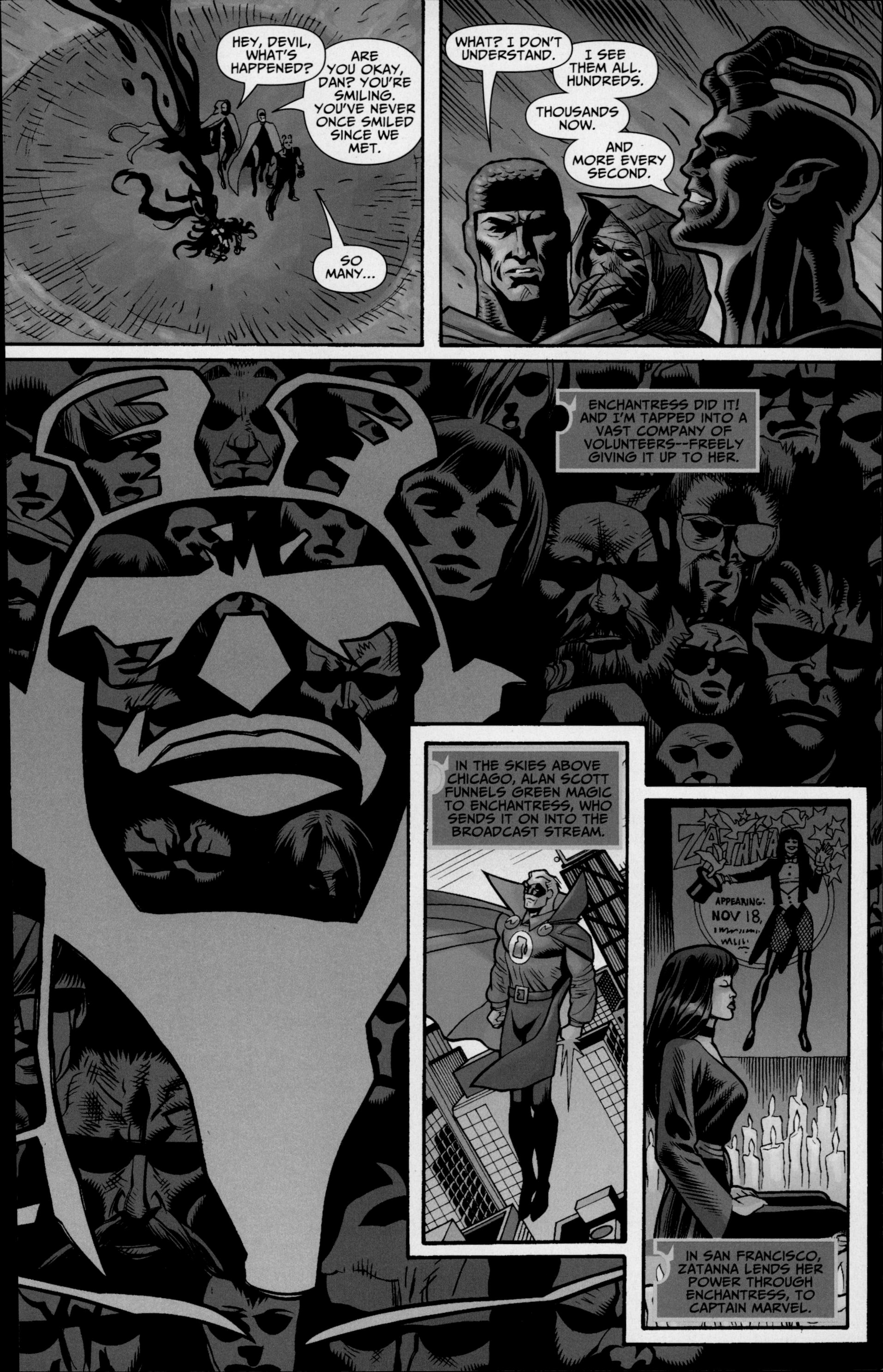
HEY, DEVIL, WHAT'S HAPPENED?
ARE YOU OKAY, DAN? YOU'RE SMILING. YOU'VE NEVER ONCE SMILED SINCE WE MET.
SO MANY...
WHAT? I DON'T UNDERSTAND.
I SEE THEM ALL. HUNDREDS.
THOUSANDS NOW.
AND MORE EVERY SECOND.
ENCHANTRESS DID IT! AND I'M TAPPED INTO A VAST COMPANY OF VOLUNTEERS--FREELY GIVING IT UP TO HER.
IN THE SKIES ABOVE CHICAGO, ALAN SCOTT FUNNELS GREEN MAGIC TO ENCHANTRESS, WHO SENDS IT ON INTO THE BROADCAST STREAM.
ZATANNA
APPEARING: NOV 18,
IN SAN FRANCISCO, ZATANNA LENDS HER POWER THROUGH ENCHANTRESS, TO CAPTAIN MARVEL.

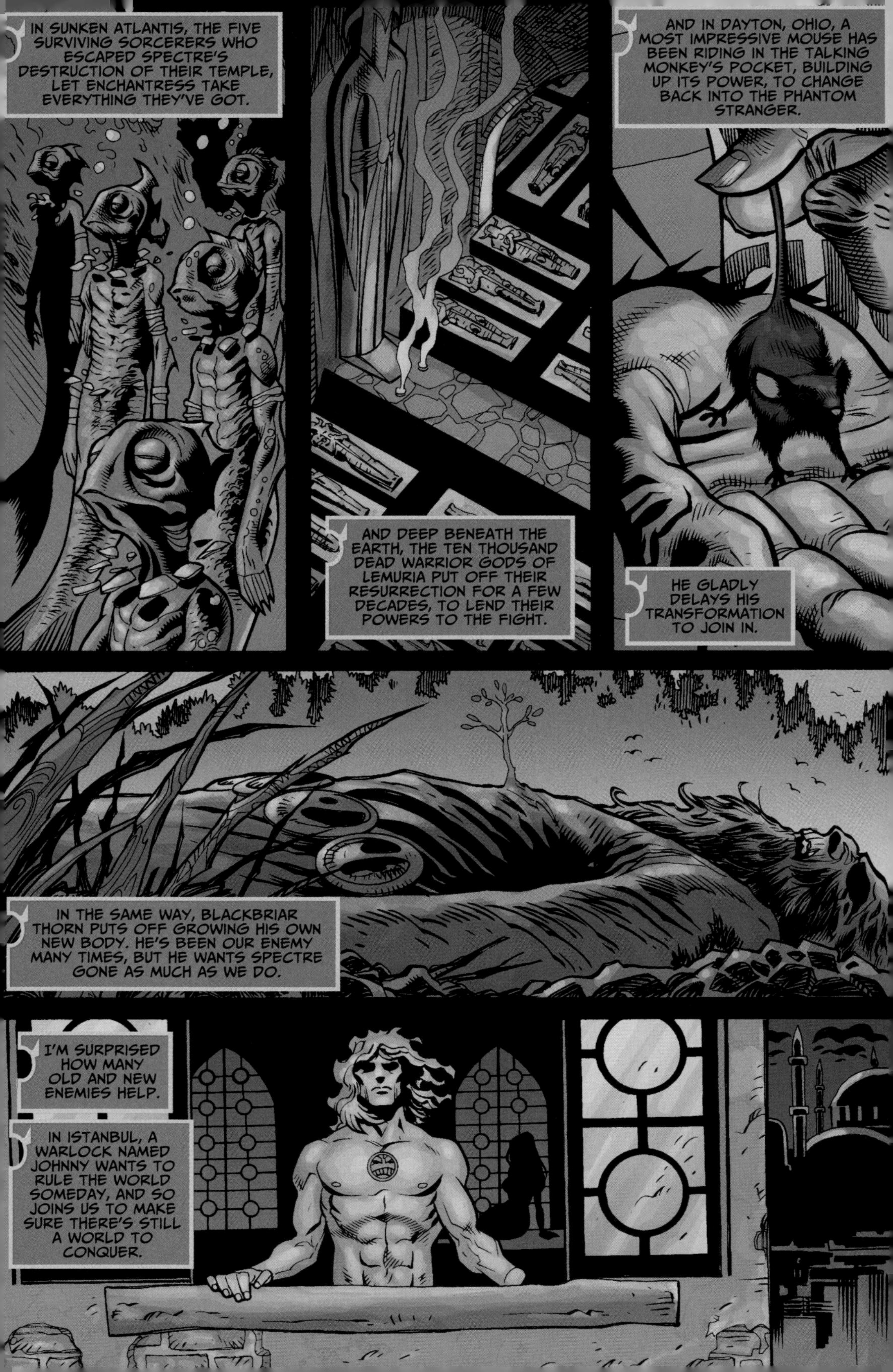

IN SUNKEN ATLANTIS, THE FIVE SURVIVING SORCERERS WHO ESCAPED SPECTRE'S DESTRUCTION OF THEIR TEMPLE, LET ENCHANTRESS TAKE EVERYTHING THEY'VE GOT.
AND DEEP BENEATH THE EARTH, THE TEN THOUSAND DEAD WARRIOR GODS OF LEMURIA PUT OFF THEIR RESURRECTION FOR A FEW DECADES, TO LEND THEIR POWERS TO THE FIGHT.
AND IN DAYTON, OHIO, A MOST IMPRESSIVE MOUSE HAS BEEN RIDING IN THE TALKING MONKEY'S POCKET, BUILDING UP ITS POWER, TO CHANGE BACK INTO THE PHANTOM STRANGER.
HE GLADLY DELAYS HIS TRANSFORMATION TO JOIN IN.
IN THE SAME WAY, BLACKBRIAR THORN PUTS OFF GROWING HIS OWN NEW BODY. HE'S BEEN OUR ENEMY MANY TIMES, BUT HE WANTS SPECTRE GONE AS MUCH AS WE DO.
I'M SURPRISED HOW MANY OLD AND NEW ENEMIES HELP.
IN ISTANBUL, A WARLOCK NAMED JOHNNY WANTS TO RULE THE WORLD SOMEDAY, AND SO JOINS US TO MAKE SURE THERE'S STILL A WORLD TO CONQUER.

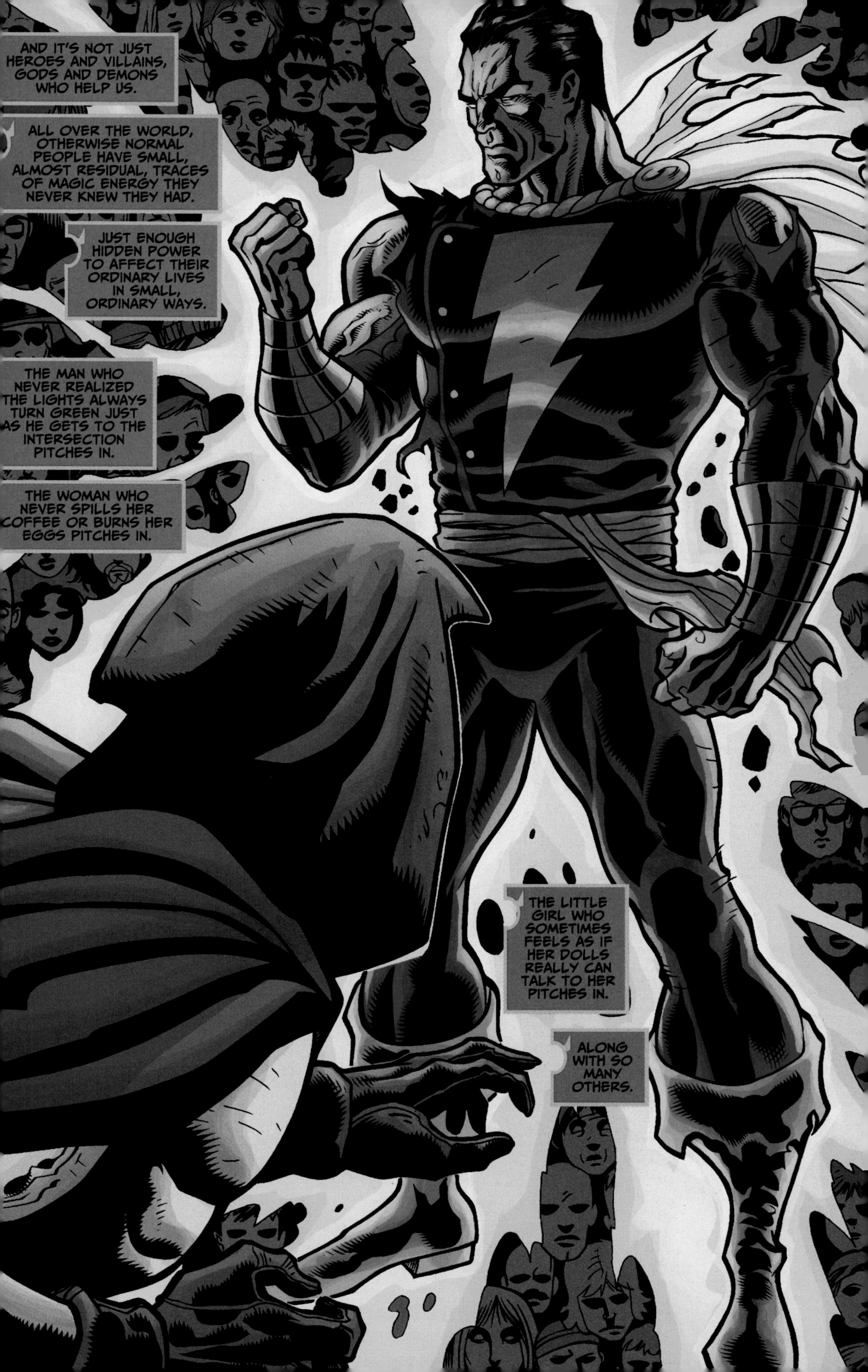
AND IT'S NOT JUST HEROES AND VILLAINS, GODS AND DEMONS WHO HELP US.
ALL OVER THE WORLD, OTHERWISE NORMAL PEOPLE HAVE SMALL, ALMOST RESIDUAL, TRACES OF MAGIC ENERGY THEY NEVER KNEW THEY HAD.
JUST ENOUGH HIDDEN POWER TO AFFECT THEIR ORDINARY LIVES IN SMALL, ORDINARY WAYS.
THE MAN WHO NEVER REALIZED THE LIGHTS ALWAYS TURN GREEN JUST AS HE GETS TO THE INTERSECTION PITCHES IN.
THE WOMAN WHO NEVER SPILLS HER COFFEE OR BURNS HER EGGS PITCHES IN.
THE LITTLE GIRL WHO SOMETIMES FEELS AS IF HER DOLLS REALLY CAN TALK TO HER PITCHES IN.
ALONG WITH SO MANY OTHERS.

ALL THAT POWER FLOWING INTO ONE MAN: CAPTAIN MARVEL!

I BEAT YOU! YOU WERE NEARLY DRAINED!

HOW--?

I DON'T KNOW, GHOST!

MAYBE A BENEVOLENT UNIVERSE HAS FINALLY HAD ENOUGH OF YOU!

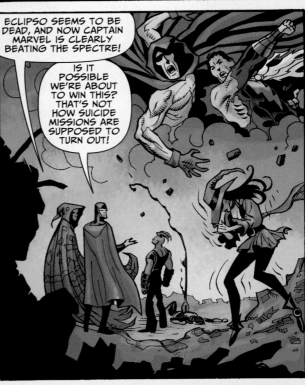

ECLIPSO SEEMS TO BE DEAD, AND NOW CAPTAIN MARVEL IS CLEARLY BEATING THE SPECTRE!

IS IT POSSIBLE WE'RE ABOUT TO WIN THIS? THAT'S NOT HOW SUICIDE MISSIONS ARE SUPPOSED TO TURN OUT!

ENCHANTRESS, YOU'RE DOING THIS, RIGHT?

YOU'RE HELPING CAPTAIN MARVEL SOMEHOW?

DON'T--TO--ME.

BARELY--HOLDING--ON.

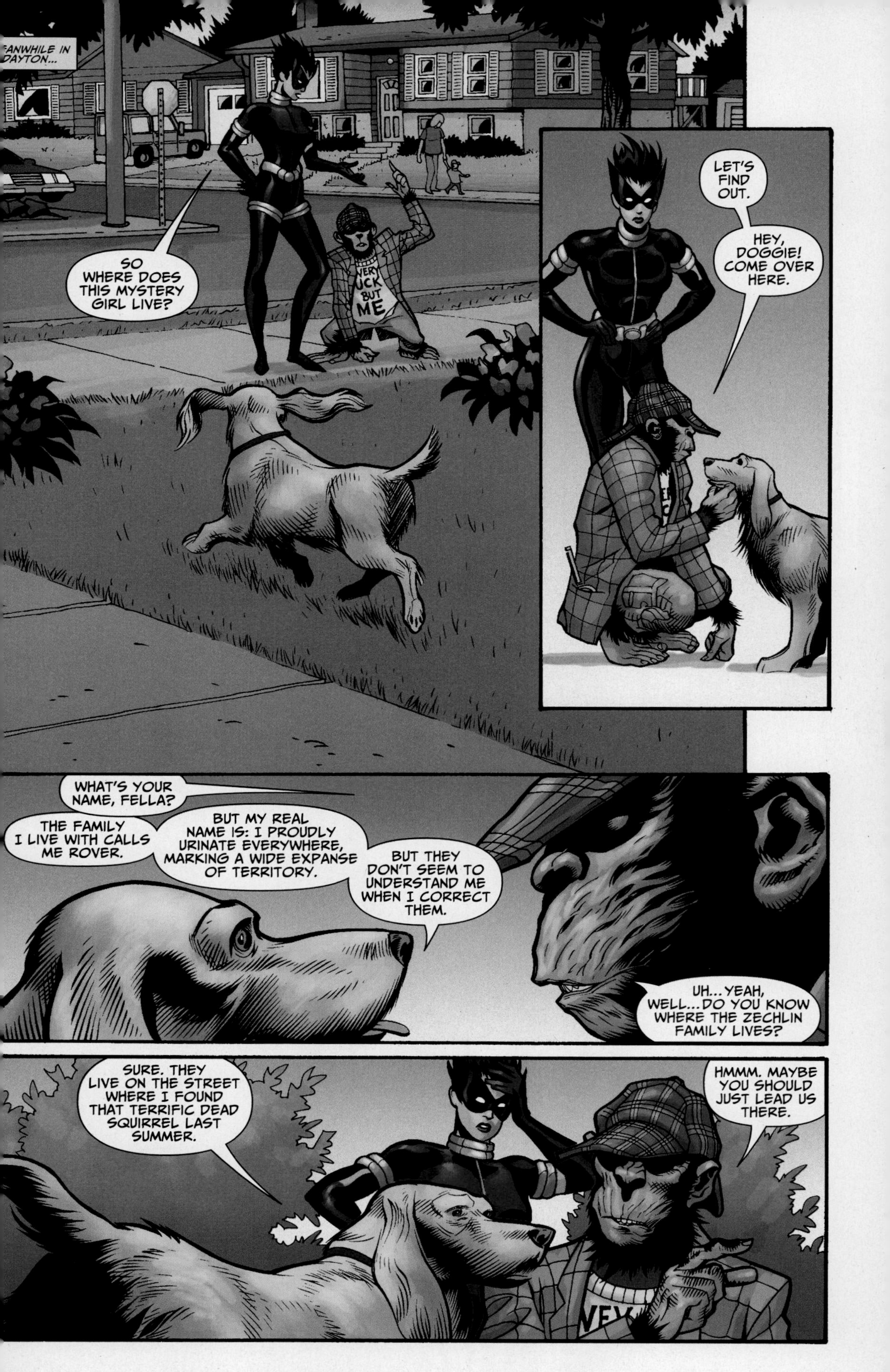
EANWHILE IN DAYTON...
SO WHERE DOES THIS MYSTERY GIRL LIVE?
LET'S FIND OUT.
HEY, DOGGIE! COME OVER HERE.
WHAT'S YOUR NAME, FELLA?
THE FAMILY I LIVE WITH CALLS ME ROVER.
BUT MY REAL NAME IS: I PROUDLY URINATE EVERYWHERE, MARKING A WIDE EXPANSE OF TERRITORY.
BUT THEY DON'T SEEM TO UNDERSTAND ME WHEN I CORRECT THEM.
UH...YEAH, WELL...DO YOU KNOW WHERE THE ZECHLIN FAMILY LIVES?
SURE. THEY LIVE ON THE STREET WHERE I FOUND THAT TERRIFIC DEAD SQUIRREL LAST SUMMER.
HMMM. MAYBE YOU SHOULD JUST LEAD US THERE.

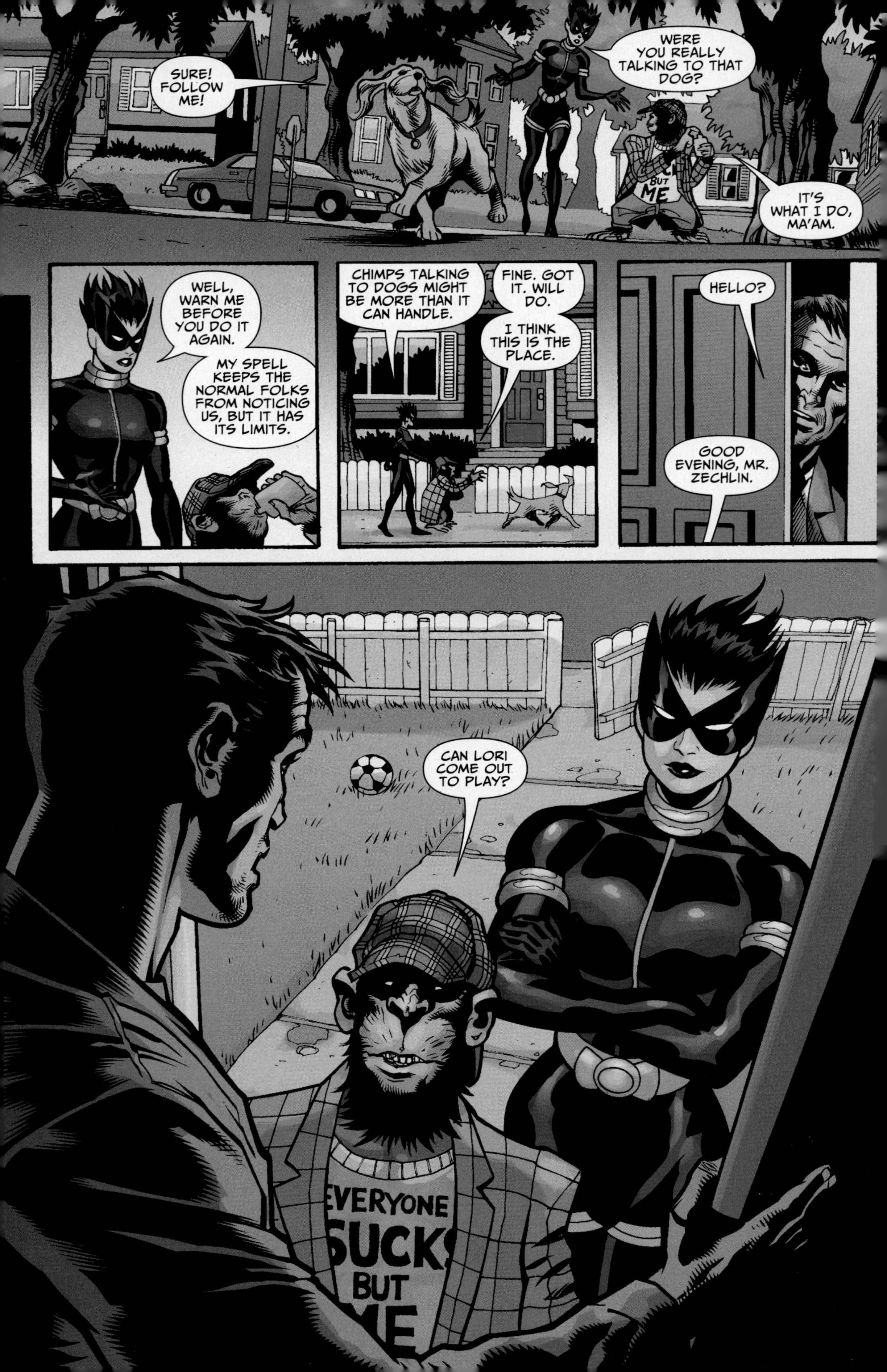
SURE! FOLLOW ME!
WERE YOU REALLY TALKING TO THAT DOG?
IT'S WHAT I DO, MA'AM.
WELL, WARN ME BEFORE YOU DO IT AGAIN.
MY SPELL KEEPS THE NORMAL FOLKS FROM NOTICING US, BUT IT HAS ITS LIMITS.
CHIMPS TALKING TO DOGS MIGHT BE MORE THAN IT CAN HANDLE.
FINE. GOT IT. WILL DO.
I THINK THIS IS THE PLACE.
HELLO?
GOOD EVENING, MR. ZECHLIN.
CAN LORI COME OUT TO PLAY?
EVERYONE SUCKS BUT ME

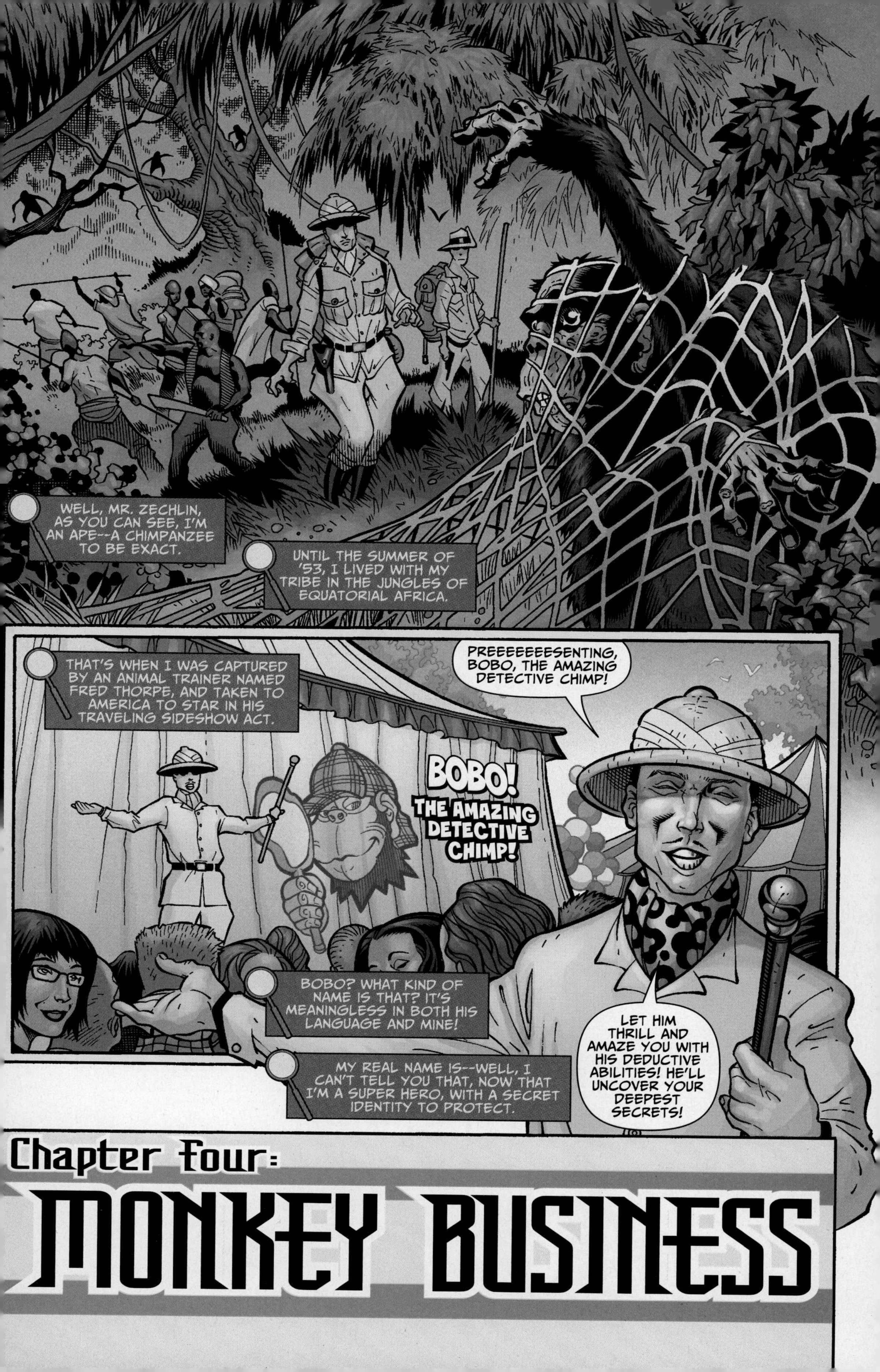
WELL, MR. ZECHLIN, AS YOU CAN SEE, I'M AN APE--A CHIMPANZEE TO BE EXACT.
UNTIL THE SUMMER OF '53, I LIVED WITH MY TRIBE IN THE JUNGLES OF EQUATORIAL AFRICA.
THAT'S WHEN I WAS CAPTURED BY AN ANIMAL TRAINER NAMED FRED THORPE, AND TAKEN TO AMERICA TO STAR IN HIS TRAVELING SIDESHOW ACT.
PREEEEEEEESENTING, BOBO, THE AMAZING DETECTIVE CHIMP!
BOBO! THE AMAZING DETECTIVE CHIMP!
BOBO? WHAT KIND OF NAME IS THAT? IT'S MEANINGLESS IN BOTH HIS LANGUAGE AND MINE!
MY REAL NAME IS--WELL, I CAN'T TELL YOU THAT, NOW THAT I'M A SUPER HERO, WITH A SECRET IDENTITY TO PROTECT.
LET HIM THRILL AND AMAZE YOU WITH HIS DEDUCTIVE ABILITIES! HE'LL UNCOVER YOUR DEEPEST SECRETS!
Chapter Four:
MONKEY BUSINESS

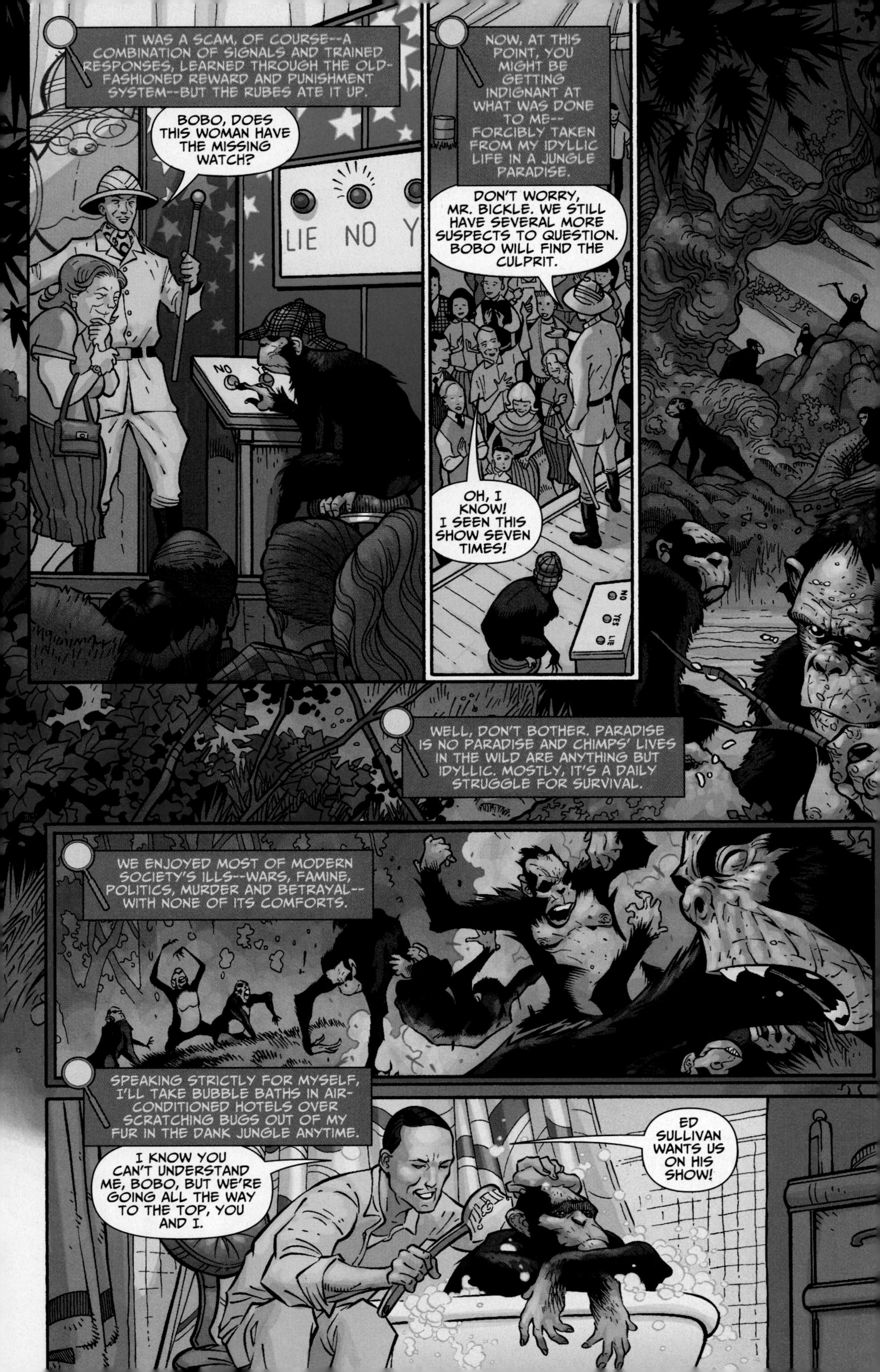
IT WAS A SCAM, OF COURSE--A COMBINATION OF SIGNALS AND TRAINED RESPONSES, LEARNED THROUGH THE OLD-FASHIONED REWARD AND PUNISHMENT SYSTEM--BUT THE RUBES ATE IT UP.
BOBO, DOES THIS WOMAN HAVE THE MISSING WATCH?
LIE NO Y
NO YE
NOW, AT THIS POINT, YOU MIGHT BE GETTING INDIGNANT AT WHAT WAS DONE TO ME--FORCIBLY TAKEN FROM MY IDYLLIC LIFE IN A JUNGLE PARADISE.
DON'T WORRY, MR. BICKLE. WE STILL HAVE SEVERAL MORE SUSPECTS TO QUESTION. BOBO WILL FIND THE CULPRIT.
OH, I KNOW! I SEEN THIS SHOW SEVEN TIMES!
NO YES LIE
WELL, DON'T BOTHER. PARADISE IS NO PARADISE AND CHIMPS' LIVES IN THE WILD ARE ANYTHING BUT IDYLLIC. MOSTLY, IT'S A DAILY STRUGGLE FOR SURVIVAL.
WE ENJOYED MOST OF MODERN SOCIETY'S ILLS--WARS, FAMINE, POLITICS, MURDER AND BETRAYAL--WITH NONE OF ITS COMFORTS.
SPEAKING STRICTLY FOR MYSELF, I'LL TAKE BUBBLE BATHS IN AIR-CONDITIONED HOTELS OVER SCRATCHING BUGS OUT OF MY FUR IN THE DANK JUNGLE ANYTIME.
I KNOW YOU CAN'T UNDERSTAND ME, BOBO, BUT WE'RE GOING ALL THE WAY TO THE TOP, YOU AND I.
ED SULLIVAN WANTS US ON HIS SHOW!

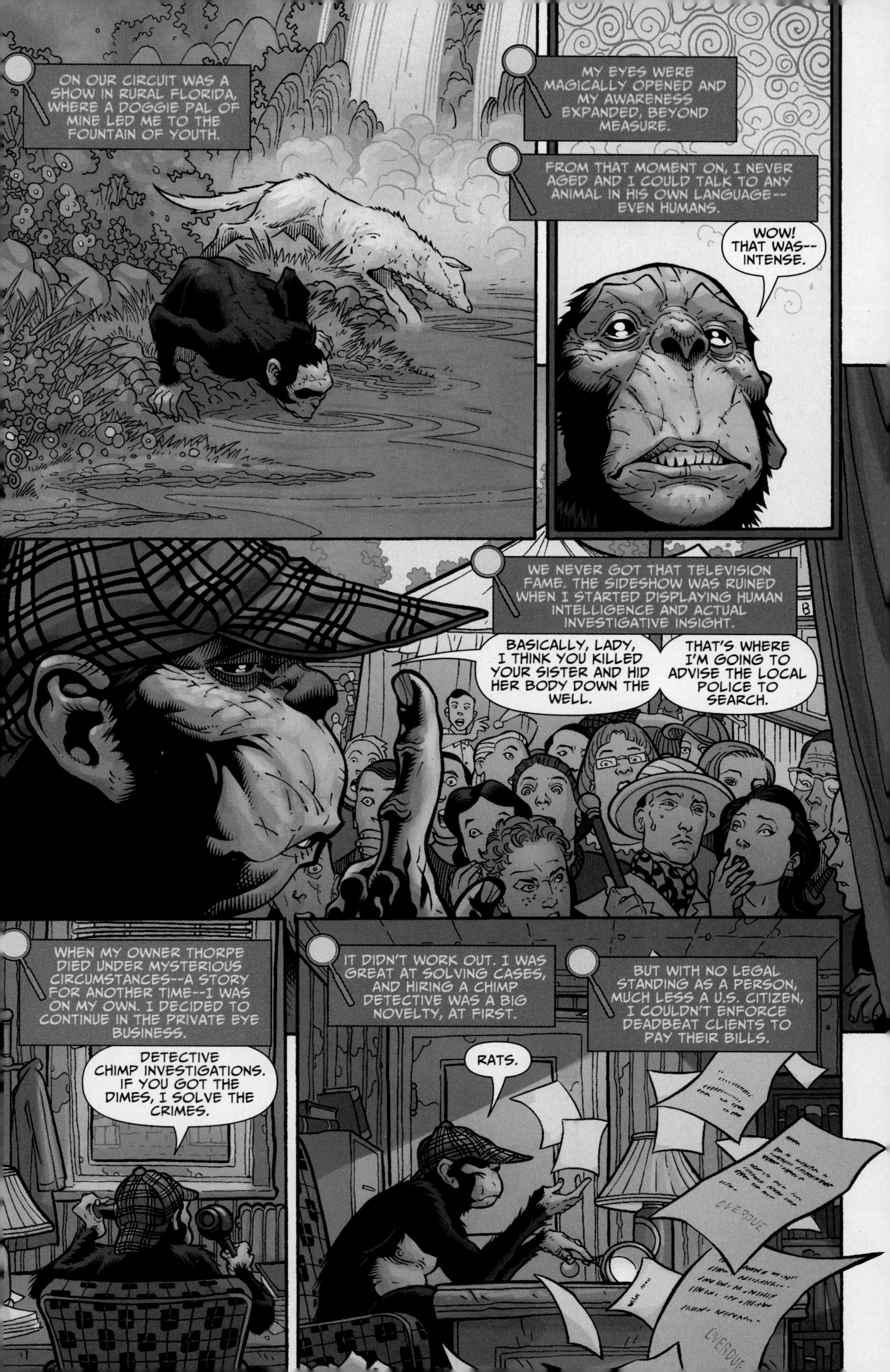
ON OUR CIRCUIT WAS A SHOW IN RURAL FLORIDA, WHERE A DOGGIE PAL OF MINE LED ME TO THE FOUNTAIN OF YOUTH.
MY EYES WERE MAGICALLY OPENED AND MY AWARENESS EXPANDED, BEYOND MEASURE.
FROM THAT MOMENT ON, I NEVER AGED AND I COULD TALK TO ANY ANIMAL IN HIS OWN LANGUAGE-- EVEN HUMANS.
WOW! THAT WAS-- INTENSE.
WE NEVER GOT THAT TELEVISION FAME. THE SIDESHOW WAS RUINED WHEN I STARTED DISPLAYING HUMAN INTELLIGENCE AND ACTUAL INVESTIGATIVE INSIGHT.
BASICALLY, LADY, I THINK YOU KILLED YOUR SISTER AND HID HER BODY DOWN THE WELL.
THAT'S WHERE I'M GOING TO ADVISE THE LOCAL POLICE TO SEARCH.
WHEN MY OWNER THORPE DIED UNDER MYSTERIOUS CIRCUMSTANCES--A STORY FOR ANOTHER TIME--I WAS ON MY OWN. I DECIDED TO CONTINUE IN THE PRIVATE EYE BUSINESS.
DETECTIVE CHIMP INVESTIGATIONS. IF YOU GOT THE DIMES, I SOLVE THE CRIMES.
IT DIDN'T WORK OUT. I WAS GREAT AT SOLVING CASES, AND HIRING A CHIMP DETECTIVE WAS A BIG NOVELTY, AT FIRST.
BUT WITH NO LEGAL STANDING AS A PERSON, MUCH LESS A U.S. CITIZEN, I COULDN'T ENFORCE DEADBEAT CLIENTS TO PAY THEIR BILLS.
RATS.
OVERDUE
OVERDUE

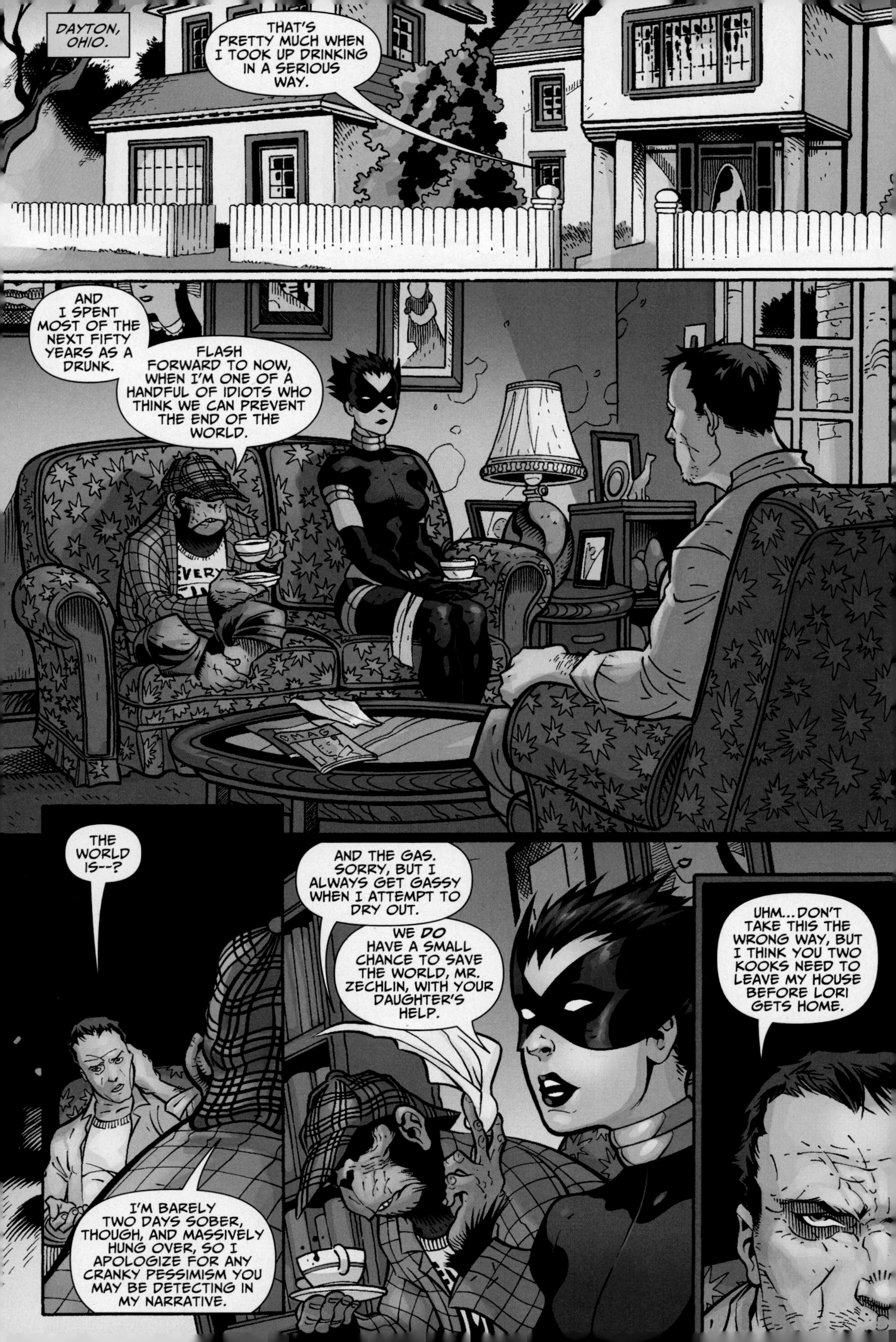
DAYTON, OHIO.
THAT'S PRETTY MUCH WHEN I TOOK UP DRINKING IN A SERIOUS WAY.
AND I SPENT MOST OF THE NEXT FIFTY YEARS AS A DRUNK.
FLASH FORWARD TO NOW, WHEN I'M ONE OF A HANDFUL OF IDIOTS WHO THINK WE CAN PREVENT THE END OF THE WORLD.
THE WORLD IS--?
I'M BARELY TWO DAYS SOBER, THOUGH, AND MASSIVELY HUNG OVER, SO I APOLOGIZE FOR ANY CRANKY PESSIMISM YOU MAY BE DETECTING IN MY NARRATIVE.
AND THE GAS. SORRY, BUT I ALWAYS GET GASSY WHEN I ATTEMPT TO DRY OUT.
WE *DO* HAVE A SMALL CHANCE TO SAVE THE WORLD, MR. ZECHLIN, WITH YOUR DAUGHTER'S HELP.
UHM...DON'T TAKE THIS THE WRONG WAY, BUT I THINK YOU TWO KOOKS NEED TO LEAVE MY HOUSE BEFORE LORI GETS HOME.

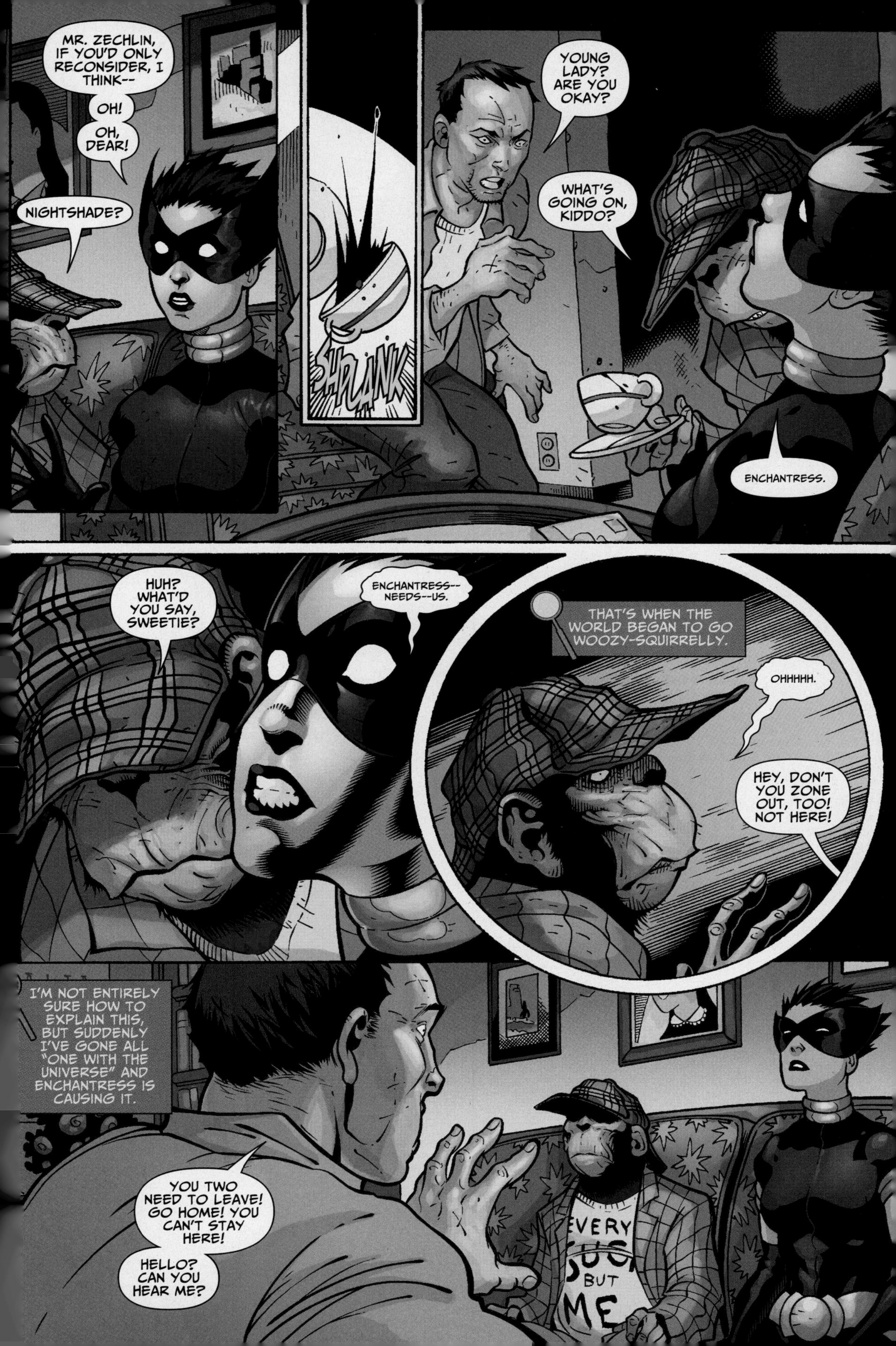
MR. ZECHLIN, IF YOU'D ONLY RECONSIDER, I THINK--
OH!
OH, DEAR!
NIGHTSHADE?
SHPLANK
YOUNG LADY? ARE YOU OKAY?
WHAT'S GOING ON, KIDDO?
ENCHANTRESS.
HUH? WHAT'D YOU SAY, SWEETIE?
ENCHANTRESS-- NEEDS--US.
THAT'S WHEN THE WORLD BEGAN TO GO WOOZY-SQUIRRELLY.
OHHHHH.
HEY, DON'T YOU ZONE OUT, TOO! NOT HERE!
I'M NOT ENTIRELY SURE HOW TO EXPLAIN THIS, BUT SUDDENLY I'VE GONE ALL "ONE WITH THE UNIVERSE" AND ENCHANTRESS IS CAUSING IT.
YOU TWO NEED TO LEAVE! GO HOME! YOU CAN'T STAY HERE!
HELLO? CAN YOU HEAR ME?

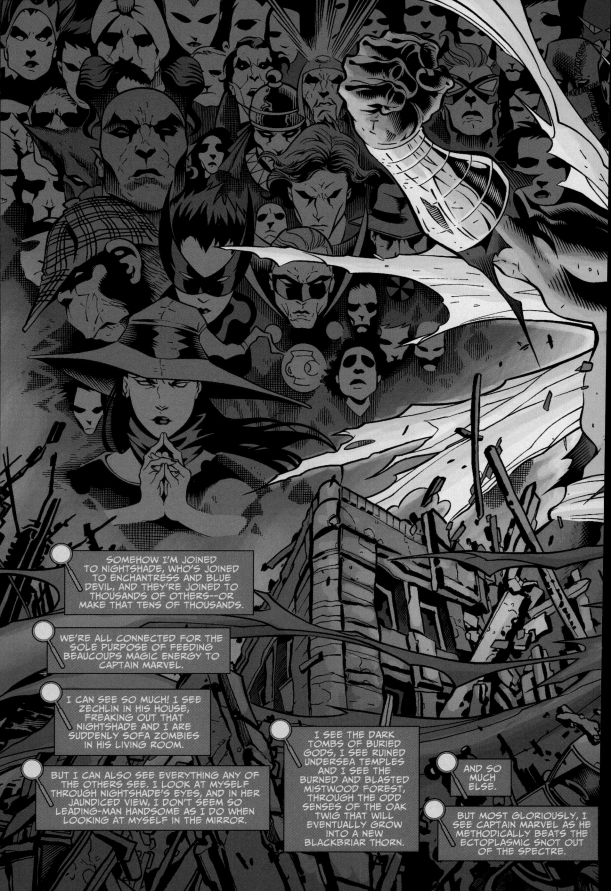

SOMEHOW I'M JOINED TO NIGHTSHADE, WHO'S JOINED TO ENCHANTRESS AND BLUE DEVIL, AND THEY'RE JOINED TO THOUSANDS OF OTHERS--OR MAKE THAT TENS OF THOUSANDS.

WE'RE ALL CONNECTED FOR THE SOLE PURPOSE OF FEEDING BEAUCOUPS MAGIC ENERGY TO CAPTAIN MARVEL.

I CAN SEE SO MUCH! I SEE ZECHLIN IN HIS HOUSE, FREAKING OUT THAT NIGHTSHADE AND I ARE SUDDENLY SOFA ZOMBIES IN HIS LIVING ROOM.

BUT I CAN ALSO SEE EVERYTHING ANY OF THE OTHERS SEE. I LOOK AT MYSELF THROUGH NIGHTSHADE'S EYES, AND IN HER JAUNDICED VIEW, I DON'T SEEM SO LEADING-MAN HANDSOME AS I DO WHEN LOOKING AT MYSELF IN THE MIRROR.

I SEE THE DARK TOMBS OF BURIED GODS, I SEE RUINED UNDERSEA TEMPLES AND I SEE THE BURNED AND BLASTED MISTWOOD FOREST, THROUGH THE ODD SENSES OF THE OAK TWIG THAT WILL EVENTUALLY GROW INTO A NEW BLACKBRIAR THORN.

AND SO MUCH ELSE.

BUT MOST GLORIOUSLY, I SEE CAPTAIN MARVEL AS HE METHODICALLY BEATS THE ECTOPLASMIC SNOT OUT OF THE SPECTRE.

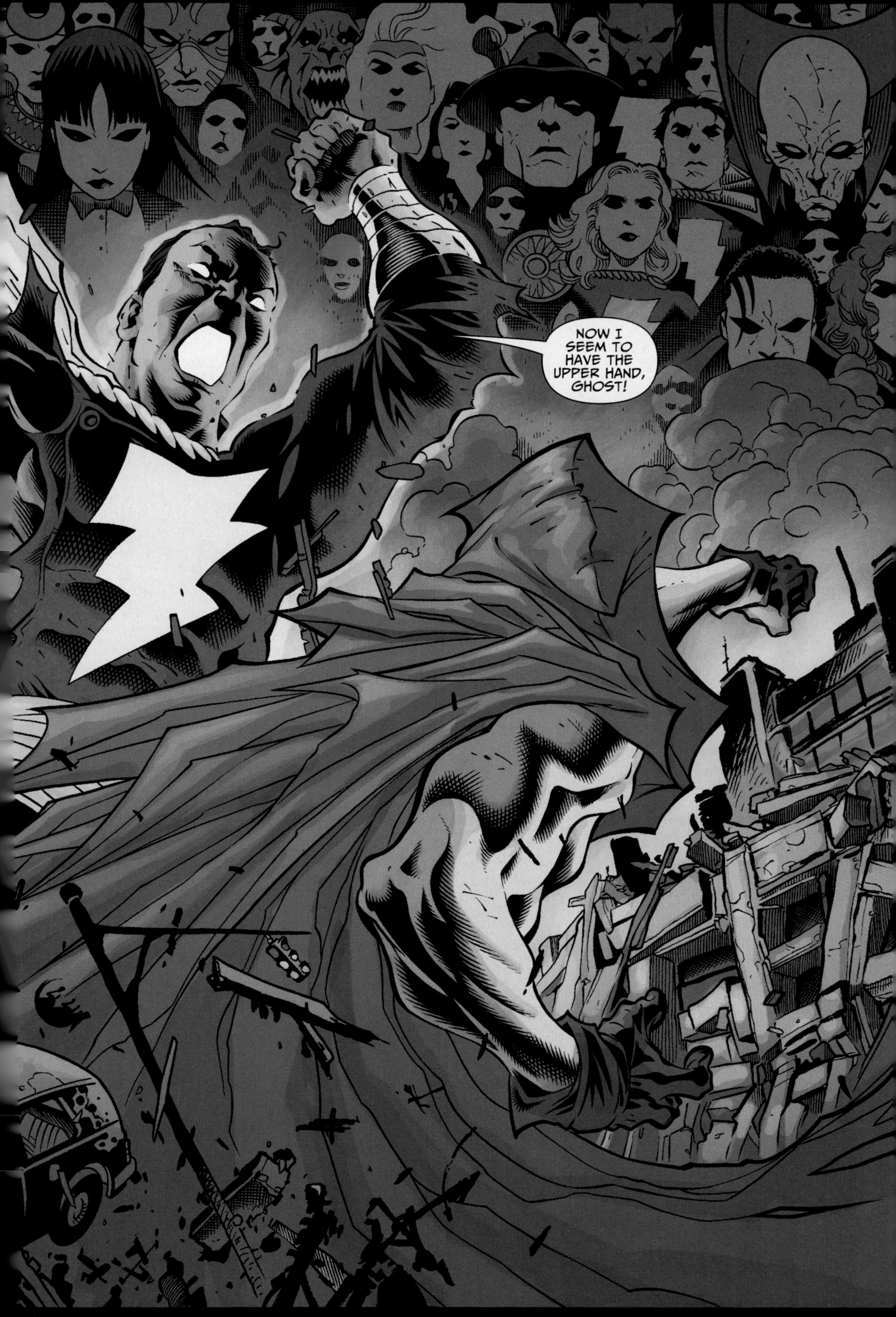
NOW I SEEM TO HAVE THE UPPER HAND, GHOST!

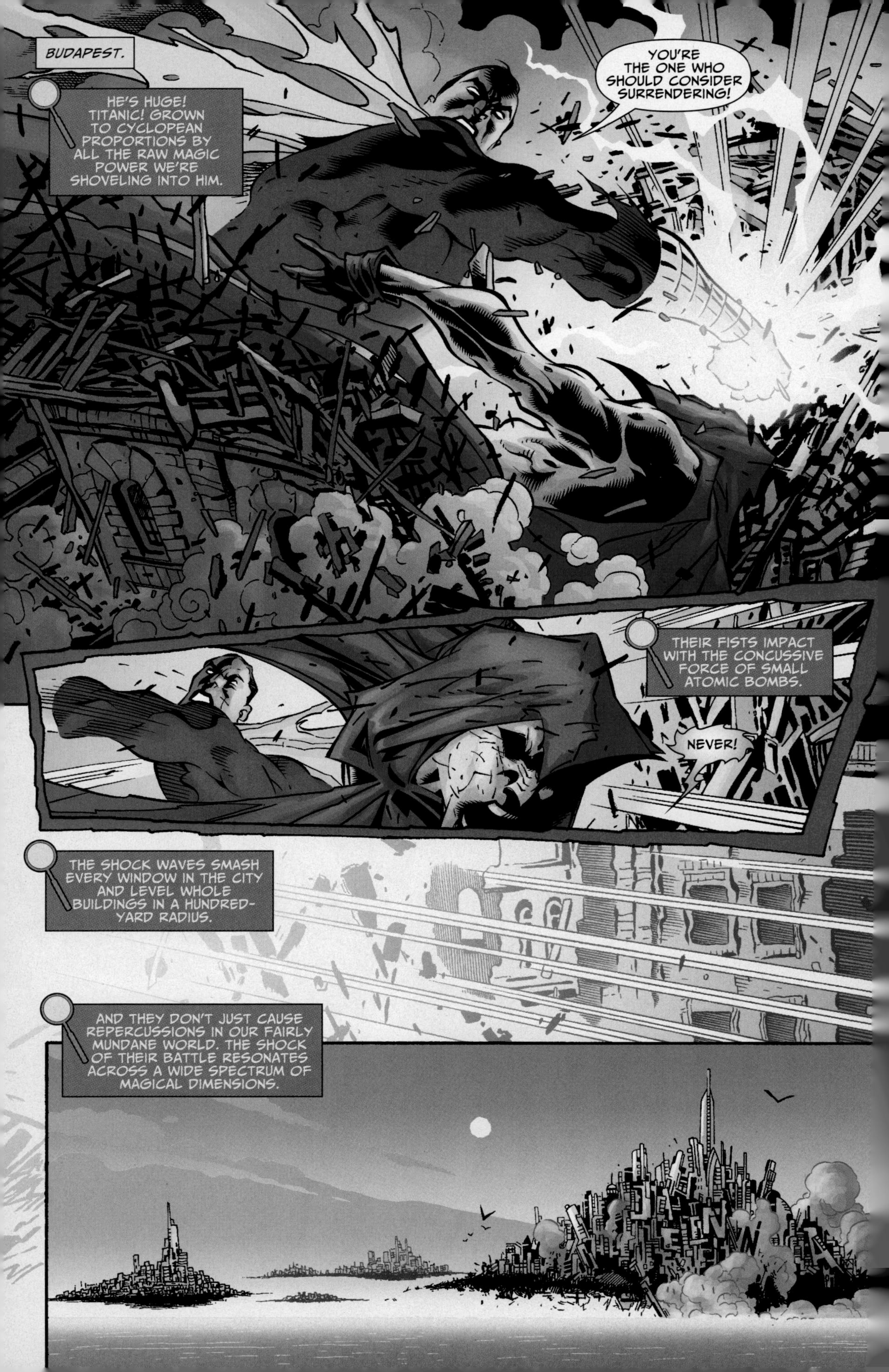
BUDAPEST.
HE'S HUGE! TITANIC! GROWN TO CYCLOPEAN PROPORTIONS BY ALL THE RAW MAGIC POWER WE'RE SHOVELING INTO HIM.
YOU'RE THE ONE WHO SHOULD CONSIDER SURRENDERING!
THEIR FISTS IMPACT WITH THE CONCUSSIVE FORCE OF SMALL ATOMIC BOMBS.
NEVER!
THE SHOCK WAVES SMASH EVERY WINDOW IN THE CITY AND LEVEL WHOLE BUILDINGS IN A HUNDRED-YARD RADIUS.
AND THEY DON'T JUST CAUSE REPERCUSSIONS IN OUR FAIRLY MUNDANE WORLD. THE SHOCK OF THEIR BATTLE RESONATES ACROSS A WIDE SPECTRUM OF MAGICAL DIMENSIONS.

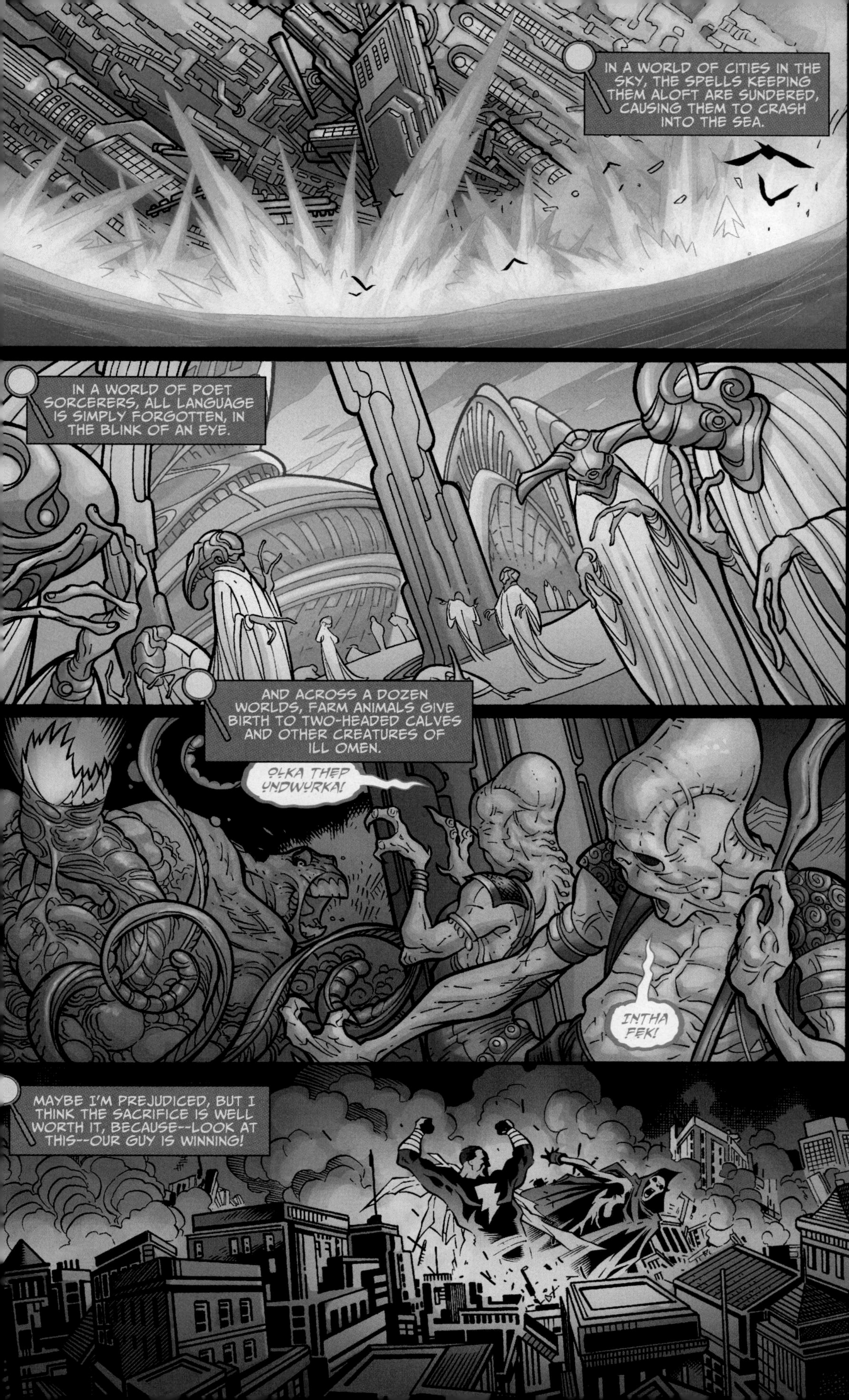
IN A WORLD OF CITIES IN THE SKY, THE SPELLS KEEPING THEM ALOFT ARE SUNDERED, CAUSING THEM TO CRASH INTO THE SEA.
IN A WORLD OF POET SORCERERS, ALL LANGUAGE IS SIMPLY FORGOTTEN, IN THE BLINK OF AN EYE.
AND ACROSS A DOZEN WORLDS, FARM ANIMALS GIVE BIRTH TO TWO-HEADED CALVES AND OTHER CREATURES OF ILL OMEN.
OLKA THEP UNDWURKA!
INTHA FEK!
MAYBE I'M PREJUDICED, BUT I THINK THE SACRIFICE IS WELL WORTH IT, BECAUSE--LOOK AT THIS--OUR GUY IS WINNING!

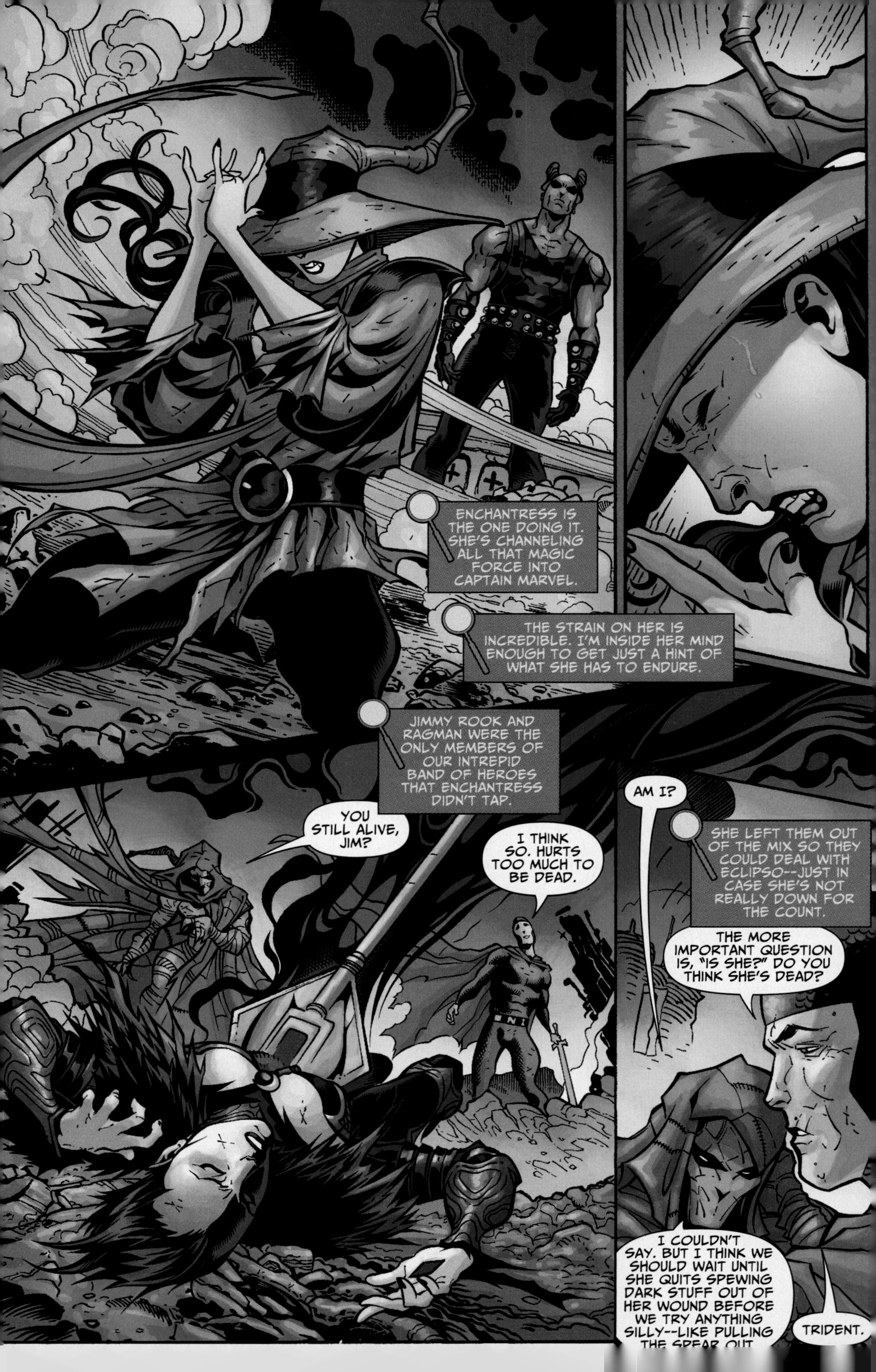

ENCHANTRESS IS THE ONE DOING IT. SHE'S CHANNELING ALL THAT MAGIC FORCE INTO CAPTAIN MARVEL.
THE STRAIN ON HER IS INCREDIBLE. I'M INSIDE HER MIND ENOUGH TO GET JUST A HINT OF WHAT SHE HAS TO ENDURE.
JIMMY ROOK AND RAGMAN WERE THE ONLY MEMBERS OF OUR INTREPID BAND OF HEROES THAT ENCHANTRESS DIDN'T TAP.
YOU STILL ALIVE, JIM?
I THINK SO. HURTS TOO MUCH TO BE DEAD.
AM I?
SHE LEFT THEM OUT OF THE MIX SO THEY COULD DEAL WITH ECLIPSO--JUST IN CASE SHE'S NOT REALLY DOWN FOR THE COUNT.
THE MORE IMPORTANT QUESTION IS, "IS SHE?" DO YOU THINK SHE'S DEAD?
I COULDN'T SAY. BUT I THINK WE SHOULD WAIT UNTIL SHE QUITS SPEWING DARK STUFF OUT OF HER WOUND BEFORE WE TRY ANYTHING SILLY--LIKE PULLING
TRIDENT.

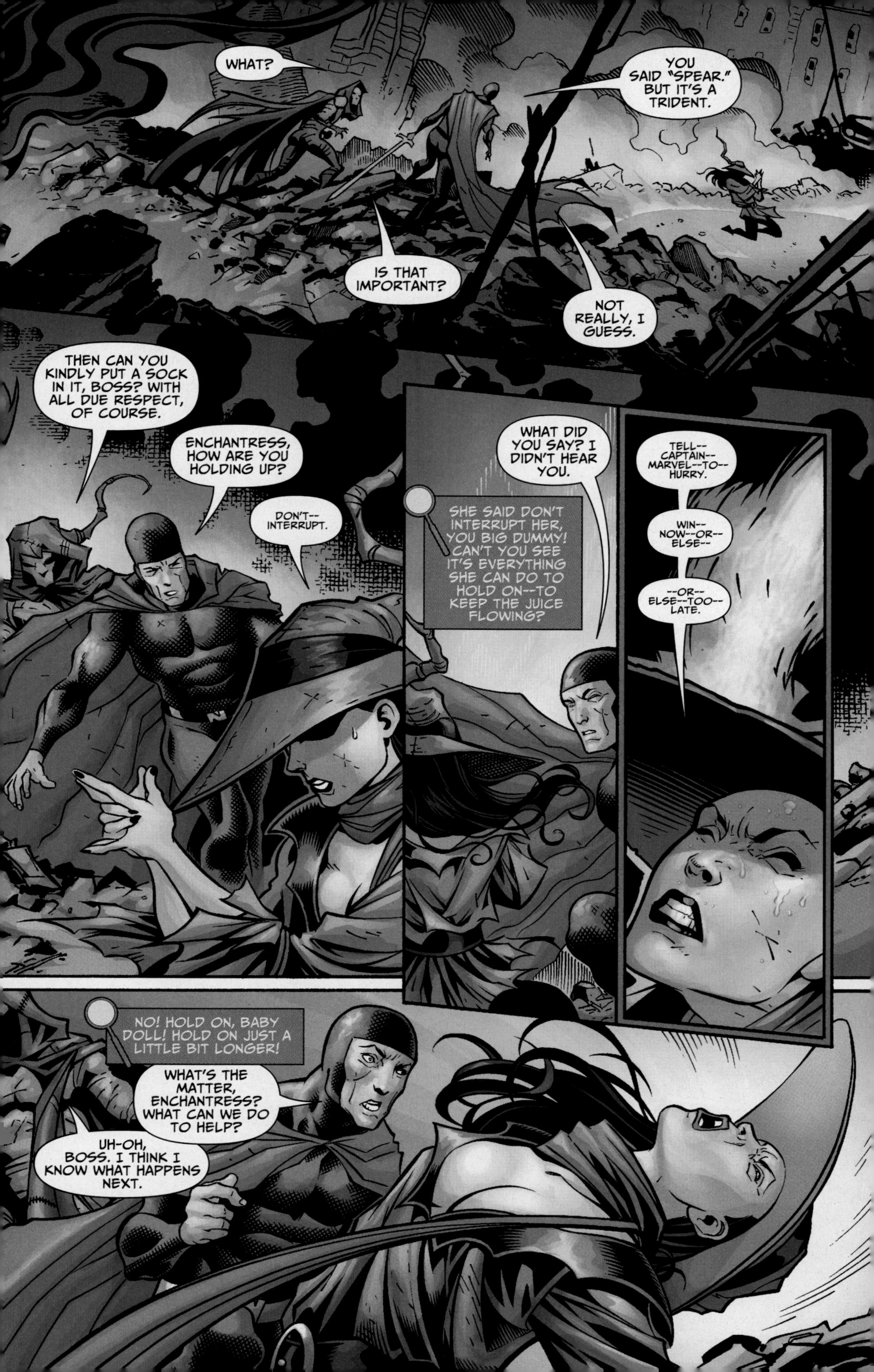
WHAT?
YOU SAID "SPEAR." BUT IT'S A TRIDENT.
IS THAT IMPORTANT?
NOT REALLY, I GUESS.
THEN CAN YOU KINDLY PUT A SOCK IN IT, BOSS? WITH ALL DUE RESPECT, OF COURSE.
ENCHANTRESS, HOW ARE YOU HOLDING UP?
DON'T-- INTERRUPT.
WHAT DID YOU SAY? I DIDN'T HEAR YOU.
SHE SAID DON'T INTERRUPT HER, YOU BIG DUMMY! CAN'T YOU SEE IT'S EVERYTHING SHE CAN DO TO HOLD ON--TO KEEP THE JUICE FLOWING?
TELL-- CAPTAIN-- MARVEL--TO-- HURRY.
WIN-- NOW--OR-- ELSE--
--OR-- ELSE--TOO-- LATE.
NO! HOLD ON, BABY DOLL! HOLD ON JUST A LITTLE BIT LONGER!
WHAT'S THE MATTER, ENCHANTRESS? WHAT CAN WE DO TO HELP?
UH-OH, BOSS. I THINK I KNOW WHAT HAPPENS NEXT.

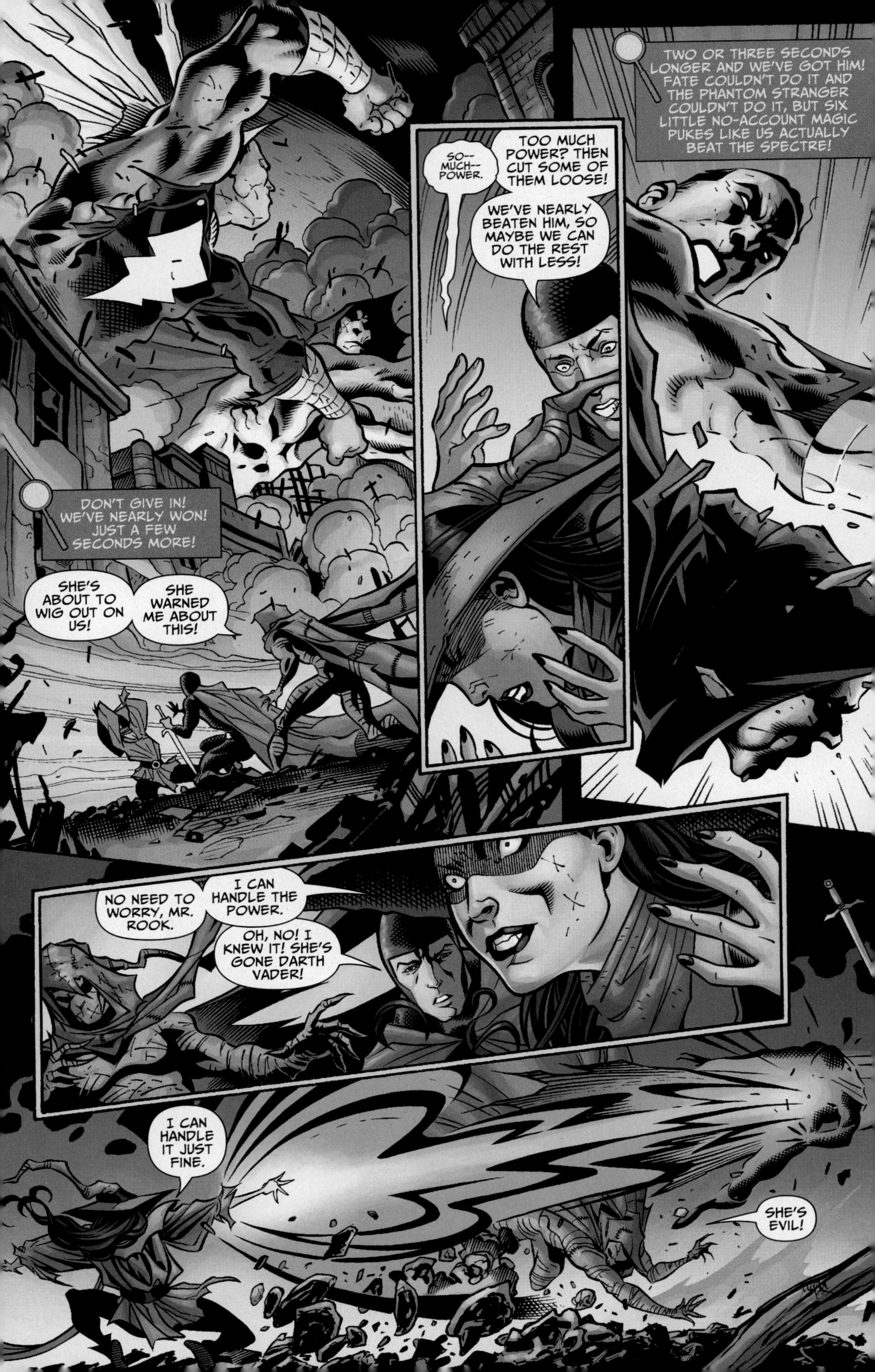

DON'T GIVE IN! WE'VE NEARLY WON! JUST A FEW SECONDS MORE!
SHE'S ABOUT TO WIG OUT ON US!
SHE WARNED ME ABOUT THIS!
SO-- MUCH-- POWER.
TOO MUCH POWER? THEN CUT SOME OF THEM LOOSE!
WE'VE NEARLY BEATEN HIM, SO MAYBE WE CAN DO THE REST WITH LESS!
TWO OR THREE SECONDS LONGER AND WE'VE GOT HIM! FATE COULDN'T DO IT AND THE PHANTOM STRANGER COULDN'T DO IT, BUT SIX LITTLE NO-ACCOUNT MAGIC PUKES LIKE US ACTUALLY BEAT THE SPECTRE!
NO NEED TO WORRY, MR. ROOK.
I CAN HANDLE THE POWER.
OH, NO! I KNEW IT! SHE'S GONE DARTH VADER!
I CAN HANDLE IT JUST FINE.
SHE'S EVIL!

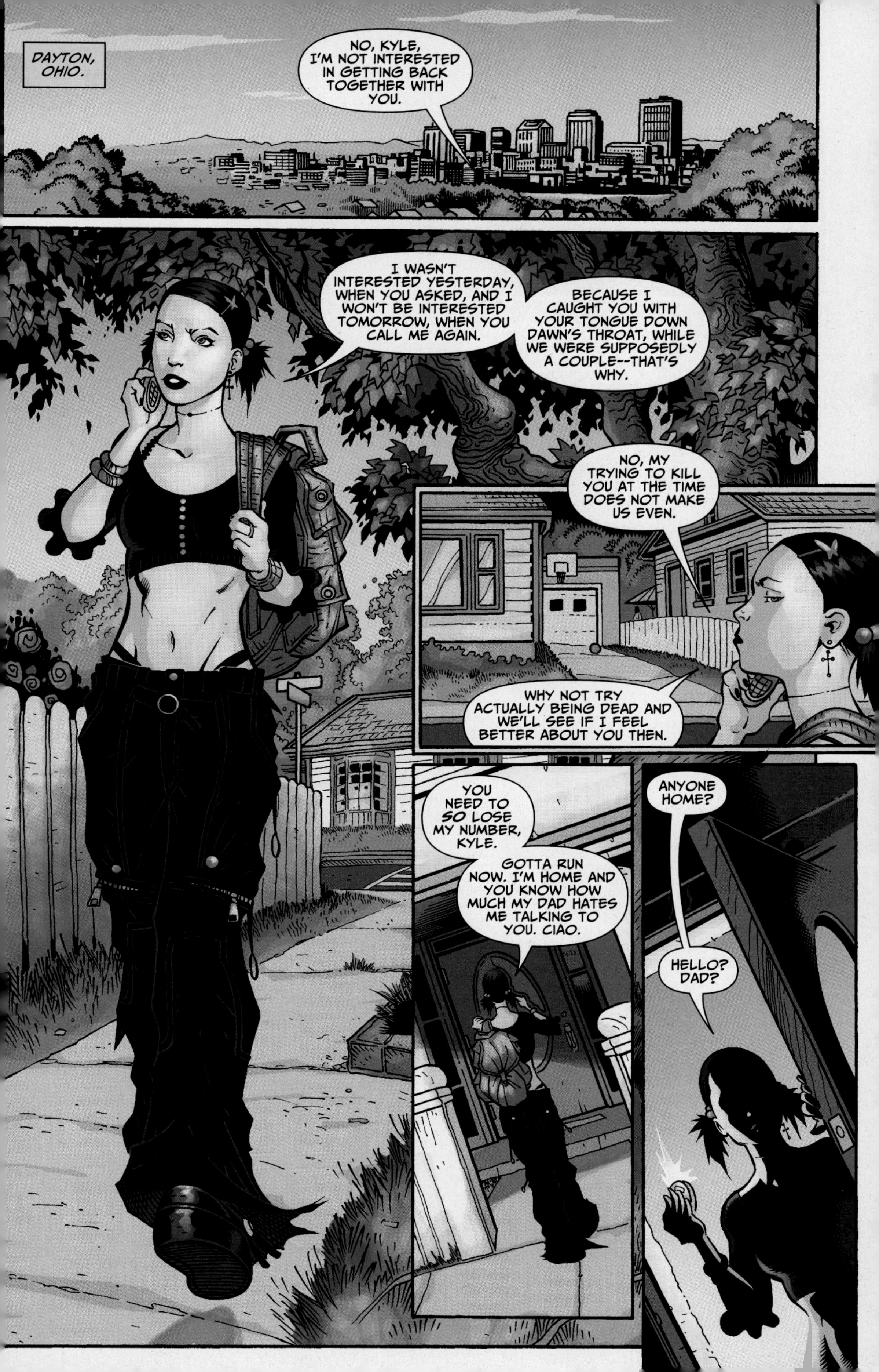
DAYTON, OHIO.
NO, KYLE, I'M NOT INTERESTED IN GETTING BACK TOGETHER WITH YOU.
I WASN'T INTERESTED YESTERDAY, WHEN YOU ASKED, AND I WON'T BE INTERESTED TOMORROW, WHEN YOU CALL ME AGAIN.
BECAUSE I CAUGHT YOU WITH YOUR TONGUE DOWN DAWN'S THROAT, WHILE WE WERE SUPPOSEDLY A COUPLE--THAT'S WHY.
NO, MY TRYING TO KILL YOU AT THE TIME DOES NOT MAKE US EVEN.
WHY NOT TRY ACTUALLY BEING DEAD AND WE'LL SEE IF I FEEL BETTER ABOUT YOU THEN.
YOU NEED TO SO LOSE MY NUMBER, KYLE.
GOTTA RUN NOW. I'M HOME AND YOU KNOW HOW MUCH MY DAD HATES ME TALKING TO YOU. CIAO.
ANYONE HOME?
HELLO? DAD?

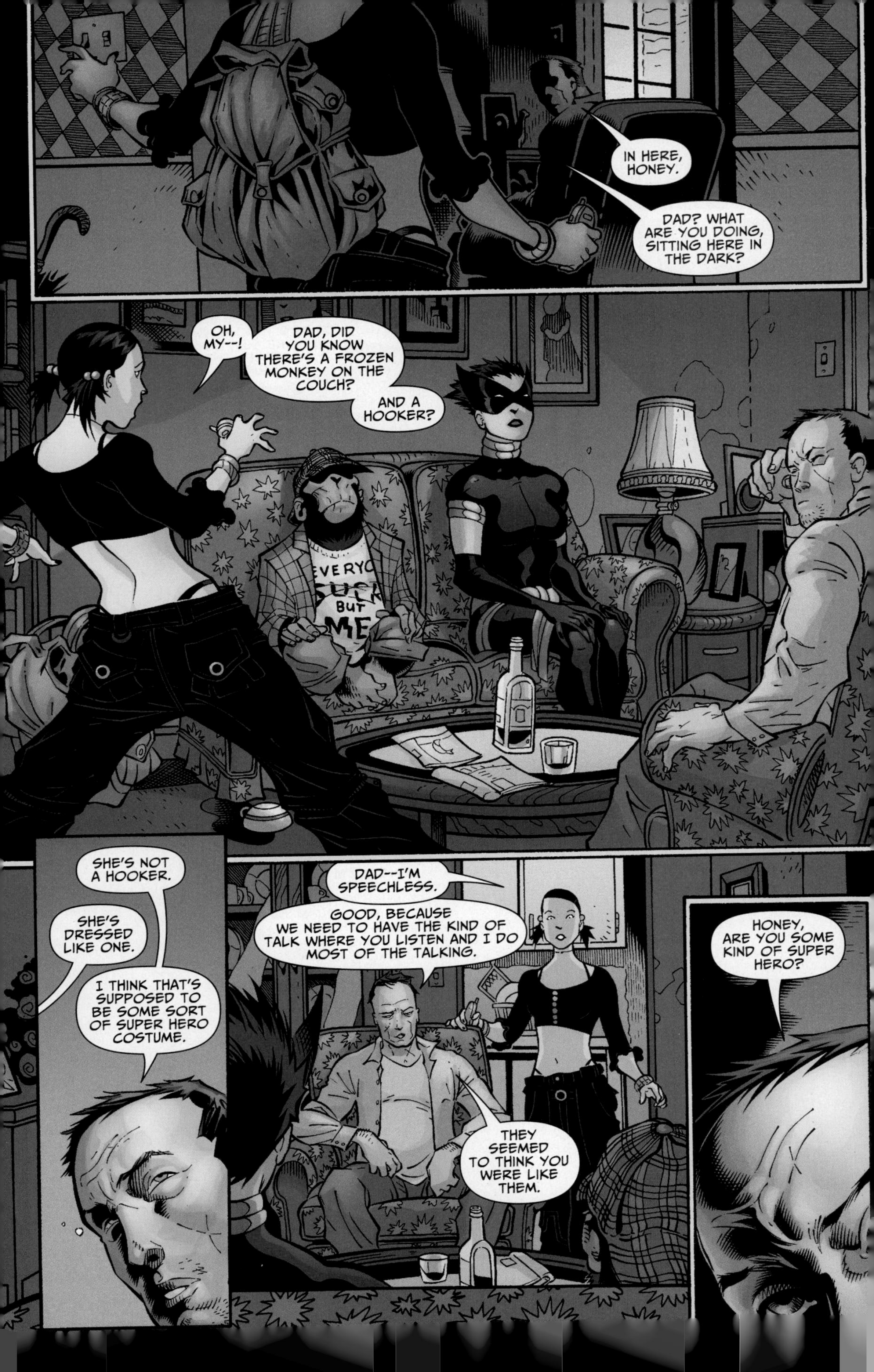
IN HERE, HONEY.
DAD? WHAT ARE YOU DOING, SITTING HERE IN THE DARK?
OH, MY--!
DAD, DID YOU KNOW THERE'S A FROZEN MONKEY ON THE COUCH?
AND A HOOKER?
EVERYO SUCK BUT ME
SHE'S NOT A HOOKER.
SHE'S DRESSED LIKE ONE.
I THINK THAT'S SUPPOSED TO BE SOME SORT OF SUPER HERO COSTUME.
DAD--I'M SPEECHLESS.
GOOD, BECAUSE WE NEED TO HAVE THE KIND OF TALK WHERE YOU LISTEN AND I DO MOST OF THE TALKING.
THEY SEEMED TO THINK YOU WERE LIKE THEM.
HONEY, ARE YOU SOME KIND OF SUPER HERO?

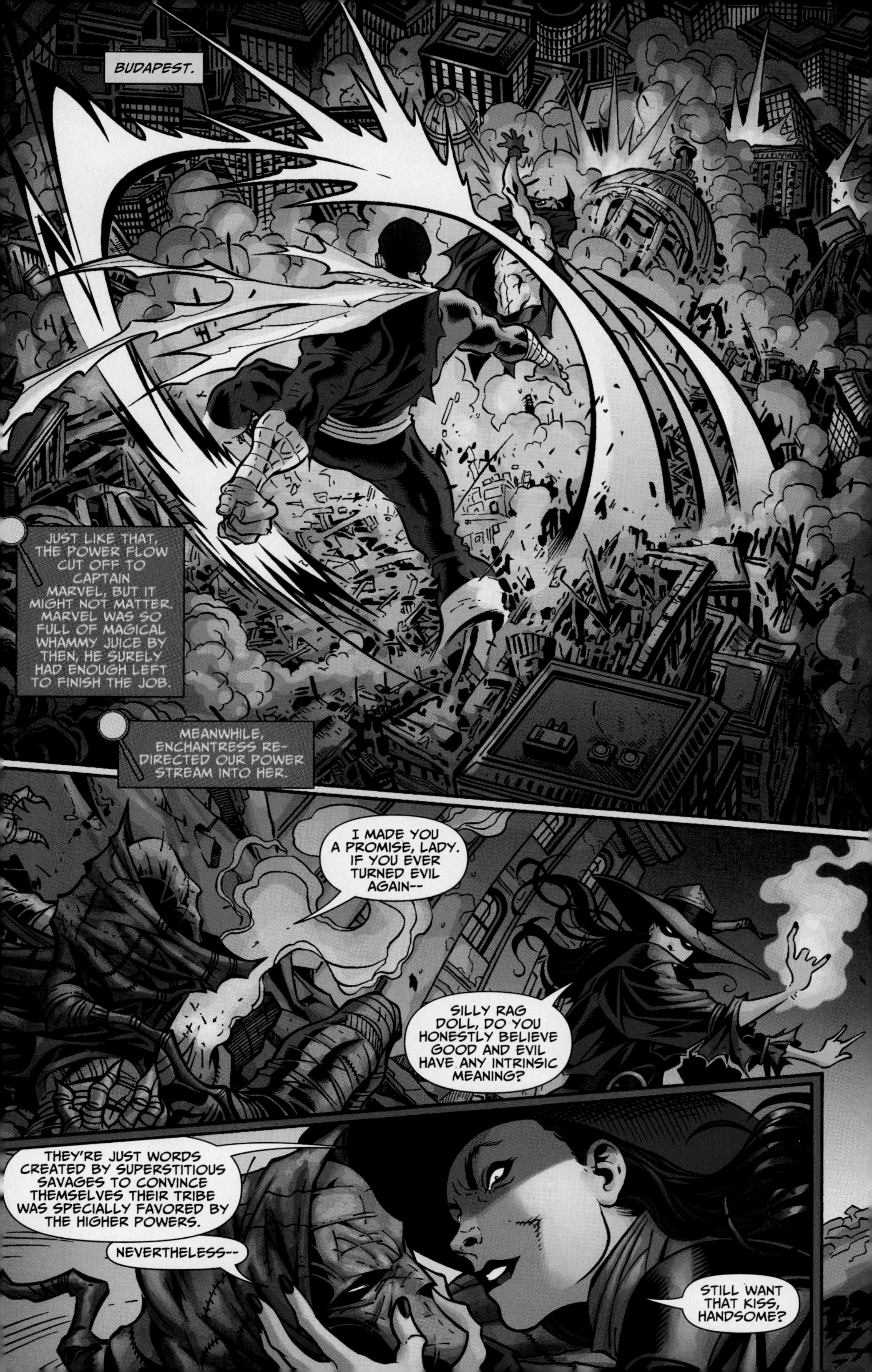
BUDAPEST.
JUST LIKE THAT, THE POWER FLOW CUT OFF TO CAPTAIN MARVEL, BUT IT MIGHT NOT MATTER. MARVEL WAS SO FULL OF MAGICAL WHAMMY JUICE BY THEN, HE SURELY HAD ENOUGH LEFT TO FINISH THE JOB.
MEANWHILE, ENCHANTRESS RE-DIRECTED OUR POWER STREAM INTO HER.
I MADE YOU A PROMISE, LADY. IF YOU EVER TURNED EVIL AGAIN--
SILLY RAG DOLL, DO YOU HONESTLY BELIEVE GOOD AND EVIL HAVE ANY INTRINSIC MEANING?
THEY'RE JUST WORDS CREATED BY SUPERSTITIOUS SAVAGES TO CONVINCE THEMSELVES THEIR TRIBE WAS SPECIALLY FAVORED BY THE HIGHER POWERS.
NEVERTHELESS--
STILL WANT THAT KISS, HANDSOME?

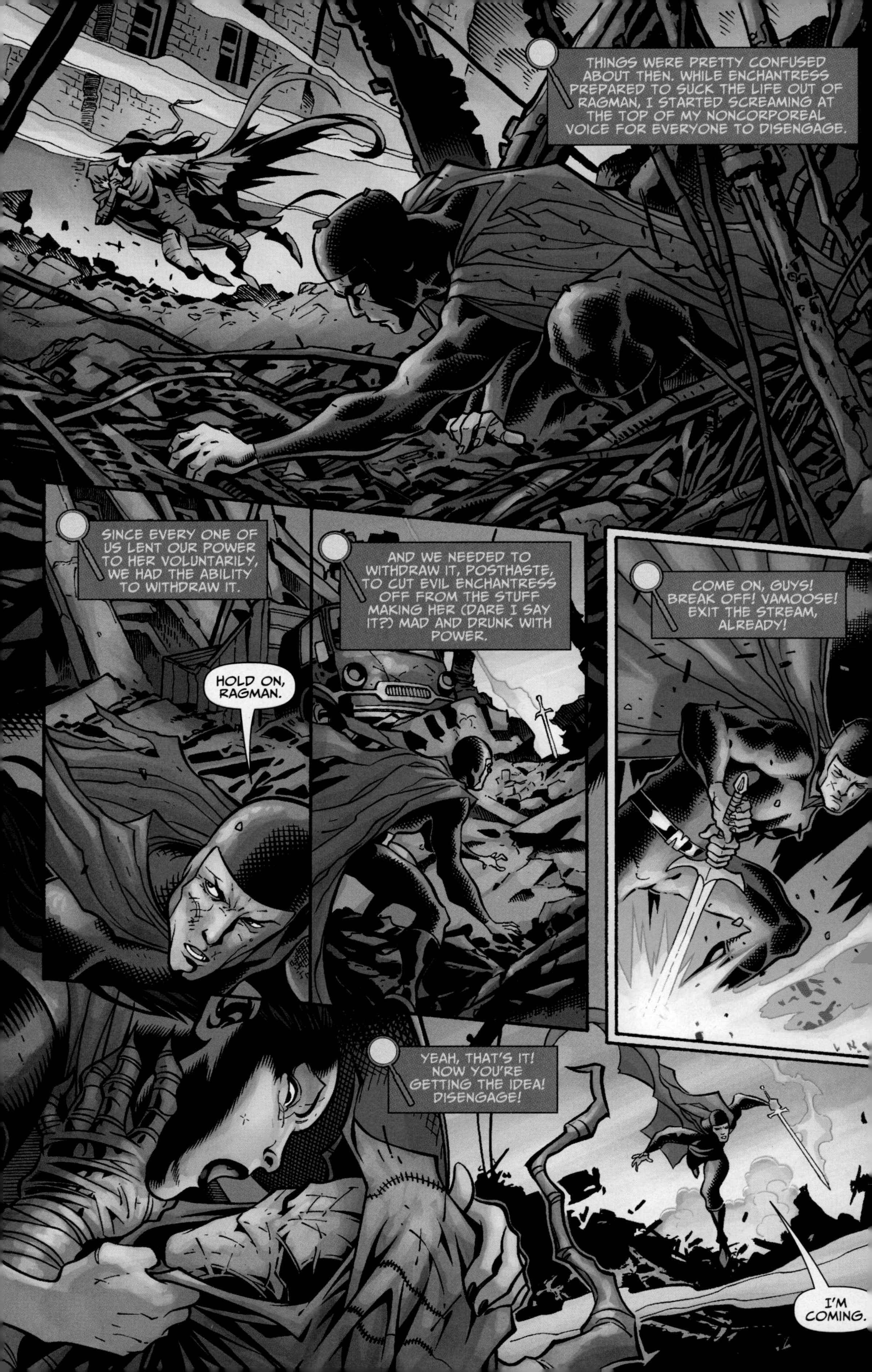
THINGS WERE PRETTY CONFUSED ABOUT THEN. WHILE ENCHANTRESS PREPARED TO SUCK THE LIFE OUT OF RAGMAN, I STARTED SCREAMING AT THE TOP OF MY NONCORPOREAL VOICE FOR EVERYONE TO DISENGAGE.
SINCE EVERY ONE OF US LENT OUR POWER TO HER VOLUNTARILY, WE HAD THE ABILITY TO WITHDRAW IT.
HOLD ON, RAGMAN.
AND WE NEEDED TO WITHDRAW IT, POSTHASTE, TO CUT EVIL ENCHANTRESS OFF FROM THE STUFF MAKING HER (DARE I SAY IT?) MAD AND DRUNK WITH POWER.
COME ON, GUYS! BREAK OFF! VAMOOSE! EXIT THE STREAM, ALREADY!
YEAH, THAT'S IT! NOW YOU'RE GETTING THE IDEA! DISENGAGE!
I'M COMING.

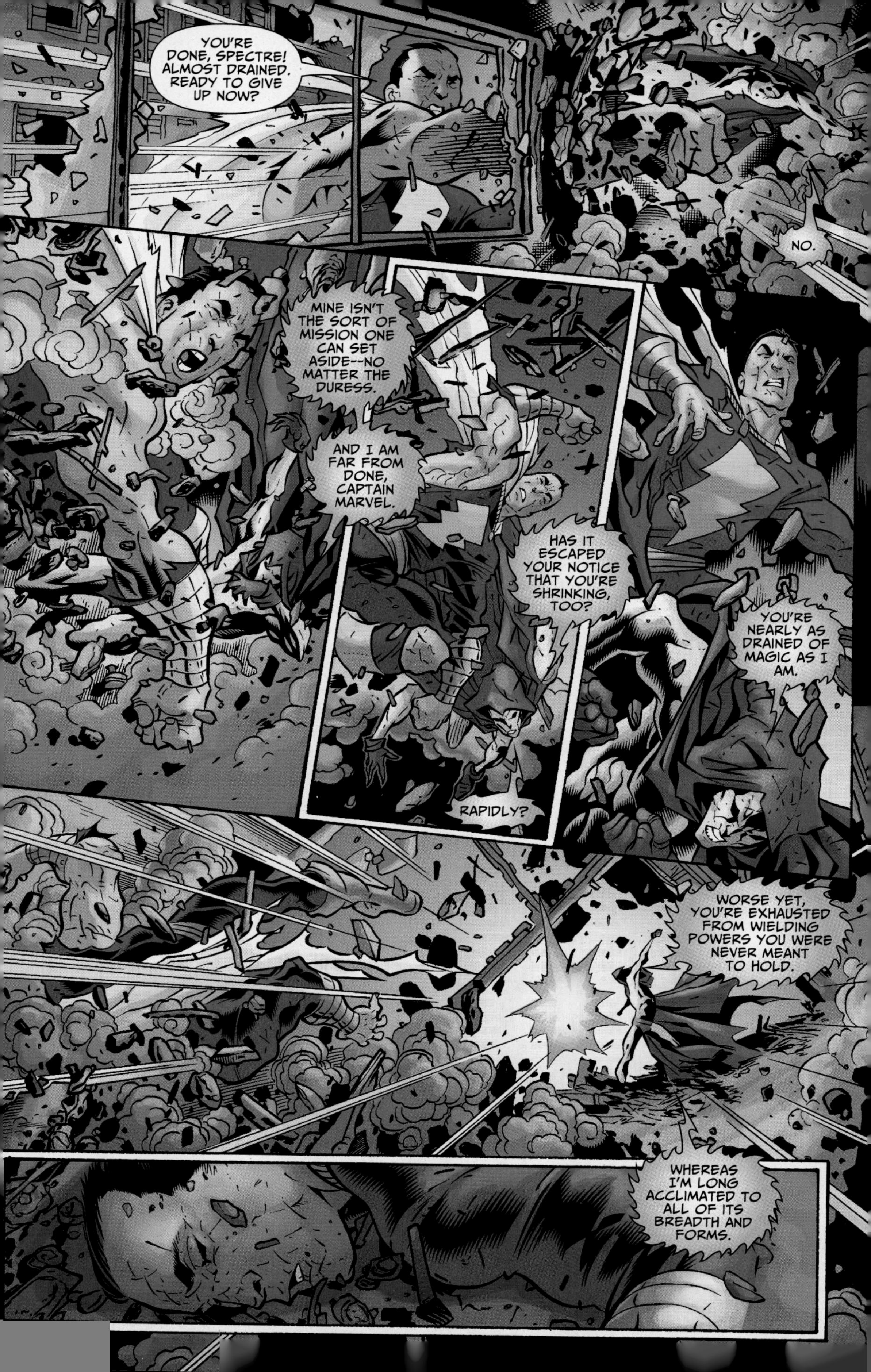
YOU'RE DONE, SPECTRE! ALMOST DRAINED. READY TO GIVE UP NOW?
NO.
MINE ISN'T THE SORT OF MISSION ONE CAN SET ASIDE--NO MATTER THE DURESS.
AND I AM FAR FROM DONE, CAPTAIN MARVEL.
HAS IT ESCAPED YOUR NOTICE THAT YOU'RE SHRINKING, TOO?
RAPIDLY?
YOU'RE NEARLY AS DRAINED OF MAGIC AS I AM.
WORSE YET, YOU'RE EXHAUSTED FROM WIELDING POWERS YOU WERE NEVER MEANT TO HOLD.
WHEREAS I'M LONG ACCLIMATED TO ALL OF ITS BREADTH AND FORMS.

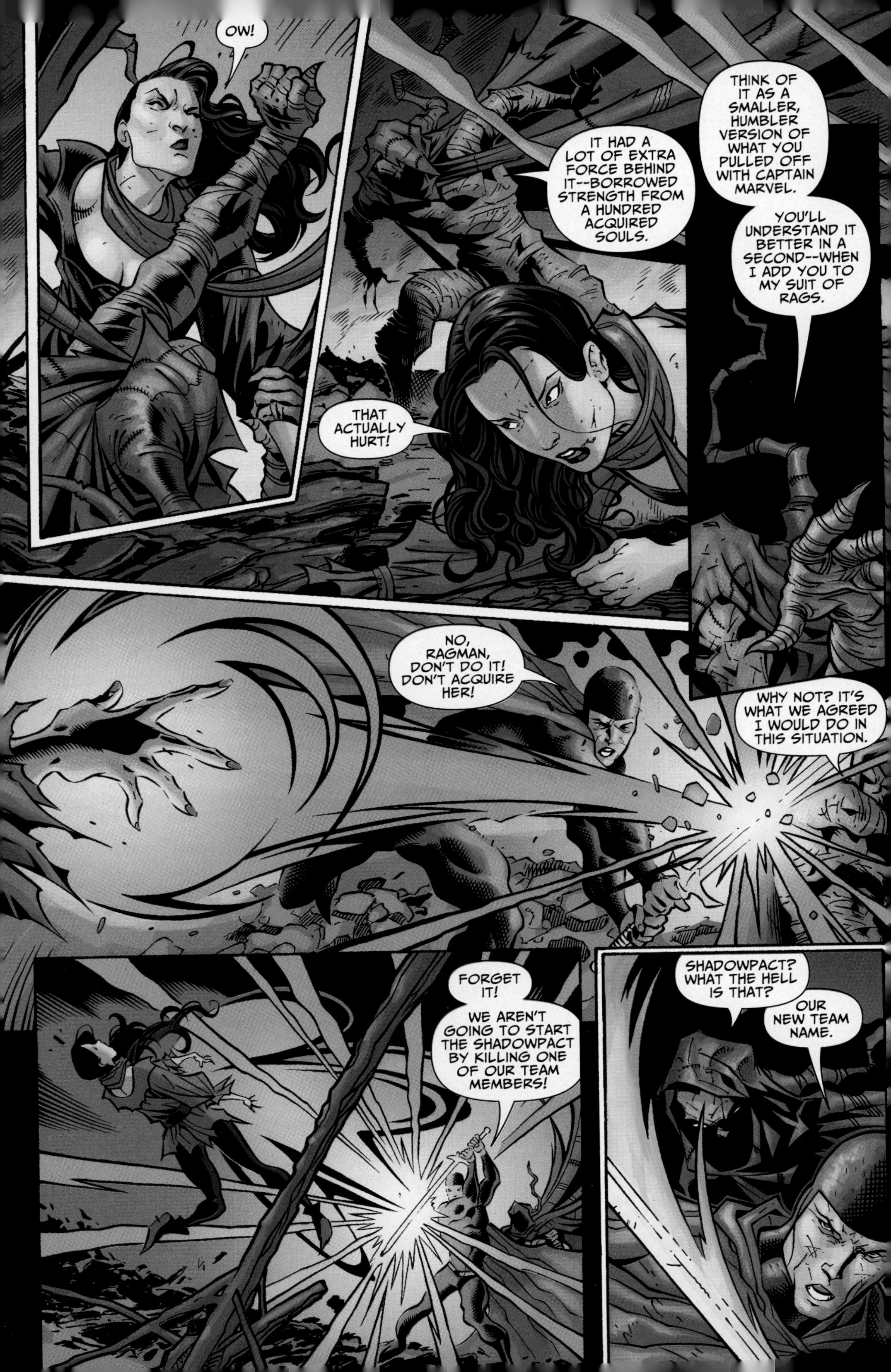
OW!
IT HAD A LOT OF EXTRA FORCE BEHIND IT--BORROWED STRENGTH FROM A HUNDRED ACQUIRED SOULS.
THINK OF IT AS A SMALLER, HUMBLER VERSION OF WHAT YOU PULLED OFF WITH CAPTAIN MARVEL.
YOU'LL UNDERSTAND IT BETTER IN A SECOND--WHEN I ADD YOU TO MY SUIT OF RAGS.
THAT ACTUALLY HURT!
NO, RAGMAN, DON'T DO IT! DON'T ACQUIRE HER!
WHY NOT? IT'S WHAT WE AGREED I WOULD DO IN THIS SITUATION.
FORGET IT!
WE AREN'T GOING TO START THE SHADOWPACT BY KILLING ONE OF OUR TEAM MEMBERS!
SHADOWPACT? WHAT THE HELL IS THAT?
OUR NEW TEAM NAME.

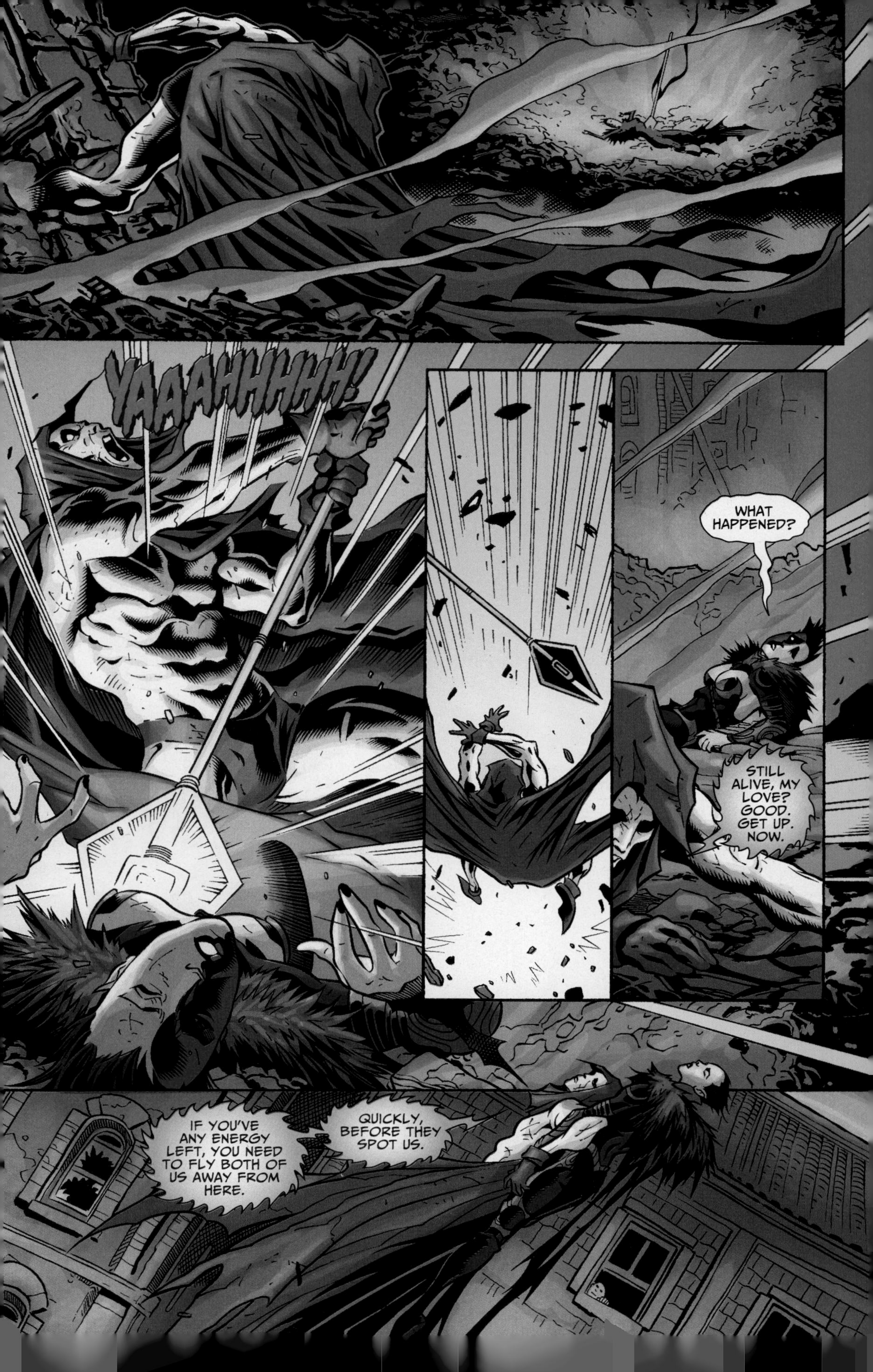
YAAAHHHHH!
WHAT HAPPENED?
STILL ALIVE, MY LOVE? GOOD. GET UP. NOW.
IF YOU'VE ANY ENERGY LEFT, YOU NEED TO FLY BOTH OF US AWAY FROM HERE.
QUICKLY, BEFORE THEY SPOT US.

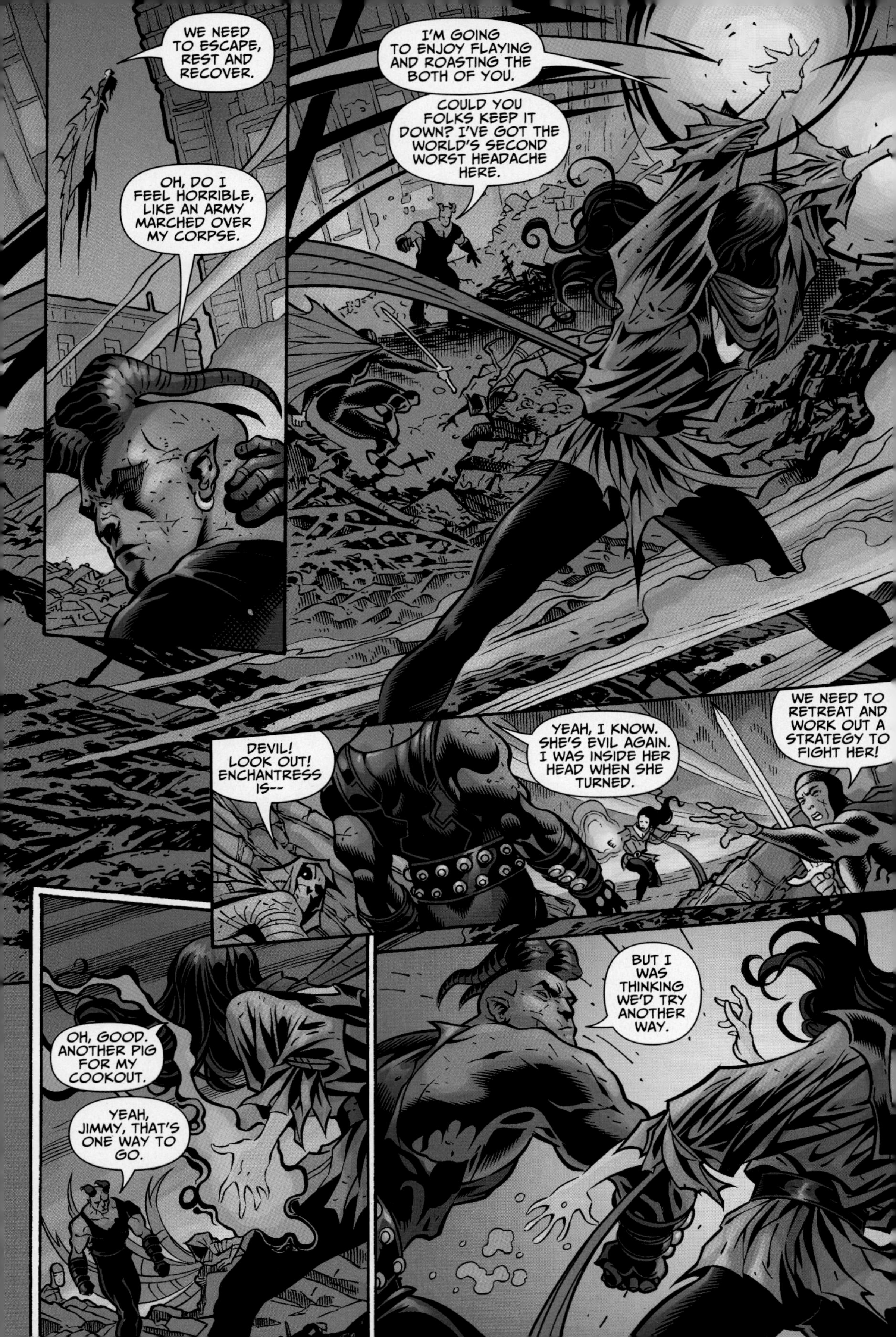
WE NEED TO ESCAPE, REST AND RECOVER.
OH, DO I FEEL HORRIBLE, LIKE AN ARMY MARCHED OVER MY CORPSE.
I'M GOING TO ENJOY FLAYING AND ROASTING THE BOTH OF YOU.
COULD YOU FOLKS KEEP IT DOWN? I'VE GOT THE WORLD'S SECOND WORST HEADACHE HERE.
DEVIL! LOOK OUT! ENCHANTRESS IS--
YEAH, I KNOW. SHE'S EVIL AGAIN. I WAS INSIDE HER HEAD WHEN SHE TURNED.
WE NEED TO RETREAT AND WORK OUT A STRATEGY TO FIGHT HER!
OH, GOOD. ANOTHER PIG FOR MY COOKOUT.
YEAH, JIMMY, THAT'S ONE WAY TO GO.
BUT I WAS THINKING WE'D TRY ANOTHER WAY.

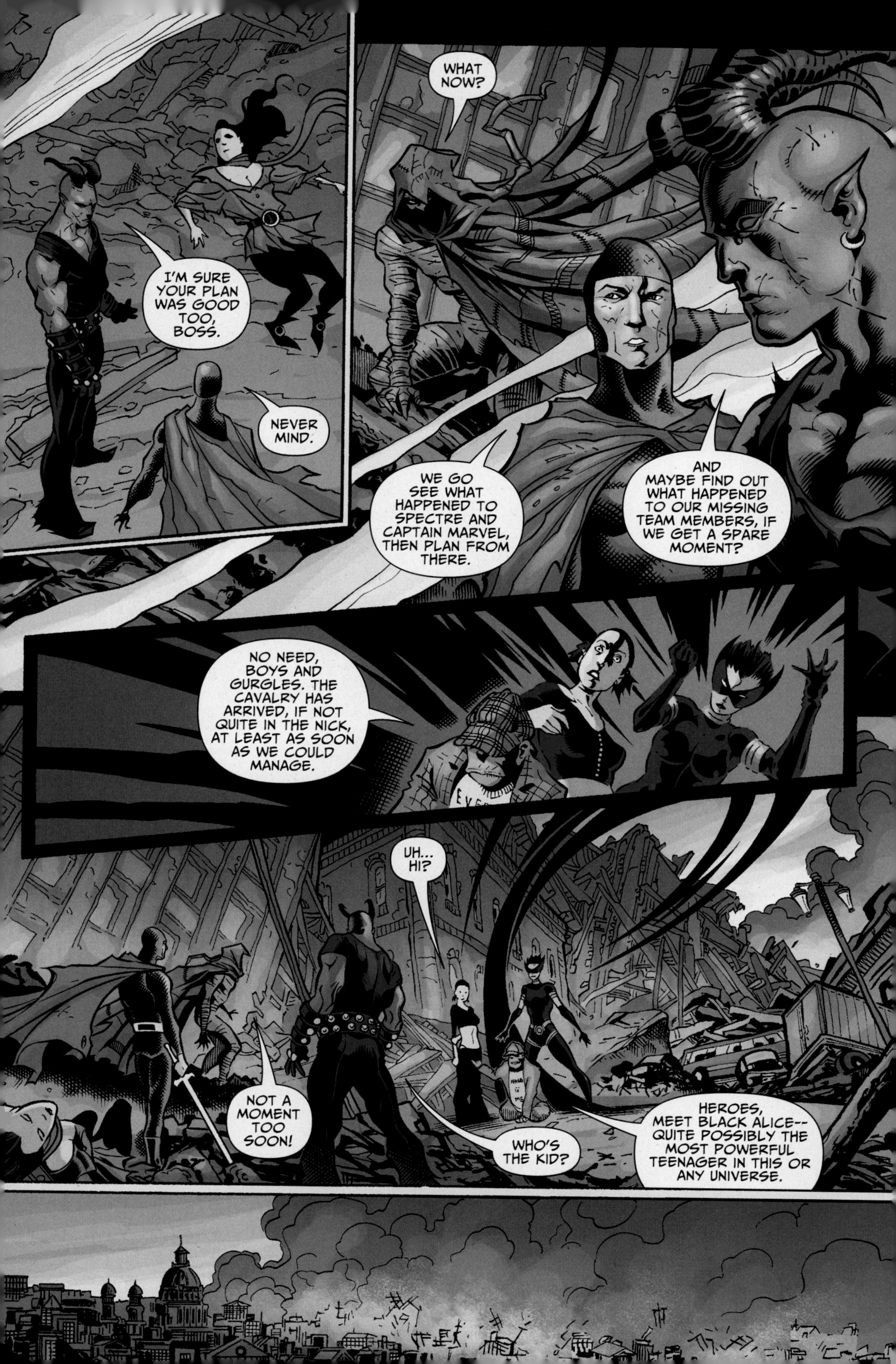
I'M SURE YOUR PLAN WAS GOOD TOO, BOSS.
NEVER MIND.
WHAT NOW?
WE GO SEE WHAT HAPPENED TO SPECTRE AND CAPTAIN MARVEL, THEN PLAN FROM THERE.
AND MAYBE FIND OUT WHAT HAPPENED TO OUR MISSING TEAM MEMBERS, IF WE GET A SPARE MOMENT?
NO NEED, BOYS AND GURGLES. THE CAVALRY HAS ARRIVED, IF NOT QUITE IN THE NICK, AT LEAST AS SOON AS WE COULD MANAGE.
UH... HI?
NOT A MOMENT TOO SOON!
WHO'S THE KID?
HEROES, MEET BLACK ALICE-- QUITE POSSIBLY THE MOST POWERFUL TEENAGER IN THIS OR ANY UNIVERSE.

DAY OF VENGEANCE

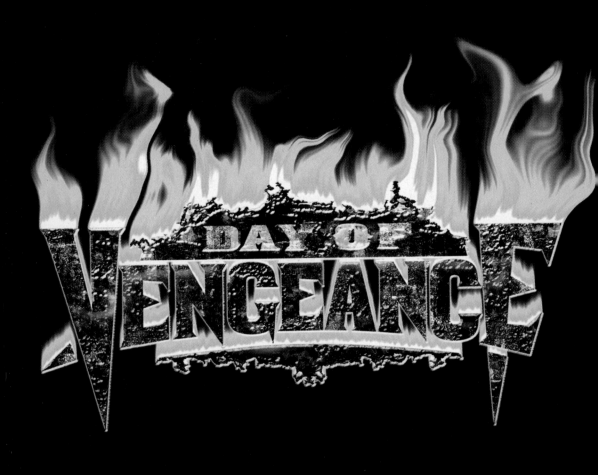

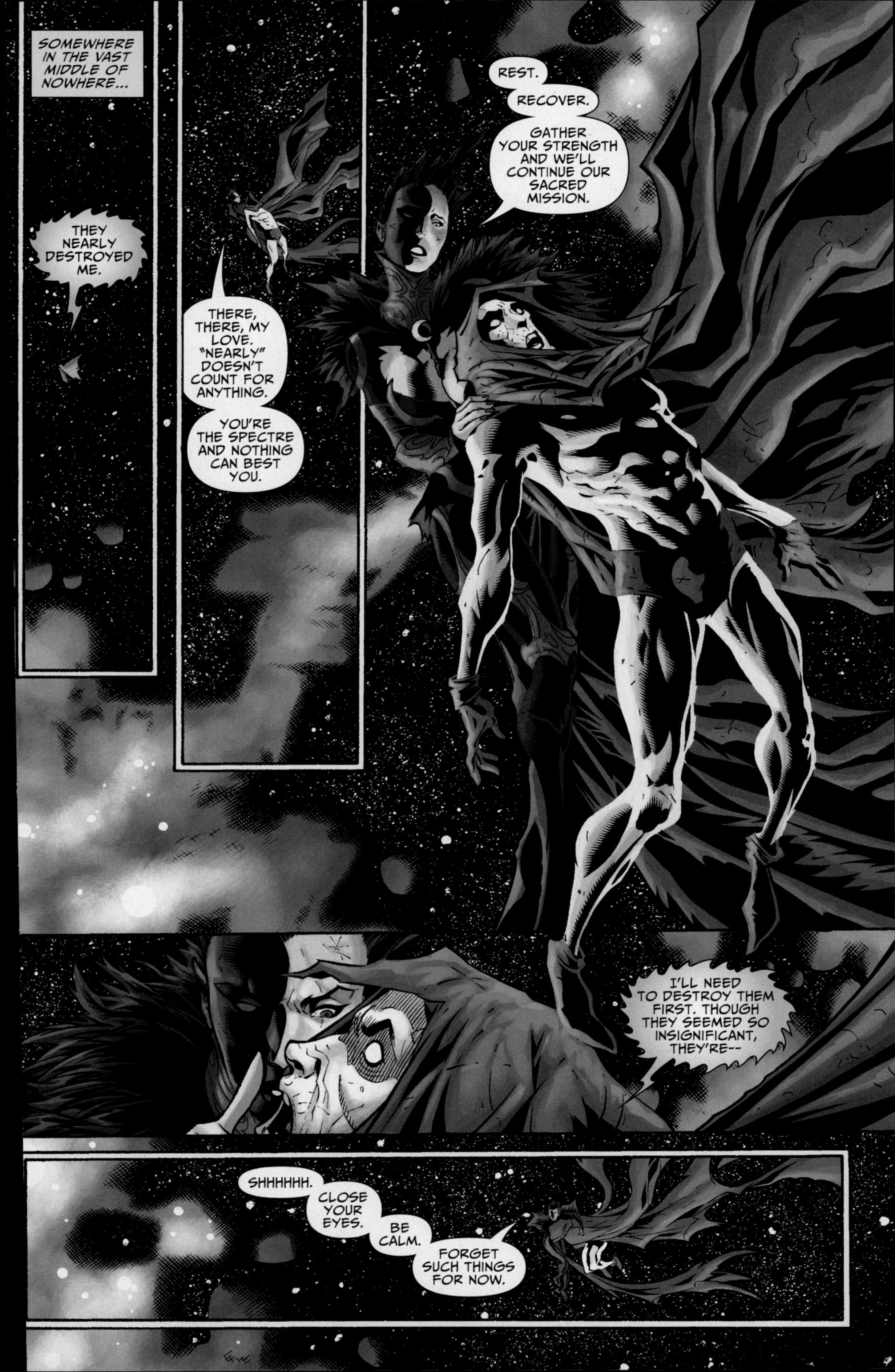
SOMEWHERE IN THE VAST MIDDLE OF NOWHERE...
THEY NEARLY DESTROYED ME.
THERE, THERE, MY LOVE. "NEARLY" DOESN'T COUNT FOR ANYTHING.
YOU'RE THE SPECTRE AND NOTHING CAN BEST YOU.
REST.
RECOVER.
GATHER YOUR STRENGTH AND WE'LL CONTINUE OUR SACRED MISSION.
I'LL NEED TO DESTROY THEM FIRST. THOUGH THEY SEEMED SO INSIGNIFICANT, THEY'RE--
SHHHHHH.
CLOSE YOUR EYES.
BE CALM.
FORGET SUCH THINGS FOR NOW.

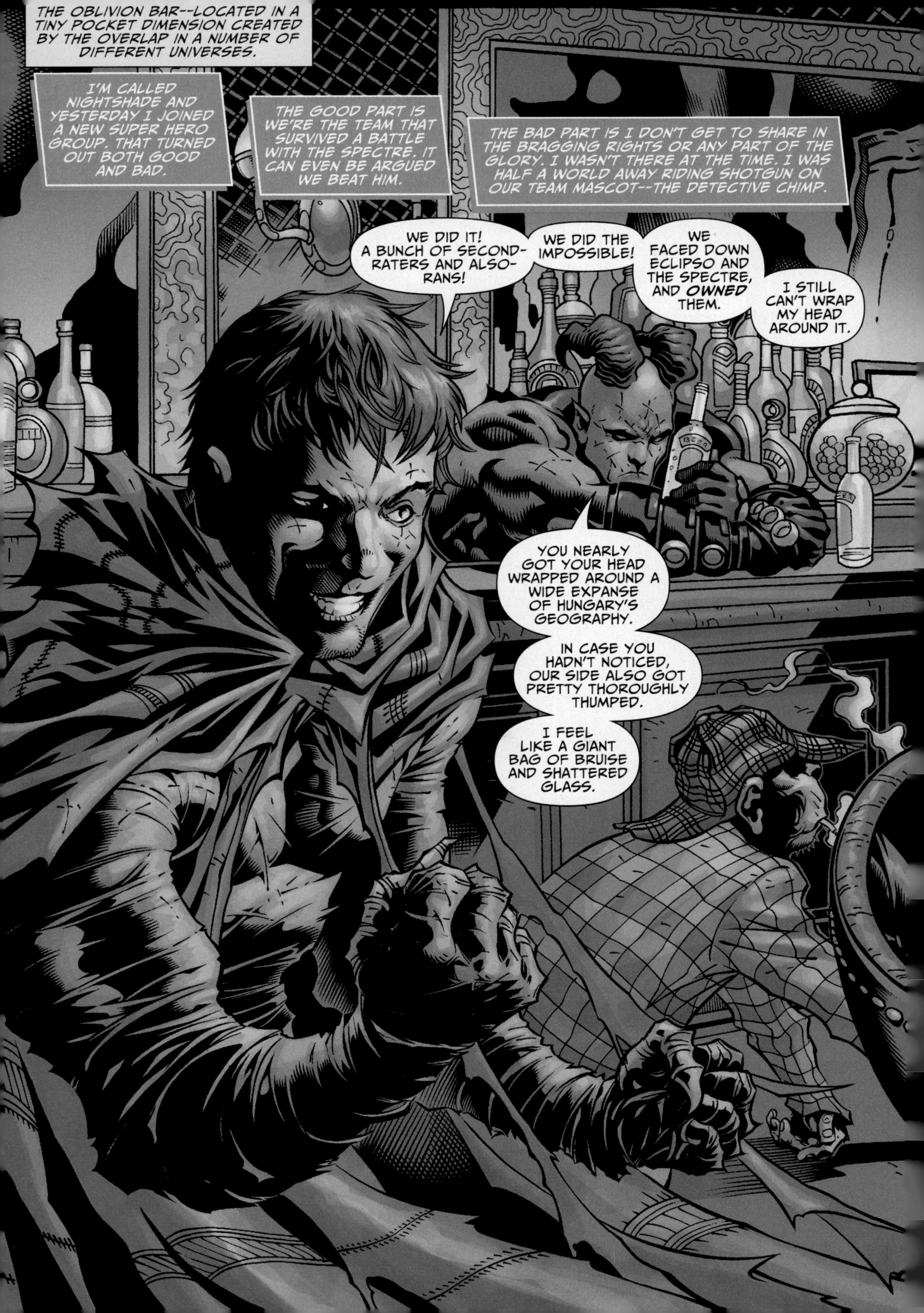
THE OBLIVION BAR--LOCATED IN A TINY POCKET DIMENSION CREATED BY THE OVERLAP IN A NUMBER OF DIFFERENT UNIVERSES.
I'M CALLED NIGHTSHADE AND YESTERDAY I JOINED A NEW SUPER HERO GROUP. THAT TURNED OUT BOTH GOOD AND BAD.
THE GOOD PART IS WE'RE THE TEAM THAT SURVIVED A BATTLE WITH THE SPECTRE. IT CAN EVEN BE ARGUED WE BEAT HIM.
THE BAD PART IS I DON'T GET TO SHARE IN THE BRAGGING RIGHTS OR ANY PART OF THE GLORY. I WASN'T THERE AT THE TIME. I WAS HALF A WORLD AWAY RIDING SHOTGUN ON OUR TEAM MASCOT--THE DETECTIVE CHIMP.
WE DID IT! A BUNCH OF SECOND-RATERS AND ALSO-RANS!
WE DID THE IMPOSSIBLE!
WE FACED DOWN ECLIPSO AND THE SPECTRE, AND **OWNED** THEM.
I STILL CAN'T WRAP MY HEAD AROUND IT.
YOU NEARLY GOT YOUR HEAD WRAPPED AROUND A WIDE EXPANSE OF HUNGARY'S GEOGRAPHY.
IN CASE YOU HADN'T NOTICED, OUR SIDE ALSO GOT PRETTY THOROUGHLY THUMPED.
I FEEL LIKE A GIANT BAG OF BRUISE AND SHATTERED GLASS.

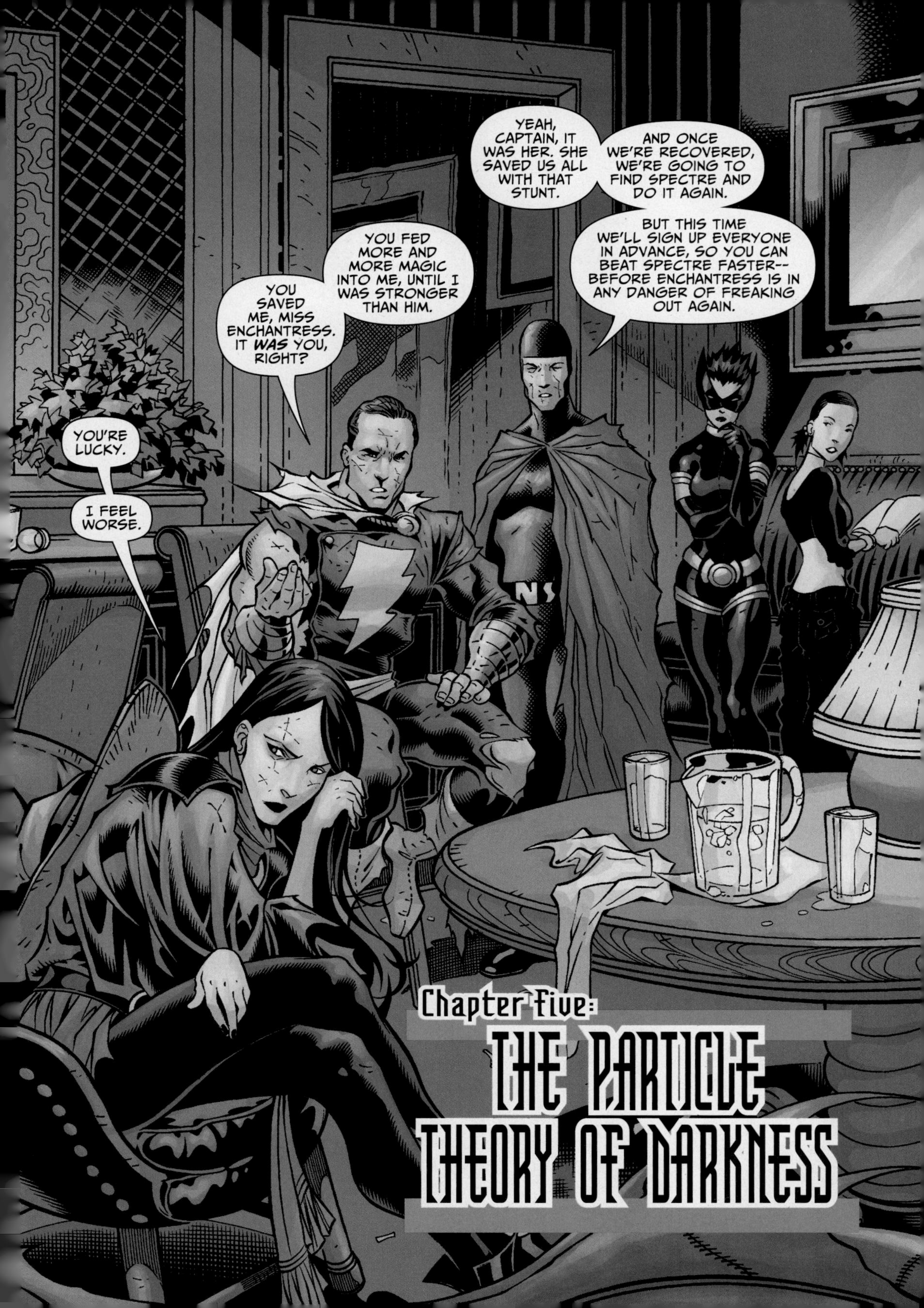
YOU SAVED ME, MISS ENCHANTRESS. IT **WAS** YOU, RIGHT?
YOU FED MORE AND MORE MAGIC INTO ME, UNTIL I WAS STRONGER THAN HIM.
YEAH, CAPTAIN, IT WAS HER. SHE SAVED US ALL WITH THAT STUNT.
AND ONCE WE'RE RECOVERED, WE'RE GOING TO FIND SPECTRE AND DO IT AGAIN.
BUT THIS TIME WE'LL SIGN UP EVERYONE IN ADVANCE, SO YOU CAN BEAT SPECTRE FASTER-- BEFORE ENCHANTRESS IS IN ANY DANGER OF FREAKING OUT AGAIN.
YOU'RE LUCKY.
I FEEL WORSE.
Chapter Five:
THE PARTICLE THEORY OF DARKNESS

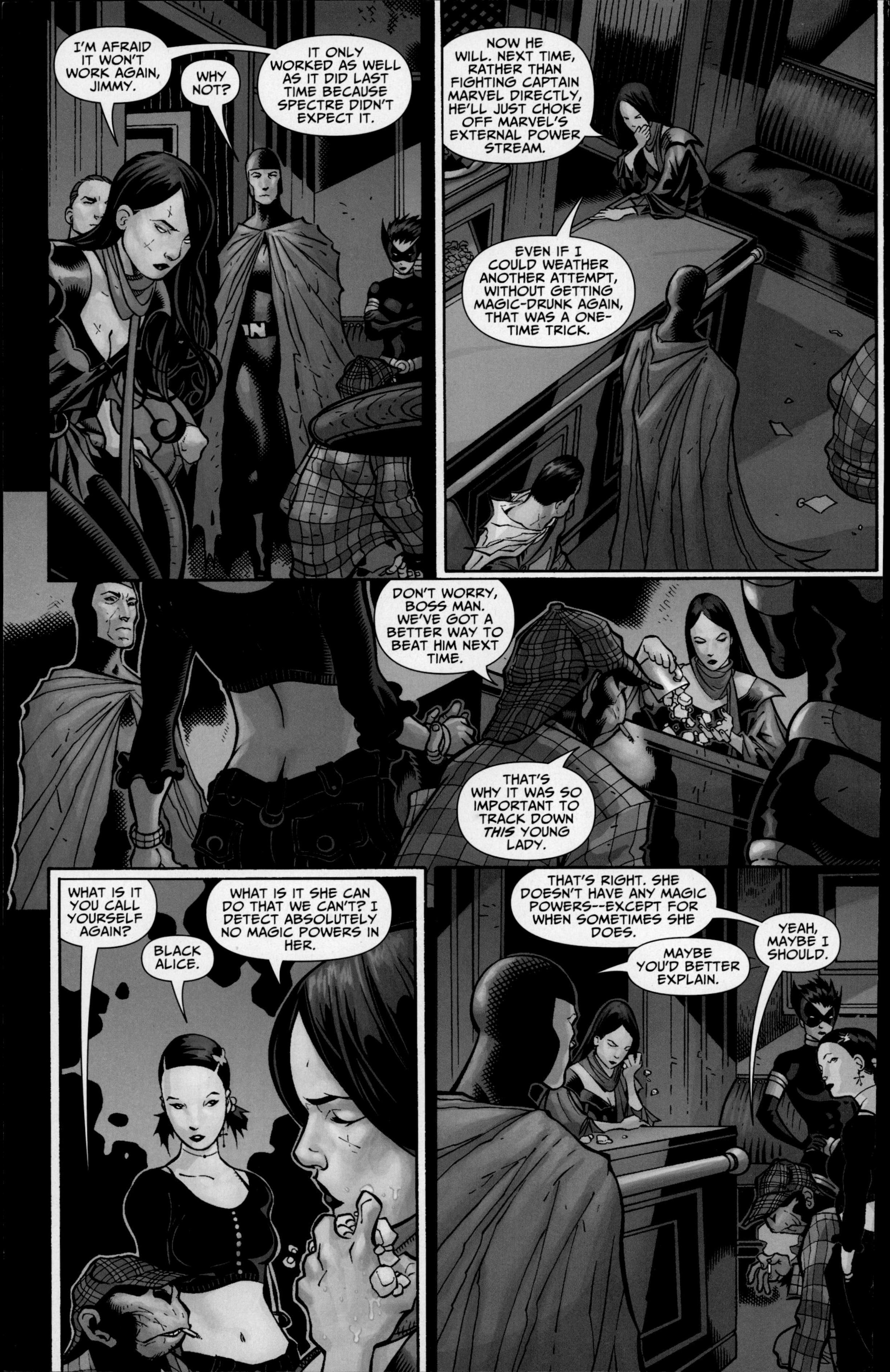

I'M AFRAID IT WON'T WORK AGAIN, JIMMY.
WHY NOT?
IT ONLY WORKED AS WELL AS IT DID LAST TIME BECAUSE SPECTRE DIDN'T EXPECT IT.
NOW HE WILL. NEXT TIME, RATHER THAN FIGHTING CAPTAIN MARVEL DIRECTLY, HE'LL JUST CHOKE OFF MARVEL'S EXTERNAL POWER STREAM.
EVEN IF I COULD WEATHER ANOTHER ATTEMPT, WITHOUT GETTING MAGIC-DRUNK AGAIN, THAT WAS A ONE-TIME TRICK.
DON'T WORRY, BOSS MAN. WE'VE GOT A BETTER WAY TO BEAT HIM NEXT TIME.
THAT'S WHY IT WAS SO IMPORTANT TO TRACK DOWN *THIS* YOUNG LADY.
WHAT IS IT YOU CALL YOURSELF AGAIN?
BLACK ALICE.
WHAT IS IT SHE CAN DO THAT WE CAN'T? I DETECT ABSOLUTELY NO MAGIC POWERS IN HER.
THAT'S RIGHT. SHE DOESN'T HAVE ANY MAGIC POWERS--EXCEPT FOR WHEN SOMETIMES SHE DOES.
MAYBE YOU'D BETTER EXPLAIN.
YEAH, MAYBE I SHOULD.

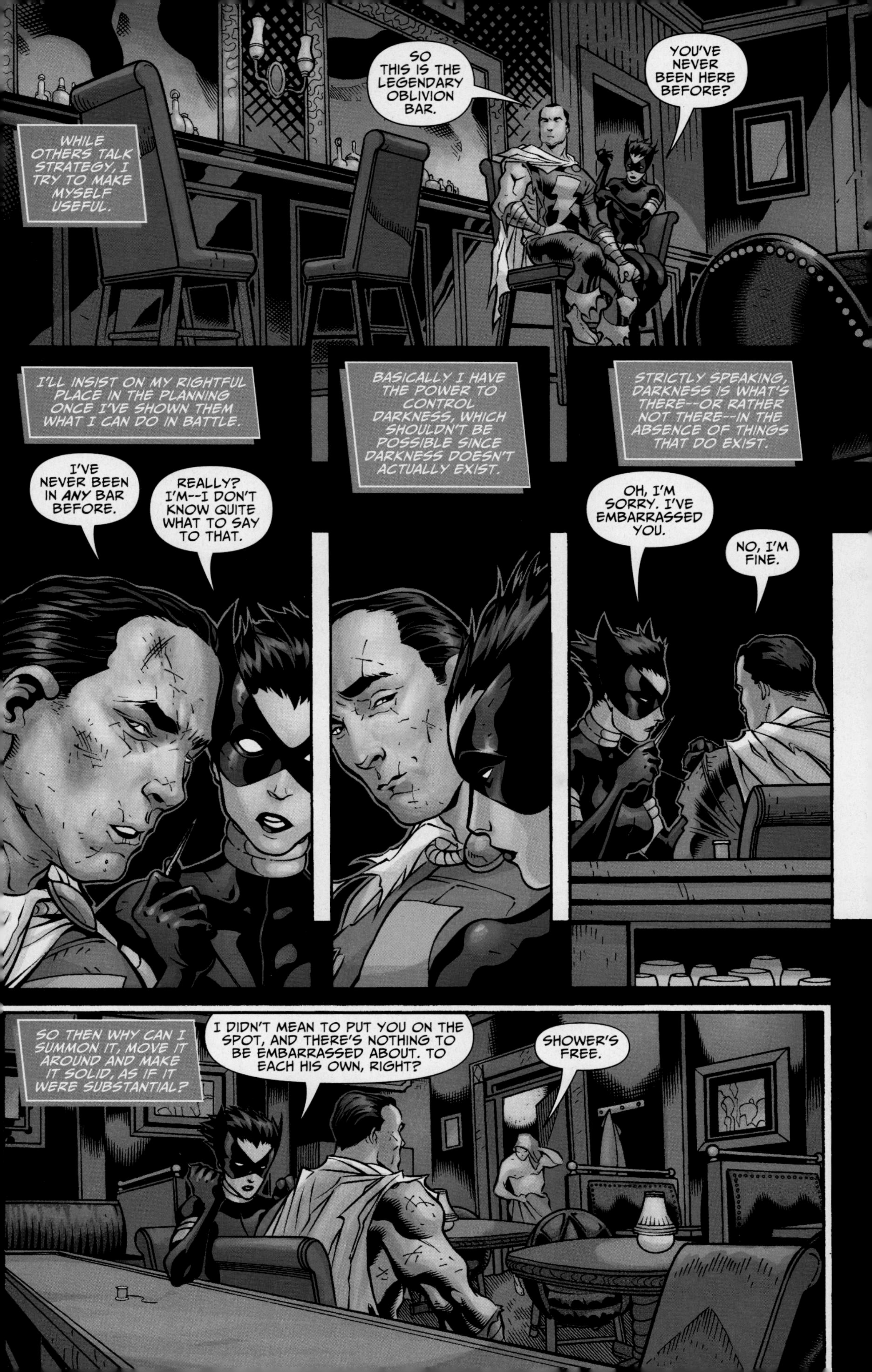
WHILE OTHERS TALK STRATEGY, I TRY TO MAKE MYSELF USEFUL.
SO THIS IS THE LEGENDARY OBLIVION BAR.
YOU'VE NEVER BEEN HERE BEFORE?
I'LL INSIST ON MY RIGHTFUL PLACE IN THE PLANNING ONCE I'VE SHOWN THEM WHAT I CAN DO IN BATTLE.
I'VE NEVER BEEN IN ANY BAR BEFORE.
REALLY? I'M--I DON'T KNOW QUITE WHAT TO SAY TO THAT.
BASICALLY I HAVE THE POWER TO CONTROL DARKNESS, WHICH SHOULDN'T BE POSSIBLE SINCE DARKNESS DOESN'T ACTUALLY EXIST.
STRICTLY SPEAKING, DARKNESS IS WHAT'S THERE--OR RATHER NOT THERE--IN THE ABSENCE OF THINGS THAT DO EXIST.
OH, I'M SORRY. I'VE EMBARRASSED YOU.
NO, I'M FINE.
SO THEN WHY CAN I SUMMON IT, MOVE IT AROUND AND MAKE IT SOLID, AS IF IT WERE SUBSTANTIAL?
I DIDN'T MEAN TO PUT YOU ON THE SPOT, AND THERE'S NOTHING TO BE EMBARRASSED ABOUT. TO EACH HIS OWN, RIGHT?
SHOWER'S FREE.

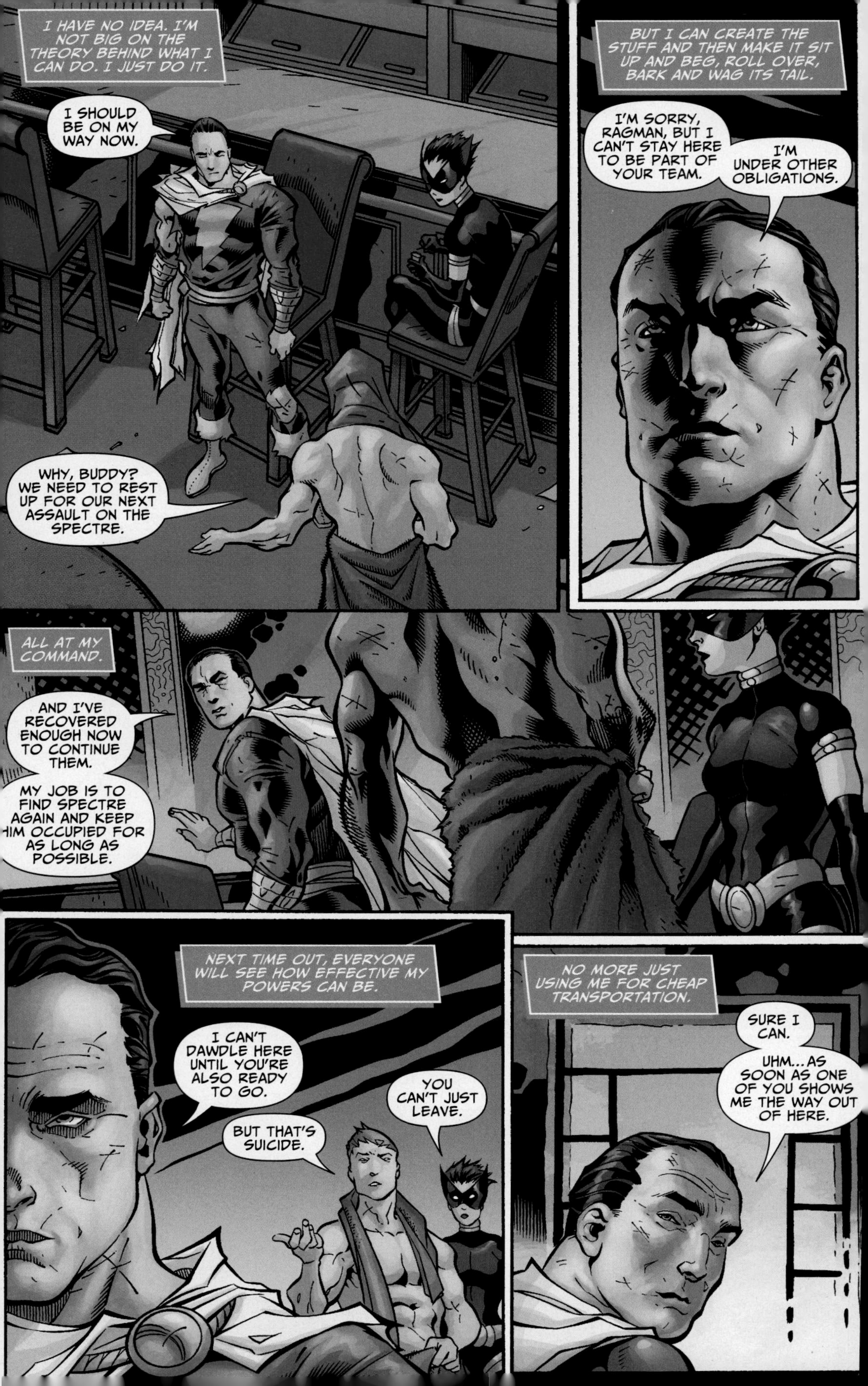
I HAVE NO IDEA. I'M NOT BIG ON THE THEORY BEHIND WHAT I CAN DO. I JUST DO IT.
I SHOULD BE ON MY WAY NOW.
WHY, BUDDY? WE NEED TO REST UP FOR OUR NEXT ASSAULT ON THE SPECTRE.
BUT I CAN CREATE THE STUFF AND THEN MAKE IT SIT UP AND BEG, ROLL OVER, BARK AND WAG ITS TAIL.
I'M SORRY, RAGMAN, BUT I CAN'T STAY HERE TO BE PART OF YOUR TEAM.
I'M UNDER OTHER OBLIGATIONS.
ALL AT MY COMMAND.
AND I'VE RECOVERED ENOUGH NOW TO CONTINUE THEM.
MY JOB IS TO FIND SPECTRE AGAIN AND KEEP HIM OCCUPIED FOR AS LONG AS POSSIBLE.
NEXT TIME OUT, EVERYONE WILL SEE HOW EFFECTIVE MY POWERS CAN BE.
I CAN'T DAWDLE HERE UNTIL YOU'RE ALSO READY TO GO.
BUT THAT'S SUICIDE.
YOU CAN'T JUST LEAVE.
NO MORE JUST USING ME FOR CHEAP TRANSPORTATION.
SURE I CAN.
UHM... AS SOON AS ONE OF YOU SHOWS ME THE WAY OUT OF HERE.

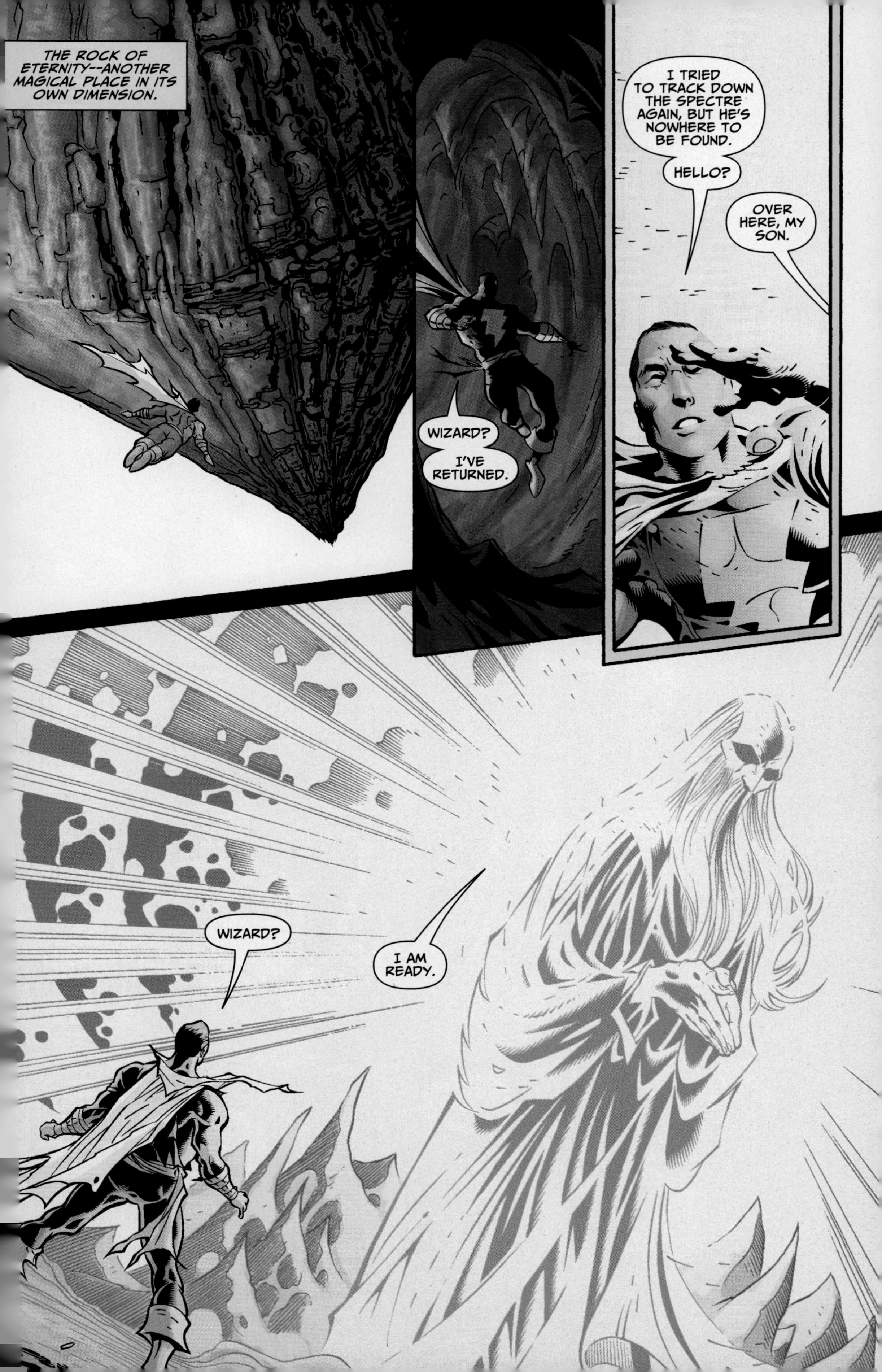
THE ROCK OF ETERNITY--ANOTHER MAGICAL PLACE IN ITS OWN DIMENSION.
WIZARD?
I'VE RETURNED.
I TRIED TO TRACK DOWN THE SPECTRE AGAIN, BUT HE'S NOWHERE TO BE FOUND.
HELLO?
OVER HERE, MY SON.
WIZARD?
I AM READY.

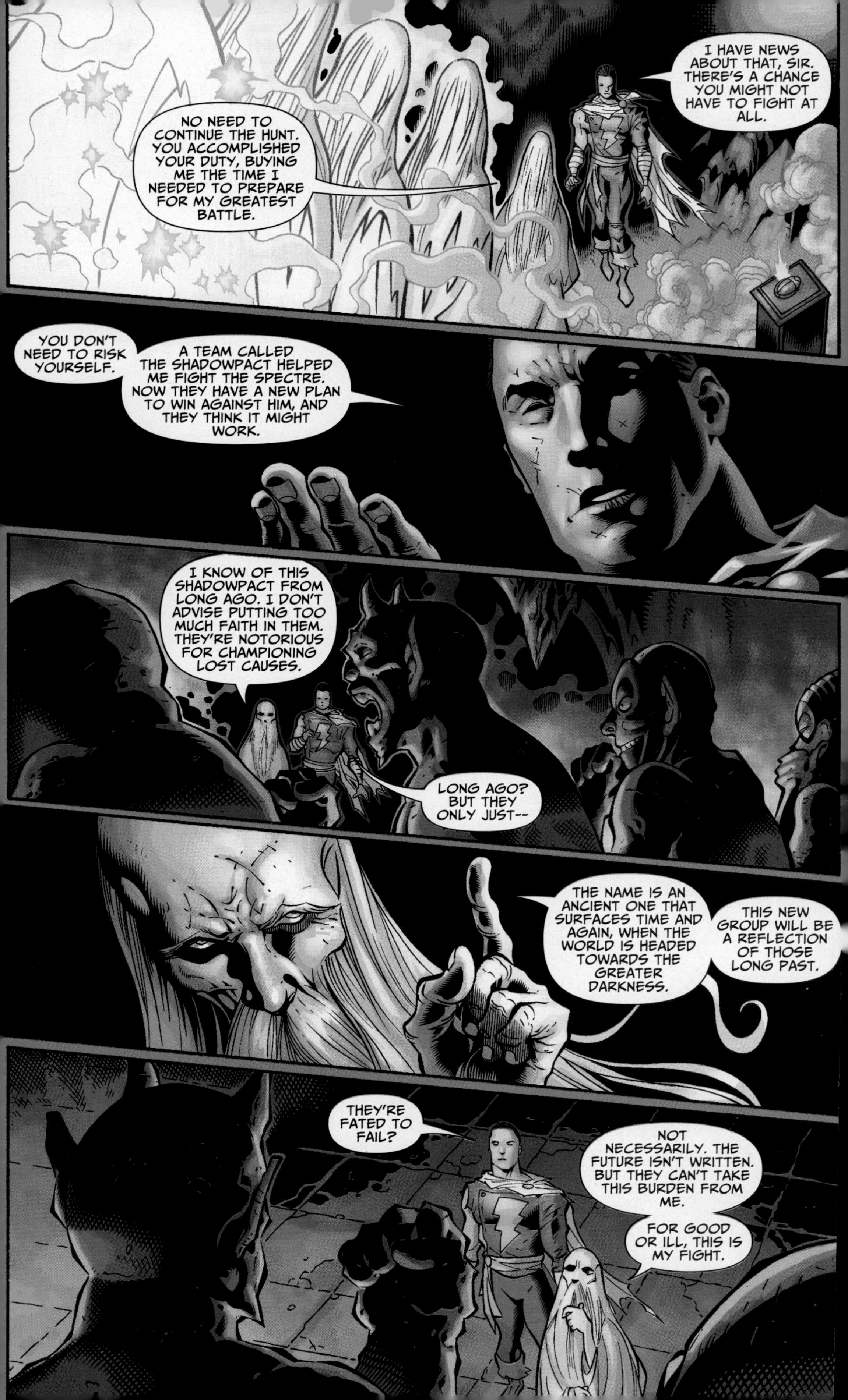
NO NEED TO CONTINUE THE HUNT. YOU ACCOMPLISHED YOUR DUTY, BUYING ME THE TIME I NEEDED TO PREPARE FOR MY GREATEST BATTLE.
I HAVE NEWS ABOUT THAT, SIR. THERE'S A CHANCE YOU MIGHT NOT HAVE TO FIGHT AT ALL.
YOU DON'T NEED TO RISK YOURSELF.
A TEAM CALLED THE SHADOWPACT HELPED ME FIGHT THE SPECTRE. NOW THEY HAVE A NEW PLAN TO WIN AGAINST HIM, AND THEY THINK IT MIGHT WORK.
I KNOW OF THIS SHADOWPACT FROM LONG AGO. I DON'T ADVISE PUTTING TOO MUCH FAITH IN THEM. THEY'RE NOTORIOUS FOR CHAMPIONING LOST CAUSES.
LONG AGO? BUT THEY ONLY JUST--
THE NAME IS AN ANCIENT ONE THAT SURFACES TIME AND AGAIN, WHEN THE WORLD IS HEADED TOWARDS THE GREATER DARKNESS.
THIS NEW GROUP WILL BE A REFLECTION OF THOSE LONG PAST.
THEY'RE FATED TO FAIL?
NOT NECESSARILY. THE FUTURE ISN'T WRITTEN. BUT THEY CAN'T TAKE THIS BURDEN FROM ME.
FOR GOOD OR ILL, THIS IS MY FIGHT.

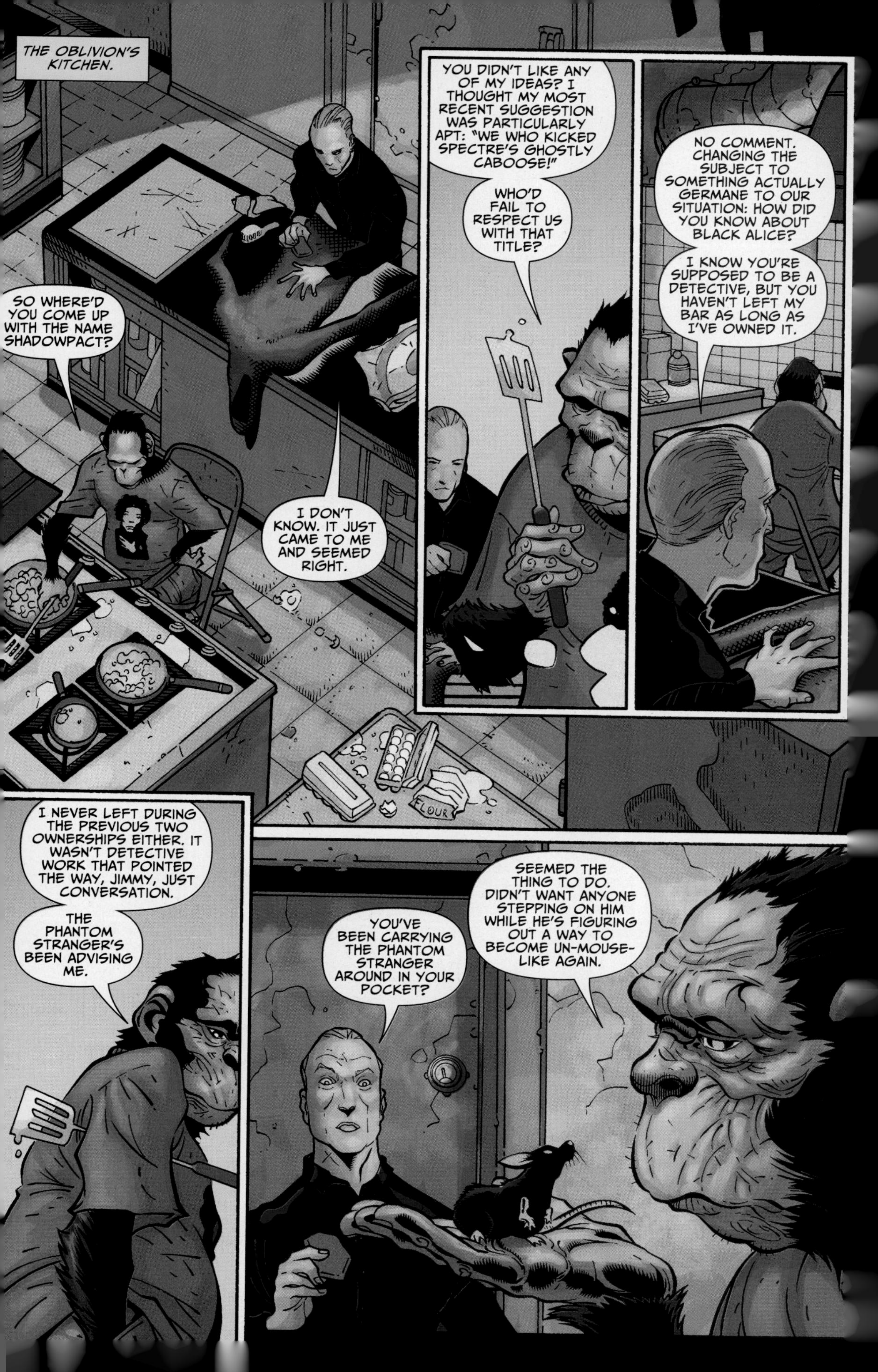
THE OBLIVION'S KITCHEN.
SO WHERE'D YOU COME UP WITH THE NAME SHADOWPACT?
I DON'T KNOW. IT JUST CAME TO ME AND SEEMED RIGHT.
YOU DIDN'T LIKE ANY OF MY IDEAS? I THOUGHT MY MOST RECENT SUGGESTION WAS PARTICULARLY APT: "WE WHO KICKED SPECTRE'S GHOSTLY CABOOSE!"
WHO'D FAIL TO RESPECT US WITH THAT TITLE?
NO COMMENT. CHANGING THE SUBJECT TO SOMETHING ACTUALLY GERMANE TO OUR SITUATION: HOW DID YOU KNOW ABOUT BLACK ALICE?
I KNOW YOU'RE SUPPOSED TO BE A DETECTIVE, BUT YOU HAVEN'T LEFT MY BAR AS LONG AS I'VE OWNED IT.
FLOUR
I NEVER LEFT DURING THE PREVIOUS TWO OWNERSHIPS EITHER. IT WASN'T DETECTIVE WORK THAT POINTED THE WAY, JIMMY, JUST CONVERSATION.
THE PHANTOM STRANGER'S BEEN ADVISING ME.
YOU'VE BEEN CARRYING THE PHANTOM STRANGER AROUND IN YOUR POCKET?
SEEMED THE THING TO DO. DIDN'T WANT ANYONE STEPPING ON HIM WHILE HE'S FIGURING OUT A WAY TO BECOME UN-MOUSE-LIKE AGAIN.

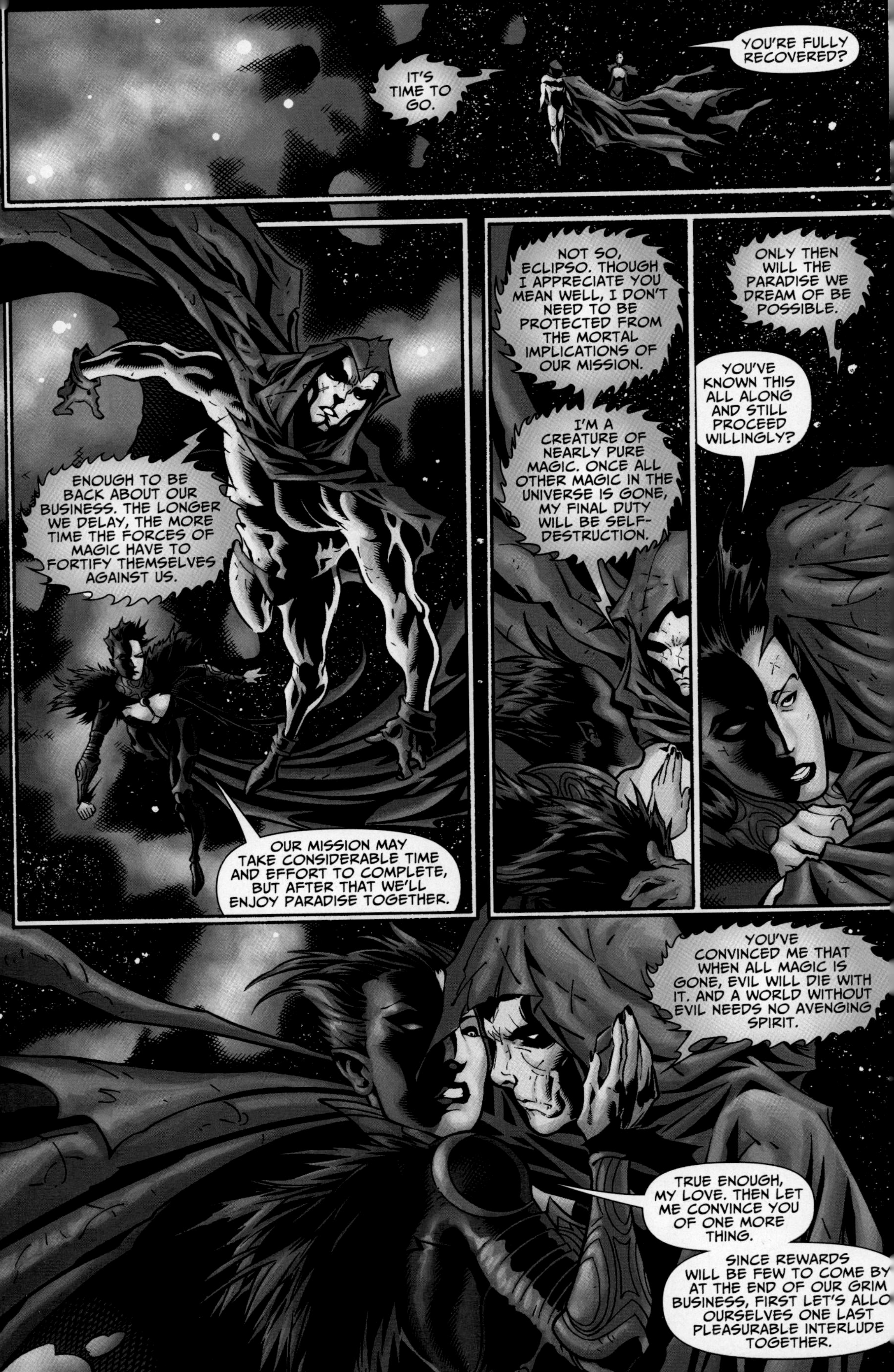
IT'S TIME TO GO.
YOU'RE FULLY RECOVERED?
ENOUGH TO BE BACK ABOUT OUR BUSINESS. THE LONGER WE DELAY, THE MORE TIME THE FORCES OF MAGIC HAVE TO FORTIFY THEMSELVES AGAINST US.
OUR MISSION MAY TAKE CONSIDERABLE TIME AND EFFORT TO COMPLETE, BUT AFTER THAT WE'LL ENJOY PARADISE TOGETHER.
NOT SO, ECLIPSO. THOUGH I APPRECIATE YOU MEAN WELL, I DON'T NEED TO BE PROTECTED FROM THE MORTAL IMPLICATIONS OF OUR MISSION.
I'M A CREATURE OF NEARLY PURE MAGIC. ONCE ALL OTHER MAGIC IN THE UNIVERSE IS GONE, MY FINAL DUTY WILL BE SELF-DESTRUCTION.
ONLY THEN WILL THE PARADISE WE DREAM OF BE POSSIBLE.
YOU'VE KNOWN THIS ALL ALONG AND STILL PROCEED WILLINGLY?
YOU'VE CONVINCED ME THAT WHEN ALL MAGIC IS GONE, EVIL WILL DIE WITH IT. AND A WORLD WITHOUT EVIL NEEDS NO AVENGING SPIRIT.
TRUE ENOUGH, MY LOVE. THEN LET ME CONVINCE YOU OF ONE MORE THING.
SINCE REWARDS WILL BE FEW TO COME BY AT THE END OF OUR GRIM BUSINESS, FIRST LET'S ALLO OURSELVES ONE LAST PLEASURABLE INTERLUDE TOGETHER.

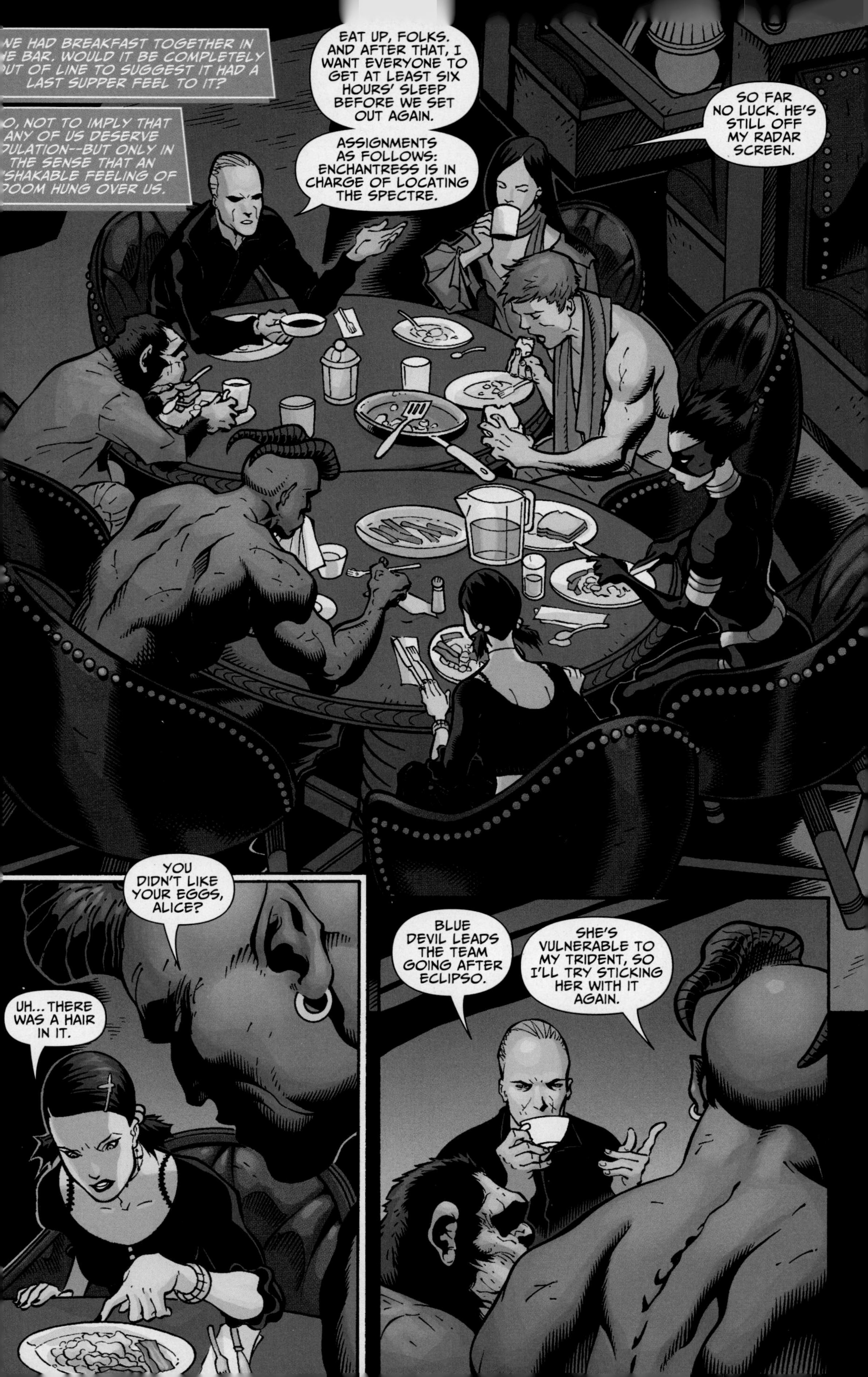

NE HAD BREAKFAST TOGETHER IN HE BAR. WOULD IT BE COMPLETELY UT OF LINE TO SUGGEST IT HAD A LAST SUPPER FEEL TO IT?
O, NOT TO IMPLY THAT ANY OF US DESERVE ULATION--BUT ONLY IN THE SENSE THAT AN 'SHAKABLE FEELING OF OOM HUNG OVER US.
EAT UP, FOLKS. AND AFTER THAT, I WANT EVERYONE TO GET AT LEAST SIX HOURS' SLEEP BEFORE WE SET OUT AGAIN.
ASSIGNMENTS AS FOLLOWS: ENCHANTRESS IS IN CHARGE OF LOCATING THE SPECTRE.
SO FAR NO LUCK. HE'S STILL OFF MY RADAR SCREEN.
YOU DIDN'T LIKE YOUR EGGS, ALICE?
UH... THERE WAS A HAIR IN IT.
BLUE DEVIL LEADS THE TEAM GOING AFTER ECLIPSO.
SHE'S VULNERABLE TO MY TRIDENT, SO I'LL TRY STICKING HER WITH IT AGAIN.

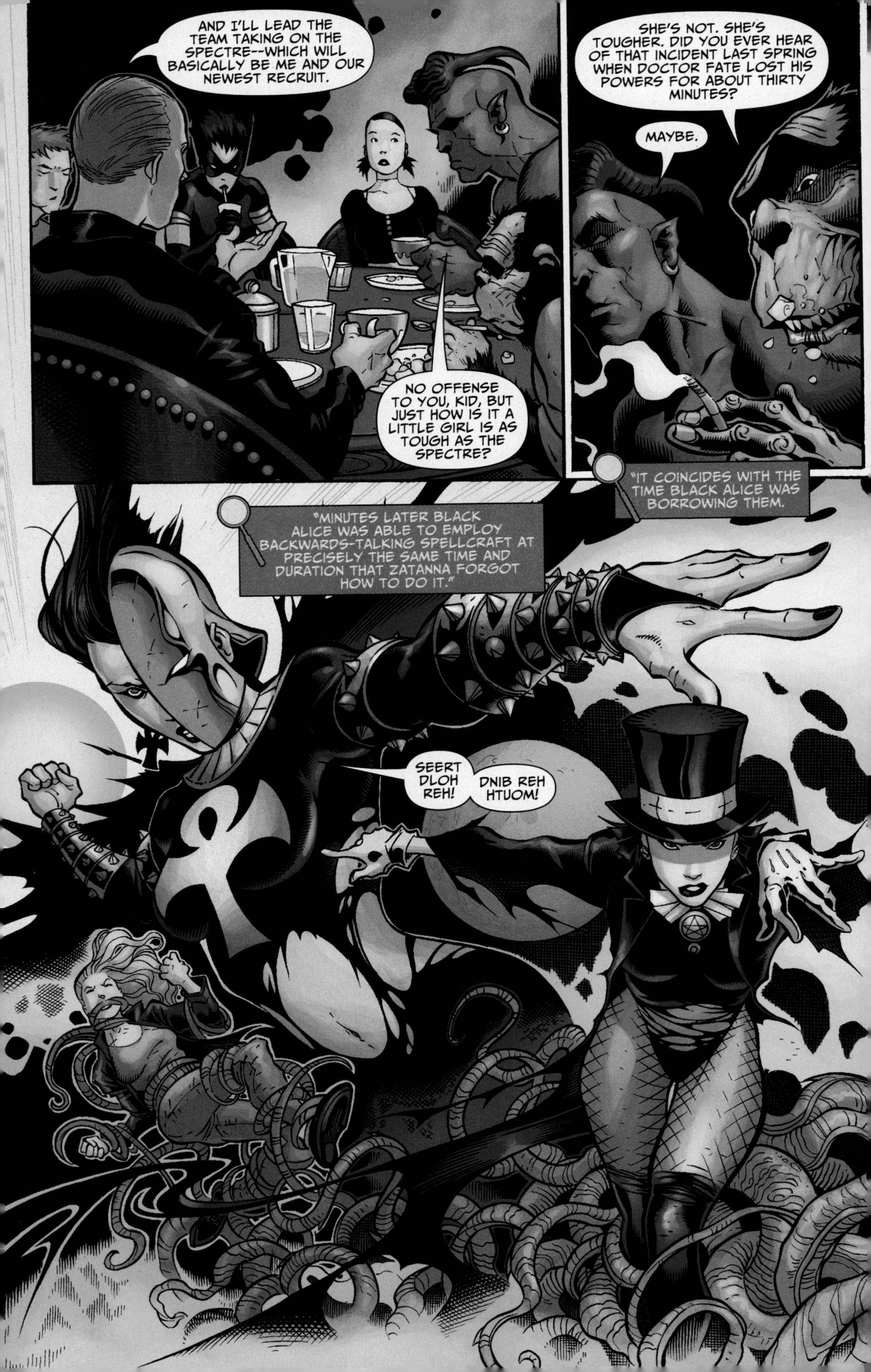
AND I'LL LEAD THE TEAM TAKING ON THE SPECTRE--WHICH WILL BASICALLY BE ME AND OUR NEWEST RECRUIT.
NO OFFENSE TO YOU, KID, BUT JUST HOW IS IT A LITTLE GIRL IS AS TOUGH AS THE SPECTRE?
SHE'S NOT. SHE'S TOUGHER. DID YOU EVER HEAR OF THAT INCIDENT LAST SPRING WHEN DOCTOR FATE LOST HIS POWERS FOR ABOUT THIRTY MINUTES?
MAYBE.
"IT COINCIDES WITH THE TIME BLACK ALICE WAS BORROWING THEM.
"MINUTES LATER BLACK ALICE WAS ABLE TO EMPLOY BACKWARDS-TALKING SPELLCRAFT AT PRECISELY THE SAME TIME AND DURATION THAT ZATANNA FORGOT HOW TO DO IT."
SEERT DLOH REH!
DNIB REH HTUOM!

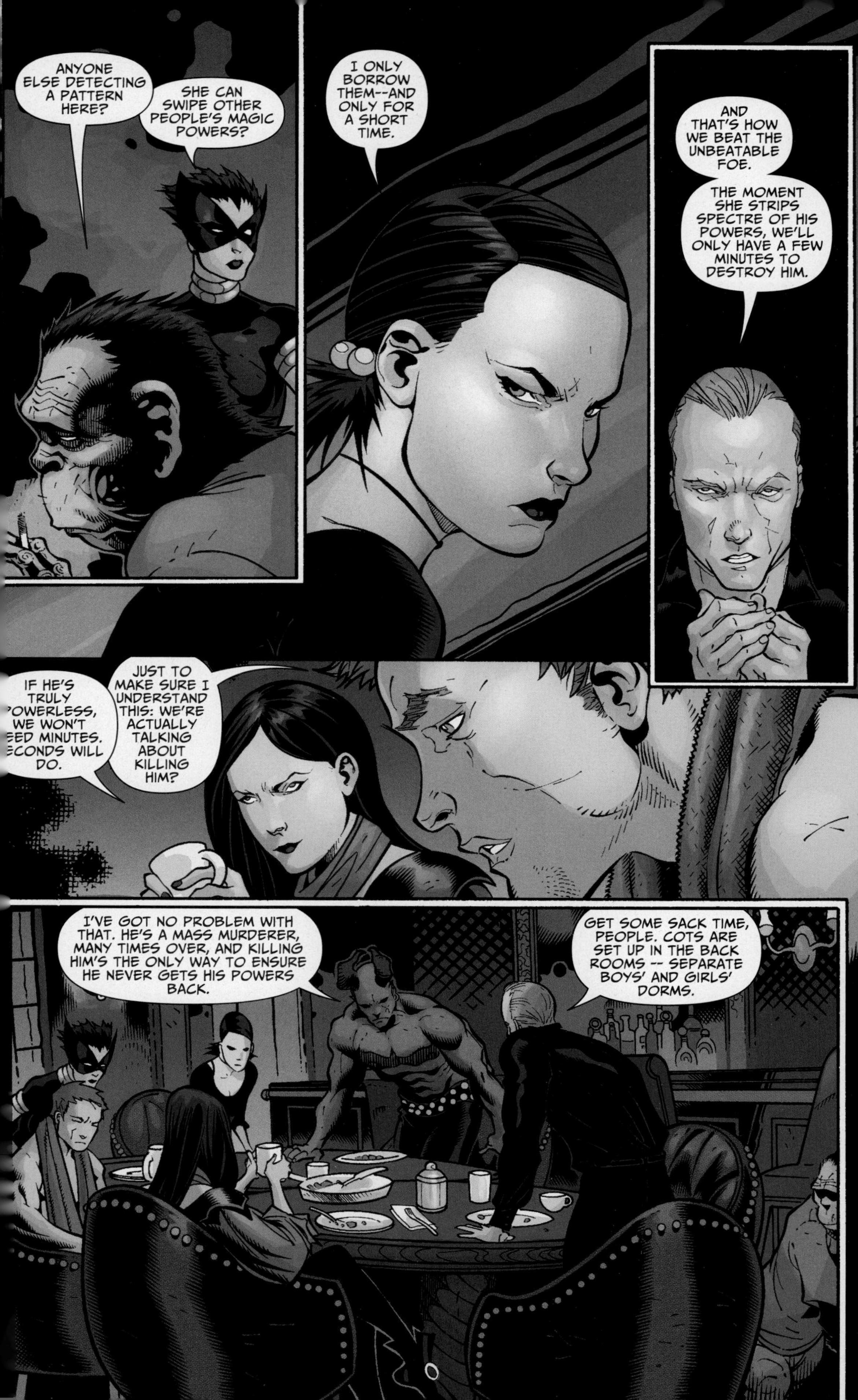

ANYONE ELSE DETECTING A PATTERN HERE?
SHE CAN SWIPE OTHER PEOPLE'S MAGIC POWERS?
I ONLY BORROW THEM--AND ONLY FOR A SHORT TIME.
AND THAT'S HOW WE BEAT THE UNBEATABLE FOE.
THE MOMENT SHE STRIPS SPECTRE OF HIS POWERS, WE'LL ONLY HAVE A FEW MINUTES TO DESTROY HIM.
IF HE'S TRULY OWERLESS, WE WON'T EED MINUTES. ECONDS WILL DO.
JUST TO MAKE SURE I UNDERSTAND THIS: WE'RE ACTUALLY TALKING ABOUT KILLING HIM?
I'VE GOT NO PROBLEM WITH THAT. HE'S A MASS MURDERER, MANY TIMES OVER, AND KILLING HIM'S THE ONLY WAY TO ENSURE HE NEVER GETS HIS POWERS BACK.
GET SOME SACK TIME, PEOPLE. COTS ARE SET UP IN THE BACK ROOMS -- SEPARATE BOYS' AND GIRLS' DORMS.

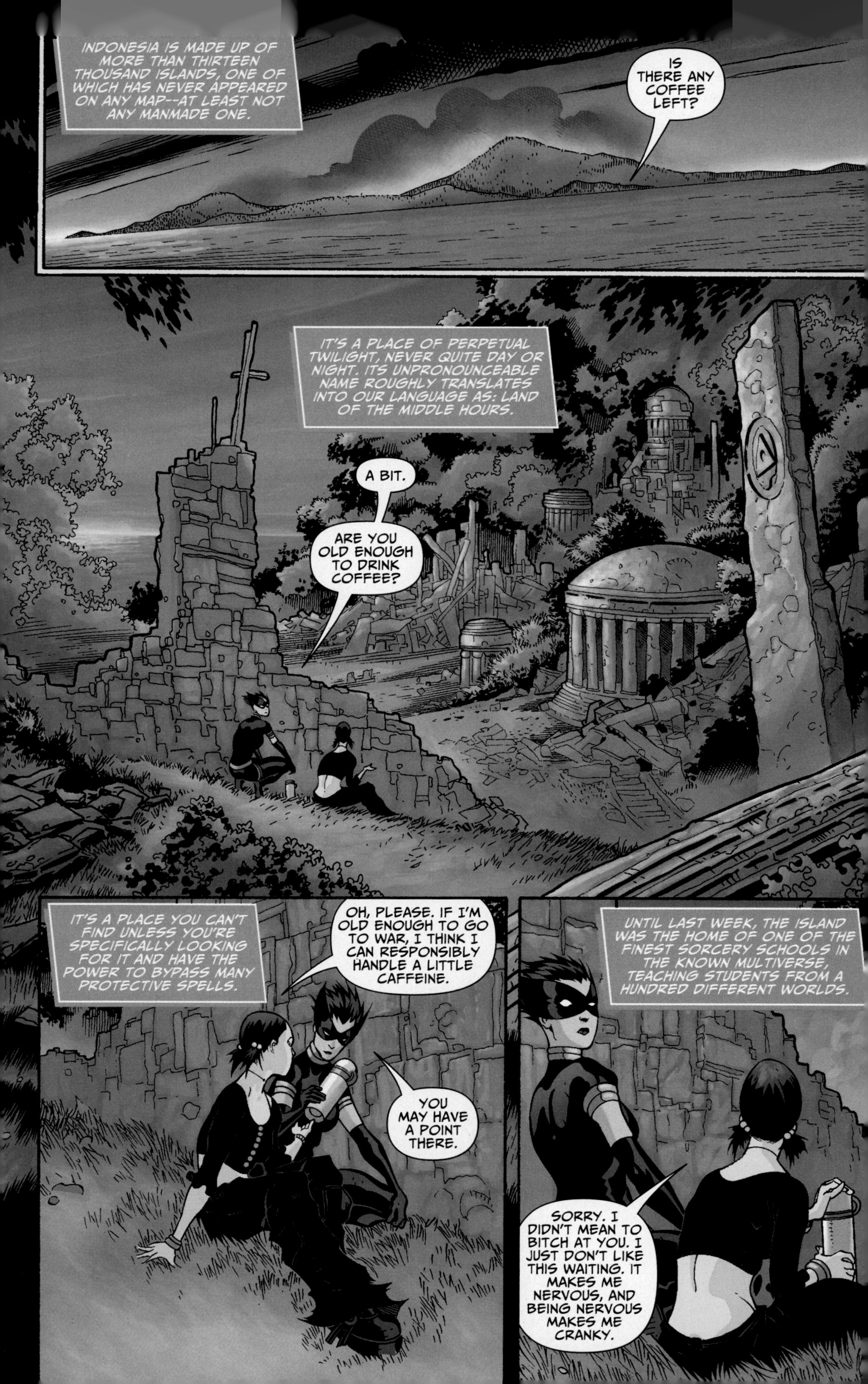
INDONESIA IS MADE UP OF MORE THAN THIRTEEN THOUSAND ISLANDS, ONE OF WHICH HAS NEVER APPEARED ON ANY MAP--AT LEAST NOT ANY MANMADE ONE.
IS THERE ANY COFFEE LEFT?
IT'S A PLACE OF PERPETUAL TWILIGHT, NEVER QUITE DAY OR NIGHT. ITS UNPRONOUNCEABLE NAME ROUGHLY TRANSLATES INTO OUR LANGUAGE AS: LAND OF THE MIDDLE HOURS.
A BIT.
ARE YOU OLD ENOUGH TO DRINK COFFEE?
IT'S A PLACE YOU CAN'T FIND UNLESS YOU'RE SPECIFICALLY LOOKING FOR IT AND HAVE THE POWER TO BYPASS MANY PROTECTIVE SPELLS.
OH, PLEASE. IF I'M OLD ENOUGH TO GO TO WAR, I THINK I CAN RESPONSIBLY HANDLE A LITTLE CAFFEINE.
YOU MAY HAVE A POINT THERE.
UNTIL LAST WEEK, THE ISLAND WAS THE HOME OF ONE OF THE FINEST SORCERY SCHOOLS IN THE KNOWN MULTIVERSE, TEACHING STUDENTS FROM A HUNDRED DIFFERENT WORLDS.
SORRY. I DIDN'T MEAN TO BITCH AT YOU. I JUST DON'T LIKE THIS WAITING. IT MAKES ME NERVOUS, AND BEING NERVOUS MAKES ME CRANKY.

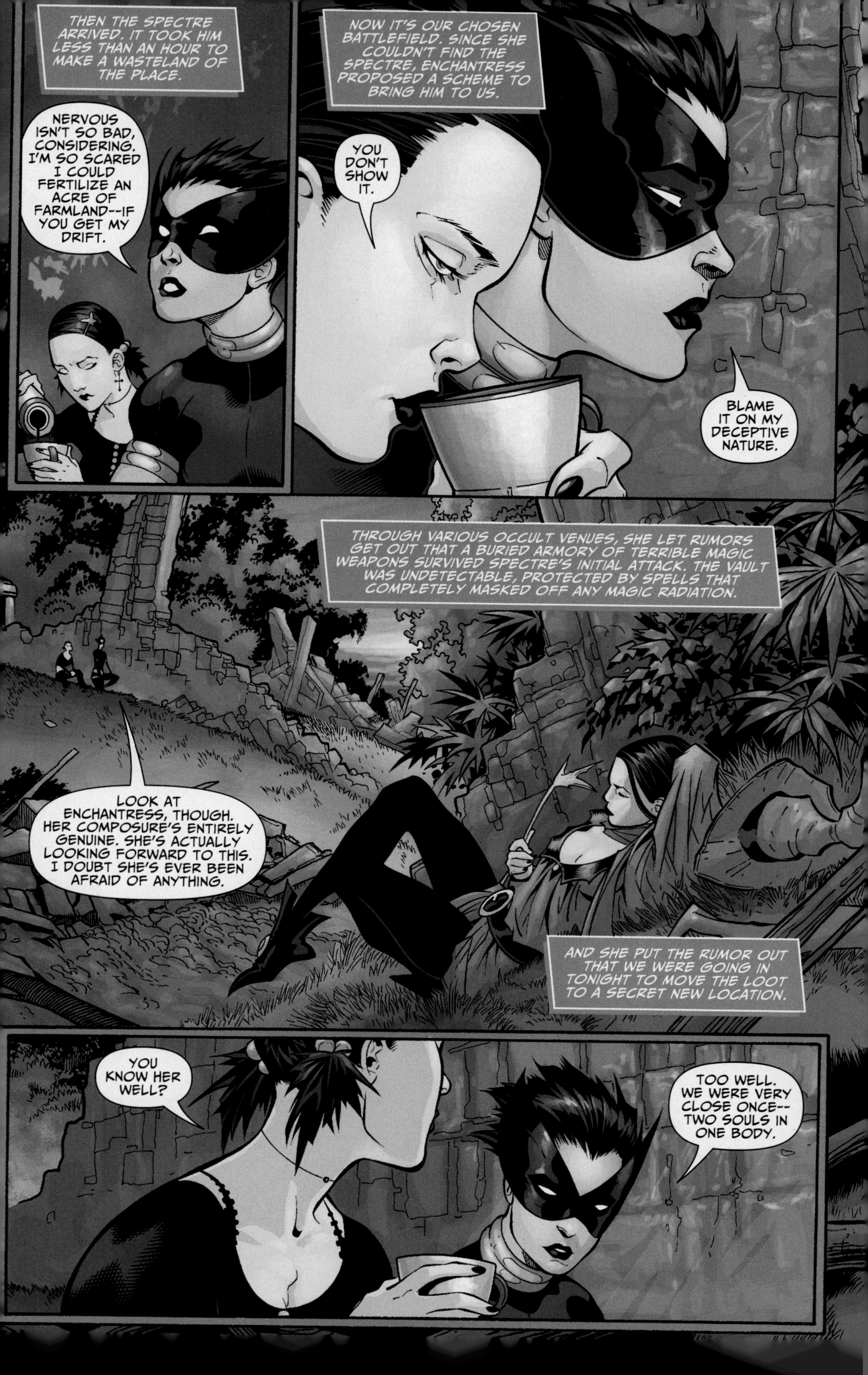

THEN THE SPECTRE ARRIVED. IT TOOK HIM LESS THAN AN HOUR TO MAKE A WASTELAND OF THE PLACE.
NERVOUS ISN'T SO BAD, CONSIDERING. I'M SO SCARED I COULD FERTILIZE AN ACRE OF FARMLAND--IF YOU GET MY DRIFT.
NOW IT'S OUR CHOSEN BATTLEFIELD. SINCE SHE COULDN'T FIND THE SPECTRE, ENCHANTRESS PROPOSED A SCHEME TO BRING HIM TO US.
YOU DON'T SHOW IT.
BLAME IT ON MY DECEPTIVE NATURE.
THROUGH VARIOUS OCCULT VENUES, SHE LET RUMORS GET OUT THAT A BURIED ARMORY OF TERRIBLE MAGIC WEAPONS SURVIVED SPECTRE'S INITIAL ATTACK. THE VAULT WAS UNDETECTABLE, PROTECTED BY SPELLS THAT COMPLETELY MASKED OFF ANY MAGIC RADIATION.
LOOK AT ENCHANTRESS, THOUGH. HER COMPOSURE'S ENTIRELY GENUINE. SHE'S ACTUALLY LOOKING FORWARD TO THIS. I DOUBT SHE'S EVER BEEN AFRAID OF ANYTHING.
AND SHE PUT THE RUMOR OUT THAT WE WERE GOING IN TONIGHT TO MOVE THE LOOT TO A SECRET NEW LOCATION.
YOU KNOW HER WELL?
TOO WELL. WE WERE VERY CLOSE ONCE--TWO SOULS IN ONE BODY.

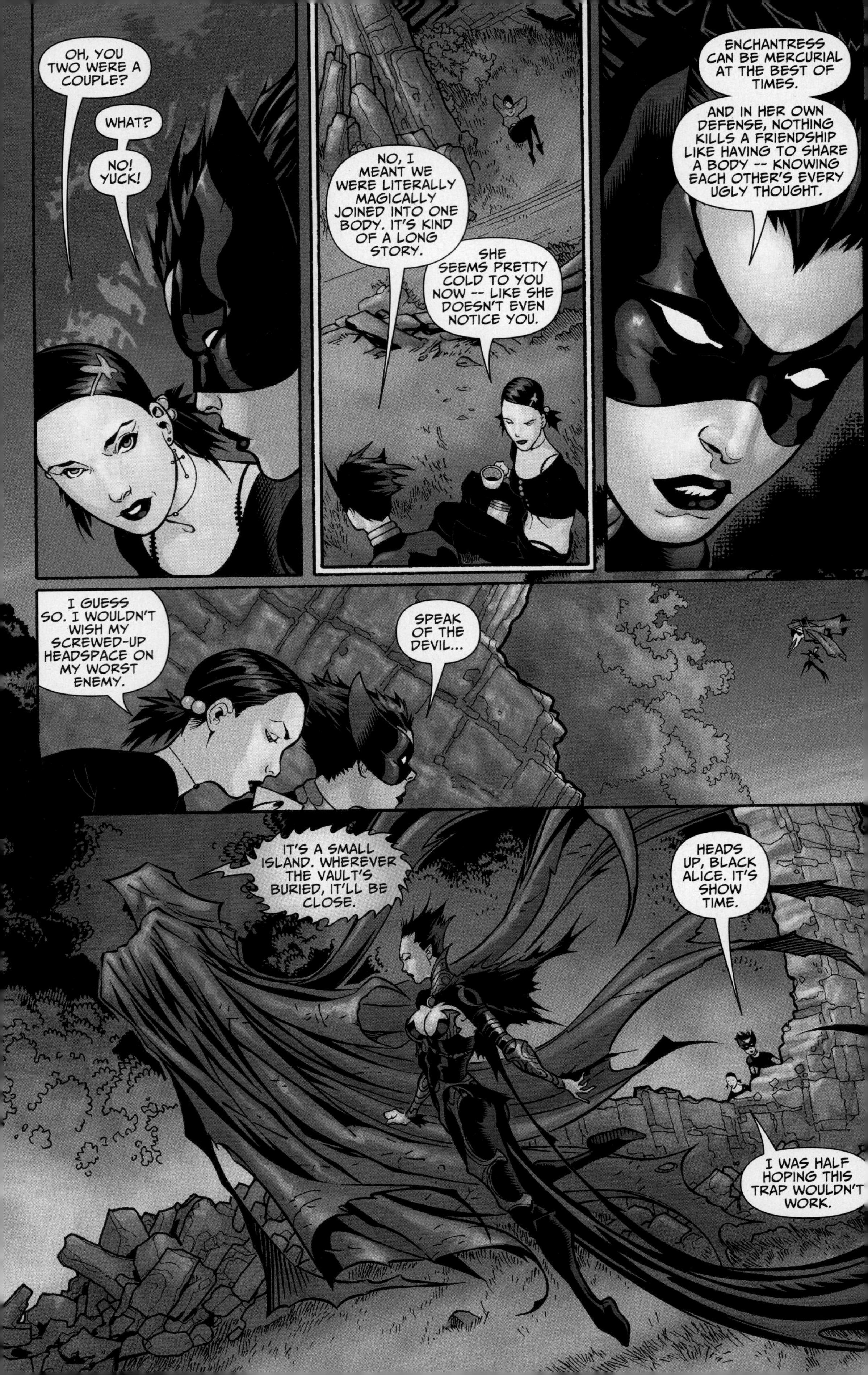

OH, YOU TWO WERE A COUPLE?
WHAT?
NO! YUCK!
NO, I MEANT WE WERE LITERALLY MAGICALLY JOINED INTO ONE BODY. IT'S KIND OF A LONG STORY.
SHE SEEMS PRETTY COLD TO YOU NOW -- LIKE SHE DOESN'T EVEN NOTICE YOU.
ENCHANTRESS CAN BE MERCURIAL AT THE BEST OF TIMES.
AND IN HER OWN DEFENSE, NOTHING KILLS A FRIENDSHIP LIKE HAVING TO SHARE A BODY -- KNOWING EACH OTHER'S EVERY UGLY THOUGHT.
I GUESS SO. I WOULDN'T WISH MY SCREWED-UP HEADSPACE ON MY WORST ENEMY.
SPEAK OF THE DEVIL...
IT'S A SMALL ISLAND. WHEREVER THE VAULT'S BURIED, IT'LL BE CLOSE.
HEADS UP, BLACK ALICE. IT'S SHOW TIME.
I WAS HALF HOPING THIS TRAP WOULDN'T WORK.

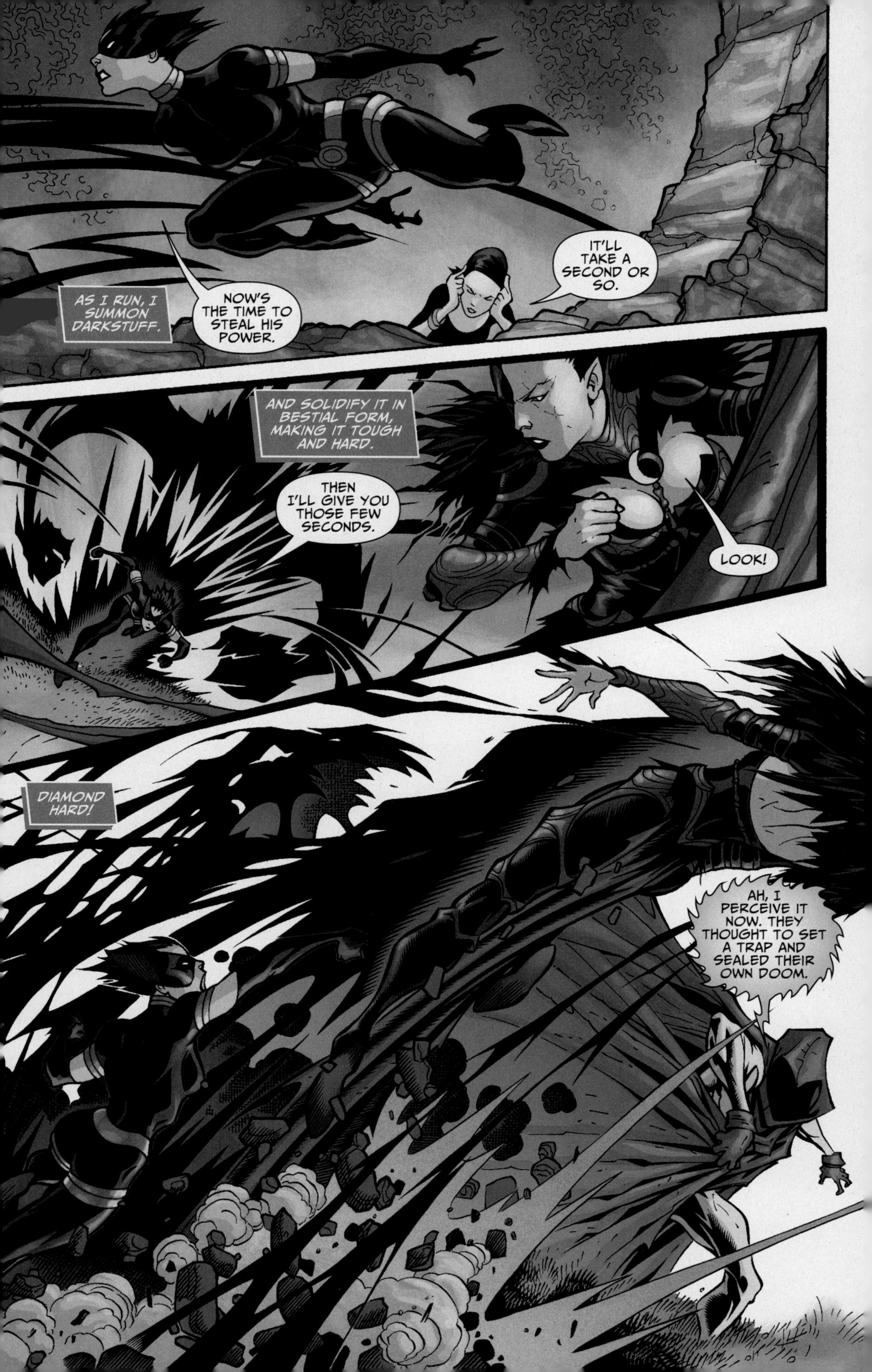
AS I RUN, I SUMMON DARKSTUFF.
NOW'S THE TIME TO STEAL HIS POWER.
IT'LL TAKE A SECOND OR SO.
AND SOLIDIFY IT IN BESTIAL FORM, MAKING IT TOUGH AND HARD.
THEN I'LL GIVE YOU THOSE FEW SECONDS.
LOOK!
DIAMOND HARD!
AH, I PERCEIVE IT NOW. THEY THOUGHT TO SET A TRAP AND SEALED THEIR OWN DOOM.

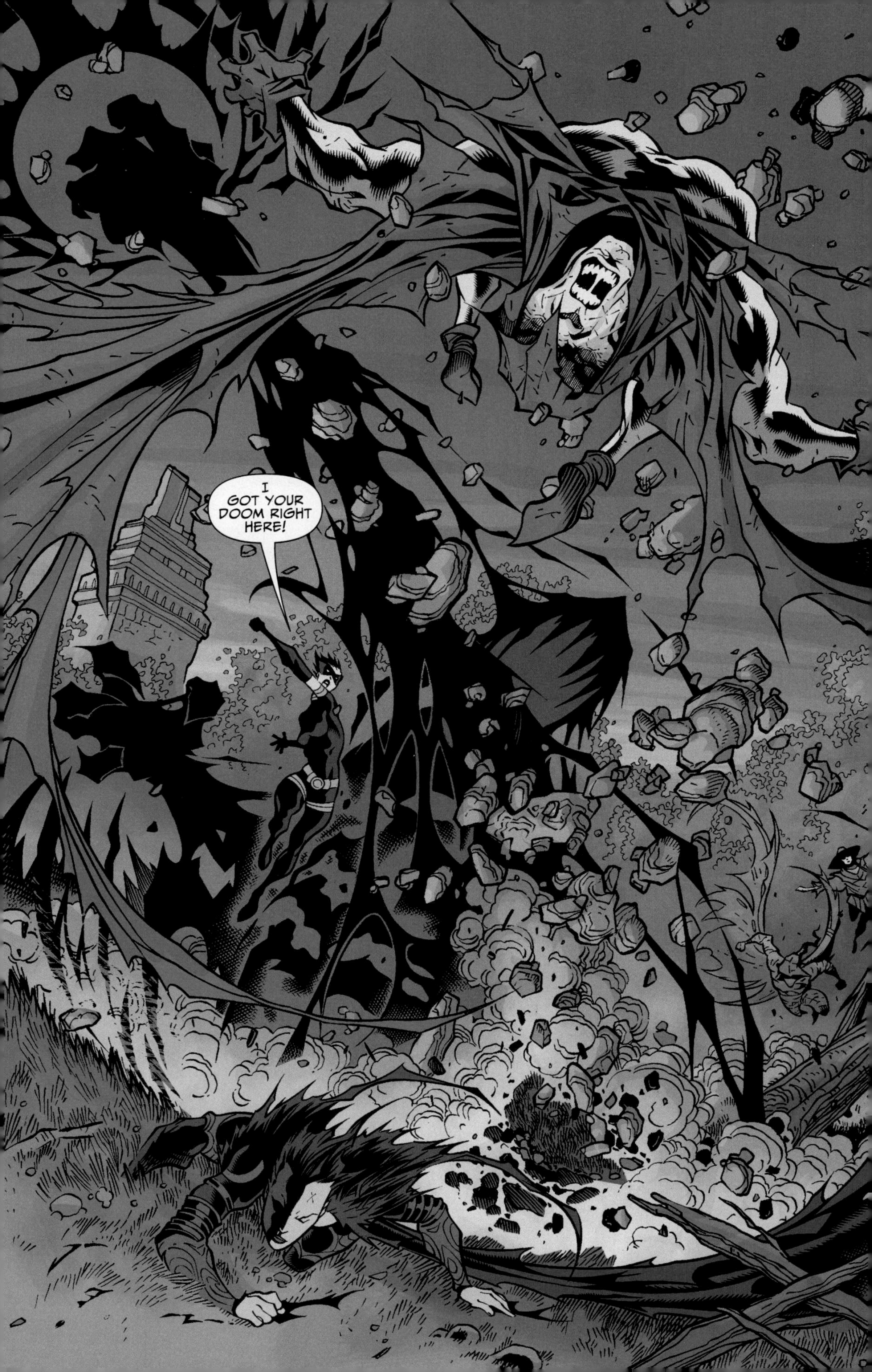
I GOT YOUR DOOM RIGHT HERE!

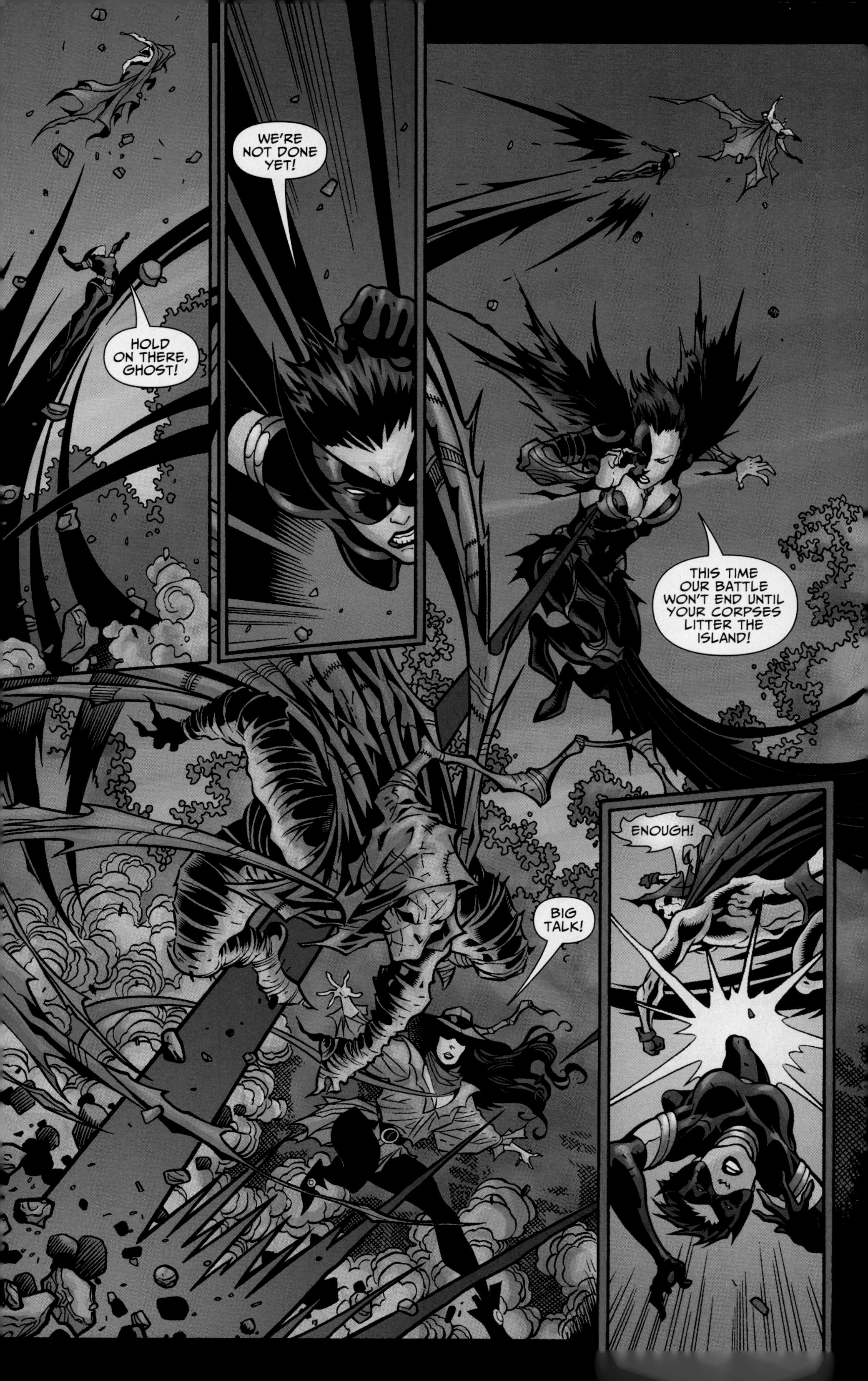
WE'RE NOT DONE YET!
HOLD ON THERE, GHOST!
THIS TIME OUR BATTLE WON'T END UNTIL YOUR CORPSES LITTER THE ISLAND!
BIG TALK!
ENOUGH!

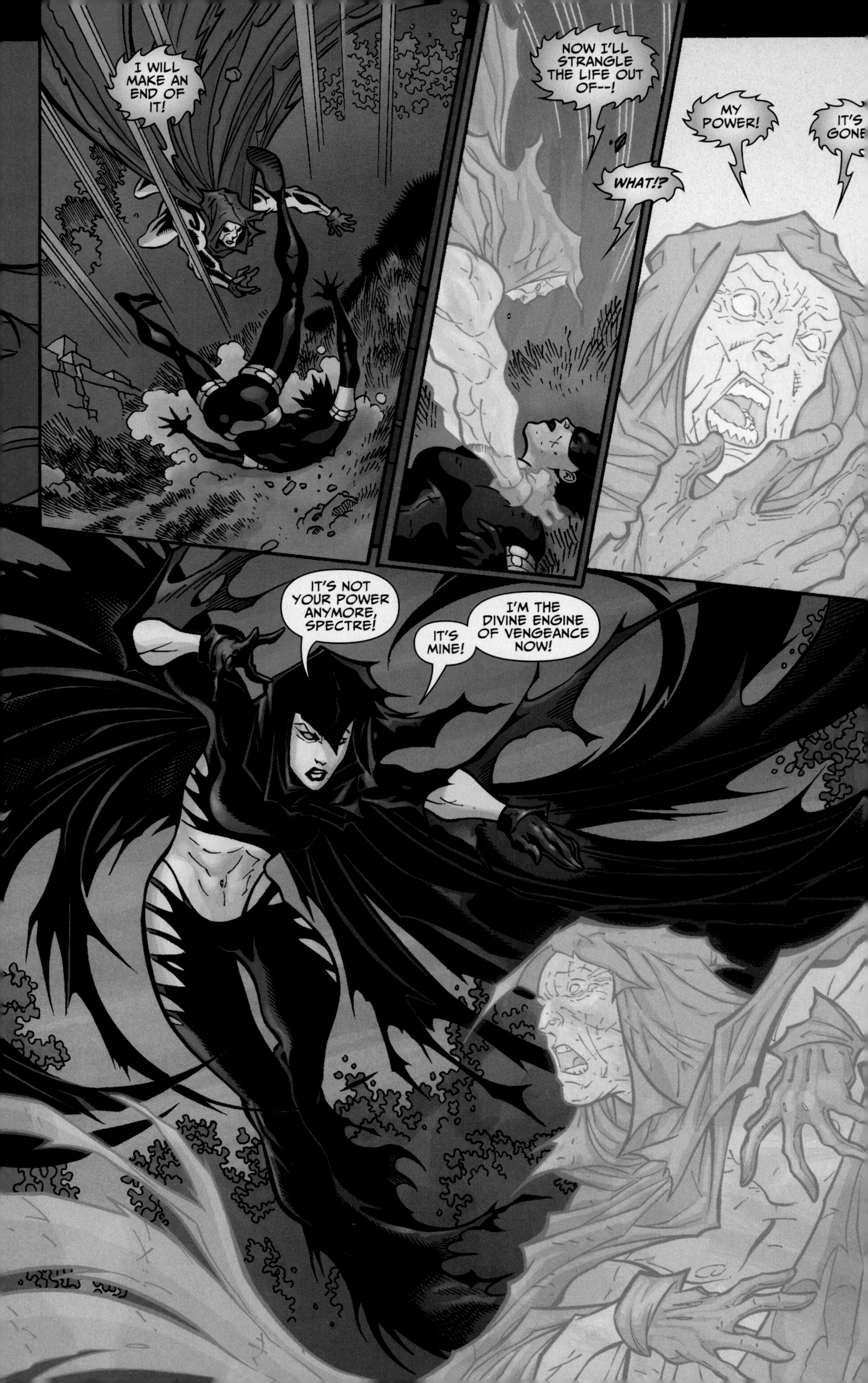
I WILL MAKE AN END OF IT!
NOW I'LL STRANGLE THE LIFE OUT OF--!
WHAT!?
MY POWER!
IT'S GONE
IT'S NOT YOUR POWER ANYMORE, SPECTRE!
IT'S MINE!
I'M THE DIVINE ENGINE OF VENGEANCE NOW!

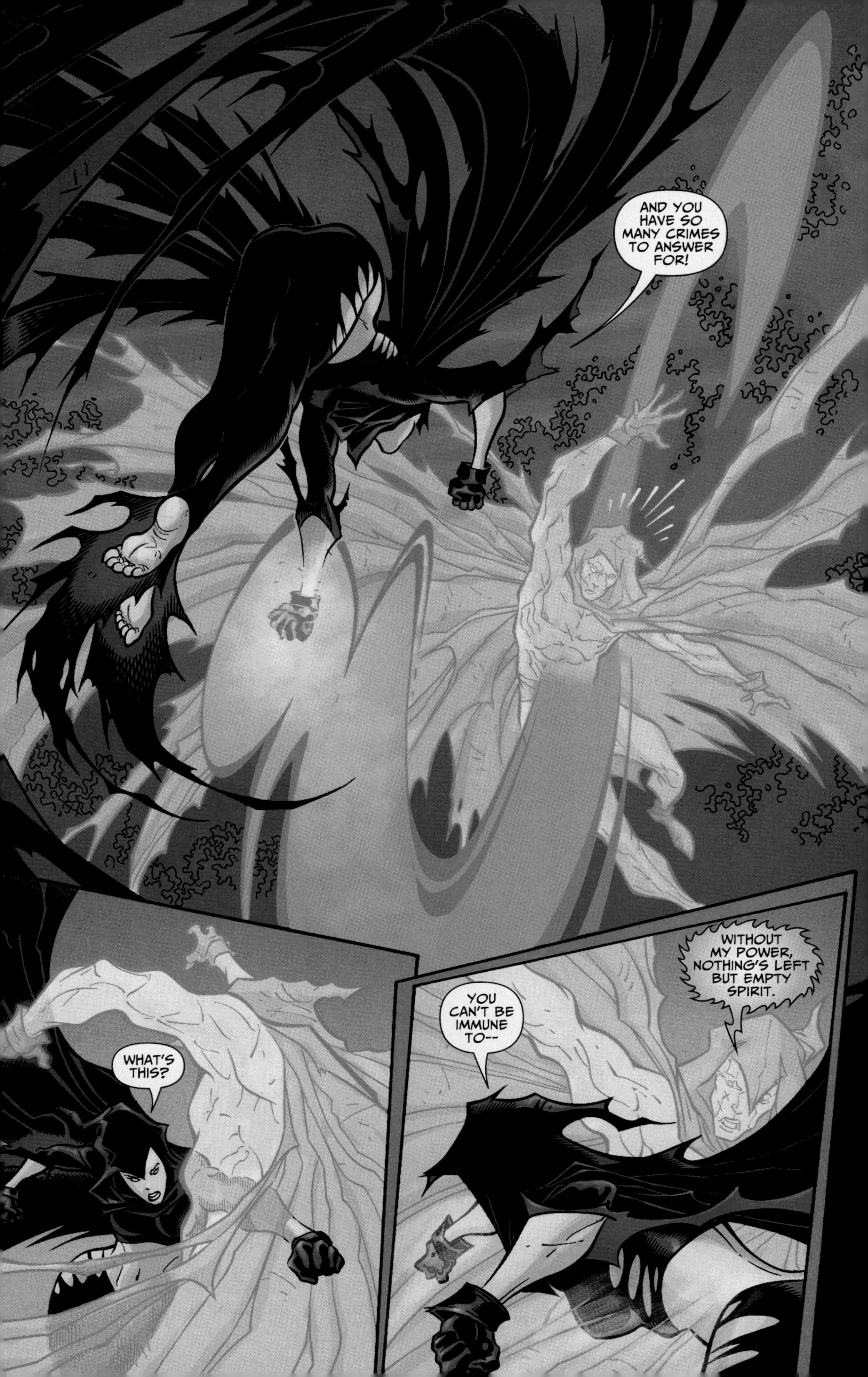
AND YOU HAVE SO MANY CRIMES TO ANSWER FOR!
WHAT'S THIS?
YOU CAN'T BE IMMUNE TO--
WITHOUT MY POWER, NOTHING'S LEFT BUT EMPTY SPIRIT.

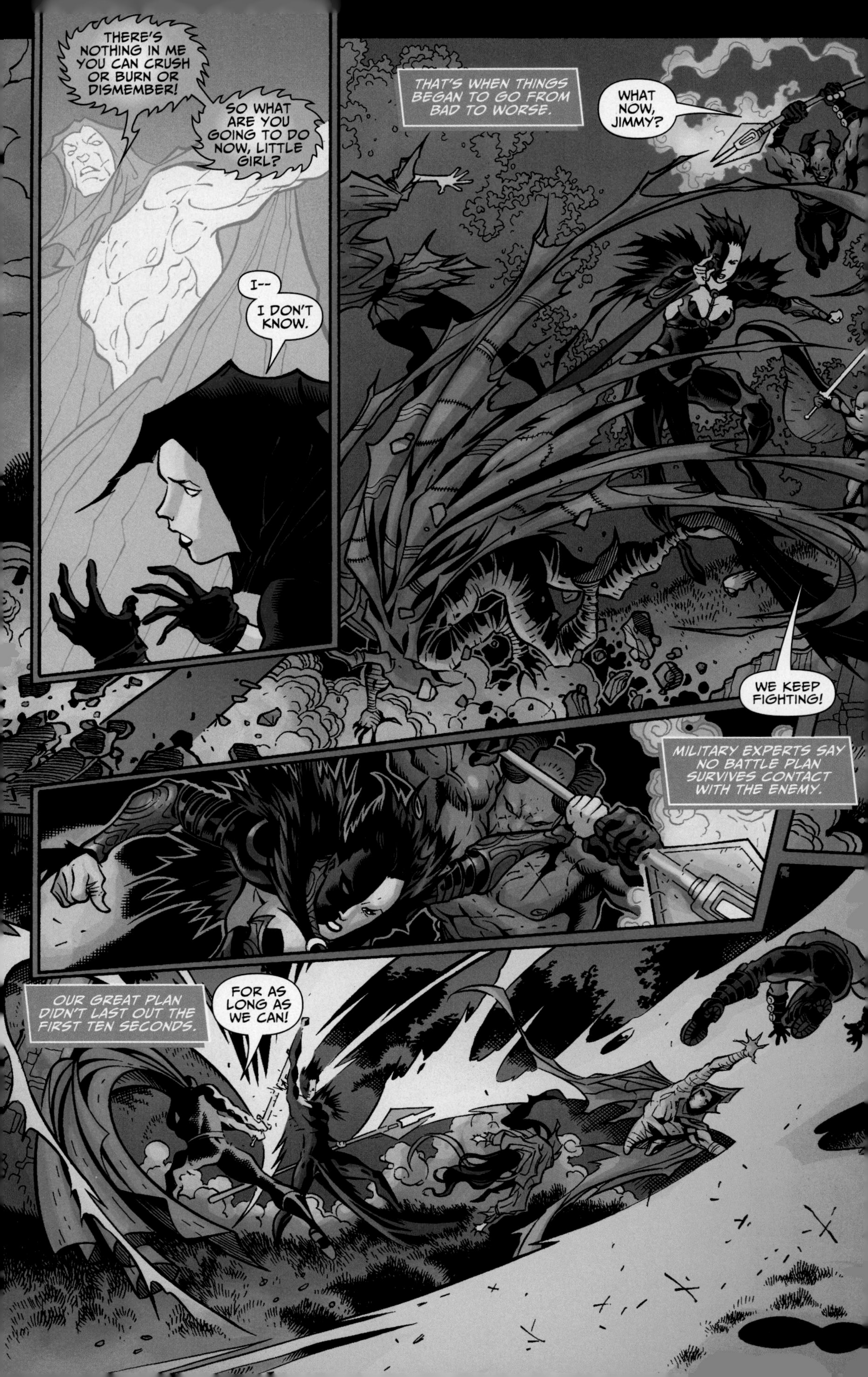
THERE'S NOTHING IN ME YOU CAN CRUSH OR BURN OR DISMEMBER!
SO WHAT ARE YOU GOING TO DO NOW, LITTLE GIRL?
I--
I DON'T KNOW.
THAT'S WHEN THINGS BEGAN TO GO FROM BAD TO WORSE.
WHAT NOW, JIMMY?
WE KEEP FIGHTING!
MILITARY EXPERTS SAY NO BATTLE PLAN SURVIVES CONTACT WITH THE ENEMY.
OUR GREAT PLAN DIDN'T LAST OUT THE FIRST TEN SECONDS.
FOR AS LONG AS WE CAN!

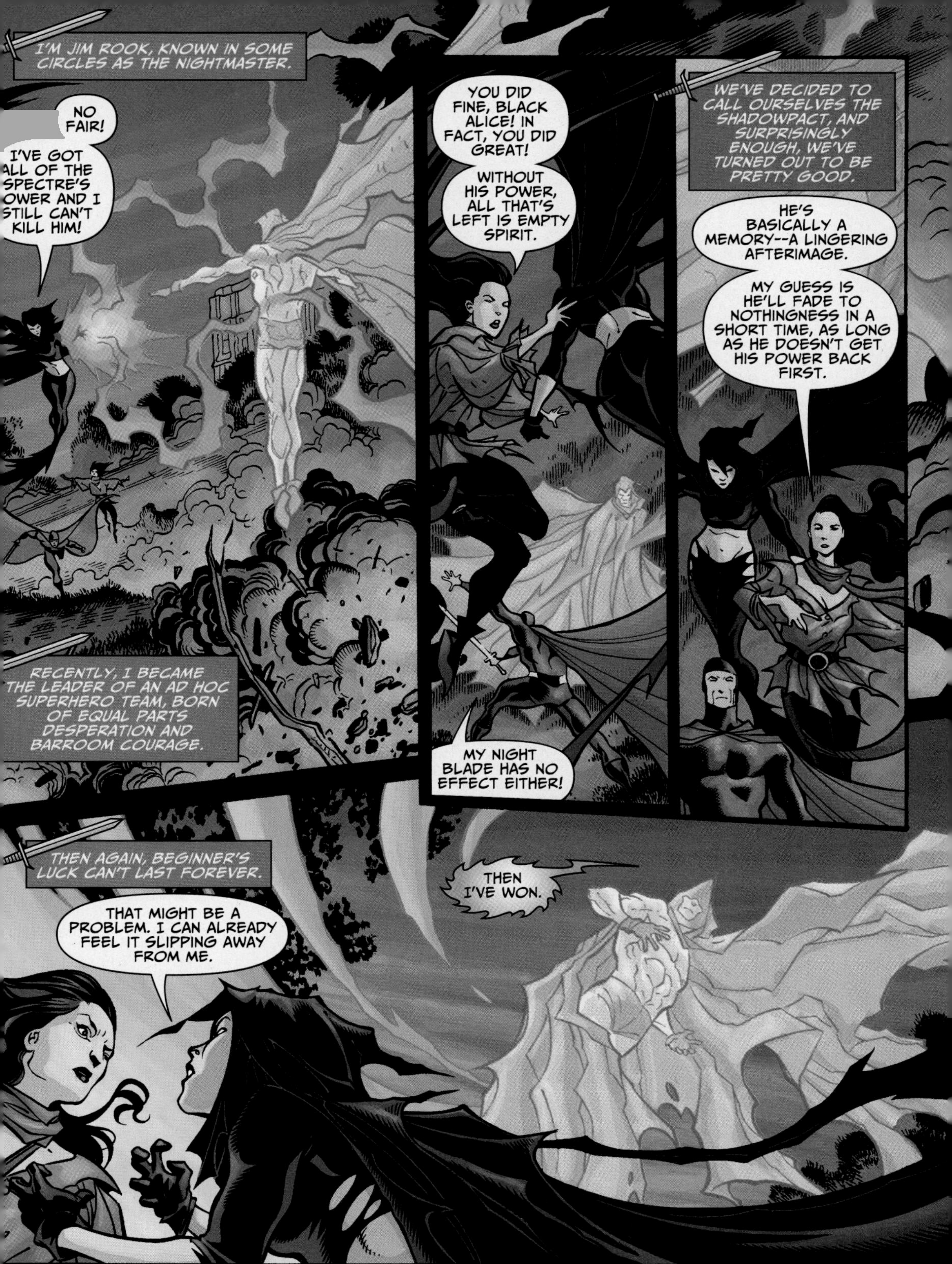

I'M JIM ROOK, KNOWN IN SOME CIRCLES AS THE NIGHTMASTER.
NO FAIR!
I'VE GOT ALL OF THE SPECTRE'S OWER AND I STILL CAN'T KILL HIM!
RECENTLY, I BECAME THE LEADER OF AN AD HOC SUPERHERO TEAM, BORN OF EQUAL PARTS DESPERATION AND BARROOM COURAGE.
YOU DID FINE, BLACK ALICE! IN FACT, YOU DID GREAT!
WITHOUT HIS POWER, ALL THAT'S LEFT IS EMPTY SPIRIT.
MY NIGHT BLADE HAS NO EFFECT EITHER!
WE'VE DECIDED TO CALL OURSELVES THE SHADOWPACT, AND SURPRISINGLY ENOUGH, WE'VE TURNED OUT TO BE PRETTY GOOD.
HE'S BASICALLY A MEMORY--A LINGERING AFTERIMAGE.
MY GUESS IS HE'LL FADE TO NOTHINGNESS IN A SHORT TIME, AS LONG AS HE DOESN'T GET HIS POWER BACK FIRST.
THEN AGAIN, BEGINNER'S LUCK CAN'T LAST FOREVER.
THAT MIGHT BE A PROBLEM. I CAN ALREADY FEEL IT SLIPPING AWAY FROM ME.
THEN I'VE WON.

Chapter Six:

THE DEATH OF MAGIC

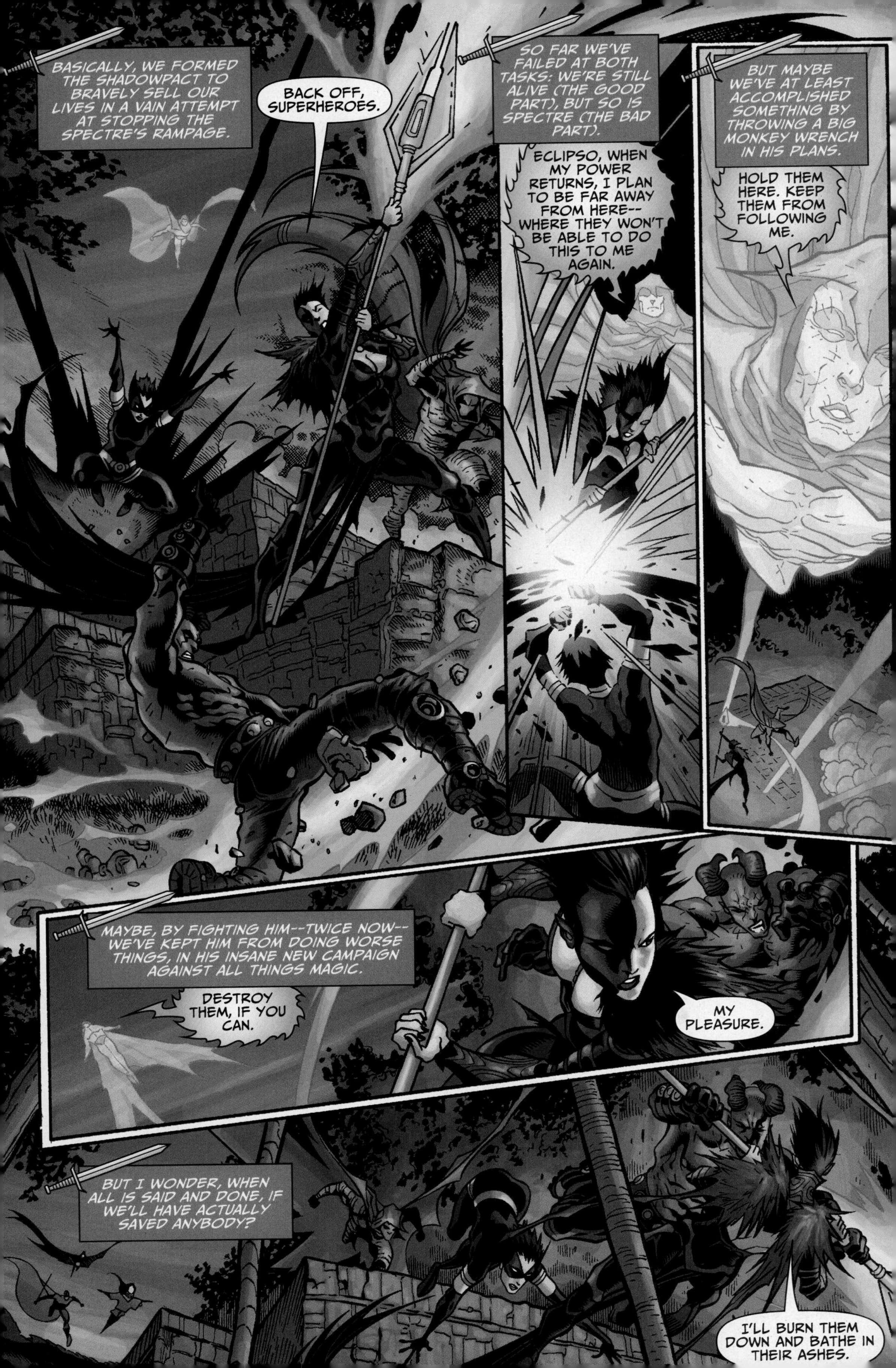
BASICALLY, WE FORMED THE SHADOWPACT TO BRAVELY SELL OUR LIVES IN A VAIN ATTEMPT AT STOPPING THE SPECTRE'S RAMPAGE.
BACK OFF, SUPERHEROES.
SO FAR WE'VE FAILED AT BOTH TASKS: WE'RE STILL ALIVE (THE GOOD PART), BUT SO IS SPECTRE (THE BAD PART).
ECLIPSO, WHEN MY POWER RETURNS, I PLAN TO BE FAR AWAY FROM HERE--WHERE THEY WON'T BE ABLE TO DO THIS TO ME AGAIN.
BUT MAYBE WE'VE AT LEAST ACCOMPLISHED SOMETHING BY THROWING A BIG MONKEY WRENCH IN HIS PLANS.
HOLD THEM HERE. KEEP THEM FROM FOLLOWING ME.
MAYBE, BY FIGHTING HIM--TWICE NOW--WE'VE KEPT HIM FROM DOING WORSE THINGS, IN HIS INSANE NEW CAMPAIGN AGAINST ALL THINGS MAGIC.
DESTROY THEM, IF YOU CAN.
MY PLEASURE.
BUT I WONDER, WHEN ALL IS SAID AND DONE, IF WE'LL HAVE ACTUALLY SAVED ANYBODY?
I'LL BURN THEM DOWN AND BATHE IN THEIR ASHES.

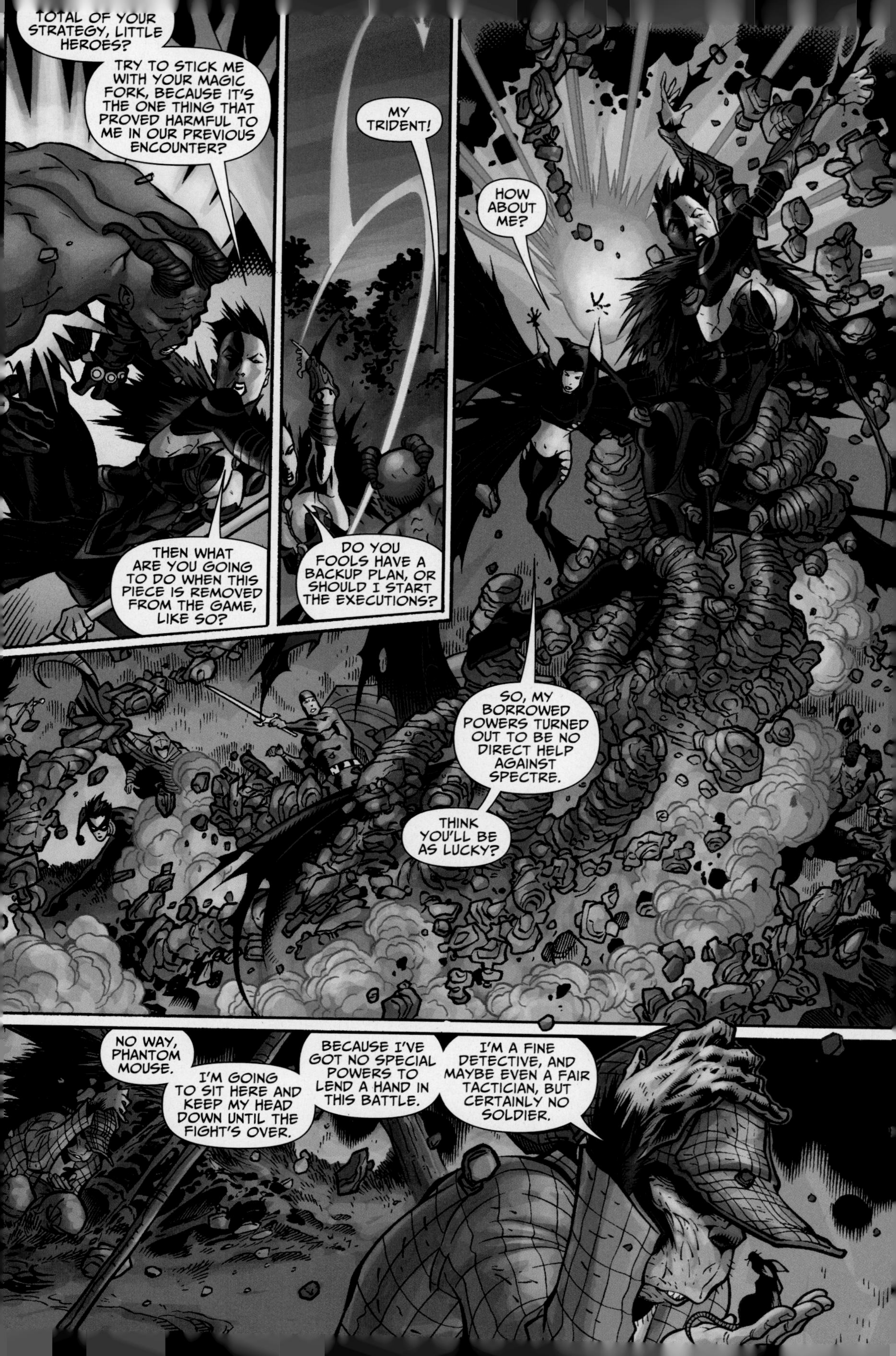
TOTAL OF YOUR STRATEGY, LITTLE HEROES?
TRY TO STICK ME WITH YOUR MAGIC FORK, BECAUSE IT'S THE ONE THING THAT PROVED HARMFUL TO ME IN OUR PREVIOUS ENCOUNTER?
THEN WHAT ARE YOU GOING TO DO WHEN THIS PIECE IS REMOVED FROM THE GAME, LIKE SO?
MY TRIDENT!
DO YOU FOOLS HAVE A BACKUP PLAN, OR SHOULD I START THE EXECUTIONS?
HOW ABOUT ME?
SO, MY BORROWED POWERS TURNED OUT TO BE NO DIRECT HELP AGAINST SPECTRE.
THINK YOU'LL BE AS LUCKY?
NO WAY, PHANTOM MOUSE.
I'M GOING TO SIT HERE AND KEEP MY HEAD DOWN UNTIL THE FIGHT'S OVER.
BECAUSE I'VE GOT NO SPECIAL POWERS TO LEND A HAND IN THIS BATTLE.
I'M A FINE DETECTIVE, AND MAYBE EVEN A FAIR TACTICIAN, BUT CERTAINLY NO SOLDIER.

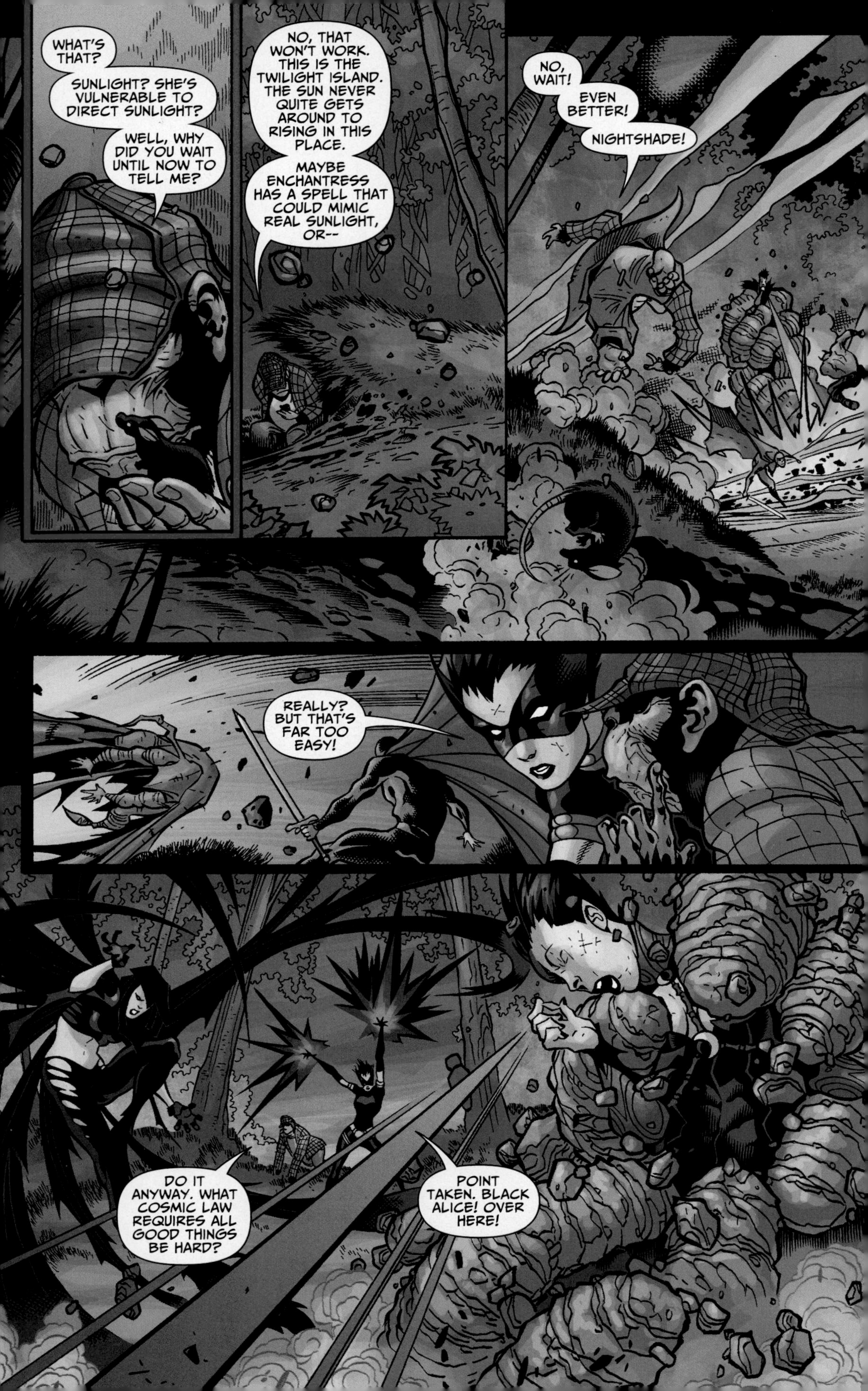
WHAT'S THAT?
SUNLIGHT? SHE'S VULNERABLE TO DIRECT SUNLIGHT?
WELL, WHY DID YOU WAIT UNTIL NOW TO TELL ME?
NO, THAT WON'T WORK. THIS IS THE TWILIGHT ISLAND. THE SUN NEVER QUITE GETS AROUND TO RISING IN THIS PLACE.
MAYBE ENCHANTRESS HAS A SPELL THAT COULD MIMIC REAL SUNLIGHT, OR--
NO, WAIT!
EVEN BETTER!
NIGHTSHADE!
REALLY? BUT THAT'S FAR TOO EASY!
DO IT ANYWAY. WHAT COSMIC LAW REQUIRES ALL GOOD THINGS BE HARD?
POINT TAKEN. BLACK ALICE! OVER HERE!

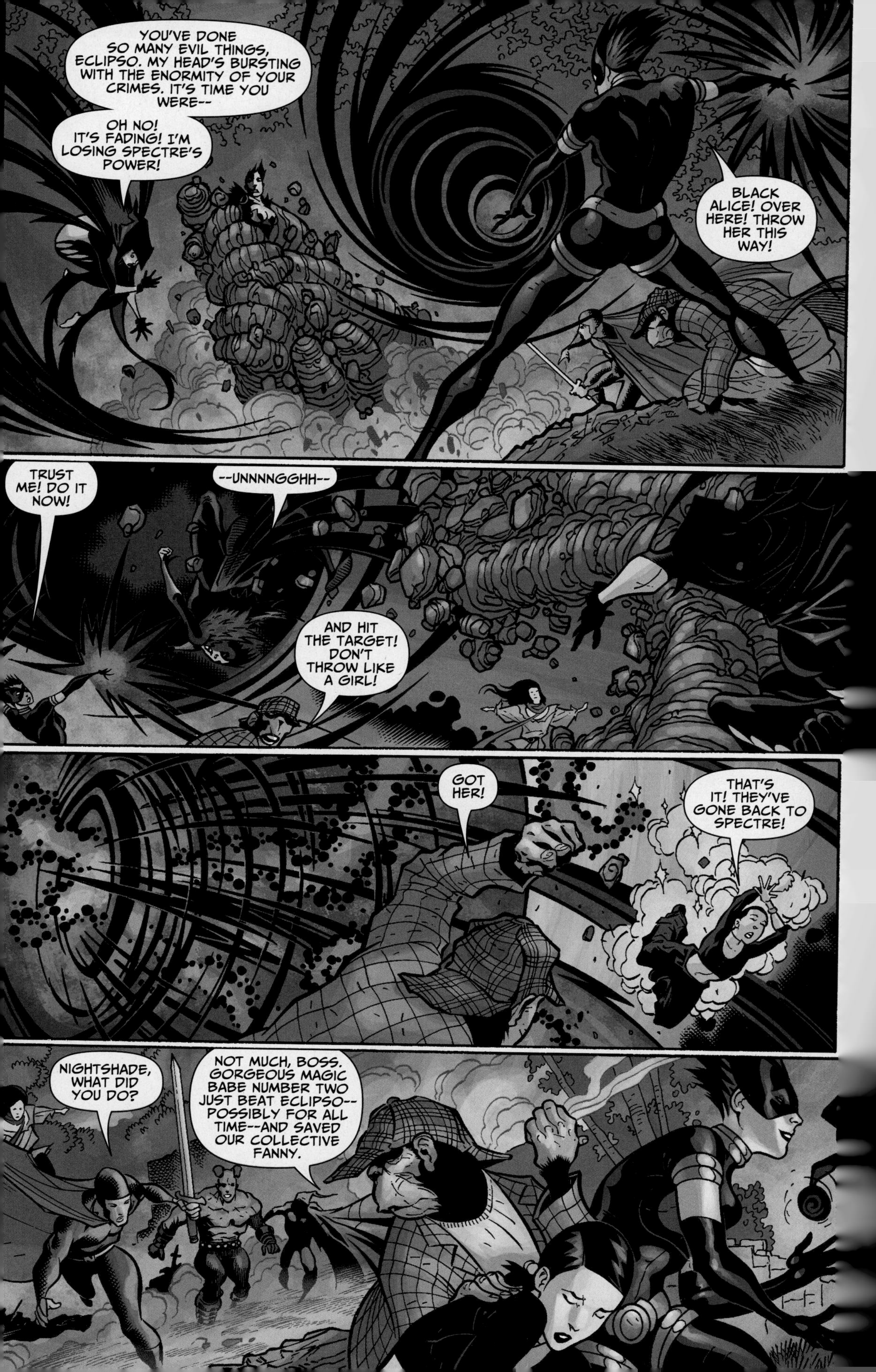
YOU'VE DONE SO MANY EVIL THINGS, ECLIPSO. MY HEAD'S BURSTING WITH THE ENORMITY OF YOUR CRIMES. IT'S TIME YOU WERE--
OH NO! IT'S FADING! I'M LOSING SPECTRE'S POWER!
BLACK ALICE! OVER HERE! THROW HER THIS WAY!
TRUST ME! DO IT NOW!
--UNNNNGGHH--
AND HIT THE TARGET! DON'T THROW LIKE A GIRL!
GOT HER!
THAT'S IT! THEY'VE GONE BACK TO SPECTRE!
NIGHTSHADE, WHAT DID YOU DO?
NOT MUCH, BOSS. GORGEOUS MAGIC BABE NUMBER TWO JUST BEAT ECLIPSO--POSSIBLY FOR ALL TIME--AND SAVED OUR COLLECTIVE FANNY.

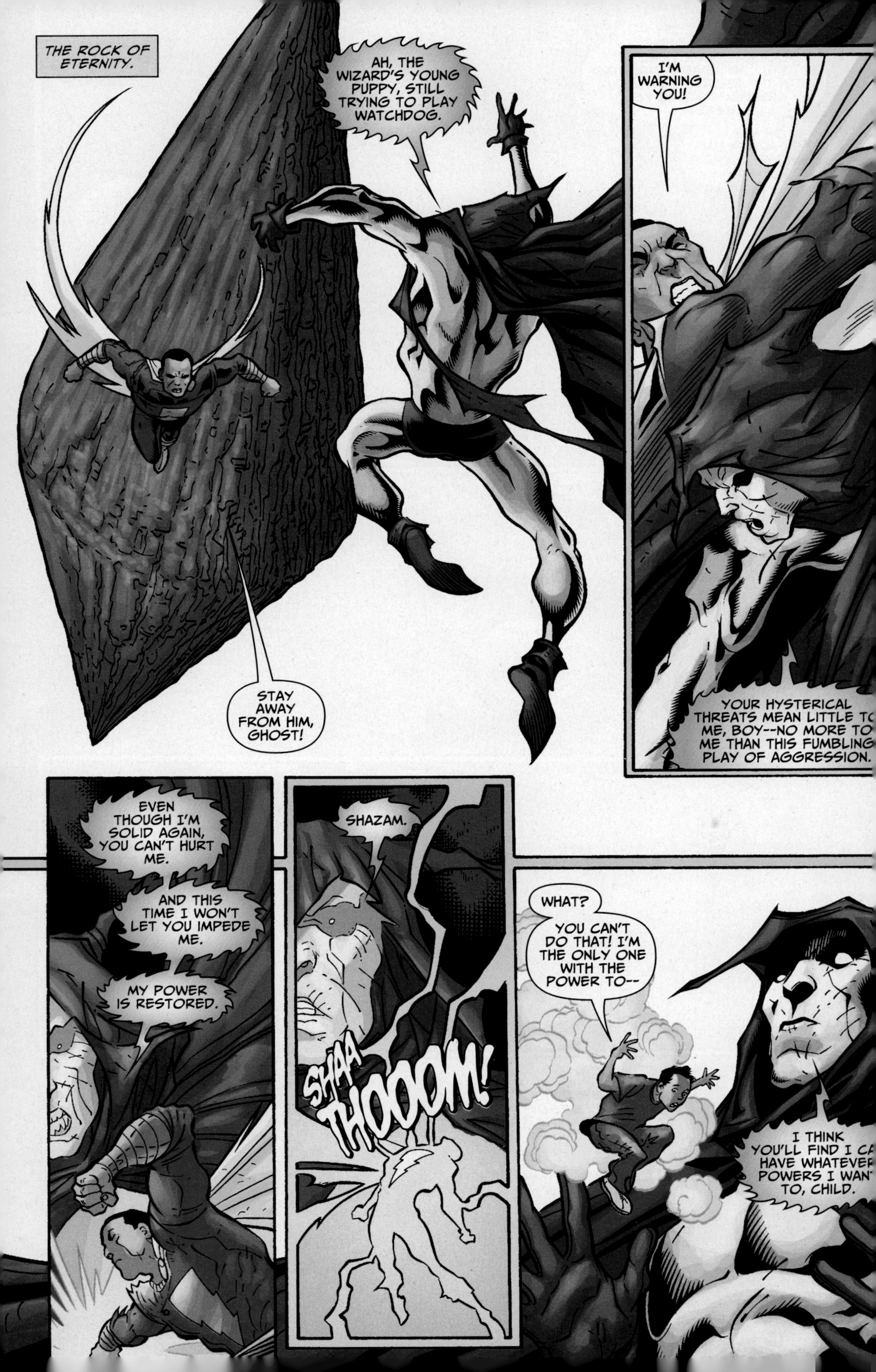
THE ROCK OF ETERNITY.
AH, THE WIZARD'S YOUNG PUPPY, STILL TRYING TO PLAY WATCHDOG.
STAY AWAY FROM HIM, GHOST!
I'M WARNING YOU!
YOUR HYSTERICAL THREATS MEAN LITTLE TO ME, BOY--NO MORE TO ME THAN THIS FUMBLING PLAY OF AGGRESSION.
EVEN THOUGH I'M SOLID AGAIN, YOU CAN'T HURT ME.
AND THIS TIME I WON'T LET YOU IMPEDE ME.
MY POWER IS RESTORED.
SHAZAM.
SHAA THOOOM!
WHAT?
YOU CAN'T DO THAT! I'M THE ONLY ONE WITH THE POWER TO--
I THINK YOU'LL FIND I CA HAVE WHATEVER POWERS I WAN TO, CHILD.

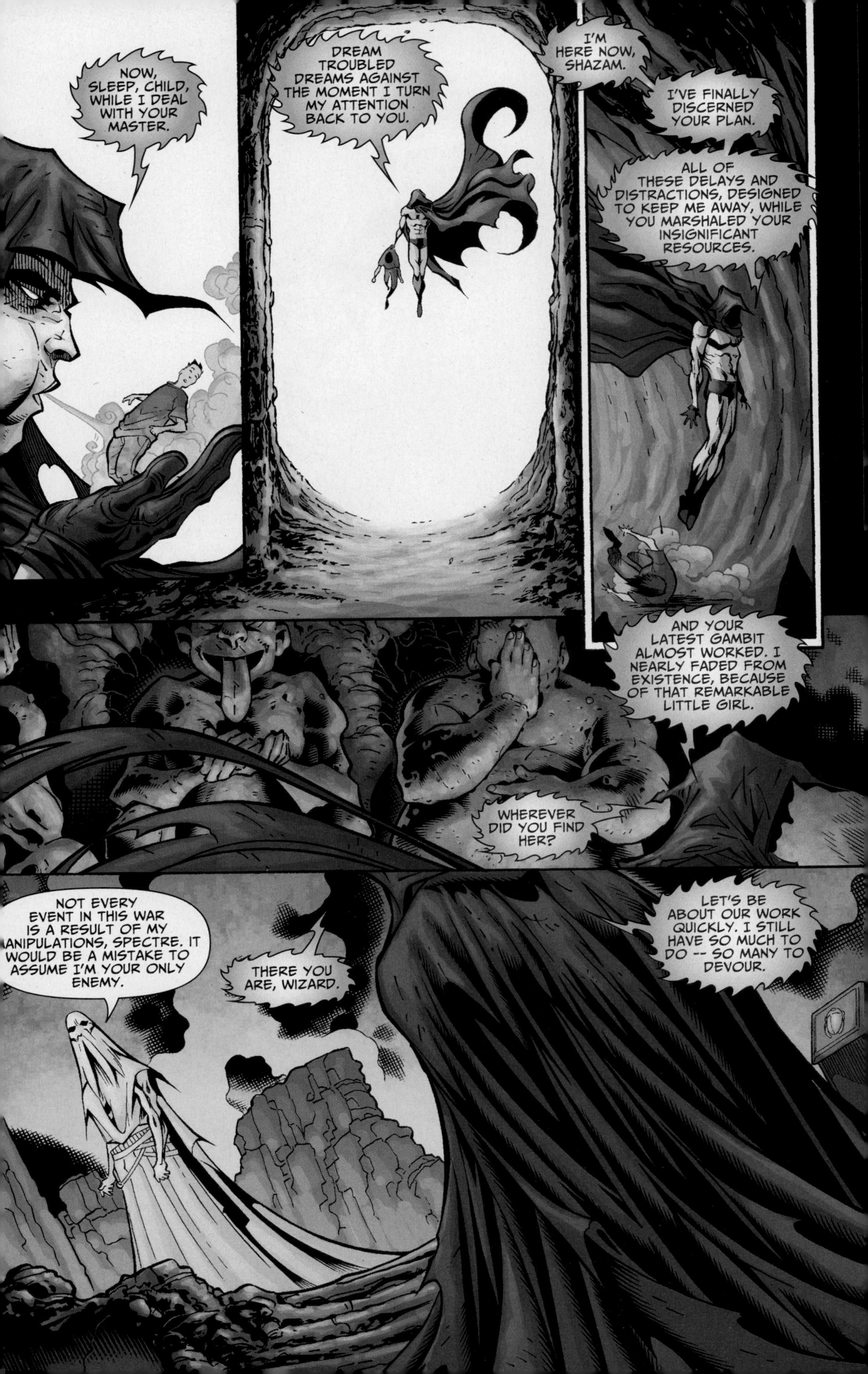

NOW, SLEEP, CHILD, WHILE I DEAL WITH YOUR MASTER.
DREAM TROUBLED DREAMS AGAINST THE MOMENT I TURN MY ATTENTION BACK TO YOU.
I'M HERE NOW, SHAZAM.
I'VE FINALLY DISCERNED YOUR PLAN.
ALL OF THESE DELAYS AND DISTRACTIONS, DESIGNED TO KEEP ME AWAY, WHILE YOU MARSHALED YOUR INSIGNIFICANT RESOURCES.
AND YOUR LATEST GAMBIT ALMOST WORKED. I NEARLY FADED FROM EXISTENCE, BECAUSE OF THAT REMARKABLE LITTLE GIRL.
WHEREVER DID YOU FIND HER?
NOT EVERY EVENT IN THIS WAR IS A RESULT OF MY MANIPULATIONS, SPECTRE. IT WOULD BE A MISTAKE TO ASSUME I'M YOUR ONLY ENEMY.
THERE YOU ARE, WIZARD.
LET'S BE ABOUT OUR WORK QUICKLY. I STILL HAVE SO MUCH TO DO -- SO MANY TO DEVOUR.

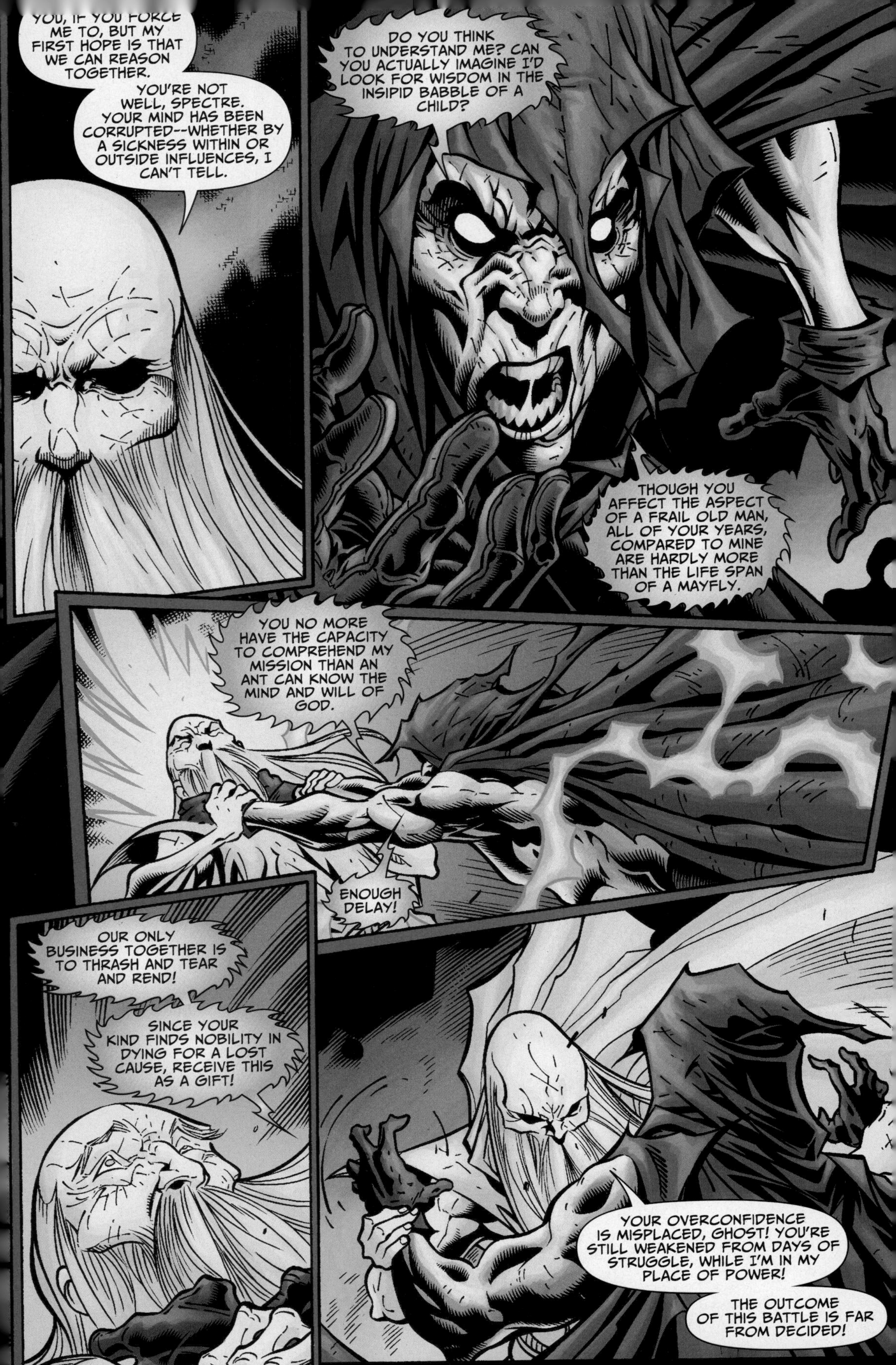
YOU, IF YOU FORCE ME TO, BUT MY FIRST HOPE IS THAT WE CAN REASON TOGETHER.
YOU'RE NOT WELL, SPECTRE. YOUR MIND HAS BEEN CORRUPTED--WHETHER BY A SICKNESS WITHIN OR OUTSIDE INFLUENCES, I CAN'T TELL.
DO YOU THINK TO UNDERSTAND ME? CAN YOU ACTUALLY IMAGINE I'D LOOK FOR WISDOM IN THE INSIPID BABBLE OF A CHILD?
THOUGH YOU AFFECT THE ASPECT OF A FRAIL OLD MAN, ALL OF YOUR YEARS, COMPARED TO MINE ARE HARDLY MORE THAN THE LIFE SPAN OF A MAYFLY.
YOU NO MORE HAVE THE CAPACITY TO COMPREHEND MY MISSION THAN AN ANT CAN KNOW THE MIND AND WILL OF GOD.
ENOUGH DELAY!
OUR ONLY BUSINESS TOGETHER IS TO THRASH AND TEAR AND REND!
SINCE YOUR KIND FINDS NOBILITY IN DYING FOR A LOST CAUSE, RECEIVE THIS AS A GIFT!
YOUR OVERCONFIDENCE IS MISPLACED, GHOST! YOU'RE STILL WEAKENED FROM DAYS OF STRUGGLE, WHILE I'M IN MY PLACE OF POWER!
THE OUTCOME OF THIS BATTLE IS FAR FROM DECIDED!

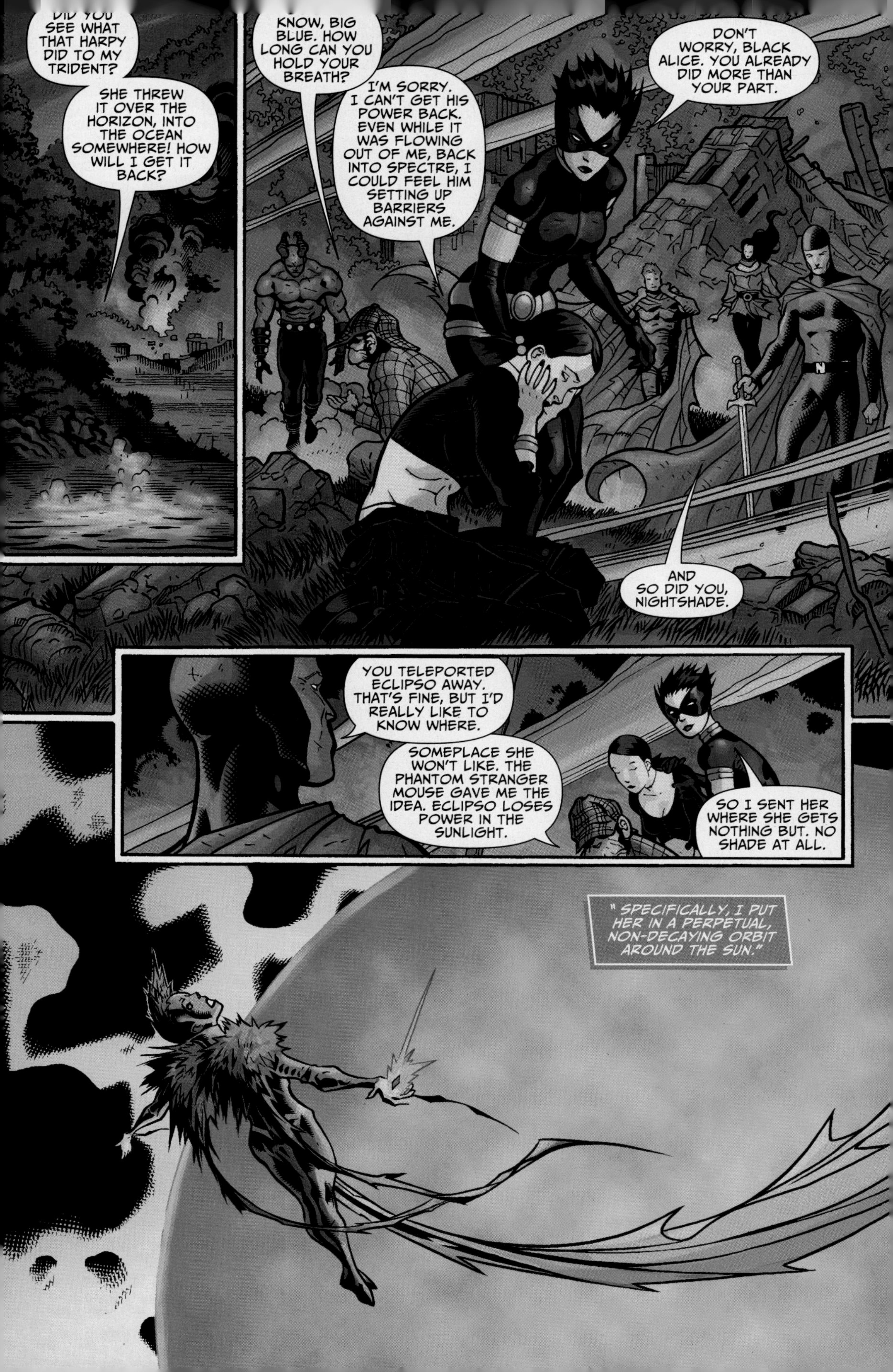
DID YOU SEE WHAT THAT HARPY DID TO MY TRIDENT?
SHE THREW IT OVER THE HORIZON, INTO THE OCEAN SOMEWHERE! HOW WILL I GET IT BACK?
KNOW, BIG BLUE. HOW LONG CAN YOU HOLD YOUR BREATH?
I'M SORRY. I CAN'T GET HIS POWER BACK. EVEN WHILE IT WAS FLOWING OUT OF ME, BACK INTO SPECTRE, I COULD FEEL HIM SETTING UP BARRIERS AGAINST ME.
DON'T WORRY, BLACK ALICE. YOU ALREADY DID MORE THAN YOUR PART.
AND SO DID YOU, NIGHTSHADE.
YOU TELEPORTED ECLIPSO AWAY. THAT'S FINE, BUT I'D REALLY LIKE TO KNOW WHERE.
SOMEPLACE SHE WON'T LIKE. THE PHANTOM STRANGER MOUSE GAVE ME THE IDEA. ECLIPSO LOSES POWER IN THE SUNLIGHT.
SO I SENT HER WHERE SHE GETS NOTHING BUT. NO SHADE AT ALL.
"SPECIFICALLY, I PUT HER IN A PERPETUAL, NON-DECAYING ORBIT AROUND THE SUN."

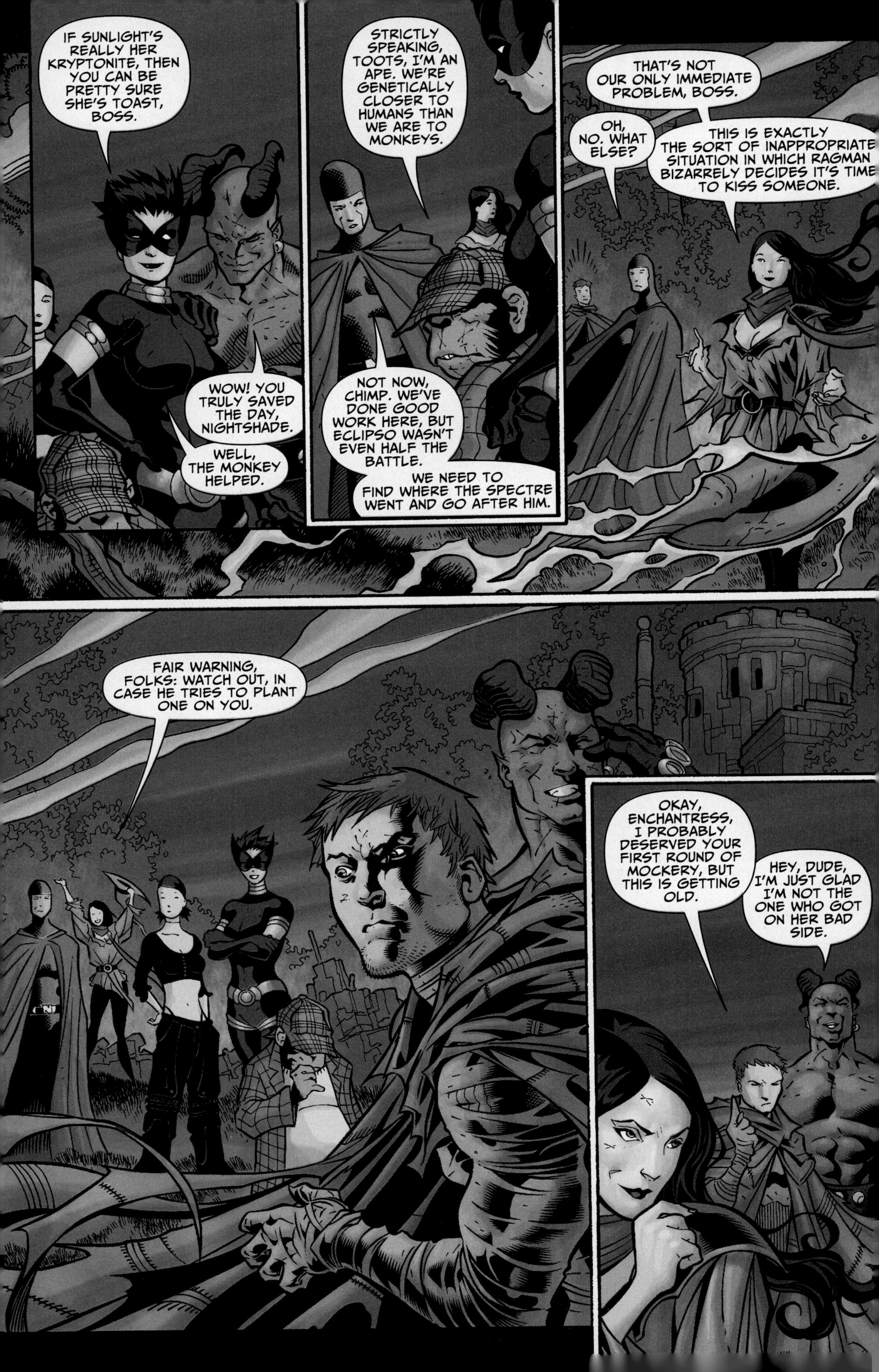
IF SUNLIGHT'S REALLY HER KRYPTONITE, THEN YOU CAN BE PRETTY SURE SHE'S TOAST, BOSS.
WOW! YOU TRULY SAVED THE DAY, NIGHTSHADE.
WELL, THE MONKEY HELPED.
STRICTLY SPEAKING, TOOTS, I'M AN APE. WE'RE GENETICALLY CLOSER TO HUMANS THAN WE ARE TO MONKEYS.
NOT NOW, CHIMP. WE'VE DONE GOOD WORK HERE, BUT ECLIPSO WASN'T EVEN HALF THE BATTLE.
WE NEED TO FIND WHERE THE SPECTRE WENT AND GO AFTER HIM.
THAT'S NOT OUR ONLY IMMEDIATE PROBLEM, BOSS.
OH, NO. WHAT ELSE?
THIS IS EXACTLY THE SORT OF INAPPROPRIATE SITUATION IN WHICH RAGMAN BIZARRELY DECIDES IT'S TIME TO KISS SOMEONE.
FAIR WARNING, FOLKS: WATCH OUT, IN CASE HE TRIES TO PLANT ONE ON YOU.
OKAY, ENCHANTRESS, I PROBABLY DESERVED YOUR FIRST ROUND OF MOCKERY, BUT THIS IS GETTING OLD.
HEY, DUDE, I'M JUST GLAD I'M NOT THE ONE WHO GOT ON HER BAD SIDE.

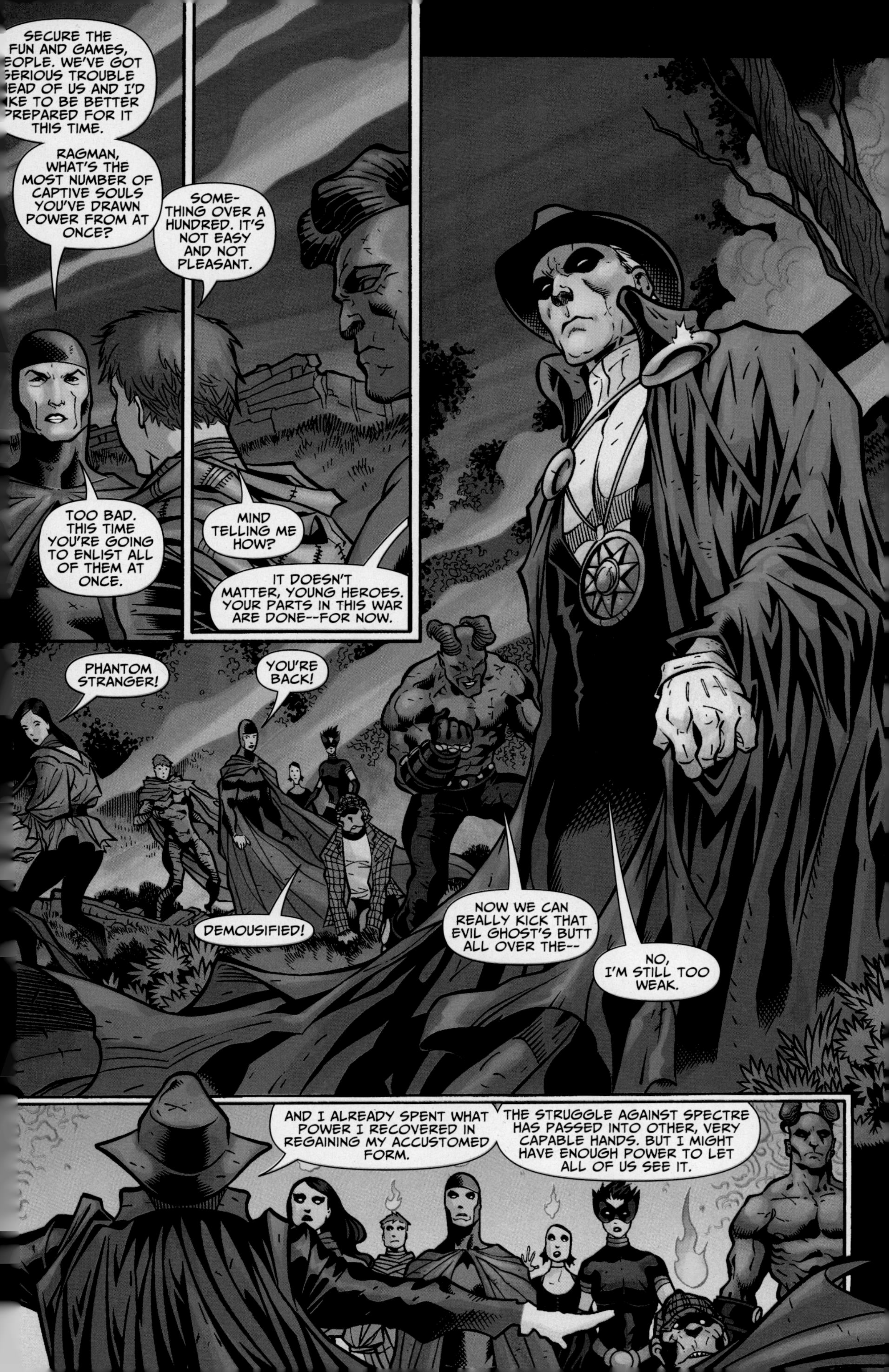
SECURE THE FUN AND GAMES, EOPLE. WE'VE GOT ERIOUS TROUBLE EAD OF US AND I'D IKE TO BE BETTER PREPARED FOR IT THIS TIME.
RAGMAN, WHAT'S THE MOST NUMBER OF CAPTIVE SOULS YOU'VE DRAWN POWER FROM AT ONCE?
TOO BAD. THIS TIME YOU'RE GOING TO ENLIST ALL OF THEM AT ONCE.
SOME-THING OVER A HUNDRED. IT'S NOT EASY AND NOT PLEASANT.
MIND TELLING ME HOW?
IT DOESN'T MATTER, YOUNG HEROES. YOUR PARTS IN THIS WAR ARE DONE--FOR NOW.
PHANTOM STRANGER!
YOU'RE BACK!
DEMOUSIFIED!
NOW WE CAN REALLY KICK THAT EVIL GHOST'S BUTT ALL OVER THE--
NO, I'M STILL TOO WEAK.
AND I ALREADY SPENT WHAT POWER I RECOVERED IN REGAINING MY ACCUSTOMED FORM.
THE STRUGGLE AGAINST SPECTRE HAS PASSED INTO OTHER, VERY CAPABLE HANDS. BUT I MIGHT HAVE ENOUGH POWER TO LET ALL OF US SEE IT.

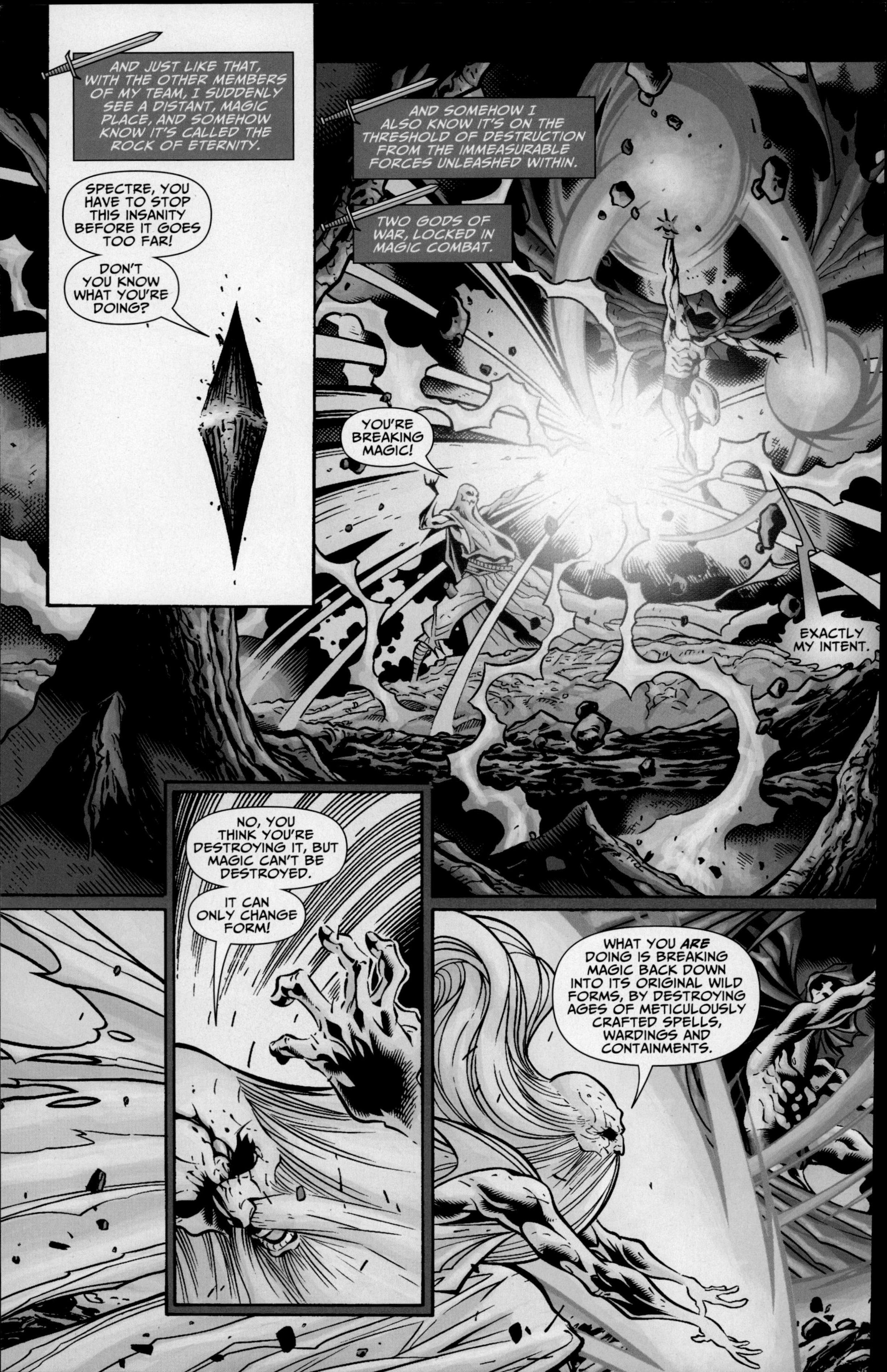
AND JUST LIKE THAT, WITH THE OTHER MEMBERS OF MY TEAM, I SUDDENLY SEE A DISTANT, MAGIC PLACE, AND SOMEHOW KNOW IT'S CALLED THE ROCK OF ETERNITY.
SPECTRE, YOU HAVE TO STOP THIS INSANITY BEFORE IT GOES TOO FAR!
DON'T YOU KNOW WHAT YOU'RE DOING?
AND SOMEHOW I ALSO KNOW IT'S ON THE THRESHOLD OF DESTRUCTION FROM THE IMMEASURABLE FORCES UNLEASHED WITHIN.
TWO GODS OF WAR, LOCKED IN MAGIC COMBAT.
YOU'RE BREAKING MAGIC!
EXACTLY MY INTENT.
NO, YOU THINK YOU'RE DESTROYING IT, BUT MAGIC CAN'T BE DESTROYED.
IT CAN ONLY CHANGE FORM!
WHAT YOU *ARE* DOING IS BREAKING MAGIC BACK DOWN INTO ITS ORIGINAL WILD FORMS, BY DESTROYING AGES OF METICULOUSLY CRAFTED SPELLS, WARDINGS AND CONTAINMENTS.

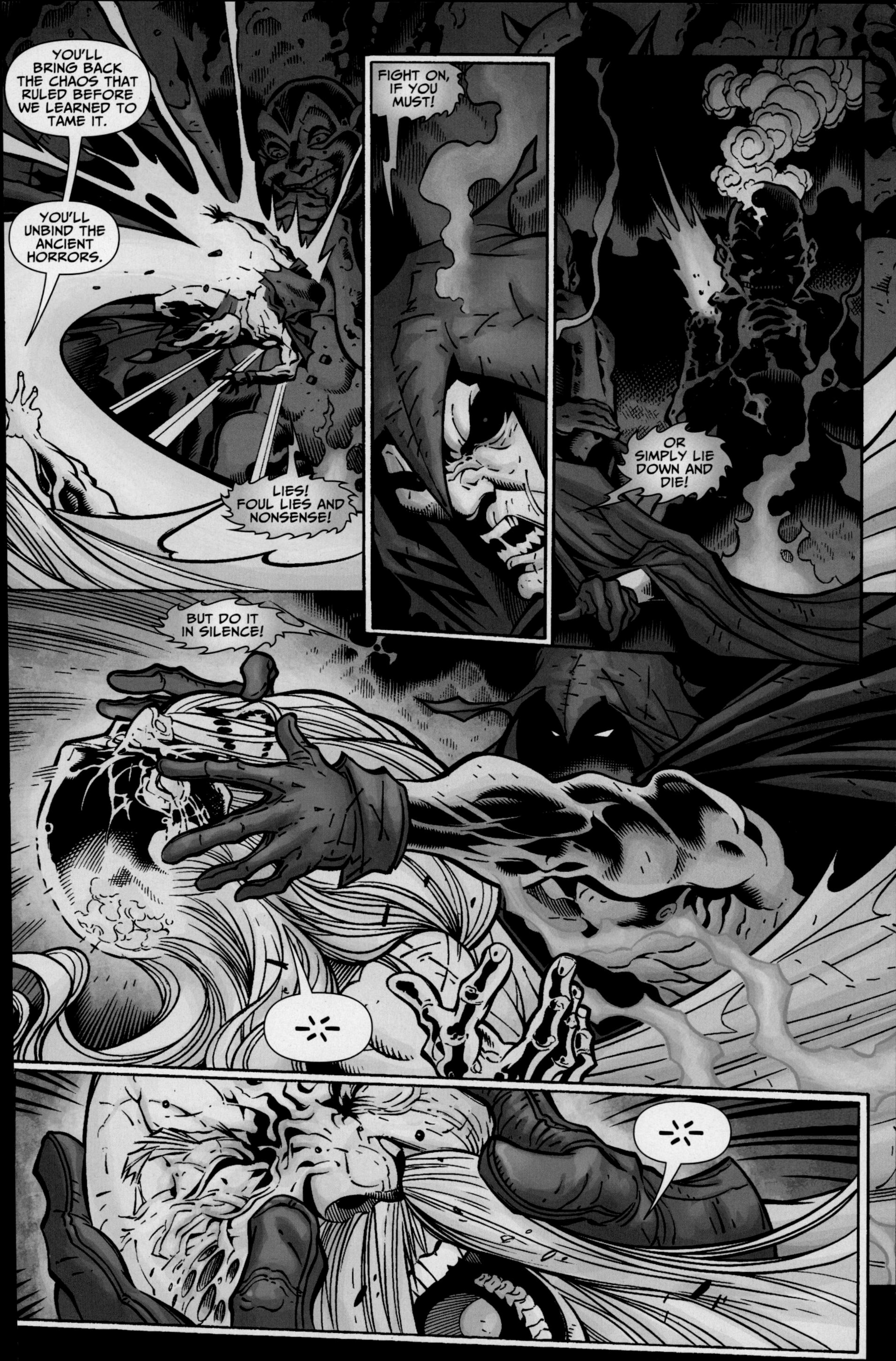
YOU'LL BRING BACK THE CHAOS THAT RULED BEFORE WE LEARNED TO TAME IT.
YOU'LL UNBIND THE ANCIENT HORRORS.
LIES! FOUL LIES AND NONSENSE!
FIGHT ON, IF YOU MUST!
OR SIMPLY LIE DOWN AND DIE!
BUT DO IT IN SILENCE!

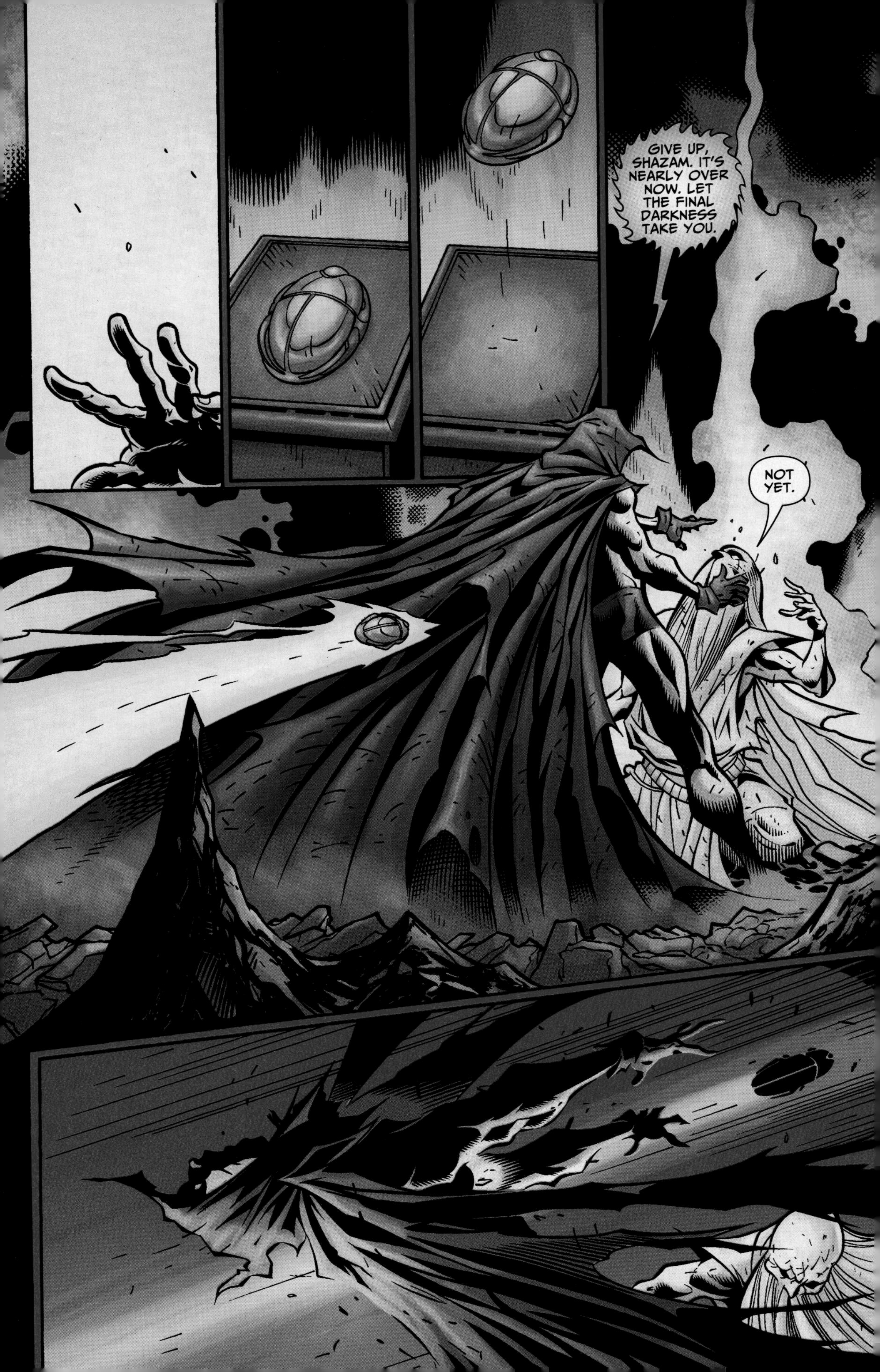
GIVE UP, SHAZAM. IT'S NEARLY OVER NOW. LET THE FINAL DARKNESS TAKE YOU.
NOT YET.

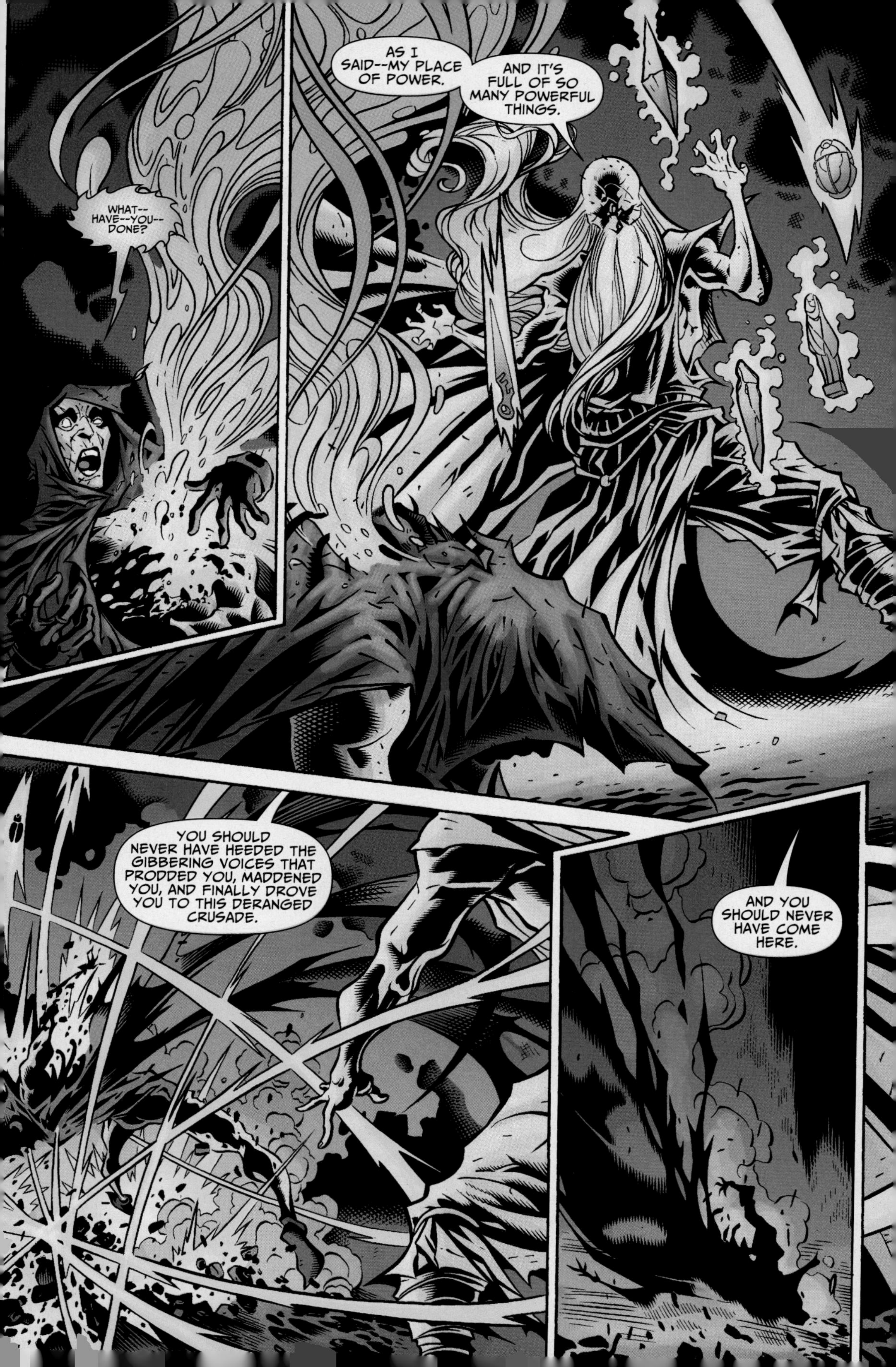

WHAT--
HAVE--YOU--
DONE?
AS I SAID--MY PLACE OF POWER.
AND IT'S FULL OF SO MANY POWERFUL THINGS.
YOU SHOULD NEVER HAVE HEEDED THE GIBBERING VOICES THAT PRODDED YOU, MADDENED YOU, AND FINALLY DROVE YOU TO THIS DERANGED CRUSADE.
AND YOU SHOULD NEVER HAVE COME HERE.

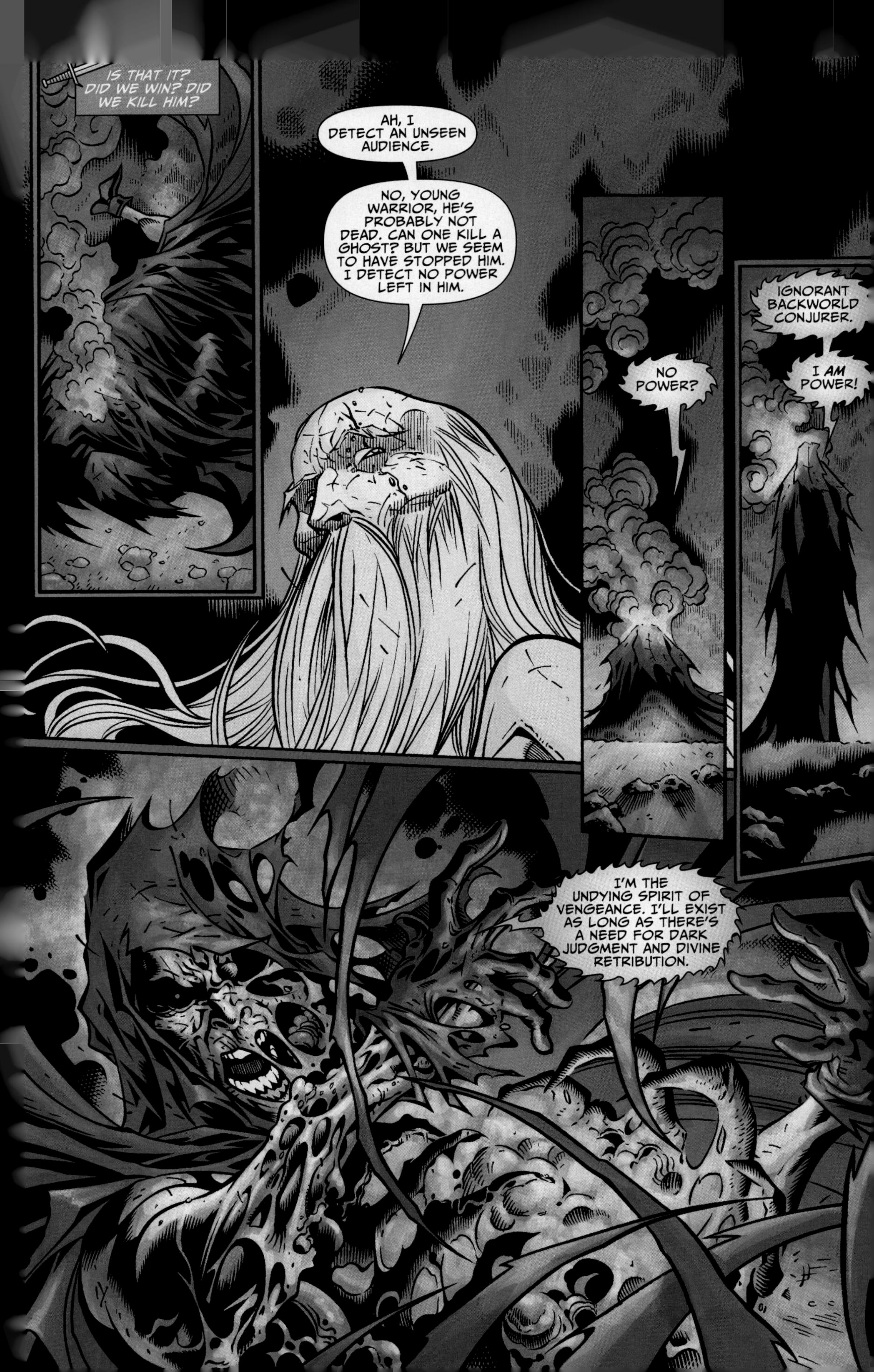
IS THAT IT? DID WE WIN? DID WE KILL HIM?
AH, I DETECT AN UNSEEN AUDIENCE.
NO, YOUNG WARRIOR, HE'S PROBABLY NOT DEAD. CAN ONE KILL A GHOST? BUT WE SEEM TO HAVE STOPPED HIM. I DETECT NO POWER LEFT IN HIM.
NO POWER?
IGNORANT BACKWORLD CONJURER.
I AM POWER!
I'M THE UNDYING SPIRIT OF VENGEANCE. I'LL EXIST AS LONG AS THERE'S A NEED FOR DARK JUDGMENT AND DIVINE RETRIBUTION.

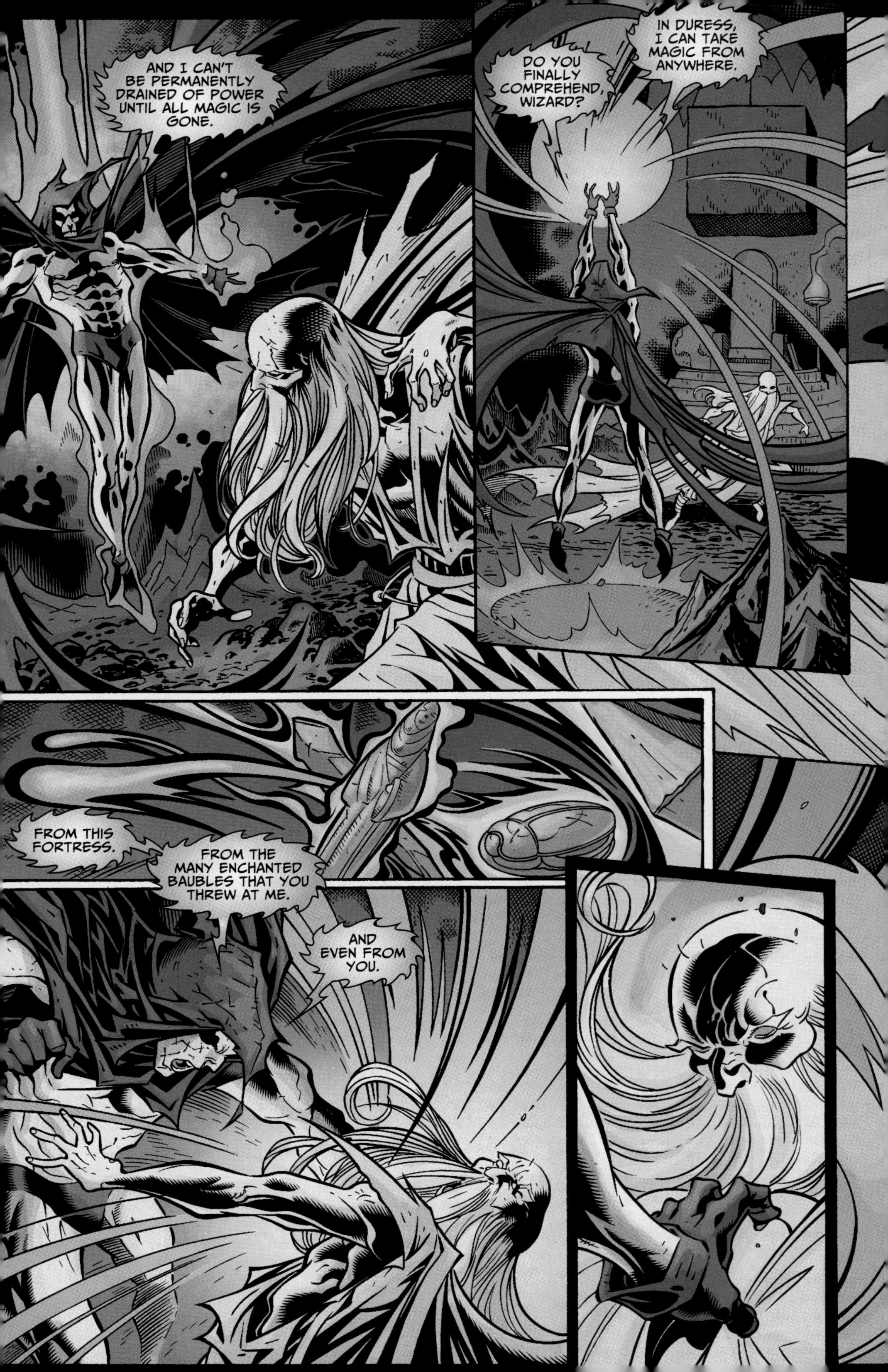
AND I CAN'T BE PERMANENTLY DRAINED OF POWER UNTIL ALL MAGIC IS GONE.
DO YOU FINALLY COMPREHEND, WIZARD?
IN DURESS, I CAN TAKE MAGIC FROM ANYWHERE.
FROM THIS FORTRESS.
FROM THE MANY ENCHANTED BAUBLES THAT YOU THREW AT ME.
AND EVEN FROM YOU.

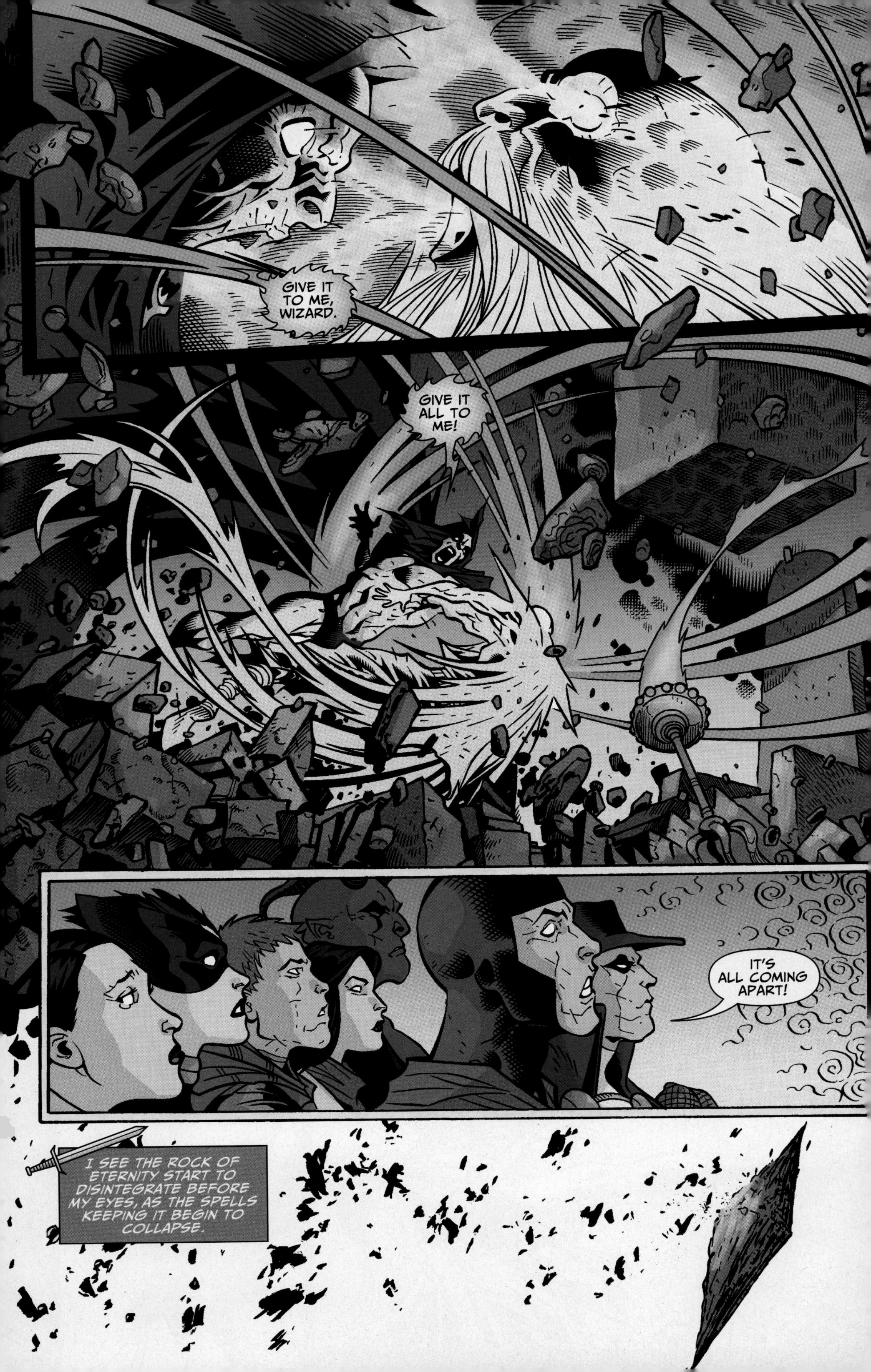
GIVE IT TO ME, WIZARD.
GIVE IT ALL TO ME!
IT'S ALL COMING APART!
I SEE THE ROCK OF ETERNITY START TO DISINTEGRATE BEFORE MY EYES, AS THE SPELLS KEEPING IT BEGIN TO COLLAPSE.

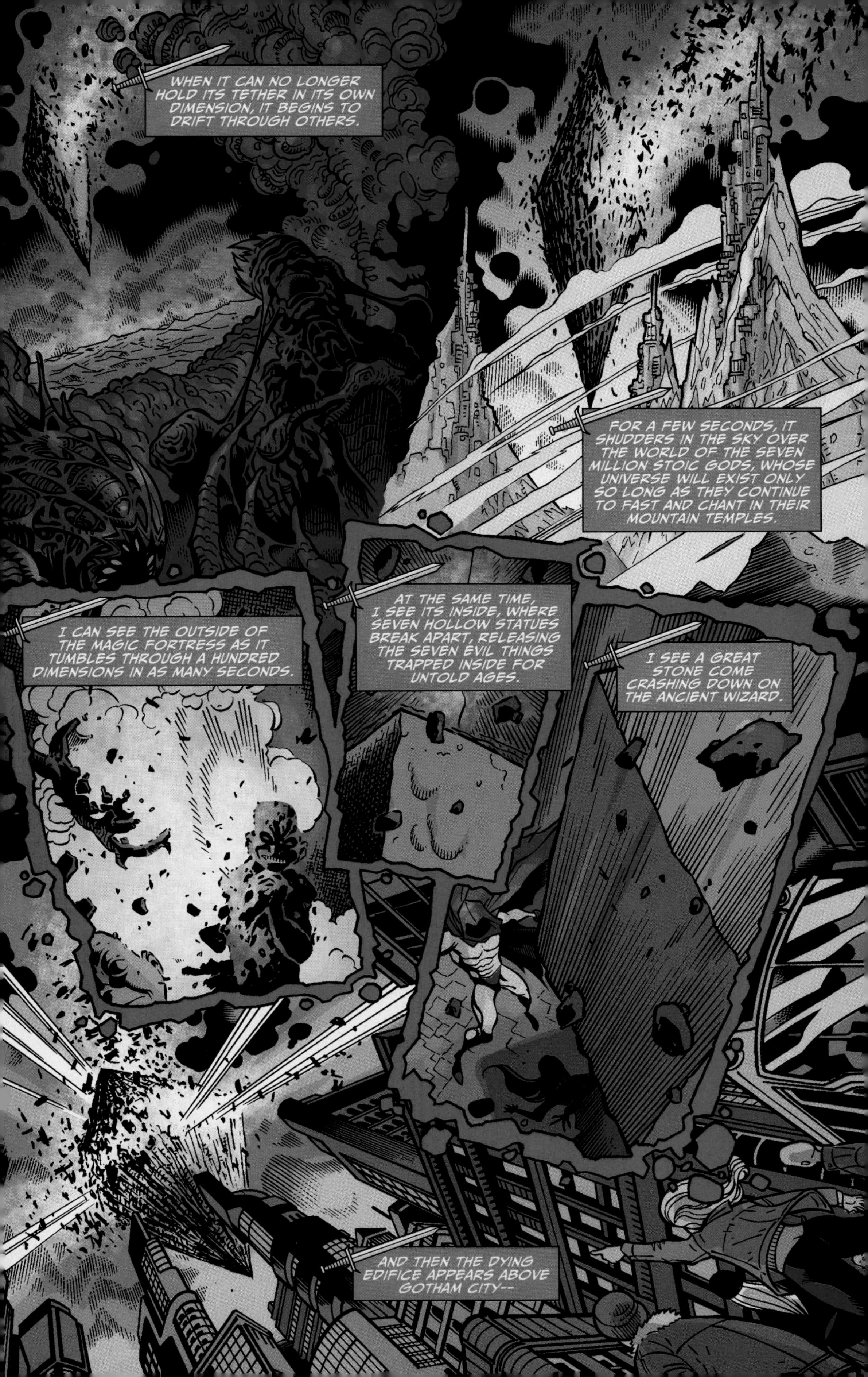
WHEN IT CAN NO LONGER HOLD ITS TETHER IN ITS OWN DIMENSION, IT BEGINS TO DRIFT THROUGH OTHERS.
FOR A FEW SECONDS, IT SHUDDERS IN THE SKY OVER THE WORLD OF THE SEVEN MILLION STOIC GODS, WHOSE UNIVERSE WILL EXIST ONLY SO LONG AS THEY CONTINUE TO FAST AND CHANT IN THEIR MOUNTAIN TEMPLES.
I CAN SEE THE OUTSIDE OF THE MAGIC FORTRESS AS IT TUMBLES THROUGH A HUNDRED DIMENSIONS IN AS MANY SECONDS.
AT THE SAME TIME, I SEE ITS INSIDE, WHERE SEVEN HOLLOW STATUES BREAK APART, RELEASING THE SEVEN EVIL THINGS TRAPPED INSIDE FOR UNTOLD AGES.
I SEE A GREAT STONE COME CRASHING DOWN ON THE ANCIENT WIZARD.
AND THEN THE DYING EDIFICE APPEARS ABOVE GOTHAM CITY--

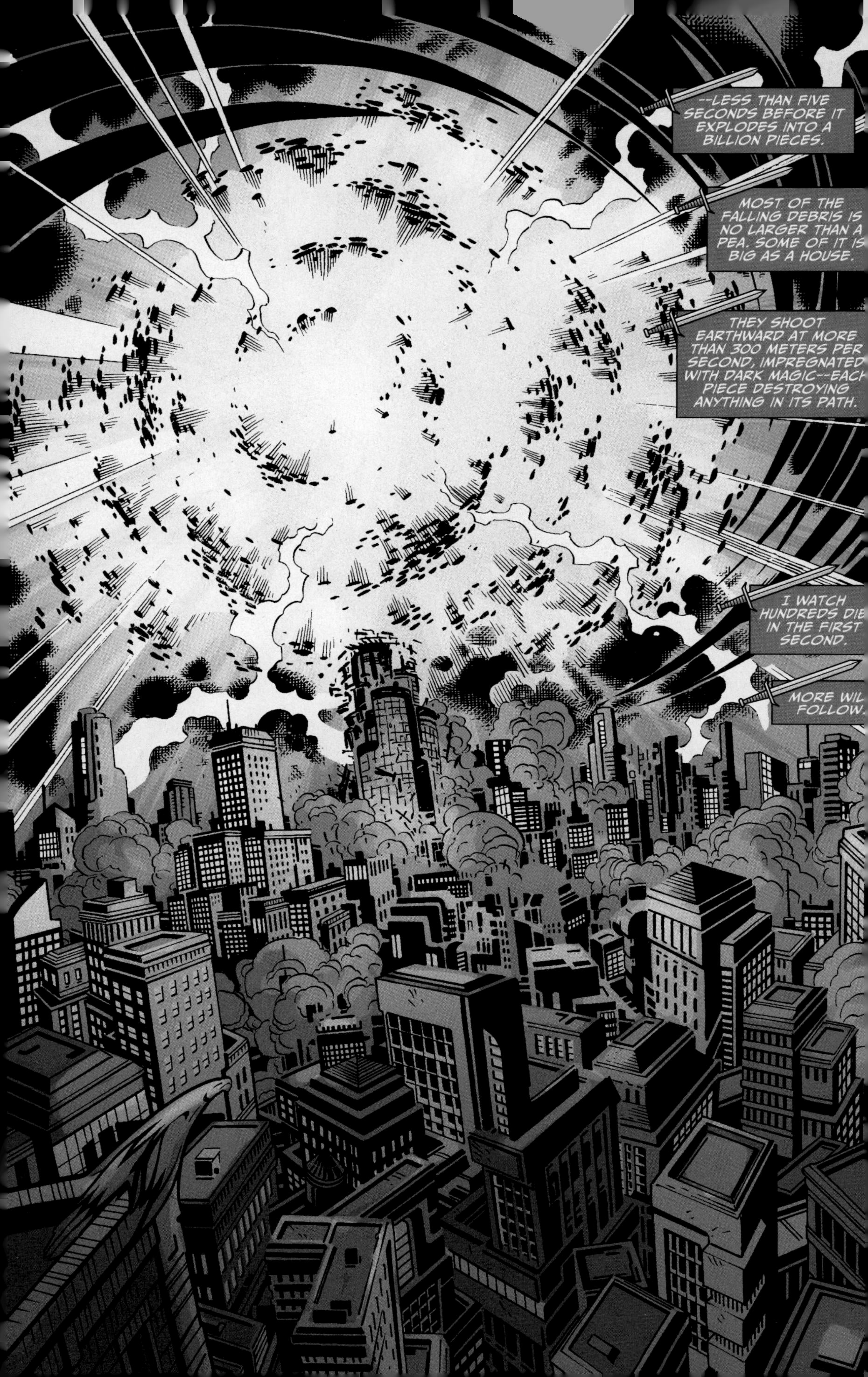

--LESS THAN FIVE SECONDS BEFORE IT EXPLODES INTO A BILLION PIECES.
MOST OF THE FALLING DEBRIS IS NO LARGER THAN A PEA. SOME OF IT IS BIG AS A HOUSE.
THEY SHOOT EARTHWARD AT MORE THAN 300 METERS PER SECOND, IMPREGNATED WITH DARK MAGIC--EACH PIECE DESTROYING ANYTHING IN ITS PATH.
I WATCH HUNDREDS DIE IN THE FIRST SECOND.
MORE WIL FOLLOW.

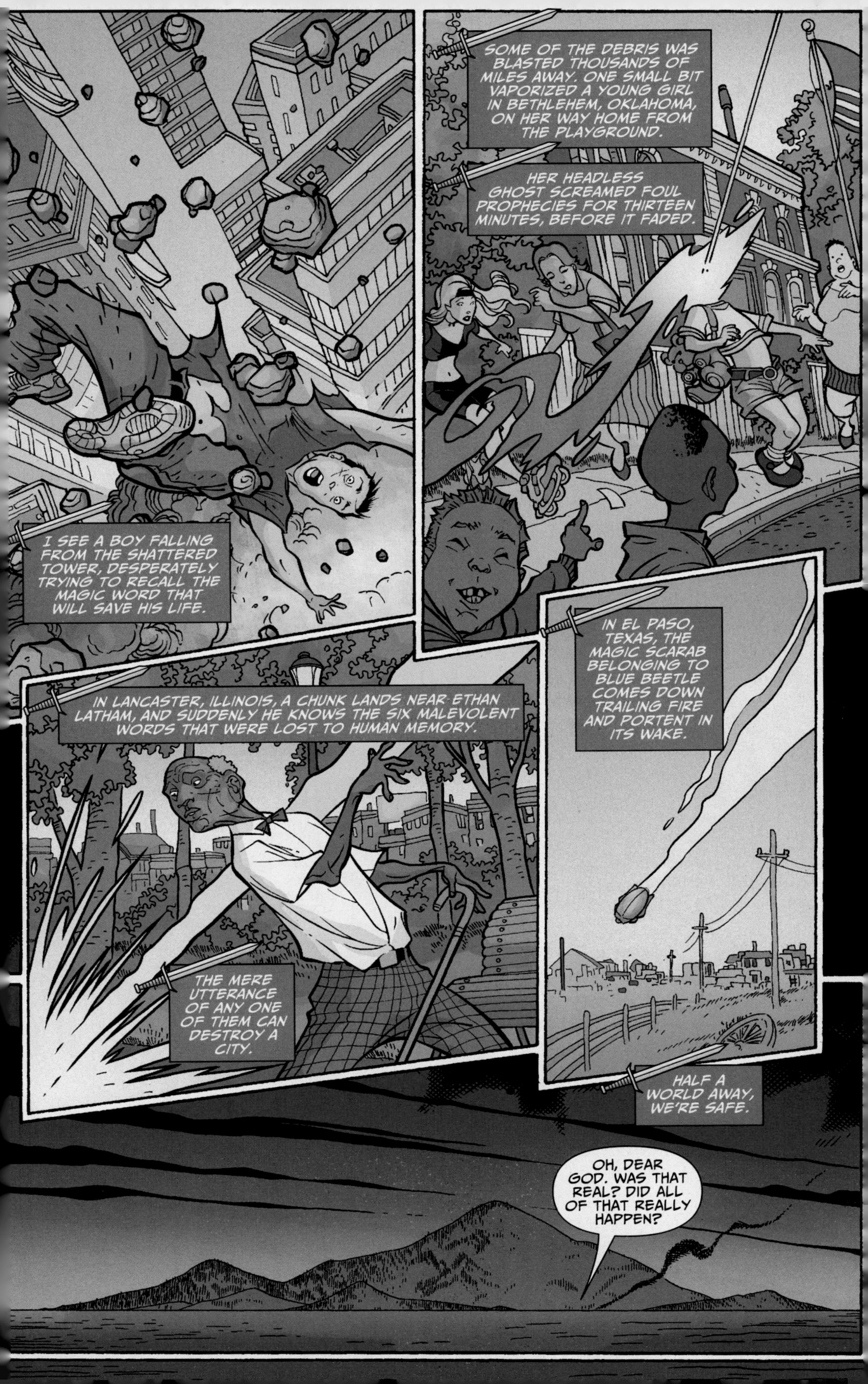
I SEE A BOY FALLING FROM THE SHATTERED TOWER, DESPERATELY TRYING TO RECALL THE MAGIC WORD THAT WILL SAVE HIS LIFE.
SOME OF THE DEBRIS WAS BLASTED THOUSANDS OF MILES AWAY. ONE SMALL BIT VAPORIZED A YOUNG GIRL IN BETHLEHEM, OKLAHOMA, ON HER WAY HOME FROM THE PLAYGROUND.
HER HEADLESS GHOST SCREAMED FOUL PROPHECIES FOR THIRTEEN MINUTES, BEFORE IT FADED.
IN LANCASTER, ILLINOIS, A CHUNK LANDS NEAR ETHAN LATHAM, AND SUDDENLY HE KNOWS THE SIX MALEVOLENT WORDS THAT WERE LOST TO HUMAN MEMORY.
THE MERE UTTERANCE OF ANY ONE OF THEM CAN DESTROY A CITY.
IN EL PASO, TEXAS, THE MAGIC SCARAB BELONGING TO BLUE BEETLE COMES DOWN TRAILING FIRE AND PORTENT IN ITS WAKE.
HALF A WORLD AWAY, WE'RE SAFE.
OH, DEAR GOD. WAS THAT REAL? DID ALL OF THAT REALLY HAPPEN?

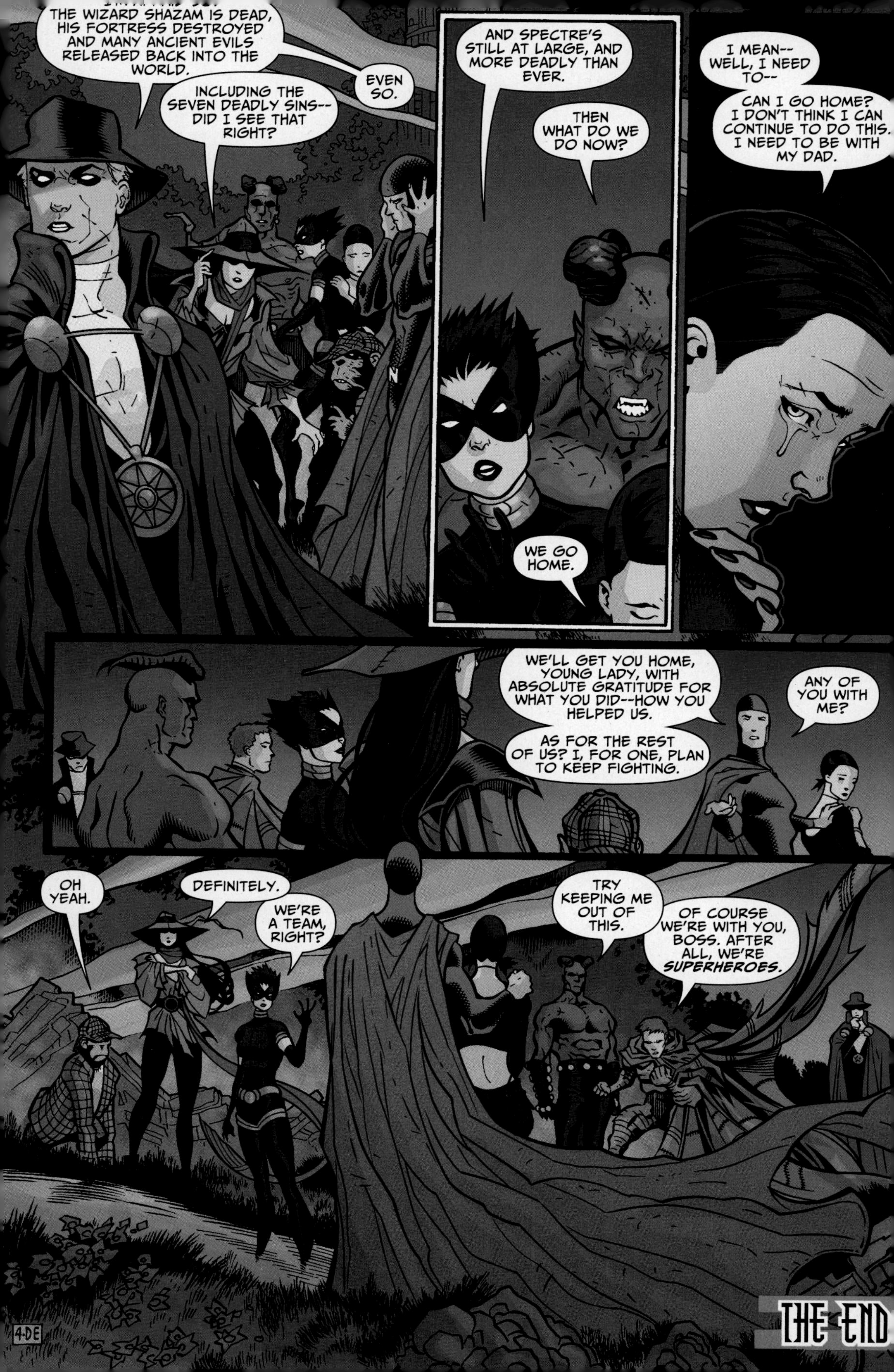
THE WIZARD SHAZAM IS DEAD, HIS FORTRESS DESTROYED AND MANY ANCIENT EVILS RELEASED BACK INTO THE WORLD.
INCLUDING THE SEVEN DEADLY SINS--DID I SEE THAT RIGHT?
EVEN SO.
AND SPECTRE'S STILL AT LARGE, AND MORE DEADLY THAN EVER.
THEN WHAT DO WE DO NOW?
WE GO HOME.
I MEAN--WELL, I NEED TO--
CAN I GO HOME? I DON'T THINK I CAN CONTINUE TO DO THIS. I NEED TO BE WITH MY DAD.
WE'LL GET YOU HOME, YOUNG LADY, WITH ABSOLUTE GRATITUDE FOR WHAT YOU DID--HOW YOU HELPED US.
AS FOR THE REST OF US? I, FOR ONE, PLAN TO KEEP FIGHTING.
ANY OF YOU WITH ME?
OH YEAH.
DEFINITELY.
WE'RE A TEAM, RIGHT?
TRY KEEPING ME OUT OF THIS.
OF COURSE WE'RE WITH YOU, BOSS. AFTER ALL, WE'RE *SUPERHEROES*.
THE END

AT THE OBLIVION BAR

Sharp-eyed readers enjoyed trying to identify the major and minor mystics who bellied up to the pandimensional Oblivion Bar in the early chapters. Artist Justiniano created mages, mystics, and sorcerers of his own to fill out the bar. For the uninitiated, here's a guide:

ISSUE #1 PAGE 17
FIRST PANEL: (from left): Timothy Raven (in top hat), Unnamed (in green, with ruffled collar), Unnamed (woman at table with jewel on forehead), Unnamed (in purple cape), Jennifer Morgan (green dress, sorcerer from Skartaris), Jim Rook, Unnamed (wizened man with hood and staff), Cicada, Nightshade, Arion Lord High Mage of Atlantis, Animal Man, Claw the Unconquered (holding drink), Vixen, Unnamed, Unnamed, Unnamed (cat, creature and woman at table).

SECOND PANEL: Black Orchid, Deadman, Jason Blood, Bobo.

THIRD PANEL: Zauriel (golden helmet), El Muerto, Deadman, Black Orchid, Dr. Occult, Andrew Bennett.

PAGE 18
SECOND PANEL: Jennifer Morgan, Jim Rook, Mongrel.

FOURTH PANEL: Ragman and Enchantress, backed by the Ghost Patrol.

FIFTH PANEL: Vixen, Unnamed, Animal Man, Nightshade, Arion, Unknown (red cape), Unnamed, Unnamed, Unnamed, Valda the Iron Maiden, Freedom Beast.

PAGE 19
FIRST PANEL:
Ragman, Enchantress, Corona (in back).

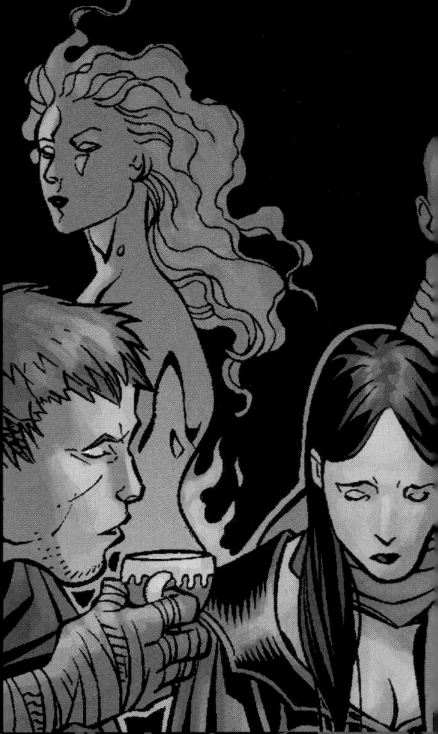

PAGE 20:
FIRST PANEL:
Witchfire, Janissary, Cicada, Claw the Unconquered, Enchantress, Deadman.

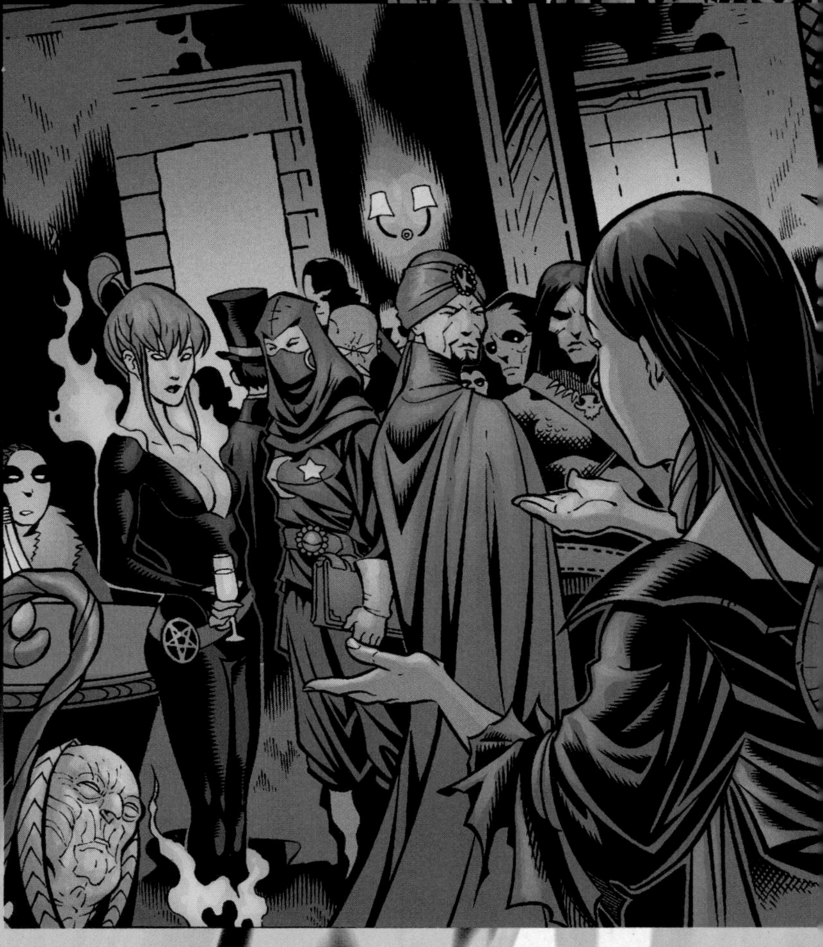

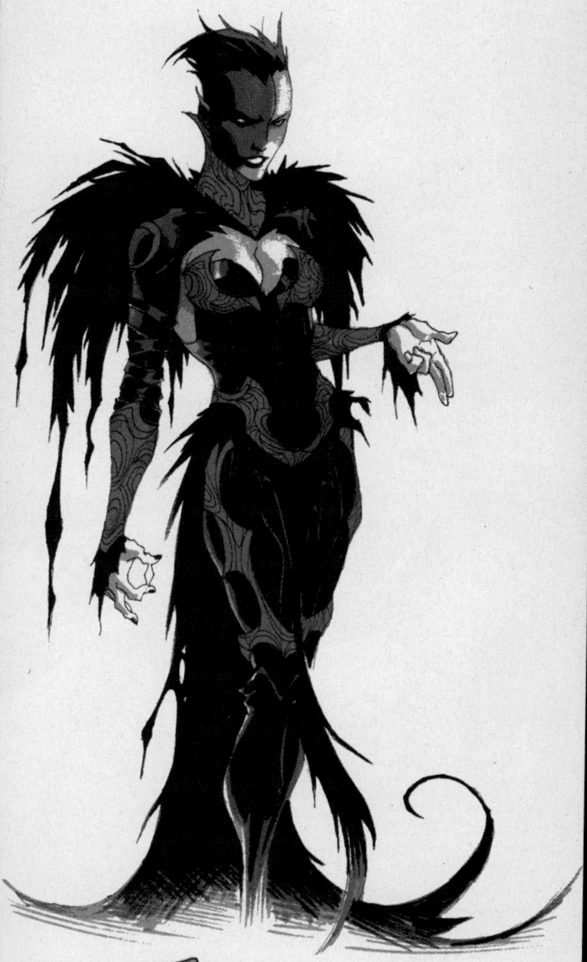

Eclipso, since his 1964 debut, has looked like no other character in the DC Universe. While the evil spirit has moved from body to body, this is the first time Eclipso's primary form has been female, and artist Justiniano wanted her to look distinctive. Here's a treatment he did in full color before beginning to draw the story.

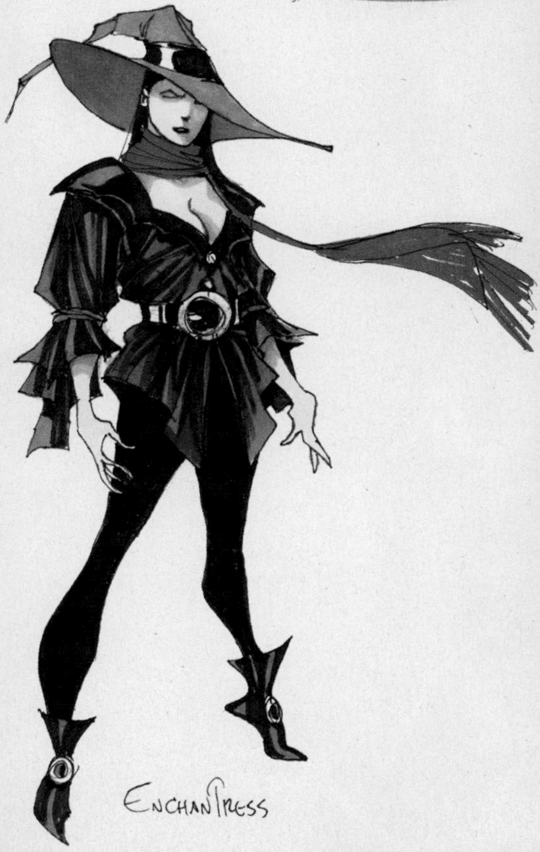
ENCHANTRESS

Enchantress's original witch-inspired outfit had a classic look to it, but again, given her prominence in the series, Justiniano wanted her to look special. The treatment he drew more than accomplishes the task.

ACTION COMICS 826

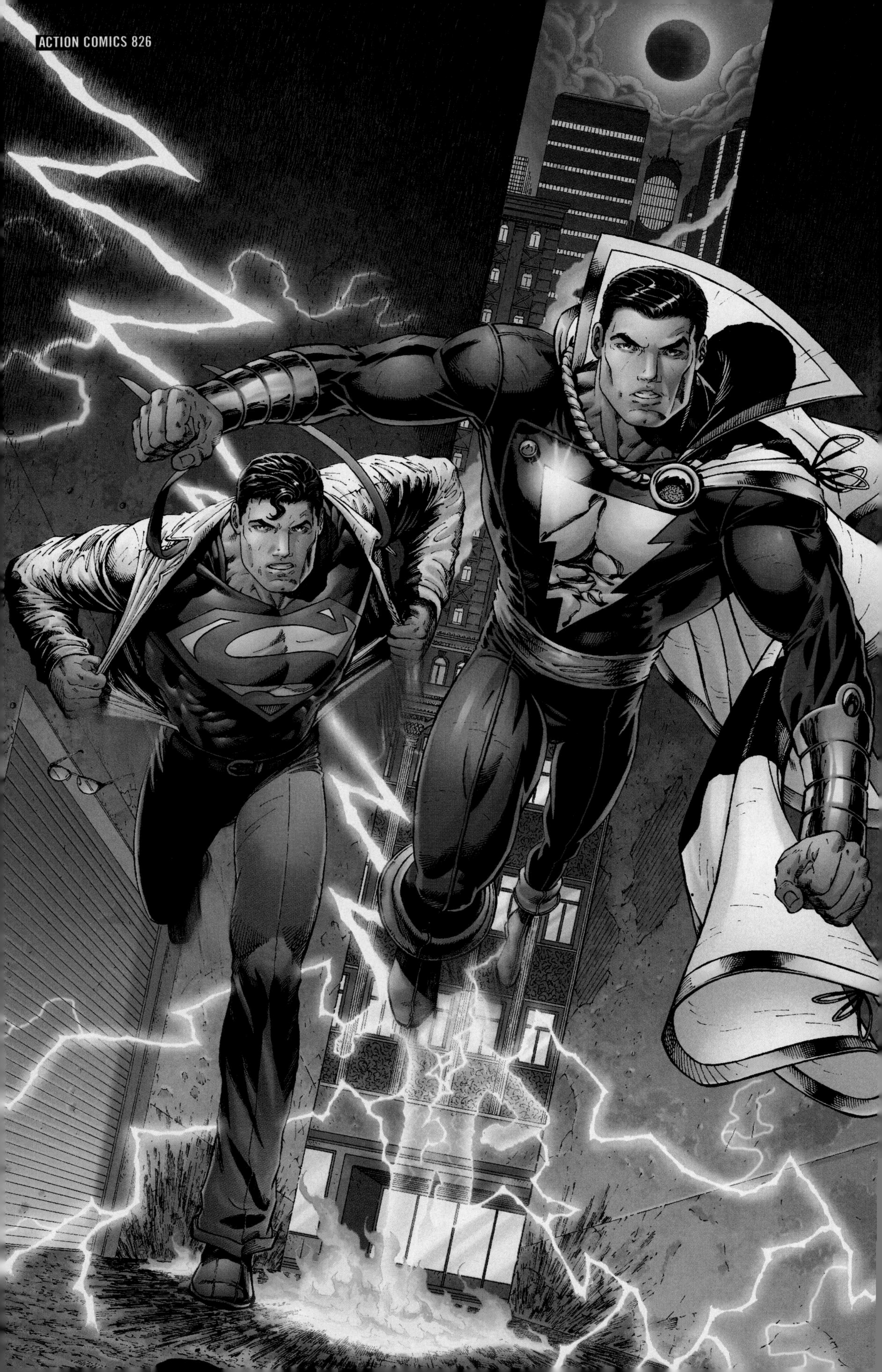

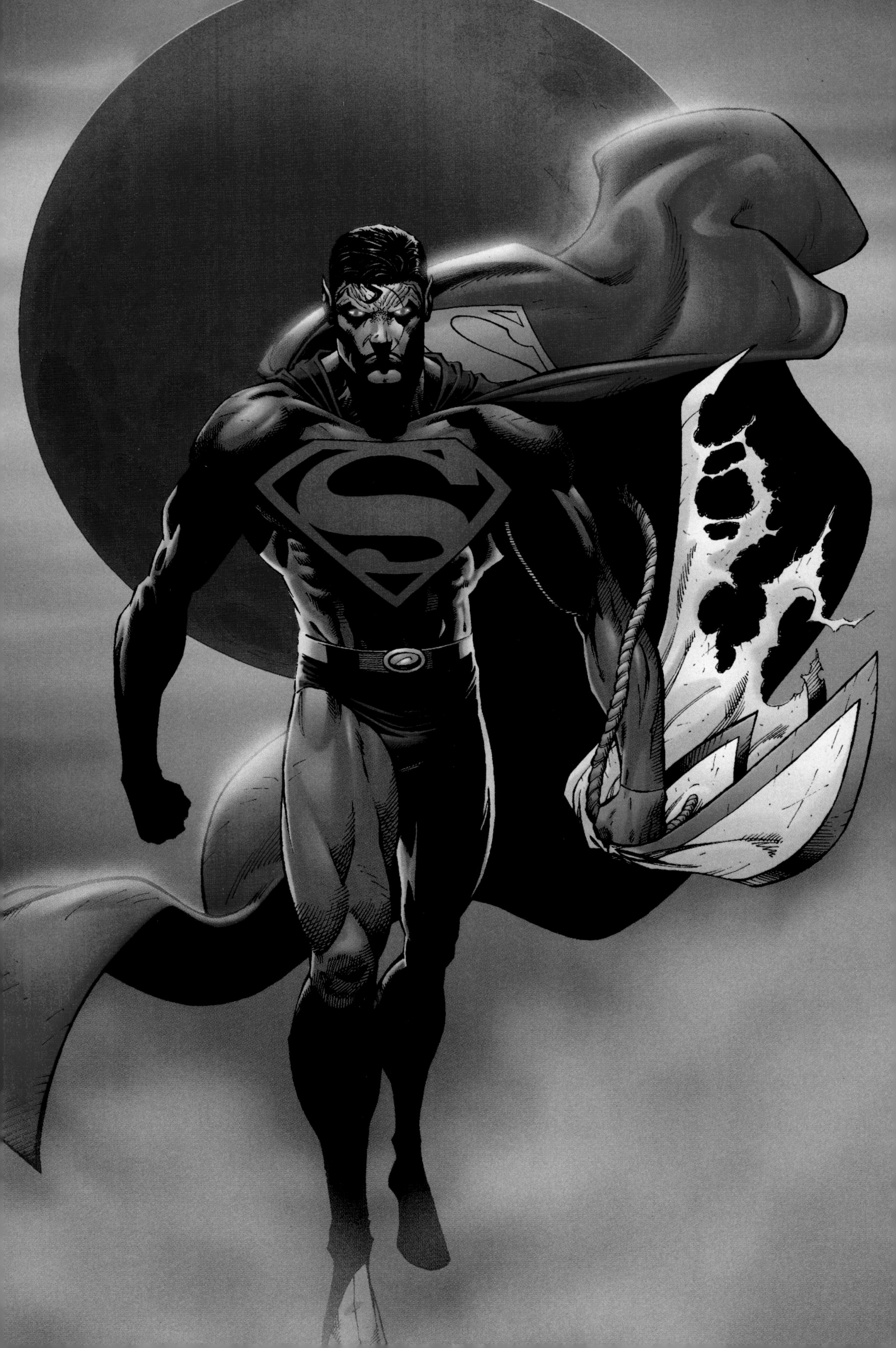

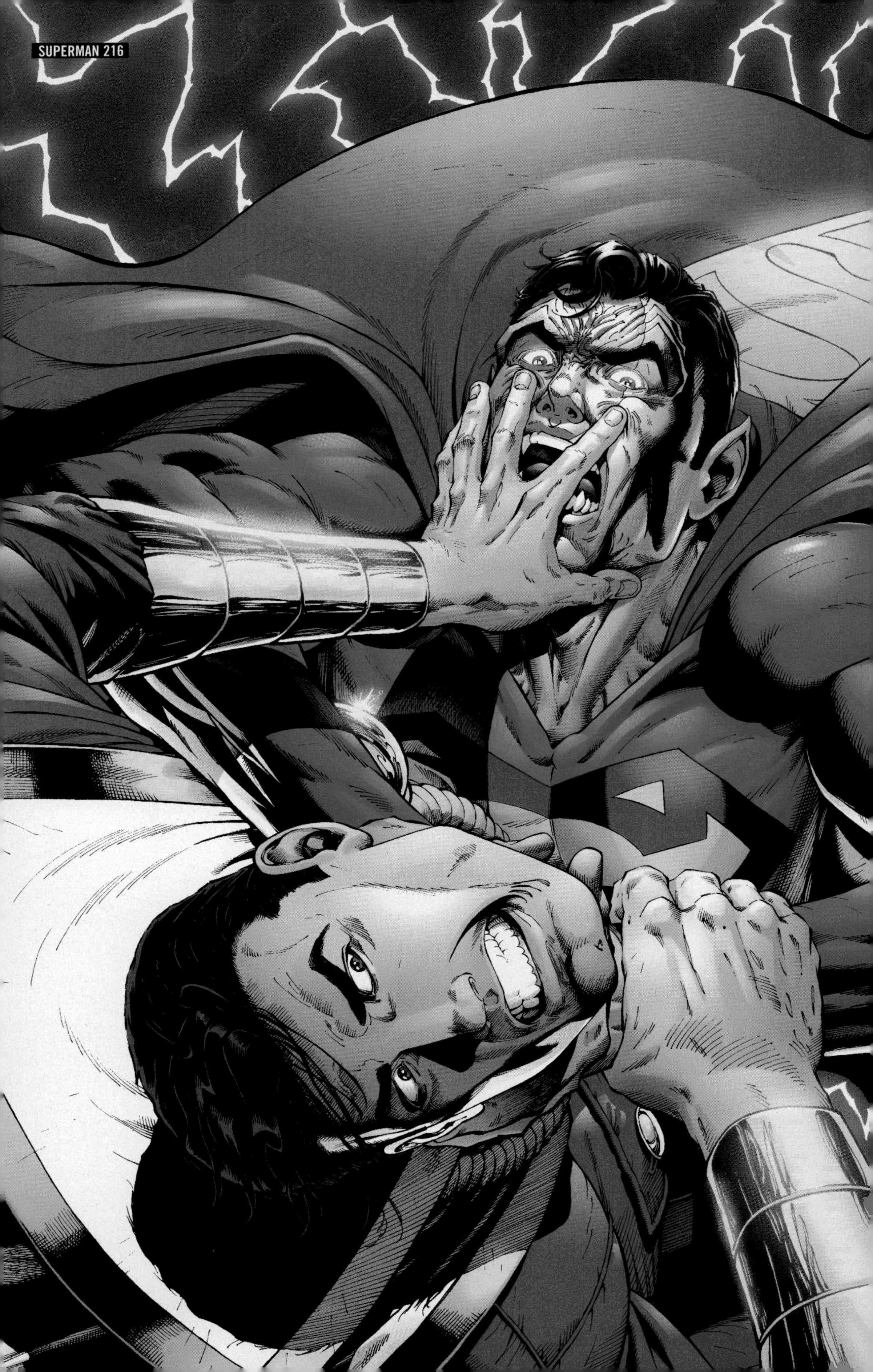

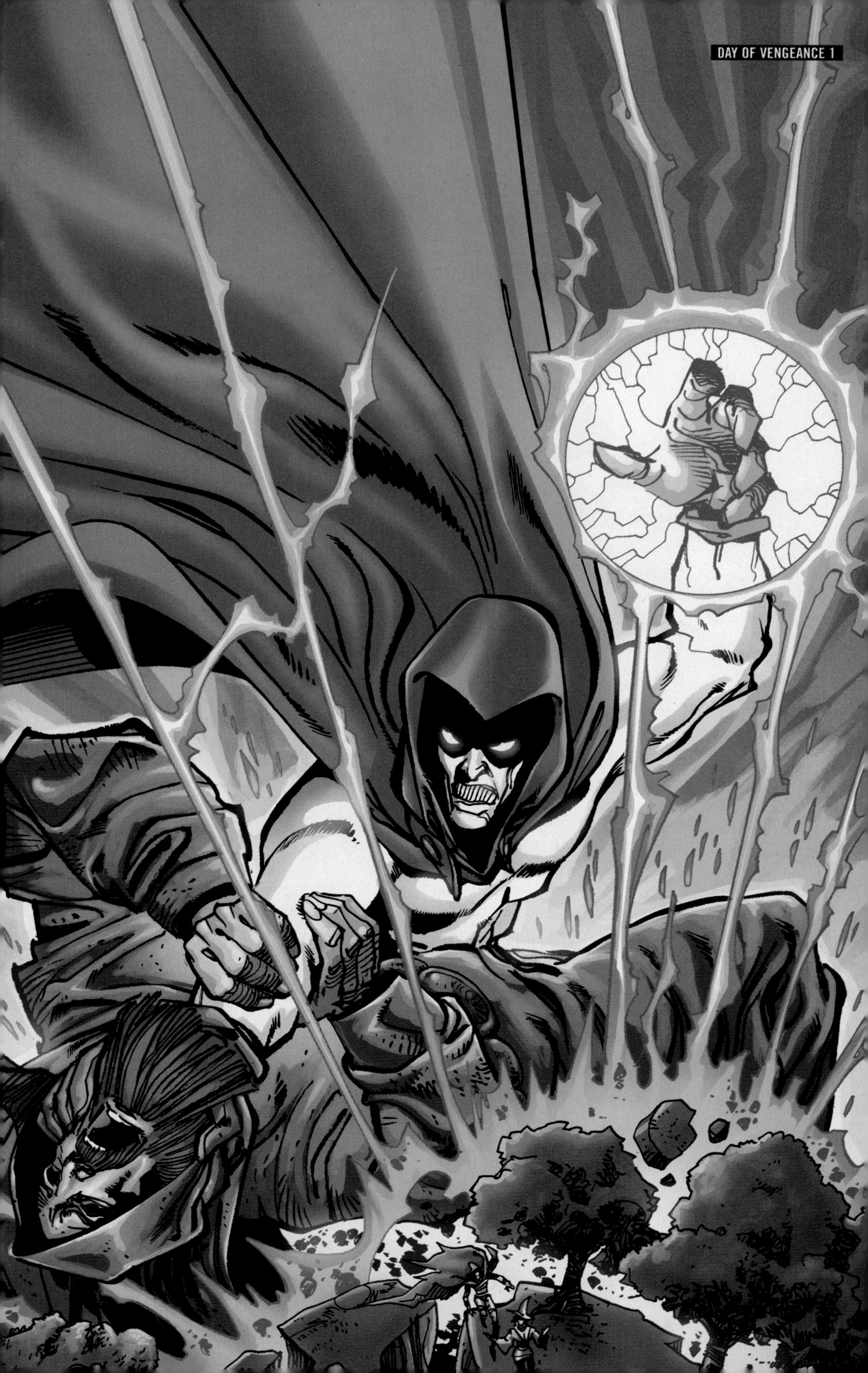

DAY OF VENGEANCE 1

DAY OF VENGEANCE 1
SECOND PRINTING

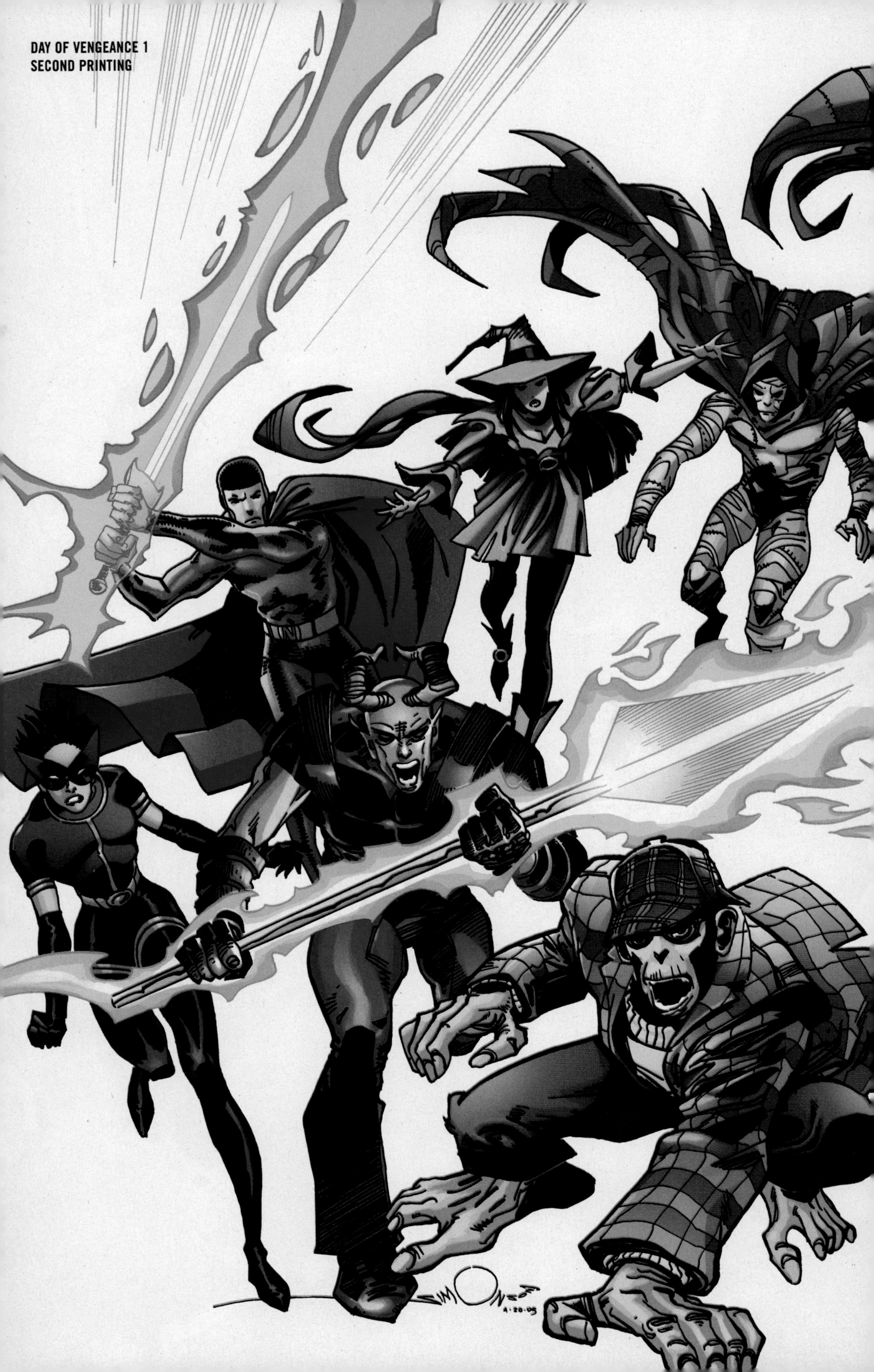

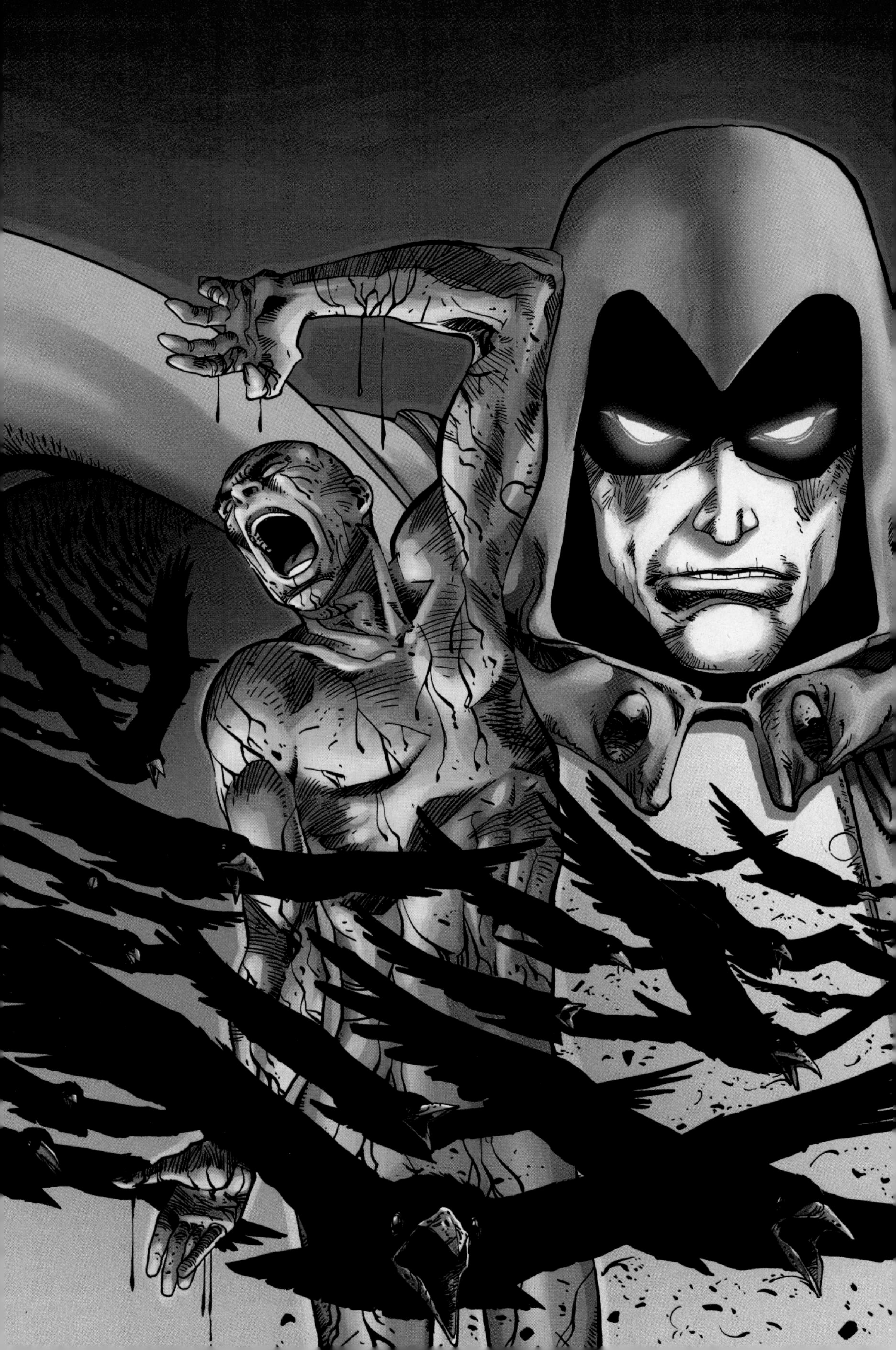

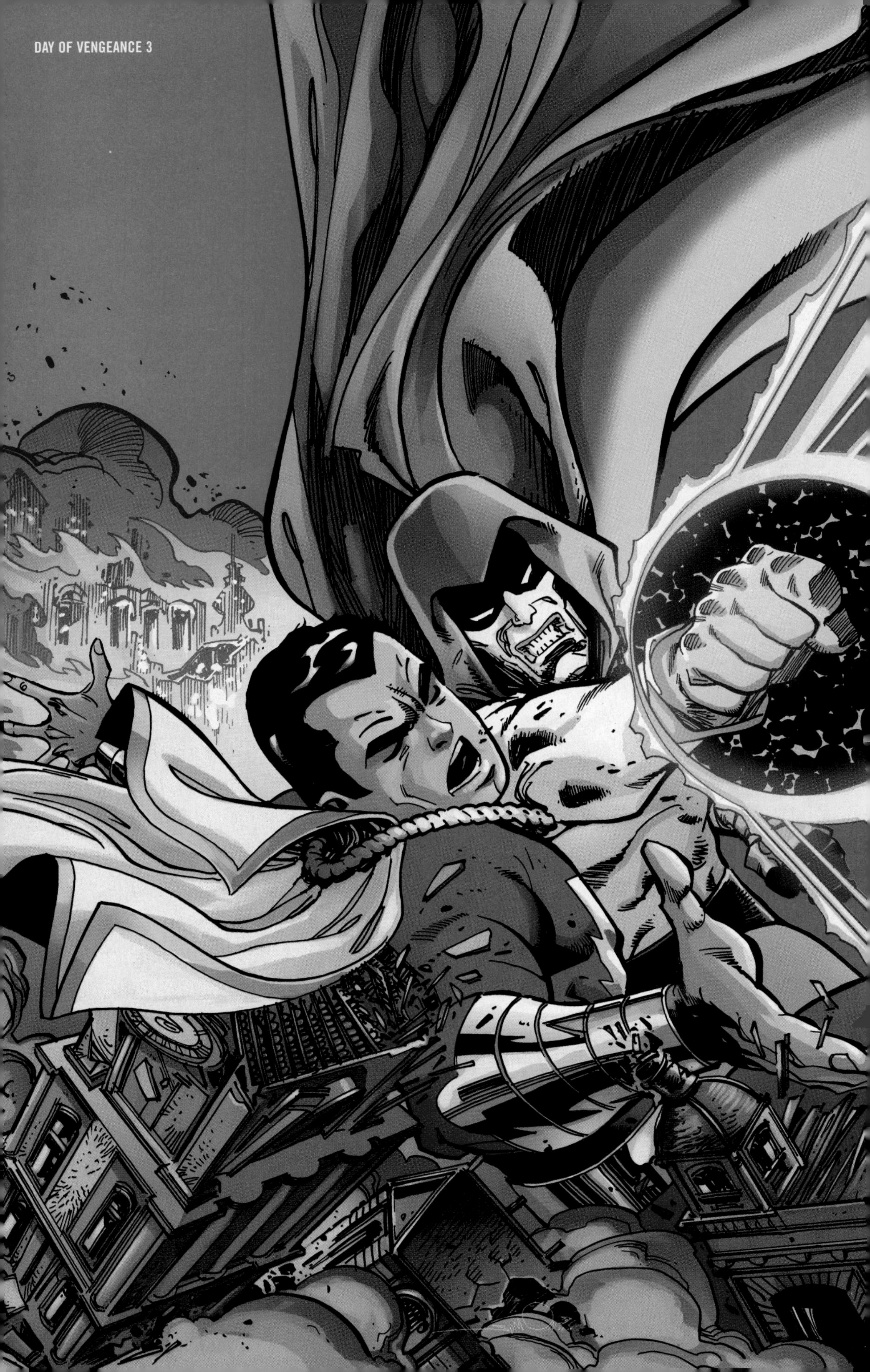

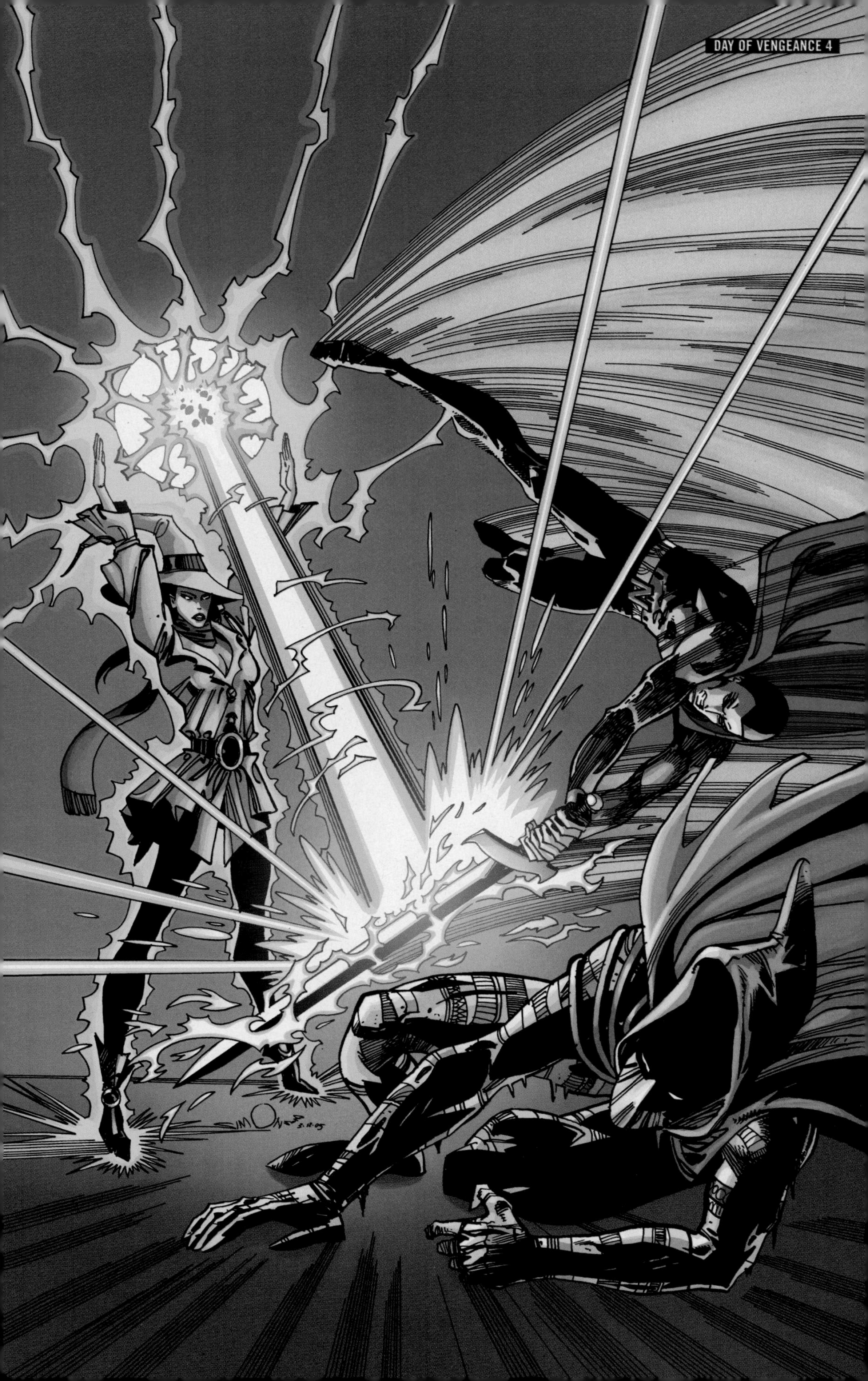

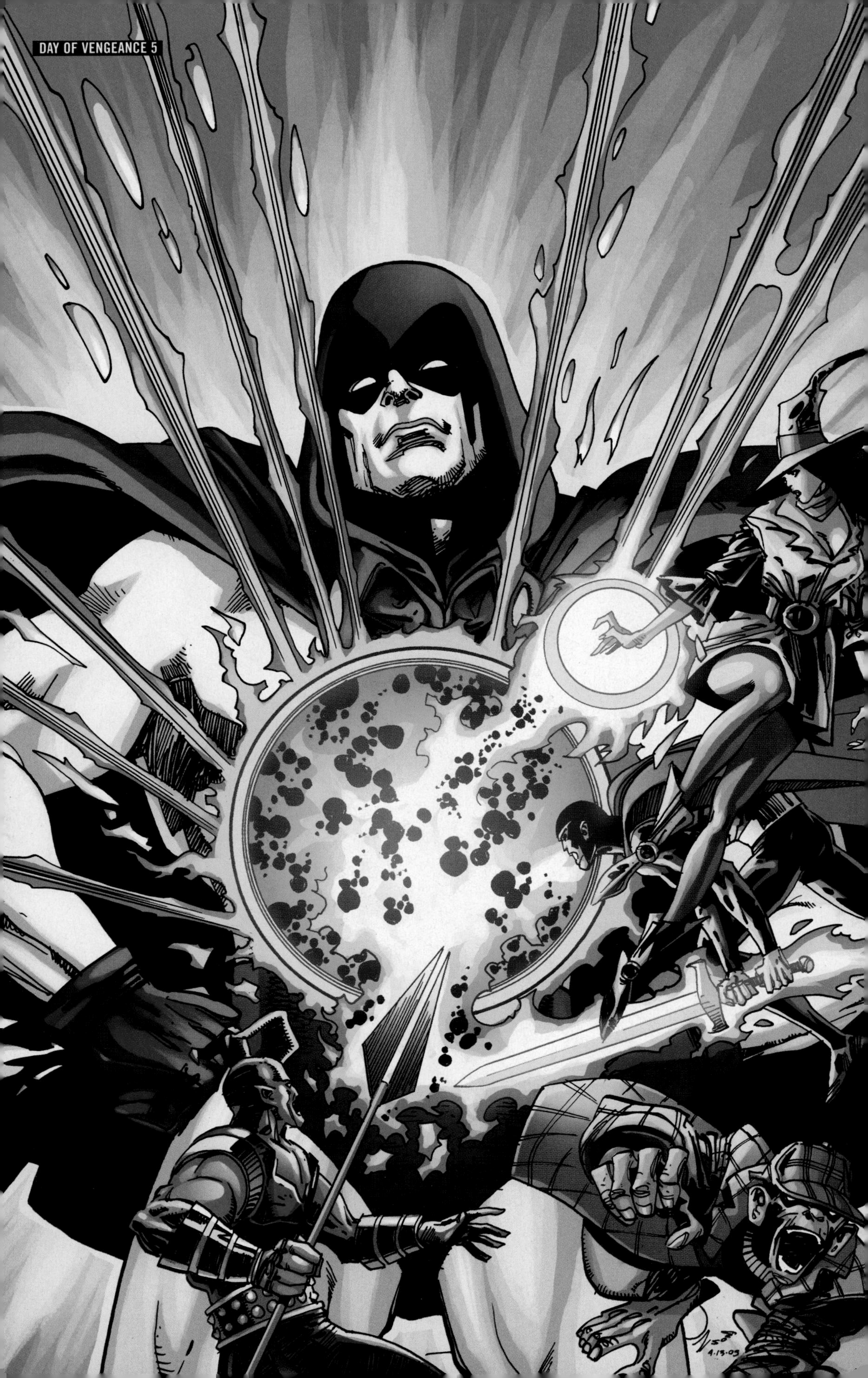

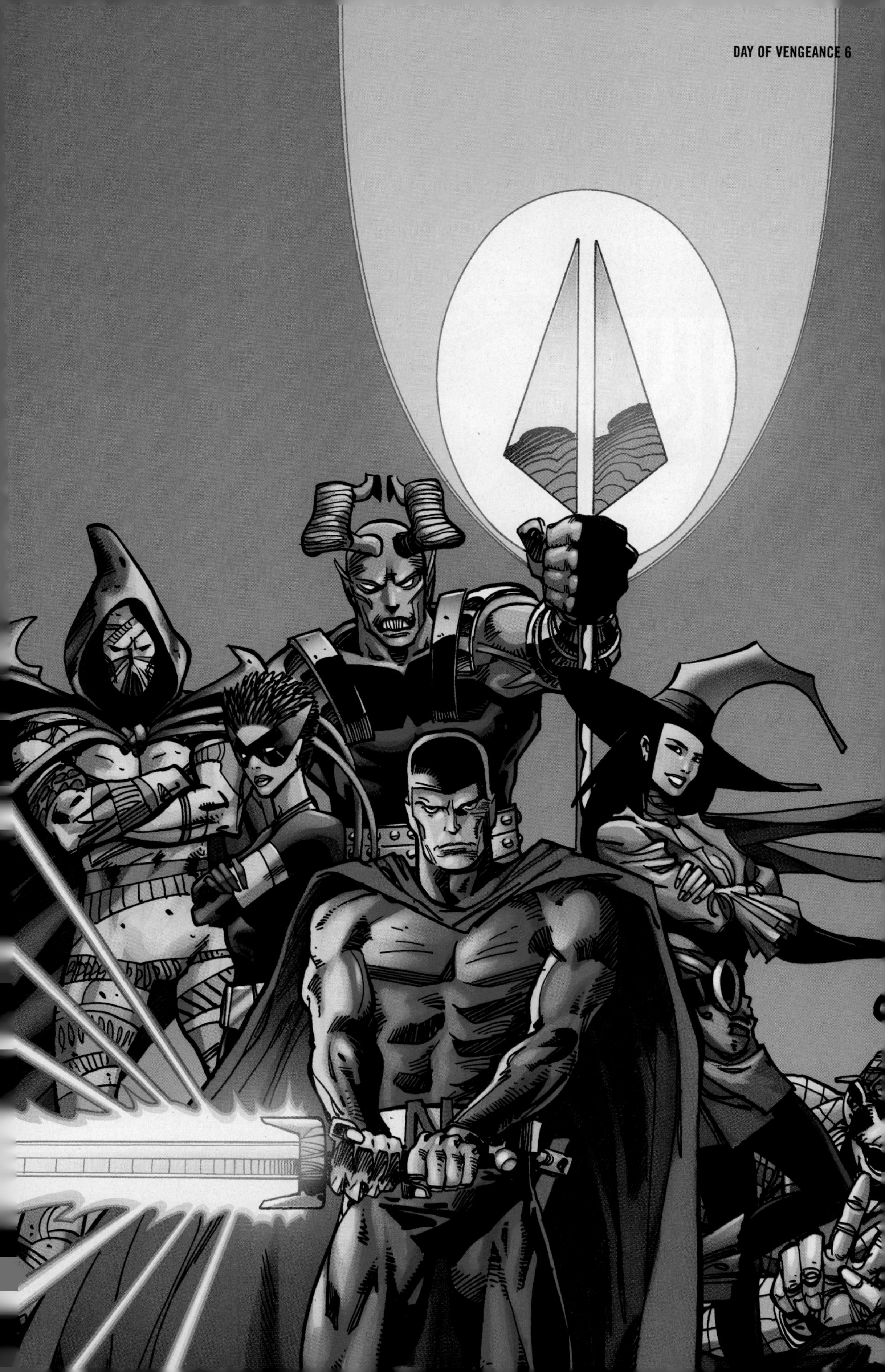

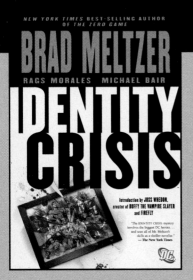 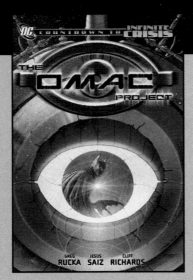